The *Paralogs* of Phileas Fogg

Columbiad, the Gem of the Ocean!

James Downard

Copyright © 2016 by Rulon James Downard.

The Paralogs of Phileas Fogg: Columbiad, the Gem of the Ocean!

All rights reserved. No part of this book may be reproduced in any manner whatsoever without written permission except in the case of brief quotations embodied in critical articles and reviews.

Inquiries should be addressed to

Rulon James Downard
4033 N. Belt St.
Spokane, WA 99205

First Printing: 2016
ISBN 978-1533544506

In life, as often as in art, things are not always as they appear to be....

1. IN WHICH PHILEAS FOGG AND PASSEPARTOUT ACCEPT EACH OTHER, BUT WHO IS MASTER, AND WHO IS MAN

Phileas Fogg of London is a man of mysterious background. Even his chronicler, the famed Mr. *V.* of France, conceded how no one knew where, or by what means, Fogg had made any of his fortune, nor were any other particulars known concerning his family or origins. He looked to be in his later thirties or early forties by age, but even that was mere speculation. He was so knowledgeable about the world, though, it was assumed he must have traveled widely, yet for many years was known exclusively as a London habitué, and a rather monotonous one at that: taking luncheon and dinner without fail at the Reform Club, of which he was a member only by virtue of having been recommended to it by someone at Barings Bank (where Fogg had on deposit a most attractive £20,000).

To what extent such disparities and lacunae reflected mere discretion or bald reportorial incompetence is uncertain. It must be recalled that, however great the virtuosity of his prose and imagination, Mr. *V.* often succumbed to suspicious confusion and inaccuracy in his written entertainments. The rampant geological implausibility of *Journey to the Center of the Earth* comes readily to hand, while the inexcusably obtuse chronological anachronism of *The Mysterious Island* recounting adventures taking place after *Twenty Thousand Leagues Under the Sea*, yet set years previously in the American Civil War, has often been noted by querulous commentators.

Similarly, I. Barbicane's experiments presented in *From the Earth to the Moon* transpire some years after that American convulsion, but required fresh investigation to finally ascertain a truer sequence of events and their intimate correlation with Mr. Fogg's well-publicized global escapade, activities over which a hitherto secure veil of secrecy was ultimately drawn by many individuals and governments, to their own purpose and intent, until disclosure in this present narrative.

To commence, it is true that young James Forster was indeed dismissed as Fogg's valet on account of providing shaving water for his unusually fastidious employer at 84° Fahrenheit rather than the scrupulously specified 86°. What has not been previously appreciated is that Jean Passepartout had handsomely paid the lad to commit this breach of instruction, deliberately to provoke his precipitous replacement on the 2nd of October, 1872, by Passepartout himself.

Passepartout duly presented himself at Fogg's fine Savile Row residence early that Wednesday morning by appointment, carrying only a small valise of personal belongings, and rather nervously fussing with his hair during the interview, fingering a large toothed comb, one beautifully made of ivory inlaid with what appeared to be delicate cloisonné, suggesting an earlier prosperity in contrast to the distinctly shabby character he featured presently.

While Fogg read his brief letter of introduction in silence, Passepartout vigorously recounted his many prior occupations, from singer and circus acrobat to tight-rope walker, gymnastics instructor to fireman, none of which seemed notably useful for anyone seeking position as a gentleman's valet, especially for one so demanding as Phileas Fogg. Moreover, although Passepartout had already served as valet in ten British houses over five years (the last being Lord Longferry, an MP more disposed to taverns and early morning police escorts than legislation or statesmanship), none of that was offered to Fogg for its persuasive effect.

Without further inquiry, Fogg pocketed the letter and declared, "You are well recommended to me."

Fogg then commanded they calibrate their watches to the exact minute, Passepartout's being four behind that of Fogg's, kept precisely to Greenwich Time. Fogg's was an elegant timepiece, its face decorated by six exquisite bezels circling the face, each ring but one bearing a tiny letter finely inscribed in black, beside a jewel of varying hue that glinted to one degree or another as they glided independently, shifting as Fogg did. Standing still now in his London drawing room, they stopped so that one bearing "**?**" rested by the *IX*, its gem flashing bright. An "**O**" and "**I**" were crowding *X*, with the jewel for the former glowing while that beside the other was not. One labeled "**N**" hugged *XI*, its gem also dim, as was that of the "**A**" resting at *III*. Below *VI* one lacking a mark altogether looked most dull, its jewel not scintillating either.

That synchronization accomplished, the Jean Passepartout who said he came from France was expeditiously engaged as Mr. Fogg's man as of 11:29 AM, and a minute later Fogg departed (as per his invariant schedule) for the Reform Club.

The now unemployed James Forster was about to leave No. 7 Savile Row for good when Passepartout took him aside. "Your cooperation is most appreciated. You must *never* tell how I came to be employed here, or even that I am at all." With a nod, Forster was on his way, many pounds richer than before. Passepartout stood at the door, looking up and down the street while Forster descended the steps.

And there she still was, the Woman who had been following Passepartout ever since America, casually strolling along the avenue, twirling a dark turquoise parasol that matched the skirts peeking out from under her fur-trimmed coat. He supposed she was pretending to admire the many tailors that had taken to Savile Row of late. He also knew she had several associates, who kept track of him while she presumably slept or dined, changing clothes but not tenacious manner, though presently she was unescorted.

That he had been followed meant somehow he had blundered, been spotted and assessed despite his precautions. By whom he had no idea. He had yet to exchange a word with the Woman, as she most carefully kept her distance, but that she was still on his tail here in London was a frustration he didn't yet know how to resolve in a way that would not make matters worse.

2. IN WHICH PASSEPARTOUT THINKS HE MIGHT AT LAST HAVE FOUND SOMETHING OF IMPORTANCE, IF ONLY HE COULD GET TO IT

Being now alone in the residence of Mr. Phileas Fogg, Passepartout embarked on a full inspection of the premises. The house was immaculately kept, served by a profusion of electric bells and speaking-tubes for easy communication. Fogg's suite was finely furnished but not ostentatious, a most modern electric clock humming away on the mantel. Passepartout later discovered its mate on the mantel of what he assumed was the valet's room on the top floor, perfectly synchronized with the one in Fogg's room. A card hanging above the clock summarized all of Fogg's precise needs, from his punctual rising at 8 AM until his return home at midnight on the dot.

A check out the window of the valet's room showed the Woman still on solitary patrol below.

Having surveyed the accommodations, Passepartout worked his way down the servants' stair to ground, where he discovered in the kitchen a door opening onto a small courtyard, dimly lit as walled on all sides by the adjoining buildings. Passepartout noticed that the stone pavement of the courtyard was clean, not even a stray leaf. Someone must be brooming it occasionally.

Unlike the structures to either side, though, that immediately opposite also had a door to the courtyard, one which Passepartout found to have a most unusual lock: a set of combination tumblers with no slotted provision for a key. Bright and shinning, no sign of wear to them, of precise craftsmanship and fitting. Nothing on Fogg's card alluded to this.

Passepartout did not like the coincidence of it. One does not put so special a lock on a door that does not need to be specially used. And who apart from those dwelling in No. 7 Savile Row would be in a position to unlock it?

There was a lone window to the right of the door, glass blacked out from the inside, as were all the windows on the several floors above. Passepartout noticed there were a few windows on the other buildings to the left and right, but none of them were blacked, only curtained. The darkened window offering an adequate reflection, Passepartout pulled out his comb, only to pause momentarily, eyes shut in thought, then swaying a bit as if suddenly faint. Opening his eyes, he scowled, and tucking his hat briefly under one arm, gave his hair a proper combing before returning through the kitchen door to do further thinking.

At that moment, Passepartout would have dearly liked to know what lay beyond that locked courtyard door. And had the Woman only not been there to certainly follow, he would have slipped out to explore the avenue beyond to find out what frontage that building had there. Was it a commercial establishment, or another remnant residence such as Mr. Fogg's? Yes, he would have done all that, if only the Woman weren't there.

Passepartout might have been somewhat consoled to know that the Woman had taken no great notice of the gentleman who had left the house at 11:30, intending to identify him at a later convenience. So Phileas Fogg had walked out of her attention as a seeming irrelevancy, to stroll on through Piccadilly to the Reform Club just off Waterloo Place, but a few blocks west of Trafalgar Square.

Not that Fogg appeared particularly interested in his own surroundings, from the cloudy autumnal weather, threatening rain, to the day's news boards, where the £55,000 Bank of England robbery was fast crowding out lesser mysteries, such as the presumed abduction in Paris of the noted French scientist, Professor Aronnax.

But with Phileas Fogg, no less than Passepartout, appearances could be most deceiving, for the moment Fogg stepped into the Reform Club, he stopped at the desk to have a telegram sent to an address in Paris: URGENT DETERMINE PARTICULARS ARONNAX DISAPPEARANCE. REPORT FINDINGS AT PLM STATION CAFE 8AM 3 OCT.

3. IN WHICH A CONVERSATION TAKES PLACE EXACTLY AS PHILEAS FOGG PURPOSES

Fogg's routine at the Reform Club was sufficiently clockwork that any deviation from it might have drawn more attention than had he suddenly burst into flame. As it was, he took his luncheon exactly as he always had, and afterward went (as he always did) upstairs to the reading room, one of many fronting the large skylight-brightened nave that occupied the center of the building, its balustrade punctuated by tall Corinthian columns, to read through the latest *Times* and *Standard* before dinner. He looked in particular for further reportage on the Aronnax matter, but nothing new had transpired beyond the fact of his evident kidnapping from his apartments in Paris on the 30th of September, about which anxious inquiries were flooding the Continent owing to his prominence in the scientific academy.

After dinner, Fogg returned to the reading room to digest the *Pall Mall* gazette, and around 6 PM familiar personages were settling by the warm coal fire: the noted engineer Andrew Stuart, the brewer Thomas Flanagan, and a trio of lofty bankers: Samuel Fallentin, Gauthier Ralph, and John Sullivan. Ralph being a Director of the Bank of England, the robbery was naturally prominent in their fireside banter, with much speculation on whether the thief was a professional jobber, and a gentleman or not. Word having been sent out to many ports and cities, with a £2000 reward promised, all but Stuart seemed confident the detectives of the world would eventually nab the culprit, wherever he may have fled.

Stuart was thus a natural contrarian, a temperament which Phileas Fogg now counted on.

By now Stuart and Flanagan had partnered against Fogg and Fallentin for some whist, Fogg's only discernable public passion. When Stuart suggested how easily any thief could disappear, the world being big enough for it, Fogg inclined the conversation in a desired direction with a quiet comment between deck cuts, "It was once." In short order the bank robbery was forgotten, and the card players were speculating how fast one could travel these days.

Ralph ventured how one could go all the way around the world in only three months, which Fogg then refined to an explicit eighty days. He had read the *Daily Telegraph*, you see, where just such an itinerary had been set out, steamship and rail connections intimated. Sullivan had read that account as well, and obligingly nurtured Fogg's planted seed by sprinting over to retrieve that very issue.

Fogg's whist partner that evening, Samuel Fallentin, recounted the *Daily Telegraph* itinerary for them all with some fascination:

From London to Suez via Mont Cenis & Brindisi, by rail & steamboats	7 days
From Suez to Bombay, by steamer	13 "
From Bombay to Calcutta, by rail	3 "
From Calcutta to Hong Kong, by steamer	13 "
From Hong Kong to Yokohama (Japan), by steamer	6 "
From Yokohama to San Francisco, by steamer	22 "
From San Francisco to New York, by rail	7 "
From New York to London, by steamer & rail	9 "
TOTAL	80 days

While Stuart could accept the numbers, he was certain it couldn't be done in reality. He offered a litany of plausible delays: bad weather, accidents, even truculent natives, to which on each Fogg replied with a deliberately smug, "All included."

It did not take long to goad Stuart into wagering £4000 that Fogg could not possibly travel around the world in only those eighty days.

That seemed audacious enough, but Fogg went further, offering his entire Baring's account of £20,000 as stake for any who would take it. That dangling prize summarily brought Fallentin, Flanagan, Ralph and Sullivan into a bet so profligate that it could not possibly elude general interest.

Which was exactly as Fogg intended. The wager was the most perfect excuse Fogg could contrive on short notice to do what he was about to do: break his inviolate routine in order to be in certain very distant places at certain very specific times, and be openly seen to do so, without arousing the slightest suspicion because he was, after all, only hurtling along in pursuit of a bet. It had taken Fogg only the time to walk from his home to the Reform Club to have meshed all his mental gears on this and see the scheme entire. That the *Daily Telegraph* had supplied him with the particulars so conveniently was but a serendipitous coincidence Fogg was most happy to exploit.

Thus it was that Phileas Fogg of London became committed to travel around the world and return to the Reform Club at 8:45 PM on Saturday, the 21st of December. As it was only 7 PM, Fogg insisted they finish out their hand of whist. He and Fallentin's play netted Fogg twenty guineas.

4. IN WHICH PHILEAS FOGG CONFOUNDS PASSEPARTOUT, WHO EXPECTED SOMETHING ALTOGETHER DIFFERENT

Having left the Reform club at 7:25 PM, and not being expected back until midnight, Fogg had to call Passepartout twice to bring him downstairs, to inform him that they would be leaving for Dover in ten minutes. Passepartout did not initially realize that meant the two of them. He expressed even more surprise when Fogg explained they would be going all the way around the world, and in eighty days.

"By the end of November we are certain to be crossing the Pacific Ocean. Later we will be traversing much of America."

"Later?" protested Passepartout.

"That *is* how America is located," Fogg declared with the merest smile. "Don't worry. All is planned."

They would be traveling *lightly*. Passepartout was instructed to pack Fogg's carpetbag with shirts and stockings, some stout shoes for walking (though Fogg doubted they'd be doing much of that) and coats suitable for varied conditions. Anything else they needed, they'd buy along the way.

Passepartout discovered the carpetbag already contained a small traveler's toiletry case, featuring miniature shaving implements and other related gear. To that he quickly packed the specified items, to which he added but one of his own treasures: an exceptionally unblemished copy of an American newspaper recounting the impending flight to the Moon by Impey Barbicane. And, of course, he had his own comb.

It was just coming on 8 PM when Passepartout returned downstairs, the packed bag in one hand, Fogg's mackintosh and cloak on the other arm. With a copy of *Bradshaw's Continental Railway Steam Transit and General Guide* tucked under his own arm, Fogg briskly dropped a very plump roll of Bank of England notes into the carpetbag, £20,000 worth he had released from his own wall safe, with which they would lubricate their progress. Passepartout was enjoined not to lose sight of it.

Although after sunset now, there was still some twilight as Fogg double locked the door of No. 7, and lead the way to the end of Savile Row, giving a deferential nod at the Royal Geographical Society occupying No. 1, to hail a cab to Charing Cross station. Passepartout caught sight of the Woman following them, and doing likewise.

Their cab pulled up at the railroad station and its grand hotel frontage at twenty past eight, the Woman's conveyance close behind. When a bedraggled beggar woman holding a child appealed to Fogg for charity, without hesitation he gave her the twenty guineas he had won at whist the hour before. Passepartout was most moved by Fogg's generosity, learning more of his human nature by the moment.

While Fogg bought two First Class tickets to Paris, Passepartout surveyed the station for the Woman. He had to admit she was not easily spotted, even with the benefit of her fairly distinctive attire that day. He finally located her eclipsed by a portly gentleman whom she had likely engaged in conversation as fortuitous camouflage.

Proceeding to the trains under their huge iron arch roof, Fogg and Passepartout found the Reform Club quintet of Fallentin, Flanagan, Ralph, Stuart, and Sullivan, there to see them off, Stuart taking pains to be absolutely clear as to when Fogg was expected to be back at the Reform Club in order to win his bet. This delay afforded Passepartout an opportunity to confirm that the Woman was also on the platforms, ricocheting casually from one human cover to the next. She was still evidently alone.

Settled finally into their compartment, the boat train to Dover set out at 8:45 PM, the light drizzle now playing along the windows adding to the gloom of Passepartout's disposition, though not the imperturbable Fogg's.

Roundabout Sydenham, Passepartout blurted out that he'd left the gas on in his new room back at Savile Row.

Fogg smiled oddly, "I wish I had known that," and advised Passepartout that it would burn at his expense.

Arriving in due course in Dover, it proved exceedingly challenging for the Woman to remain invisible aboard the ferry across the channel, as the rain made a promenade by the rails rash, forcing her to frequent the common room along with the other passengers, though she managed to position herself as far as practicable from Passepartout and his stranger sitting at one of the tables. At one point the needs of biology must have triumphed over those of surveillance, as she removed herself to the Ladies' privy.

Fogg promptly pulled an envelope from his coat pocket, extracted a blank sheet from it, and set that and a pen down before Passepartout. "Specify as many as you can of those in Baltimore and Tampa most worthy of independent investigation. Quickly, before the lady returns."

Passepartout arched an eyebrow at that, but did as he was told, scribbling and thinking in succession. Though the ship's lantern lighting was far from adequate, Passepartout showed no difficulty seeing. After he had put down some half dozen names, he silently slid the paper and pen over to Fogg, who positioned the sheet behind the other in the envelope, and dropped it into the carpetbag.

All done before the Woman returned.

"What do you know of her?" Fogg asked Passepartout.

"Nothing, unfortunately. She's made no attempt to speak to me, nor have any of those I take to be her confederates. Not that I was stopping long enough to investigate."

"And now she has pressed on alone," Fogg said. "No chance to signal any of them, or retrieve any of her luggage. That could be to our advantage. Clearly, though, great incentive to her not losing you."

"And now *you*, monsieur," Passepartout reminded.

Fogg shrugged, "If it relates to Barbicane, they will likely become very confused soon enough."

Once they had resumed the Paris train at Calais, early on October 3rd, Fogg permitted himself a nap. While Passepartout's eyelids closed on occasion, not long passed before he opened them again, ever holding tight to the fortune-laden carpetbag.

The rain was letting up when the train arrived in Paris, on schedule at 7:20 AM. With all the globe yet to traverse, here at least they were punctual.

Just as they pulled into the grand *Gare du Nord*, Fogg's watch quietly chimed twice. He found its six rings largely unchanged: "**?**" still held court by *IX*, "**O**" and "**N**" hovered between *X* and *XI*, "**A**" was still static at *III*, while the blank ring by *VI* had been joined by "**B**", both their jewels still dull. He snapped shut the watchcase firmly.

As they alighted from their car, Passepartout saw the Woman doing the same farther on. He wondered whether Fogg had as well, impressed by now with how much he apparently apprehended without seeming to see anything. The Woman duly followed them from the station, to hail a carriage to follow Passepartout and Fogg wherever they would go.

None of them had noted the elderly but surprisingly agile gentleman who had watched the Woman following Passepartout and Fogg, and now took his own cab to the *Chemins de fer de Paris à Lyon et à la Méditerranée* railway station, or PLM for short.

Fogg and Passepartout were already seated at a table at the station café, the Woman ensconced a few chairs away, when the gentleman, a man in his middle sixties, dapperly dressed, arrived and set himself down without invitation.

"Ah, Dupin," Fogg said flatly, "I expected you here already."

He smiled. "Boat-train schedules being what they are, your departure from London must have been precipitous."

"Passepartout, this is Auguste Dupin." Turning to Dupin, Fogg explained, "I am travelling around the world as part of a wager, my new servant in tow. We have a short time to take breakfast, while you recount what you discovered."

"I did as you asked, despite the short notice, and assume you will be appropriately appreciative." Fogg nodded, and Dupin reciprocated,

"*Merci.*"

Dupin drew in a breath, his expression drolly animated, fingers often waving as he recounted: "The Professor lives on the upper floor of his residence. Witnesses (neighbors, servants. including his presently inconsolable valet Conseil) saw nothing untoward, all doors and windows having been properly secured for the night. It being moonless, not much could be seen, though many heard to some degree a mysterious whining vaguely exterior. My inspection of the apartment confirmed the signs of forced entry through the doors of a rooftop terrace—which the Paris police had previously observed, and attributed to some team of gymnastic ruffians dexterously scaling drainpipes from the ground."

Disdain for the unimaginative dripped. Dupin's fingers flicked.

"The superficial similarities of this case to other midnight invasions in my experience I dismiss, in favor of a more intriguing solution that perhaps explains why you have consulted me, and with such haste. The police did not sufficiently appreciate two long parallel indentions along the roof, quite consistent with something of considerable weight, approximately ten meters in length and almost that in width, alighting temporarily on the roof, abrading it as if repositioned before its full bulk came to bear, thus stressing its tiles and rafters, which I confirmed by further inspection of the attic."

Dupin paused, "I am led to presume the Professor was abducted by some manner of very advanced airship, nothing at all so flimsy as the familiar balloon gondola." Tossing a wary smile at Fogg, "So *curious* an episode to come so soon after his other curious episode, don't you think, his recently chronicled adventures with that revenge-minded Captain you too cannot quite let go of."

Without further word, Fogg extracted £2000 from the carpetbag, along with the envelope which he placed atop it. As an impoverished chevalier, Dupin was grateful for the former, but it was the puzzle presented by the letter addressed to him that properly set his mind racing. "America," his lips pursed as he read on.

Passepartout had plopped his hat on the table and aimlessly managed his hair, smiled, and returned the comb to his pocket with a shrug.

"Interesting," Dupin offered pensively, "Maryland ... Florida."

Seeing Dupin turning to the second page, Fogg spoke. "Inquire of the names appended on the last page discretely, *unobserved*. You have our itinerary and shall apprise us of your progress as indicated, bearing in mind the public nature of telegrams."

Dupin nodded, replaced the letter in the envelope and slipped that and the money into his inner coat pocket, only to lean in to offer, oh so casually, "And what of the determined woman in turquoise who followed you from the *Gare du Nord*, now so insouciantly taking coffee nearby?"

Fogg suppressed a smile, but appreciated not only the difficulty of putting anything over on Dupin, but how effortlessly he would end up well ahead of you, winking. No better man for the critical challenge ahead.

"Passepartout is her lodestone," Fogg said, "We'll see how long she sticks to him." Then he warned Dupin, "See to it no one sticks to *you*."

Dupin replied with a confidently charming smile.

With dispatch, Fogg paid the breakfast bill and he and Passepartout set off to buy tickets for the next leg of their journey (to Turin via Mont Cenis, the train leaving at 8:40 AM). Dupin awaited the inevitability of the Woman gracefully sweeping after them, nibbled on the last of his food, and only then went on about his own business. Unobserved.

For the first time since leaving London, Passepartout felt oddly calm as the train pulled out of the station, even as he knew the Woman was aboard, as though Fogg's preternatural complacence were finally rubbing off on him. Still, Passepartout's curiosity did get the better of him, "You have a professional detective on retainer?"

Fogg chuckled, "Ah, Dupin. I engaged him some years ago to inquire how one might go about learning to build a submarine boat. It is not the most common of knowledge, even for a brilliant mind. The French being pioneers in that area currently, Dupin was a propitious choice. According to his investigation, nearly twenty years ago there were several foreigners attentively following the work of Borgeois and Brun. The elusive Nemo turned out to be one among them."

5. IN WHICH SEVERAL MATTERS OF IMPORT, KNOWN AND UNKNOWN, BECOME CLEARER TO PHILEAS FOGG

The rail journey through southeast France into Italy was uneventful. The Woman kept her distance, even at their station stops, for brief sprints to the privy or hastily nabbed food. Fogg slept as they rolled through the Alps that night, in and out of the new Mont Cenis tunnel without a thought. Once more, Passepartout flirted with napping now and then.

The train arrived at the imposing new Porta Nuova station in Turin at 6:35 AM that Friday, October 4th. There being almost an hour before the connection to Brindisi, Fogg took advantage of the time to have a professional shave, then strolled out to the columned entrance for some air and to see what little he could of the city (no longer a capital since its removal to Florence in the recent flux of Italian political unification).

Passepartout remained inside, observing at prudent remove the Woman spending some minutes at the telegraph office, sufficient to have dispatched several messages of substantial length, but not tarrying to receive any replies. By now Passepartout found tagging her whereabouts almost a parlor amusement. Almost—since it plagued him that he did not know who had employed her or what all they might know about him. Or whether entangling Fogg in this adventure so precipitously would be bringing the Englishman into hazard as well.

Fogg and Passepartout were ensconced in their train compartment, ready for its 7:20 AM departure, when three light chimes struck on Fogg's watch. A smile crossed his face, and he opened the case to inspect its circuiting bezels. Then he started, bolt upright in his seat, and swung around so that the timepiece's XII was directed whence they'd come.

That "**N**" lay just past *VII* far away and the dim unmoving "**A**" was now by *XI* did not surprise Fogg in the least, nor that the equally static "**?**" rested just past *XII*, and the blank ring and "**B**" continued to hug *VI*. No, it was the "**O**" that galvanized his interest: located now between *XI* and *XII*, its gem sparkling more brightly than ever before. This one had definitely been on the move, and was now back behind them, likely somewhere in France. Doing what?

There was a whole day for Fogg to speculate on that as the train cut across Italy to proceed down the Adriatic coast, and the longer they traveled the more pensive Fogg became. Whatever thoughts he had on any of it he did not communicate to Passepartout.

The scenery was agreeable, at least—it was Italy, after all—and there were several stops at various stations along the way, for food and relief, all in varying states of new as the full line had only recently been completed. The Woman was still occasionally to be seen.

Fogg was at his quietest just before falling to sleep that night. Passepartout did not know what to make of it.

The Adriatic train arrived at Brindisi at 4 PM that Saturday, October 5th. An English language newspaper among those at the station caught Fogg's attention with a long front page account of how Fogg's Reform Club wager had rocked the London scene. He purchased the piece to learn that dozens of major papers had declared his endeavor the purest folly, including the *Daily News*, *Morning Herald*, the *Standard* and, most portentously, *The Times*. The *Daily Telegraph* (whose itinerary Fogg had expropriated) stood alone on his side.

Traffic in wagering on the journey escalated so quickly that there were already "Phileas Fogg Bonds" on the Exchange.

Fogg tucked the paper under his arm as they took a carriage to the piers to catch the SS *Mongolia* for Suez and Bombay beyond, scheduled to sail at 5 PM. Tickets bought, boarding accomplished, and from the railing Fogg and Passepartout could see the Woman striding up the gangway. A most persistent lady.

Awaiting the ship's departure, Fogg plopped into a chair in the lounge to finish his paper while Passepartout accompanied a steward to attend to their suite. Midway down the third page, Fogg broke into the driest knowing smile. There was a curt announcement that Professor Aronnax had suddenly turned up at his residence. His dutiful valet and assistant Conseil resolutely assured the press and gendarmes that the Professor had not been kidnapped after all, but had only undertaken an investigation of certain rare marine invertebrates, whose specialized nocturnal breeding habits were as yet improperly known to Science, committing the oversight of not rigorously communicating beforehand his intent to his temporarily nonplussed associates.

After completing the rest of the paper, Fogg got up and added it to those on a nearby reading table, already stocked with examples in many languages, there to benefit their fellow passengers. Fogg had strode away to familiarize himself with the lay of the ship by the time the Woman glided by to scoop up the paper. In her furtive observance of Passepartout's new companion, the earlier purchase of it stood out as the only time he had shown an interest in the public press, so she resolved to be as equally apprised.

Passepartout rejoined Fogg as the liner steamed from the harbor, bearing a review of their suite as unexpectedly spacious and comfortable. He had also inspected the grand dining saloon, which served four meals daily (breakfast, lunch, dinner, and a supper at 8 o'clock) and was well-appointed with fine table runners and plush chairs. Passepartout had arranged for them to have a table to themselves (leaving a chair for the essential carpetbag) rather than be seated at the long common tables running parallel down the middle of the hall, where safeguarding the bag's contents from prying neighbors and elbows might be considerably less easy.

"Very good," Fogg said.

The dinner was agreeable. From their table to starboard they could not adequately identify the Woman among the sea of bobbing heads around the hall, a colorful mix of civilian passengers and a sizable contingent of British troops deploying to India. Both Fogg and Passepartout were confident she'd turn up eventually, which indeed she did, in a manner that surprised them both.

Fogg was, remember, enamored of whist, and scouted out available players after dinner in the lounge on the deck above the dining saloon. Sir Francis Cromarty, resplendent in his army uniform, turned out to be a fellow enthusiast, and with Passepartout recruited as third they lacked only a fourth.

"In need of a partner?" sang a most ingratiating voice. It was the Woman, now attired in a refined rose dress, courtesy of her having worn a garment with reversing qualities, a seamstress trick she'd learned from prior experience in the theatre, but unable to make use of these last few days until she had a cabin to perform the transformation. A hurried canvas of other ladies aboard ship had further secured fresh undergarments and toiletries by trade.

Fogg invited her to sit with an extended hand to the empty chair opposite his. Introductions commenced.

"I'm Marie Hammond."

"Sir Francis Cromarty, Brigadier-General."

"Phileas Fogg, and my man Passepartout."

Play commenced, with Cromarty and Passepartout partnered opposite Fogg and Hammond, revealing all to be at least adequate whist players. After a few hands, Hammond inquired, "So, where are you gentlemen bound?"

"Off to join my corps in Benares, ma'am," Cromarty ventured, "That would be in India."

"So far away." Hammond smiled to Fogg, "And you?"

Passepartout interjected, "This is the celebrated Monsieur Fogg, who has wagered to traverse the entire globe in but eighty days. I am his humble servant in this enterprise."

Hammond was momentarily thrown off at that, having been so intent on following Passepartout that she had no opportunity (or cause) to keep up with any of the hubbub mounting on *L'affaire Fogg*, and had yet to read the newspaper she had retrieved from the reading table.

"Eighty days? Is that possible?"

Fogg offered a casual, "So we shall ascertain."

Back on point, Hammond asked, "You are continuing all the way through then to Bombay?"

"And thence across India," Fogg replied.

Hammond turned to Passepartout, "Your loyalty to your master will doubtless be of great service to him in this. You're an employee of many years?"

"Oh no, ma'am, Monsieur Fogg only engaged me on the very morning of his wager, our departure most impromptu."

Fogg put in, "And you, Miss Hammond, what campaign are *you* embarking on?"

"Mrs.," she corrected. "My husband always wanted to go and see the wonders of the Orient, the Pyramids of Egypt, or even farther. On a caprice we have decided to carry out that dream. I'm to meet him in Suez."

"So traveling alone now?"

"Like you, Mr. Fogg, it was a *whim*."

Cromarty turned paternal beside her, "Well madam, no offense, but a lady skirts danger without at least a maid or better, like this Queen I shall play on your Knave."

"I am thus advised," Hammond smiled, "Thank you."

Later that night, in the seclusion of her small Second Class cabin, Mrs. Hammond finally got around to reading the newspaper she had seen Fogg carry aboard and had read so attentively. The accounts of Fogg's impact on the London markets earned her grudging admiration. Fogg, the creature of habit, was capable of sudden audacity. Was it just accident, then, that Passepartout had caught onto his coattails?

She had been tasked with following Passepartout because a most distant and generous personage (known to her only discretely as a certain "Mr. M.") had come to employ the former Confederate Colonel who knew of her own background and experience, and what it would take to overcome her reluctance to resume it. It was nice to have visited London again, but now she was on a ship headed for Egypt, and if Mr. Fogg was indeed intent on traveling around the world, Passepartout with him, that was farther than she was prepared to go, especially with her luggage and hired assistants still back in London, awaiting her return.

Although she had read the same newspaper as Fogg, Mrs. Hammond had not been struck by the brief announcement concerning Prof. Aronnax. Had she realized its full significance, she might well have shrunk from further encounters with any of those who *did* know of its full significance.

Such being the pitfalls of limited information.

6. IN WHICH MRS. HAMMOND, CONFOUNDED AS AN OPERATIVE, BETRAYS A VERY NATURAL IMPATIENCE

During the four day journey across the Mediterranean to Egypt and the Suez Canal, there was ample opportunity for whist, played without stake long into the night in the lounge, purely for the pleasure of it—at least for Fogg and Cromarty. Though there were other card players aboard, Passepartout was more than willing to balance out Mrs. Hammond. He seemed genuinely intrigued by the very idea of playing cards as a human social pastime so trivial, yet capable of engendering such intense focus and participation, while how much of Hammond's interest was to keep close to Passepartout was impossible to tell from her consistently genial manner.

After a few days of this, it could hardly have escaped her attention how Passepartout never partnered with Fogg in her presence. By this arrangement, the servant could deposit their carpetbag on the floor between himself and Fogg, out of anyone else's convenient reach. That they never left it unattended in their cabin further precluded any surreptitious inspection.

Given how many hours the quartet whiled away in this manner, punctuated by comments on cards well or poorly played, tricks blundered or triumphed, little more could have been said about either Fogg or Passepartout afterward than before. Cromarty actively reminisced about his military experience, family heritage, and concerns for the future of the Raj in India, but however she probed, Hammond could extract from Fogg and Passepartout nothing beyond that one was an Englishman traveling around the world, and the other was his newly acquired French servant.

Nor had the steward who attended to Passepartout and Fogg revealed anything of moment when she pumped him on it. To all observation, Fogg and servant were polite and circumspect travelers, free enough with gratuities to ensure the smiling cooperation of any livery they encountered.

That defense also meant Hammond was unable to obtain seating at Fogg's dining table in any manner that would have not been accounted effrontery or intrusion. Hammond turned that failure over in her mind as she stood at the large balcony that overlooked the dining saloon, watching as the luncheon crowd filtered in. She caught the briefest glimpse of Fogg and Passepartout, the latter lugging their carpetbag, to take up their accustomed table down to her left, hidden from view by the decks that split into two galleries flanking the central high vault of the saloon. Once again she'd have to go down alone, take up a seat beside some voluble stranger, and while away the time until she could resume her next assault on Mount Whist.

Their arrival at Port Said slowed their naval progress, as night sailing was not permitted in the canal itself. The traffic here consisted mainly of steam vessels, for the new canal not only rendered the long Cape of Good Hope route obsolete (hurting British warehouses that had thrived on the slower African route)—it discouraged sailing ships who found the Egyptian short cut impractical because the prevailing winds once in the Mediterranean blew as westerlies. Such were the unintended economic consequences of technological progress.

The *Mongolia* proceeded in the leisurely queue, stopping on the 7th in Lake Timsâh halfway through. There was a surreal counterpoint in the dark silence of the lake to the tunes played on the ship's pianos by passengers musically skilled or not, sometimes accompanied in song by those who could or could not actually sing, but surely took pleasure in the effort. A cascade of sonatas and popular ditties of the swarm of European regimes ascendant in these lands of ancient heritage and simmering colonial resentment.

However many passengers gawked at the bleak grandeur of this artificial river through the desert, the dedicated whist players in the lounge were not among them. Mrs. Hammond counted it an accomplishment of Pyrrhic character to be Passepartout's partner that night, allowing her to sit closer to Fogg at his right, while observing the servant's expression in something other than profile. That didn't help. And they lost most of the hands to Fogg and Cromarty besides.

On the following afternoon they traversed the appropriately named Great Bitter Lake, as scenic as any body of water could be, ringed by searing sands and bare rock devoid of vegetation. The canal veered east at this point, and the card playing resumed that evening as they stopped in the Little Bitter Lake.

With the port of Suez to be reached the following morning, Hammond was back as Fogg's partner and pressed her game to the limit. Finessing one of Cromarty's aces with a lowly trump, she exclaimed, "Like winning a battle! I feel like Napoleon—or better, Ulysses Grant, since he's their President now. You know, my husband, although English, fought for the Union over in America. Have *you* ever been to America, Passepartout?"

His being the next card to play, Passepartout tossed in his lowliest of the lost ace's suit. He decided then to concede something the woman already knew: "I have been in many places, madam, including America."

"Oh? Were you a valet there?"

"Nothing so serene. Laboring has often been my fate. It is something you quickly tire of, however, and flee when able. Being a valet is much cleaner, I assure you."

"Will you be stopping to see anyone you know when you and Mr. Fogg get to America?"

Fogg put in, "I foresee no time for that. Catching the next train or boat will be our sole object."

Cromarty looked disappointed. "Seems too bad a rush you're in, Fogg. Mrs. Hammond at least intends to marvel at something in Egypt. You'll only have the sooty windows of railroad cars and ship railings to remember when you get back home."

"That *is* one way at least to keep from getting into any trouble," Hammond said, "So many places in America can be wild and dangerous, especially to those unfamiliar with them."

"You speak from experience?" Fogg asked.

Most seriously—and even honestly—Mrs. Hammond replied, "I do Sir. Yes, I do."

7. IN WHICH EVENTS AT THE PORT OF SUEZ OCCASION SEVERAL CHANGE OF PLANS

The SS *Mongolia* completed the 103 miles of the Suez Canal on Wednesday morning, October 9th, turning west and briefly doubling back north to drop anchor at the port of Suez at 11 AM, a half hour later than expected. Since the liner had thirteen hundred miles ahead of them, south through the Red Sea—then into the Gulf of Aden and on another sixteen hundred across the Indian Ocean to Bombay—voluminous coal loading commenced over the next four hours, while small boats pulled up like anxious gnats to the liner to convey passengers to and from the main quay.

Fogg instructed Passepartout to take his passport to the British consul to have it visaed for Bombay. This was not actually required of a British traveler, but Fogg wanted an official stamp in place to verify their passage through Suez regarding the wager. He watched from the ship's railings as Mrs. Hammond boarded Passepartout's launch just as it was about to set out.

With Passepartout and Hammond on their way, Fogg crossed to the other side of the liner and targeted one of the smaller boats, a little steam launch, offering its pilot a fine reward if only he could convey him and his carpetbag to whatever spot on the quay lay closest to the telegraph office, doing so without waiting for any other passengers, and then return him to the liner. A fee was agreed on and Fogg set off.

While Fogg's boat slipped off from port, Passepartout's launch arrived at the quay. Mrs. Hammond for once did not hover, but set off on her own, while Passepartout looked around the crowded pier asking where he might find the consul in order to have a passport visaed. Finally a short fellow intervened to see if he might be of help, and learning Passepartout's intent, told him the gentleman of the passport would have to appear in person before the consul at his residence (which was not far from the quay at the corner of a square) to be properly certified.

The man had not identified himself to be a certain Detective Fix, one of the many broadcast to the world in search of the Bank of England thief. Fix had become convinced that he had the very culprit in his sights, Passepartout's Mr. Fogg. Enticing Fogg from the *Mongolia* on this pretext of the consular stamp, he had only to arrange for his sequestration until a warrant could be obtained from London.

Fix felt confident as he watched Passepartout meander back through the throng to catch one of the launch boats.

By this time Fogg had landed farther down the quay, and made for the telegraph station to see if anything had arrived for him. The plain structure had a fresh sign announcing it belonged to the new Eastern

Telegraph Company, a consolidation occasioned by the recently completed submarine lines to Aden and Bombay laid by such vessels as the giant *Great Eastern* (whose old Atlantic captain was now a General Manager of the ETC).

Having been away from London for a week now, Fogg expected several messages and was not disappointed: Dupin had sent a succinct RECEIPT 6TH from Paris, and SAILING 8TH subsequently from Le Havre.

Both pleased Fogg, and he turned around to find himself tête-à-tête with Marie Hammond.

Fogg quickly buried the telegrams in his coat pocket, nodded pleasantly and started to go, but Hammond caught his arm. "I fear to intrude, but how much do you know about your new man, Passepartout?"

"I beg your pardon?" Fogg gripped the telegrams tight.

Hammond turned melodramatic, waving her furled parasol at him, "Call it ladies' intuition. I sense *secrets* in him. Just take care with him, Mr. Fogg."

"I appreciate your concern. Do give your *husband* our regards, and enjoy your trek to the Pyramids." He started off, then offered as afterthought, "Though strenuous, I understand the view from the summit of Cheops can be quite inspiring."

Fogg not unreasonably surmised that Mrs. Hammond was about to send a telegram or two herself, but otherwise planned to hold no further interest in her unless she reappeared to follow them on to Bombay. He returned to his waiting boat, and they set off for the *Mongolia*. As the little steamer chugged across the harbor, Fogg took out the telegrams, resolutely tore them into repeatedly smaller fragments, and sprinkled them like confetti into the water.

Because Passepartout had to wait for a boat to fully load before it set out, it was utter coincidence that his launch and Fogg's were simultaneously docking on opposite sides of the liner, unknown to the other. Encountering one another in a gangway passage, Passepartout reported that he had failed to obtain the requisite visa and that Fogg must report in person for that formality. Fogg, as familiar with regulations as any mortal of similar temperament might be, thought that odd, but duly complied.

Catching the next starboard boat, Passepartout also informed Fogg that Mrs. Hammond had earlier followed him.

"Yes, I know. I saw her from the *Mongolia*. She was adequate at whist."

To Fix's consternation, the consul visaed Fogg's passport without objection. Fix fidgeted silently from an alcove as the consul did his duty, having no legal authority to do other than stamp it, once the nominal fee was paid, and unwilling to take the suspicions of Fix as justification for holding the traveling Englishman or his servant.

Outside the consul's residence, Fogg squinted in the Egyptian sun. "Our shoes and shirts are proving inadequate, for climate or terrain. See if any are available hereabouts, for yourself as well. There's ample time before sailing, three PM—one Greenwich. If you like, you might also see if Mrs. Hammond is still on your trail, or about to abandon you for her postulated spouse. Don't dilly, though, in case the ship steams early."

After Fogg set off for the *Mongolia*, Fix emerged from the consular house to attach himself to Passepartout with no less guile than Mrs. Hammond had. Except in Fix's case, it was Fogg who had his attention and Passepartout merely the conduit to it. But Fix was no more successful than she had been in extracting from Passepartout any genuine information.

As they made their way to a shop where shirts and shoes might be obtained, Passepartout transparently regaled Fix with nothing that wasn't actually true: that Mr. Fogg was traveling around the world, and quickly, keeping their watches to Greenwich not local time, and possessing sufficient funds to accomplish all this with ease. Passepartout even admitted how the gas burning in his room would, over those eighty days, more than exhaust the salary he was due as Fogg's valet.

By now Fix wasn't listening. All that Passepartout had said only confirmed his unyielding deduction that Fogg was the fleeing thief, using his ill-got gains to finance his escape, and Fix bid his leave to arrange for the only response open to him. Since the consul would not exceed his powers to hold Fogg until an arrest warrant could arrive, he would have to follow the miscreant himself, telegraphing London to request a warrant and hoping to bring writ and Fogg together somewhere ahead, on some soil where British jurisdiction held scepter. Fortunately, Britain ruled near half the world in one way or another, and great swaths of it were certain to be crossed by Mr. Fogg.

Aboard the *Mongolia*, Fogg awaited Passepartout's return in the reading lounge, where he found a recent English news sheet that reported the latest about his own circumnavigation. A Royal Geographical Society report released on the 7th had been so highly critical of his chances that the Fogg bond values plummeted, waves of bettors abandoning his cause. A lonely exception was the aged and paralyzed Lord Albermarle, who stood by his £5000 bet even as the odds against soared.

Fogg let out a sharp exclamation, loud enough to have startled

Passepartout had only he been there to witness. Then he turned morose, tossing the paper on the table. Of all people, now to be dependent on Fogg's success, one old man showing what must have seemed to those who knew him to be the most unwarranted of confidence in a complete stranger.

An hour to spare before sailing, Passepartout returned to the liner with the new provisions, which Fogg deemed satisfactory, but noted Passepartout had bought nothing new for himself.

"I saw nothing to suit me." Passepartout paused. "I caught no sight of Mrs. Hammond. No way to know if she has a husband."

"It may be that simple, and the Hammonds are off north to Giza. But if not, we have made no secret we are sailing to Bombay. If her masters have not lost interest in us, we should assume they will arrange for someone to resume the trail there."

"Or someone to replace her here, aboard this ship. She may have had the time, while I was buying shirts."

"We'll look for new arrivals, then," Fogg decided.

Among those in the last boat landing passengers on *Mongolia*, mere minutes before it blasted its horn for departure, was the stolid detective Mr. Fix bearing one small piece of hastily arranged luggage.

8. IN WHICH PASSEPARTOUT REMAINS ADRIFT OVER FOGG'S UNDERTAKING

By the eight o'clock supper as the *Mongolia* plowed south through the Red Sea, Fogg and Passepartout had come to suspect that Mrs. Hammond had indeed quit the chase at Suez, leaving Passepartout the luxury of forgoing the play of whist, which he had judiciously concluded was a pastime of striking pointlessness.

Passepartout found more to challenge his observational acuity trying to remember which of the ship's passengers were holdovers from Brindisi, and which were fresh travelers at Suez. The uniformed men seemed largely interchangeable to him, despite minor variations in whiskers or eye color. The women were somewhat more distinctive in their often bright frocks, except that custom and propriety dictated they change their attire several times in a day, soon confusing his attempts to associate a particular configuration of smile or hairstyle with a readily recallable couture.

Fogg and Cromarty found two more whist partners. A Mr. Andrade was heading to the tiny but wealthy Portuguese colony of Goa, some three hundred miles south of Bombay, to take up a post as tax collector. The other was the Rev. Decimus Smith, returning to his parish in Bombay. Neither had boarded the vessel at Suez.

Fix initially kept to himself, catching glimpses now and then of his quarry, until the following day when Passepartout spotted him and immediately recalled their encounters on the Suez dock. They exchanged introductions and pleasantries, Fix dissembling by identifying himself as an agent of the Peninsular Company that operated their vessel, and quizzing Passepartout whether Fogg's claimed trip around the world might not "conceal some secret errand—perhaps a diplomatic mission?"

Though he seemed unprepossessing, as Passepartout couldn't rule out Fix being Hammond's replacement, he welcomed his company after that, especially after Fix began to generously spot Passepartout a whiskey or ale in the ship's bar, an assist to idle conversation which Passepartout found a more stimulating novelty than whist. Judging by Fix's reaction to the ship's inevitable rolling in the waves, the alcohol may have served him more functionally as a restorative distraction.

Several days were spent in this manner, Passepartout strolling about deck, chatting later aimlessly over a drink with Fix, while Fogg and his carpetbag gravitated to the evening's card play.

Mongolia passed the ruins of Mocha at the south end of Arabia that Sunday the 13th, traversing the "Bridge of Tears" into the Gulf of Aden the following night, and turning eastward. On Tuesday afternoon they stopped for four hours at the line's large coaling station at Steamer

Point by Aden, part of a ring of settlements hugging the remnants of an ancient volcano that now operated as a broad sheltered portage.

Fogg and Passepartout braved the day's heat to hike eastward across the headland escarpment and down into Aden itself, to have the passport visaed. Fix doggedly followed, successfully unobserved, while trying not to succumb himself to the temperature, hovering by then in the lower nineties Fahrenheit.

Passepartout didn't mind the dry heat at all, and found the bustle of Aden's twenty-five thousands most exciting, exotic compared to the ethnic uniformity of London or Paris, so many peoples from different places, going about their commerce. The Eastern Telegraph Company was certainly contributing to the city's growth, with a new three story station as large as a hotel, to shepherd the escalating cable traffic coursing along their new line to Bombay.

While Fogg and the carpetbag returned to the *Mongolia*, the Fix shadow not far behind, Passepartout delayed his return for a while to soak in all this variety.

No use wasting this visit to a place he might never set foot in again.

Passepartout seemed invigorated by this solitary excursion when he did board the liner, which steamed away from Aden at 6 PM. The schedule put the *Mongolia* to arrive at Bombay in a week. Seven more days to do pretty much what they'd been doing for the last six.

The weather grew most favorable to their voyage after Aden, *Mongolia* picking up speed and the passengers making merrier for it, the gangs at the pianos growing so boisterous on the night of the 16th that it began to erode the Olympian seclusion of Fogg's whist players, who broke up early as a result.

Thus unoccupied, Fogg strolled out onto the deck, a rarity for him so far. There was a full Moon that night, though, which did render the passing ocean and landscape particularly scenic. Passepartout, keeper of the carpetbag that evening, soon joined him.

"Mr. Fix's tab at the bar run out?" Fogg inquired dryly.

"He's retired for the night. I'm not sure he has a calm stomach for the sea."

"Hmm," Fogg mused softly.

Passepartout could contain himself no longer. "How much of your intentions do you plan to let me know about, preferably a little in advance?"

Fogg took on the manner of a firm schoolmaster educating a bright but insufficiently knowledgeable pupil. "You invited me to this task. We have only to be in the right places at the right times, with the right tools in hand. The Pacific comes before America, and we are still a long way from either. I am still working on the first; I will rely on you to fulfill the second."

"You will pardon me if I am not reassured."

Fogg collected his thoughts before replying. "It's unwise to commence a gambit without knowing where all the pieces are. I realize now there is a very big one still missing here, Passepartout, one that moves fast and in great stealth, and somewhere in India I hope to find it."

9. IN WHICH THEIR SPEEDY PASSAGE ACROSS THE INDIAN OCEAN PROVED ADVANTAGEOUS TO PHILEAS FOGG

The *Mongolia* drew within sight of the Indian coast around noon on Sunday, the 20th of October. The pilot intercepted them two hours later, and they steered around the rocky Malabar Point headlands, before turning north into Bombay Harbor. From the railings, Fogg's party were witness to a procession of grand public structures and residences, of a kind that would have done London proud—all raised up over the last half century on what had once been a set of low disconnected islands.

By 4 PM the liner had docked, passengers disembarking into the humid swelter of the city a full two days ahead of schedule.

Fogg was satisfied at that, though saddened to be parted from his challenging whist partners, save for Cromarty, who accepted Fogg's invitation to share their railway compartment at least as far as Benares. As the Calcutta train wouldn't be departing until 8 PM, there would be ample time for Fogg to attend to the visa stamping at the passport office while Passepartout acquired fresh shirts (the temperature and humidity presaging to Fogg what toll would be taken on their supply from Suez) and some proper boots (their Aden hike suggesting they might be doing more strolling on rugged or otherwise unpaved ground than he had initially anticipated). The world of 1872 was less like the refinement of London or Paris after all.

Indicating he'd be taking dinner at the *Great East Indian Peninsula Railway* station afterward, there to await the train and Passepartout, valet and Fogg went their separate ways.

Mr. Fix, meanwhile, disembarked from the *Mongolia* and set out at once for the police station, where he learned not only that no warrant had appeared from London regarding Mr. Fogg, but that the authorities here were no more willing to detain him than their consular counterpart in Suez. Fix doubted Fogg would stay obligingly in Bombay until a warrant did arrive, though, so resumed his tailing. His inclination to hit the passport office first proved spot on, finding Fogg and carpetbag exiting just as he arrived. Staying, as he imagined, fully out of Fogg's observation, Fix resolutely followed man and luggage all the way to the railroad station, both parties equally impassive to the burgeoning city's varied architecture and scenery passed along the way.

The Bori Bunder station was substantial but not grandiose. Fogg bought two tickets, and Fix swooped in after to confirm with the agent that Fogg's party was booked through to Calcutta. While Fix was thus occupied, Fogg moved to the telegraph office, where the clerk was greatly relieved to learn this was the Mr. Fogg for whom a message had been festering on yesterday's pending spindle. As Fogg expected, it was from Dupin, this time from New York: DOCKED 18TH.

Excellent, Fogg thought, pocketed the telegram and made for the restaurant. Once seated, he bent to the proprietor's recommended specialty, purporting to be local rabbit, but it proved not at all to his palate, and likely not rabbit. Fogg suspected something of a feline provenance, an animal he understood was once held sacred in India, and summoned the owner to chastise the man with his unsatisfactory culinary review.

Fix took a brief meal himself, parked in an inconspicuous corner of the restaurant, and watched Fogg not enjoying his giblet of "rabbit" from afar.

The older city west of the harbor was thick with bazaars, from which Passepartout could pick and choose where to secure the new shirts and boots. That done, though, he felt disposed to explore some of Bombay's further avenues before surrendering to the monotony of the railroad station and the impending locomotive prison. The city, named for a Hindu goddess, Bambai Mumba, sprawled around a rocky half-moon peninsula that jutted out to sea. It was only a few miles out to that far promontory, which they had sailed by earlier that morning, and Passepartout was up for the exercise and resolution of his curiosity.

Along one road, some festival was going on, and Passepartout stopped to watch the procession of brightly clad celebrants, accompanied by percussive musicians and many dancing-girls, all most animated and so presumably acclimated to the heat and humidity that otherwise sapped the enthusiasm of many a European coming to this region.

To the very west lay Malabar Hill, which over the last half century of British authority had come to be a favored district of residence for those with the money for it. Nearby was the Walkeshwar Temple dedicated to Shiva, served by a large open pool, the Banganga Tank, built over eight hundred years ago but donated to the shrine in the previous century by a wealthy merchant who had piously undertook its repair.

Strolling along the stone steps that fronted one long side of the pool, his parcel tucked underarm, he noted several people sitting reverently there, even as crowds thronged by, a mix of tranquility and bustle. The customs of this place differed so from those of Aden, or London, or America, yet shared the intensity and certainty of their disparate inhabitants' attention to rituals and conventions.

Passepartout was drawn to explore the temple beyond, its tall narrow tower trying to peek past the walls of so many intervening structures. The stairs that led up from the water opened onto a small plaza, where stood a tall and beautifully carved column set on a wide platform. Stairs to the right continued up between the buildings to the temple proper: a richly decorated steep pyramid that had been destroyed by the Portuguese but rebuilt at the time of the pool's restoration. Its interior proved not very large, but Passepartout admired as any imaginative tourist might the elaborate carvings within.

It had not crossed his mind that some temples were forbidden for non-believers to enter, buttressed now by the fist of British legal sanction, or that those who were allowed in were required to remove their shoes first.

Almost at once Passepartout was set upon by a trio of affronted priests, who drove him to the stone paving, pulling off his shoes which they hurled aside, and proceeded to beat the infidel for his disrespect. At least that was their intention, for Passepartout was quickly back on his feet, deflecting two of his assailants with precise jabs of hand and foot, hurtling them to the ground, and avoiding the third by beating a hasty retire, losing himself adroitly in the throng outside.

As he walked shoeless back into town to find the railroad station, Passepartout realized he no longer had his hat or the shirts and shoes he had bought. He was not about to go back for them, obviously, but dreaded the reaction of Fogg all the more when he tried to explain what had happened.

And what *had* happened? Passepartout thought about it all as he walked, on what it told about the beliefs people held and the actions they undertook based on them. How mere footgear could be deemed a religious insult worthy of violence, not by any intrinsic property of it, but solely by arbitrary tradition. Responses triggered as unreflectively as if jostling an automaton.

Thus was Passepartout's initial pleasure at his stroll through Malabar Hill dissipated as he trod on toward the *Great East Indian Peninsula Railway*. When his path brought him up Kalbadevi Road, past the gaudily painted Monkey Temple, the blue primates carved into the second floor pilasters grinned down, as if to remind the valet of the dangers in ignoring the superstitions of their ambitious and loquacious cousins, who so cleverly built temples and railroad trains.

Though Passepartout had one consolation: he still had his comb.

Bare minutes before the train was to depart, Passepartout lumbered into the station and sought out Fogg, who was annoyed at his tardiness, then looked down at his unshod stocking feet. Fix managed to sidle into an adjacent spot to overhear the gist of what had happened at the temple, which the detective found most interesting. While Fogg had yet to commit any infraction sufficient to allow his detention, his servant had apparently done just that. Which was why Fix, who was set to board one of the carriages for Calcutta himself, decided at the last moment to remain behind a while longer in Bombay.

Soon after, Cromarty found Fogg's compartment and took a seat, a porter positioning his tack in the rack above. The engine's whistle blew at eight, and the train slowly pulled from the station. Passepartout draped a traveling blanket over his throbbing feet. Fogg wondered whether they could avoid sweating through their remaining stock of shirts before the next main station stop. Cromarty conceded that the climate of India could be unsettling for those new to it.

One thing pleased Fogg, though: as they crossed a fine long arched stone bridge to the mainland, a check of his watch showed the fleet "**O**" bezel had come to a stop half past X, somewhere off ahead of them, to the northeast. How far it was beyond the mountains they'd be traversing that night, his instrument was insufficiently precise to say.

10. IN WHICH SEVERAL DEDICATED TRAVELERS FIND WAYS TO GET WHERE THEY NEED TO GO

In Bombay on the morning of Monday, October 21st, the rail terminal was soon crowded with that day's patrons. Waiting for the train to Calcutta were two men of steely resolution: William Gratton and Crawford Fox.

The early arrival of the *Mongolia*, while certainly agreeable to Phileas Fogg and affording Passepartout opportunity for international blasphemy, had confounded those picking up where Mrs. Hammond had left off regarding Passepartout. It had taken a little time for those shadowy personages who had employed Mrs. Hammond to find someone locally with her balance of discretion and capability, someone who knew how to follow instructions but could also improvise intelligently should the need arise.

Gratton, a hardened veteran of the British Sepoy Rebellion—with a slightly game leg to prove it—had found his recent work as the intimidating collection agent for a prosperous Glasgow engineering firm remunerative but pedestrian. Seeing to it that entrepreneurs (however speculative or competent) contracting for boilers or cranes paid promptly and without fuss seemed less challenging than this new assignment: to watch—and if necessary, apprehend and even deal with—a suspicious foreigner who may well be thinking to thwart the tide of British Imperial ambition. Or at least the ambition of those now commissioning his loyalty on their behalf.

Just as Mrs. Hammond had a month before and continents away, Gratton called on others he knew and trusted to give number to his strength. Fox he knew already here in Bombay, while Frank Stanish enthusiastically fell to post in Calcutta. All they'd need do was be on hand to follow the Frenchman called Passepartout when he arrived on the 22nd. Gratton had even befriended several dockyard denizens to alert him if the *Mongolia* came in unexpectedly early.

Very careful, indeed—except that he had not entertained the idea that "early" could have been the 20th.

Gratton's tripwire had worked, though. A native porter had taken note of the distinctive foreign travelers who had only a lone carpetbag between them, but by the time news of *Mongolia*'s precipitous arrival was conveyed to Gratton at his temporary rooms, and the presence of Passepartout confirmed, the 8 PM train had chugged on east.

So here they were, bright and early on the morn, ready to take up the scent. Gratton telegraphed Stanish from the station to come north to Allahabad and stand watch there. Provided this Passepartout stayed on the train, which he seemed liable to do as manservant to the audaciously rapid celebrity Fogg, they'd have him pocketed at both ends. That done, Gratton crossed into the waiting lounge to take a seat next to Fox, a younger ex-British Army in India man—a fellow bachelor who also pined for some adventure in his life. Alas, they would all be getting it.

Gratton extended his often worried left leg out onto the floor for more comfort, which obstacle Mr. Fix darted around as he went to buy four tickets for that same next train to Calcutta, a First Class ticket for himself and three Third Class fares for the affronted Brahmin priests of the Malabar Hill temple.

ര ഇ

Three hundred miles ahead of them, Fogg's train was progressing along the north bank of the Tapti River, which ran through a broad valley. Around half past noon they stopped at Burhampoor, where a quick breakfast was taken, and Passepartout bought a resplendent pair of Indian slippers, decorated with costume pearls. They were absurd but serviceable, and amused him a bit as well.

The train pressed on through more mountainous terrain all that day and into the night. Passepartout pondered whether Fogg and Cromarty felt pangs of frustration at not being able to shuffle cards all those hours. At eight the next morning, Tuesday, the 22nd of October, the train stopped at the village of Kholby. And by *stopped*, it was to say absolutely concluded, for there was no more track ahead. The newspaper accounts of the line's completion being, as the saying goes, somewhat premature.

Passengers were instructed to disembark.

Sir Francis and Passepartout were incredulous at this, while Fogg remained unperturbed. A conductor officiously reminded them that the line's schedule, clearly posted at their various stations, had a proviso (admittedly not in the largest of typeface) advising travelers that, for the time being, they were responsible for providing their own transportation for the fifty miles separating Kholby from Allahabad, whereupon their purchased ticket would once again be conjoined with an actual train.

Those passengers who *were* aware of the line's hiatus were among the fastest in dispersing among the village's huts and farms to procure the limited means of transport, from wagons to ponies. Fogg's party joined the hunt, but discovered nothing further available for hire. A knowledgeable villager advised them that there might be some conveyances arriving later that day, bearing passengers going the opposite direction, here to take up the train that would be returning to Bombay. That prospect was rather too vague for Fogg, though. As they were two days ahead of schedule, he was up for walking it, a prospect which appalled Passepartout in his charming but not very durable slippers. Fortunately, the valet had identified a possible transport in the tame elephant kept by a nearby resident.

Elephants were actually becoming a rarity in 19th century India, especially males, prized by would-be Barnums around the globe. This one, named Kiouni, was being trained as a war elephant, though not very successfully. Still, the owner was reluctant to let his prospective livelihood be rented, even at a princely £40 per hour. But Fogg was now hot on this task by then, and over Cromarty's objections offered to buy the animal outright. At a mesmerizing £2000, Kiouni's owner relented.

Hiring a guide proved considerably easier, as a local Parsee lad by the name of Omeed volunteered his own howdahs of novel design to carry passengers on the animal's flanks—though seeing how free Fogg was with his money may have played a part, of course.

While the howdahs were being rigged, Passepartout was sent into the village to acquire provisions for their journey, and Fogg offered to take Cromarty along as guest. When Passepartout returned, Fogg and Cromarty climbed into the not very comfortable howdah seats, their respective bags crammed in with them, while Passepartout (now with a new hat bought at Kholby—a curious round-topped chapeau that took his fancy) straddled the saddlecloth on the animal's back, and the Parsee guide directed from the neck. At 9 AM they began jostling along through the acacia forest towards Allahabad.

Their guide diverted from the meandering railroad line being constructed to gain twenty miles by going straight through the forest, which was accomplished at a surprisingly fast gait that caused the howdahs and their passengers to lurch constantly. Riding atop the back, Passepartout's previous experience as a circus acrobat proved of utility after all, and he found the experience actually exhilarating. It was certainly not a dull train ride.

At 11 AM they stopped for an hour to rest, Kiouni taking water at a spring and then foraging on the vegetation. All were impressed with the animal's stamina and retained docility. Cromarty warned that they were nearing the still independent principality of Bundelcund, a land convulsed recently by violent adherence to the not fully suppressed murder cult of Kali, and that they should be on their guard until they reached Allahabad.

The landscape of forest gave way that afternoon to open dry plains, dotted by shrubs, making it easier to see longer ways, but likewise easier to be spotted from a distance themselves. Belligerent-looking Indians were occasionally seen, but none made a move on their fast-striding beast. That speed produced a hint of a breeze that compensated slightly for the great heat and bright sun.

଼ ଼

Back at the village of Kholby, Gratton and Fox found better luck than Fogg when their train to Calcutta pulled to a stop at dusk. A large group of passengers venturing in the other direction were just arriving in the village and readily gave up their horses to the more insistent travelers. Mr. Fix and his priestly witnesses also availed themselves of this fortuitous resource, and when they learned of Gratton's plan to press on along the railroad construction line through the night to Allahabad, arranged to accompany them.

The other passengers were very wary of this scheme—who knew what banditry or peril might await them in the dark? But Gratton, Fox and Fix were all armed, Gratton and Fox knowing much of the lay of the land (the Brahmins were not actively consulted), and the resolute band set off along the forest path, relying on the light of the waning half Moon for navigation.

By that time, Fogg's elephant was crossing the Vindhias Mountains, an expanse of lightly vegetated aired plateaus of fairly low elevation. Nearing the edge of the range, they encountered what was left of an ancient building, broken walls and mostly roofless, which could have been some old fort outpost or even someone's modest residence. Their guide had them take shelter in it for the night. "We have done well today," Omeed announced. "Twenty-five miles covered, half way to Allahabad."

The Parsee cobbled up a small fire, the night turning cold at this altitude, and Cromarty was grateful to warm himself by it. But Fogg was in less hurry to join him, walking off past the ruin to stand on a promontory, watch in hand, peering out at the dark landscape below. Occasionally the growls of some distant reptile or owl call broke the stillness up on the slopes.

Leaving Fogg alone to his reverie, Passepartout hiked along a circuit away from their encampment, stopping to almost comb his hair several times. Looking back at Fogg from some dozen yards distance, the Englishman in urban coat and formal hat struck an incongruous silhouette in the moonlight, perched on a rock like some commander surveying a battlefield from high ground.

Passepartout whispered quietly, "What are you able to see, that I cannot?"

They resumed their journey at six the next morning, Wednesday the 23rd of October. Progressing down into the valleys below, at noon they skirted around the village of Kallenger on the Cani, a tributary of the great Ganges. Omeed thought it advisable to avoid moving through populated settlements. They were now but twelve miles from Allahabad.

Stopping later beside a banana tree, they plucked off several as a welcome snack. The weather was turning cloudy, which shielded them more from the direct sun, but did not ameliorate the heat. Still they pressed on. Fogg had taken to consulting his watch more frequently, and seemed increasingly pleased with the time.

At 2 PM they entered a sizable forest, which shade the guide found a convenience. But two hours into the vale, the Parsee suddenly stopped. Listening intently, the sound of approaching music could be heard, a grand Brahmin funeral procession with musicians and singers escorting a ceremonial cart bearing a fierce red statue of the goddess Kali, pulled by four zebus. A most extraordinary sight.

Their now highly troubled guide had them all disembark and remain as quiet as possible, while he led Kiouni farther into the woods, hoping to keep their company unobserved while the priests and their attendants passed.

Among the band was a richly adorned young lady, so heavily laden with jewels and gold that she seemed to have trouble walking. Behind her a squad of men, menacingly large swords swinging from their waists, carried the remains of their raja on a splendid bier, and Cromarty at once realized they were witnessing the prelude to a suttee—the intended ritual sacrifice of the ruler's bride when his body was cremated the following dawn.

Once the procession had passed and they could speak again, Cromarty explained the prevalence of this barbaric practice, though noting that the sacrificed woman did so voluntarily, or at least insofar as failing to comply would have left her so ostracized and reviled that her survival would have counted for little were she to remain among her community.

Omeed then objected that in this case the victim was *not* going to her death voluntarily. She was a Parsee like himself, by the name of Aouda, and had heard she was under extreme duress, even now possibly under the controlling intoxication of hemp or opium.

Fogg resolved on the spot to rescue the woman.

☙ ❧

While Kiouni and his passengers were thus preoccupied in the perilous forest of Bundelcund, Gratton's equestrian band had made excellent progress along the incomplete railway line. No miscreants had taken notice of them in the moonlight, and they had exchanged nothing beyond the most perfunctory of grunts by way of conversation. Stopping for only the briefest of watering for their steeds at dawn, and forgoing both food and sleep for themselves thereafter, they were now arriving at Allahabad sorely in need of both.

Fix was happy to discover from the stationmaster that Mr. Fogg had apparently not yet arrived to resume his journey to Calcutta. Fix arranged for his quartet to take the next train there, on which he planned to finally sleep, and obtained for himself a meal in the restaurant to assist his hard-earned slumber with palliative digestion. The Brahmins fasted and prayed outside beside a tree.

Gratton and Fox were met by Stanish, who had reached Allahabad on the afternoon of the 22nd without delay. Telling those at the station he was awaiting friends from Bombay, he had camped out in the waiting room, napping, getting quick meals, and relieving himself as rapidly as he could to keep dutifully on watch of the quaint little locomotives coming and going. And so he could report no one matching the description of Passepartout had appeared.

They were ahead of their quarry at last.

Gratton and Fox were soon asleep in their waiting room seats.

11. IN WHICH PHILEAS FOGG LEARNS MORE ABOUT AN UNSEEN CONVEYANCE AND THOSE ASSOCIATED WITH IT

Phileas Fogg uncountered no difficulty in persuading his three companions to undertake a rescue of the endangered Parsee widow Aouda. How to go about that was not so obvious.

Omeed was confident the woman would be held in the Pillaji temple lying only some score yards from the funeral pyre, which was situated beside a small stream, and which they reconnoitered cautiously at dusk. The overcast had grown more complete by 6 PM, obscuring the remnant moonlight, so they were able to move invisibly beyond the flickering pools of light of the processionals' own torches. The raja's body now lay atop the pyre, covered by a fine white shroud.

By now many of the celebrants littered the ground from pyre to temple, their guide suggesting they were likely intoxicated on liquid opium or hemp, surely to remain so until aroused for the suttee at dawn.

The temple was an unassuming box of plastered brick and wood, with only a lightly decorated roof and a single entrance, reached up short stairs now guarded by two of the sabre-wielding pallbearers. Although Brigadier-General Cromarty carried a pistol and loaned Fogg a large knife from his kit, these lone armaments and their limited numbers had to be counted against the many sharp instruments and unassessed (but presumably sufficient) skill of those they had seen among the opposing camp.

The Parsee did not think they could prevail in any direct engagement.

It was now eight o'clock. As it was possible the balance of power might shift in their favor were the guards to grow tired or depart for sleep, Fogg's company waited things out. Four hours on and it was evident that the situation at the temple had not changed in the slightest.

That left one other prospect: they had seen no guards anywhere beyond those two at the door. Most importantly, none were on patrol, leaving the rear of the temple fully unobserved from the front. Would it be possible to excavate an entry to the temple there? They had only Omeed's pocketknives available as tools, but the brick of the old edifice might prove tractable.

A half hour later, the Parsee and Passepartout were carefully scraping at the plaster on the back wall, striving to be as silent as possible as they worked to pull out brick after brick, exposing more and more of the interior plaster behind them—which they could then punch through easily once a large enough hole were made, reckoned at several feet.

Fogg and Cromarty coolly kept watch from either side, peeking around the temple corners periodically, lest any wandering priest or guard step their way and interrupt the scheme.

Suddenly cries came from inside the temple, men's voices by the sound of it. Passepartout and Omeed quickly abandoned their digging and retreated into the safety of the dark forest, Fogg and Cromarty close behind. A prudent precaution, as several guards appeared and circuited the temple. Somehow they managed not to see the bricks stacked along the base of the building, or the incipient hole in its back wall.

Passepartout worked off some of his frustration at this discouraging turn of events by climbing a tree, from which vantage he could see the temple, and more dimly, the pyre beyond it. Glancing below, Fogg, Cromarty and their guide were in unresolved conclave concerning whether they had any options left, save a direct assault (despite the risks) on the pyre at dawn, once the princess made her appearance.

None of them could sleep any over the hours that followed, and as the sky began to lighten their apprehensions only grew. The crowd of celebrants were now rousing from their lethargy. Musicians began to work their instruments, others commenced wailing songs. The doors of the temple were opened, the light inside revealing Aouda between two of the guards, her countenance appearing most nervous and fearful.

As the guards escorted her down a path to the pyre, on the opposite side, Fogg and Cromarty followed Omeed closer to the back of the crowd, who in their growing ecstasy and focus on the spectacle ahead took little notice of anything or anyone behind them. The princess was compelled up a wood stairs onto the pyre platform and laid out beside the raja's covered body. The wails and music grew more frenzied then as a priest brought a torch forward and set the oil-soaked wood ablaze, a thick cloud of choking smoke soon obscuring the growing flames, forcing those on the stair side to disperse as the fumes were blown onto them by a light westerly breeze. The guards, swords in hand, prodded those closest to the pyre to retreat to a more prudent distance.

Cromarty and the guide grabbed Fogg's arms as he was about to lunge forward on his own. It would have been folly to let him go now.

Passepartout was not behind them. In the flush of that dreadful excitement, his companions had not realized he'd slipped away, circuiting with great speed around the mob, putting his Indian slippers to the fullest test. Under the cover of that smoking cloud, Passepartout dashed up the steps, just then starting to burn, quickly pulled the raja's body from under the shroud, tossing it on the ground below like a giant rag doll, and slid up under the cloth. Such circus panache, it was all coming back to him.

To Passepartout's surprise, Aouda's head was covered by an odd cloth cowl with a clear visor in it. He could see her blink at him, and Passepartout brought a finger to his lips to signal that she remain silent. She pulled the cowl back and was about to speak, but immediately coughed in the acrid smoke. Passepartout pressed his spread hand across her forehead, sensing a slightly fevered brow, whereupon she fell into a faint.

Fogg was turning back to Cromarty and Omeed to demand they release him, when the sounds of the wails changed into screams of anguish. The shrouded raja was standing up, and bearing his unconscious wife in his arms, strode forward and began to step down the other side of the pyre, from one level of logs to the next, through the smoke and mounting flames. Some of the cultists fell to their feet, abased in prayer; others fled in panic.

Once he reached the ground, Passepartout picked up his gait, bearing Aouda in his arms without showing any strain. As he passed Fogg's company in a clip, they spun around to join him, and all broke into a fast run into the forest to rejoin their elephant Kiouni.

Passepartout handed the princess into Fogg's arms, climbed quickly onto the elephant's back, then motioned for Fogg to hand her up to him. Cromarty and Omeed assisted, though Passepartout showed such strength that he finished the task easily. Fogg and Cromarty hauled themselves back into their respective howdahs, the Parsee bounded on Kiouni's neck, and they were off.

They could hear the sounds of the suttee crowd changing then, and Fogg suspected Passepartout's ruse had been discovered. Suddenly a red flash caught his peripheral attention, accompanied by a coarse pop heard over his left ear. Pulling off his hat, Fogg found an elliptical hole now cut into it, which he surmised to have come from a passing bullet—though in the tumult of the moment he couldn't recall having heard a proper report.

They were all grateful that none of the suttee acolytes were following them. Perhaps it was all that opium they had consumed. Or the need to finish burning the raja's body. Or the swift pace of their most reliable and worthy elephant.

Passepartout held his charge gently, but most firmly, on his lap while trying to maintain his balance as the elephant plodded on into the forest and ahead to Allahabad. Investigating her cowl, he noticed it was part of a larger piece of clothing worn under her shimmering silks, of denser milky-colored fabric than any he'd have expected from a princess, Indian or otherwise. Within the limits of propriety and his need to keep good hold of her on the bobbing elephant's back, Passepartout ascertained how it apparently covered all her body, like some odd practical pajama, with the cowl and clear visor attached at the neck and now draped down along her back.

When Fogg next checked his watch, he discovered the "**O**" quivering unexpectedly at *XII*, and its gem flashing brightly but intermittently. That was novel, and Fogg turned his gaze upward, peering into the clouds, but could see nothing. At the pace they were going, little could be heard beyond the whining drone of insects and the slap of foliage they brushed past along their path.

Around seven that Thursday morning, the 24th of October, Omeed felt confident enough of their escape to stop by a small stream for a rest. Fog checked his watch again, which read 2 AM Greenwich, and the "**O**" now lay beside *III*, its jewel no longer flashing, but still as bright.

The Parsee decided a swig of brandy and water might revive his countrywoman, which it did.

Aouda shook her head, surveyed her surroundings, then her disparate companions: one fellow native with an elephant, one man in fashionable European street attire, one older man in a British uniform of fairly high rank, and the casually dressed jackanapes in those preposterous slippers who had appeared unexpectedly on the funeral pyre along with her raja's corpse. No apparent weapons.

She turned to Passepartout sternly, "Did you render me unconscious?"

He bowed and nodded, "*Pardon.*"

Aouda paused to ponder the implication of that. "You must teach me how."

"What was that commotion in the temple?" Fogg interjected, snapping his watchcase shut.

"That was an assassin. One of those allied with the *late* raja saw me putting on my protective garment, which we'd secreted in the temple beforehand—that's how I intended to withstand the flames, long enough to effect my escape in the smoke, to seemingly perish. No one would ever look for a puff of smoke after, would they? I acted quickly before he could spread further alarm. Fortunately, the guards were there to corroborate my story: that the priest accidently fell upon his blade while blundering in his opium stupor."

"The guards were your partisans?' Cromarty was now thoroughly confused, as was their guide after him.

"Of course. Only a fool would march to their own suttee pyre alone." Aouda continued resolutely, "They were faithful men, who respected the tradition of their rank, hated how the new raja, my now *late husband*, had so corrupted it after Prince Dakkar fell in the Rebellion. They were there to protect me; I counted on their swords should my plan fail. I didn't count, though, on being 'rescued' by

44

you."

Fogg nodded, "I apologize, for Passepartout's initiative."

Aouda surmised from dress and manner the relation between the two men as something akin to master and servant, and smiled, "I do appreciate the audacity of your man's trick at the pyre, it was clever."

"We were on our way to Allahabad when we came across your peril, madam, and Mr. Fogg here inspired us all to action," Cromarty explained, turning then to Fogg, "She can hardly be returned to her people."

"Of course not," Fogg said plainly, then leaned in to whisper to Aouda, "Do you have some connection with a rather unusual mode of transportation, which I believe lies presently off in that direction," pointing south.

Aouda startled, and this time it was Fogg putting a finger to his lips, continuing in a low tone, "Discretion. We shall have need to talk more later, I think, after we've taken leave of Sir Francis in Benares."

When they resumed their journey, Aouda once more joined Passepartout atop Kiouni, resting her back against his chest, thinking about her situation. Fogg called up to them, "I doubt we shall encounter many funeral pyres in the next days, so when we reach Allahabad, whatever you may need in the way of fresh toilet and dress I shall have Passepartout acquire for you. The city has 140,000 people; I'm sure there are proper shops."

"Perhaps the Princess would like to select her own couture, Mr. Fogg," Passepartout objected.

"Are you not are a follower of fashion?" Aouda asked with a smile, which he did not see as her back was to him.

"I see many clothing, some more interesting than others. Would this not be a matter of your own taste?"

"I think, Passepartout, I am curious what clothing you would buy for me."

"As you wish, madam."

The slipper of Passepartout's left foot bobbing by his head, Fogg added, "Include a new pair of shoes for yourself, Passepartout."

They arrived at the *Great East Indian Peninsula Railway* station before ten that morning, the train to Calcutta puffing at the ready. The sight of the travelers appearing by elephant, though not unprecedented for Europeans, was sufficiently unusual in these modern times to warrant some gawking from those around the station, including the Gratton party, who had come over the last few day of inactivity to fear that Passepartout was about to disappear into legend.

While the description of the man and his English companion tallied, there had been no mention of a woman, and Gratton dashed into the train station to send a hasty telegram off to America apprising those higher up of this addition, and acquire three tickets for the train to Calcutta.

Phileas Fogg, meanwhile, settled his account with their excellent guide, offering as most generous and appreciated gratuity Kiouni himself (the animal no longer being of any utility to Fogg, of course). When Passepartout dashed off on his clothing buying errand, Crawford Fox, loitering with Stanish outside in the eighty degree heat, told the latter to follow him.

A protective Cromarty accompanied Fogg and Aouda into the station, followed by Fox, who crossed casually to Gratton to let him know he had set Stanish on Passepartout's tail.

"Good man," Gratton said, though he was worried that Passepartout might be doing a bolt on them. As for Fogg and the oddly dressed Indian woman who had ridden in beside Passepartout, Gratton didn't know what to make of them. Had they picked her up along the way as a native diversion, a courtesan to alleviate their natural desires in between stations? She was pretty enough for it.

"I need to send a telegram," Aouda was telling Fogg.

"At my expense, please," Fogg smiled.

"To Hong Kong."

"No matter the distance, Aouda."

"I have some relations there."

"Someone you could stay with, good," Cromarty put in.

At the station telegraph window, Aouda quickly penciled: TELL R AMETHYST SECURE. D TO DIADEM, AWAIT FURTHER A.

Fogg was pleased to discover he had another message from Dupin, from the American prairie city of Chicago, which had been held for him since its arrival the previous day: 22 OCT WABASH DEPOT & WAREHOUSE, IN WALKING DISTANCE.

Meanwhile, Passepartout searched the adjacent avenues of Allahabad in vain for some counterpart to the shops of Regent Street, finally encountering an elderly Jewish second-hand merchant, who had on hand a workaday dress, fur coat, jacket and toilet articles he thought might be adequate for Aouda—and a pair of shoes for himself. A rapid negotiation settled on £75.

On the dash back to the railroad station, Passepartout noticed the equally fleet man following him. Fogg, Aouda and Cromarty were waiting at one end of the train carriage, Gratton and Fox at the other, when Passepartout and Stanish bounded on board the train in unison.

Passepartout was saddened that, once again, he hadn't opportunity to visit any of the sights of this Holy City, laying at the juncture of the sacred Ganges and Jumna rivers. From their compartment window, he caught a tantalizing glimpse of the nearby towers and domes of the walled garden of Khusro Bagh, a grand collection of red sandstone mausoleums of the old Mughal style. So many different ways among these people to make buildings, he mused, built for worship of their gods, their dead, or their locomotives—but train windows seldom the best way to see them.

Aouda inspected Passepartout's clothing haul. "You're a shrewd judge of size, Passepartout."

"Are the garments too antique? There was little time. The coats you will probably not need in this heat, as yet, but I follow as commanded," shooting a glance at Fogg.

"On this day I shall take utility over fashion. Thank you."

Once the train was chugging along, Aouda asked a favor: that the gentlemen stand and turn their backs to allow a change from her suttee regalia to the new attire. They obliged with alacrity, the more portly Cromarty standing in the middle, while Passepartout and Fogg posed on either side, one knee on the seat cushion, the other on the floor, as the train crossed the long double-decked truss bridge spanning the Yamuna River.

When finished, Aouda handed Passepartout his new shoes with a smile. The Indian slippers were finally retired to Fogg's carpetbag, along with her old frock and peculiar pajamas.

The eighty miles to Benares were expediently covered in two hours. It proved much warmer here than at Allahabad to the east, though only Cromarty showed a reaction to the hundred degree heat. The city offered a splendid collection of temples and mosques, and was famed for the saris and gold-embroidered cloth of its bazaars—where shopping for Aouda might have been most productive had they only been stopping long enough.

While the Brigadier-General was anxious to fulfill his regulation resolve to rejoin his corps near the city, met by an orderly who took hold of his kit, bidding farewell to Fogg, Passepartout and Aouda was not undertaken without its deep emotion. Sir Francis would certainly never forget his adventure in the forest of Bundelcund that October of 1872. He gave them a quick salute, on the brink of being tearful, and disappeared with his orderly into the throng.

William Gratton darted inside the station to send a telegram off to his distant clients, reporting that the (to him) unidentified British Brigadier-General had now taken leave of Passepartout, Fogg, and the (to him) unidentified Hindu woman.

Aouda, strolling roundabouts on her own, took note of that stranger's activities, and of the attitude of her traveling companions concerning him, who even now appeared to be just as attentive on the sly to those same three men who had boarded the train with them back at Allahabad.

"I think there stand Mrs. Hammond's successors." Passepartout told Fogg softly.

"Yes, I saw the one racing after you. That was clumsy of them."

"He was certainly not buying dresses," Passepartout agreed.

Aouda joined her companions by the car and commented, "Sir Francis is now departed. You had something momentous to say to me?"

Fogg smiled. "As soon as we're on our way."

True to his word, the train had barely begun moving again when Fogg turned to Aouda in their compartment to bluntly ask, "Why did you abduct Aronnax in Paris? And I know of his safe return."

This was astonishingly more than Aouda anticipated. Realizing Fogg clearly knew too much to make any subterfuge worthwhile, she replied honestly: "To learn what he knew of my brother, things that might not have been revealed in any of the public accounts."

"Nemo your brother?" Fogg nodded, "Yes—that explains much."

She sensed Fogg's sympathy. "We visited what little remained of his island base. He'd begun setting it up before his fall—somewhere to carry out experiments of a more dangerous character. But I didn't know its exact location until I spoke to Aronnax. We searched far for any sign of his vessel after that, but found nothing. Even were he submerged, my craft could have followed, had we only found some trace." Aouda looked forlorn.

Fogg's mood was her opposite, positive and confident. "A submersible that can fly, most interesting. I think our mutual cooperation is in order, for I know *exactly* where *Nautilus* is, now and at all times, and can lead you there with confidence whenever you so choose. I can even build a suitable detector, in my London laboratory—where I intend to be on the 21st of December, I should stress. In exchange for which, I believe your craft could be of great assistance to our enterprise," indicating himself and Passepartout.

"And what might that 'enterprise' be?"

"Do explain it, Passepartout."

Since candor now seemed the order of the moment, Passepartout drew in a breath. "The American Impey Barbicane plans to send a projectile to the Moon next month. There are many reasons why this must not succeed, ones sufficient to enlist Monsieur Fogg in my plan to intercept his *Columbiad* in the Pacific Ocean, utilizing if possible your brother's celebrated *Nautilus*."

Aouda thought on that, then nodded, "I can see where my ship might be of use too."

Fogg turned more serious, "It should be noted, we have already encountered agents of as yet unidentified malefactors who might be quite opposed to what Passepartout and I have in mind. Three new ones we believe to be aboard this train. Any involvement you elect to make from this point on cannot be promised to be free of potential danger."

Aouda paused a moment. "I have just disposed of a vile and treacherous husband, and contrived to appear to be burned on his funeral pyre. I think I may be up to whatever perils lay ahead." Aouda paused again, "Pacific, you say. Is Hong Kong on your itinerary?"

"It is indeed," replied Fogg, "We aim to be there roundabout the 5th of November."

Aouda bowed and smiled, "Then we have but to proceed."

12. IN WHICH THE BRITISH RAJ REVEALS THE PRACTICAL COST OF MANY THINGS OF VALUE

The *Great East Indian Peninsula Railway* train pressed east from Benares, covering hundreds of miles in a gentle arc that eventually turned southeast through the night for yet more hundreds of miles on to Calcutta, that great port on the Ganges delta founded by a bold East India Company man, and capital of British India these last hundred years.

Before going to sleep, Phileas Fogg checked his watch and found the "**O**" bezel now around *X*, its gem growing dimmer by the hour. On the move once more, it would seem, like the still more distant but slower "**N**" coincidentally beside it near *XI*. A matter now of just bringing the two together in reality, a prospect which seemed increasingly feasible, thanks to their meeting the now slumbering Aouda.

Fogg had to concede this was a welcome improvement on what he originally hand in mind, which had depended perhaps too heavily on things being as expected in Chicago, a place Fogg had never been before, and as yet knew little about. Not that he doubted his own capacity to have accomplished it, just that this opportunity seemed simpler and superior.

Fogg appreciated any more elegant resolution to a problem.

The train pulled into Calcutta at 7 AM, Friday the 25th of October, the weather an almost balmy eighty. The SS *Rangoon*, their necessary connection to reach Singapore 2200 miles away to the south on the 31st, and thence another 1300 back north to Hong Kong, wouldn't be departing until noon. Ample time to even dawdle, thought Fogg as they exited the new Sealdah Main Station.

Passepartout glanced back at its imposing but unattractive façade—a cumbersome admixture of Italian Renaissance side buildings and central glass pediment suggesting some angular Crystal Palace—partly out of architectural curiosity, but more to catch sight of the new trio doing their best not to appear to be already on their tail.

The Gratton gang pulled up short, though, when they saw a police constable meet Fogg and Passepartout outside the station. Both were ordered to accompany the officer, without further explanation, and prodding a more reluctant Passepartout with his stick—though he did permit Aouda to join them in the carriage.

Gratton consulted with his fellows. Would their further activity (and prospective promised rewards) be rendered unnecessary via such official intervention? Only one way to find out. Gratton quickly bundled his men into another carriage so they could follow at a circumspect distance. Over the next twenty minutes, this attenuated parade traversed the narrow dismal alleys of the city's native poor, then into the broader tree-lined boulevards of manicured European prosperity, passing many a confident British equestrian out for a morning's ride in their domain, to stop finally at a building Stanish recognized with a wince was a municipal law court.

This was the fruit of Mr. Fix, who had labored ever since arriving in Calcutta to exploit Passepartout's Malabar Hill outrage. Judge Obadiah, a rotund juridical stickler, as concerned with wearing only his assigned wig in court as any issue of legal consistency, heard the case promptly at 8:30, before a crowd of spectators that now included Gratton, Fox and Stanish warming seats in the back row.

Fix was in the back row too, seated off to their right and striving to be inconspicuous himself, and finally realized two of them were his traveling companions out of Kholby. That seemed a rather odd coincidence to him.

Gratton and Fox eventually identified Fix as well, as the man from Kholby with the three wog priests in tow. Strange his turning up here, thought Gratton.

Until informed of the charges, Fogg and Passepartout were suspecting their detainment was on account of their activities at the suttee—especially when they discovered three Brahmin priests were on hand as complainants. So they were rather surprised to learn this concerned the Malabar Hill trespass. One of the priests had even retained Passepartout's offending shoes as evidence.

Passepartout chided himself that he had not recognized those who had assaulted him in Bombay, confusing them by their garb and swarthy features for those seen in the night and smoke around the Pillaji temple—though in fairness, both incidents had happened quite quickly and he had other things on his mind. In any event, Passepartout and Fogg were caught dead to rights. Passepartout was summarily sentenced to fifteen days in prison and fined £300; the complicit Phileas Fogg earned a week in jail and a £150 fine. Mr. Fix could not have been more delighted.

"I offer bail," Fogg said. And he was within his rights under British law. Judge Obadiah perfunctorily set bail at £1000 each for them, which Fogg paid at once from his carpetbag. At the back of the court, Fix was livid.

Passepartout even got his shoes back, though at a ransom of £2000 they had come rather costly. Besides, he had a new pair on already, which didn't pinch nearly as much as the old.

The parade of carriages soon resumed outside: Fogg's party in one, Fix hailing the next (only now taking note of their newfound lady companion), and Gratton's brigade pulling up the rear, wondering how

Fix fitted into the picture, as boon or obstacle. Since Passepartout was sitting facing to the rear in this carriage, he could appreciate the view, and couldn't suppress a smile at the artifice of it. He almost combed his hair, but since Fogg was sitting opposite beside Aouda, decided the effort would be unproductive.

Fogg's carriage and vehicular retinue arrived at the quays at 11 AM, less a harbor proper than a vast line of masts and funnels, stopped as they could parallel to the broad riverbank, reached by waves of small skiffs and boats. The SS *Rangoon* was moored half a mile out in the Ganges, its departure flag already raised to signal an impending sail. A launch took Fogg, Passepartout and Aouda out to the liner. The next boat included Fix and several Portuguese and Ceylonese travelers. When Fogg's boat returned to pick up the last stragglers, a mix of Indians, Malays and Chinese aimed for Second Class, Gratton, Fox and Stanish were among them—and not especially comfortable to be sharing the small launch with a crowd of so many non-Europeans.

The *Rangoon* was not so large or luxurious a vessel as the *Mongolia*, nor its cuisine so competent, but by way of compensation Fogg and Passepartout now had a personable guest. With the carpetbag filling out the table, for the first time on their trip, Fogg and Passepartout dined that evening with another, Aouda.

"I wonder how many whist players are aboard," Fogg mused between courses.

"Mr. Fogg is most dedicated to it," explained Passepartout.

"I know of the game. It requires four, does it not?"

"Invariably," confirmed Fogg.

"Are you hoping to play with the men from the train?" Aouda asked.

"Not if it can be avoided."

Passepartout smiled.

Fogg added, "If they didn't take First Class tickets, we may not bump into them at all."

Passepartout amended, "And if we do, it will be by their design."

The "men from the train" dining just then down in Second Class were not, as it happens, players of whist. Gratton enjoyed a game of backgammon now and then, and Stanish likewise for dominos, but Fox took no pleasure in any pastime beyond hunting for game worthy of a shot. Not that any of the three were inclined to whiling away their time aboard the *Rangoon* in anything other than calculated pursuit of their captain's mission.

"Our first task will be to reconnoiter their cabin," Gratton briefed as he slurped on a stew. "Belongings must be searched fully, but returned precisely after, so they'll know of no intrusion. Any luggage or case locks will be your job, Frank."

Stanish nodded. He was aware only of a carpetbag, usually lugged by this Passepartout.

"You think he'll be carrying anything on him?" Fox asked.

"Possible, but we'll check on that after we find out what they're holding onboard."

Fox again, "And what of the Fogg bird, and their woman?"

"Best guess, he's running under their cover," Gratton said. "We may get news on the woman when we stop at Singapore. Until we can corner him alone, though, we'll have to be careful."

"And the man at the court?" Stanish asked.

"He called himself Fix at Kholby. We'll have to find his cabin, too, see if he's given the same name to the stewards. I'll telegraph from Singapore for background. Until then, we'll have to hold back until we learn more of him."

"You can't expect any answer until we're at least to Hong Kong," Fox protested. "Then what?"

"Ask me again in Hong Kong," Gratton replied.

Hong Kong was on the mind of Mr. Fix as well. He had made a point of staying out of the view of Fogg's party at dinner. Though he was now aboard with them, he realized a dire inevitability: Hong Kong lay ahead as the only British possession remaining on Fogg's claimed itinerary where he could bring a warrant to bear for the Bank of England robbery. Fail there, and he did not know what he would—or *could*—do next.

As for violating the privacy of a fellow passenger's rooms and belongings, Gratton's team could not be faulted for lack of executive skill. Over the next twenty-four hours they successfully located the bail-flaunting Fogg's cabin, found that the Hindu woman (identified by the stewards as one of those unpronounceable Indian surnames) occupied a room of her own on another deck entirely, while the man they knew as Fix was traveling under that name still, his cabin tucked in a corner not that far from that of Fogg's woman.

On Saturday afternoon, the 26th of October, while Gratton and Fox acted as spotters following the Fogg party, Stanish invaded first the Fogg cabin, and after thorough search, found nothing. Nothing. No luggage, cases, personal items. The place was so tidy, beds made and tables empty, it might as well have been awaiting its first occupant.

The woman's cabin was only slightly different: on a dressing table a small bundle of slick white cloth contained a brightly colored native sari dress, which Stanish recalled she had been wearing when they rode into Allahabad on the elephant two days before. Atop the bundle rested a delicate toilet case, which Stanish inspected quickly and found contained nothing out of the ordinary.

Strolling just then out on the *Rangoon*'s deck, Fogg asked Aouda, "I have been able to work out a little of what I think happened regarding your brother. You may correct me if in error. His interest in applying his motive power to a submarine vessel came after—an application of necessity?"

"Yes, our work was on the principle of it, proving it, harnessing it. We speculated on ways to apply it to propulsion, but that had to wait until we had mastered it safely. It's very dangerous, you know. That's how I came to have such protective gear, to use at the suttee. It took years to work it all out. My brother and I had ample means to carry out our experiments, though. We're related to the late Sir Jametsee Jeejeeboy—odd what our share of that opium fortune could buy. Not that obtaining pitchblende in quantity was expensive, just cumbersome. You can't imagine the *volume*. It was the refining, purifying—and developing shielding once we learned how penetrating its distillations could be."

She put her hands tight on the railing, staring out southwest to the rolling sea, and shuddered. "We were both so focused on the science of it, making it *work*, that we never thought others might take note of all that effort, want it for themselves—do *anything* to get it." Turning around to Fogg, "One day, Srikar and his wife and son disappeared. I was still so young, they overlooked *me*. I think they must have imagined I was just playing with my brother in his laboratory of melted rocks."

"Srikar, so that is Nemo's name?" Passepartout asked.

"Yes. It is right to say his name again. Srikar is one of Vishnu's thousand names, you know, when consort to the goddess Lakshmi. Except Srikar's goddess was his wife, Himadri—it means a peak of Himalayan snow. She shared no interest in his science, but was a sweet and deep oasis for his dark moods. And there was their son, Ajit—Invincible in Sanskrit. He was too young to be invincible, the last I saw him. I wept when Aronnax told me what Srikar said happened to them." Aouda was almost weeping now.

"There was a small band of Englishmen responsible for what happened to my brother and his family. Of that I am sure. Two, maybe three—people too much to be feared to mention their names, and with money enough to silence the rest. That too, I know. I did find the Raja of Bundelcund helped them in this betrayal. Nothing I prize more than to find the rest of them."

"I cannot be certain," Passepartout said, "but I sense your Englishmen may be just as curious about Barbicane's *Columbiad*."

"If so, Passepartout, we are fully in league."

"You continued your brother's experiments alone?" Fogg put in.

"Hardly alone," Aouda laughed. "But more secretively after that, most definitely. Srikar's faithful 'oak', Robur, escaped with us. You'll meet him in Hong Kong. My cousin Jeejeeh opened his mercantile company and heart to us, and several years ago he retired to Holland, leaving us to expand there at our need. That's where I completed the *Deimos*."

"Named for the moon of Mars?" Fogg asked.

"What?" Aouda looked puzzled, not a follower of astronomical minutiae. "No, the Greek mythology, twin of the god Phobos. Partly for him, but also for its meaning: *terror*. I confess to a terrible purpose for it, Mr. Fogg. I shall make no secret of that."

13. IN WHICH SEVERAL DISCERNMENTS OF AOUDA GREATLY IMPRESS PASSEPARTOUT AND FOGG

When Passepartout awoke on Sunday, the 27th of October, he stayed awhile in bed as the *Rangoon* heaved to and fro, attending to the ship's engine throbbing away below (in which he detected a far from reassuring inconsistency in its muffled vibrations resonating up from deep in the vessel's hull). Fogg was already up, adding entries to a small log he kept of their progress around the world.

Passepartout finally called to Fogg, "I think Aouda should see plans of the *Columbiad*, to know what we are fetching so she may organize accordingly."

"That is reasonable. How long will it take you to sketch them?"

"I can do better than a sketch. Perhaps we may meet in her cabin before we go to breakfast?"

Fogg gave an assenting nod, and not long afterward they appeared at Aouda's door and were admitted at the knock. "Passepartout has something to show you."

Lowering the carpetbag to the floor, Passepartout retrieved two sheets of newsprint sized paper from it, laying them out on a nearby table. Fogg arched a brow.

The first displayed a meticulous plan of the *Columbiad*, showing its bullet-shaped pilot compartment, and the multiple circular service cars connected behind it, resembling a tubular aluminum worm, annotated with full dimensions and many cross sections. Aouda turned the sheet over, to reveal a much enlarged plan of the front section alone, with correspondingly more detail.

"*Pardon*, the captions are in French," apologized Passepartout.

The second sheet showed the giant launching tube, its dimensions and metallurgical specifications for the various components; its reverse, a map of the relative location of the front capsule, showing how it was to be brought to the firing cannon along a short rail line.

Passepartout extended his index finger to the *Columbiad*'s passenger compartment on the first sheet, "It is this which must be detached from the others, and compelled along a course to bring it down close to where *Nautilus* and *Deimos* may be stationed. That will not be your task." He then indicated a chart beside the drawing, "You need to accommodate the *weight* of the craft, to see whether your machine can lift it, either from the water or fly with it over distance, and help us to decide how best to involve the *Nautilus* in its retrieval or subsequent transport. These are things, I think, best pondered at leisure—which we have in abundance before reaching Hong Kong."

"These are amazing," Aouda complimented. "How did you come by them?"

"I undertook an extensive reconnaissance of the facility. My studying too much of this may have led to my being followed."

Aouda was examining the prints closely, holding one up to the light. "I've never seen paper quite like this. It doesn't seem to tear."

"A useful quality that enhances its durability," Passepartout offered.

Fogg looked at Passepartout with eyebrow arched even more.

"It will take some time to study," Aouda said.

"They are yours," Passepartout responded. "Just guard them close."

That evening Fogg finally scraped together some whist partners, so he could while away the night hours even as Aouda remained cloistered in her cabin, pondering what her *Deimos* might do with the *Columbiad*, as yet known to her only by Passepartout's wonderfully crafted drawings.

It befell Crawford Fox to be the one to survey Fogg's nightly whist tournaments, since Stanish was dedicated to cabin ransacking, and Gratton thought his own limp might make him too memorable to be consistently inconspicuous. They were Second Class passengers, after all, and while presentable enough by appearance, clothing and manner to fit in for short excursions above, including an occasional visit to the ship's bar for some welcome fortification, they could wander around the premier areas of the *Rangoon* for only limited times lest they be discovered by some knowledgeable steward and rightly ejected from where they did not belong.

Stanish's resistant problem was Mr. Fix's disinclination to leave his cabin, apart from the briefest ventures to the privy and his dining—and not always even then, as Fix was not immune from bouts of seasickness that made the *Rangoon*'s middling fare even less attractive to his traveling stomach. Finally, Stanish had to forgo one of his own meals to conduct a search during one of Fix's sporadic appearances in the dining room. Finding only a small traveling case within, though, with nothing of revealing content—no personal photographs or letters—Fix's accommodation proved as uninformative as Fogg's and the Hindu woman's.

That left the one remaining uninspected object: Fogg's carpetbag. But whether in the custody of Passepartout or Fogg, Gratton and his men could contrive no reliable way to get near enough to it up in First Class, and alone for sufficient time, to open it and learn whether it was filled with Aladdin's treasure or merely another barren well.

Gratton was not as disappointed in this aspect as Fox and Stanish feared. "There may be something of value in the carpetbag," he explained, "but whatever is of importance to *our* commission will be in

Passepartout's *head*. What has he seen? Why did he run? Who does he follow? What does he believe? Is he radical, some Parisian Communard? He's certainly not *British*."

Fox was adamant, "I'd teach him what British means. Get me alone with him."

"That may yet come," Gratton said.

Over dinner in the First Class saloon the following evening, Tuesday the 29th of October, Aouda patted her blouse where Passepartout's *Columbiad* plans were sequestered in an inner pocket. She had discovered they could be folded repeatedly without difficulty, retaining no discernable crease, resembling more a slick fabric than any paper she knew of.

"I've decided we'll have to make a grappling truck for *Deimos*." She picked up a salt cellar with her left hand, the fingers closing around it as example, shifting it above the table but not dispensing any salt, then returned it to the tablecloth. "Tight enough to grip, but not puncturing the capsule. I'm relying on your metallurgical figures, Passepartout."

"And the weight?" the valet asked.

"It will slow us down, as much from the air resistance than the mass. And the *size*—if it were any bigger around, it would obstruct even the lateral thrusting vanes, and we wouldn't be going anywhere. As it is, *Deimos* will be less maneuverable."

Left elbow propped on the table linen, Fogg rubbed a finger on his upper lip. "How long will it take to build, and attach?"

"Days at least. Maybe more." Aouda smiled, "Robur will tally my sums in Hong Kong. I'll be sure then."

As Wednesday, the 30th of October, was the day before the *Rangoon* was due at Singapore, Mr. Fix girded his queasy stomach and dragged himself from his cabin with the object of encountering Passepartout. Fix had decided he must enlist him as a confidant, hoping somehow this could be used to his advantage should a warrant not be on hand in Hong Kong.

Once more, Fix drew Passepartout into conversation over a good gin in the ship's bar—still pretending to be crossing Fogg's path yet again by mere coincidence. Passepartout freely recounted more of what was publicly knowable (including matters about which Fix knew all too well enough): the trouble at the Bombay temple and subsequent court appearance over it, their elephant ride to Allahabad and rescue of Aouda, and their ostensible intention to bring her safely to Hong Kong.

Fix and Passepartout's nursing shots at the bar had an altogether different effect on Frank Stanish when he spotted them together, taking his own drink just then at a corner table. Was Fix somehow apologizing to Passepartout for the proceedings at the Calcutta court? Stanish quickly reported this unexpected development to Gratton, who was equally troubled by it.

The actions of Mr. Fix at his point were illustrative of the manifold uncontrollable happenstances of history. Fix was, if a belabored pun be allowed, by now too *fixed* on Phileas Fogg to properly function at what he was supposed to be, a detective. His peripheral recollection of Gratton and Fox at the law court faded the farther the *Rangoon* sailed from Calcutta. Had Gratton and his men taken First Class passage (and there had been a few empty berths still available for that), or had Fix's stomach been more possessed of sound sea legs, allowing him to stalk the *Rangoon*'s decks more diligently, their presence aboard might have been harder to conceal from him, and Fix the investigator might have been prodded to plumb the even more strained coincidence of their being on the same ship to Hong Kong.

Had Fix thought to send off inquiries about them from Singapore, would others above his rank have begun poking at the hornet's nest themselves, connecting one name with another, and others still, so that the whole house of cards would come tumbling into the harsh light of official scrutiny, Scotland Yard and the Foreign office jockeying for jurisdiction and grappling over which facets of the case were to be hushed up, and which exposed? Might such broader observation have even come to dissuade Gratton and his men from doing all that they had become grimly persuaded to do?

Instead, Fix could not even perceive how the otherwise inexplicable attention he lavished on Passepartout from one ship to the next weaved his path ever more inextricably into the travelling schedule set out in the *Daily Telegraph* barely a month before.

14. IN WHICH THE TELEGRAPH OFFICE IN SINGAPORE GREW BUSIER ON ACCOUNT OF THE *RANGOON*'S PASSENGERS

The *Rangoon* had made good time, steaming into the port at the island of Singapore (a Sanskrit word meaning "city of the lion") at the tip of the Malay Peninsula half a day ahead of schedule, at 4 AM on Thursday, the 31st of October. Aouda awoke when the ship's engines stopped, quickly dressed and went up to Fogg's stateroom to arouse them. She wanted to send another telegram to Hong Kong, which there should be time to do while the steamer was taking on coal for the long journey north across the South China Sea, their departure now scheduled for 11 AM.

After taking a quick breakfast, Fogg, Aouda and Passepartout joined the parade of passengers disembarking here, taking one of the many sampans that darted back and forth serving the ships dotting the bay, some forming strings of boats abutted one to the next, only the first of which actually touched a vessel's side. The temperature at seven was only in the middling seventies, though climbing, but feeling almost a chill presently compared to the previous Indian heat, and Aouda was happy to be wearing the jacket Passepartout had bought her in Allahabad.

Fix scrambled to follow Fogg in another sampan, needing to work in a telegram to Hong Kong warning them of his arrival and the imperative need of that warrant. Fix did not notice Gratton, Fox and Stanish shouldering their way aboard another sampan working an open gangway aft, though they spotted Fix, and skillfully stayed back, especially when they reached the quay and found Fix too was heading to the Eastern Telegraph Company office.

Passepartout was just strolling away from the station as Fix arrived, but the detective was relieved to find Fogg at least inside, his carpetbag in hand and waiting as Aouda finished her message: R ABOARD RANGOON WITH NEW FRIENDS WHO INTEND CARNATIC SAIL A.

Seeing Passepartout leaving in a saunter, Gratton told Fox and Stanish to keep on him, then worked his way toward the queue at the telegrapher's window, trying to keep out of sight of either Fix or Fogg and that woman of his.

Fix raced through his telegram to the Hong Kong police, hurrying back outside afterward to see if Fogg was anywhere in view. His heart skipped a beat when he saw Fogg in a fine carriage nearby, and the Indian woman sitting casually beside him, which then set off down a tree-lined byway. Fix hastily arranged a carriage of his own to follow them at a discrete distance.

Gratton was just then sending his telegram asking about the man

Fix, while receiving one from his American contact concerning the woman Fogg had picked up somewhere before Allahabad, reporting that nothing could be said about her identity or circumstances. That was a minor disappointment for Gratton, already inclined to relegate her to a peripheral status as an inconsequential native dalliance of Mr. Fogg.

As Fogg's carriage ride with Aouda penetrated deeper into the forests covering the island, the air became rich with the scent of the flourishing nutmeg trees. Mindful of the fact that they had a driver who may be all too fluent in English, Aouda leaned into Fogg to ask in a soft voice, "How long has this Mr. Fix been following you?"

Fogg replied in circumspect kind. "Since Suez. He's approached Passepartout many times, but not me. Neither of us know what to make of him. Passepartout thinks he might be from the Reform Club, seeing to it I'm not cheating in my journey. If so, I've never seen him there."

"Couldn't Fix have been assigned to follow you alone, leaving the three new men to keep after Passepartout?"

"Yes, possible." Fogg sighed, "There are too many possibilities. But so long as they don't interfere with our plans, they are an irrelevancy."

"Are you prepared to deal with them if they do 'interfere'?"

"We're not carrying an arsenal, if that's what you mean. I'm drawing on our speed, and the fact that we travel by public means, surrounded by others, all in plain view. It's a bold, if not foolhardy villain who resorts to violence while observed by others."

"And yet the world is full of people willing to do exactly that, Phileas. Assassins, and fanatics, who don't care how many see their villainy. My brother and his family are testament to that."

Fogg assessed that all too accurate observation in thoughtful silence.

Aouda finally said, "I am not without an 'arsenal', Phileas. Or at least will be, once we get to Hong Kong." She smiled, in a way Mr. Fogg was finding increasingly congenial to his accumulating sentiments.

While Fogg and Aouda rolled through the gardened outskirt avenues of Singapore over the next two hours, followed by the attentive Mr. Fix, Passepartout strolled up and down the several low hills of the city proper, followed by the equally attentive Fox and Stanish on foot.

Passepartout drank in the city's buildings and diverse population of mainly Chinese, but also many Malays, Indians and Europeans, all nominally under the government of the Straits Settlement reached with the distant Sultan of Johore—British and yet not quite British. So much of the city seemed to be very new, though, thrown up over the last half century since the days of Sir Stamford Raffles, albeit with a reverent nod to the charm and dignity of the region, trees and foliage abundant all about.

Apart from the occasional public edifice or church of obvious European inspiration, the bulk of the city's private buildings seemed an indistinct melding of the needs of tropical ventilation, overlain with hints of elements of the architectures of the many peoples living there, and the inclination to manifest their mounting prosperity in size and practical comfort, if not obvious opulence.

On his way back to the harbor to catch a sampan out to the *Rangoon*, Passepartout stopped at a vendor to buy several dozen fresh mangoes, a purchase of such volume that the seller deposited them with a smile into a fine net bag allowing him to carry them as a bunch. Fox and Stanish observed the transaction from behind a stout pillar of one of the crush of shops forming a wall of busy commerce along the quay.

By 10 AM, Passepartout was on the deck of the *Rangoon*, eating some of his mangoes (which he found quite enjoyable) and awaiting Fogg and Aouda's return, along with looking for Fix and the Allahabad trio presumably following them. The Allahabad men arrived first, consistent with their being on his own tail and not Fogg's, while Fix was in the next sampan docking after the one bearing Fogg and Aouda. All falling true to Passepartout's expectation.

Passepartout offered Aouda and Fogg some of his mangoes when they crossed to him on deck, which Aouda accepted with much thanks. "I was followed by two of the men," Passepartout explained as he chewed on the delightful fruit.

Fogg smiled. "Mr. Fix took a carriage through the forest after us."

"They're afraid we're going to slip away," Aouda decided between mango bites. "Not stick to the schedule."

"Or consort with people of mysterious character the moment we are out of view," Passepartout joked.

"Which, as it happens, we intend to do," Fogg said. "But not today."

The *Rangoon* departed for Hong Kong as promised, at 11 AM, steering eventually north by northeast, and sails were put up to take advantage of a strong southwesterly wind.

"This ship will need it," one of Fogg's whist partners declared that night, joined by a new fourth culled from the passengers boarding at Singapore, who asked what the man meant. Being a regular passenger on the Malay run, he explained as he shuffled for their next rubber, "As maritime construction goes, the *Rangoon* is not pride of the line. Its engines strain even in good weather. If we hit a squall, expect the pumps and wrenches to get their work."

The smooth sail coaxed Fix out of his cabin more, and sharing liquor again with him in the bar on the first night of November, Passepartout couldn't resist chiding Fix on his ever-changing destinations: "You were only going to Bombay, and here you are in China."

Feigning unalloyed pleasure at his company, Passepartout suggested then how fine it might be if only Fix would not stop in Hong Kong as he repeatedly insisted to be his plan now, but instead journey on to America and beyond with them. Fix did not express a great deal of enthusiasm for such a prospect, adding that he was not traveling at his own expense.

As they progressed north towards the French colonies of Anam and Cochin China, they encountered heavier seas and concomitant ship rolling. This made dinner more interesting that Saturday, the 2nd of November, as Fogg chased some aggressively migrating new potatoes across his plate with a fork. Passepartout began to hear the pitch of the *Rangoon*'s engines changing as well, and called this to the attention of Fogg and Aouda.

"One of my whist players is not of the highest opinion of the ship's fitting," Fogg noted.

"It would not be desirable if we *stopped* before reaching Hong Kong," Passepartout complained.

Aouda would have agreed with that, but still found his anxiety amusing. "I'd offer to take a peek at the engine room with you, Passepartout, but I doubt they'd appreciate my meddling. Not that we'd be in a position to do much about anything we *did* see. I left my foundry in my other dress."

Clouded by his worry, Passepartout missed the humor of it. "Well, I will go look, nonetheless."

The lurching of the ship seemed only to intensify as Passepartout set off for the engine room below. Passing through the domain of Second Class, he strode right past a nonplussed Frank Stanish, who turned about in the passageway and started to follow him at a distance. Lower into the *Rangoon*'s hull, Passepartout traced the sound of machinery until he reached the reciprocating leviathan at the ship's heart.

The engineers were too frantically attending to the galloping engine to pay much notice to the two passengers invading their nearly deafening sanctum. The heat and steam in the engine room prompted Passepartout to pull off his coat, draping it over one arm. Just then a great wave brought the ship's propeller momentarily out of the water, accompanied by screams of steam from the engine. Passepartout shook his head and shouted over the din, "The valves are not sufficiently charged!" He then turned to Stanish, who he knew had come up beside him at the railing. "We are not going. Oh, these English! If this was an American craft, we should blow up, perhaps, but we should be at all events go faster!"

Passepartout tried to assess the man's reaction to his calculated rant about the English, but Stanish only stood there, briefly dumbfounded. Not a hair-trigger temper, at least, that one.

The *Rangoon* splashed through the waves until its propeller once more encountered water and they resumed a semblance of powered motion. Passepartout and Stanish both grabbed at a railing until the ship steadied, when Passepartout smiled at him and headed off, slipping his coat back on once he had retired from the engine room's warmth. Stanish (who had kept his coat on) declined to follow, and returned to the Second Class passenger area to recount his mechanical adventure to Gratton.

By the evening, the gale had flipped about to a northeast headwind, noticeably slowing the ship and beginning to worry the passengers—though not Fogg, who continued his whist game without evident concern, even as some of the cards slid off the table when they hit the next huge wave.

While the dealer attended to the hand following, Fogg checked the time. It was just on 2 PM Greenwich (being 10 PM locally there in the China Sea). As for the watch's rings, all settled into anticipated positions, including the "**O**" at *XII*—until he noticed that its jewel was flickering brightly. He was not about to quit his whist game to assay the heavens out on deck, especially not in this weather, but did throw a quizzical look at the ceiling paneling and smiled. Never quite alone, it would seem, even out here in the churning sea.

Fix was by then utterly seasick in his cabin, though happy in his own way, once he learned from a passing steward who looked in on him that the *Rangoon* had fallen a day behind schedule.

The storm in the South China Sea only grew worse on Sunday, November 3rd, forcing the sails to be pulled in altogether, the masts heaving in the wind as the crew undertook the dangerous reefing. Passepartout braved the deck to observe it all, impressed with their skill and daring, then pestered everyone from the captain to the crew about how long the storm would last (an efficient subterfuge to allow him to wander all about the ship, taking note of the Allahabad trio as best he could).

Fogg played more whist that night aboard *Rangoon*, Aouda on hand this time, watching sometimes from a nearby sofa; at others, strolling around the players, trying to work out the strategy of the game

Phileas Fogg seemed so enamored of.

The bad weather abated considerably the following day, Monday the 4th of November, allowing them to unfurl the sails again and make up some of the time lost, though by Tuesday it was looking bad for their being able to make their connection to the *Carnatic*, set to sail that next morning from Hong Kong for Yokohama.

None of these concerns had any visible effect on Fogg's whist playing, as Fox confirmed on his latest fast sortie into the privileged world of the *Rangoon*'s First Class lounge. The effete monotony of it was on his mind as he left. This might be their last night at sea, so he decided he needed to grab a fast, but long overdue, drink in the bar. After downing a whiskey, then another, Fox headed for the stairs. He was just starting his descent when who should be coming up from the deck below but Fogg's woman. On impulse, he pointedly blocked her progress, planting himself on the tread above hers and stretching out his left arm to rest his hand on the railing. "I've seen you. You rode into Allahabad on an elephant, all *grand*, with your *friends*. What are you riding here on this ship, hmm?"

Aouda assessed her surroundings. No one else was in view; they were alone, potentially vulnerable. There were no lanterns or other functional protrusions on the staircase walls at anything like a convenient height, just the railings. But the man stood above her, putting gravity in her favor, and his apparent intoxication might further impair his physical reaction. If she pulled him down and around properly, quickly enough, she could possibly break his neck on the paneling, or trip him against the railing itself, the opportunity to crush his skull in the fall.

She was considering all these options, and the obvious hazards of being so rash here aboard ship, when Passepartout suddenly bounded into the stairwell from the deck above. He stopped short, and the noise prompted Fox to turn around. The look of disdainful menace on the man's face could have melted glass, but Passepartout was quite impassive, only asking deliberately, "Is it your intention to block the stairs, sir? These are *premier* class, you know. Are you lost from your proper station? Should we hail a steward to assist you?"

"I'm quite capable of finding my way myself," Fox replied finally, shaking off the alcohol's buzz enough to recover his self-possession, to dart past Aouda and disappear down the flight.

Passepartout turned to Aouda with great concern, "Was he threatening you?"

"I think he was about to. Good thing you came along though, Passepartout," she smiled, "to rescue him."

15. IN WHICH THE ENVIRONS OF HONG KONG REVEAL DIFFERENT THINGS TO PASSEPARTOUT AND PHILEAS FOGG

As preface, it must be noted that the vivid accounting of what happened in Hong Kong by the otherwise scrupulous Mr. *V.* deviated in many critical respects from the facts assembled here—most notably concerning the seeming passivity of Aouda at the (apparently fictitious) "Club Hotel" where his narrative situated Fogg's party. Whether *V.*'s more innocuous farrago was due to the intervention of any of the many persons or governments who had reason not to have more of the full story known, is of course a matter of ample historical interest, but regrettably beyond conclusive settlement as of this time.

As best as the events may be reconstructed, land was sighted by the *Rangoon* in the dim light of dawn at five o'clock on Wednesday, the 6th of November. An hour later the pilot arrived in his boat, boarding and joining the captain to guide them around the mountainous Hong Kong Island and through the narrow strait to the port on its sheltered north coast. As they were still five hours from the harbor, the *Carnatic* was expected to have already sailed for Japan.

The *Rangoon*'s stopping to take on their pilot awoke Aouda, Fogg and Passepartout, who promptly dressed for what promised to be an eventful day. Showing no apparent deference to authority or the ship's routine, Fogg approached the pilot on the bridge to ask him when a steamer would be leaving next for Yokohama. The pilot replied that one would be departing at high tide the following morning: the *Carnatic*, which had delayed her departure to make repairs to one of her boilers.

Fogg's luck had struck again.

Steaming in from the west along the estuary, the liner passed the imposing Praya Reclamation Scheme, a parade of new buildings (many complete, but others still under construction) along a massive concrete esplanade that considerably extended the city's rentable waterfront. Observing their nearly identical façades from the deck, Passepartout wasn't sure he liked these three story stacks of vaguely Mediterranean arches, but it was clear from the profusion of similar structures that this was proving to be the popular Hong Kong edifice *ala mode*.

The *Rangoon* was small enough to pull up to the quay jutting out in the middle of the old port. After some inquiry, it was learned that the *Carnatic* was docked farther on in Victoria harbor, and set to sail at five on the morrow.

"Sixteen hours." Knowing how advisable it was to appear merely the visiting tourist while in the port, Fogg turned to Aouda, "Do you know a good hotel?"

"The Hong Kong is just up Peddar Street," Aouda replied, pointing towards the avenue off to their right leading south. "Quite new and deluxe, good food."

The hotel was adjacent to another recent addition to the skyline: a tall campanile clock tower just chiming one. That would be 5 AM Greenwich, Fogg noted on his watch, along with the "**O**" now resting half past *I*, its gem exactly as bright (and not flashing) as he expected it to be.

The mild seventies temperature and the trees shading Peddar Street made for a pleasant stroll up to the hotel, a four story structure which Passepartout found to be yet another built in the city's trademark faux Mediterranean. Fogg arranged for two quite adequate rooms on the third floor. Both were spacious, some forty feet long by twenty-four wide, one corner near the door screened for a bedroom, the rest appointed with tables and sofas as a sitting room, opening in turn onto a balcony with a charming view of the clock tower in the square—and a somewhat less charming view of two of the Allahabad men, loitering casually at its base: the man with the limp and the surly fellow Passepartout and Aouda knew from the *Rangoon*'s staircase.

"I surmise the third is inquiring about us at the hotel desk," Fogg said to Passepartout.

Aouda rapped at their door and entered, crossing to their balcony as Fogg motioned for her. "Admiring the view? Oh, I see," she said when she followed Fogg's gesture to the pair below. "We'll need to hire a carriage to my Diadem. Do we want them following?"

"We still need tickets for Yokohama," Passepartout said. "If *I* went for them, they would likely follow me."

Aouda nodded, then crossed to a table where she saw some writing paper, pulled a pen from her jacket pocket, and commenced drawing. "Here, directions to my building. You must *not* be followed when you come."

"Buy three cabins, two if necessary," Fogg said. "We'll watch you go out by the tower from here, see if they follow."

Which they did, Stanish joining his fellows by the campanile, conversing a moment, then setting off after Passepartout, Gratton pressing on with commendable animation given his dodgy leg.

Not long after, Aouda, Fogg and carpetbag stepped out of the hotel lobby, past the line of willing but far too slow human-carried sedan chairs, and sought out the first serviceable wheeled vehicle for hire.

ଓ ଛ

Passepartout took his diversionary journey in his stride, giving him a chance to see more of Hong Kong's scenery, even as he was pursued by the Allahabad trio. Throngs of Chinese, Japanese and Europeans darted on their business, including every so often an old native gentleman attired in bright yellow robes, standing out in the crowd in a manner which struck Passepartout as oddly funny, reminding him of wizened canaries.

The urban western half of the harbor had now given way to still forested hills off to his right, one capped by a modest cathedral (something at least to break the architectural uniformity of the place, he thought), another promontory ascended by the four massive parallel buildings of the Victoria Barracks, martial symbol of the importance now accorded this burgeoning and strategic port city.

Continuing on east to the piers, Passepartout saw a barber and stopped for a shave, though truth be told his stubble was only slight. While keeping an eye on the Allahabad men outside, he asked the barber about the yellow-clad old fellows he had seen, and learned that wearing that Imperial color was an honorific privilege of those over eighty. A reminder of how rare living to over eighty could be among these people. How such transience must have affected their culture and attitudes, he thought.

Eighty years. Eighty days. Eighty minutes—which, realized Passepartout, was an adequate estimate of the time he'd be devoting to his ticket-buying mission, before he made for Aouda's unique facility.

ಚಿ ಸಿ

Fogg and Aouda's carriage was by then approaching her cherished Diadem, which lay on the outskirts of the city, one among many buildings flirting with the slopes of the small mountain on the southwest side of town, well beyond the posh new Praya Reclamation Scheme. Aouda had the driver stop a few blocks short of their destination, though, which they walked to only after the carriage pulled away.

"Jeejeeh & Cie Ltd" was a sprawling structure bearing faint traces of that arched Hong Kong building fashion, featuring a row of what used to be shops along its street arcade, shuttered now but not unoccupied. Aouda entered by way of the old main company entrance, finding a wiry old Chinaman seemingly nodding in slumber inside, but he immediately roused and smiled a toothy greeting to see her.

"My friend, Phileas Fogg," she introduced, then knelt beside the old man and took his hand gently in her own, as she continued to Fogg, "Xie here has been a great treasure, staying on from my cousin's days. I learned so many skills of physical defense from this 'frail' old man." Then she asked him, "Is Robur here?"

"In the Sanctuary with the Beast, safe and sound. I believe he has much to tell you."

"And I him." Aouda took Fogg toward a rear door, then turned back to Xie, "Phileas' man Passepartout should be visiting us later. Put a friendly lamp in the window to welcome him, ring when he arrives, and send him on."

The rooms beyond the door had been taken over by all manner of machinery, lathes and foundries—and other equipment he could not easily identify in the shadows, some of which were attended by workers, who traded satisfied nods with Aouda as they passed. She led the way out back into a wide courtyard, across which was the larger of the buildings, bearing a pair of massive closed doors fully two stories high. Aouda went in by a normally scaled portal to their right, which opened onto a chamber more akin to a railroad terminal, full of tall clear space, in the middle of which, positioned directly behind those huge doors, squatted Aouda's *Deimos*, its beluga whale white hull gleaming in what Fogg immediately recognized to be some very proficient electric lighting, arrayed in diverse ceiling fixtures.

Aouda spotted a tall man attired in a nautical looking uniform, *sans* identifying decoration, examining some instruments nearby with a grave expression, the sort of man who had seen much in a life to forget, and perhaps some also to regret. "I must speak to Robur," Aouda said. "Do inspect my 'unusual mode of transportation', Phileas."

Fogg deposited the carpetbag at the bow of *Deimos*, which was unlike any vessel he had ever seen. As Dupin had so correctly deduced back in Paris, it was some ten meters in length and almost that wide. From the front it resembled an oval tube rolled onto its broad side, and ribbed by an x-shaped set of flanged metal runners curving out from nose to tail, the lower ones functioning like skids, obviously responsible for the marks on Aronnax's apartment roof—the ones above of the same proportion. Both pairs of skids evidently functioned as a protective guard, as their outside edges were trimmed in a black rubbery ribbing, slightly giving to the touch.

Both runners and the general hull had many small covers along them, hinting at the doubtless ingenious mechanisms hiding inside, presumably requiring access for servicing or repair. At the moment, the machine did not rest on the side skids, but was raised from the ground on four wheels positioned just inboard of them, each much smaller around than a carriage or train wheel, and covered by thick black rubber similar to the flange trim. Standing that close, down on his haunches, Fogg could hear a distinct low hum from within, again of a character unlike that of any engine of his acquaintance. Reaching out to lay a hand on the metal, he could feel it vibrating slightly, while noticing the striking absence of seams or protruding rivets.

Aouda watched Fogg looking over her creation, while Robur told her, "I didn't know at first what to make of your rescuers. I took a shot at one of them on the elephant, my apologies. Then I saw some of the priests running after you. Dispatched them. The ones behind them thought better of that and retreated."

Getting to his feet, Fogg peered at the windows up above the flanges on *Deimos*' front, dimly seeing a thicket of gauges and levers amid the ducting on its cabin ceiling inside, some instruments alight with more electric glow. Stepping around the craft to its port flank, he observed about halfway back a large closed hatch with a smooth porthole, the door small enough to not interfere with the runners above and below it, the bottom skid featuring a flattened section that clearly functioned as an entry step.

All over the hull were slits, each a few inches wide and about a foot in length, with vanes inside them, reminding Fogg of a shark's gill flaps. In addition, there were perhaps a dozen small apertures, some three inches in diameter, all covered by tiny covers like metal eyelids.

Fogg stepped away then to get a better view of *Deimos*' profile, where a broad horizontal fin formed out of its hull aft of the side hatch, and several others emerged dorsally from its rear. At the back, the flanking fins flared into two long tubes over a foot around, bearing vertical vanes positioned behind them, putative rudders in Fogg's estimation. From here he could also see there was an angular windowed cupola on the very top, right ahead of where the side hatch was, and what looked to be another entry hatch on the back of the cupola. Apart from the wheel handles on the hatches, some mounting cleats visible on the upper aft deck, and the functional main skids and fins, the *Deimos* was strikingly free of external protrusion.

Aouda brought Robur to meet Fogg. As they shook hands, Robur declared, "I was concerned about the storms, so followed your course with *Deimos* to see the *Rangoon* was all right."

Fogg smiled, recalling his observation of that very thing from his whist game watch checking four days before.

"He also had some of our men slip aboard the *Carnatic* yesterday, to sabotage her boiler," Aouda put in.

Robur said modestly, "Nothing perilous for them. It only delayed a few hours, I imagine, but figured that could help."

"It did indeed," agreed Fogg, who now knew much about this Robur's independent initiative, and Aouda's justifiable reliance on her 'oak'. Turning to the craft, "You appear to have developed an entirely new form of propulsion." Indicating those shark flaps, "You use the same both in air and under water?"

"Yes. It's something like Mennons' Caloric Engine, if you're familiar with that."

Fogg nodded, "A turbine."

"Except much faster, and no blades, magnets doing the job. In that way gases and fluids can be accelerated equally well. *Deimos* can fly at two hundred miles an hour, hover almost effortlessly, and go a hundred and fifty even on land, on its wheels."

"There are very view places with pavement suitable for that," cautioned Robur.

Aouda laughed. "True. We mostly keep the wheels down to roll *Deimos* in and out of the courtyard, where we can fly out or land, discretely. I've given Robur a sketch of the grappling truck I have in mind for the *Columbiad*, along with the metallurgical tolerances from Passepartout's plans." Turning to Robur, "The best place I can see to attach it is in the wheel openings."

"Flying with the covers down could pose a problem settling in water."

"I know," Aouda said. "You'll have to check all my figures, to see the weight and mountings don't over strain the seals inside."

"Also see that our rope ladder will drop long enough to reach the ground if we have to land with the craft in tow."

"I hadn't thought of that. Thank you, Robur." Aouda turned to Fogg, "Now for a question to you, Phileas: how do you know where *Nautilus* is?"

Fogg pulled out his watch, opened the cover and motioned for them both to attend to it, holding the timepiece facing *Deimos*.

"Eight o'clock?" wondered Robur.

"He keeps his watch on Greenwich time," explained Aouda.

"It's the rings around the face I call your attention to." Fogg pointed at *XII*, "The 'O' is your *Deimos*, right here, which is why its gem is so bright."

"'O', for what?" asked Aouda.

"Orient," replied Fogg. "And the 'N' is Nemo's *Nautilus*, here by the ten hour. Given our direction, it means he's well east of us, out in the Pacific, beyond the Philippines I'd say, possibly exploring the ocean depths in that region." A faraway look flashed in Fogg's eyes, "There is so much to explore." Pulling back to his point, "You see, even though you're all relying on the same energy, making it in much the same way, you've assembled the engines to do it in different ways, changing the number and strength of certain tiny particles thrown out in the process, variations as individual as a signature. My watch shows where they are."

Aouda grew alarmed, "*All* the rings on your watch are measuring them? There are so many others?"

"Two I know only by their emanations, though I think before I reach London I'll know more about them both. The ones not lit, are not *lit*."

"You don't perceive any of them as a danger?" Robur asked.

"No. I don't. Not if they belong to who I think they do."

That seemed to satisfy Aouda, who then mused, "So, Srikar is in the Pacific."

"Yes. Passepartout's plan is to bring *Columbiad* down farther north, though, somewhere between Japan and the Hawaiian Islands. That would be," Fogg calculated, "some two thousand miles from here, a ten hour flight at your full speed."

"And out and back," noted Aouda. "A day just for that. Time, time, time. We still have to locate my brother, persuade him to help us—and we still need to construct a lifting carriage that won't break our egg or the *Deimos* carrying it."

"We have *two* weeks," Fogg reminded.

Robur put in decisively, "The grappler is novel, so should be begun first. *Deimos* has to be kept close to test its mountings, correct any mistakes. Time lost to contact Nemo."

"Can your craft pick us up from a ship at sea?" Fogg asked Aouda.

Aouda furled her eyebrows, "The *Carnatic*. If calm enough, I suppose so," then broke into a broad smile, "We've never done that."

"The problem would be coordination," Fogg said, "Doing so unobserved by the passengers, and knowing when and where exactly to rendezvous. Unless *Deimos* were following us, like a leopard."

Aouda couldn't resist looking smug. "We have a way to communicate at sea, Phileas. A telegraph without wires."

Fogg showed no surprise, started to say, "Ah, Mar—." Then he thought a bit, and said, "Yes, very good."

16. IN WHICH SEVERAL CONSEQUENTIAL DECISIONS ARE MADE ON THE SPUR OF THE MOMENT

Arriving finally at the *Carnatic*, Passepartout was by now not surprised to see a disconsolate Mr. Fix pacing around the pier. He asked Fix whether he was there to continue on with them to America, and Fix replied with no trace of pleasure that he would be doing so after all. Fix and Passepartout even went into the shipping office together to obtained their cabins, one for Fix and three for Fogg and party, and the agent told them brightly that the ship's boiler had been expeditiously repaired, allowing the liner to depart that evening, at half past six—and not at tomorrow's high tide, as planned.

Passepartout was about to leave to inform Fogg of this welcome news, the prospect of gaining back some of their time lost on the *Rangoon*, but Fix insisted on talking with him over a drink. Out the corner of his eye, Passepartout saw the limping man enter the shipping office, leaving the other two associates outside to track after himself, as he followed Fix off to a nearby tavern. And opium den.

The establishment was surprisingly well decorated, little of the "cheap dive" about it. Several dozen men were inside, drinking as well as smoking balls of opium paste from red pipes available on all the tables. A few patrons were already laid out unconscious on a large cushioned bed at the back of the room, and as others dropped off, attendants dutifully added their somnolent frames to the mass.

The two men who had been accompanying the limping man entered and ordered a beer and brandy.

Fix bought a bottle of port for himself, and one for Passepartout, and began to dangle the prospect of bestowing on Passepartout a £500 share from a reward he claimed he was due, if only the servant would help him delay Fogg two or three days more in Hong Kong.

Not a gentlemanly thing for the Reform Club men to do, Passepartout objected, prompting Fix finally to admit that he had nothing to do with the Reform Club, but was actually a police detective trying to apprehend the elusive Phileas Fogg for the £55,000 stolen from the Bank of England on the 28th of September. The warrant he had been trying to get from London had eluded him all the way around the world, and here they were.

Passepartout had to concede that latest story explained a great deal about Fix's behavior. And, given how much money Fogg had been spending this last month, and how Fogg's physical description had so agreed with the bank thief's particulars, it was not even an unreasonable conclusion for Fix to have jumped. He wondered what Fogg would make of it, though, when he told him. As for Fix's generous offer to reward Passepartout for betraying Fogg, he would have none of that, and told Fix so.

He realized then, that would have been true even had Fogg been only what he appeared to be, someone intent on going around the world in eighty days, just on an absurd bet. In only this one month, Passepartout had found Phileas Fogg to exemplify much that was held admirable among human folk, his generous and good nature, coupled with a mind of a cleverness and calm that counted a great deal with him too.

The limping man had by now entered the tavern and had joined his fellows at their table, though not ordering a drink. Fix was sounding most conciliatory over his rejection of the detective's attempt to suborn him, and was now offering him one of the red pipes from the table. Not unlike his inspiration at the temple of Pillaji two weeks before in India, Passepartout had an idea.

He accepted the pipe, and Fix too casually lit it for him, dripping conviviality. Soon enough Passepartout's head dropped to the table, eyes shut, his left hand still holding the pipe tight, his right below the table, clutching at his heirloom comb that he had taken from his pocket. Seeing Passepartout thus disposed, Fix summarily left the table to pay his bill and depart the tavern.

Just then, a band of rowdy Dutch sailors swept in for excitement on their leave, momentarily obscuring the view Gratton and his men were trying to get of Fix going out, or Passepartout sprawled head down on the table.

At exactly that moment, Passepartout's eyes popped open. He shot up from the table, slipping the pipe into one pocket, the comb in the other, as he darted with great speed out into a rear hallway, so that by the time the Dutch sailors had dispersed to several tables, restoring Gratton's line of sight to where Passepartout was laid out, Passepartout was not there.

Passepartout sped through the dark back halls of the tavern with swift determination but no sense of haste or panic. He swept open a door on the right, closing it behind him, and stepped into a preparation room, lined with bottles of liquor and two old men working on bags of opium. No one paid the pleasantly smiling European more than a passing glance, perhaps too jaded by their routine to care. Within moments he was into the next room, out a back door there, and into the languid afternoon air of the alley behind.

Seeing Passepartout's absence, Stanish had jumped up and worked across to the now unoccupied table, looked off to the camp bed, getting full at the end of the room, but did not see Passepartout among them. He went to the entrance to the back hall, very dimly lit and empty of traffic, turned to give a shake of his head to Gratton and Fox across the room, and returned to their table.

Gratton stayed cool, "The attendants probably took him to a back room."

"I could see lots of doors, all shut," Stanish agreed, then asked, "Should we *search* for him now?"

Gratton mistook Stanish's tone to mean their taking charge of Passepartout with the purpose of interrogating him, an activity they were fully prepared (if not even anxious) to do, if given leave by their paymasters, but shook his head. "It's a crowd here, even if half conscious."

"Will we have to carry him aboard the *Carnatic*?" Fox offered sarcastically.

That too was a prospect he hadn't recognized until Fox brought it up. "We may have to be his friends, yes," Gratton half smiled. "Wait a while, then poke around as much as you can in the back—no trouble. I have to check the telegraphs. Stick close here till I return."

By then Passepartout was retracing at speed his path through the city, past the Victoria Barracks, until he found a carriage in the commercial zone to convey him near enough to walk in prudent anonymity the final blocks to the address on Aouda's map.

Reaching the Eastern Telegraph Company, Gratton informed his higher ups that Passepartout and his own men were all booked on the *Carnatic* for Yokohama, but also found a sheaf of telegrams waiting for him, several reporting more on Mr. Fix. Or rather *detective* Fix, as his sources had learned he'd been hectoring London the last month for a warrant to arrest Phileas Fogg regarding the notorious Bank of England robbery. Could that card playing popinjay actually have robbed the Bank of England, Gratton wondered—and. if so, could Passepartout somehow have a connection to it?

One of Gratton's telegrams went beyond mere information: AT YOUR DISCRETION ENQUIRE FULLY, CARTE BLANCHE. Now *that* was more to his liking. Clearly, those above were losing patience with this cat-and-mouse, and were ready for hound-and-hare. Or maybe more. At his discretion.

Gratton headed back for the tavern by the pier with more jump to his gait, leg be damned.

෪ ෨

Across town, Passepartout was fairly certain no one was observing his arrival in the neighborhood of Jeejeeh & Cie. When the watchful elder Xie rang an electric bell sounding over in the *Deimos* hall, Aouda and Fogg stepped out into the courtyard to greet him as he crossed.

"How did you fare on your stroll?" Fogg asked.

"I am intact. But many developments. Tickets purchased,

including by Mr. Fix, who he now says is a police detective, following you because he thinks you robbed the Bank of England." Fogg raised his eyebrows at that. "I am inclined to believe him—that he is a detective, not that you are a thief," Passepartout continued as they walked toward the hanger door, "News on the *Carnatic* too: her boilers are repaired and she will be sailing *tonight*, at half past six, not tomorrow morning, so we cannot tarry."

Aouda opened the door and motioned for the two men to enter, Passepartout going first, and Fogg strolling after, hands clasped behind his back.

"Fix took me to an opium den, the Allahabad men following, and—*mon Dieu!*" Passepartout could now see Aouda's *Deimos*. Indicating the carpetbag still plopped down in front of it, he turned to Fogg with a smile, "Your offering to the gods?"

Passepartout immediately began a circumnavigating walk around the craft, from the carpetbag, circuiting along the starboard side to aft, fingering his comb in his pocket as he walked, pausing briefly at a windowed hatch central on that starboard side, matching the one to port. Finally reappearing around the tail fins on the port side, Passepartout stepped up to the hull, rapped gently on it with his knuckles at several spots—then felt the surface, back and forth, "Impressive. How did you achieve its uniformity?"

Robur explained, "Fusing the metal at high heat."

"We found a new way to ignite Berthelot's acetylene a few years ago," Aouda commented. "Very intense if you mix equal parts oxygen."

"What was that you said about an opium den?" Fogg asked.

"Fix wanted me to help him delay you a few days here in Hong Kong, until a warrant could arrive for you. I refused. By that time the Allahabad gang had arrived, watching us. It was then I thought of your trick in India, Aouda, creating an illusion and disappearing in a puff of smoke. In this case, Fix thought to put me into an opium stupor—an interesting sensation, that. Instead—poof! I am gone, and made my way here." Passepartout smiled, but added no further details.

"So Fix thinks we won't know the *Carnatic* will be sailing early," Fogg said.

"*Exactement*. I suspect the Allahabad men are of the same opinion."

"Perhaps it's time to find out who is following whom. Passepartout takes the *Carnatic*, and we find our own way to Yokohama. The *General Grant* will only leave for San Francisco when the *Carnatic* arrives. All we'd need is a fairly fast boat with a master trustworthy enough not to notice things at the proper time, such as an absence *en route* when *Deimos* rendezvous with us—as Aouda and I have just discussed. Anyone trying to follow us would have to hire their own boat, and that might be rather conspicuous."

"Bunsby of the *Tankadere*," Robur suggested, "No pilot boat's faster. He's helped us before; keeps a secret." Seeing Aouda's agreeable nod, he added, "I'll send word ahead," and made away to do so.

"If we are to be separated, I think Passepartout should have one of my portable telegraphs." Aouda stepped away to an office, and quickly returned with a beautiful little snuffbox, a bit darker than robin's egg blue, with delicate tendrils of foliage painted on it. She flipped open its case, "When the switch is engaged, the button on top operates as a telegraph. The lamp in the lid will glow if there's sufficient power, which is limited, so make messages short. It will flash for signals received."

"Dash dash dash, dot dot dash, dot dot," Passepartout replied in the international Morse spelling out *oui*, eliciting a broad grin from Aouda. "I will only signal from the *Carnatic* if there is some untoward emergency," he added.

"Signal when you're safely aboard and the ship underway. Then take care, Passepartout," Aouda ventured.

"We will see you in Yokohama," was all Fogg would say.

After Passepartout left, Aouda turned to Fogg, "Excuse me. I need a change of clothes."

When she returned she had a look equally distant from the sari of Pillaji or the passé secondhand dress Passepartout had found for her. Aouda's walking dress was nearer the latest fashion, with pleats and folds aplenty, concealing sundry pockets and their contents. She wore a most complementary tall hat, held in place by stout hairpins, and a colorful beaded purse was slung on a long sash over one shoulder. Both wrists were adorned with elegant metal bracelets, suggestive of her exotic background, which were easily concealed by her blouse cuffs. She also carried two cases: one large for the old dress and additional clothing, the other quite small, of red leather, which she implored Fogg to hold in his carpetbag along with the coat from Allahabad.

"Now I'm ready to travel, Phileas. Things I couldn't keep at hand while the raja's wife—and now I shall not let go of."

Fogg and Aouda bid farewell to Robur, and several others, on the way out. In the building across the courtyard, Aouda crossed to a short figure in brown protective garments, including a hood with blackened visor, working a searing white flame (so bright Fogg had to avert his eyes) along a piece of metal held in a vise. The technician stopped when Aouda approached, and pulled away the hood to reveal an Asian woman's round face beneath.

"Kim, Robur will be getting with you shortly about a new project, an attachment for the *Deimos*. It must be made *very* quickly. I'll be relying on you to assign whatever workers we'll need to achieve it." Then Aouda's voice broke with passion, "I'm also going to be meeting my brother."

The woman put out a leather gloved hand to touch her shoulder, nodding and smiling.

"Soon," Aouda said in parting, and Kim went back to her work on the metal plate.

Passing the quiet Mr. Xie on their way out, Fogg and Aouda, carpetbag and luggage in hand, set off to find a carriage to take them back to their rooms at the Hong Kong Hotel.

 octurn; so

When Gratton returned to the tavern by the pier, itching for the adventure ahead, he found a downcast Fox and Stanish outside, the latter reporting, "We can find no sign of him."

"What?" Gratton was incredulous. "Did he *crawl* out?"

"We looked in as many rooms as we could," Stanish protested.

"Until they threw us in the street," Fox amended.

"So we don't know he isn't in a room you *didn't* check. Fine." Gratton stroked his chin, took in a few breaths. "The ship will be sailing soon. If he isn't on it, *we* don't go."

A check with the ship's purser, a calm and careful man by the name of Collingwood, established that the Frenchman was not yet aboard. They were about to give up hope when Passepartout appeared on the pier a quarter past six that evening (a lean fifteen minutes before the ship was to sail), seeming most dazed, struggling up the gangway, only to collapse on deck. While stewards rushed to his aide, Gratton and his men dashed on board, just catching sight of the purser inspecting the groggy Passepartout. Finding his tickets on his person, the understanding officer arranged for Passepartout to be taken to the second of the three booked cabins, there to sleep whatever it was off.

Bon voyage Carnatic.

17. SHOWING WHAT HAPPENED CONCERNING VOYAGES NORTHWARD FROM HONG KONG

Although the narrative of Mr. *V.* was inaccurate regarding the provenance of Aouda's new clothing obtained on the evening of November 6th (attributing it to an extensive Hong Kong shopping foray), he was fully correct in recounting how the two had a fine meal afterward at their hotel, and that Phileas Fogg stayed up after Aouda to catch up with some of the world in the hotel's copies of *The Times* and *Illustrated London News*.

Mr. *V.* had far more difficulty imbuing even a scintilla of dramatic plausibility to Fogg and Aouda's otherwise inexplicable lack of concern over the absence of Passepartout, that night at the hotel, or the following morning when they left the hotel without him and arrived at the pier at 8 AM, now laden with luggage and coats, in the feigned expectation of sailing on the already departed *Carnatic*.

Their seeming indifference becomes clear, of course, once it is recognized that neither had absentmindedly misplaced Passepartout, but instead envisaged him already on that vessel heading north (though not perhaps fully anticipating what Passepartout might be capable of, or provoked to do, in their absence).

Nor were Fogg or Aouda surprised when Mr. Fix showed up on the pier like a bad penny, for the first time approaching Fogg directly, asking—with considerable gall, in their view—about the whereabouts of his acquaintance Passepartout. Fix felt at his cockiest right now, as the next boat for Yokohama wouldn't be leaving for another week, but began to deflate as Fogg decided to search out another craft to transport them before then. Fogg and Aouda also took note of the apparent absence of the three men from Allahabad.

☙ ❧

By that time, the *Carnatic* was 150 miles up the Chinese coast. Passepartout had awoken some hours before, fully refreshed, but remained in his cabin longer, estimating the time it would take to fulfill any suspicion that he might have been sleeping off the lingering ill effects of an opium daze.

He sat down, brought out Aouda's snuffbox from his pocket and set it on the table. Then retrieved his comb, which he proceeded to pass back and forth over the box, some of the tines of the comb quivering and turning out of alignment with the others. Passepartout smiled. A very ingenious mechanism, he thought, with a surprisingly powerful and compact electric battery inside, something involving the element known as lithium, as near as he could tell.

Passepartout returned the box to his pocket and stood up. The space in the cabin was not great, but enough. Closing his eyes he held the comb out at near arm's length and began to wave it back and forth, slowly turning in place until he had completed a full circle. At some times in this strange waltz, the comb fell temporarily motionless relative to the ship, all the while various tines swung out and back again. There was no great sound to it, though if one listened very closely, there was the faintest pulsing throb accompanied by a kind of subliminal crackling. This was the sort of activity that would have looked most peculiar were anyone there to see it, but Passepartout was alone.

He left the cabin then, crossing to a stair to go up onto the open deck, where he commenced a great show of searching for Fogg and Aouda, exploring fore to aft and back again, port and starboard, past strolling passengers, crossing to the railing to touch the stays to the sails running up to its three masts, looking up at the black cloud belching from the single funnel amidships, dodging around the occasional crewman intent on some task, feeling the sudden shade walking beneath one of the eight lifeboats suspended in their davits over the deck. All with the hidden object of ascertaining the presence of those he truly was interested in: the Allahabad trio.

Finding no sign of them, Passepartout entered a door on the starboard side and descended the stairs to the main public rooms. He moved more slowly now, unlike on deck when his line of sight was broad, and stopped altogether at the entrance to the ship's bar. Ring the bell, success! There they were, working on drinks, and at not yet eleven in the morning.

Retreating from the bar entrance, Passepartout immediately made for the *Carnatic*'s dining saloon, where he inquired after the ship's purser to ask for the cabin numbers of Fogg and Aouda. He was told no one by the name of Fogg was aboard, and there were no women passengers at all. Passepartout now frothing with Gallic skepticism, the purser insisted he look over the passenger list to see for himself. Passepartout did so, acknowledged the truth of the officer's statement, and thanked him for his kind assistance.

Passepartout now had the names of those aboard and their cabin assignments, though not yet which ones were the three. He could see all were single berths, meaning they'd have taken three rooms, just as he'd done for Fogg. The names of foreign derivation might logically be excluded for the moment, along with Second Class passengers—assuming their bar visit *en mass* was more likely if they actually belonged there for a change. Had he had the foresight to have obtained a list of the *Rangoon*'s passengers he could have compared names and usefully narrowed the field, but *c'est la vie*, as he knew so well from the French language.

Knowing the three were in the *Carnatic*'s bar, Passepartout undertook a stroll down the passageways to familiarize himself with what cabin numbers were associated with which physical space on the overall deck plan, translating his mental picture of the labyrinth into as clear a sense of the ship's interior as the backrooms of the much smaller Hong Kong opium den had been the day before.

ଔ ଓ

Trudging along the docks of Hong Kong, Detective Fix had gradually regained his hopes about thwarting Fogg's intentions, as over three hours he had followed Fogg and Aouda in fruitless quest of a boat for hire. Aouda occasionally motioned Fogg along with a gesture to take a preferred direction, while Fogg requested Fix stand with Aouda as protection for her and their luggage, while he scrambled down boarding planks or conversed with captains bobbing up and down on their decks. One vessel after another proved either unsuitable by speed or accommodation for Fogg's purpose, had a master unwilling to oblige the quixotic Englishman's need to sail *immediately*, or showed no confidence that they could cover the 1600 miles to Yokohama in time for their necessary connection with the *General Grant* on the 14th.

ଔ ଓ

Aboard the *Carnatic*, a fine buffet luncheon was just being assembled, which by now Passepartout was much in need of. Gathering up a broad sampling of their fare, hot (a curried lamb, some spaghetti in cream, onions and potatoes) and cold (sausage, a tomato salad, some cheese and a presentable looking pastry), he caught sight of the Allahabad men entering the saloon. *Premiere* Class after all.

Passepartout found a partially occupied table to land his plates, and swept back to obtain a cup of tea. Back at his seat, he smiled at the other men at the table, then began to wolf down enough food to settle his immediate cravings. Slowing down after that, Passepartout drank some of the now cool enough tea, dabbed his napkin to his lips, and smiled again pleasantly at his companions as he draped the cloth beside his plate, while he took out the snuffbox and lay it on his lap, fully out of view of anyone at the table.

Switching it on, he pressed the button to send by Morse: *SAFELY ABOARD CARNATIC, JEAN P*, feeling a slight tingle on his leg as he tapped each keystroke. To his surprise, only bare seconds elapsed before the light on the lid flashed a reply, again felt on his leg: *BON, AOUDA*. When nothing else followed, he turned the mechanism off, returned it to his pocket, and resumed emptying his plate.

ଔ ଓ

Continuing their catalog of Hong Kong junks and launches, Aouda stepped forward to offer Fogg a helping hand as he navigated up another narrow gangplank to the dock, and leaned in to whisper,

"Passepartout is on *Carnatic*, safe." Then more loudly, pointing off to their left, "I think we should try down here."

Soon after, Fogg, Aouda and Fix were maneuvered to Captain John Bunsby's sleek twenty-ton Pilot Boat No. 43, the two-masted *Tankadere*. Bunsby, a skilled mariner well-tanned by years at sea, in his middling forties and of evident jovial disposition, initially resisted Fogg's offer of £100 a day (with a bonus of £200 should they reach Yokohama in time), noting the impossibility of it—until he was inspired to recall for them what the *General Grant* did *before* Yokohama.

Bunsby explained that its schedule touched at Nagasaki at the southern end of Japan before that. But more opportune, on the 11th it would be stopping at Shanghai, only 800 miles away, and not leaving that port for Japan until 7 PM, so just barely feasibly reachable in time by his boat, which could make eight or nine knots on sail. As they'd be hugging the China coast, they'd also find the currents running favorably northward. They'd have to depart the moment they were provisioned, though, which would take an hour or so, and have to sail on through the night. Nor could Bunsby promise that they'd encounter only calm seas—not this time of year.

All risks Fogg was perfectly amenable to accept, giving Bunsby £200 on the spot as a show of good intent. Fix was in a dither now, and was girding up his courage to ask whether he might sail with them, when Fogg preemptively invited him.

While Fix sheepishly boarded the *Tankadere*, and Captain Bunsby stowed their assorted luggage in compartments under the cots in the small cabin below, Fogg concluded the charade by striding off to the shipping office, where he arranged to have word sent to the police and French consulate to keep an eye out for their missing passenger Passepartout, along with establishing a £100 reward.

So it came to be that at ten past three o'clock that Thursday afternoon, the 7th of November, the pilot boat *Tankadere* took sail and braved east out of Hong Kong harbor with her three passengers, just as bravely out on deck, feeling the sting of the salt sea air as they raced on toward the horizon.

Aouda stayed back at the stern, at one point turning around and pulling out from one of her secluded pockets a small but very powerful binocular glass to survey the south for any sign of a pursuing ship. Though there were some junks heading to the coast or passing from the other direction up ahead, nothing was in view behind.

Fogg sat next to her, "Clear sailing for us?"

"It would seem so." She turned to Fogg, "Robur's making great progress with the truck, by the way. We had all the metals to hand, putting everyone to it."

Fogg was curious. "How do you receive your telegraphs?"

Aouda touched her bracelets, and beamed. Seeing Fix pacing to and fro up by Bunsby at the wheel, she asked, "Why did you invite Fix? Not just to keep an eye on him?"

"No, he's turning into a nuisance. But he's someone who has been with us all the way since Suez, so if ever there was an unbiased witness, to the fact of my traveling around the world, Mr. Fix is the man."

"I could *fly* you to London in two days, Phileas."

"I'm sure you could. But nonetheless, quite apart from what else we may do on the way, *I* must travel around the world in eighty days—and be *seen* to do so." Fogg was smiling, and said no more.

At dusk, as they would be sailing on in the dark, Bunsby brought lights out. There was still the half Moon's illumination, but clouds crowding in to the east would soon end that, and not being seen in time in these busy seas could result in a collision no one aboard desired.

Fix was by then planted at the bow, leaning on the small brass cannon used for signaling in fog, sulking in thought. Here he was, traveling at the generous expense of the very man whose arrest he sought. That was a garb of ironic obligation he did not feel comfortable wearing.

Still more ill-fitting when Fogg invited Fix to partake of their dinner of cold hen, cheese, biscuits and beer. Fogg was not especially fond of beer, but there was no provision for tea. Fix wondered what manner of meal he was missing aboard the *Carnatic*.

଍ ଎

On that topic, the Allahabad gang could have attested to its comparative sumptuousness. Sitting some tables away from Passepartout, who once again had seated himself among other passengers, Gratton surveilled their target and his present resources. By this time they were confident that neither Fogg, his woman, nor the police detective Fix had made it aboard. They were still trying to identify which cabin Passepartout occupied, though from the lack of luggage they saw when he'd staggered up the gangway, Stanish's expertise would likely be wasted this trip.

They couldn't assume Passepartout didn't have a firearm or knife, of course, but as they still carried their own pistols, and were proficient in using them, cornering the Frenchman should be just a matter of applying military discipline to a properly timed moment, and not losing their nerve.

଍ ଎

The wind picked up still more for the *Tankadere* around ten o'clock, but Captain Bunsby knew his boat and its limits and kept to his sail plan. Fix retired below not long after, taking one of the cots arrayed around a table, its swinging lamp only reminding him of the pilot boat's rolling and his stomach. Fogg and Aouda did not retire to the cots until midnight, while Bunsby and his crew of four remained on duty all through the night.

By their efforts, the *Tankadere* had covered a hundred miles by sunrise, Friday the 8th of November, and continued to make steady progress under good wind the rest of the day. Captain Bunsby was now able to take some sleep below, while another of his mariners stood the wheel. The scenery of the Chinese coast, while not dull, was not terribly distracting, a passing succession of low wooded lands visible far off to port. The temperature remained in the low eighties Fahrenheit.

Fix accepted Fogg's hospitality once more when they took an afternoon meal. This time Fix insisted on paying for his passage, but Fogg rejected this, accounting his presence as merely another of his "general expenses." Fogg's attitude made Fix's mood even more bilious.

By that evening, the *Tankadere* had traversed another 120 miles, and as the temperature fell into the less torrid sixties overnight, they entered the Formosa Strait, where the seas turned rougher from conflicting currents. The condition of Fix's stomach did not improve.

                              ଔ ଓ

Aboard the *Carnatic* that night, Passepartout felt in an experimental mood, and went for a gin in the ship's bar, a nod of bitter homage to the many beverages the absent Fix had treated him to while at sea, but choosing a time when he might well bump into the Allahabad men. When they did indeed appear on the scene, Gratton saw this as an opportunity to press his mission.

While they ordered their drinks, then crossed toward him, they noticed Passepartout grooming his hair (how very French of him), then stuffing his comb into his pocket as they sat down at his table, uninvited. Gratton pulled a chair from a nearby table, sitting down to Passepartout's right, and extended his troubled left leg up under the table for comfort. "You're quite a traveling gentleman," Gratton said.

"Oh, how so?" Passepartout sounded unconcerned.

Gratton took a drink of whiskey. "You're a long way from America, Passepartout. And we do know your name."

"I am honored," Passepartout replied. "And your names?"

Fox, sitting to Passepartout's left, put his ale down. "None of your concern."

Gratton pressed ahead, seeing no need to identify themselves.

"What were you looking for there? Who was paying you to do it? Simple enough questions."

Passepartout looked puzzled, "*There*? America is very large. I *can* tell you, no one is paying *me* to do anything, apart from Mr. Fogg, to be his valet. Is someone paying *you* to wander after me? That seems frivolous. If it is to be our game to be questioning, and answering—I too have questions."

"Are you trying to be *funny*?" Fox snapped.

"Often unintentionally," Passepartout said, not at all lightly. "English is far from my native language."

Gratton motioned Fox to simmer down, and the man took solace in his ale. "We're thinking of your stay in Florida. Right after Baltimore. Is that clearer?"

"I remember inquiring about jobs. And seeing that amazing cannon. Have you heard of it?"

"And then you rushed off," Gratton added.

"No job for me." Passepartout spread his hands, and smiled.

Following the exchange from directly opposite Passepartout, Stanish put down his brandy, and asked wide-eyed, "Take anything *with* you?"

"I put all the knowledge of the universe in my pocket, young man, and strode away with it," Passepartout said to him, then pointed at Fox with a smile, "There, I *am* being funny."

"You'll pardon me, but *I* don't believe you," Gratton said sternly, and worked more on his whiskey.

"That I am being funny?"

Gratton shook his head and snorted. "May I remind you, your friends are no longer on board, to protect you."

"Do I have something to be protected *from*?"

"Us," Gratton hissed.

"That is very honest of you," Passepartout nodded. "And I have honestly answered your questions, anonymous trio. No one is paying me, I took nothing but my curiosity from Florida—or Baltimore. All completely true, I assure you. You should accept that, and enjoy your voyage to Yokohama."

"It's a long trip to Yokohama," Gratton warned, downed the last of his drink, and got up, his fellows rising as well. "Good day to you," and he led them out of the bar.

Passepartout smiled after them, sipped more on his gin. It would have been polite of them to at least have given him their names, since they were hard laboring to intimidate him, and when he was being so honest.

But no matter, it was enough that they had come forward, to sit only a few feet away from him, all together, so confident in their number. No one aboard ship but them carried the distinctive pistols concealed in their pockets, and each of the weapons informatively different from the other. As they had been in their respective staterooms when he waved his comb about yesterday morning, he already knew which room contained which man with gun. Now he could place the guns with the faces, and by the passenger list now knew his adversaries by their booked names: William Gratton, Frank Stanish, and Crawford Fox.

And by the deck layout, Passepartout also knew the three did not share adjoining berths, and the hothead Fox's was not on the same deck as the other two. That displacement might be turned to his advantage.

Passepartout also knew of at least three cabins aboard ship not presently in use (those booked for Fogg. Aouda, and Mr. Fix). He could easily slip into any of those to nap, in the event the Allahabad men were already aware of which cabin he had been assigned. In fact, he would commence that juggle tonight, though taking the precaution of slipping into his stateroom periodically to muss up the bedsheets and reposition furniture there, so that the stewards each day would still deem it occupied.

18. IN WHICH PHILEAS FOGG, AOUDA, AND PASSEPARTOUT EACH GO ABOUT THEIR BUSINESS

At daybreak on Saturday, November 9th, a typhoon was building to the south, threatening the *Tankadere* with worse seas but putting the gusting winds even more to their favor, if they had the courage to stick out the squall. Bunsby and Fogg were of that character, and the Captain pulled in the regular sails, to hoist the storm jib to take the wind alone. Despite the worsening weather, Fogg, Aouda—and even Fix—resolutely remained on deck, lent appropriate coats from the *Tankadere*'s stock, as the temperatures were dropping into the fifties, and would continue in that range the farther north they sailed.

Aouda took leave to go below once, pulling out her luggage case, then a plain small pillbox from one of her pockets. Opening the box, there was but one tiny lever atop a mechanism; which she turned to its other position, shut the cap and placed it in her luggage. She then availed herself of the chamber pot, and returned to the open deck.

Another cold dinner (this time of sausages, bread and cheese) was taken around five o'clock, Fogg carving the sausage slices, Aouda attending to the bread and cheese. Fix once more accepted Fogg's hospitality, though he seemed increasingly ill from the sea and retired below deck a bit later.

"I sprinkled an herbal condiment on his cheese," Aouda told Fogg. "He should be indisposed shortly, and remain so for many hours." Seeing Fogg's arched reaction, she added, "Robur is confident he can finish the truck later, so he's ready to fly now."

"We begin," Fogg smiled.

Aouda was more circumspect, "No, we *wait*."

೦೩ ೫೦

The change of weather that was bearing down on the *Tankadere* was but an impending trouble for the *Carnatic* farther north, but enough that the purser Collingwood took pity on the luggage-less Passepartout, who seemed unable to resist openly strolling on deck at all hours, and scavenged the man a coat. Passepartout expressed his gratitude.

Piecing together conversations he and his men had with the stewards, Gratton was finally able to discover the number of Passepartout's assigned cabin, which Stanish was dispatched to search while everyone was occupied during dinner that evening. He wasn't especially surprised when Stanish appeared shortly at their table to report a hapless, "Nothing."

Gratton wondered now whether Stanish might have missed anything, overlooking something obvious, because there were no bags to riffle through. It might be like that American tale of the "Purloined

Letter" he'd heard tell of, things hidden in plain sight. He was still thinking that when they headed up to the bar together for some drinks, especially as Stanish continued to express his conviction that Passepartout couldn't have been such a worry to their commissioners unless he'd taken away more than just his observation.

"Nobody can remember everything," Stanish insisted, "He must've written something down, or taken something."

"Have *we* been told everything?" Fox asked.

Gratton said to Stanish, "Show me his cabin. If he isn't there," he turned to Fox, "see if you can find him."

When Gratton and Stanish got to Passepartout's cabin, and a knock elicited no response, they looked either way down the passageway. Finding it empty, they pulled out their firearms and entered. A quick inspection revealed they were alone.

Stanish started to say, "I looked—," but Gratton shushed him, and began his own perusal. The room seemed undisturbed by human occupation. He labored down onto his knee and probed under the bed mattress, worked back to his feet and felt over the undersides of all the furniture, hunting up any medium of concealment. There were no papers or letters, purloined or otherwise, to his assessment. The cleanest of whistles.

Strolling aft along the starboard side of the liner after dinner, Passepartout pondered what might be happening with Fogg and Aouda. There was no provision for the snuffbox to activate itself to signal him if there were some disaster at their end, and he had not used it since his lunchtime message two days before. Aouda was quite correct, that it held enough power for only a few short messages, so best not waste them. And while he could imagine ways to circumvent that limitation, right now he felt no need, having come to believe that of all people on the Earth, Fogg and Aouda were ones especially agile at taking care of themselves.

Passepartout was just coming out from under the third starboard lifeboat when Crawford Fox came up to him rapidly from behind. Assisted partly by their drinks, Fox had misconstrued Gratton's instructions as a command to bring Passepartout to his cabin, where he supposed Gratton and Stanish would be assembled. When Passepartout wheeled quickly about, Fox pulled a pistol from his left pocket, waved it to the right and said firmly, through a confident sneer, "You're to come with me."

As he was now looking forward, Passepartout could see there was not a passenger or crewman in sight, few being inclined to stroll the deck on this increasingly foul evening. The man he now knew to be named Fox had likely considered that very circumstance in choosing this moment to act. There was no window in the superstructure there either, so no one would see whatever took place between the third and fourth starboard lifeboats.

Fox was just returning the pistol to his coat pocket, instinctively looking down for an instant, when Passepartout strode a step forward, and his right hand shot out to grab the man's left forearm in a vicelike grip, while his left arced up to strike the man's neck with the side of his palm, then flashed down to grab his pant leg, and in one swift motion Passepartout had hurled the winded man over the rail and into the China Sea.

Another fractioned second and a faint splash might have been heard as a flailing Fox hit the water, had anyone on board been in a position to have done so—and Fox had taken such pains to have assured exactly that seclusion. Not many seconds after, the ship had steamed on tens of feet, and tens of feet more, and tens of feet more, so that soon no commotion the drowning man might have made could have arrested the *Carnatic*'s steady churning progress for Yokohama.

Passepartout resumed his promenade.

ଓ ଚ

By eight o'clock, the storm was raging around the *Tankadere*, the crew all working the flailing storm jib. Aouda carefully made her way up to Captain Bunsby, ever steady at the helm, and shouted over the rain and wind, "Whatever you or crew may think they may be seeing these next few hours, I'm sure by the cold light of day tomorrow, you'll all dismiss as mirage, or dream."

Bunsby winked, "I'd reckon so, Miss Aouda."

Aouda returned aft to Fogg. An odd whining sound could be heard now, quite loud, were it not mixed in with the shrieking wind. "Ready," Aouda extended a hand to Fogg, who stood up and turned.

Suddenly, with the precision of a great pendulum swinging into view, the *Deimos* appeared out of the rain, flying sideways, putting its portside across the stern of the *Tankadere*, just above the heaving rail and staying skillfully clear of the second mast's stays and rigging. The side hatch flung open just then, a flood of light from inside brightening the pilot boat's stern. An older Asian man extended his right hand, while clinging tenaciously to a handle on the bulkhead wall behind him with his left. Aouda motioned Fogg to climb up first, and she followed, the Asian man hauling each forward into the *Deimos* with a sharp tug.

"*Habis!*" the man shouted once Aouda was inside, and immediately the craft pulled up and tilted sharply to starboard, causing Fogg and Aouda to briefly tumble onto one another against a bulkhead (an experience neither of them found in the least way uncongenial), while the old man yanked the hatch shut and secured it.

The brightness of the illumination from the open hatch was only relative to the darkness aboard *Tankadere*. Once the hatch was closed, the electric lighting aboard *Deimos* proved to be pleasant, not harsh, of comparable intensity to mellow gaslight.

Once they had regained their feet, Aouda asked, "Phileas, we need a heading to *Nautilus*."

Fogg consulted his watch, "Your ship is pointed almost in the right direction already. I'd say ... four or five degrees further to your right should do, for the time being."

Aouda climbed a short ladder to convey the information to Robur, who sat in a pilot's chair up in the cupola.

Almost at once the ship accelerated, and inclined as they climbed, the pitch and pulsing sounds of the *Deimos*' engines keeping to pace. Bracing himself against interior panels and instruments, Fogg worked his way to the front windows to see what he might, and Aouda joined him just as the floor was returning to level.

"Not much to see in a storm, at night, flying at a thousand feet," Aouda conceded.

Fogg turned about, leaning back against the railing at the window, and looked at her with calm reflection, while the machinery hummed and sang.

"Can you tell how far away we are?" Aouda asked then.

"A rough speculation, this far out. A thousand miles, perhaps more. And I can't say how deep."

"My metallurgical improvements should mean we can match *Nautilus*."

The old fellow from the hatch stepped up. "Robur thinks the weather should clear farther east. If so, and he can hold us steady, I'll try for some tea. China black, if that is agreeable to Mr. Fogg—no cream. We brought desserts too."

"Thank you, Niru," Aouda smiled.

Moving carefully as the ship heaved in the turbulent air, Niru flopped down a pair of leather upholstered seats that were mounted flat on a panel of the bulkhead underneath the pilot cupola, and then flipped up a small table between them. Spartan, but comfortable, Fogg thought as he sat in the starboard one, putting Aouda across the table to his left.

"How do you manage a *kettle*?" Fogg asked.

"Electric. Likewise for hot food. One does like the amenities."

"The future dawns," Fogg observed.

Robur's forecast proved correct, *Deimos* flying more smoothly once the storm abated, and around ten o'clock Niru appeared with a black lacquer tray bearing a pair of small green Chinese-style cups, an equally scaled squat charcoal gray teapot with a sculpted dragon rampant on it, and a rectangular plate with an assortment of delicate desserts, spirals and cubes of sugared fruits appearing like miniature works of art. And all quite delicious.

"You've flown to Paris and searched for Nemo. Have you done much other exploring?"

"Ah! That is an indulgence I have never added to my vocabulary, Phileas. Too many years of worry, and work." Looking around the cabin of her *Deimos*, Aouda said, "I suppose that would be the best use of a ship like this, wouldn't it? To travel, just for the pleasure of it. To bring people together, rather than to hunt them down." She looked wistful, "Maybe someday."

After midnight, now Sunday the 10th of November, Fogg began to attend more closely to his watch, which he placed on the table with the *XII* facing north. In this way, Nemo's "**N**" fell around *III*, while the "**O**" had fixed at *XII* and was flickering repeatedly, as he expected. When they were directly over *Nautilus*, its ring would jump to *XII* also and commence to flash. That took place around 2 AM, and Fogg signaled by pointing straight below.

As Robur brought *Deimos* gently down toward the dark sea, he turned on several navigation lamps, and Aouda changed places with him so she could pilot. Aouda could feel the wave intensity now, and was pleased that the sea was fairly calm; hoping it remained thus should she be successful in finding her brother's great submarine boat.

As they submerged, Fogg asked, "Do you have a way of seeing *down*? We wouldn't want to collide with it."

"Our periscopes survey dorsal and ventral," Robur reassured him. *Deimos* also had an acoustic resonator to estimate the proximity to nearby objects, which Robur could follow on a small electric display (the particulars of which he did not explain to Fogg).

The interior of *Deimos* felt cooler now, and soon electrically heated air began to flow in compensation. The descent took somewhat longer than Fogg anticipated, perhaps forgetting that the *Nautilus* was a moving object, but also because the exact diving protocols for submersibles were not among his most salient fields of interest. Every so often Fogg glanced up at the windows, his eye caught by the shimmering of passing fish reflecting *Deimos*' glow.

Fogg and Robur independently alerted Aouda when they were nearing the *Nautilus*, some two hundred feet below the waves. Fogg rose from his seat and crossed to the windows to get a better view as bits of the vessel came into view, illuminated by their lights, as Aouda was by now using *Deimos*' maneuverability to sail sideways parallel to the submarine, gradually edging closer and forward until her lamps shone directly on the large glass orbs of *Nautilus*' wheelhouse.

Impossible for them not to see.

SRIKAR SURFACE PLEASE AOUDA she began to signal repeatedly using the lights, in the international Morse she hoped would be understood clearly enough by those aboard.

After what seemed to her a terribly long time, *Nautilus* stopped.

The *Deimos* continued to move forward, drifting so that the submarine's saw-tooth ram fell into their lamps, and Aouda promptly shifted *Deimos* back, but by now the *Nautilus* was also rising. Aouda's heart was racing as she began to surface as well, pacing *Nautilus*' ascent.

It was nearing three o'clock in the morning when the *Nautilus* and *Deimos* surfaced, there in the trackless freedom of the Pacific Ocean. Fortunately the sea had remained *pacific*, though coming beside the submarine in safety was still no simple matter. The *Nautilus*' hull bulged out from her central platform, making any approach along most of her two-hundred foot length perilous for both vessels. Aouda decided the best spot lay aft, between the submarine's rudder fin and the visible terminus of the top deck, where a small covered dinghy was moored.

Aouda felt anxious as she steered *Deimos* ever closer to the *Nautilus*, her nose aimed at the submarine's tail fin sticking up some twenty feet ahead, just visible by *Deimos*' lamps. Feeling her way along, Aouda finally heard the gentlest of percussion as the skids encountered the *Nautilus*' hull. Then she switched on a mechanism designed to keep her craft at a set distance from a target, and soon her ship was bobbing and heaving on its own in close synchrony with the much larger *Nautilus*.

By now a cover on the *Nautilus* between her bridge and its dorsal fin had retracted, exposing the hatch and stairs beneath. Aouda, meantime, had come down from her pilot's seat and, taking Fogg's hand, headed for the ladder to their upper hatch, which Robur was already opening, the smell of salt air rushing in.

Captain Nemo strode forward along *Nautilus*' deck, others of his crew remaining behind in the hatch well. As he cleared the fin, Nemo could now see Aouda emerging from *Deimos*' hatch ahead, climb down to the starboard lateral fin, then work her way forward, past the dorsal fin jutting out, to get close enough to make a jump the few feet to *Nautilus*, and Nemo's inviting hand.

The proffered hand quickly turned into a long embrace, which Robur and Fogg watched as they duplicated Aouda's path along *Deimos*' hull. Fogg was greatly touched by the emotion of their reunion, and found Nemo quite as he imagined he would look, on this November day in 1872.

Srikar finally broke the silence, tight with emotion, "I thought you were dead."

Aouda looked into his eyes with deep consolation, "I know about Himadri and Ajit. I've spoken with Aronnax."

Nemo's frame shuddered. "Did you ever learn who lay behind our being taken to *Kalapani*? I never could."

"No, but I think we have stumbled on a fresh trail, Srikar, thanks to my friend Mr. Phileas Fogg, the man who has made it possible for me to find you, and who has a favor to ask of us both."

Aouda motioned for Fogg and Robur to jump aboard.

"Welcome to *Nautilus*, Mr. Fogg." Nemo turned to Robur, clasping his hand in his, "And you. Still our truest oak."

Nemo was keen to show Aouda and her companions the *Nautilus*. The hatch stair led down into an instrument laden chamber beneath their steering room, its interior lit by electric lighting, though somewhat more glaring than *Deimos'*. Nemo led the way down a short stair aft into a grand salon that filled the center of the ship port to starboard. Inside were many plush red upholstered settees, book shelves crowded with volumes of science and art, whose titles Robur began to check out of curiosity, along with display cases with marine specimens living and not. The far end of the salon was dominated by a pipe organ, on which was emblazoned a rather ostentatiously prominent "N" on a gold medallion.

There were two observation alcoves on either side of a central fountain (a strange thing for a submarine, Fogg thought as he walked past). Large telescoping metal irises covered their giant convex lenses, and Nemo stepped down into the starboard alcove, turned a control to open it, inviting Aouda to appreciate the view. From here Nemo could just see the stern of Aouda's craft thirty feet away to their right, its lights shining on *Nautilus'* hull. He began to peer intently.

"How are you keeping it so stable?" he asked Aouda.

"I improved on your thrust vane idea. They can be switched to independently react, automatically, using instruments on our bumpers."

"Magnificent!" Nemo declared with a smile. Shutting the window iris, Nemo said, "I fear you'll be disappointed with my engine room," but took them on aft even so.

Fogg was admiring the pipe organ, and was unable to resist poking out a short melody on it to hear its tone: C, G, C an octave higher, followed more quickly by an E, then E-flat. Nemo didn't appreciate that concluding dissonance and gave him a disapproving look as they exited the room, taking a steeply inclined ladder to the deck below.

Nemo pointed out all manner of devices and techniques to Aouda, Fogg and Robur following, from their underwater diving chamber, to the strangely glowing furnace that powered the great ship. Entering the area that turned *Nautilus*' propeller, amid the churning pistons and distinctive pulsing vibrations of Nemo's propulsion, he conceded to Aouda, "Not the most elegant of mechanics, but it was the best we could fashion with what we had at hand on my island."

"Professor Aronnax and I flew over what remained of it all last month. We did not stay long, for obvious reasons."

Nemo didn't catch that allusion to flying, more concerned about her mentioning Aronnax again. "How *is* the Professor?"

"Well," Aouda assured him. "What he told about his voyage made me realize you were still alive. The *Nautilus* had all your art about it."

"Have you other facilities, now that your island is—," and Fogg spread the fingers of one hand while making a low explosive sound.

"That's not where we built *Nautilus*, though I did replace her old coal-fired engines once we got there. I still have my original secret island, and not a few supply depots roundabouts. There are still many isolated places around the world, Mr. Fogg, though how long they may remain so I now have considerable doubt."

"Any you secure to your satisfaction, Srikar, whatever supplies you call on may be brought to you," Aouda promised.

Having looked over the mechanics in the meantime, Robur interjected, "Magnetic fluid control would eliminate the need for pistons, reduce weight, increase range and efficiency."

"My thought exactly," Aouda agreed, then turned to Srikar, "Now, I should like you to see *my* vessel."

Returning to that steep access ladder, Nemo led the way out the hatch above to *Nautilus*' deck. It was now coming on to dawn. The traces of clouds could be seen far off to the west. Aouda told Nemo, "We'll have to be leaving soon. Wouldn't want a passing ship to catch us on the sea."

"Either of us," Nemo added.

Although surely invited, when about to cross over to the *Deimos*, Robur held Fogg back and shook his head, knowing the two needed to be alone. Aouda caught that gesture as well, and as they boarded, she told Niru, "Please stay with Robur."

Niru closed the hatch behind him, and crossed over to join Robur and Fogg on the *Nautilus*.

"Welcome aboard my *Deimos*," Aouda was saying to Srikar.

"The *Terror*. So we burn with the same vengeance."

"It's been my reason to exist these last few years," Aouda called as she climbed up to settle into the pilot's chair, rubbing the arms proudly, "See what I have built."

Disengaging the station keeping mechanism, Aouda pulled *Deimos* away from *Nautilus*. "You saw how deeply it can dive and maneuver, that's just a matter of containing pressure. Where I moved ahead was to apply magnetic fields to fluid control, both liquid and gaseous, enabling *this*," and with a rush of water ejecting from the vents, to be replaced by even more swiftly moving air, flaming in the darkness, *Deimos* lifted off the sea.

Nemo was flushed with excitement as Aouda bought the ship higher, the surging sounds being made reminding him at times of his own engine, while others were utterly unfamiliar. Keeping his balance, Nemo went to the windows as Aouda circled the *Nautilus* from fifty feet in the air, *Deimos*' lights playing dimly along its hull as the dawn continued to brighten.

"In a day we can span continents, or oceans," Aouda called from her chair.

Nemo returned to a spot where he could look up at her, full of admiration, "You were always the brightest light, now you're brighter still."

Aouda frowned, "You would have done far better, if you'd not been taken."

"That, dearest sister, I cannot claim. But *thi*s, is *splendid*!" Srikar paused. "Now, what is this *favor* Mr. Fogg asks through you?"

Aouda swung the ship around to near where she had positioned *Deimos* before, and settled into the water. The whine of the engines diminished.

"It involves Barbicane. You were right to think him capable of working through at least some of the problem. He's uncovered enough to shoot a ship to the Moon, Srikar, ten days from now, an innocent lark that may have attracted the same spider that tried to claim you."

Nemo stiffened, "Go on."

"There are several agents already after Fogg's man Passepartout— he and Fogg are adamant Barbicane must not reach the Moon. I'm sure they're not telling all, even to each other, certainly not to *me*, and yet I've caught their resolve, Srikar. And besides, it should be quite exciting."

"You have put your trust in them, then?"

"Yes, and it's a mystery to me why. Something about them both doesn't *belong* here."

The morning light was increasing by the moment as Aouda returned *Deimos* close to *Nautilus*' hull so Srikar could depart and Fogg, Robur and Niru rejoin her. Niru boarded first, temporarily replacing Aouda at the pilot's chair so she could go out for her parting with her brother.

Nemo now carried a small metal case under one arm (a bit over a foot wide but not that deep), and declared to Phileas Fogg, "It seems my sister has ensnared me in your scheme. I have the time and place where *Nautilus* must be, and there I shall be."

"My thanks to you, sir. It is no small confidence you grant us, all the more given how little we have been able to confide in return."

"Aouda has put my hand in yours. That is enough."

Aouda instructed Robur, "You must fashion an electric so Srikar may signal us in future."

"It can be made ready by the time needed, but cannot be used when they are underwater."

Aouda nodded in understanding, telling Srikar, "We've found a way to send telegraphs through the air."

Nemo smiled, "Brighter *still*!"

While Robur and Fogg disappeared down *Deimos*' hatch, brother and sister embraced, silently. Then Aouda darted back up to the hatch, tossing a last smiling wave before it closed.

Nemo stood on deck watching as *Deimos* pulled away from the *Nautilus*, and then the sudden surge of power as it rose from the sea, spinning around so beautifully, with such control, finally dashing away to disappear into the early light, the whine of its engines now replaced by the lap of waves on the submarine's iron hull.

The *Nautilus*' taciturn First Officer had come up beside him now, and Nemo let a sigh, "I had thought such feelings lost." He quickly regained his manner, though, "Prepare to submerge. I have to sketch and then build a rig to hold a Moonship."

19. IN WHICH GRATTON AND STANISH CONTINUE TO TAKE TOO GREAT AN INTEREST IN PASSEPARTOUT, AND WHAT COMES OF IT

The remaining two Allahabad men only began to have worries about their compatriot when Fox failed to show for breakfast that morning. The pair glared over at Passepartout across the saloon, who was working through a hearty fortification of cutlets, fish, toast, eggs and coffee.

Surmising that Fox might have taken ill, after breakfast Gratton and Stanish descended to his cabin. They knocked, though the engine noise on this lower deck did make that harder to hear. Gratton opened the door, and entered to find his kit and other clothes, but no Crawford. Parenthetically, their comradely concern may be contrasted with the aforementioned oddity of Mr. *V.*'s opposite attribution of temporary apathy to Phileas Fogg and Aouda regarding Passepartout's absence in Hong Kong.

There was nothing to it but to inform the purser, who sent word out through the officers and stewards to keep an eye out for the missing man.

☙ ❧

Phileas Fogg and Aouda had five hours to nap on the leather seats during their flight west, and the storm had lessened considerably by the time *Deimos* intercepted the *Tankadere* around 10 AM, when Niru gently roused both with shakes of the shoulder. Robur reconnoitered the vicinity from altitude first before descending, Aouda checking their lower periscope to confirm there were no other vessels nearly close enough to apprehend anything of moment. Seeing only Bunsby and crew on deck, Robur swooped down to perform the same maneuver as the night before, except in broadest of daylight, this time Aouda and Fogg exiting out the starboard hatch.

Two of *Tankadere*'s mariners plainly saw this visitation, calling the others' attention to it. Bunsby turned around at the wheel and grinned—this *was* something you didn't see every day.

Deimos had shot up vertically and was flying away to the southwest as Aouda and Fogg ambled up to the wheel, but Bunsby spoke first, "Can you build one of those to suit?"

"Are you richer than Croesus and can handle what fuels it?" Aouda replied with a smile, and the captain laughed. "How did Mr. Fix fare overnight?"

"Never poked his head from the cots."

By noon the weather was clearing further, the crew were hoisting more sail, and Fogg and Aouda were ready for a lunch. Retrieving their victuals from the cabin below, Fix began to waken at their commotion. "Did you stay on deck all night?" he wheezed, "I don't think I saw you down here."

"Quite invigorating, the sea, don't you think, Mr. Fix?" Fogg said.

Aouda was retrieving the pillbox from her luggage, flipping its switch down again, and returned it to her pocket, before helping Fogg gather up their luncheon.

"Care to join us, Mr. Fix?" Fogg asked.

"Not just now," Fix replied with great certainty.

ଓଃ ଯୋ

Gratton and Stanish went to the purser before lunch to see if any news had come of Fox, but there had not.

By now both men had a more than passing suspicion about who might have been involved in Fox's disappearance, but Gratton could think of no better way to direct that cloud but to cast the shadow wide. "There are a lot of foreigners on board, aren't there? Have you looked into that?"

Collingwood sought to be diplomatic. "There are many foreigners aboard, Mr. Gratton. But non-foreigners have been known to commit offense before—and we have no knowledge of any offense having been committed. The weather was poor yesterday. Perhaps he grew too adventurous, and fell overboard. It does happen."

The First Officer was passing by and approached to ask the purser, "Something the matter, Mr. Collingwood?"

"It's about that missing passenger, Fox. It's possible he lunged overboard, intentionally—or not."

"If any intention, it wouldn't be *his*," protested Stanish.

"Did he travel on ships often?" the officer asked.

"Not to my knowledge," Gratton had to say.

"Well, there you have it. Land legs trying to weather a bad sea. *Hazard*," the officer harrumphed, and returned to the bridge and his productive duty.

As the purser knew Passepartout was prone to deck strolls, it occurred to him that the Frenchman might have seen something, so when he spotted Passepartout seated in the saloon later, Collingwood crossed to ask him softly, "Could we have a word, after luncheon?"

"Of course," Passepartout replied.

Gratton raised an eyebrow to see that from across the room, calling it to Stanish's notice. "Look, they may be investigating after all."

"If he *did* do something, what do *we* do?" Stanish asked worriedly.

"*Carte blanche*, Frank. Whatever we need to."

Once the luncheon patrons had thinned out, Collingwood went over to Passepartout. "We have a missing passenger, a Mr. Fox. He's nowhere aboard ship, and his two friends are most concerned about him. Knowing how often you've been out on deck, perhaps you saw something."

"Can you describe him?"

"Young man, English, late twenties—early thirties, somewhat long hair, bit unkempt, no beard, thinner than you, a bit of a sallow face."

"Oh, I think I may have spoken to the man, in the bar. Yes, he and his two friends—did one have a limp?"

Collingwood nodded, "Yes, that's the one."

"They had taken the same train as Mr. Fogg, Aouda and I in Allahabad, way back in India. It was quite a coincidence being on the same boat with them from Calcutta, to Hong Kong. And then again on this, to Yokohama. We chatted briefly about our travels. The gentleman—Fox? He seemed of a nervous temperament."

"But you never spoke to the man anywhere out on deck?"

"No, no words to him out on deck." Which was technically true, as what conversation Passepartout had with Fox had taken place on another ship's deck, and on the *Carnatic*, Fox had only managed to get five out, while Passepartout had spoken none.

It had been a straw grasped, and the purser added (as a conclusion, not a question): "And you saw no one leap overboard, or fall accidentally," chucking his lips after.

"No—I saw no one *leap* overboard, or fall *accidentally*."

When Collingwood took leave of Passepartout, Gratton and Stanish kept close on him, obliged (if only for Fox's sake) to carry this through to the end. Passepartout whiled away the rest of the day in public view, as well observed by his fellow passengers and the crew as he could contrive.

After a few hours of watching Passepartout continue to enjoy his sea voyage in a way they were not, Gratton and Stanish retired to the bar to reconsider their situation over a few drinks.

"He's a dangerous man, but we can't be put off by that," Gratton said. "We need to get him alone, without being seen at it. I think half an hour would do, if we're not interrupted. Much can be muffled by pillows and blankets."

"Could we wait to Yokohama?" Stanish wondered.

"A whole city for him to run off into? I'd prefer to have it done by then. Be rid of it."

"Fox's stateroom will be empty."

Gratton nodded, realizing the irony of it, but also cautioned, "We still have to mind the noise. Best done when most people are above deck."

"Winging him could make him more agreeable, do you think? Shoulder, leg. Not the torso, for bleeding."

"Risky, for the noise. Can't be in a place where anybody would hear the shot, raise an alarm. Then still to get him back to the room."

"It was noisy as hell in the engine room on the *Rangoon*," Stanish reminded.

"Yes, he went down there, didn't he? How far is that from Fox's room?"

"I'm not sure. Have to reconnoiter."

"Must be closer, we could hear the engine more there. Let's find out about that, eh?"

Gratton and Stanish went down to Fox's stateroom, poked inside to see it unoccupied and dark, then began to explore the passageway in both directions, looking for any crew entries to the engines, which they could hear were somewhere forward. It was odd, Stanish thought, how easy it was not to think about such acclimated sounds, until a person consciously took note of them.

Apart from doors to the other staterooms and several small storage rooms, there were only the stairs they had used to come down, which both now followed to the deck below. Here Stanish finally found a crew hatch forward, which on opening revealed a forest of pipes and equipment, and confirming sound of the churning engines within. He motioned Gratton to join him there. Hearing footsteps approaching from the stateroom hall, Stanish shut the hatch just as a steward carrying bedding flitted past.

Gratton tossed a friendly nod at the steward, but wasn't pleased after the man had gone. "We've got a passageway, and a stair, and another hall between here and Fox's room. Might as well have the Crystal Palace along the way, trying to parade a wounded captive along this—especially a protesting or fighting one—without people like him seeing or hearing. This is not high ground, Frank."

Such tactical considerations were still vexing Gratton and Stanish as they ate dinner that night. Passepartout was an adversary all the more elusive and frustrating by being one of the crowd, all too visible and yet so unapproachable. And yet—if they could only contrive to be in the right place with him, and for just long enough without intervention, both were sure the flag could be taken after all.

After dinner, Passepartout embarked on a venture that surprised himself a little: he decided to seek out some card play in the lounge, knowing by Fogg's experience how efficiently that could fritter away endless hours, all in public view. There were passengers gambling at a game Passepartout understood to be called poker, which he avoided as he had neither the money nor understanding for it, but none playing anything like whist.

Catching Gratton and Stanish out the corner of his eye,

Passepartout came upon a pair of burly but glum businessmen hailing from the Hapsburg's Austria-Hungary, lonely for a knowledgeable player to join them in one of their country's pastimes, for which they had brought a deck of the curious picture cards used for it, laying out its five suits face up on the table in separate stacks as advertising enticement. Passepartout recognized the spades, clubs, diamonds and hearts familiar from whist, but the card topping the fifth stack placed prominently between the blacks and reds bore lightly colored drawings of two churches, St. Gilgen and St. Wolfgang, arranged so that one could be seen right side up depending on how the card was oriented, each with a number XI at its leftmost corner.

"That is interesting," Passepartout pointed at the churches, "What manner of game is this?"

"Tarock," one of the men enthused, motioning him to take a seat, which Passepartout did. "*Diese karten*—," he began, then stumbled slowly into English, "These cards are for them. We *komme aus* Salzburg, and the trumps have all *bilder* of our city. Ah—playing reminds of home."

"Trumps? Like the whist?" Passepartout asked.

"*Ja*, like." Tapping the picture stack, "*Abe*r this suit *immer* trump. May we teach you to play?"

"With only three?"

"*Tarock spielt mit drei*," the other man grumped, fluent enough to understand English, but less motivated to use it, and skeptical that Passepartout would quickly learn its refined rules. Fortunately his partner was a patient, if labored, tutor.

The game shared many features with whist, where players were obliged to follow any suit led, but could only play one of the twenty-two picture card trumps were they void in that regular suit, or trumps being led—the highest here being an unnumbered one called the *Sküs* (showing a bearded soldier, holding a doll-sized vaguely Asiatic counterpart in his left palm). Each played alone, not partnered. The four regular suits had fewer cards than in whist, and in a most idiosyncratic combination. A fourth equestrian figure had been added to royalty, but there were but four numbered cards below them: *ten* to *seven* for the spades and clubs; *one* to *four* in the diamonds and hearts—and Passepartout was informed that those red cards ranked the "wrong" way, such that the *four* counted lower than the *three* above it.

Passepartout shook his head at such an irrational convention, but accepted that was how the game was played. Three cards were set aside in the deal as a talon, variously available for replacing cards in the winning bidder's hand. There were points accrued for tricks taken, as in whist, but also for capturing any of the court cards and three of the trumps (collectively called *Matadors*)—novel features compared to whist, which Passepartout found provocative and challenging, particularly the enormous benefit to any player who could bid an intention to take the final trick with the lowest of the trumps, the *Pagat*, and then hoard that card through the seventeen tricks to carry out this extremely difficult *pagat ultimo*. How so many Italianesque phrases had come to be attached to this eccentric Austrian game, Passepartout could not fathom.

And so did Passepartout learn to play a new (yet very old) game there in the lounge of the *Carnatic*, as it steamed along through the night toward Yokohama, observed by Gratton and Stanish, who otherwise had no game at all. Passepartout and the two Salzburgers were still at it at two in the morning, when the Allahabad duo were losing the battle with their eyelids and had to retire to their staterooms.

After some time, Passepartout's gaming partners were worn out too, after which Passepartout had to decide which of the unoccupied staterooms he would take short slumber in that morning, after jostling the sheets and chair in his own cabin first, and move his hat about.

 ☙ ❧

By dawn that Monday, the 11th of November, the *Tankadere* was in sight of the Chinese coast again, more rugged and green in this region, and now less than a hundred miles from Shanghai. The sea air remained cold, though, with the added chill of Mr. Fix, having recovered from his indisposition and joining Fogg and Aouda more frequently on deck.

The wind and weather were at their best, and Bunsby put up the remainder of their sails so they now raced along at full reach.

"Nothing more from Passepartout," Aouda sighed as she sat down beside Fogg on deck.

"Are you concerned?"

"I dislike not knowing."

Fogg smiled. "He's a resourceful fellow. And no message means *no message*. Nothing else."

"I know many a Buddhist who thinks that way, Phileas. It surprises me, from an Englishman."

"It's all a way of managing one's ... time," Fogg told her.

 ☙ ❧

When Passepartout appeared as usual for breakfast on the *Carnatic*, Gratton and Stanish were not sure what to make of it. They didn't wait for Passepartout to finish when Gratton asked the purser, "Any developments concerning our associate Fox?"

"Nothing to report. Sorry." Thinking of what Passepartout said about his conversation with them in the liner's bar, he added, "What's the occasion for your trip to Yokohama?"

"Business in Japan, selling cranes and other shipping gear. Here's their card," which Gratton fished from his wallet. Good that he'd kept that, from his prior employment.

"Stuart and company, Glasgow. I think I've heard of them." Collingwood handed the card back. "You sailed all the way from Scotland?"

"No, India. An agent for them there," Gratton smiled, and he and Stanish repositioned to be ready to follow Passepartout when he was done.

After a good comb of his hair in a mirror by the saloon entrance, Passepartout resumed his strolls around the ship, this time increasing his speed. Back in Hong Kong he had initially wandered about at only a casual pace, calculated so that his pursuers might not be lost too easily, but now he endeavored to gauge more precisely at what rate and under what conditions Gratton might fall by the wayside (he did not question the much younger and fitter Stanish's capacity to keep up).

Those doorways with a sill (often involving a hatch that could be closed in inclement seas) naturally slowed the man, as did stairs in general, but not as much as one might have thought. From his carefully judged backward glances, Passepartout soon could see Gratton and Stanish were increasingly unappreciative of the merry chase, but stuck it through all the way to the luncheon bell. Everyone by now had considerable appetites.

Passepartout resumed his perambulations after lunch, pressing forward until he reached the forecastle stairway beside the foremast. Sitting down on one of the middle steps, he surveyed the panorama from this added height. The Allahabad men were not in view, affording him a welcome respite from thinking about them.

Just then, Passepartout's Austrian tarock instructor happened by. "You use the walking for fitness?" The man's build did not suggest he indulged in that much himself.

"*Ja*," a use of the German that pleased the fellow. "And to get where I want to be."

"I hope we may play more cards tonight," the man said.

"We shall see," Passepartout smiled.

Seeing the smoke churning out of the funnel, Passepartout was reminded that the *Carnatic*, like the *Mongolia* and *Rangoon*, was one of those ships built in the older style, where all the steam machinery was situated directly beneath their funnel (unlike the new way, especially preferred for the heavily trafficked Atlantic service, where the mechanical workings were cleverly displaced so that First Class passenger accommodations could be situated there, where there was less roll to the ship). Having heard no variations in the sound of the *Carnatic*'s engines, Passepartout grew curious to see how they differed from the *Rangoon*'s.

Gratton and Stanish were in the bar, working on their third round of beverage, appearing to the barman's jaded opinion as two lonely bachelors drinking away their frustration on a ship with no women. When Gratton and Stanish spied Passepartout passing one of the windows, though, the latter darted out on deck while the former followed more slowly.

"He took a door down ahead," Stanish reported. Gratton was in less of a hurry this time, feeling steadier now, more resolute. He led the way into the corridor, which spanned the deck and carried an access way into the ship's engineering on their right. Gratton rapped his knuckles softly on that door and indicated with a thumb gesture that Passepartout may have gone below. Stanish's expression suggested he agreed.

"Let's go explore," Gratton said.

Gratton and Stanish proceeded carefully into the gangway, discovering a steep stair working around the base of the funnel along its starboard face, which Gratton negotiated slowly but successfully. Both men listened for any crewmen so as to avoid encountering them if possible, while also keeping an eye out for whether Passepartout was a fellow interloper here.

Pressing forward, they found themselves before an open railed gangway which spanned aft; from it, they could see down many decks. Here, the piping leading up to the funnel was in a roar from the boilers far below, tended by sweating gangs feeding the insatiable monster its diet of coal, but not visible from where they stood. Aft of that, the engine proper transformed the steam into reciprocating motion via two great walking beams, cycling as the pistons relentlessly rose and fell, in turn powering the ship's propeller shaft far to the rear. Two levels of transverse gangways gave precarious access all around to the machinery's sides, for lubrication or repair.

Stanish tapped Gratton's shoulder and pointed down off to a corner, decks below, where Passepartout's head could be seen, bobbing back and forth, apparently in conversation with some engineer, whose cap occasionally slipped into view.

"If he goes out the back way," Stanish shouted into Gratton's ear, "I think he'd have to come *up* to the hatch we saw yesterday."

Pressing ahead on the gangway to where there were stairs to the walkways below, Gratton motioned for Stanish to take the port way, while he headed down the starboard stair beside him. The faster moving Stanish crossed between the two piston beams and gamboled down the stairs, from where he could now see Passepartout and the engineer more clearly, still at their chat, though quite impossible to make out in the din. Passepartout seemed jovial, moving his hands in animation, causing the coat he'd taken off in the engine room heat (and which now he held on one arm) to flop about, one flailing sleeve almost slapping into the machinery. Passepartout looked apologetic, and began to groom his hair.

A few moments later, Gratton reached the lower gangway and could just see Passepartout leaving the engineer. Gratton looked around for the best way to proceed, but Stanish was already on it, reaching the end of the port side gangway on the far end of the second piston beam, giving him a good view below as Passepartout darted into his view, heading up a stair to the level just below the one Stanish was on, which he figured was that leading to the exit hatch.

With Passepartout's back being to him, the white shirt an invitingly contrasting target, easily within his practiced marksman's range at this distance (even after a few drinks), Stanish impetuously pulled out his revolver and fired. The report was all but unheard over the rattle and rumble of the engines, but he apparently got the Frenchman in his right arm, as Passepartout tossed a quick look back and then proceeded up the stairs more quickly, signs of blood finally appearing around the spot.

Stanish was now racing to a stair down to that gangway, committed to keep hot on his prey. He saw Gratton working in from the starboard side on the catwalk above, paused to wave to get his attention, motioning to his own right arm where he'd hit Passepartout, before running for the hatch himself. He was just seeing Passepartout's back disappearing through the door of the passenger stairs at the far end of the hall as he emerged from the crew hatch.

Picking up speed, Stanish bolted down the hall for the stair himself, bounding up one flight and around the corner and headlong into Passepartout, who had stopped on the step next up from the landing, comb in his right hand. Without a moment's pause, Passepartout barreled down onto him, forcing him back against the wall, his left hand dislodging the gun from Stanish's right with what must have been a most painful snap, but Stanish offered no cry as Passepartout's right forearm was now rammed into the man's neck. Stanish could clearly see the blood around the wound he'd inflicted.

"This is *absurd*," Passepartout said sadly, "You should have stopped."

And with precision, Passepartout flung the man back down the stairs, grabbed his gun from the floor, pocketing it along with his comb. Continuing up the stairs to the next deck, Passepartout did not stop to hear the sound Stanish's neck made as it slammed into the landing below. He now appreciated why Aouda had not been more alarmed at Fox on the *Rangoon*'s staircase, recognizing how fragile the human frame could be when propelled with sufficient momentum in such a confined space.

Striding out the stair door on the deck above, Passepartout made for one of the staterooms, which he knew belonged to a man of his approximate build, and was presently not containing its occupant. Slipping inside, he fished out the least distinctive shirt from the man's luggage, then quickly left with it and crossed to a door just down the hall, one of the unoccupied staterooms. Tossing his coat and the expropriated shirt down on the bed, Passepartout began to remove his own shirt, with its splotch of blood around the bullet hole, draping it over a chair back so that its stain did not bleed through to the wood or upholstery.

At just that moment, William Gratton had reached the staircase, and found on the next landing the body of young Frank Stanish sprawled there. He immediately sought out a steward or officer to report this latest outrage.

In his borrowed stateroom on the deck above, Passepartout crossed to the washstand and lifted up his right arm, pulling the forearm back and clenching his hand into a fist. Closing his eyes, his muscles tensed and quivered, and eventually a sharp plink was heard as the bullet fell from his arm into the bowl. Without opening his eyes, Passepartout turned slightly to the right, the fingers relaxing, extended his arm and put his left hand up under the wound, remaining so for some time.

At length, with the surface of the wound adequately mended, Passepartout took a deep breath, put on the fresh purloined shirt, removed the gun from his coat pocket, setting it beside the stained shirt on the chair, and crossed to the porthole wall. Taking out his comb he held it up, its tines shifting back and forth, then returned it to his pocket. Passepartout then bundled up Stanish's pistol in the damaged shirt, added the bullet from the bowl, opened up the porthole and chucked the lot into the East China Sea.

Passepartout then put his coat back on and left for a stroll. He was quite hungry now, but there were still some hours to fill before dinner.

The officer who Gratton brought to Stanish's body on the stairs took note of the alcohol on both the men's persons, the breath of the alive one and the palpable reek on the face of the one no longer, and presumed this a misstep and tumbling occasioned by that regrettable indulgence. None of Gratton's direct testimony could count against it (since he could hardly admit to having stalked Passepartout just previously, without that information being taken rather the wrong way).

⋙ ⋘

The *Tankadere* reached the mouth of the Shanghai River at six that evening, their captain skillfully working through the currents and winds that threaded the vine choked hilly islands there. Beyond that barrier, the broad open port of Shanghai itself, with its European buildings and imposed colonial manners, was situated twelve miles further up the estuary, and an hour later they had still three miles to go.

The Captain's expression turned crestfallen, as he pointed away to a paddlewheel steamer just working its way downriver towards the sea—it was the Pacific Mail's *General Grant*, already departing Shanghai. They were too late.

Fogg advised they lower their flag to half-mast, a recognized signal for naval distress, and fire the *Tankadere*'s cannon as further warning. Bunsby complied, and by that means managed to attract the attention of the steamer, Pilot Boat No. 43 performing, in a manner of speaking, its customary role of making contact with a ship—only 800 miles from its regular service and acting outside its typical function, conveying no pilot but only several new passengers.

Settling what he owed the good captain (£400 for their four-day voyage to Shanghai, minus the £200 advance, but sweetened by another £500 as bonus for general appreciation), Phileas Fogg quickly persuaded his way onto SS *General Grant*, with Aouda and Fix and baggage soon aboard, impromptu cabins arranged, and the paddles given tacit leave by the unstoppable Mr. Fogg to resume their flap-flap-flap-flapping northeast across the East China Sea to Japan.

⋙ ⋘

William Gratton was not comfortable as he took dinner alone aboard the *Carnatic* that evening, not helped even by having taken another drink in the bar in honor of his slain comrade. He was especially furious to see Passepartout dining as calm as you please, as if nothing had happened. Finishing early, Gratton marched over to the purser to demand, "I saw you questioning that Passepartout yesterday. Didn't you learn anything?"

"I was not *interrogating* him, Mr. Gratton."

"Isn't he suspicious? Traveling alone, no baggage. Says he's a Frenchman. He's been following us all the way since India, you know."

"Has he really?"

"Yes. He was even arrested in Calcutta, for blaspheming a Hindu temple. Check that."

"You seem to know a great deal about someone you weren't following."

"Are you going to search him, or not?"

"We'll do what we deem appropriate, sir."

The purser had a most conciliatory expression when he sought out Passepartout, Gratton hovering ominously nearby. "I must apologize, but Mr. Gratton—that man with the limp—has demanded you be searched, regarding the Fox matter, and now the death of his other man, this afternoon, Stanish. He's most agitated."

"Another? What happened?"

"Fallen down a stair, drunk apparently, heading for his cabin likely."

"My—tragic. But why does this man concern himself with me?"

"It is ... *complicated*. He seems ... *obsessed*. You have every right to refuse a search."

"*Merci*. But, no. You must do your duty. Freely search my stateroom, and my person. To allay all doubt."

Collingwood found another ship's officer to assist, but seeing Gratton trying to follow, he turned back to warn, "Please, Mr. Gratton. Stand down." Gratton frowned, but did so, watching in mounting frustration as the purser and the officer took Passepartout below to his cabin—which he had not actually occupied for several days, apart from his hat now and then, and which naturally exposed nothing of suspicion.

Passepartout pulled out the contents of his pockets onto a table: a few coins of modest value, his watch, the charming little snuffbox, and, of course, that beautiful comb. "These are heirlooms greatly dear to me," he said of the comb and box, passing his hand by them. "My only possessions to cherish." He scooped up the telegraph, leaving Collingwood to take up the comb.

Flipping the case open, Passepartout did something he did not like doing: he invented a tale. "This is the tiniest of music boxes, or used to be. It has not worked in years. The little lever winds the mechanism, but as you can hear, it no longer plays when you press the button," making a point of tapping it with his right thumb, without having moved the switch from its off position, lest the lamp light in the cover—or worse, the purser pick it up and paw at it, flip the switch and inadvertently start signaling Aouda's receiver in what would likely have been incoherent Morse, in turn running the risk of eliciting a singularly quizzical response on the light that, by all odds, could not be unsuspiciously explained.

"A tune of opera, Rossini—a great favorite of someone I knew," Passepartout concluded wistfully.

Quite moved by Passepartout's emotional prevarication, the purser returned the comb to the table and inspected the watch.

"Twenty past eleven?" Collingwood wondered, it being some three hours earlier presently.

"The watch is kept on Mr. Fogg's London Greenwich time, at his stipulation," Passepartout explained. "It is in the late morning there."

Finding no weapons or articles of thievery on Passepartout's person or in his stateroom—least of all anything linking him to Fox, Stanish, or Gratton—Collingwood justifiably concluded, "I think we've learned enough. Thank you."

Whereupon Passepartout decamped to the lounge, where he brightened the night of the two Austrians by joining them for cards once more, playing tarock well into the morning hours. Passepartout found he was getting rather good at it.

20. IN WHICH PASSEPARTOUT RESOLVES AN IMPEDIMENT, WHILE LEARNING NOT ENOUGH BY IT

Although paddlewheel propulsion had become rather *passé* for modern ocean craft of the 1870s, the *General Grant* was a swift enough vessel, making good time toward Nagasaki all that Tuesday, November 12th.

After breakfast, Phileas Fogg and Aouda commenced an exploratory survey of the public decking, with the object of ascertaining the crew and passenger habits (including those of Mr. Fix), as well as which locations might be most suitable for the discrete comings and goings they had in mind for the *Deimos* next week. The stern appeared promising, with two lifeboats stowed on each side of the rear deck, and a small deck lounge between them.

Leaning against the railing by the fantail flagpole, Fogg and Aouda could only see the deck forward in slices, around the boats or deckhouse, suggesting anyone standing forward of those obstacles might not take much note of anything back here, especially at night. Moreover, Aouda called Fogg's attention to the waterline, far enough below to allow the *Deimos* to glide up under the bulwarks, popping up to the deck height only briefly.

Altogether, satisfactory enough.

Now, if only there were some aboard proficient in whist.

ଓଃ ଛୀ

Aboard the *Carnatic*, just then working east along the southern stretch of the Japanese archipelago, William Gratton was anxious and angry. In the space of a few short days both of his compatriots, armed as he was, and as skilled as any commander could hope, whom he had known for their military valor and unshaking loyalty to the Crown, were gone. And the vile Frenchman, of the land of Republics and Scientific Reason, whom men above his station regarded as a danger to be squashed (and had hired him to accomplish that very purpose), continued to promenade and dine and amuse himself at foreign cards with complete impunity.

He was the only one left now. The sort of bold action he had envisaged when there were three of them, or even two, now seemed less considerate. How could he achieve *alone* what the three of them had so miserably failed to do in concert? And given what had happened to Fox and Stanish, should he not also be in fear for his own fate, with no one aboard *Carnatic* knowing what threat this Passepartout represented? No one he could confide in, or trust—least of all that useless excuse for a purser, Collingwood, who could not be made to act the British officer.

Gratton's appetite was declining by the mile, from breakfast through lunch and on to dinner—though not so his solace at the *Carnatic*'s bar, where he drank more that day than he had all the voyage, trying to work out what he might—or even *could*—do next.

଴ ଺

The stateroom suite Fogg arranged aboard the *General Grant* was actually their best, capacious and well-decorated, with two bedrooms for complete propriety, not always booked due to its cost (and certainly not by any of the large number of Chinese coolies the ship was conveying to California this trip, striving for a better life there in spite of the great distance and even greater domestic prejudice).

This was the first time Aouda had a proper room for sleeping since they'd left Hong Kong, which she now made the most of. Obtaining from Fogg the small red leather case she had him keep in his carpetbag, Aouda opened it to reveal three felt-lined compartments. The left contained many thin black cords, like slightly stiff shoelaces. The one in the middle held an intricate miniature engine. In the third, adjoining a small funnel, a glass flask fit very tightly, in which a clear liquid sloshed.

Aouda set the machine on a table near her bed, below the swinging kerosene wall lamp, and adjusted set screw pads at each corner until a tiny level built into its base marked to her satisfaction. A walking beam about four inches in length connected two shining brass pistons, between which lay a cylinder with an inlet valve which Aouda now filled from the flask, a pungent perfume of alcoholic distillation wafting the air. She then removed her bracelets, and took the pillbox from a dress pocket; to each of these she attached a cord via tiny circular openings, the other ends affixed in like manner to the engine, over which a row of tiny gauges and lights were arrayed.

After turning a switch on one side of the mechanism, she tugged a small lever on its front, back and forth three times, then flipped a switch beside it—a dull electric crackle snapped, but nothing else. Aouda frowned, pumped the lever thrice again, and once more raised the switch. This time, a flick of flame shot from a straw-sized exhaust tube as the pistons began to cycle, chugging softly—and once the boiler had warmed, sped up to a governed rate, the gauges' needles (now illuminated in a pale green glow) reporting the electric flow along the several cords.

"Does that have to be done very often?" Fogg asked.

"It depends on how we use them. My bracelets, most frequently. I'll need to replenish with some perfume or other combustibles eventually."

When a red lamp lit over the cord to the pillbox some time later, Aouda pulled it from the still running engine. The red lamps over the two linking her bracelets took considerably longer to light, after which she returned all the devices to their compartments, and the case back to Fogg's carpetbag.

☙ ❧

Excitement mounted for the tarock players aboard *Carnatic* that evening.

Having been dealt a surfeit of trumps but not void in any of the standard suits (which would have forced him to play them too quickly), Passepartout had felt confident enough to bid his first *pagat ultimo*. He now held the only two trumps not yet played: the low *Pagat*, primed for taking the last trick, and the VI showing two of Salzburg's nearby crags of *Schellenberg* and *Berchtesgaden*, scenery of such bucolic innocence.

Retaining the lead, Passepartout had just taken the penultimate trick with the VI, and was about to sweep up the other captured plain suit cards (including a nice Queen of spades for points), when Gratton appeared by their table.

"You're not going to catch me on a stair, do you understand?" Gratton warned Passepartout, who did not acknowledge him apart from a silent glance.

"You know this gentleman?" the Austrian facile in English asked, not satisfied at this interruption or the man's manners.

"Not really," Passepartout told him, refusing to turn from the card table. "He has mislaid some of his friends, I understand."

"*Mislaid?*" Gratton was now flush, a vein in his neck throbbing.

"Misled, perhaps?" Passepartout still not turning to look at him, "My English is not always so perfect."

Gratton stepped behind Passepartout's chair, planting his hands on either side, looking fit to try and rock the chair clear off its front legs. Staring down at the top of Passepartout's oft-combed hair, "You *know* what you say—and I know what you have *done*. Not forgetting, not for me."

Now Passepartout's partner definitely did not like this man's card room etiquette, and he rose, as did his fellow Austrian to support him, a woolen-suited wall looming cross the table, the non-English speaker brandishing his score-keeping pencil like a defensive pike.

"Your company might be better spent at some other *Tisch, bitte*," the first said, "We vill *spiel* here."

Gratton removed his hands from Passepartout's chair, pursed his lips, and quit the lounge.

After the Austrians resumed their seats, Passepartout flung the *Pagat* onto the table, capturing the remaining cards and earning grunts of admiration from them both.

☙ ❧

Phileas Fogg and his unprecedented rush around the world were by now well known to those aboard the *General Grant*, and he found no trouble partnering up for whist. They were keen at it still when the ship steamed into the harbor of Nagasaki late that night. The temperature had dropped to around fifty Fahrenheit, and the stay was short, just long enough for passengers to leave or come aboard, effected by boats coming out to them, as at Suez or Singapore.

"It's a pretty city, worth the view if it were day," one card player offered. "Mountains all around, terraced fields, old temples and castles. The Nagasaki River gorge is filled with giant boulders like pebbles, very Japanese."

"Starting to change, though," Fogg's partner ventured from across the table. "They're a long way from where they were half a century ago, when their engineers used to make only mechanical toys for the aristocrats of Kyoto. The new Meiji government's running the old Dutch shipyard here now. Military expansion is their official policy, army and navy."

"I doubt Nagasaki will ever be famed for anything violent," the first replied skeptically. "Giving up rice paper walls and deferential politeness for iron plate seems against their nature."

Fogg shuffled the deck for the next hand without comment.

ෲ ෩

When Passepartout retired that night on the *Carnatic*, he went through his cautionary ritual: going first to his assigned cabin to disturb the bedding and reposition isolated furniture, flopping his hat on a wall peg, then checking the way out with a wave of his comb, before proceeding to the stateroom he'd slept in last night (which happened to be Fogg's). Retrieving the opium pipe from deep under the mattress, Passepartout repeated his comb maneuver, slipping away to Fix's intended room once the way was clear.

Tonight, though, Passepartout did not let go of his comb, nor put the pipe under the mattress. Mr. Gratton was, as one saying might put it, at the end of his tether. His accosting Passepartout in the ship's lounge, accompanied by an even stronger scent of liquor about him, put the valet on heightened guard. If Gratton—or rather, Gratton's *gun*—went strolling this night, Passepartout resolved not to remain unaware of it, and be prepared to move himself at the menace.

So it was, that when Gratton did leave his stateroom later that night, gun in his pocket, Passepartout was awoken by his instrument's pervasive apprehension.

Gratton went straight to Passepartout's booked cabin, looked both ways to see that no one was out in the hall, then pushed inside without knocking, his pistol brandished at the ready. It took some minutes in the dark to find the room empty, no Passepartout on the bed or hiding in some corner, only his hat on the peg. Gratton didn't leave, though. He sat on a chair and began to think—finally realizing what had not occurred to him before, that Passepartout hadn't been sleeping there, and possibly hadn't been for many days.

It meant Passepartout was even more cautious than he had thought, and that he had no idea where he might be aboard ship.

Passepartout was thinking, too. Tomorrow they would be arriving in Yokohama. Whatever Gratton planned to report to his masters, whoever they may be, could have no effect if he never reported it. The logic of it was all too obvious, and he decided it was time to conclude this dismal conflict.

When Gratton did return to his own room, he had a guest. By the dim kerosene lamplight, Passepartout forced an elbow into his side, and spun Gratton around to the floor, the cabin door swinging shut from a measured kick from Passepartout's right foot. In a moment, Passepartout had dropped down to plant his right knee across the man's chest, and lay his left hand across his forehead.

"You cannot—," Gratton started to say, but soon was teetering toward unconsciousness. But not completely, not yet.

Passepartout began to slide his hand across Gratton's forehead. Attending to every eye flicker and muscle twitch the man made, Passepartout looked him in the eyes, speaking deliberately. "You all have hunted me, stupidly. Someone must have *ordered* it. Did you know the person who *ordered* it? Or that person who only hired *you*. Just *that* person, no one else. No one else." Passepartout seemed puzzled now. "Did you not ask them *why*, no curiosity to ask them *why*? Waving your guns without asking *why*?"

Gratton's eyelids were fluttering now, his breathing more labored, muscles showing the slightest of quivering even to his limbs. Passepartout finally shook his head with disappointment, "No, no—no curiosity. Nothing there. Foolish. I don't think you knew *anything*."

The fingers of Passepartout's hand splayed wider, and he concentrated more intently. Gratton's eyes stayed shut now, his breathing becoming more measured. Passepartout took the opium pipe from his pocket, pressed Gratton's fingers onto it, then lay it by the man's left hand, knowing exactly what it would imply once the scene was found—relying on the human nature, people so often taking their expectations for the real.

Ideally, by then Passepartout would already be off the ship.

Passepartout conducted one final wave of his comb before leaving, looked back at Gratton's chest, rising and falling in a sleep he would be unlikely to arouse from anytime soon, whatever the stimulus, and went out into the hall. This time, Passepartout landed in his own booked stateroom, where for once on this worrisome voyage he could fall into something like an untroubled slumber.

21. IN WHICH PHILEAS FOGG RUNS GREAT RISK OF LOSING ACCOUNT OF PASSEPARTOUT, AND WHAT WAS DONE ABOUT IT

The *Carnatic* reached the broad Yokohama harbor at dawn on Wednesday the 13th of November, somewhat ahead of schedule, making way through the many ships anchored around the bay, to settle at the quays of the European quarter near the customs house. Passepartout awoke once the engines stopped, and fetched out Aouda's snuffbox to report: *ARRIVED YOKOHAMA EARLY, ALLAHABAD MEN DEALT WITH, JEAN P.*

The pulsing of her left bracelet awoke Aouda. She had caught only the last few words of Passepartout's message, but fortunately she had the prescience to have adapted the repeater telegraph idea of the clever American, Mr. Edison, so that she could hear again whatever message may have last been received. After feeling that repeat of Passepartout's pulse on her left wrist, she quickly replied: *ABOARD GENERAL GRANT, ARRIVING YOKOHAMA 14TH AM, WHAT WILL YOU DO IN MEANTIME? AOUDA.*

Passepartout wondered how they managed to get aboard the very ship they were intending to meet only there in Yokohama, but he would learn that in due course. Unfortunately, Aouda's response was incomplete at his end, getting only so far as *YOKOHAMA 14T* when the lamp in the snuffbox lid gave out.

One day to occupy himself in the foreign metropolis of Yokohama, it would seem, among people whose language he did not know, provisioned with only a few coins in his pocket (none of them Japanese), one snuffbox (as inert now as his music box fiction)—and, of course, his comb.

Passepartout resolved to make the most of his last paid-for breakfast aboard ship before leaving.

Aouda waited some time for Passepartout to answer her query. When she heard nothing further, she rightly deduced Passepartout's telegraph had run out of power, and informed Fogg of her concern later.

"Well, he should be waiting at the Pacific Mail's pier for the *General Grant*," Fogg predicted affably.

CS SO

The morning air of Yokohama had remained cool, laced with the salty bite of the sea, when Passepartout strolled down the gangway to occupy himself for the next twenty-four hours or so until Fogg and Aouda reached the port. For the very first time since leaving America, and particularly so for the six harried weeks he had known and accompanied Phileas Fogg from London to this place, he could explore an unfamiliar land without anyone following. No Mrs. Hammond, or Mr. Fix, or the Allahabad men now welcomed to their respective peace.

The promontory on the south side of Yokohama harbor, originally given by begrudged treaty as a settlement for the foreigners forcing their entry into Japan two decades before (including even the many Chinese locating here for work), was now a maze of low buildings outwardly looking not excessively European, but whose interiors notably adhered to their homelands' various esthetics.

There were gardens in the western fashion, and even their own cemetery. The narrow streets were already thick with pedestrians and rickshaws, people of many nations, many languages—not Japanese.

But the European influence did not end at the low fence circuiting the enclave, as Passepartout discovered as he made his way north along the bay. The Meiji Restoration had done more than acknowledge the new openness with the west; they were embracing the Europeans' architecture, clothing, industry and science, with the object of making it their own and by that means transcend that foreign humiliation—beating them at their own game. A sign of this were the several clothing shops he passed in which western fashions were prominently on display along with that of their own culture.

One local tradition had not been usurped: the many stalls offering food of all kinds—the Japanese seemed resolutely dedicated to their own cuisine and little other. Unfortunately, he lacked local coin for any of it. Still less for another of the city's institutions: the famous Jinpuro ("Nectarine") brothel that had recently opened an enlarged facility at its new location, *Takashima-cho 2-chome*, covering a whole block on three floors, rows of prostitutes sitting or standing at its windows, inviting their own aspect of commerce with expressions Passepartout found more impassive and harried than demure or enticing.

Strolling still farther into Yokohama, Passepartout came upon their new railroad station, designed by an American architect in a stolid Beaux Arts style that would have been equally at home in Des Moines or Albany, where squat little British locomotives pulled quaint boxlike passenger cars on the pioneering line to Tokyo. That American style was reflected in how the tracks simply appeared on the cleared soil of the street, no intent to hide them or the long platform behind from public view or access.

Passepartout noted more of the passengers were still in traditional Japanese attire than those not, while mixed in were knots of newly minted soldiers, proud and swaggering in their crisp uniforms (dark blue in mimicry of the American Union model), the latest product of the mandatory military service recently instituted by the Meiji.

Just then he was about the only European among those outside the railroad station, standing out by his height and features. Several people at the station took note of his clothing, though, some women in a party pointing at his quaint round hat and giggling.

ఴ ఞ

The unsettling discovery that morning of a comatose passenger in his stateroom by one of *Carnatic*'s stewards provided a melancholy denouement to what was adding up to be an ill record for that installment of the company's Hong Kong to Yokohama run.

"A rash of intoxicated falling," Collingwood offered as gallows humor to a representative of the line who appeared early that afternoon to assess the situation for the company. "One overboard, we think. Another down stairs, both drunk apparently. And our opium smoker," indicating Gratton, just then being carried off on a stretcher. "We thought to take him to the new American Naval Hospital up on the Bluff. Someone there may be able to revive him—or look after him, at least, until the British Consul weighs in. We had an envelope for the Consul anyway, so gave the messenger a note to carry on this Gratton matter."

"Rather rum luck for you, all on one sail?" the company man said.

"Yes. Odder still, they were traveling together. Suspicious, three that way, knowing one another. Something for the authorities to look into, anyway. My money, the limping man could have been responsible, the one with the opium pipe. Fits of rage, perhaps. He was the one who discovered the man's body on the stairs, or so he said. An arrogant bully, paranoia for foreigners, too—he even conjured some grudge against one of our First Class, a French valet. No end, the sort of people you encounter on the sea."

Two Japanese men were also watching the departure of the litter, just as they had discovered that the *Carnatic* had arrived early in Yokohama (in this way, unknowingly retracing the same miscalculation the now indisposed Gratton had tumbled over back in Bombay three weeks prior). Both men were strong and wary, one a fellow in his mid-thirties, his companion somewhat older—and well attired in understated European suits with manners tailored to match.

The younger man, a Mr. Inagi, in black, came up to the purser, asking deferentially, "Excuse me. Is that a Mr. William Gratton? He is come for business. I am to meet."

"Yes, I'm sorry to say. That is Mr. Gratton—a mishap."

"He was traveling with two others also, no?"

"More mishaps there, I'm afraid," Collingwood said slowly, thinking how much he ought to reveal to a stranger. "The Yokohama prefecture, or the ship's agents may be at liberty to tell more. If you might leave your name—."

"I must seek instruction," the Japanese man smiled, nodding in retreat. "Thank you."

The older man, Mr. Tanabe, in dark blue, waited a bit before making his own inquiry of the purser, choosing his words very carefully. "Officer Sir, a passenger from France, sailing alone, do you recall him here?"

"His name?"

"Passepartout. I convey message."

"He's already disembarked. I'm sorry."

"Thank you," the man nodded, and left to rejoin Inagi, now out on the quay. They commenced an extended conversation in their native tongue.

It might have seemed an easy task to spot an isolated foreigner like Passepartout, towering over so many of the local population, dressed differently, in every way behaving out of place. But the two Japanese men had only a general description of the man to go on—and had been dispatched to the *Carnatic*'s pier merely to provide whatever assistance may have been required by Gratton and his team.

So much for that plan. And so much for Mr. Gratton, and his men. This grim and unexpected development put their own mission in a completely different light. They went to the telegraph office (another burgeoning project of the new Meiji regime of the Rising Sun) to report what had happened to the *Carnatic* venture.

That left Passepartout at large. But he was not the only foreigner in Yokohama that morning. There were so many now that the two Japanese men could find no one among those working down by the docks who could recall much of anything about that one particular passenger who had disappeared into the throng some hours before, other than that he had done so, and carried no luggage. His little round hat was somewhat unusual, though—several remembered that.

Which left to them the task of thinking like a European, reasoning out what Passepartout might be doing, or where he may have gone in pursuit of it. Food first? Shelter later? Meeting those basic needs, before doing—what? A canvas of rickshaw operators along the harbor began to suggest that the foreigner with the odd chapeau might have remained on foot, which would greatly restrict the territory open to him—unless, of course, he had hired one somewhere else. Or had not—exactly because any rickshaw driver might then have recognized him.

There was the train to Tokyo, though.

That they knew well, the British company whose affiliate they worked for here having supplied so much of the pipe and iron used to build both the station and the railyard. The two men took rickshaws there, where they found a few Europeans among those headed for Tokyo, but none corresponding to Passepartout's particulars (certainly not the two portly Austrian businessman up from the *Carnatic*).

Careful inquiry of the workers lent no support for Passepartout having taken the train, but several recalled a man of his description (that hat again) walking there earlier, talking with no one, but looking at the people and the trains and the buildings with evident interest. As near as one could recollect, the foreigner's hat had set off in the general direction of Noge Hill.

Noge Hill was a favorite place of residence for the city's wealthier merchants, its broad winding avenues undulating up and down, thickly lined with cherry trees, growing bare now in the autumn. There was a great Shinto shrine here, *Iseyama Kotai Jingu*, built just three years ago by the Meiji government on this high hill, where it would be plainly visible to all the Christian foreigners over on their promontory across town, silent affirmation of the youthful emperor's ascendance, and of the Shinto religion whose promotion was now a matter of political and cultural policy of his Enlightened Rule.

Could this Passepartout have been acting as the *tourist*? Something so simple, so banal?

Mr. Tanabe stopped his rickshaw at the steep steps that led up to the shrine, as did Inagi, who darted to the ground and up the path to investigate. The shrine was thronged with admiring faithful, strolling among its serene pavilions, stone lanterns, and tall narrow pylons carved with Japanese characters, the view of Yokohama and the harbor quite fine from here.

And indeed, some among the visitors remembered the looming (to their eyes) European with the little round hat, showing great pleasure in the sights, though not going too close to the temple itself (who there could have known of his experience at Malabar Hill in faraway India?).

Returning to the rickshaw, the two men speculated further. They had not passed Passepartout on the way from the train station to the shrine, so he had either wandered out into the countryside or … might be working his way back into town, perhaps towards the European enclave on the harbor.

Passepartout had come to Yokohama alone because he was separated from this Phileas Fogg he had been traveling with. Could he just be waiting to reconnect with him here? They had not been told of any of the Frenchman's booking intentions beyond Japan, but Mr. Fogg was traveling around the world—he was in all the papers, even their brand new daily newspaper, the *Mainichi*, as a recurring curiosity of note. That was at least a path they might follow, and the man in blue directed their rickshaws for the European quarter, where they learned the *General Grant* was the first available ship out for America, due in sometime tomorrow.

Their next move, then, come the morning—watch for that vessel, and who might be boarding it.

☙ ❧

Passepartout had covered a lot of the byways and gardens of Yokohama by the time night fell, the glow of lanterns now spilling dim slots of light into the streets. In the native quarter, Passepartout saw an old robed man with a telescope set out, a younger assistant standing beside at a folding table, and holding a lamp that he could open to bring illumination on it as needed. The telescope caught Passepartout's interest, and he edged closer, smiling and nodding all the while, his expression redolent of curiosity. Neither of the men seemed to mind his approach, smiling in return.

Once he was near enough, though, Passepartout realized these were not astronomers, working to extend the field of Japanese science for the Meiji, but an astrologer and his apprentice, the table dangling amulets and charms. A wooden *shikiban* divination board set on the table, painted an auspicious yellow and displaying a Big Dipper constellation in its raised center, around which were rings of Japanese characters allowing the hours of the day and night to be calibrated to the many magical influences.

Passepartout knew none of that arcane content, though he imagined it was as arbitrary and useless as the astrology found in Europe, among the many occult beliefs steeped in the old Second Empire of Napoleon III and showing no sign of waning in popularity even in the restored French Republic, that domain of professed empirical Reason. While Europe deemed the times AD 1872, here it was another Year of the Monkey, a land where the number *four* should be shunned because it shared its name with *shi*, the word for death, and astrologers like this fellow plotted with great precision which animal governed the subdivision of the hour.

He looked up at the stars where the astrologer's telescope was aimed. Had he been conversant in their language, he might have asked how far away they thought those twinkling sparks were above, or speculate on what sublime fires caused their light. Or whether Beings with even bigger telescopes might be looking back at them from invisible planets circling still more distant suns, far beyond any to be seen in this night sky.

And supposing a few of those Beings to be of a judgmental character, what might they make of such people as the astrologer or the protective priests of Malabar Hill, or the often marshalled armies and navies of a world childishly emboldened with their mastery of steam, if only they were made known to them?

But Passepartout did not know their language, so went on his way, back to the harbor to sit down among the seamen to await the dawn of Thursday, the 14th of November. There was less than a week to go before Impey Barbicane would be flying to the Moon, and here he was, plopped by himself on the quays of a city in Japan, like so much jetsam.

Every so often he could see another ship come into the bay, or even a few smaller boats settling up to the shore in the dark, faint lanterns swinging from bamboo stanchions. The chill of the night air didn't seem to bother him, though he was getting hungry. Thinking on that, he wondered whether his hat or coat might fetch enough in trade to cover a meal—obtaining some Japanese counterpart to render him simultaneously less conspicuous and serve as a souvenir of his visit here, like his Indian slippers.

After sunrise at quarter past six, some of the shops began to open, and Passepartout made his way back into town to find some dealing in used clothes. He eventually found a vendor partially communicative in French and English, and discovered his hat and coat were enough of a marketable novelty to exchange for a Japanese coat and a turban-like head covering, both well worn, with enough in change to handily finance a breakfast.

As he switched the contents of his pockets, the shopkeeper avidly sought to persuade him to part with his watch, snuffbox or comb as well, but Passepartout was adamant on those belongings.

Passepartout used his newfound Japanese coins to buy a hearty bowl of rice and some fried bird from a stall nearby, which was actually quite flavorful and fortified him for the walk back to the harbor. Working through the rousing activity along the dock, Passepartout did not initially attend to the two Japanese gentlemen in their European suits, who were asking things of the native stevedores and ship men, passing right by them at a steady clip.

But at length Passepartout noticed the man in the black suit gesturing out with his right hand, his palm upraised to above the man's own height, followed by a move to the top of his head, mimicking the shape of a hat with rounded top, after which the fellow he was addressing this performance to shook his head. The black suited man and his blue suited companion both looked disappointed, and moved farther down the pier in his direction, soon to repeat this pantomime.

The combination of the gestured height and curved headgear, while not conclusive, was nonetheless an indication he could not dismiss, and his mood damped at once. Not alone, after all, Passepartout lamented.

Before they had a chance to run into him down at the end of the pier, Passepartout would have to work back the way he had come, through the throng and past them, to find some safer location to await the *General Grant*'s arrival. Bringing out his comb, Passepartout determined as quickly as he could the lay of things: that among the assorted armaments filling the pockets of those on the pier, small pistols and some odd metal rings were on the persons of those two well-dressed Japanese gentlemen. The one in the blue suit also carried a sizable knife in a tubed scabbard, concealed under his long coat.

Looking for some moving combination of taller Europeans for cover, and hoping his new Japanese coat and headgear might provide further camouflage, Passepartout began to worm along the pier. He didn't look back as he passed where the two men were—and had progressed some dozens of feet successfully, when Mr. Inagi happened to look in his direction and was struck by the mismatch of European trousers and shoes, with a familiar local style of coat and head wrap above, only to be worn by someone rather too tall, and moving away too resolutely. Even from the back, he didn't like the look of it.

By the time Passepartout reached the streets and felt it safe to cast back, he saw the two men now approaching through the crowd, eyes clearly on him. He quickly and calmly turned, proceeding north, not knowing what the men might have in mind were they to reach him, but intending for that not to occur. He realized that his height put him at an irreversible disadvantage, so had to seize some other opportunity.

Farther down the street, Passepartout could see a clown outfitted as a rustic sage in flowing red robes tied with a bright blue sash, wearing a placard over his shoulders that announced front and back that the Japanese acrobatic troupe managed by one William Batulcar was ending its run of shows in Yokohama, then to be departing for America. Surrounded already by an entourage of enthusiastic children, and some curious adults, the clown's tall soled boots added considerably to his height, putting his head slightly higher than Passepartout's own. That too was convenient.

Passepartout pressed closer to read more of the placard. "LONG NOSES! LONG NOSES! UNDER THE DIRECT PATRONAGE OF THE GOD TINGOU!" the advertisement promised, confirmed when the clown turned his head to show him in a fierce red Japanese mask with a tubular nose almost a foot long. Tingou, once a Chinese mountain god, had become in the Shinto faith a birdlike slayer of vanity, and that popular folk tale provided the theme for their entertainment.

The Tingou-blessed clown was leading the throng on a long circle through parts of the native town, then back into the European settlement and the Gaiety Theater where they would be giving their performances. Passepartout followed all the way, as did the two Japanese men, always remaining well back in the street crowd—thereby sealing his surmise that they were a third set of people sent after him.

The Batulcar troupe's show was scheduled for three that afternoon, but Passepartout wasn't about to retire outside to wait for it, not with those two new pursuers about—and with likely not enough money to pay for any ticket himself. So he continued along beside the clown, right up to the stage door entrance, where the performer began to extricate himself from the placard.

"Please, may I help you off with this burden," Passepartout offered jovially, "You must have been carrying it for miles."

The clown pulled off his mask, revealing a Japanese visage, and one who spoke English, "Thank you."

"I'm a man of the circus myself," Passepartout said as he helped carry the placard inside, glancing back to see the two other men silhouetted against a brighter European plastered wall across the street. "Might I speak with your manager, Mr. Batulcar?"

With almost the speed with which he had come to be taken on as Mr. Fogg's valet in London, Passepartout parlayed employment on the spot as an acrobat capable of acting as the key support for their challenging showpiece: a great human pyramid. Their keystone performer for this having come to suffer from back tremors of late, Passepartout's size and manifest strength outweighed his obviously not being in any sense Japanese—a disguise further facilitated by those garish Tingou masks.

Studying the Gaiety Theater's advertisement poster outside, and its notification of the production's impending departure for America, the two Japanese men had to recognize the possibility that Passepartout had found some other means to travel to that destination, no longer in need of the mobility of Phileas Fogg. In either event, telegraphs would have to be dispatched reporting all, requesting and advising, after which some further action might be intended. They were debating now whether they should attend the show that afternoon, or otherwise ascertain what Passepartout was doing there at the theater.

ఴ ಜ

The SS *General Grant* steamed into Yokohama bay later that morning. Instead of mooring out in the harbor and using launches, though, the paddlewheel liner fell to American recklessness and sidled its stern hatches directly up to the end of the pier. Informed that the *Carnatic* had successfully disgorged her passengers the night before, the *General Grant*'s captain had only to await their connecting patrons while they took on fresh supplies, resolving to sail for San Francisco at half past six that evening.

Mr. Fix availed himself of this interlude by roaring down the gangplank and off to the British Consul, where he learned that at last his arrest warrant for Fogg had caught up with him (carried aboard the *Carnatic*, ironically enough), albeit of no use here. He would have to nurse it in his pocket until Phileas were back on British soil—*if* they were ever so.

Seeing no Passepartout roundabouts, though, Phileas Fogg and Aouda sought out the *Carnatic*, still at its pier, to inquire after him.

"Your servant, yes, fine chap—spoke about you both. Glad to meet you," purser Collingwood told Fogg. "He left ship yesterday morning. Didn't the Japanese fellow tell you?"

"No," Fogg said slowly, the pit of his stomach sinking. "Japanese fellow?" Aouda was already suppressing alarm.

"Yes, he was asking after your man, by name. Said he had some message for him. I assumed he was representing *you*."

"I'm sure he's representing *someone*," Fogg smiled thinly. "Thank you."

Down the gangplank and plopping their luggage on the pier, Fogg planted his left hand behind his back and sternly surveyed the maze of buildings and coursing people filling the panorama, none of them his valet. This would not do. Passepartout *must* be found—and before reaching Chicago.

"Where *are* you, Passepartout?" he sighed.

"We have six hours till sailing," Aouda reminded. "Though, however far we go, we still must return to the pier. That limits our spread."

"Now, if we only had the slightest idea where to search. Confound the man." At this moment, Fogg wished Auguste Dupin were there.

☙ ❧

Although Passepartout had some experience in this area, it took a bit of practice for him to learn the gymnastic routine he would be performing that afternoon for Batulcar's troupe, as did his fellows, having to adjust their actions to the increased stature of their central supporting man. In due course, all grew comfortable with the cooperative moves needed above and to either side of Passepartout. Fortunately, the lead artistes were already adequately fluent in their manager's American brand of English, and a few even spoke a smattering of French.

Once the actions were becoming routine, Passepartout graduated to the costuming, trying on his robe (red with stylized wings attached at the shoulders) and Tingou mask for fit, finding they easily covered his own coat and turban without need of removing them, then seeing how they operated in concert as he gestured and flexed.

The show was about to commence, and he couldn't help but be struck by the incongruity of it, yet another odd interlude between Mr. Fogg's placid Savile Row residence, the rescue of an Indian princess with her own flying carpet, and Mr. Barbicane's threatened cannonade to the Moon out in Florida. Oh yes—and the unpleasantness aboard the *Carnatic*.

What *tableaus fantastique* he had come to be a party to, and all within two months, having taken up with that amazing pair, Mr. Fogg and Aouda ...

Idiot!

Passepartout had fallen so completely into his preparations for the show over the last hours, he had forgot that his traveling companions *had no idea where he was*. Nor did he know *their* whereabouts, or when the *General Grant* would be sailing.

Absurd, ridiculous, pathetic.

He was about to reach for the snuffbox, but caught himself. No way around it, Passepartout thought. Looking around for somewhere reasonably secluded, he finally found a bench along a side wall where he could sit, nestled beside rows of costumes and theatrical props. He removed his mask and lay it to his right. Undoing the blue sash on his red robe so that he could fish into his own coat, Passepartout pulled out the comb, held it in both hands and shut his eyes—looking almost as if in prayer.

Aouda and Phileas Fogg had explored much of the European enclave by then, including uninformative stops at the French and English Consuls, and were far into the native section, walking down yet another street some distance from the harbor (knowing they were nearing the time when it would take as long to proceed back to the pier as they had up to this point), when Aouda's left bracelet hummed to life: *BEING FOLLOWED BY TWO JAPANESE MEN. I HAVE TAKEN REFUGE IN W BATULCAR ACROBAT SHOW, GAIETY THEATER. HAVE YOU SAILED? JEAN P.*

The physical intensity of the signal surprised her, the feeling from the bracelet almost a literal shock. Fogg noticed her reaction, but Aouda waved him to remain silent, moving her left hand to work the right bracelet: *OF COURSE NOT SAILED, 6 3 0 PM, LOOKING FOR YOU. THOUGHT BOX POWER GONE. WILL FIND YOU NOW. AOUDA.*

MERCI, WILL KEEP BUSY HERE, JEAN P.

Fogg and Aouda immediately sought out rickshaws to take them to this Gaiety Theater.

Passepartout opened his eyes, but only briefly to see no one taking note. Closing them again, he extended his right hand, waving the comb back and forth several times slowly, as the tines bent in and out and the merest of buzzing could be discerned. When he opened his eyes again, and returned his comb to his pocket, Passepartout was not pleased (though also not in the least surprised) to know that the same mix of weaponry that he had detected down on the Yokohama pier were now situated in the pockets of two figures reposed along the back row of the Gaiety Theater.

ભ જ

The Tingou spectacle began promptly at three o'clock, the opening acrobats leaping onstage in a swirl of vivid fabric and motion, accompanied by a din of celebratory percussion from the orchestra's gongs, wood clappers and blocks, *kokiriko* beating sticks, hand held bell trees, long *shamisen* banjos, bamboo flutes and seashell horns.

Mr. Inagi waited until several scenes had concluded before leaving his seat to make his way backstage to find whether Passepartout was indeed among their company—adopting the confident unthreatening pose of someone who looked exactly like the sort of person who belonged wherever they happened to be. Mr. Tanabe, meanwhile, remained seated to continue his observations from the spectator side (and it was a rather entertaining show, too, he thought, harboring quite a fondness for those skilled in such things as spinning tops).

The nature of the activity transpiring in the back of that theater in Yokohama would be familiar to any thespian of any land or time. The American William Batulcar was scurrying about like a harried mother hen, dividing his attention between peeking from a screen to see the current performers and assessing the audience's reaction to them (a satisfying mix of westerners and local people in traditional dress, he found), and glancing back at those preparing for the next act to make sure nothing went amiss there.

Sliding scenery for the pending tableaus were being shifted into place, performers scheduled for a later display were practicing their moves or chatting lowly with their fellows on matters having little to do with their profession, some others were seated on what few chairs or benches were available around the backstage aisles—and all accompanied by the dramatic reverberating harmonies of their grand Nipponese orchestra out in the pit.

Inagi skillfully circulated through this hubbub, trying to spot the Frenchman—or at least any persons falling within Passepartout's physical parameters, masked or not.

A prudent qualification, for Passepartout had by now put his leering red mask on and returned to the bench along the wall, reckoning that, sitting thus, it might be harder for others to tell how tall he was.

Batulcar came up to Passepartout, squinting down, "Which of my Tingou are you?"

Passepartout pulled his mask away enough to reveal his identity.

"Ah, sitting things out till your act is up, saving your strength! You looked good in the rehearsal; I'm confident."

Batulcar plopped down beside Passepartout, and began to rub his hands along his pants legs nervously, "Hope the show plays as well in America. You know, *none* of this is Japanese," waving an arm around him. "*We* brought the circus here, we Americans. Found a lot of Japanese who took to it, though, adding on their own ways. This Tingou thing is so exotic, and that *band*—have you ever heard anything *like* it?" Batulcar smiled, "Should shock the bustle off many a lady back home. Or at least, enough for them to buys lots of tickets, eh?" Batulcar jabbed Passepartout lightly with his elbow.

Passepartout hummed and nodded agreement. At just that moment he had glimpsed out of his mask eye openings the Japanese man in black, gliding coolly by across the building, the fellow glancing this way and that, obviously intent on locating him. Passepartout was about to point out this stranger to Batulcar, asking whether he knew the man and so perhaps set in motion his proper ejection from their midst—but the moving acrobats and stagehands soon eclipsed him and that opportunity slipped away.

"Well, don't miss your cue," Batulcar slapped Passepartout's robed leg, and got up to worry over something else.

Assessing all those he saw, eavesdropping on their chatter in Japanese and English, Inagi singled out a promising one to ask where he might find the "new Frenchman." While the man couldn't say exactly, he assured him there was plenty of time before the human pyramid. Thus had Mr. Inagi confirmed Passepartout was somewhere among these entertainers, and would have to move to the front ensemble eventually.

While Passepartout had been correct in thinking it would be more difficult to evaluate his height were he sitting down, he had forgot that it also made his trousers and shoes more visible as the bottom of the robe pulled up—which William Batulcar inadvertently accentuated by his innocent warning touch. Once Inagi took note of them, from off to Passepartout's right, he worked closer, as carefully as he could, anxious that the figure on the bench not fly off at his approach, until at last he settled down beside him.

"Mr. Passepartout, now the Tingou god." When the figure said nothing, he went on, "Your cuffs and shoes are not hidden by that long nose." More silence (save for the orchestra's adjacent accompaniment). "There were three men on the *Carnatic* boat I was to meet yesterday. On account of you, no one to meet. Messages have been sent on that, Mr. Passepartout, of your arrival *here*—you *must* know that. Where do you plan to run next? You have offended someone with very long reach."

Passepartout stood up, adjusted his robe and retightened his sash, and strode off away from Mr. Inagi, who arose and followed, first at a distance, then gradually closer. As Passepartout slid among the racks of costumes and scenic props, his pursuer taunted, "They must have got *very* close, those men on the *Carnatic*—to what you *know*?"

Passepartout stopped, removed his mask and laid it on the roof of a pagoda lantern, and turned back to declaim, "You say I have offended someone—"

Inagi took Passepartout's turn as an opportunity to move in even closer, putting one of his legs in between Passepartout's own, and arranging his arms for bodily attack to exploit his leg maneuver once the Frenchman was unbalanced and commenced to fall. Only Passepartout wasn't falling, not unbalanced at all, and Inagi's limbs found no more purchase or effect than had he attempted to waylay a great Sequoia tree.

"—but never say whom. Or is it *who*? Umm. No matter." Even as the man switched moves, trying alternative attacks, Passepartout continued to speak, all the while parrying each of Inagi's escalating efforts. "I suppose you will not tell me who has hired *you* for this, and for what purpose they have told you?" The man's expression, full of puzzlement and mounting frustration, did not look supportive. "No? I thought not."

Mr. Inagi paused, took a breath and girded to try another set of moves, none of which interrupted Passepartout's discourse. "Your movements are *amazingly* rapid," he smiled, eyes wide in genuine admiration now for the Japanese man, "You must have trained *years* for that."

When the Japanese started to reach down into his coat pocket, Passepartout chided, "You aren't thinking of using that metal ring of yours, are you? Not the gun—that's in your other pocket." Passepartout shook his head and sighed, "A shame your skills turned to such service."

Now quite disconcerted, Inagi abandoned his plan to put the dangerous *kakushi* (with its three short triangular spikes) on his middle finger. He resolved to prevail by his unaided limbs, honorably.

"Those men on the *Carnatic*," Passepartout went on, unperturbed by the Japanese's renewed assault, "do you not realize they made the same blunder as you—they *misunderstood*." Passepartout pressed the man back through the racks and props, closer to the brick wall of the theater. "Do those nameless wraiths you say I have offended want *you*, your Japan, to be a competitor in *their* world, an equal? Or only a compliant servant, dressing as *they* do, acting as they wish *you* to? I don't think you're ready for *that* role, a heavier mask than I am to wear today."

At Inagi's next attack, Passepartout ended his response by throwing the man against the wall and in a moment brought his left hand up across the man's brow, his right gripping the Japanese man's left wrist. The Japanese's free right hand flailed momentarily as he slumped to his feet, quickly unconscious.

Passepartout pulled a cloak from a rack of costumes and draped it over the man. Then he checked his watch, just after 6 AM Greenwich, "Almost time for the pyramid." Retrieving the Tingou mask from the lantern, Passepartout made his way to join his acrobatic fellows, then commencing to gather in full number, and stretch in anticipation of their turn on the stage.

ൠ ൡ

The sun was setting as Fogg and Aouda's rickshaws reached their destination, prompting some pique from Phileas Fogg as he realized that the Gaiety Theater was so near the pier they could have walked to it at ease, had they only known beforehand.

Since the show inside was nearing its conclusion, the ticket agent was at first reluctant to sell them seats at all, and worried they might make too much noise on entering, possibly spoiling the attention of those already enjoying. But Phileas Fogg is not one easily deterred, and the man eventually accepted money for himself and Aouda.

Mr. Tanabe was among those who tossed a quick glance at Fogg and Aouda when they entered, but even he returned his attention to the stage almost immediately. The settings were being readied for the grand human pyramid, in which the legion of red-nosed demons writhed around a *papier mâché* forest before assembling with grunts and leaps into their towering ensemble. The magnificent sight had just been achieved when Passepartout saw Fogg and Aouda seated in the back row. Plucking off his mask, he shouted "Mr. Fogg!" and pulled away from his position at the base.

As the other acrobats tumbled to the mats and several unsettled musicians momentarily lost track of their place in the scheduled accompaniment, Passepartout bounded from the stage, racing up the center aisle to where Fogg and Aouda were now standing. Tanabe was on his feet as well, not knowing what might have happened to his companion, but resolving to keep track of Passepartout at least.

A fuming William Batulcar showed how quickly he could move in a crisis, as he appeared to verbally accost Passepartout (just then removing his robe and respectfully placing it across an unoccupied seat) for his abject failure at his post, but Fogg summarily alleviated the man's outrage with £200 withdrawn from his carpetbag.

Exiting the Gaiety Theater then, Passepartout dashed abreast of Fogg, "One of the two is following us."

"So it would appear," Fogg agreed, then asked, "Where ever did you find those clothes? We'll have to find new for you before we sail."

It was growing increasingly dark, and street lanterns were just being lit.

"Head this way," Aouda called, motioning off to a path leading left into a small public garden, heading in the general direction of the harbor, and showing few evening pedestrians presently about, apart from themselves. Aouda had by now buried her right hand in one of her pockets as they strode along, carefully casting glances around so that she might attend to the man in the blue suit, who was not only keeping pace but striving to work closer.

The Japanese man was scarcely twenty feet behind them when Aouda wheeled around. Tanabe at once reached under his coat and was pulling his *tantō* blade from its scabbard as he burst into a run toward them. In Aouda's hand was the small pistol-shaped device she'd taken from her pocket, a mechanism of polished copper and steel and much else harder to make out in the waning light.

Firing directly at the Japanese man's torso, a greenish-yellow flash emanated from its "barrel" in a thin filament of electric energy which instantly felled the man, who briefly convulsed on the ground before going limp, his right hand dropping the handle of the short sword. There had been no loud report, only the most modest of crackling thrums, and that only during the moment while the beam was visible.

"Part of your arsenal?" Fogg inquired, as he assessed the fallen man, who seemed uninjured apart from his unconsciousness.

"Talk later," Aouda said, and urged Fogg and Passepartout forward, out of the glade and into the harbor avenues.

"Now for your clothes," Fogg declared.

Passepartout was a bit peeved at this instruction, but relented and led them to the shop where he had pawned his old coat and hat that morning. Fortunately it was still open and the garments were still there—and, despite quizzical looks from Fogg, Passepartout bought them anew (though he did retain his Japanese coat for memory of his Yokohama experience).

After which, Phileas Fogg, Aouda and Passepartout set out for the pier to board the *General Grant* and arrange for Passepartout's included passage to America (the settee in Fogg's suite proving quite adequate for that purpose).

Mr. Fix had already returned to the ship, his warrant for Fogg's arrest safely tucked in his pocket, but very much remained out of

Passepartout's way when he saw him boarding with Fogg and Aouda. He had no idea how much the man may have told them regarding their activities in the Hong Kong opium den. Such uncertainty promised to make Fix's Pacific voyage over the next three weeks interesting, to say the least.

After the Fogg party had gone below, Fix returned to the deck to stand at the railing and watch as the *General Grant* dropped her lines and began to paddle free of the pier. As the distance separating the vessel from the dock increased, Fix saw a pair of Japanese gentlemen sprinting toward them. Both were well-attired in suits of black and blue, carrying no luggage, but stopping in evident displeasure at their failing to reach the ship in time.

Bad luck for them, thought Mr. Fix.

22. IN WHICH TRANQUIL DAYS WERE SPENT ABOARD THE *GENERAL GRANT* IN THE PACIFIC

After the undeniable excitements of that day's layover in Yokohama, it was relaxing for Phileas Fogg and party to sit down for a genteel evening's meal aboard the SS *General Grant*. Aouda and Passepartout were tabled opposite Fogg and the carpetbag.

Fogg laid out their itinerary on the cloth. "Twenty-one days yet to San Francisco, putting us there on December 2nd possibly," representing that by a salt cellar. "If so, we should be reaching New York by the 11th," dropping a pepper grinder farther on, then sliding his teacup to the far starboard of the table, "Making London on the 20th, a day ahead of the wager." He smiled.

Passepartout took out the snuffbox and reached around Aouda to land it before the salt, "Let us not forget *Columbiad*, on the 20th." With a nod to Aouda, "Thank you for its use."

Aouda took up the box, quickly determined it was indeed in need of power, which prompted a question, "How did you send the message from the theater? That was *very* strong."

"*Pardon*, I will diminish the intensity should I do that again."

"Do *what* again?" Aouda pressed.

"The trick I did, that did not harm your snuffbox. I must not say more," Passepartout smiled defensively.

"We must assume more of those gentlemen may await us here," Fogg interposed, tapping the top of the salt cellar.

"How did you deal with the *Carnatic* ones?" Aouda asked.

"Not peaceably. They all had guns—the *bullet* kind," Passepartout winked at Aouda. "I warned them to stop, though. It was an irony, how hard I had to work not to be blamed for any of it after, aboard ship. Since I *was* fully responsible."

Fogg considered that admission, and whether to probe further, but said instead, "Were you able to learn anything about our shadowy nemesis?"

"*That* was a regret—no. The *Carnatic* man was certain I was hired by someone. It makes me think none of them were their associates. But so many *countries*—America, India, now Japan. People must know people. There are connections we must be missing. Something that threads them all together."

"Dupin may shed light on it," Fogg said.

"'Doo-*pan*'?" Aouda asked.

"That is Mr. Fogg's detective. We met in Paris—oh, on my second day of employment."

"I have sent him on to Barbicane to investigate. If there are figures hiding behind screens, Aouda, Dupin is the man to expose them."

Aouda very much desired that would turn out to be true.

Having retrieved her snuffbox telegraph from Passepartout, there were two more machines to attach to Aouda's chugging miniature engine that night in their suite, the electric pistol requiring more even than the snuffbox.

Passepartout marveled at the little mechanism. "Is it affected much by the ship's roll?"

"It hasn't so far. These are new conditions for it," Aouda admitted. "It seems to be working fine. I expect I'll be needing fresh alcohol from the bar soon, though."

"Does your machine prefer any particular proof or flavor?" Passepartout asked with a wry smile.

"Whatever *burns*—and not too viscous."

Late on Friday morning, November 15th, Aouda received telegraphic word from Robur that he had finished installing and testing to his satisfaction the grappling attachment for the *Deimos*. Aouda discussed the import of this with Fogg and Passepartout later, siting in the public lounge.

"We'll have to leave here at least five hours before the *Columbiad* does. It's three hours just to reach the rendezvous with Srikar, and I'd prefer a wide leeway. Since we'll be some thirteen hours away from Diadem by then, *Deimos* will have to leave there that much earlier still. Long flights."

"Niru will have to pack some lunch," Fogg offered dryly.

Aouda smiled, appreciating that Phileas has remembered his name.

"I look forward to flying in your machine," Passepartout said.

"It's not so luxurious as the *Nautilus*, if only by size, but certainly serviceable. It traversed turbulent air most proficiently." Fogg began to pensively rub the philtrum of his lip with his left index finger, "We still have to find whist players—I think my previous ones disembarked here."

"Just two," Aouda proposed, "if you'll consent to be partnered with me."

"Two it is, then," Fogg said.

Passepartout did not volunteer to be a third, but he did resolve to be on hand to observe their card play. There happened to be two East Indian army officers aboard (embarked back in Shanghai, but in civilian dress) who were open to mixed card play with a native woman—possibly overlooking that aspect because Mr. Fogg had come to be so popularly known aboard ship as the fellow racing around the world on a wager, and they were eager to make his acquaintance.

"Archie Bennett, Major of Her Majesty's," the first man introduced, turning to his fellow, "Timothy Sinclair, my generally quiet

Captain. And you must be the world-girdling madman, Phileas Fogg."

"None other," Fogg agreed.

"I am Aouda. Accompanying the madman," she smiled.

"We're going around the world too, you know," Bennett said brightly, "only not so fast. Went to Australia first, then China. Off to the Americas now. North, maybe South, too—then to see Africa, Europe and the Levant last, the Holy Land, before rejoining the regiment."

"Assuming we don't die from some jungle fever or native uprising along the way," Sinclair offered pessimistically.

"Has traveling around the world been a long ambition?" Aouda asked.

"Very much," Bennett said. "Read all about these exotic places—books, and tales of family. When we finally saw service in India, though, we could see how pictures or words never caught them proper, so figured a look-see trek was in order for the rest."

"I envy you, seeing so much of the scenery," Passepartout put in from a seat nearby, there guarding Fogg's carpetbag.

"For once, we had time free for leave—our Colonel was called away suddenly, left our whole company a shambles."

"Helps having the pull of a father who's an ambassador," Sinclair said.

"Your father is an ambassador?" Aouda asked.

"No!" Bennett snorted, "Our Colonel's. Sinclair here has not the greatest admiration for our Colonel Moran, do you?"

Sinclair made a face, and gave the cards a further thorough shuffle.

Watching Fogg and Aouda playing cards with Bennett and Sinclair that evening, Passepartout wondered whether the reason why he had enjoyed playing with the two Austrians more involved the fact that whist involved *partners*. In whist, two people were drawn into transient alliance against two others, creating an artificial social relationship of necessary cooperation or exclusion. Passepartout had never played as Fogg's partner, either—the need to protect the carpetbag from the prying attention of Mrs. Hammond. Yes, that could have been it: he'd felt uncomfortable having to play as Fogg's adversary, even though only at cards.

Aouda and Fogg appeared to be quite compatible card partners, though, and held their own most admirably against the two English soldiers.

The following morning after breakfast that Saturday, the 16th of November, Phileas Fogg was the keeper of the carpetbag, allowing Passepartout to stroll off on his own, and where he might conduct an experiment unobserved. Crossing to the very prow of the steamer,

Passepartout turned back and pulled out his comb to perform a competent sweep of the *General Grant*. The fidelity of its detection fell off abruptly in the vicinity of Fogg and Aouda, then pacing out on deck well back along the starboard rail.

There could be no doubt about it, thought Passepartout—it was Fogg's *watch*. Or, at least, the contraption that resembled a watch in every respect, by size and appearance, save that timepieces did not read as a black *nothingness* where gears and springs ought to be—or show increasing distortion to his comb's perception the closer he stepped to it (as he had been encountering at various distances since first meeting Mr. Fogg at No. 7 Savile Row).

Nothing Passepartout knew of could provoke such a response in his instrument. Absolutely nothing. And yet there it was.

Over the next few minutes, Passepartout tested various configurations of his comb's tine movements, to see which had any effect on the phenomenon. A few minimized that strange ellipsis, though if he moved forward or to the side in even the slightest degree, the quality at once dissipated, so that he had to hit on a new combination to achieve comparable results. And with no obvious pattern to the why or how if it, this was a most perplexing circumstance, he had to admit.

What then was Mr. Fogg's "watch"—and how ever had that Victorian gentleman come by it? Or that something not unlike it that lay somewhere in the building behind Fogg's courtyard—a *something* his comb had found even less discernable than Phileas' modest chronometer. Passepartout hoped—no, *expected*—in time he might learn a few answers on that.

Phileas Fogg and Aouda were then continuing their stroll on deck, Aouda's arm comfortably entwined in Fogg's, enjoying the warming sun (the temperature now in the middle seventies Fahrenheit) as the *General Grant* steamed ever eastward.

"What will you be doing with *Columbiad* once you have it? Or have you pondered that?"

"You mean, supposing we're successful in persuading Mr. Barbicane to part with it, without fisticuffs?" Aouda joked. "Not put it on a shelf. It's not a trophy. Robur and I will want to disassemble it for study—carefully, given its engines. From what I can make of Passepartout's drawings, he has far too much power for just light and heat inside, but if he's using some of it for propulsion, in some way, I can't make out just from those schematics."

"So you must take it apart."

"I am curious," Aouda admitted. "Though we may do that at our leisure, Phileas, once I return to Hong Kong." She paused as they continued to perambulate. "I was thinking that it might be an amusement ... to continue on with you and Passepartout, to America ... and England—see your quest fully done. Robur can easily follow along with us, in the *Deimos*, in case we need it."

"If it would not be an inconvenience to you. I should like that."

Below deck, in his stateroom, Mr. Fix was in a quandary. So far he had taken only light meals, sometimes only broth and tea, brought to his cabin by a sympathetic steward, as his stomach remained unsettled—and not just from the ship's roll.

Fix had behaved in a most mercenary manner regarding Passepartout, who seemed intransigently loyal to his master, Mr. Fogg. And Fix himself had repeatedly observed and even benefitted from the man's generosity and decency of character. Still, here he was, stalking after him with a warrant for his summary arrest the moment he set foot on his native soil. To accomplish that purpose—and Fix had no doubt he must do that—he would not only have to continue to follow Fogg, but actively conspire to help the daring thief make good his bet, not bolt in some other direction at the last moment.

He dreaded so meeting Passepartout again, though, let alone Fogg, that his only solace was to remain in his stateroom as much as practicable, there to while away the days until they arrived in San Francisco. When he did go out, for the necessary bath and privy duties, he was most careful to check the public rooms above for what he might learn of Fogg's whereabouts, and was not surprised to see Fogg had resumed his customary evening pursuit of whist—though now joined by Aouda, as his card partner. When Passepartout was occasionally spied, Fix beat a hasty retreat to the safety and seclusion of his cabin.

Phileas Fogg endured a minor inconvenience on the evening of November 17th, however, when Misters Bennett and Sinclair were not on hand to play whist, it being the Sabbath (it was Bennett who was most particular on this point, with those gentlemen attending the ship's religious service in the lounge). Passepartout took note of that as yet another example of how people could be so deflected from even their favored activities, provided the dictates were based on what other people had done long before, and especially were they of a religious sentiment. Passepartout was relieved at least how this present instance didn't involve shoes.

Fogg and Aouda found card players that evening anyway (this time among the Americans aboard), but come Monday the 18th, they were back with the two British officers, reminding Passepartout of how often familiar faces could preempt novelty in such matters.

Mindful of the date, though, Passepartout had grown restive assessing the manifold permutations of the English and their social proclivities, and waylaid Fogg that evening just before his nightly round was to commence.

"We are in the Pacific, which is most opportune, but what shall have been happening in America?"

Fogg remained both imperturbable and inscrutable. "Exactly the point! Shall be, and done. You have been using *your* secrets, Passepartout—even Aouda noticed. Do leave me mine."

Passepartout shrugged as Fogg took his seat across from Aouda, the ebullient Major Bennett shuffling the deck and chiding Captain Sinclair for their weak showing the night before against Aouda and Phileas Fogg. Passepartout and the carpetbag retired then to Fogg's suite.

Some hours later, Aouda was just marking down the latest rubber's score (they were up by two games) when Fogg's watch let out two gentle chimes.

He flipped the case open briefly to inspect it, and smiled to see all as it should be. Among the several shifting bezels: a shining "**O**" fell just past *III*, the "**?**" more dimly near it at *IV*, the blank ring and dark "**B**" unmoved at *VI*, beside a faint "**A**" at half past *VII*, while a much brighter "**N**" lay across the face between *X* and *XI*. And the time: just approaching noon Greenwich.

"Two o'clock?" Bennett cried. "It's not that late, is it?" Peering over to a wall clock above a side table, he was puzzled (then relieved) to see it was not yet eleven.

"Mr. Fogg keeps his watch to London's time," Aouda explained.

"Oh," Bennett sighed. "Doesn't that cause confusion?"

"Only for those easily confused," Fogg said. "Your deal, isn't it, Sinclair?"

Fogg and Aouda did splendidly at whist that night, and both were in fine spirits when they retired to the stateroom, at nearly one that morning, on Tuesday the 19th of November.

Passepartout eyed their arrival horizontally from where he lay on the suite's settee, bobbing in and out of slumber while he clutched the carpetbag for safety, all too mindful of the hours relentlessly ticking down, before *Columbiad* took sky at noon on the 20th in distant Florida.

That datum may have been weighing on Passepartout's mind when he did finally drift off to sleep, for he found himself awakening not that many hours later, just around dawn, bearing the oddest of feelings about that—not quite a dream (for that was not a manner of slumber his consciousness was naturally prone to), but rather a strange apprehension regarding the drawings of Barbicane's *Columbiad* he had given Aouda.

Passepartout was not prone to such presentiments, so this feeling struck him all the more for its atypical character. It came very deeply, as though something of importance concerned them, something he ought to take note of, and yet whatever it was eluded him.

He continued to be preoccupied all that day, through more meals and cards and forced inactivity, and by November 20th—on what looked to be a most cheerful Wednesday out there in the broad Pacific—he was quite downcast.

Just after breakfast that morning, at 10 AM, Aouda reported that *Deimos* was taking flight. It would be reaching them that night, around eleven. Any whist game would have to be curtailed.

Despite that impact on the sacrosanct card playing, Fogg remained phlegmatic all the day, though Aouda and Passepartout were considerably more animated as they anticipated what they were about to do, acting on their own initiative to brazenly capture what was, after all, humanity's very first halting venture into celestial space.

What right had they to preempt that potential landmark of scientific exploration?

Passepartout and Fogg both knew what they were about, but kept to their own council. Aouda had her own ideas, but likewise held her tongue. At this point, it was enough that they trusted one another, feeling a comradery they could neither explain nor disregard.

After locating her tiny electric pillbox in the bottom of her luggage aboard the *General Grant*, flipping its switch on, Aouda joined Fogg, Passepartout and carpetbag for a deck promenade just before eleven. The Moon was not yet quarter past full, so there was considerable light—and a few passengers and crew were out as well. Fogg and Aouda strode arm in arm, while Passepartout ambled to and fro, all the while working farther aft. For those attentive enough to filter out the sound of the ship's paddlewheels and its aggressively churning engines, a rising whining might be discerned away to the stern.

"*Deimos* is here," Aouda reported, and they circled past the *General Grant*'s rear lifeboats to the fantail rail.

And there she was, hovering right above their wake about a hundred feet back, no running lights on, but the moonlight rendering her visible enough, plus some glow from within the cupola and front windows, and occasional flickering gasps of flame from her many thrusting ports. The grappling attachment hung underneath *Deimos* like a collapsed metallic spider.

Passepartout, standing back as watch by the boats, darted forward to say, "No one near."

Aouda nodded and signaled for *Deimos* to come for them, the engine noises mounting as the craft rose up over the end rail. The flyer's side struts gently bumped the *General Grant*'s flagpole, whose banner fluttered obligingly out of their way from a slight breeze from starboard, while the dutiful Niru pushed the port hatch open.

Fogg climbed up and into the machine first, Passepartout handed the carpetbag ahead and followed himself. Aouda had dropped to her haunches, looking at the undercarriage attachment. Pleased with how it had turned out, she stood up and entered last. As Niru closed the hatch after her, Robur wasted no time in pulling away from the *General Grant*, dropping low to fly off back along her wake for some distance, until far enough from the receding ship to warrant climbing higher, and head off at speed to the east.

Master Xie sat cross-legged on the floor in front of the main window, eyes closed. Aouda climbed up the cupola ladder to ask Robur, "You brought Xie. Expecting trouble?"

"To be sure there is not," Robur answered.

Aouda crossed to the elderly Chinese, who opened his eyes at her approach. "You did not want to fly with us before."

"I still do not," Xie said flatly, bringing a sympathetic smile from Aouda.

Passepartout had deposited the carpetbag in a corner and was now intently exploring the interior, much as he had *Deimos*' exterior a fortnight ago. Phileas Fogg was talking sympathetically with Niru, about how the lengthy flight had been from Hong Kong.

Had old Mr. Xie not been with them, a man of fearless nature who nonetheless found being thousands of feet in the air unsupported a disquieting place to be, the import of Passepartout and Fogg's behavior might not have struck her quite as it did at that moment.

Unconcerned, casual—the both of them. As though flying over a hundred miles an hour and half a mile in the sky was something one simply *did*. Now was that the way for a typical English gentleman and his French valet to act?

All the more interesting, Aouda decided.

23. IN WHICH THE FIRST HUMAN TRAVELERS TO THE MOON FIND THEIR DESTINATION UEXPECTEDLY CHANGED

Just after two that Thursday morning, the 21st of November, the *Deimos* approached the area where they were to meet Captain Nemo, settling onto the ocean to await his arrival. They had specified a latitude and longitude, of course, but Phileas Fogg also apprised them of the *Nautilus'* approach as measured by his watch. Robur came down from the cupola and opened up the top hatch, surveying the sea roundabout with a larger pair of the sort of binocular glasses Fogg had seen Aouda use aboard the *Tankadere*.

The Moon was still up at the first light of dawn when *Nautilus* surfaced around fifty yards from *Deimos*. Robur could see two X-shaped mounts had been attached to the submarine's hull, between its central serrated fin and the covered skiff, suitably spaced to accommodate the putative dimensions of Barbicane's *Columbiad*.

By the time the *Nautilus* had come to a stop, Aouda had climbed up into the pilot's chair and soon guided *Deimos* beside the vessel as she had done previously. Nemo had appeared on deck, and this second meeting when his sister emerged from her craft was almost as emotion filled as their first eleven days before.

Phileas Fogg jumped across to *Nautilus'* deck shortly thereafter, followed by Passepartout and Mr. Xie. Inspired by the comparative warmth of these latitudes, Fogg, Passepartout and Aouda all had removed their hats and left them aboard *Deimos*, which Niru arranged in a neatly-spaced row along the rail of the front windows, a sartorial shrine above Fogg's carpetbag: Phileas Fogg's top hat (with Robur's blast hole) on the left, Passepartout's shorter round hat beside it, and Aouda's tall chapeau placed third for visual balance.

Fogg soon had his watch out, studying it attentively and gazing off to the west, while Xie began to pace out in broad strides all the decking of the submarine available above water, forward around the pilot house, dodging under the grim saw-tooth bar that protected the front ram—then back down the port side, all the way aft and around the X mounts. Passepartout found that most amusing, and tagged along after him, his hands clasped behind his back.

Robur, meanwhile, had brought the special wireless telegraphic device aboard, which Nemo directed him to take up to his second in command in the pilot house and instruct him on its operation (Nemo intending to learn what he needed to about it later). This Robur did, stressing to that crewman that no communication could be sent or received by it while they were submerged. While the machine had considerable range, that could be extended further if used out on deck with an accompanying thin metal tube extended.

When three distinctive chimes rang on Fogg's watch (each stroke sounding a different bell) not long after, he turned around to face east, looking on the timepiece's face as the "**B**" ring spun in response, coming to settle by *XII*, its gem finally aglow.

"They've turned on *Columbiad*'s engines," Fogg called out.

Aouda, Nemo, Passepartout and Robur gathered around Phileas Fogg then. Niru's head could be seen poking up from *Deimos*' hatch, while Xie perched on the hull above the opening to *Nautilus*' main deck opening, from where he had quite a fine view all about.

At 5 AM Fogg announced, "It is noon in Florida now. Time to trust—if *monsieurs* Newton and Laplace are correct—in three quarters of an hour, the *Columbiad* should be coming down somewhere about *there*," pointing off to the west horizon.

Fogg alone seemed calm as those minutes dragged on. None spoke, each expectantly peering at the increasingly bright horizon, so that the gentle lapping of the waves on the two craft and the mechanical sounds they made were all that could be heard. The stillness was such that when Fogg's watch chimed again forty minutes on, three times identically, it startled Aouda and Passepartout most of all.

"Not long to wait now," Fogg said, and as if on command, an increasing bright streak appeared at the farthest horizon, high in the sky, "There!"

Robur and Aouda did their best to follow the approaching trail with their glasses, Robur interposing darkened lenses on his instrument when the meteoric flame grew too intense to see directly.

"I can see flashes laterally," Robur reported, "rockets possibly."

"Slowing—yes, I can see it from here," Aouda said.

Nemo was as attendant on how his sister and Robur were conducting themselves as he was curious about the flaring streak bearing down on them.

Gradually a sharp rumbling could be heard, growing louder as *Columbiad* neared on its descent. The rocket blasts from the bottom of the capsule were occurring more frequently, too, as Aouda could see even through her unprotected lenses, and were still more plainly *heard* and increasingly very much *felt* by those on board *Nautilus* when the capsule roared directly overhead, causing necks to spin and bodies to swivel, as the flaming vessel dropped and decelerated until it splashed into the sea some miles to the east.

"Come, Robur—our turn." Aouda and Robur proceeded to *Deimos*, which swiftly set off to retrieve Barbicane's moonship.

Passepartout looked over to Fogg, and was struck by his expression of supremely assured accomplishment. Fogg had been asked by Passepartout to do this very thing, intercept the *Columbiad* here in the Pacific Ocean. And here it was, done.

And yet—what had happened in faraway Florida to achieve this *fait accompli*? Passepartout didn't know. And, he realized with a disconcerting mental plop, it was possible neither did Fogg. Things had been set into motion, with a cool aplomb that took Passepartout's breath away. Could there ever be so smug a man on this Earth as Mr. Phileas Fogg? But Fogg would not be one to brag about it. No, not merely out of conspiratorial silence—though he suspected there was that, too—but because Fogg *didn't know either*.

What a marvelous daring thing to think on, what had just happened around them this morning—and how frightening.

ଔ ଞ

Although surfaced in the shining metallurgical rarity of an alloy of aluminum, not much of *Columbiad* was gleaming in the morning sun when *Deimos* reached it, because little of that craft was visible above the waves, her windows on either side fully under water.

Aouda had correctly reckoned that the *Columbiad* was balanced so that its hatch would turn up when in the water, but seeing how low the ship was, Robur called from his periscope, "She's still laden with all her supplies, too heavy, looking to sink."

Leaning by the main windows, Niru looked very concerned at this development.

Activating the grappling mechanism, its three pairs of arms opening like dangling metal fingers, Aouda maneuvered *Deimos* so they would embrace *Columbiad*'s cylinder at its widest, some fifteen feet. Seawater was already sloshing over the foundering craft's hatch, though, when Aouda achieved attachment of it, tightening the grip slightly before lifting the *Columbiad* from the sea.

"Handles the weight well," Aouda shouted down to Robur, as they flew back to the *Nautilus*, and gently began to lower toward the waiting X frames—an arrangement deemed necessary by Aouda as *Columbiad*'s hatch would rest directly under *Deimos*' grapplers, requiring someplace on *Nautilus* to land it if its occupants were to get out.

Nemo and the others watched this process with great admiration. Mr. Xie turned out to have the best vantage of all, sitting so far above even their sightlines.

Once *Deimos* let go of *Columbiad*, Nemo and several of his crew swept forward to affix temporary lashing to hold the vessel in place. "Mind don't touch it, parts will be *hot*," Nemo shouted.

Deimos settled down into the water and Aouda and Robur were crossing to *Nautilus* when the hatch on *Columbiad* swung open.

Due to the size and curvature of the *Columbiad*, Impey Barbicane could see little of the *Nautilus* under him as he poked his head up, standing on a ladder arranged now to reach a hatch which had become the roof due to the reclined position of the capsule on the support frames. The hatch itself obscured the view from the starboard side, such as the bobbing *Deimos*. He could see the two stout strapping ropes holding the craft in place, as well as the broad sea all around, and *Columbiad*'s tapered front permitted some view of *Nautilus*' imposing armored pilot house off to his right, where the sight of an elderly Chinaman placidly sitting there only added to Barbicane's disorientation and puzzlement.

Barbicane rubbed a gloved hand along the metal around the hatch seals, discovering it to be cool enough not to be felt through the leather. After a few moments, Barbicane had attached a rope ladder to the hatchway, which he flopped out to unroll down the side of the ship, disappearing over the edge. Once he had clambered out and climbed down to that point, Barbicane could see there was a solid iron decking below, with assorted people milling about, none looking immediately belligerent.

As he worked his way down to the deck, past the small observation window on that face, he could also see the X mounts and how the arrangement held his craft.

Passepartout approached him, Fogg and Aouda behind. "You are Impey Barbicane," Passepartout declared. "Welcome to safety."

"English—all right. Were you responsible for what happened up there?"

Passepartout was genuinely curious, "*Pardon*, what *did* happen up there?"

"We lost all our priming stages at once, forcing us to Earth prematurely." Seeing Passepartout's complete attention and evident understanding of what he had just said, Barbicane continued, "At least we were over the ocean by then—I'm assuming, the Pacific." Barbicane then strode aft to the back of *Columbiad*, inspecting the surface, feeling the heat still present there. "We barely had time to flop around, light the slowing rockets. Only this protected end could take the brunt of the atmospheric heat, which was intense," Barbicane indicated the scorched and discolored metal there.

Reaching the back of *Columbiad*, Barbicane could now see the *Deimos*, and Niru's head and shoulders, arms folded and leaning on the hatch rail.

"Barbicane?" a Southern drawl shouted from *Columbiad*'s hatch.

"Down here, Nicholl," Barbicane shouted back. "We're on some sort of iron boat."

Barbicane had turned back to his own concerns, peering closely at one bent and burnt section of the hull when Nemo came around the other side of the *Columbiad*, from the starboard, and Barbicane's expression suddenly brightened in recognition, "Srikar!"

Nemo was surprised and touched by the immediacy of Barbicane's recollection, "After so many years? Do I look so unchanged?"

"You're not a man easily forgotten. We had good days back then. So all this is yours?"

"This is *Nautilus*. I am more widely known—and notorious—by the name of Nemo."

Fogg had joined them, crowding the limited space where the skiff was docked, and brought Nemo back to the needs at hand, "Perhaps your guests would welcome the comforts of the ship below, after their certainly harried adventures."

Aouda had remained by Passepartout at the rope ladder, attending to the man descending, who asked with a very quizzical expression, "Where are we?"

"The Pacific Ocean, *monsieur*," Passepartout replied, as he steadied the man's departure from the swinging ladder. The man seemed tense, and reluctant to be helped by anyone right then.

A third man was also working down the ladder. Neither so burly and open a fellow as Barbicane—nor as wiry and suspicious as Nicholl—Michel Ardan was younger than both, coolly taking in all that he was seeing, struck by the presence of a dark skinned woman here on this strange vessel, exotically beautiful and so well dressed and ... something else he couldn't quite put his finger on.

Both Nicholl and Ardan could see how familiar and friendly Barbicane was being with the swarthy bearded stranger in the unmarked naval uniform.

"We have to talk about *this*," Nemo was telling Barbicane, indicating the *Columbiad* with a nod, as they made their way around Passepartout, Aouda, Nicholl and Ardan.

"Come along gentlemen," Barbicane said to his fellow voyagers, who followed him and Nemo forward, around *Nautilus*' fin, to the open stairs below.

Nicholl and Ardan both took notice of the strange Chinese man, sitting above them and smiling like some scrutinizing spirit made flesh. Nicholl seemed less pleased by this sight than Ardan, especially when he heard Aouda tell Robur, "You and Xie, back to *Deimos* and be ready to go."

Going below, Barbicane and Ardan were struck by the electric lighting within. Barbicane stepped up to one of the lamps, touching its glass covering, reacting with a wince as he found it quite hot. Nicholl showed less interest in this marvel of internal illumination.

Nemo approached his second officer, pointing to Ardan and Nicholl, "Find cabins for these two gentlemen, separately, and see to it they have company until I've decided what pleasantries to engage in."

While the officer and several crewman escorted Nicholl and Ardan below, Nemo conducted Barbicane, Passepartout, Aouda and Phileas Fogg into *Nautilus'* salon.

"Quite the digs here," Barbicane declared of the chamber. Turning to Passepartout, Aouda and Fogg, he explained, "Srikar and I met long ago, our mutual interest in Bohemian mine tailings."

Nemo smiled, recollecting, "Remember Otto Lidenbrock's paper? *On the Properties of Pitchblende Undergoing Fluorescence by Nitric Acid.*"

Barbicane returned the smile. "We poured over every word of that, speculated into the night hours on what it meant. The silver mines just threw the useless stuff away, happy for us to take all we wanted. So this is what you did with it! Stupid of me not to have made the connection."

"There turned out to be too many prying eyes in Joachimsthal, my friend, I paid the price for that."

Aouda put in, "I repaid the Raja for that, Srikar, fully. And found fresh and slightly safer ore, too, in Kazakhstan."

"Yes," Nemo nodded thoughtfully, then turned very serious, "You have had no ... *accidents*?"

"*None.*" Aouda sounded proud. "And your island refuge—an intentional 'accident'?"

Nemo nodded gravely.

"I feared as much," Aouda said.

"Have I stumbled into something?" Barbicane asked.

"Only *us*," Passepartout said. "You are not here by accident."

Barbicane turned to Nemo, "Was it your plan then to bring us down?"

"Not mine. I'm a conscripted conveyance only." Nemo indicated Passepartout, Fogg and Aouda, "These three you need to talk to."

"I apologize for our anonymity, but it is necessary." Passepartout motioned for Barbicane to take a seat down in the port observation window, Fogg and Aouda following. Nemo stepped down as well, but remained standing before the open viewing lens, arm's crossed, light from the rippling waves playing on them all.

"I have observed your experiments in Baltimore and Florida, most extraordinary. But most dangerous, also." Passepartout decided to be blunt, "It is unwise for Power X to be so flaunted at this time."

"Flaunted?" Barbicane was puzzled. "Don't you stand for progress? Exploration?"

"Were you able to get this *progress* without any accidents, strange illness?" Aouda asked.

"Oh, I see. The little burns. We took every precaution after that, not a single lasting injury. Is that all you're worried about? Or were you afraid we'd damage the Moon?"

"Here I have a special experience," Nemo put in. "I alone know what it means to fashion those elements for their full explosive power."

Barbicane showed surprise. "That can be done? All I've seen is heat."

"I assure you, my friend, it can be done, and with no more fuel for it needed than what powers my *Nautilus*. Prince Dakkar asked me to build a bomb of it, before his fall. Should I have done that?"

Aouda recognized at once the horrid implication of what her brother just said. Long ago, when she was but a child, Dakkar had been told enough of their work to imagine an explosion from it, and what he thought to be possible, others may have learned from him since—an offhand boast or taunt under duress, it didn't matter. Someone must have learned of this dream and embraced it, for their own ends; sought to make it real, at whatever cost. Their nemesis who hunted Srikar and destroyed his family.

"There are people who desire all knowledge of Power X," Aouda said. "They persecuted Srikar for it, and would me also if they knew of my role in it. Srikar used it to destroy his island base to prevent their obtaining it."

"My island vanished in a second," Nemo said with great intent. "I had become Death, the Destroyer of Worlds, as the scripture of my country puts it."

"Mr. Barbicane, I have seen what remains of that island, blasted, poisoned, where even visitors like me could stay only briefly to evade those 'little burns'." Aouda leaned close. "Would you put that power into the hands of those for whom war is second nature?"

Phileas Fogg now spoke. "It may well be that a Freemasonry of Science, or something of that nature, can be contrived someday to husband such knowledge, to forestall bleak futures." Fogg's expression grew distant, repeating, "Very bleak futures." Then he roused, more resolute, "Perhaps you can help in that pursuit. But until we better know who craves that power for evil intent, I urge you to keep your door to it firmly shut."

"Plain speaking," Barbicane said, and thought some on it. "What are your plans for us now, or are we to be your extended guests?"

"My *Nautilus* is neither hotel nor prison. I'll take you three to America, in what comfort we can offer. You may consider yourself temporary cargo."

"And my *Columbiad*?"

"That will be *my* guest," Aouda said. "I shall be studying how it works."

Barbicane thought further. Resigned now to their intentions, he offered, "We have a Berthon collapsible boat aboard, which we would have used to row ashore."

"I'll have it moved to my ship," Aouda said. "When *Nautilus* is positioned, we'll come and take you to Florida."

"Where you may paddle to land and tell all about your amazing journey to the *Moon*," Passepartout suggested, "a dramatic story that you will have had much time to think of on the way there in this inspiring vessel."

 C3 80

The *Columbiad*'s small boat and remaining provisions were being removed from the craft to *Nautilus* when Aouda, Fogg and Passepartout gathered on deck to bid thankful farewell to Nemo.

"No value crowding your ship with Barbicane's boat," Srikar said. "We'll hold it till needed in the Atlantic."

"I feel better now that we have a way to signal," Aouda said.

"As do I." Srikar and Aouda embraced once more, then parted.

Aboard the craft soon after, just before resuming the pilot's chair, Aouda told Robur, Niru and Xie, "*Deimos* has to fly us to the *General Grant*, then back here to pick up the *Columbiad*, and take it to Diadem. Then remove the lifting carriage. You will all deserve a rest after that—a good one, because you'll be needed then to come to America, be on hand there for the flight to wherever *Nautilus* has come to surface."

Mr. Xie had folded onto the deck by the windows, again in meditation, as they flew west to locate the *General Grant*. At Fogg's urging, Niru and Robur took the folding seats, heads quickly drooping in a well-earned nap, while Fogg and Passepartout sat on the deck by the side hatch crossway.

"Why do we not fly all the way in *Deimos*, stopping wherever we may, Chicago, London?" Passepartout asked.

"Aouda suggested that. But there are features to this I must appreciate. First, the wager must be won—properly, witnessed even by Mr. Fix. And something else. I learned from Dupin that sometimes, the best way to remain hidden is to do so in plain sight. Our adversaries either have to send the same faces time and again, risking identification by their repeated conspicuous presence, or dilute their numbers by sending fresh antagonists each and every time. We are fewer in number but very mobile, and not without our unique resources, are we?"

Robur was again in the cupola when they approached the *General Grant* around eleven o'clock, circling high for Aouda to check how many were on deck. All the hats were again on the designated heads, save Aouda, who was occupied at the telescope. She could see there were a few passengers and crew about, but none by the stern, and Robur piloted *Deimos* along a descending arc that brought the craft once more up behind the ship. Aouda donned her hat and secured it with the hatpins.

Because the full bulk of the flyer might have been easier to spot were they to disembark from the side hatches, a more challenging and thrilling maneuver was undertaken this time. Spinning around at the last moment and rising just enough to back the aft tail platform over the *General Grant*'s rails, Fogg, Aouda, Passepartout and the carpetbag exited by the top hatch, down between the two fins, and jumping off between the engine tubes.

Niru signaled Robur of their success, and quickly closed the hatch while the *Deimos* jumped forward clear of the rails, allowing it to sink below the bulwarks and race back along the *General Grant*'s wake before taking high flight off east toward *Nautilus*.

Fogg and party were soon settled into the dining saloon for luncheon. A cheered Bennett and Sinclair crossed to their table.

"Missed you at breakfast," Bennett said. "Glad you're over your indisposition. Hope you'll all be up for fresh cards tonight, umm?"

"I should think so," Fogg declared, turning to Aouda with an invitational look.

"We expect you at your best, gentlemen," Aouda smiled.

Ensconced down in his stateroom, Mr. Fix had not taken breakfast, either, being sick to one degree or another, so was none the wiser as to the absence of Fogg &c these past hours.

In this regard, as it was the case that in his account of the SS *General Grant*, Mr. *V.* modestly averred, "Nothing of moment happened on the voyage," it is entirely possible that the author had relied too extensively on the restricted testimony of Mr. Fix in assembling his précis.

And there was even a kernel of truth to it, since those events of moment that had taken place, strictly speaking, had not taken place on the *General Grant*.

24. DURING WHICH PHILEAS FOGG AND PARTY CONCLUDED THEIR JOURNEY ACROSS THE PACIFIC OCEAN

At breakfast on Friday morning, November 22nd, Aouda conveyed that she had received a telegraphic message from Robur earlier around five, reporting the successful transport of the *Columbiad* to the Diadem facility in Hong Kong. While the journey had taken longer due to the added weight, it was effected without incident.

Phileas Fogg did not seem buoyed by this, in contrast to his assurance aboard the *Nautilus* only the day before.

"Something troubles you?" Passepartout asked.

"I am slower than Dupin at this, but approve of his method of ratiocination. We're expecting those following you to likely resume in San Francisco. That's obvious. But if they *are* after the secrets of Power X—something we are again prudently assuming to be so—what might they do once they discover something has happened to *Columbiad*? And how long might it take them to work out *what*? It is a long way still through America, to London, and we have no names to put to any behind the screens. So I ponder. Any thoughts?"

"Those plans you gave me, did you steal them?" Aouda asked Passepartout.

Passepartout grinned, "No, I did not. Though the man Stanish on the *Carnatic* thought I had done something like that. Hmm, if they were hunting me on such speculation, it may be they have nothing like that themselves."

Aouda was nodding her head. "That would leave them either to seize the inventors, as they did with my brother—which they have not done with Barbicane, *yet*. Or take the *Columbiad*—and *we* have that."

Turning to Fogg, "On *your* question, Phileas, it would have been difficult to follow telescopically, especially from close where it was fired, so anyone watching locally might have no idea anything went wrong. Do you have any way of hearing from your men in Florida on that? You mentioned Dupin—he will be commanding them?"

"Commanding is not the right word for Dupin. He works alone, as a rule."

"Well, you must have *some* there. The *Columbiad* did not dive into the sea on its own."

Passepartout's curiosity was as great as Aouda's to hear what Fogg had to say to that.

"There is an avenue of communication for me to hear whatever Dupin has to report. It is one only I may use, but it is not presently open. Suffice on that."

"You two are worse than Japanese boxes, hidden compartments at every pull," Aouda shook her head.

"That is quite correct," Fogg agreed.

"Does that worry you?" Passepartout asked Aouda.

"Not yet. You see, I *too* have secrets," Aouda smiled. "I wonder which of ours will turn out to be the grandest."

"Or the more formidable," Fogg said. "I have nothing like your electric gun."

A most alluring smile came to Aouda's face at that.

Passepartout was off on a stroll to his thoughts after breakfast when he caught sight of Mr. Fix up on deck. The detective's absence from the public scene had persisted so long that Fogg's party had all but forgot he was aboard. Seeing him thus now, though, Passepartout ran up to Fix, taking him by the throat. This naturally startled Fix, and not a few fellow passengers nearby.

Although Mr. Fix was not devoid of pugilistic prowess, he was no match for Passepartout, who also reveled in the expenditure of energy in furtherance of balancing the accounts a bit for Fix's persistent mendacity, especially after the events of Hong Kong. As more blows were exchanged, several of the Americans watching began to bet on the contest, though as all weighted the bout in Passepartout's favor, there was no money exchanged. In short order Fix was flat on the deck.

"Have you done?" Fix asked once he had the breath for it, as Passepartout loomed over him.

"For this time—yes." Passepartout turned to leave.

Fix scrambled to his feet and pleaded for him to stay. Yes, he deserved the thrashing, certainly for Hong Kong. But he took pains to tell Passepartout that he was now fine with Fogg traveling across America. In fact, he was positively dedicated for him to succeed, and would function as the most steadfast of confederates in that endeavor—for only by returning Phileas Fogg to English soil could his own warrant take effect. There were the plainest of facts, offered in full sincerity.

Passepartout was astonished by this declaration, but also impressed. As someone whose own actions might be similarly measured for their ethical ambiguity and mercenary calculation these last few weeks, he had to credit the weird honesty of the man.

"Are we friends?" Fix asked tentatively.

"Friends? No, but allies, perhaps. At the least sign of treason, however, I'll twist your neck for you." Passepartout hoped the man understood that he meant it.

It was a great burden lifted from Fix's mood to finally have had it out with Passepartout, and even endure the pummeling. His position was now clear to all, no further subterfuge, and he was able to show his face at meals with a resilient stomach to match (bearing in mind the ever present ship movements that Mr. Fix knew now he would never find to his comfort).

On Saturday, the 23rd of November, the *General Grant* reached the 180th Meridian—half way around the globe from London's Prime Meridian at Greenwich. Fix made a great fuss about that, since it had taken nearly two months for Fogg to reach this point, and had only another month to cover the same to reach Britain.

"For once, at least, our watches are correct," Passepartout joked—though he realized they were twelve hours ahead here, making the coincidence only that.

Fogg reminded that they were still to schedule, with the fleet American railroads and but one ship's step across the Atlantic to effect the remainder of their course. The *General Grant* was also making steady progress, making an early arrival in San Francisco on the 2nd a possibility (though one fewer evening of whist in consequence, should that occur).

November 24th was another Sunday, though, causing Fogg and Aouda to negotiate other card partners, then back to Bennett and Sinclair on the 25th, and 26th ... and 27th. The decks were well shuffled that trip.

The 28th was a Thursday, and the ship's dinner menu catered to their American clientele and destination by featuring the rustic specialties becoming associated with a new holiday in that land, one reverently devoted to a national Thanksgiving. There was a buffet of oyster soup and lobster salad, roast turkey and boiled ham, a cranberry sauce and cold slaw, browned mashed potatoes and sweet potatoes, roasted broccoli and canned corn, and a dessert of mince and pumpkin pies.

Fogg, Aouda and Passepartout sampled a bit of each, with overall agreement on its general edibility. Mr. Fix was less heterogeneous in selecting this exotic fare, but also found it satisfactory.

During their dessert, Aouda announced, "*Nautilus* will be going to the Atlantic by way of the Arctic Ocean. Srikar says they will be submerged for the next week, so will be out of telegraphic signal, but will see much under the ice that has never before been witnessed."

"I can imagine *Monsieur* Barbicane and his friends, pressing their noses to the glass, Nemo's great windows, watching all that too," Passepartout posed. "I wonder what they will make of it."

"I think your brother was exploring Antarctica earlier," Fogg put in. "At least, as far as I could tell from my watch readings."

"He would map all the world's seas, if given a chance," Aouda admired, "and marvel at all their wonders."

Bennett and Sinclair came up to their table, each working on a plate of pie, pumpkin and mince respectively.

"This is a joy of travel, don't you think?" Bennett enthused. "Eating things from other places, hearing of their customs. I can almost hear the Pilgrims' chanting."

"Do Pilgrims *chant*?" Passepartout wondered.

"Well, we'll find out in America," Bennett beamed. "You'll be up for cards tonight, I hope? Sinclair is keen to save the regiment's honor, since we're down five on you."

"I have learned much on the playing of whist by observing you two gentlemen," Aouda smiled.

The remaining days and hours of their voyage sped by in such halcyon dining and card play, with Sunday the 1st of December once more jettisoning the devout Major Bennett and his Captain Sinclair. But they turned out to have two more days of rousing whist with them, as the *General Grant* did not finally paddle through the Golden Gate into the harbor of San Francisco until the evening of Tuesday, December 3rd.

From their card table, Aouda silently signaled Robur to bring the *Deimos* to America, to follow them close. It would take them about a day and a half to fly across the Pacific Ocean.

25. IN WHICH SLIGHT GLIMPSES ARE MADE OF SAN FRANCISCO

The *General Grant* pulled up its night moorings and made its way to the Pacific Mail Steamship wharf on the southeast flank of San Francisco just after dawn. The city was undergoing explosive growth as its housing and buildings colonized every hill in sight, served by seven privately operated horse trollies on the lower elevations. Many large Christian churches and cathedral spires stuck up from the wood and brick—even a splendid synagogue, whose twin round towers (sporting onion domes suggestive more of the Middle East) were just visible off to the west. San Francisco was a city of rampant commerce catering to every perceived need and vice, but well punctuated by ostentatious piety.

Fogg and his party had assembled at the rail, discerning what they could of this urbanity in the dim light before sunrise, further obscured by the coal haze of the awakening city. As they neared the Pacific Mail wharf, they could see the Long Bridge jutting out of one of the streets beyond, running out across the bay as a shortcut to the southern part of the peninsula and already lined with fishermen's poles. Which reminded Fogg of food.

"We're arriving before breakfast so they won't have to serve any," Fogg observed disapprovingly. "We'll need to find a hotel restaurant, preferably close to our railroad terminal, which is on Vallejo Street, according to our purser. The Americans are peculiar, as we must purchase tickets at a different location—New Montgomery and Market, which I am told is well across town. There is supposedly a morning express, at eight, but we're likely too late for that, so we'll aim for the evening train, at six. And there's the British Consul to locate, to validate my visa."

"Always the wager," Aouda joked.

"Yes," affirmed Fogg.

The main Pacific Mail wharf would have resembled a long trident were it seen from above. A central pier jutted a few hundred feet beyond its covered section, while to either side parallel service docks permitted coal to be brought to the ship on chutes fed by railed pushcarts running along elevated tracks, their attendants letting heaving grunts as they moved the weight along, while their passengers exited (First and Second Class from the side into the roofed area, Third Class out under the coal viaduct).

Because the *General Grant* was a side-wheeler, long gangways had to be positioned fore and aft of the port paddle house once the ship had backed into to its dock and secured by hawser ropes. This took some time, and still more before the first passengers began to set foot on the soil of the Golden State—or at least the planking of the Pacific Mail Steamship Company's pier.

At least one thing could be said for the enterprising Americans: they knew how to attack a problem with sheer numbers. Just as Mrs. Hammond had a proper team of people with her to follow Passepartout from America (losing track of them only because of Phileas Fogg's precipitous departure from London two months before), the squad of observers and runners put to watching for the arrival of the *General Grant* and one of its passengers in particular were fully up to that task.

There already being a steamer docked on the northeast slot, they knew the *General Grant* would be filling its mate on the southwest. Men inside would be covering the floor view, of course, but those in charge could not resist a military tactician's urge to command higher ground. By some finagling with underlings they procured a strategic vantage atop the brick provisioning warehouse adjacent to the coal tracks. Anyone hunched by its southeast parapet could see over the roofing below to those crossing down the long gangways, before they had a chance to disappear under the arcade to the left. And from the north corner, the building extended sufficiently beyond the covered pier to see anyone emerging from its main entrance.

Four men moved along the roof, hunching down as needed, since the side facing the Pacific Mail entrance was higher than the edge overlooking the coal runners. One man equipped with a spy glass expressed his displeasure at the Chinese coolie laborers disgorging from the Third Class coal side. "Gawd, look at all them chinks. Something's gotta be done about them."

"You and your Klan friends can play the vigilante on somebody else's time. Farley says this Passepartout is aboard, still traveling with the Englishman and his squaw. Keep an eye out for *them*," nudging the underling's telescope slightly to the left, "three together, well dressed apart from the Frenchman, carrying only a little luggage between them, no steamer trunks. That should be plain enough."

The man reluctantly but quickly withdrew his telescopic circle from the offending alien invasion to those starting to filter down the gangways on the port side. In due course people matching the description appeared: the top-hatted Englishman, carrying one small piece, followed by a darker skinned woman in European dress, and the Frenchman behind, carrying a carpetbag. Once this was reported, their leader led them along the parapet to the far corner, where they could observe what happened once they left the Pacific Mail dock.

The pantomime seen from the rooftop might have seemed comical. The Frenchman dropped the carpetbag, and let out a shout of delight at finally reaching American land, causing the seabirds resting near him to take wing at the disturbance. The top hatted figure stepped away to hire a carriage from among those waiting at the street, whereupon the valet took off his odd little hat and began to comb his hair. As for the "squaw," he might have regarded her as not badly featured at all, and certainly finely costumed, were there not already too many foreigners descending on their country to permit his incipient xenophobia the luxury of flattering objective assessment.

With Phileas Fogg, Aouda, and their two pieces of luggage occupying the enclosed carriage, Passepartout climbed up into the driver's box, from where he had an excellent view of his environs, flashing a careful glance up at the heads just visible along the brick wall of the building to their left.

Once the carriage set off, the man in charge on the roof barked out orders. "Send Darby, Fenton and Grissom to follow the carriage—don't be *seen*. We'll move to the Occidental, to tell Proctor they've arrived. Grissom can report where they've landed, to us at the hotel."

Packing up themselves and their gear and departing from their temporary aerie, the agents did not take note of Detective Fix, who had scuttled down the gangplank shortly after Fogg, and was by then just one among the throng of passengers boarding cabs and proceeding to and fro to their own calling.

The sun was just officially rising as Phileas Fogg's carriage headed northwest along First Street, by a hill being demolished a block west of them, an excavation gradually expanding the city's acreage by dedicated deposition into the bay. They covered three of the long San Francisco blocks before having to steer around an oncoming horse trolley turning off the avenue at their left. Passepartout could see how broad the streets of San Francisco were, well paved but largely treeless. A utilitarian landscape so far, thought Passepartout, less pleasant than the verdant thoroughfares of Singapore or Hong Hong—or the tranquil residential glades of the elite on Noge Hill.

Dodging west onto Market Street, the driver proudly pointed back off to the right, at a modest little building wedged between two others of like design, "That's all new, built after the old fell apart in the quake of '68."

"Earthquakes—they are common here?" Passepartout asked.

"Not always—had another one last March. Not as big as the one in '68, though. That was a *rattler*." The man grinned enthusiastically.

How characteristic it was of so many people, thought Passepartout, to find excitement and even take civic pride in implacable forces of Nature that might in time engender their own doom. "This would seem a dangerous place to build a city." The driver only laughed at his evident fecklessness.

Market Street was wide enough for two lines of horsecars to run down it, one in either direction. Passepartout could see how mindful the Californians were of their traffic etiquette, with westbound carriages and wagons reverently staying on the right side of the avenue, those oncoming eastbound on the opposite, and both giving wide berth to the horsecar lines running down the middle.

The boulevards intersecting north of Market ran parallel, but veered on an angle, while those to the south simply ran parallel to it. After one very long block to their left, two short ones brought them to the Central Pacific Railroad offices. Passepartout and Aouda remained out in the carriage while Fogg darted inside with his carpetbag to buy three First Class tickets through to New York, $138 dollars each, along with $1 on impulse for an extensive book entitled *Crofutt's Trans-Continental Tourist's Guide* that was on sale there at the desk—all paid out of £100 (the considerable change retained as incentive to accept the British currency). Fogg confirmed that their departure terminus was indeed up on Vallejo Street, and that an arrival before six o'clock would be recommended.

Back outside at the carriage, Fogg called up to the driver, "We shall now need a hotel restaurant for breakfast before our train. Take us up this Montgomery Street."

A short ride brought them to a grand three story establishment on the left side of Montgomery Street. The driver scrambled down and opened the door, "Here's the Lick House. Up next block is the Occidental, and the Cosmopolitan around the corner—three of the best stays in town."

"Is the Central Pacific Railroad near here?" Fogg asked.

"No—that's a ways north. You won't find a better breakfast than here, though."

"Proximity to the railroad is our primary concern. Please find one closer," Fogg said. While the driver was resuming his seat, he told Aouda, "For asking *three dollars* a ride, the man should find what we *want*."

Aouda decided San Francisco was an expensive place to visit, and Phileas Fogg was a man acclimated to getting his own way.

The driver shrugged to Passepartout (who had remained up in the box) and pulled from the curb, crossing the trolley lines to continue north up Montgomery Street.

Looking out her window, when they passed the Occidental Hotel, Aouda could see this was even more grandiose than the Lick, a four story Victorian layer cake of arches, pediments and columns designed to show all patrons they were staying in an establishment worth the cost—and, unbeknownst to them, where the Proctor gang were assembled equally unawares inside (having been instructed to take rooms there, under the not unjustified speculation that Phileas Fogg might have planned to stay at one of the city's better inns).

A continuous line of well-decorated three and four story buildings devoted to commerce of all kinds stretched off toward another great hill in the hazy distance, some sporting awnings but most bare to the sun.

"Where are you going on the train?" the driver asked Passepartout.

"All the way to New York City, and then by boat to England. Mr. Phileas Fogg is going around the world. Have you not read of him?"

"Nope," the driver said. "But I do read about the train attacks, all the time. Those Sioux and Pawnees, always doing that. You've got some guns, I hope?"

"How many would you recommend?"

"As many as you can carry. As many as you can carry."

The blocks were shorter in this part of town, their progress steady, but when they reached the intersection of Montgomery and Sacramento streets, Phileas Fogg called out for them to stop. Darting into the First National Gold Bank on one corner, Fogg and his carpetbag were quickly provisioned with £750 converted into the American currency. Just for contingency.

While they waited, Passepartout was struck by the contrasting perspective presented by the street here. Looking off to the west, at their left, there was in the distance a steep hill (one evidently not so profitably dismantled as that down by the wharf) on which sparsely populated heights an elegant new two story mansion was being built for the Central Pacific's chief lawyer, David Colton.

Seeing Passepartout's interest in that direction, the driver said, "Some company's tearing up Clay Street to pull trolleys up Nob Hill with steam cables. Not sure how *that's* going to work out."

Passepartout turned then to face east, where far down the avenue lay the crowded Chinese section, busy with skewed awnings of varying shape and quality, fragile overhanging wood porches, bright banners and signs telling of their business in ideograms unintelligible to the untutored eye, a clutter proclaiming by its every look and manner that here were the *foreign*, strangers, the different.

Californians specifically, but also Americans generally, were having some trouble with *different* these days, banning the Chinese hair queues and restricting their places of work or residence—an ungrateful irony, given how many Chinese laborers had been enticed to these very shores by railroad baron Charles Crocker to build his share of the Central Pacific railway fortune. Then Passepartout recalled the Japanese, likewise attempting to cordon off both Chinese and Europeans in Yokohama.

Could any of these people imagine how *not* "different" they all were, at least as witnessed by the one who called himself Jean Passepartout, riding up in the box with the driver of their carriage in San Francisco that pleasant December morning in 1872?

Fogg's currency conversion was soon done, and off they went again. A few more intersections north, Fogg's driver paused for a passing horsecar before he steered his team left onto Jackson Street. All the trolleys passed so far had only white faces within, not a Chinese or Negro passenger among them (such being the practice of their companies' management in reflection of the general local prejudice).

They pulled to a stop in the middle of the block, by the International Hotel on the north side. Jumping down to the pavement, the driver opened the curbside door. Once Fogg and Aouda were out and able to appreciate it, he pointed off to the northeast, "Your railroad station is off that way, sir, half a dozen blocks or so, as the crow flies."

"Flying would be a great convenience," Fogg winkled slyly to Aouda. Consulting the *Crofutt's Guide*, Fogg found the International Hotel was rated a good establishment, through the driver had been accurate in ranking the Lick, Occidental and Continental hotels so highly.

The International Hotel was done up to European tastes, though with a large bar on its ground floor reflecting an American focus, in charging only for any alcohol purchased, the cheese, biscuits, oyster soup and dried beef laid out being freely available otherwise. There were many gentlemen (and even a few ladies) there in the restaurant drinking and nibbling. Although rather early in the day for imbibing, on a whim Aouda said, "I should like a sherry."

"Order one for me, as well," Phileas Fogg said, and while Passepartout and Aouda commenced to partake of this gratuitous bounty, supervised by many Negro waiters, he went off to consult with some of the hotel's staff to determine corroborating directions to the Central Pacific depot, ascertain the whereabouts of the British Consul, and inquire after some of the latest news.

In the meantime, Misters Darby, Fenton and Grissom had skillfully followed Fogg's carriage all this time, keeping well back and inconspicuous among the city's busy morning traffic. As had Mr. Fix behind them both—occasioning one more unscheduled parade along the avenues of San Francisco, much as in distant Calcutta with a different threesome six weeks before.

While Grissom was dispatched inside the hotel to see what could be seen within, verifying Passepartout and Aouda in the bar restaurant, and Fogg inquiring on directions, Darby and Fenton intercepted the carriage driver, who readily disclosed that his passengers had been highly partial to dining as near as may be to the Central Pacific Railroad. When a couple leaving the hotel took that carriage; the two men returned to their own, but did not depart. Standing some feet back along Jackson Street, his small traveling case beside him on the sidewalk pavement, Mr. Fix finally acted like a competent field detective, by noticing all this.

After completing his conference with the hotel staff, Fogg obtained some food of his own and joined Passepartout and Aouda, who shifted the other small wine glass toward where Fogg was sitting down, with the observation, "It is not a bad sherry."

Fogg smiled and took a sip. "No, it is not. Not my usual breakfast, but we are in America. The hoteliers were reasonably informative. It is indeed only some short distance down to the rail station, perfectly adequate for walking, if needed. *I* appear to be still in the papers, but the Barbicane expedition fell off the front pages once they flew away. I learn, though, the British Consul resides at 319 California Street, well to the south of us, which we almost rode over earlier. Another Gaiety Theater—vexing."

"More vexing," Passepartout interjected. "We are being followed. Three gentlemen, *again*, picking up after us from the wharf. One of them is loitering in the lobby, the man in the light brown coat and cap. And we have Fix, behind them." That brought a dry smirk to Fogg's face.

"You have an advantage, I see, riding up with the carriage driver," Aouda said.

"Do we divide and conquer, as before?" Fogg asked.

Passepartout thought a moment. "The driver regaled me with stories of lurid Indian attack on the transcontinental train. He suggested we should travel *armed*."

"We have *that*," Aouda patted a dress pocket.

"It could be useful to be *seen* to be armed. If I were to buy a brace of Enfield rifles or Colt pistols, making a great show of it—a deterrence to them, possibly."

"Yes," Fogg agreed. "I still have to visit the Consul; you could embark on a shopping trip. Our separate ways."

"Whoever I do *not* go with, will need *this*." Aouda set her snuffbox telegraph out on the table, and Passepartout readily reached for it.

"I know," Passepartout shook his head, "the last time we separated, a *petite* mess. But this time, everyone speaks English, no?" Then adding for Aouda, cycling his index fingers up and down, "Have you used your engine?"

"It should be fully powered."

Fogg withdrew several hundred dollars from the carpetbag for Passepartout, then considered the time. "It is twenty past eight now. We should all be returned here for an early dinner—no later than ... three o'clock? Eleven Greenwich."

Outside the International Hotel soon after, Passepartout parted company with Fogg and Aouda, setting off back along the street on foot toward Montgomery. Fogg and Aouda headed off in the other direction, intending to hail a carriage once they'd seen what happened with their pursuers. This dispersal brought Darby and Fenton out of their vehicle in a hurry, Mr. Fix observing their consternation from nearby. When Grissom arrived by their side, he was directed to take the carriage back to the Occidental Hotel to report to Proctor, while Darby and Fenton set off to catch up to Passepartout, receding in a southerly turn at the corner.

Mr. Fix stuck to the Fogg path, however, catching up with them before they reached the end of the block, and declaring what a remarkable stroke of luck that he should encounter them both again here in San Francisco, having sailed on the same vessel all the way across the Pacific Ocean with so little interaction. And might he please stroll along with them, as they explored the city?

"By all means," Fogg replied. "We are on our way to the British Consul, so were about to call on a carriage."

"Capital!" Mr. Fix said. "Please, let me pay." This time, Fogg let him, and around the corner on Kearney Street they soon obtained another $3 conveyance to 319 California Street (doing some justly earned chagrin to Fix's more attenuated pocketbook).

In the very next block they rolled into the environs of City Hall and its broad plaza of Portsmouth Square, sprinkled with recently planted saplings testifying to a city craving a patina of Old World permanence while yet spinning on a New World timetable. Some sort of festival appeared to be in the offing there, as groups of workmen were assembling platforms and tall scaffolding for banners and flags.

The City Hall had "temporarily" resided here these last twenty years in what had been the old Jenny Lind Theater. Although a sprawling replacement edifice was on the drawing table to replace this makeshift arrangement, only the most preliminary of physical foundations had yet begun on it at its planned location southwest across town, a circumstance widely known in American civic administration of this Gilded Age, where the raising of vast funds for municipal improvements by diligently corrupt public servants were not always accompanied by necessarily building them.

Incidentally, regarding San Francisco's conjectured City Hall, in his brief description of the city's governmental amenities, the creative

Mr. *V.* somehow hallucinated its completion—remarking on its "lofty tower" that did not in fact exist. Then again, he had also erroneously taken San Francisco to be the capital of the state of California, an honor long deferred to Sacramento to the northeast. Could such apparent errors have been deliberate on his part, either to distance the narrative from the actual facts—or, more intriguingly, to act as subtle clues to subsequent investigators, alerting the perceptive reader to the presence of calculated misinformation? As with the events in Hong Kong, either possibility may be entertained by those of a suspicious temperament.

Just as Phileas Fogg, Aouda and Mr. Fix were admiring the rudimentary majesty of the theater turned City Hall, Passepartout was just then on the same block but over on the Montgomery Street side, when he noticed across the way at No. 630 something of what he needed: Clabrough & Bros. (John and Joseph) gunsmiths. He considered wending his way through the morning's carriage and wagon and horsecar traffic to see what they had in store, even looking both ways up and down the street (and thereby confirming that the two tailing men were indeed close at hand), but decided to continue on further south first.

Passepartout had worked all the way back down to the corner where they had passed the Occidental Hotel, prompting some peculiar looks from his pursuers (who knew their compatriots were likely somewhere inside), but as he had spotted no further gun stores on this side of the avenue, he crossed over to the opposite addresses, to head north back toward the known quantity of No. 630. Being closer to the doors and window displays here, though, Passepartout found at No. 410 a notice that Mr. Albert Crane operated out of Room No. 1 as the exclusive Remington firearms agent for the entire Pacific coast. Most ideal, Passepartout imagined, assuming one wanted to buy only a Remington (perhaps the man dealt in bulk, he speculated).

Declining this particular purchasing opportunity, not long after Passepartout was back up at Clabrough & Bros. (John and Joseph), inspecting their ample plate window signs—proud purveyors of Colts, Smiths and Wessons among their many pistols, rifles and shot. Though not Remingtons, of course. He stepped into its entrance alcove and opened the door into a temple of projectile assurance, walls lined with locked cabinets of barrels short and long, the smell of gun oil and national confidence thick in the air.

Ding-ding went a small doorbell, the glass rattling as Passepartout shut it. Several customers were there already—joined by another ding-ding, glass rattling, as Misters Darby and Fenton ambled in to silently admire the displayed arsenal while the floorboards' creaking signaled their every movement.

Passepartout was amused by that doorbell—such a mild, diminutive tinkle to announce entry into a shop dedicated to devices designed to accelerate blobs of metal to lethal velocities. And, thanks to the late Mr. Stanish's attack aboard the *Carnatic* three weeks before, Passepartout had a keen visceral familiarity with that side of things.

The next available Clabrough brother turned his attention to the new customer with a smile and inquiring gaze.

"I am in service to Mr. Phileas Fogg, who is traveling around the world, in eighty days," Passepartout said, not too loudly, but still sufficient to be handily overheard by anyone not deaf. "We are about to embark on the transcontinental railroad, all the way to New York. I have been seriously advised that there is great risk of *attack* aboard the train. To forestall this, we seek adequate additional weaponry. And ammunition, of course. What might you recommend, for ease of use, the accuracy, and the reliability? Pistols, rifles?"

"Rifles are fine, sir, but less so for close quarters, as you'd find on a moving train. Have you hunted with long guns, or infantry experience?"

"Neither of those." Passepartout glided his fingers along the polished wood of the glass cabinet between him and this Mr. J. Clabrough, seeing within pistols of varied manufacture, so many with beautiful wooden handles and delicate engraved scrolls and whorls on their metal parts. "I have never used weapons of this type, all that wood and refined metal tubes. They are quite the novelty to me. But I have seen their use, and learn most quickly." Passepartout smiled.

"I think a revolver would best suit you," the Clabrough brother decided. "We've got some fine Colts. The Army Model here is good," pulling out a gun with a rich red wood handle, and a long 8 inch barrel. "Sixteen dollars. Colt has a new pistol in the works for the Army, but this is the current one, not the shorter barrel ones the Texas rebels bought—better quality on this Army 1860."

Still sizing up his customer, Clabrough fetched another firearm, smaller than the other and with a plainer blonde handle. "This may be better for you, though—the new Colt Open Top, bit lighter, shorter barrel. Even simpler, it uses the new Henry Rimfire cartridges. Still six shots, but easier to load. We can do … twenty-six dollars a gun here, including ammunition, four boxes." Seeing his customer showing no obvious signs of resistance or rejection at his dealer's markup, he dangled a merchant's honed close, "How many guns were you thinking to get?"

Passepartout took the Army Model in his left hand and the Open Top in his right, comparing their heft and balance and grip. Laying them down on the case, he indicated the lighter Open Top, "This will do. I should want six. You have in supply to take now? The train leaves this evening. Oh, and a case, small enough to carry them all, and the bullets—size is a consideration on our trip."

Thanks to Phileas Fogg's prescient visit to the First National Gold Bank, Passepartout was able to purchase the guns with some of those American dollars, plenty to spare. Seeing that Passepartout would be waiting for the carrying case to be crafted, Darby and Fenton realized they would either have to act like customers or retreat. Ding-ding soon sounded, glass rattling as they scouted a location outside to await Passepartout's exit.

Over the next hour the craftsman in the back rooms of Clabrough Bros. cobbled up a hinged box that previously held a dozen guns in lined slots, six on each side. By removing the sections in the lid, the cartridge boxes could be held there, adding two lacquered boards that opened like the covers of a book to hold the contents in place, clasped in the middle with brass. Passepartout studied the hinges, locking clasps and leather handle grip, tugging and assessing how well the sections held together the considerable weight.

"Most well-made and sturdy," Passepartout complimented their workmanship, "especially done at haste. Many thanks."

It was just past eleven o'clock when Passepartout departed the Clabrough establishment with his gun-laden case, casting at eye out for Misters Darby and Fenton (now striving too hard to appear unnoticed a few doors down the block). Having many hours to occupy his time, and since he had already seen something of the city south of where he was now, Passepartout set off for the sizable hill that loomed to the north.

A few blocks north of the International Hotel, Passepartout passed Broadway Street, where a deep excavation plowed the road straight through the increasingly hilly terrain off to his left, a few ramshackle houses adamantly perched on the vertical edges, looking to collapse at any moment down onto the street and horsecar line, while to his right he was on the edge of another rough precipice. From here he could see the roofs and back porches of the multistoried residences of the next streets; further on, the harbor, a sizable island poking up to the east, with some stretch of hilly land beyond in the haze.

San Francisco so often seemed to Passepartout not merely *new*, but in spots unattractively oblivious to its haphazard process of construction.

The avenue continuing north degenerated into a series of increasingly steep stairways and connecting alleys, but Passepartout pressed on, taking some amusement at how the two men following him were less adept at pounding up the many, many, many steps.

⋘ ⋙

Coming out of the Consul's residence on California Street after his passport was visaed, Phileas Fogg took in a good draught of air and declared ebulliently to Aouda and Fix, "I feel peripatetic. We have over three hours to return to the hotel, and there is much of the city we might see on the way. I reckon seven or eight turns, zigzagging our way north. Are you game for a stroll? We'd be carrying our luggage."

"I have no difficulty with mine," Aouda said. "What of you, Mr. Fix?"

As Fix's case was the smallest of the three, he could not decline without appearing embarrassingly less capable than the woman in their party. "All fine here."

Their journey northward brought them into the edge of Chinatown, where Aouda made use of her familiarity with the language to note the varied establishments whose business might not be obvious from the outside, from apothecaries to opium parlors. On occasion she stopped to converse with some of those she encountered, learning more about the people and their community, growing more sympathetic and pensive by the block.

"The people here are afflicted by prejudiced hatred and much opium," Aouda said sadly. "The fear comes in local abundance, but the opium is imported, and not by their request. They have named 1864 'the Year of Opium' for how much was shipped here—not so long ago, Phileas, and the police do nothing to stop it." Turning to their English detective, whose actions in Hong Kong she was well aware of (though he remained unapprised that she had been so informed by Passepartout), "Can you imagine any officer of the law so *vile*, Mr. Fix, to encourage such a thing?"

Mr. Fix suppressed in silence a lame swallow.

⋘ ⋙

Achieving the summit of the place locally known as Telegraph Hill, Passepartout found a quite revealing panorama of San Francisco spread out before him. He did not require use of his comb to discern that the two men had stayed back rather than tagging too close—both bending over, clutching their thighs, winded from the exertion. Passepartout meanwhile stomped up onto ever higher rocky crags, stopping every so often to survey the scene from the new vantage, since the land had so many ups and downs to it that each new spot put some further distant location into better or worse view.

In the end, Passepartout was most taken by something he *didn't* observe. No matter where he looked on this peninsula, peering out as far as the ringing sea, apart from regular roads and the spiking line of ship masts at nearly every stretch of open water around, he could see no sign of any *railroad tracks*.

Where then was this "Central Pacific Railroad" he, Phileas Fogg, and Aouda were to be boarding for points east at six o'clock?

It may have been that Misters Darby and Fenton had supposed Passepartout would most likely return the way he had come, so wanted to position themselves to take up his rear. But in drifting to the west onto the broad Filbert Street that ran down the west flank of Telegraph Hill, they found themselves suddenly located in front of him as Passepartout took that path down.

Like an ebbing tide, the two men had to retreat in front of him, throwing them off what a proper tail should be up to. After a very steep drop, Filbert began to level off as it passed a city park, another dollop of recently planted foliage and grass divided by broad paths in a great X fixed at each corner. Darby and Fenton sought temporary refuge there beside a tree at the entrance, intending to resume the tail once he had passed.

Only Passepartout did not pass. He turned at the corner and sauntered diagonally across Stockton Street toward the park, the angle of his approach putting the bright new spire of St. Peter's Episcopal Church across the street directly over his shoulder. Like an avenging angel—or devil—*he* was now following *them*.

Darby and Fenton pulled back from the tree and into the walk as Passepartout approached, the Frenchman seeming casual as you please, smiling. After brief colloquy, the two men resolved to hold their ground. Moving farther apart, by the time Passepartout grew near enough for a chat, he found it harder to face both at once.

"No closer," Darby warned, "We know you're dangerous." He pulled out a pistol from his pocket, and Fenton on his right soon brandished a knife.

"Oh, *do* you now? And who has been telling you such tales? Come, come. What do these *they* say of me, umm? I should like to know."

"Men on a steamship disappeared, or died," the man with the knife declared nervously.

At every step Passepartout took in either of their direction, Darby and Fenton pulled back, and separated more. He hardly wanted to discuss, let alone defend, the incidents on the *Carnatic* with these men, so declared instead, "I cannot fathom why you still follow me. Especially now, too late."

"Too late for what?" Darby asked.

"If you understood things, you would know."

Darby and Fenton were now positioned fully to either side of Passepartout, the one with the knife seemed more skittish, muscles tensing and lunging forward occasionally in what Passepartout took to be an effort at physical intimidation. Both men were now also consciously keeping out of arm's reach.

But their estimation of *arm's reach* had not apparently included the box the valet carried.

"I do not have the time for this," Passepartout said, and with one blindingly fast move, he spun around, letting the size and weight of the gun case act as an extension of his right hand. In a great smooth arc, the very hard corner of the wooden box caught first Darby and then Fenton flat on the face, their gun and knife flinging from their hands as they were knocked to the garden pavement unconscious.

Passepartout quickly set his case to the ground and knelt down to feel the knife-wielder's forehead with his left palm, then doing likewise with the gunman. By now two bystanders from the tight row of narrow houses fronting the park along Filbert had come up to them.

"I saw those two attack you," one man said to Passepartout, with a trace of an accent, something Mediterranean perhaps.

"They followed me from the shop. I am afraid I injured them."

"An attempted robbery, here in Washington Square," the other citizen shook his head disapprovingly. No notable accent to him.

"Both these men will need hospital, I fear," Passepartout said, quite accurately, still on the ground beside Fenton, then added in a worried way, "And I must return to Phileas Fogg at the hotel, for the train."

"You're with Mr. *Fogg*?" the Italian fellow's attitude instantly flipped from concern for the altercation to admiration for the celebrity in their midst (or at least someone associated with one). "I've read all of Mr. Fogg in the *Call*, and *La Voce Del Popolo*." He quickly helped Passepartout to his feet and began pumping his hand energetically. Turning to the other man, who though a neighbor was largely a stranger to him, "He is with the around the world man." Then he asked Passepartout, "Italia, you went through Italia—what did you see and think?"

"We were in a great hurry," Passepartout replied plainly. "The trains were all very new, the land most beautiful, but we saw very little of it. We took a boat from Brindisi for Egypt and India, and that was our last of Italy."

The Italian turned to the other, eyes wide, wagging his spread hands in unison, "Just two months ago this man was in *Italy*, with Mr. Phileas Fogg. Amazing!"

"I am concerned about the two men," Passepartout waved at the quietly breathing pair on the Washington Square paths, blood tricking from two serious head wounds.

"No, no—we will attend to it. The City and County Hospital is just down there," the Italian pointed off north, "down Stockton at Francisco, very close, four blocks."

"I'll go," the other man volunteered, catching the Italian's enthusiasm, and dashed off without further prodding.

"There, *amico mio. He* will alert the hospital; *they* will bring an ambulance. And *you* may go in peace to the wonderful Mr. Fogg, and your train."

Looking down at the two men on the ground, "We'll say to the doctors and the police how we saw these two set upon a gentleman, unknown to us, who fought honorably against the assailants—yes, the *assailants*," he pronounced slowly, "but had fled to safety before we could come where these two ruffians had fallen, North Beach justice done. *That* will read well in the papers. So go—go!" he urged.

With a thankful smiling nod, Passepartout picked up his case of guns and set off towards the southeast entrance of the square, opening onto Stockton.

Just then the distant sound of a brass band could be heard, playing *Columbia, the Gem of the Ocean*, and the Italian shouted after Passepartout, "Sir, I forgot—the election parades. There will be crowds, all around, take care. And journey well with Mr. Phileas Fogg!"

Phileas Fogg, Aouda and Mr. Fix were much closer to the band by then, which they could hear blaring away back down Montgomery Street, trying to be heard over the very crowd they were in the middle of, a lengthy mob proceeding north in such numbers that it spilled over both sides of the street and brought even the horsecars to a standstill. The musicians had been culled from one of the city's many fire brigades (serious conflagrations being far more regular a menace here than the less frequent cataclysmic earth tremors) and several elaborately decorated ceremonial fire pumps were proudly drawn along.

Many marchers waved flags or carried posters proclaiming partisan support for "Camerfield" or "Mandiboy" competing for the post of Justice of the Peace. These tended to stay well apart, since close proximity often resulted in altercations where one or the other or both of the displays ended up in tatters.

"Extraordinary," Phileas Fogg said of the passing tumult, "Some manner of political celebration."

"Quite a masculine one," offered Aouda regarding the apparent absence of any of her gender in the northward proceeding throng.

"Yes. Women's participation in the public governance is not the common feature these days, is it, even among those enamored of

Republics, as they are here—or my own England, despite being ruled by a *Queen*." Fogg proffered a wry look to Aouda.

The shouting and whooping and gunfire threatened the approaching band for volume, but too many among them were also trying to sing along. Even when they were moderately close to the tune or its key valiantly being suggested by the musicians down the street, a further discord ensued as many (especially those fortified by drink prior to joining the procession) couldn't reliably recall all the lyrics or their order. Most tended to repeat "Columbia! the gem of the ocean" to start, no matter where they thought they were, while others had jumped to "The Union, the Union forever" from the last verse. Six lines on, and fewer were declaiming the first verse's convoluted "Thy banners make tyranny tremble, When borne by the red, white, and blue" than those patriotically offering the third verse's simpler martial sentiment, "The Army and Navy forever, Three cheers for the red, white, and blue."

Such sentiments were making Mr. Fix worried. "You don't think they would resent our being English, do you? The *Alabama*'s been settled."

"Alabama?" Aouda asked. "Wasn't that an American rebel province?"

"This was a Confederacy warship, named for it," Fogg explained, "one of many, all built in Britain, secretly."

"Yes, I *did* read of that," Aouda remembered now. "The Americans were objecting. Demanded some colossal amount of money in damages."

"Two thousand millions of dollars, to be exact," Fogg said.

"Or pieces of Canada," Fix added, "They'd take that instead. Something to connect to the Alaska they'd just bought from the Russians, probably."

"No matter, there's a treaty now, and the international tribunal settled *fifteen* millions on them for recompense, minus a few for their attacks on British shipping." All the while Fogg had been assessing the parade marchers, and now looked resolute, "English or not, we'll have to wade in, if we're to get across the street—which we must, if we're to return to the hotel and Passepartout."

As the Fogg party jostled and weaved their way across the street, the human current took them up a block, where they encountered another noisy human obstacle at the intersection with Clay Street. Fresh from their rally at City Hall to the west, their hotter heads had decided to show their support for the competing candidate of Mandiboy by marching in to manifest their superior enthusiasm, flooding in on the perpendicular. Besides prancing equestrians and several beer wagons draped with smiling dancehall girls, they had a band of their own, recruited from the municipal police, and starting up *Rally 'Round the Flag* not only as loudly as they could, but intentionally in an entirely different key and significantly faster rhythm.

Compounding the escalating din, some among the Mandiboy brigade were a unit of Union veterans resplendent in their old Zouave uniforms, proudly yelling the received lyrics, "The Union forever! Hurrah, boys, hurrah! Down with the traitors, up with the star," while not a few former Confederate soldiers (prudently not in their service uniforms) tried to sneak in the version of the song they had known from the War, "Our Dixie forever! She's ne'er at a loss! Down with the eagle and up with the cross," before each got to something like "Shouting the battle cry of freedom!" in unison at the end.

One of those performing *Rally 'Round the Flag* in the Confederate mode was a stocky man with a fierce red beard, holding a Mandiboy banner high, and accompanied by a significantly more circumspect Mr. Grissom.

When the light of recognition dawned on Fix, realizing the man in the brown suit and cap passing by was one of the three so concerned about Fogg's carriage at the hotel, he tugged on Phileas's coat sleeve. "Mr. Fogg, that young man over there, marching beside the one with the red beard—I think he was following after you at the hotel, with two other men. No idea why."

"Yes, I know. Thank you Mr. Fix." Useful, after all. Fogg turned to Aouda, indicating the pair to her, "The red bearded man—his superior, perhaps?"

"The way the other cowers, and keeps up—possible. Investigate?"

"Not necessary. My object is the hotel, a filling meal, and the train east, with you and Passepartout aboard. What these local *thuggees* do in their spare time is no concern of mine."

Just then Grissom caught sight of Fogg and Aouda standing there, and startled. Like Fix, he too had reason to tug at his companion's coat sleeve, "The Fogg man and his woman are back there—no Frenchman."

The man stopped, causing the other marchers to flow around them, and turned back to stare, then glare, where Grissom pointed.

By now the police band was entering Montgomery Street, and their *Rally 'Round the Flag* was in full cacophonous conflict with *Columbia, the Gem of the Ocean* still ringing from the firehouse players just up the block. This was soon matched by actual conflict, as more of the Mandiboy partisans began to pick fights with the Camerfield faction, quickly transformed into a general melee as this stretch of the parade ground to a violent halt. Banners on both sides were being torn apart, flagstaffs turned into jabbing pikes, canes and sticks vigorously wielded, hats and even shoes tossed about, fists engaged and more guns shot (vertically, for the most part, mercifully for all present)—some quarreling almost independently of which candidate they were favoring, just for the invigorating rush of it.

The music of the two bands began to disintegrate into isolated horns and winds and drums as the tumult made it impracticable to continue, their instruments by now more useful as bludgeons to ward off attack, or to be protected for their value as their players sought refuge off the avenue.

In due course, both Phileas Fogg and Mr. Fix found themselves set upon by proxy, the brunt of others' flailing elbows and careening bodies. Aouda fared somewhat better, being perceived as a lady in a world that sought to "protect" them even while granting them little else. One man of drunken demeanor looking about to strike Fogg from behind stopped to avoid Aouda's bustle, as she strategically rotated clockwise and stepped backwards toward Fogg, transferring her case from her right hand to her left. The man doffed his cap deferentially to her when she looked back, and staggered off to assault someone else.

Handing Grissom his Mandiboy banner (causing the fellow to be quickly set upon by several Camerfield supporters), the red bearded man headed straight for Phileas Fogg. When the fellow swung his right fist at Fogg, Mr. Fix dashed forward to intercept the blow, which landed on the top of the shorter detective's head, smashing his silk hat and bringing the detective and his luggage crashing to the wide sidewalk.

As Fix scrambled to his feet, the man pulled a knife from a scabbard and sliced out at Fix, catching the suit cloth in several spots, but no flesh beneath as Fogg had pulled the detective backwards. Red beard was about to lunge again, when Aouda stabbed the back of his hand with one of her hatpins, causing him to drop the knife and turn to this distraction with fury in his eyes.

Aouda did not look cowed, clutching the hatpin in front of her chest like a defensive spike. The bearded man began to shake his head, feeling disoriented, as Fogg stepped forward. He grabbed Fogg's coat sleeve, managing to tear the fabric at the shoulder seam, but didn't continue after that, his eyes blinking and his breathing becoming less regular.

Looking down at his dislodged sleeve, Fogg declared "Yankee!" at his assailant, a punning accusation the man neither appreciated for its wit nor evidently regarded as complimentary.

"Englishman!" he spat, still wagging his head and blinking. "We *will* meet again!"

"When you please," Fogg said coolly.

Almost reflexively, increasingly groggy, red beard asked, "What is your name?"

"Phileas Fogg. And yours?"

"Ah, ah." Struck by Fogg's honesty in identifying himself, he finally replied in kind, "Colonel Stamp Proctor."

Mr. Grissom, whose clothes were now in as much disarray as Fogg's or Fix's, noticed Proctor's diminished vigor and came up to assist him. Retrieving the man's knife from the sidewalk (not waving it offensively, though), Grissom took Proctor by the arm, "Back to the hotel, Colonel, come along."

Observing the two men go, Fogg smiled to Aouda, "Remind me to stand clear of your hatpins." Then he turned to Mr. Fix, "Thanks."

"No thanks are necessary," Fix replied, "but let us go." He motioned at his own and Fogg's tattered attire, "To a tailor."

"Yes, indeed," Fogg agreed.

The street fight was starting to ebb, and Fogg led the way to a stopped horsecar that was about to resume its progress. Fogg darted up to the driver's platform, his carpetbag swinging in his hand. From this high spot he could survey the avenue, up and down and around, smiled at the disconcerted fellow, and quickly returned to the pavement.

"I see a tailor's sign a few blocks down. Across the street, but the political riot seems to be breaking up now."

The three were mindful of their safety as they crossed the street and went south, coincidentally passing Clabrough Bros. gunsmiths on their way to Wm. Sherman & Co. tailors operating at 608 Montgomery.

"Oh dear, oh dear, oh dear," the proprietor lamented as he saw his entering customers. He did not have to ask why they were there.

"Is it possible to contrive new suits for us both, *immediately*?" Fogg raised an eyebrow. "We are travelers, and on a departing schedule."

"Even without your speech I could see you're English." Sherman began to eye what remained of their garments. "My rival *Short*, down on Commercial Street, caters more to the English cloth, as I see you're wearing. We have some similar. Now if you want more the latest *New York* cut, Steinhardt on *Battery* has the standard there, but we can do you well for that too, if need."

"Lack of shreds and quickly done are our primary concerns of the moment," Fogg specified. "We have a train to catch this evening, and we still have a dinner to take, at three. If you can append some fashion to your stitching, all the better, but not essential. Will two hundred of your dollars be sufficient? In cash, of course."

"Most adequate, sir," Mr. Sherman smiled. "We shall proceed!" And Sherman & Co. did exactly so, taking measurements and putting their staff to work at fullest press.

Passepartout was by that time seated on a chair in the lobby of the International Hotel. A comb of his hair raised nothing of concern, though he was increasingly mindful of the time. Around ten before three he pulled out Aouda's snuffbox and sent a message to her: *AOUDA, WAITING FOR YOU AT HOTEL. YOU DELAY, GOOD OR ILL? JEAN P.*

Aouda could see the tailors fussing over the last details of the coats they had made for Phileas and Mr. Fix, and responded thus: *JP. PHILEAS & FIX NEEDED TAILORS, NEAR AT 608 MONTGOMERY ST, WILL BE AT HOTEL SOON. A.*

Phileas Fogg, Aouda, and Mr. Fix arrived at the International Hotel at a quarter past three.

"Thank you for buying the suit," Fix said to Fogg, heartfelt.

"You were of assistance," Fogg replied.

"I hope to see you on the train," Fix added. "I have decided to continue on all the way to New York."

Not a surprise to Fogg. "What a traveler you have become," he said to Fix, and escorted Aouda and Passepartout into the restaurant for what he hoped would be an uneventful and adequate dinner.

"Mr. Fix was of aid?" Passepartout asked Fogg once they were seated.

Aouda answered instead. "We were set upon by a man with a knife, likely the master of the one with the cap you saw here. Mr. Fix helped fight him off."

"Ah, hence the new clothes. That must have been a fight." So the detective was striving to be as good as his word, thought Passepartout—at least so long as they were not on British soil.

Seeing Passepartout's box, Fogg asked, "Would that be the new firearms?"

"*Oui*, six Colt revolvers and ammunition, thirty-five pounds total—the cost, not the weight, though nearly so—half maybe." Passepartout hefted the case to the table with a gentle thud. "This heavy thing persuaded two of the young cap's friends that they needed a stay in the hospital. It scratched the corner a bit," worrying over the damage to the finish, and returning the case to the floorboards.

"Oh, and *your* box," Passepartout added, retrieving the telegraph and placing it on the table by Aouda, who returned it to her pocket with a smile.

"Between the three of us, I think we annoyed them this afternoon," Fogg declared. "They will not like that. We must be on our guard all the trip. Especially as we approach Chicago."

That last point was purely for Passepartout's benefit.

The sun had set but there was twilight by the time Fogg hired a carriage for the trip to the Central Pacific Railroad, as by common silent agreement all had their fill of walking around San Francisco.

When the carriage turned south onto Davis Street from Vallejo at a quarter to six, depositing them at the utilitarian shed with the sizable sign proclaiming **CENTRAL PACIFIC R.R. FOR NEW YORK & CHICAGO, SACRAMENTO, STOCKTON AND SAN JOSE**, Passepartout's concern welled up anew as he could not help but notice that they were situated at the edge of the bay. "Are there supposed to be *tracks*? This is worse than Kholby, there was *land* there."

"There are ferry docks here I think," Aouda observed in the decreasing light, pointing off through the cracks in a sliding gate.

"Ah, like Dover," Fogg nodded. "A boat train, Passepartout—boat first, this time. The rail line must stop somewhere across the bay."

For a city of 150,000 people, the tenth largest in the United States, Fogg and party found the barnlike ferry terminal of the Central Pacific Railroad incongruous for what was, in fact, the California end of the nation's transcontinental railway. Calcutta had done quite better than that.

Venturing inside, there were at least porters to attend to their luggage, but Fogg would have none of that, though giving them some gratuities for their livelihood even while keeping their own cases to themselves. The building eventually gave access to the wharf beyond, where the *El Capitan* sidewheel ferry was just then easing carefully to the dock, the embayment lined with double rows of stout pilings to act as bumpers in the event of a pilot's fault of navigation. Embarkation was accomplished along a broad platform lowered onto an opening at the bow (or stern, depending on which way the boat had been steaming), along which wagon freight (but not railroad cars) could be loaded as well as pedestrians bearing tickets for the train. Inside, stairs led to a Spartan but moderately clean upper deck devoted to passenger traffic.

Arriving early as they did, Fogg and his party could assay those boarding later, which included Mr. Fix—and, at the very last minute, the red-bearded Colonel Proctor, who arrived alone, carrying one commodious valise, his head still beating from whatever it was on the tip of Aouda's hatpin. Proctor played the Mrs. Hammond thereafter by keeping well out of all of their way when the *El Capitan* set off for Oakland, its stern end now becoming the prow thanks to a second pilot house located for that purpose. Their progress was slower at night, anxious not to collide with anything in the dark of the bay, so the half hour voyage of the daytime took somewhat longer now.

Evidencing a characteristic American attention to the details of function over esthetics, the Central Pacific Railroad had constructed an enormous artificial land wharf extending two miles out into the bay from Oakland, allowing ferries from various destinations to dock for the trains. Very little of this could be seen in the dark, apart from segments lit by lanterns, the ferries already docked at the piers that splayed out at various angles, or the lamps and glow of the train cars and locomotive. At length, the *El Capitan* slowed for their approach to the piers, which were similarly lined with rows of protective pilings. This Oakland end of the journey lacked even a terminal structure, however, with disembarkation conducted in the open air, beside the few rude sheds that adjoined the docks.

Owing to the hour, the railroad cars were already being readied for sleeping. This was not done as in the British or European manner, where one dozed as one might in separate compartments, but in the American bulk way pioneered by Mr. Pullman—namely, where all passengers occupied an open car, the seats facing in alternating directions along a central aisle, with upper sleeping berths lowered on hinges from above when needed, the lower seat cushions reconfigured into the lower beds (who alone had a window view). Curtains were drawn around all this for a rudiment of privacy.

Passepartout took this delay as an opportunity to step out of the carriage and explore the length of the train, a long line of passenger and cargo cars strung out along the broad artificial archipelago jutting out into the water, the sea air bracing in the night, dim lights glimmering from the distant communities dotting the land roundabouts, and all the while, the CPRR locomotive panting gently like a slumbering beast, steam emanating from valves and lazy puffs of smoke curling over the top if its absurdly large funnel. The engineer and his helper inside the engine cab were performing last minute checks on the locomotive's gauges, and paid Passepartout no mind.

Standing by the flaring triangular "cow catcher" that decorated most every American engine, extending several meters beyond the boiler, Passepartout turned to look back at the line of cars and held out his comb before him, its tines wagging this way and that. Had he been able to stand farther away from the carriages he might have obtained a clearer reading, but he was restricted by the narrowness of the Oakland wharf. As it was, Fogg's watch stood out for its blotch of blackness and so obscured most everything along that line of sight—which was pretty much everyone and thing on the train.

Ah, well. Passepartout put his comb back in his pocket and sauntered back down along the cars to board their carriage.

Finally, sharp whistle blasts signaled, the two drive wheels on either side of the engine began to turn and gain traction, and the Central Pacific Railroad train crept forward along that exceedingly long wharf.

Once they reached actual ground, the levers were gradually let out still more to gain speed for their advance at steady steam first southward along San Francisco Bay, before turning inland and northward towards the great mountains off ahead in the night.

Now they could truly be said to be on their way, across the United States of America.

26. IN WHICH SOME PARTIES TRAVEL BY THE PACIFIC RAILROAD, WHILE OTHERS DO NOT

The curtains were all drawn and the passengers were presumed to be fast asleep when the Central Pacific train made a brief stop, pulling under a covered station just after midnight on Thursday morning, December 5th. The stoppage of the train prompted Phileas Fogg (accustomed as he was to late hours playing whist) to descend from his not especially spacious upper berth to ascertain their location from the porter dozing in a seat at the end of the car. Unlike most of the passengers, Fogg had not surrendered his shoes to the porter (not to be shined but merely for safekeeping, as fear of theft was not uncommon on the line).

"Sacramento," the man affirmed softly, and shut his eyes again.

8 AM Greenwich, Fogg confirmed on his watch—which also showed the "**O**" of Aouda's *Deimos* flashing at *XII*. He wondered how much power the craft expended were it to hover when they stopped like this—or whether the adaptable Robur had some other coping maneuver.

The locomotive labored more after the Sacramento stop, leaving the rural agricultural lowlands of vineyards and pastures for the long climb into the Sierra Nevada Mountains. Through the night they drove ever higher, the rugged landscape barely illumed by a thin crescent Moon.

Those cocooned in upper berths like Phileas Fogg or Mr. Fix (stationed above Aouda and Passepartout respectively) lacked a window view, so could not appreciate what a big American landscape it was, fit for even bigger constructions. The railroad crossed many a bridge, including one at the first glimmer of dawn that was over a thousand feet in length, formed like a single great wood-planked box under the rails, balanced on the tips of hundred-foot triangular wood pylons marching across the ravine. The track wended along around the hills for some time after that, back and forth, then on through a larger promontory via a tunnel nearly as long as the train itself.

Over a thousand feet above them, Robur telescopically anticipated where the line would emerge and gave the piloting Niru directions. The *Deimos* swung ahead over the hills and was above them again when the train appeared out the east end, where a mile further on, a great stone wall protected the tracks from burial by avalanche.

The train crossed another thousand-foot bridge, this one of a more familiar timber frame type, except that it was not straight but broadly curved off to the left. Another tunnel followed, requiring more prescient navigation by Robur. Though there was no trouble keeping up with a surface conveyance chugging along at a sixth their speed, especially in the increasing light of morning and with the instruments they possessed on *Deimos*, stray bursts of rough air could be encountered over these intermittent crags and valleys, which buffeting Master Xie felt all too well from his preferred spot on the deck.

"Will we be rising high?" Xie asked, eyes remaining shut, perceptions taut.

"They're not yet to the summit of the mountains hereabouts," Robur reported. "We'll be easily two miles altitude then."

The Central Pacific Railroad was obviously mindful of the danger of avalanche, as Robur could see long snow sheds had been built over the rails at half a dozen spots here. He called up to Niru, "The tracks have been clear so far, but they've put roofs over the railroad along here. We may need to scout ahead, see how the way forward is unobstructed."

"The horizon looks mild," Niru announced. "I can see a fine lake off to the right. A big one—beautiful. Sunrise will be soon. Will you want us higher to avoid being seen?"

"Your discretion. Maybe another five hundred."

Once over the summit, the Central Pacific train picked up speed through the Truckee valley, crossing the river there several times. Each new bridge Passepartout saw out the window of his berth appeared to be of a different design than that before. This latest one was not a high bridge where they rode atop without obstruction, but one running low across the water, through a long line of wood trusses, their angled bulk and shadows flashing by, first one then their opposite, the structure joined over the train by further cross-members. Passepartout supposed there must either be a functional justification for this variety, or a contract had been let to a rival engineer with their own favored resolution for the span.

The train entered Nevada at eight that morning, by which time most of the passengers were up, angling for their spot in the desperate queue for the lone faucet and commode per coach. There was a trickle of water available by the time Aouda had her turn, still less for Fogg later.

There was a twenty minute breakfast stop at the hamlet of Reno, affording the porters opportunity to return the carriages to their day coach configuration. The station was a large wooden barn, of two stories, with an overhang sheltering the raised platform. The temperature here was brisk, about freezing this time of morning, so all venturing outside donned what coats, hats and gloves they had. Six-team stagecoaches from the mining boom towns of Virginia City and Gold Hill were dropping and adding passengers, beside a huge stack of wood supplying the locomotive's tender and the station's several stoves. A modest diner catered to the passengers' hunger—expeditiously, given the shortness of their stay.

Colonel Proctor was by now sufficiently recovered from his Montgomery Street malady to dine fairly heartily, albeit quickly, of the buffet of fried ham and eggs, coffee or tea, and bread (somewhat stale), sitting alone at a somewhat rickety table across the room from Phileas Fogg and his companions (Passepartout going to the station's toilet since he had missed his chance earlier in the car).

Being on the train was not Proctor's idea, nor that he was aboard unaccompanied by any of his men. No word had come yet from Darby or Fenton when Grissom had conveyed him back to the Occidental Hotel, only to find a letter *sans* postage stamp waiting for him at the lobby desk, which he opened once he had regained the privacy of his room. Its contents jolted him considerably from his lingering stupor:

> *Colonel Proctor,*
>
> *Enclosed is your ticket for this evening's Central Pacific RR eastbound through to New York City. Pack lightly but sufficient for full journey; carry whatever cash for sundries as you see fit. Be adequately armed, but do NOT approach Mr. Passepartout without permit. Travel on your own name & identity; use the address known to you for any telegraphs. Person(s) signaling "Catspaw" en route will convey further instructions as needed.*
>
> <u>*Tollensque quod suus iuste nostra*</u>

Pulling the letter from his pocket, Proctor ruminated over it again at his breakfast table. Was he to be the "catspaw" here? He had Mr. Grissom telegraph what had happened with Phileas Fogg during the election parade, but as the letter had been deposited for him by then, this commitment for him to head eastward had already been made. Would he still have been so dispatched had those representing *TQSIN* known of this? Something to ask the catspaw, should any appear.

Mr. Fix crossed to Phileas Fogg's table, taking the empty one being saved for Passepartout. "The Colonel showing up here—are our new suits in jeopardy?"

"If so, Mr. Fix, he gets the tailor's bill," Fogg said in between bites of toast (whose quality and temperature he found deficient to his taste).

Passepartout appeared with a plate of ham and eggs to be quickly downed, forcing Fix to relinquish his place. Boarding the train after their hasty breakfast, Passepartout observed of Proctor, "He seems a rather conspicuous visage to send after us, no?"

"Unless a coincidence—abhorrent, but possible—just as our

meeting him in the parade," Aouda replied. "I would say, though, he is meant to be seen, by us. The question is, whether as warning or distraction."

The train made good time after leaving Reno, until around noon when they were forced to a stop before a passing herd of the American bison, animals of such disposition that interfering with their rumbling migrations was thought unwise even for so massive a mechanical thing as their train. Whenever the engineer thought he could nudge the locomotive forward without provoking them to stampede, he did so, but this did not happen often. Vendors aboard the train took this opportunity to ply the aisles with their wares, from food and drink to books, newspapers and cigars.

Aouda reported that Robur had responded to the halt by settling *Deimos* down into a mountain glade south of them.

"Prudent," Fogg said—something of an answer to his curiosity about what Robur might do when their train stopped moving.

This herky-jerky with the buffalos burned away a full three hours before the train was able to resume a regular pace.

By then, the *Deimos* had settled into one of the arid valleys in the mountains to the south, a pass that opened out onto the next equally dry valley beyond that. Robur found a glade among the scrubland and pines, an adequate enough place for concealment in this high desert, with no settlers within view and only a mere ten minutes' flight from the railroad line should they be needed. When Aouda telegraphed that the Central Pacific train was in motion once more, Robur climbed up into the pilot's chair and prepared to fly.

"It was about time. We have none for delay." Robur shook his head, "Bison here, cattle in India—sacred animals all about."

Just as they began to rise, though, an alarm bell sounded, warning of an aerial object moving nearby, which Niru pointed to at the window. Gliding into view in the gap of the wide V formed by the two hills south of their glade was the envelope of an airship—a large and dirigible one, multiple propellers spinning on engine gondolas spaced on either side of a sizable passenger cabin, suspended from a tubular gas envelope easily several hundred feet in length, of a dull reddish-brown color almost lost against the similar background of the desert expanse beyond, as well as the ruddy glow of the waning evening sunlight. The craft was flying fairly low, apparently hugging the mountains, and Robur quickly suspended his climb, sinking lower in the air and turning so as to allow them a view of the machine as it passed from right to left through the gap of the pass.

Niru went to the periscopic controls and adjusted them to give better view of it, which appeared by reflective lenses for Robur on a small screen in the cupola. Bringing the focus on the envelope, where ribbing bulged beneath the covering fabric, Niru said, "A frame beneath, so not a simple balloon for the gas."

Xie's eyes opened and he sprang to his feet, turning to look out the windows at what had aroused their attention.

As the airship neared the left side of the pass and was about to disappear beyond the rise, Niru adjusted the view lower, focusing as best he could on the gondola undercarriage. People were visible through the angled windows: several in uniforms and as many not. By now the pointed prow of the envelope was slipping behind the hill, and Niru enlarged the telescopic field so something could be seen of the rest of the craft, including its vertical rudder shifting slowly from struts affixed at its stern.

"It's doubtful they would see any of us if we were high over them," Robur called out, and *Deimos* shot vertically at nearly full ascent, until they were over a mile above the airship. Once he had gained a stable altitude and position, he signaled Aouda: *A. 30 MILES EAST OF YOU IN MOUNTAINS. SEEING UNKNOWN AIRSHIP REPEAT AIRSHIP HEADING NORTHEAST. FOLLOWING IT FROM ABOVE, NOT MUCH FASTER THAN YOUR TRAIN. ADVISE ACTION? R.*

Aboard the Central Pacific, reposed on a backward facing seat, Aouda smiled affably as she considered this development. Phileas Fogg sat opposite, the carpetbag on the floor between his legs; Passepartout occupied the next pair of seats with Fix, the detective's back to her, both looking at the scenery. All wore their coats, as the limited heat pumped from the stoves at either end of each car did not completely eradicate the cold in this elevated desert, abiding around freezing even by day. At length she dispatched her telegraphic response: *R. MOST CURIOUS. FOLLOW IF CONVENIENT TO YOUR COURSE, BUT MUST DEPART FOR NAUTILUS RENDEZVOUS BY NIGHTFALL. A.*

Robur glanced down from the gondola to see Xie had requested a paper and ink from Niru's storage boxes of plenty, and was now sketching the vessel with precise but artistic strokes, while Niru indicated salient features to include, such as details of the propeller gondolas and rudder. *A. XIE & NIRU PAINTING AIRSHIP FOR MEMORY. R*, reported Robur.

"Some news from Robur," Aouda said when Fix availed himself off the washroom. "There is another airship in our midst. Heading east, like *Deimos*. Robur is following it from on high."

That brought Passepartout's attention from the window, turning toward them, resting his left arm up on the chair back. "Have they seen your ship? And who *are* they?"

"Robur didn't say on either. But knowing him, I should think not, on being seen. As for who is piloting, that too I would like to know, but there's no time now—*Deimos* must head for Nemo."

"What are the odds of a Hong Kong flying machine, known to no one, encountering an American flying machine, known to no one, in the middle of Nevada," Fogg said. Then he took out his watch, and opened both the front and back cases, checking the face and then turning it over, using his thumb to adjust the exposed top of one of the tiny rotating disks set around the mechanism. Turning the timepiece back over, Fogg faced the window and moved it to and fro several times, then stood up, adjusting the disk again before repeating the process. Retaking his seat, Fogg fiddled with the disk one last time before snapping shut the lids.

Passepartout watched all this with great interest.

"Whatever it is, it is invisible to my watch, so not propelled by Power X." Fogg returned the device to his pocket.

Towards dusk the mystery airship glided to a halt and dropped to the ground some miles south of a sleepy town along the Central Pacific line, ahead of the eastbound train by at least an hour. Niru attended to this in the now hovering *Deimos*, using filters on the periscope that highlighted the heat emanating from the objects below, the airship's engines bright to either side of the craft, but the envelope as dull as the cooling ground about. There were warmer spots on the front and back of the envelope as well.

After a few minutes, a lone figure emerged from the airship, a blob of thermal glow that soon strode off at a good rate straight northward toward the town. After that person was well away from the airship, the heat of the engines increased as it lifted from the ground in flight again.

On board the train not long thereafter, Aouda informed Fogg and Passepartout, "The airship has dropped off a passenger up ahead. That's the last to be said, I'm afraid—*Deimos* is east for Nemo."

"Leaving us to our own for a while," Phileas Fogg said.

It was dark when the Central Pacific train stopped at the town of Elko, where an acceptable dinner proved available for $1. Misters Fix and Proctor positioned themselves as near to the antipodes from one another as they could muster in the small establishment. Passepartout came up to Fogg and Aouda's table after a short delay combing his hair some paces away from the train.

Two passengers boarded at Elko, both in stout coats owning to the freezing night temperatures prevailing. One newcomer was the imposing Elder William Hitch of the Mormon Church (an offshoot of the Christian faith exceedingly popular among the people of this region), tall with a black moustache, and attired all in black save for his white shirt and cravat. The other new passenger, carrying but a single piece of well-worn luggage in his black gloved hand, was a sturdy gentleman in his early thirties, one of middle class dress and military bearing who kept silent. Neither were to be found in the same car as the Fogg party when the train resumed its course.

On this account, Phileas Fogg, Passepartout and Aouda were on their guard when the train was set up for sleeping, and all three napped more than slumbered as the train chugged along into the neighboring state of Utah.

While the train was returned to its day coach layout the next morning, Friday the 6th of December, Passepartout stepped out to the platform between that and the next car to take some air, bracing cold and with an added chill on account of the train's motion. The new passenger, Mr. Hitch emerged from the sleeping car ahead just then, carrying a sheaf of small announcements proclaiming his intention to discourse for an hour on Mormonism in car No. 117 (one of the day coaches ahead of the smoking car) commencing at eleven. Jumping across to Passepartout's platform, the prophet of Zion tacked one of the notices onto the car door with a small hammer in his gloved hand, then entered to continue on into the next carriage.

Passepartout called Elder Hitch to Fogg and Aouda's attention when the man passed them later on the way back to his own car. "Only two hours until that man in black is to lecture on Mormonism in car 117. Do you and Aouda wish to attend with me?"

Fogg looked as disinterested as Passepartout had ever seen him.

"As I am certain you have observed, Passepartout, my sole reverence to date is a well-played round of whist. Cathedrals, even the most grand among them, hold no sway for me—still less then, the myths of Mormon delivered *ex tempore* on a moving train. Aouda may be more favorably inclined, as she wishes."

Aouda smiled. "If *you* are to hear all of it, Passepartout, we may rely on you for any questions that come to mind after."

To Passepartout's surprise, some thirty people of the hundred aboard populated the No. 117 day coach to hear Mr. Hitch's address—including the difficult-to-miss Colonel Proctor on an aisle seat, about a third of the way forward. Passepartout took a seat away by the back exit. Coming in from a car up ahead was the other new Elko passenger, who landed in an aisle spot as well, closer to the Mormon who was then lost in thought, mentally rehearsing his presentation. Passepartout gave his hair a bit of a combing, netting intelligence on the many guns and knives populating the pockets and scabbards of those in the car.

When he did begin, the Elder Hitch embarked on an impassioned recounting of the history and travails of the founders of the Mormon faith, the martyrdom of Joseph and Hiram Smith, and what he had grave suspicion would be the imminent sacrifice of their presently incarcerated leader, Brigham Young. He spoke very little about the particular tenets of their sect, which disappointed Passepartout's curiosity on the minutiae of humanity's religious convictions.

The audience began to dwindle as Hitch, and the train, rolled on. One among those leaving early was the Elko man, except he exited not the way he had come, but down towards Passepartout, along the way grabbing the seat back where Proctor sat, to steady himself as the train lurched. As he released his grip, the man deftly dropped a small folded note onto Proctor's lap (an action Passepartout did not see from his vantage), which the red-bearded man did not inspect until after the Elko passenger had departed. He recognized the hand of its penciled inscription at once.

> *Meet me in smoking car in 10 minutes, Catspaw*

Proctor slipped out as instructed, trying not to make eye contact with Passepartout as he passed him. The smoking car was directly behind No. 117, and Proctor sought out this Catspaw in the clouds of cigar smoke, finding him seated at a corner bench. The man silently offered him a small cigar from a case he pulled from his coat.

"Who is the catspaw here, you or I?" Proctor asked, while he prepared the smoke.

The man smiled. "Both of us. When the time comes for Passepartout to be taken, you're to see his Phileas Fogg is occupied, by challenging him to a duel—with the gun you brought."

"I see. I have my knife, too."

Catspaw remained focused on the firearm side of things. "I know you're a good shot, and have dueled—though I imagine not on a train."

"No, but I'll manage. Any offense in mind?"

"If you can't contrive *something*, you're not the man for the job."

"As it happens, I have already fought with Fogg," Proctor said slowly, letting its import sink in.

"Oh?" Catspaw's eyebrow arched.

"I'm part of local politics, no secret, and ran into Fogg during our march that afternoon. They recognized my man Grissom, and I tried punching Fogg but another fellow stepped in front—he's on this train *now*, by the way. I tried a knife then, but Fogg's bitch stabbed me with a hatpin, which I believe to have been drugged. It was over in a few seconds, and Grissom helped me back to the hotel. I sent a telegraph on it, which I reckon you have not received."

"The sting of slow delivery, Colonel. So, Fogg knows who you are, not good. I selected you as the one man none of them would have known by sight. Now that's given the lie. At least I know now." The man thought a moment. "Drugged hatpin? *That* we didn't expect. As for the bodyguard, I know he's on the train. His name is Fix, an English policeman who we thought was hunting Fogg as a thief. Perhaps *not*."

Catspaw then suggested, "If you need a pretext for dueling with Fogg, what his man did to your two in the park should be sufficient. The Frenchman's clearly dangerous. Two skilled men in Japan couldn't take him down, either."

"I don't understand—my men? What was that? I got no report."

"No, you might not. The Frenchman had bought something in a gun shop—guns, I assume, in a case, which he later used as a weapon on them both when they met in one of the city parks. Your two men were following him, quite well I thought—but not for this Passepartout. He led them on a merry chase, up the hills, and when he cornered them—and *he* did the cornering—he decked them both in one blow, very good move. I don't know whether they're dead, your men, or in hospital. *I* continued to follow Passepartout. Once I knew he was set for the Central Pacific train, I dropped that note to you at the hotel. And here we are."

"Darby and Fenton were good men," Proctor said.

"They may still be. As I said, I didn't see what happened to them after."

"And Farley? You sent him and a few other of my men off too—what are they up to, or am I not supposed to know?"

"You have that, Colonel. You're not to *know*." Catspaw sounded firm. "Head back to your car now, before Passepartout can tumble onto us. We'll speak more, later."

Proctor did as he was told, putting out his smoke but retaining the cigar. Entering No. 117, William Hitch was still at it, with only two others and Passepartout listening to his narrative. Passepartout gave his hair a comb as Proctor pressed up the aisle, having to ease around the Elder going on about the oppressive policies of the Federal government regarding Mormon polygamy.

In due course, Passepartout was the sole remaining auditor for Elder Hitch's litany of religious persecution, and the man ended his talk to mop his sweat with a linen handkerchief.

By half past noon, the Central Pacific train was skirting the northernmost reach of the Great Salt Lake, its inhospitable briny waters sheltered by little in the way of scenic vegetation. A bit later they passed the Promontory Point where the Central Pacific and Union

Pacific railroads were joined three years before. To cater to the increasing tourist traffic, an extensive four story Wahsatch Hotel was under construction, the framing showing the promise of the mansard roofs and crowning multi-domed tower to come. Shortly thereafter, the train stopped at a stout cylindrical tank beside the tracks to take on water before crossing the low trestle over the Bear River.

The lack of the car rattling and engine noise struck Passepartout like a pall.

"The Mormon lecture depress you?" Fogg asked.

"No, but the absence of the airship concerns me." Passepartout turned to Aouda, "Are they, like your *Deimos*, engaged on some further mission?"

"The man joining us, part of a larger scheme? Not implausible. Robur said it was much slower, if that helps—more limited range, or taking longer away if it is sent on for more distant action."

"They must not want it to be *seen*, otherwise they'd be flying it over us," Fogg offered.

"A good point, Phileas. And our man, acquiescent to being let off in what may be an unfamiliar desert, confident enough for a long walk alone to the Elko station on a cold night. A measure of the man, perhaps."

The *Central Pacific Railroad* tracks did not pass through Salt Lake City, but stopped for six hours at the town of Ogden 25 miles away, where the train was turned over to their partner line, the *Union Pacific Railroad*, locomotives and cars switched out or added, luggage transferred as needed. Fortunately, a new connecting line had recently linked the two settlements, and many passengers availed themselves of the opportunity to see the Mormon capital, nestled at the foot of some fine mountains filling the eye to the east. This sortie included Phileas Fogg's party, carrying their luggage, and the Elko man not carrying his. The Elder William Hitch departed the train at Ogden, making for Brigham City.

The excursion train pulled into the small Salt Lake station a quarter before three o'clock—its return departure set for four. Aouda asked whether there was a hotel nearby, and she was told the new Walker House lay a few blocks south of Temple Square, though it was operated by a wealthy ex-Mormon who was spurned locally for his apostasy. Passepartout arched a brow at this information.

"A hotel?" Fogg asked Aouda.

"Yes, I am in need of running my electric engine. Nowhere on the train to do that in privacy, but if we may take a room here, it won't take long."

Some twelve thousand residents lived in Salt Lake City by the last census, but growing fast, now big enough for a mule-drawn streetcar line along one of their very regular Cartesian grid of wide avenues and exhaustingly long blocks. Fogg's trio headed east toward the newly built Tabernacle, peeking over a wall like a neat loaf of bread elevated on stone pilings, a line of trees bare of leaves ringing the perimeter. Though open to public view, Aouda was keen to get to the hotel so they missed this opportunity to see its celebrated interior, one of the largest unsupported roofs of its type in the world. They could hear its grand organ, though, as someone within was playing a tune of Handel on its two thousand pipes.

Also to be glimpsed was a much larger temple being begun within the palisade, while the absence of conventional church steeples around the town reminded one of the prominence here of Mormonism. In this regard, Passepartout noticed the many modestly dressed women scuttling about in clusters, some certainly the communal spouses of the local Mormon men.

Turning south along Main Street, between Second and Third South, the four story Walker House fronted the west side of the block. Retrieving her case from Fogg's carpetbag, Aouda declared at the entrance, "I am about to be very faint, and will be in need of a room to rest before resuming our exertions."

Inside, the desk agent was disapproving of the idea of letting one of their rooms for only a short time, until Fogg assured him they would be paying the full day's rate, and Aouda now appearing the very picture of frail feminine indisposition.

"We're thinking of putting in one of those elevators," the desk man said as he helped Fogg shepherd Aouda up the stairs to one of their second floor rooms, while Passepartout waited below in the lobby with their luggage. A reconnoiter at the hotel's large plate windows showed no one near, but after a comb of his hair Passepartout confirmed the presence of the man's short-barreled firearm some distance away up the block on the other side of the street. A professional tail, indeed.

In the room, Fogg found it easy to act as the doting gentleman, setting the case on a table before cradling Aouda's hand as she reclined on the bed. "There, my dear. Rest your eyes and restore yourself. We shall await your revival downstairs in their restaurant."

When Fogg returned, he and Passepartout found the Walker House restaurant quite adequate, and prompt in assembling a fillet of fish with fruit for them. As Fogg sipped on some tea, he said of what he imagined Aouda was doing up in their impromptu room, "When all buildings are equipped with electricity, this sort of thing will be much easier."

Twenty minutes later, a fleet Aouda trotted down the stairs with the case to rejoin Fogg and Passepartout. "There, done," she smiled, and together made their way back up to the train station.

All the while, Passepartout was impressed at how far away the Elko man stayed from them. He must have excellent vision and even stouter nerve and tenacity.

Back at the station, on the stroke of four o'clock the train blew its whistle and started to depart for Ogden. A young man appeared, running headlong after the train, jumping onto the back platform with such gymnastic skill that Passepartout stepped out to ask him what had been the cause for this great maneuver.

"Domestic troubles," the man said.

Supposing him to be a Mormon, Passepartout asked how many wives he had.

"One sir. One, and that was enough!"

27. IN WHICH DISTRACTION IS SOUGHT AMONG PHILEAS FOGG'S PARTY BY RESUMING THE PLAYING OF WHIST

There being time in Ogden before the Union Pacific train departed, Fogg, Aouda and Passepartout took a meal there. Thus fortified, they tried to see what they could of the scenery out the windows in the dark when the train headed east that Friday night into the mountains.

The Weber Canyon was considered most beautiful, littered with many notable rock formations given evocative names like Finger Rock, Witches' Rock, and the Devil's Slide, but apart from glints from the river to their left and glimpses of the telegraph poles sticking out at all angles, very little of this splendor could be discerned from their seats. Nor was it appreciably more interesting when they crossed a short truss bridge over the river and into a 770 foot tunnel, one of the longer on the line—just a different intermission of dark.

There was a thirty minute dinner stop at Wahsatch, whose Trout House had some reputation. Since they had eaten some earlier in Ogden, a light meal was had here suitable for the time available, as well as taking advantage of the lavatory.

The Union Pacific train crossed into Wyoming Territory around half past ten o'clock, encountering more snow sheds and fences (though less employed here than on the more mountainous Central Pacific, even though blizzards were as common here on the plains), and some light snow along with it.

Just after midnight on Saturday, December 7th, they traversed another long truss bridge (the length necessitated by the meandering character of the streams, fluctuating in low broad channels) and stopped at the Green River station for fifteen minutes, a quite extensive facility with a new roundhouse among its two dozen buildings. Both Passepartout and Aouda awoke at the stop, peering out their windows at the passengers going out for a stretch despite the cold and slushy snowfall. Both saw Colonel Proctor strolling solitarily up and down the platform, looking like a man gearing himself up for some endeavor and needing time for it alone.

Come the morning, while Phileas Fogg still slept, Aouda and Passepartout found they had differing, yet parallel, concerns about seeing Proctor gamboling about that night.

"I think we need to be together as much as practicable so long as the Colonel and the other man are aboard," Aouda said. "*Deimos* won't be back here till at least tomorrow evening."

"I'm thinking also of Barbicane," Passepartout responded. "I'm sure Robur will conduct them safely from the *Nautilus*. What I worry about is what happens to them after that. If men are being dropped on us by airship here, who may be dropping down in Florida? Whoever

Mr. Fogg has on hand there with Dupin may not expect any trouble, or be up to whatever occurs."

"And Phileas stays vague on how he is to get in touch with them." Aouda looked dour.

After Fogg was up, and the coaches being switched to the day, Aouda and Passepartout presented their worries.

"Colonel Proctor conducted what looked to us like a fretful pacing last night at the station stop. Passepartout and I think something may be about to happen, here and possibly also in Florida. If there are airships doing things here, Phileas, there may be others there."

Fogg laced his fingers together and thought a bit. Just then, his watch chimed twice softly. Checking the timepiece, it properly showed 4 PM Greenwich. Smiling placidly, Fogg declared, "Another contingency to be addressed."

While Aouda looked perplexed, Passepartout drew in a breath, having a sudden idea of what Fogg meant, but quite unable to communicate any of his suspicion to Aouda, lest he betray a strict confidence. Only time would tell if what he imagined were true.

Mr. Fix happened by then from his morning turn at the faucet and toilet, and seeing their taciturn expressions, commented, "I diagnose your problem. No cards for you to play here, as you did on the steamers."

Aouda perked at that—Fix had hit on the ideal solution, by which they could easily remain in close proximity for hours on end, and not be bored to perdition by it.

But Phileas Fogg offered the objection, "We have neither cards nor a fourth for partners—and no tables I can see."

"Cards are easily had," Fix countered brightly. "I think some of the wandering vendors have decks for sale. As for partners, I myself have some pretensions to playing a good game."

Aouda pressed Fix's suggestion, "Passepartout, see if you can find us some cards, and a table or board to play on."

Passepartout sought out a porter and in short order had acquired several packs of cards (they seemed rather flimsy and so might wear out quickly if relying on only the one), some scoring tokens, and a cloth covered board for just that purpose, one among several kept on the train for the pleasure of Americans anxious to play their poker or faro. To something of Fix's surprise, Passepartout accepted him as a partner, as Fogg and Aouda were by now quite naturally inclined to their pairing unbidden.

The pines of this area had supplied much of the Union Pacific's railroad ties, but the landscape out the windows evidenced little of that, and the most scenic thing visible as the train chugged past the Medicine

Bow watering station and their five-stall roundhouse was the low but wide snow-capped Elk Mountain off to the south of the line.

Not that the card fiends were paying much attention to that, more concerned with how they would be sitting. Aouda and Mr. Fix being the smaller of the four, the most comfortable arrangement was for Fix to sit beside Fogg in Aouda's rear-facing seat, while Passepartout and Aouda reposed opposite. The upholstered board balanced on their knees, the first deck was opened, shuffled with a modicum of ease on it, and gaming commenced. True to his assertion, Mr. Fix was indeed a competent and canny player, and even Passepartout seemed to have taken up the spirit of the thing this round.

They were just completing their first rubber when the train came to an unscheduled stop. There was no station or even settlement visible to either side of the train. Passepartout got up, "I will go inspect."

Dozens of passengers were following Passepartout's lead, including Colonel Proctor and even the young non-polygamist who had joined the passengers at Salt Lake—and the train's engineer, one Mr. Forster, with their conductor—proceeding up to the locomotive's cowcatcher, to encounter a railroad employee with a safety flag, blocking the way ahead to the bridge crossing several hundred feet of boggy expanse known as Medicine Creek.

The structure was of the suspension type, done in imitation of Mr. Roebling's celebrated steel railroad bridge of 1855 spanning the far broader Niagara River away in New York. This bridge was not so accomplished nor successful, several of the iron cabling having actually snapped, while overall the metalwork showed unsettling traces of deterioration. "The bridge's not safe," the signalman declared obviously.

"Why no flag up at Medicine Bow?" The engineer looked peeved, "Electric blocks not working?" The Union Pacific had expended great effort that year electrifying their signal block system for improved safety and warning of just this character.

"Just found the failed stays, Hank. Sent Dunninger on to Como to warn the line."

The engineer snorted, "This has been rusting from the start. Should have torn it out and put in a Howe truss, like the rest of the stretch."

"Well, until they do, it's not safe to cross."

Colonel Proctor did not like the sound of that. "We're not going to *stay* here, and take root in the snow?"

"They'll telegraph for a fresh train, Colonel," the conductor said, "but coming all the way from Omaha, that will take six hours, at least."

"Six hours!" Passepartout exclaimed, recognizing how that could unsettle Fogg's constrained itinerary (and Robur still being far away to intervene with the *Deimos*), but also paying close attention to the expression on Proctor's face, which was consistent with Aouda's idea that there was something in the offing, something whose execution might be thrown off were they not where their train was supposed to be.

"Certainly," the conductor was explaining, "besides, it will take as long as that to reach Como on foot."

"But it's only a mile from here, isn't it?" a passenger asked.

"Yes, but it's on the other side of the river. The nearest ford is north, ten miles more on that."

The engineer had stamped off to the bridge, eying the damage. Passepartout watched, and stepping away from the pack around the cowcatcher, took out his comb to see what might be discerned by that means. The results did not promote confidence in the bridge's continuing structural integrity.

But returning to the signalman and the crowd gathered about, Forster announced something quite opposite, "If we back up and lay full steam, I think we can make it over."

Neither the conductor nor signalman looked convinced, but the passengers marshalled immediate enthusiasm for the plan, especially Colonel Proctor.

"Might I suggest we cross the bridge on foot first, let the train come after," Passepartout suggested, "To be prudent."

"Prudent!" Colonel Proctor responded, as if Passepartout had just called him a Yankee. "Are you afraid?"

"I afraid." Passepartout shrugged his shoulders, "Very well. A Frenchman can be as American, whether we crash into the stream or not."

Once the anxious passengers were aboard, Forster let three short blasts from his whistle and began to back the train up. This was unexpected by Fogg and the others.

Passepartout explained, "The suspension bridge ahead is considered unsafe, but our engineer decided we may be over it, if only traveling fast enough."

"Is that prudent?" Fogg asked.

"That is what I tried to pose, but the opinions of French valets are not heeded." Passepartout added carefully, "I think the bridge *may* hold. We will find out." He paused, arching a look at Aouda, "Of greater interest, perhaps: the Colonel Proctor seemed particularly agitated at the prospect of our train being delayed, some six hours."

Engineer Foster retired the train over a mile, tooted the whistle twice more for a longer duration, and gave the engine all he could.

Truth told, the acceleration was exhilarating—or terrifying, depending on one's familiarity with such things (or agreeableness to the careening of the cars from side to side as the tracks were hardly plumb bob smooth enough for such speeds).

Fogg looked out the window at the landscape closest to the track, flitting by at increasing rate. Just as they reached the bridge, he decided, "A hundred miles per hour, I think."

The west pair of suspension towers flashed past the windows, followed a mere second and a half later by those on the eastern end of the bridge two hundred feet on. The sound of breaking cables and collapsing girders behind them might be heard by the discerning ear—though not for long, as the train did not stop to attend to the disaster accumulating in their wake. Gradually the train slowed down to its normal speed, while Fogg and company resumed their whist.

Such were the circumstances of the failure of the Medicine River Suspension Bridge in December of 1872—an incident recounted fairly accurately by Mr. *V.*, though nothing on its subsequent expungement from the historical record, as no photographs or accounts of the bridge (even its Howe truss replacement so hastily erected afterward) survive for examination. There had been no loss of life, after all, or even damage to rail property apart from the span itself—though the reputation of its overly ambitious but insufficiently skilled designer was much jeopardized. Given the several issues of liability, from the bridge's contractors to the railroad's subsequent ratification of their engineer Forster's brave (or foolhardy) resolve to run the train over it despite the warning from the signalman, the historical silence on the incident was, in retrospect, a fairly politic one.

As for the whist players, they were still at it at eleven o'clock when the train veered southward and stopped on the west outskirts of the town of Laramie, Wyoming, for what was an unusually long half hour interlude for eating.

"Well, this is rather substantial," Fogg observed when they stepped to the ground, "Compared to San Francisco."

Although there was no platform, the train occupying one of several parallel tracks there on the open ground, it could be seen that the *Union Pacific Railroad* had invested considerable effort in this district of the prairie. Directly ahead to the east, the two story Laramie Station depot included a restaurant and hotel adjacent, with fenced paths to the hotel entrance door sprouting a sapling tree (bare now in the season) suggesting an intention to lay a decorative lawn.

Off down the tracks to their right was the biggest windmill any had seen on the line so far, easily twenty-five feet around, acting as the pumping agent for the comparably scaled water tank used by the locomotives. Beyond that lay a roundhouse, and multiple large brick machine shops, their many rectangular smokestacks hinting at the foundries and mills smoldering within.

The meal was better than average, improved if only by the slightly longer time accorded the ingestion of it. Mr. Fix took his own table, once again in a spot where he could watch Colonel Proctor from afar, who appeared more sanguine now that the train had resumed its course. The Elko man and the Salt Lake monogamist likewise stayed apart and to themselves.

In their own seats, Phileas Fogg seemed lost a bit in thought, offering finally, "As we speak, Robur must be flying across the Atlantic Ocean, bearing the Barbicane party. Makes one think, doesn't it?"

"I may say, Phileas, so far at least, all is transpiring to plan at Robur's end. I continue to receive messages from *Deimos*, all appears to be well."

Fogg's attention then turned elsewhere, "Mr. Fix is not a bad card player, do you think."

"Not enough yet to beat you and Aouda," Passepartout put in, "though the deficiency is probably more mine."

"Practice, Passepartout," Aouda smiled. "To make the perfect."

They had yet more time for whist after leaving Laramie, as the train slowed to a crawl climbing up the pass towards Sherman—at over 8200 feet altitude the highest on the Union Pacific route, and reached at great physical challenge, including over a mile dug and blasted through a granite peak. The winds were often fierce though the canyon which the line crossed by the massive High Dale Creek Bridge, a 650-foot wooden span (the longest on the UPRR line) costing $200,000, yet so contagious to breeze that trains traversing it were limited to four miles an hour. Even at the lightest of zephyr, the span creaked and swayed unsettlingly, though for those not reduced to seat arm clutching dread and keeping their eyes open, the view from 130 feet was accounted impressive.

The region directly around Sherman itself was not visibly mountainous, despite its measured altitude, though once over the summit, it was a faster downhill haul—or would have seemed such, but the train continued to steam fairly slowly, under twenty miles per hour. Looking down at the more leisured march of rail ties below the window, Fogg eventually suggested, "It is not impossible that our engineer taxed the locomotive on his rush over the bridge, further aggravated on the grade over the summit."

The state of the engine was on the Fogg party's minds when they stopped for dinner at the Cheyenne station. The two story hotel lay a short stroll down the dirt from the small depot, all fronting the three tracks that ran along a raised embankment in what was otherwise a barren wilderness. Passing the locomotive, the Union Pacific's No. 2 engine, a "4-4-0" (respectively designating the number of wheels beneath the front carriage, the drive wheels, and any beneath the cab) that had served the railroad for seven years, Fogg stepped up to the engineer's window, "How is your engine, sir? Are the rails here unsuitable for thirty?"

Engineer Forster turned away from his gauges with a look that only confirmed Fogg's suspicion, though all the man said in reply was an overconfident, "McPherson here's still got mileage in him. He'll get us to Omaha."

Back aboard the train and in slow motion again, the broad expanse of the plains floated by the travelers, with less of the native wildlife (from grazing elk to warrens of "prairie dogs"—the large rodent domestic to this region) on show amidst the varying snow cover—attractions given only cursory glances anyway by Phileas Fogg and his dedicated whist partners.

When their play was finally curtailed by the porters preparing the car for sleeping, Aouda took Fogg and Passepartout aside. "Robur has safely landed the Barbicane party off Florida, and will be headed back our way after they've had a chance to rest."

Phileas Fogg didn't seem as pleased with that as one might have expected, smiling wanly at the news. In fact, he remained awake long into the night as the train pounded on through Wyoming and into Nebraska. Finally, early on the morning of Sunday, December 8th, three chimes sounded on his watch.

Opening the case, the glow of the various gems in the bezels were sufficient to show it was 9 AM Greenwich, which translating to their 3 AM local time meant, for once, the bells were coincidentally true. As for the rings, the "?" resting at X and "**B**" beside VI, no longer alight, were as expected—the skill at Diadem having apparently discovered how to safely dampen down *Columbiad*'s Power X engines. "**N**" at XI was rather more interesting: Nemo must still be sailing south—while the "**O**" at half-past I heralded *Deimos*' approach from the southeast. And then there was that "**A**" almost to XII, straight ahead and inching closer by the mile. Passepartout would be delighted.

Fogg closed his watch. Now he could go to sleep.

28. IN WHICH PASSEPARTOUT IS RESCUED FROM A PREDICAMENT OF SORTS

The engineer had apparently cured some of *Major General McPherson* UPRR Locomotive No. 2's afflictions, since their speed picked up into the dawn and day of Nebraska, perhaps so that they might honorably pass at a forty mile per hour clip the McPherson Station (for which military figure the spot was similarly named). This was at eight o'clock in the morning, still some 350 miles from Omaha.

While the porters converted the sleepers back into their day coaches, passengers could admire out the right hand windows the broad but often muddy Platte River, little fed this time of year by the many trickling streams coming in confluence from the north, unless it were snowing—which it began to do. For those enamored of frequently flat brown landscape uncluttered by forests primeval or Alpen glacier grandeur, the addition of a blanket of white only enhanced the sublime. Or, like Phileas Fogg, one could play a lot of cards and scarcely notice it.

At 9 AM there was a brief stop at the town of North Platte, an old Pony Express station before the railroad steamed it up into a rambunctious "Hell on Wheels" (as it was known hereabouts) six years ago. Expanding much like Laramie, there were similar brick machine shops today, and even another of the giant windmills (the tank hidden within a sloping box shed adjacent). Several nearby military posts were recently relocated here as well, and the community was now the proud County Seat.

A very quick breakfast was had here by all those fast enough on the order, dashing in and out through the freezing cold and intermittent snow. Then aboard the train once more, which headed off east, crossing a tributary river by a long low span of many hundreds of feet. Although it looked quite rustic, the bridge was surprisingly flat, Fogg thought, so that there was scant jostling to affect the whist play.

Forty minutes later, Fogg was triumphantly about to lay a ten of spades on the trick (voiding that suit and so preparing to sweep the next three with hearts trump, rendering it certain to take the last with a six of diamonds), when a Southern drawl unfurled from behind his back, "I should play a diamond."

Passepartout and Aouda looked up to see Colonel Proctor, leaning on the seat back from the space forward. When Fogg turned around to face him, the Colonel declared, "Ah! It's you, is it—Englishman? You, about to play a *spade*?"

"And who *play*s it," which Fogg did.

"It pleases me to have it diamonds," Proctor's tone intentionally insulting, and he reached over the seat back for the card. "You don't understand a *thing* about whist."

Fogg laid his fingers on the trick to forestall that. "Perhaps I do, as well as any other."

"Just try, you son of a John Bull."

"You forget, you must deal with me, sir," Fix screwed his neck around, unable to rise because of the card board on their knees. "For it was I whom you not only insulted, but struck!"

Aouda reached across the board and lifted it from either side, standing up and stepping smoothly out into the aisle, giving Fix free passage to move himself. As the seats behind were not presently occupied (those being allotted to Fix and Passepartout), she landed the board between the cushions like a bridge, freeing her own hands (and pockets, containing so much of interest for those who knew of them).

"Mr. Fix, pardon me, but this affair is mine, and mine only. The colonel has again insulted me, by insisting that I should not play a spade, and he shall give me satisfaction for it."

"When and where you will," the Colonel replied, "and with whatever weapon you choose."

Standing behind Fogg, Proctor could not see him give a smile to Aouda, as if saying to her, dare I ask to borrow your electric gun? Though she would have to relinquish *two* to their endeavor, were it to be honorable.

Passepartout looked about to step around to the next seats and hurl the Colonel out the window, but Fogg gestured for him to calm. "We have pistols available," which elicited an angry flinch from Proctor (recalling what Catspaw had said of the Frenchman's gun case). "Now, as to the time. Six months hence? When I am able to return to America, my business in England concluded."

"Why not ten *years* hence?" Proctor objected.

"Feasible for me, easily enough—but I say *six months*," Fogg countered. "I shall be at the place of meeting promptly."

"All this is an evasion," Proctor exclaimed, "Now or never!"

"Very good," Fogg conceded. "You are going to New York?"

"No," Proctor said, belying the ticket from Catspaw residing in his own pocket.

"To Chicago?" Fogg tossed a wry look in Passepartout's direction.

"No."

"To Omaha, then?"

"What is that to you?" Proctor was showing exasperation at Fogg's interest in his itinerary. "Do you know Plum Creek?"

"No," Fogg replied, the station not among those noted on his general map of the Union Pacific he recalled from page twenty-two of *Crofutt's Guide*.

"It's the next station," Proctor explained. "The train will be there in an hour, and will stop there ten minutes. In ten minutes several revolver shots could be exchanged."

"Very well, I will stop at Plum Creek."

"And I guess you'll stay there too," the Colonel promised.

"Who knows?" Fogg replied with a smile. "Well, till then, Colonel Proctor." Turning to his companions, "We have our hand pending, do we not?"

While Proctor stomped back to his own car, Fogg resumed his seat, motioning for the others to do likewise. Aouda repositioned the board, not a card out of place.

"You *are* a cool customer, Mr. Fogg, I'll hand you that!" Fix marveled.

"Are you sure on this, Phileas?" Aouda was quite concerned, scooping up the trick they had taken, and trying to direct her mind back to the task of selecting which of her own to play next.

"It will be an interesting experiment." Fogg then smiled in an oddly satisfied way, "To see if it is possible for Colonel Proctor to successfully shoot me dead this day in December."

Fogg and company played several more hands over the next hour, though it may fairly be said that only Phileas Fogg seemed genuinely casual about it. He did have Passepartout fetch out the *Crofutt's* at one point so he could see what, if anything, it had to say about Plum Creek.

Consulting its contents table while Mr. Fix shuffled, Fogg read out, "Ah, yes, page thirty-seven. Plum Creek, 230 miles from Omaha—during the last year has improved very much. Hmm, 'At this point many of the most fearful massacres which occurred during the earliest emigration were perpetrated by the Sioux, Cheyennes, and Arapahoes'—ominously fitting."

A passing porter overhead Fogg's mention of the Plum Creek massacres. "All too true, sir, back then. Eight years ago, the big massacre on the bluff, before the railroad. Five years ago, a locomotive toppled, men killed, some scalped. All terrible, terrible. But nothing near so bad now. I shouldn't worry."

"Enough to frighten our driver in San Francisco, at least," Passepartout reminded, as Fogg handed back the *Crofutt's* for return to the carpetbag, and Fix began to deal the next hand.

Come eleven o'clock, Colonel Proctor entered the car accompanied by a second culled from the other passengers—a fellow not recognized by any at Fogg's seat, but evidently a dentist and medical man by profession, whose skills might prove of value however the outcome.

"Passepartout, your case please. And Mr. Fix, my second?"

Fix nodded gravely, which appeared to satisfy the Colonel. Fogg looked at the Colt Open Tops, taking two out, while Passepartout opened the covers over the ammunition cache, withdrawing a box of the Henry cartridges. Seeing how Fogg handled the weapons and recalling the similar manner of the San Francisco gun shop proprietor, Mr. Clabrough, Passepartout inferred that Phileas Fogg was not a man unfamiliar with firearms.

Fogg handed Proctor one of the pistols for his inspection, which he deemed acceptable, and the Colonel waved for their dueling participants to go out onto the platform and await the station stop. One long blast came from the steam whistle, signaling they were nearing Plum Creek, and the train was slowing when two short whistle blasts followed, warning of an occurrence not otherwise provided for.

The conductor appeared on the platform of the car ahead, "You can't get off, gentlemen!"

"Why not?" the Colonel asked.

"We're twenty minutes late. Anyone getting on off at Plum Creek may do so, but we'll be steaming ahead at once."

"But I'm going to fight a duel with this man." Proctor seemed greatly perturbed. "It's arranged."

"I am really very sorry, gentlemen. Under any other circumstances I should have been happy to oblige you." The conductor was quite apologetic, then suggested, "But you're both here—why not fight as we go along?"

"That wouldn't be convenient, perhaps, for *this* gentleman," Proctor sneered at Phileas Fogg.

"It would be perfectly so." Fogg told the conductor, "All we need is an unobstructed space."

"The last car's only lightly filled, come along." While the train continued to slow, the cars' couplings clanking as each abutted the one ahead, the conductor stepped across to their car's platform and led Fogg, Fix, Proctor and his second through to the day coaches added at Ogden. Passepartout and Aouda followed anxiously after.

"The seconds and the rest may stand guard out here," Proctor declared, and followed the conductor and Fogg into the tailing car.

The conductor commanded the attention of the dozen passengers there, "Excuse me, an announcement. Would you all be kind enough to vacate the car for a few moments? Two of our gentlemen have an affair of honor to settle."

The people supportively trundled out, passing through the gauntlet of Aouda, Passepartout, Fix and the second on the platform,. As the train eased to a stop at the Plum Creek station, the conductor advised the combatants, "The car's long enough for, oh, eight to ten paces from the middle. Once shots are heard, we'll wait two minutes, take out whoever is not walking."

Down on the tracks, the stationmaster had crossed to the locomotive, responding to the two added whistle blasts. Bundled in his coat and hat from the cold and snow, he asked, "What's the matter?"

"No one boarding here?" When the man shook his head, Forster called out, "Then we'll be off—we're running late."

The engineer pulled two long whistles, and set the train in motion again.

Proctor was peering out the window at the station, dangling the Colt revolver from his left hand, "We'll wait till the train's steady, up to speed."

"As you wish," Fogg said.

But the train had no more than cleared the vicinity of the station when they were set upon by a large band of horsemen appearing from stands of trees down by the river—the limbs spare of foliage, to be sure, but sufficiently many trunks to act as adequate blind for their purpose, enhanced by the snowfall. By some hanging back to await the train's passing, they were able to come at the tracks from both sides, and all along its length, clear to the engine, shooting and yelling in the manner of the Native Americans.

The steeds flashing past the platform brought immediate alarm to Passepartout, Aouda, Fix and Proctor's second.

"Your pistols, Passepartout!" Aouda waved them on into the car to extract and load two for her own use, tossing two cartridge boxes into her pockets, Fix taking the last of the guns for his hand. They found Phileas Fogg and the Colonel had suspended their dueling venture, Proctor having been precipitously shot in the groin by a ricocheting bullet, an injury over which he seemed especially furious. While the Colonel's second saw to his wounds with what he had in his bag, Mr. Fix and Aouda defended the doors at either end from invasion—Fix admiring Aouda's cool head and keen aim, with either hand and in both directions in swift ambidexterity.

Phileas Fogg and Passepartout, meanwhile, followed the conductor forward through the cars, acting as his bodyguard, amid a blur of action—passengers rushing for their own guns to return fire at those visible through the windows, or repel boarders at the platform doors. All together the body of attackers numbered in the dozens, some assailing the baggage car, intent on whatever booty lay within. They were dressed in a polyglot of American and Indian attire, some featuring slashes of war paint on their faces, but many others not—though in the flurry of activity, such distinctions were not readily appreciated.

Suddenly the train lunged forward, and the conductor exclaimed, "Damn! They must have got the engineer. If we—," but was struck then by a bullet in the shoulder cracking a window, and fell. "We'll overshoot the stations, must be stopped...." The conductor's eyes fluttered, the wound soaking through his uniform.

"It shall be stopped," Fogg assured him, and turned to press to that purpose.

Passepartout grabbed his arm, "Stay, *monsieur*, attend to him. I will go."

Surrendering the carpetbag and gun case to Phileas Fogg, Passepartout set off. Resolving to avoid the obvious path through the cars (with their dangerous windows supplying framed targets), he went ahead to the platform, tucked the Colt under his belt after shooting one of the attackers who had jumped from his horse (now being drawn away on the reins by one of his compatriots), and slipped down under the cars. All very hectic.

Utilizing his acrobatic skills and physical strength, Passepartout ably worked his way along the train, catching sight of the horses' hooves coming closer or going farther away, depending on the lay of the brush and occasional trees near enough to the track. The snow continued to fall.

As he reached the baggage car, Passepartout could see some luggage and boxes being hurled away (whether intentionally or by savage confusion he could not tell) to the ground passing at thirty miles an hour. The tender was just ahead now, but as he was about to work up to the platform he discovered two of the attackers there: one straddling the couplings, working at the linking pin as the shaking of the cars haphazardly tightened or loosened the alignment—the other, holding onto his shoulder to steady him from the tender platform.

Seeing them at closer view, despite their weathered dark faces and costume, they did not appear to be all that "Indian" under the war paint, Passepartout thought. This attack of the train was not as it seemed.

Passepartout scrambled up to the baggage car's platform, pulling out the revolver but using it to smash across the first man's face, propelling him headlong off the coupling to the moving ground beside. Unfortunately, at that very moment the man had achieved perfect hold of the linking pin, which pulled out along with his fall. At once the weight of the cars increased the distance from the man on the tender, whom Passepartout now shot in the neck, causing him to plummet off the car to be crushed by the still moving carriages.

The valet was about to leap across to the receding tender, when he was caught by two new attackers who had come out from the baggage car behind him, one grabbing each arm in a tight grip. As they swung him around, he could see a third man, holding a pistol now aimed inches from the valet's heart. A fourth darted from behind to take the Colt revolver from Passepartout's reluctantly relinquishing hand.

◌ ◌

The terrain being on a gentle downgrade overall, it took some while for the Union Pacific cars to settle to a stop, just west of the lonely station at Elm Creek, named for the red elm woods hereabouts (unusual on the high plain, though liable to become less plentiful owing to their being vigorously harvested for their lumber). The absence of the accustomed chuffing of the steam locomotive compounded the sudden silence of the continuing snowfall.

The band of attackers had disappeared as quickly as they had come, racing off towards the east and south into the trees. Several passengers declared how they had slain numbers of the enemy, though no bodies were about to affirm or refute their convictions. The dental medical man had patched up Proctor as best he could (whose injuries proved serious enough to require proper doctoring elsewhere), then the conductor, and was attending to Mr. Fix, who had a slight wound to his non-shooting arm. Phileas Fogg had suffered not a scratch, nor had Aouda.

The conductor and porters did what they could to assess the damage, inside and out, their footfalls splaying the light snow. Phileas Fogg paced along after them, seeing how many windows were broken, adding to the leakage of heat from the cars. Up ahead, a veteran attendant reported from the open sliding door of the baggage car, "The raiders took a strongbox, some luggage. Looked more like a robbery to me than an Indian attack. I know the tribes—some were dressed to look like it, but not good enough."

"We're missing two day coach passengers," a worried porter informed the conductor. "Young Mr. Wilson, up from Salt Lake, and the Colonel Moran, boarded Elko."

Aouda, meanwhile, had undertaken her own tour of the train. She now strode up to Phileas Fogg with tears in her eyes. "I do not find Passepartout."

Phileas Fogg grew very serious, folding his arms. "I will find him, living or dead." Aouda clasped her hands on his arms. "Living," Fogg added, "if we do not lose a moment."

Just then, some riders approached from the east along the track. They turned out to be the stationmaster from Elm Creek ahead, panicked by the locomotive that had sped by earlier. He was accompanied by some of the lumbermen who were preparing a shipment of logs there—and two cavalrymen riding back to the North Platte garrison after taking a leave to attend, of all things, a piano recital of German music given that Friday by the *Grand Island Liederkranz* at their new two story clubhouse. Such were the range of people one might meet on a stretch of American railroad.

The cavalry Lieutenant was dismayed to hear about the "Indian attack" from the conductor, and of the three passengers kidnapped, or worse. Though word would be sent on to the soldiers at North Platte, the Lieutenant warned that it might be some time before a search party were mustered, if at all.

That did not suit Phileas Fogg. "The lives of three men are in question, sir, including one whom I will not abandon. If I may obtain a mount, I will search alone."

"No, sir, you shall not go alone," the Lieutenant said firmly. "I've got two days left. I can come with you."

"*Ich auch*," affirmed his Sergeant Hoffmann, a fellow especially fond of Beethoven, and the spirit of *Eroica*.

"Now, about a horse," Fogg said.

"We've got a reserve at the station you can borrow," the trainman volunteered.

Fogg turned to Aouda, "I must put this in your care," giving her the carpetbag and gun case. "And leave you to get your other case and follow us, on down to the station." Leaning in close, "We may need your *Deimos*, sooner."

Aouda could not agree more.

"Will you let me go with you?" Mr. Fix asked.

"Do as you please, sir. But if you wish to do *me* a favor, you will remain with Aouda. In case anything should happen to me."

Mr. Fix could still feel his warrant for Phileas Fogg's arrest rubbing against his coat pocket, a dead weight out here in this American wilderness. "I will stay."

Fogg turned to the men on horseback, loud enough for all to hear, "My friends, I will divide a thousand pounds among you, if we save the prisoners."

Their enthusiasm thus spurred, Phileas Fogg set out at a pace, down the quarter mile to the Elm Creek station, his kingdom for a horse—for only the missing Passepartout knew what might be done, if only they might succeed in getting to Chicago, as they must. A place both distant, and inevitably ahead.

ଔ ༀ

The snow continued to flurry over the next hours as Aouda sat with Mr. Fix and their luggage in the modest Elm Creek station house parked on the south side of the Union Pacific rails. One could measure the passing time even without the station's clock as metronome, as increments of snow piled up on the logs assembled across the way for freight shipment. The snow began to shift, however, when the wind picked up, rattling the station's windows.

This was a lonely place to be. And Mr. Fix entertained the horrid prospect that Phileas Fogg had taken this occasion to slip away from him, to his freedom as a runaway thief. And yet another part of him knew all the while that his intention to rescue Passepartout and the others rang true. Nor could he imagine Fogg lightly abandoning the scintillating jewel that was Aouda, in whose presence every moment seemed improved.

The stationmaster and his telegrapher felt deeply for the foreign woman and her stolid English companion. He offered them both cups of coffee, which the gentleman accepted graciously, while the woman declined equally so. They didn't even have the other passengers for company—that assembly remaining in the comparative comfort of the carriages until a new locomotive could be obtained.

Just before two o'clock that afternoon, though, the silence was broken by the blast of a steam whistle. Everyone in the station roused, rushing out just as the tender and *Major General McPherson* UPRR Locomotive No. 2 backed to a stop in front of them.

Engineer Forster leapt down from the cab, scrunching across the new-fallen snow, and into the station. Over a cup of coffee offered him, he explained, "Me and the stoker were overpowered and knocked out by two of those 'Indians'—in my opinion, anything but. When we came to, those two were gone, and so was the train. We'd slipped past Kearney. When we made it back there, learned the cars were here—and some wounded." Forster slurped the coffee, "All the passengers stay with the carriages?"

"All but these two," the stationmaster pointed at Aouda and Mr. Fix.

"Well, thanks for the coffee. I'll stop back here once I recouple. This is a trip to mark down," the engineer glowered, and returned to his locomotive. Two long whistles and No. 2 backed away to the left.

Twenty minutes later, No. 2 returned to Elm Creek with the train attached. The conductor, arm in a makeshift sling cobbled up from a bedsheet, came into the station with a porter (carrying the luggage of the Salt Lake and Elko passengers, which he deposited with the stationmaster). That left the two remaining passengers sitting in the depot.

"Our party is incomplete," Aouda reminded. "Mr. Fogg has not returned, nor his valet and the other two prisoners. Are you not to stay for them?"

"I cannot interrupt the trip," the conductor lamented. "We're already three hours behind time. And the Colonel needs a doctor, madam—nearest will be in Grand Island, two hours down the road. There will be another train here, tomorrow evening." (The conductor in his injured condition having completely forgot how their engineer had demolished the bridge back at Medicine Creek, thus precluding any following trains from the west until the deficiency were repaired.) "But if you're to come with *us*, *we* leave now."

"So it must be, then," Aouda emanated resolution, "I will not go."

Nor did Mr. Fix depart—though he had great misgivings as he watched the cars roll past and be gone, since he had almost jumped aboard to leave with them. But he just couldn't do it. He had to see it through, damn him—and at the moment, his only connection to Phileas Fogg was Aouda and their luggage still here at the Elm Creek station of Nebraska.

Such a lady of repose, Fix thought, seeing her resume her seat at the station with manifest dignity and calm. Then the fine lady grew very still, shut her eyes, and crossed her arms. At intervals her fingers tapped rhythmically against the ornate bracelet on her left wrist. At one point, Aouda rummaged down in her luggage, recovering a small pillbox. She did not appear to remove any of its contents, and after a few moments returned the object to the case. Closing her eyes again, Aouda resumed her nervous finger rapping.

In due course, the detective surmised she may have fell to prayer, taking solace in some ancient invocation welling up from her native land and beliefs, and considered ingesting some nostrum from the pillbox in service of this ritual, only to eschew it.

Mr. Fix could not have imagined how mistaken he was.

ᘔ ᘓ

A mile in the sky, the *Deimos* glided eastward, now following the line of rail and river at a measured ten miles per hour. The snow was letting up at least.

"According to Aouda, the horsemen disappeared off to the southeast. That means crossing this river." Robur was studying every clue from his telescopic view of the terrain immediately below, the Platte River a brownish shimmer threading through a skein of wind-tossed drifts of white.

"This seems a good spot here," he declared, "separating stream beds, shallow, maybe frozen. Bear to starboard, ninety," Robur called firmly, then ratcheted the periscope lenses several notches until he obtained a broader view, but not one where he'd lose all perception of moving equestrian bands. "Not many people live in this land. That may help us in spotting them."

"Two trails to follow, and but one eye," Xie sighed, peering intently out the windows at the landscape ahead and still far below. He was not liking this altitude, but he was getting used to it. "Captors and Fogg—no telling if they may have crossed paths."

"It will be dark in a few hours. Better chance to catch their heat if we haven't found either by then." Robur called up to Niru at the helm, "Keep an eye on any airship you see. If they fly too low or slow, they might not trigger the meter. My attention's all below, trying to keep a steady fix in this wind." With some exasperation, he swore, "Needles in haystacks."

☙ ❧

The hours crept by at the Elm Creek depot, the stationmaster adding more wood to the stove as the temperature sank below freezing. The rising winds had propelled the blizzard away to the north, at least, and at length the snowfall concluded. But despite the cold, Aouda felt compelled to step outside every so often, in the hopes that somewhere on the horizon Phileas Fogg might be returning with Passepartout.

One of the few local residents, a Mr. Mudge, had heard of the train attack from some of the lumbermen, and came by the station to talk with Mr. Fix about how they might employ his ingenious wind sled to head east, if they did not want to await tomorrow's train. Later, the man returned with some hot stew for Aouda and Mr. Fix (who had not eaten since breakfast back at North Platte). Aouda thanked the man for his generosity, another friend made.

Aouda had that effect on people—or, at least, those of considerate character.

The sun set around five o'clock, which would have given more than an hour of helpful twilight had the sky not been so gray with clouds and moonless besides. The scene mirrored Aouda's present disposition exactly.

☙ ❧

Once the railroad raiders had taken leave of that part of their company only cajoled to assist them by the enticement of the baggage car's loot, their more specialized kidnapping subsidiary found refuge for the night at a small encampment they had prepared for this purpose, among a brake of red elms (ironically some dozen miles nearly due south, though slightly west, of the railroad station named for them). A fire was commenced for warmth and food for the captors, but nothing else—no tents sheltered them from the cold, though blankets were distributed to all.

Several of the band acted as ominous silent sentinels, shotguns and revolvers at the ready, offering little beyond inarticulate grunts as they stood close by the three men taken from the Union Pacific train that day, now seated three along a not very comfortable fallen tree trunk by the fire.

"Well, this is a place to end up, isn't it? Prisoners," the gentleman from Elko declared. "Sebastian Moran, here. Colonel, British Army."

"T-thomas Wilson. A s-sergeant, in the Union—once." Wilson was visibly shivering.

"Jean Passepartout. Of no army at all."

Wilson asked, "D-do you ... think we're here for ransom—torture?"

"I didn't bring a valise of money," Moran said. "Any of you? Things to barter, parlay for our lives? If it comes to that."

Wilson put his hands out, looking penniless, then went back to rubbing them together before the fire.

Passepartout smiled. "I have only my comb. An heirloom I shall not part with."

"Even for your life?" Moran asked.

Passepartout thought on that. "Is there nothing *you* hold that dear, Mr. Moran?"

"Colonel," Moran reminded. "Honor, duty."

"Ah, intangibles of the mind. Actions, not objects, umm," Passepartout said. "Could you not *pretend* to give them up, though?"

"You either do your duty, sir, or you don't. There's nothing in the middle."

"What a clear vision you have," Passepartout said. "So, what is your duty here tonight, with us?"

"To see the morning."

"Very practical," Passepartout agreed.

"W-we don't even know w-where we are," Wilson said plaintively.

"Nebraska, is it not?" Passepartout replied factually.

"You sound a joker, sir," Moran said. "But this is no joke. These savages may do anything. We need to stick together, if we're to make it through. And if we *don't* all make it out of here, gentlemen ... anyone you need told? Anything said or done?" After a silence, Moran volunteered, "I'd want my father to know, that I never gave up."

"M-my wife," Wilson said finally, looking toward Passepartout, "Just t-the one—you know." He turned to Moran, "S-she should be told." Then he got a distant look to him, "A m-man does a lot of t-things to support a f-family."

"I envy you your families," Passepartout said, and meaning it.

Moran let a low snort, thinking of his father, of whom he had to admit he was not always on the best of terms. But he was a man you did not say "no" to.

Wilson was more sympathetic, "D-don't you have anyone?"

"None. Not on all the Earth."

"I thought I saw you with people, on the train," Moran said.

"Ah—that is Mr. Phileas Fogg. He is journeying around the world, in eighty days. Have you not heard of this? I am his valet."

"More than just you. A woman. And some other Englishman." Moran tiptoed ahead, "I think I saw you all playing cards, through a window, from one of the depots. No care for any of *them*?"

"Mr. Wilson asked if I had relations, family, like your own. They do not qualify."

"So there's nothing you'd want said, or done? For them, or anything, in case you don't … make it out?"

"Everything that has happened so far on Mr. Fogg's journey has been satisfactory. Whatever I may still add to it," Passepartout tossing a nod to each, "Colonel, young Wilson—may not be added *here*."

❦ ❧

Had he been asked, Robur would have freely confessed to what may at times have been an overly methodical mind, skilled at such things as sabotaging the *Carnatic*'s boiler to delay its departure, but not so freely capable of anticipating the movements of people tracking other people through an unfamiliar landscape, and as viewed from a mile in the air. But neither would he willingly disappoint Aouda, not so long as he had a breath.

Robur had initially taken the *Deimos* south from the possible river fording, examining almost twenty miles along a good day's horse ride without encountering a human soul, let alone ones matching the collective numbers of the railroad attackers or Fogg's rescue party. He had then swung around to the north, heading back toward the river and tracking further east on that pass, but around dusk had again found nothing of need.

So, if neither parties had headed *east* (or at least as far he could discover under his path), the course would be to swing back around and survey the land he had missed, when he had elected to fly left rather than right. By now it was dark, his filters supplemented with the thermal lens, which could reveal any animal of a horse's bulk even at this altitude. He directed Niru to swing in a broad clockwise arc, until they were headed west again.

Two hours along this fresh heading and something at last looked of interest: half a dozen horses were likewise trotting west, closely packed. Adjusting the periscope's angle to see where they might be going, there was the slimmest glimmer ahead of a campfire, which the horsemen might reach in perhaps another quarter of an hour. Robur ordered *Deimos* to speed, reaching the area of the campfire in under a minute.

Hovering over the place, Robur could see a dozen people, and almost that many horses. Three figures were in a close line beside the fire, five more arrayed around them, two stood off by the horses, and two further standing away from the encampment. Niru was told to bring the *Deimos* down to ground, deep enough into the elm forest for their engines (vented now to their quietest) would not call dangerous attention to their descent.

As they glided to land, Robur toggled to the upper periscope, and checked to see if their arrival had disturbed any of the figures by the fire—it apparently hadn't. Robur telegraphed: *A. FOGG & OTHER PARTIES POSSIBLY FOUND, AROUND TEN MILES SSW OF YOU, INVESTIGATING NOW. R.*

Aouda's response was immediate: *R. THRICE EXCELLENT. A.*

Master Xie had taken a small metal case from a storage cabinet, and opened it on the folding table across from the windows. Most of its interior was filled by another of Aouda's electric mechanisms, this one attached to leather strapping, with a thick tubular cord running from its right side to the butt of a larger version of the electric pistol. Xie quickly had it out and positioned so that Robur might slip his arms into the harness, the energizing machinery resting then on his back. Robur turned around, and while Xie buckled the hasps securing the front, he activated the device and adjusted softly glowing dials on the barrel while low hums and clicks and throbs cycled resonantly from the box on his back.

"Stand guard for our return," Robur called up to Niru, who descended to close the port hatch after them, as Robur and Xie stepped down onto the snows of Nebraska.

Neither man spoke—nor needed to—as they proceeded from tree to tree toward the encampment, their perceptions heightened to every sound they made and those they could gradually hear from the people ahead.

Two of the villainous company had stepped well away from their fellows, and that drew Robur's interest first. Finally they were close enough to overhear their conversation, both of the men's backs to them.

"This smells, Farley, no matter what the pay." The man on the left shook his head. "They're not gettin' the Frenchman to say a damned thing. I say we should bail out, not wait to be picked up at the fort."

Before the other on his right could speak, the rough tumult of approaching horses broke the quiet, coming from the east. "Damn," the man called Farley said. "We gotta' move!"

Robur motioned for Xie to deal with the man on the left. Raising the weapon's barrel, a small red dot appeared on Farley's back, and in an instant the electric bolt followed, bringing him to the ground, dead. Almost at once, a flash of Xie's blade dispatched the other man.

Back by the fire, Passepartout had seen those two men stride away, too far to be overheard, but close enough to see them both suddenly tumble to the snow just as the galloping hooves overwhelmed the camp. He realized this was the moment for initiative, and with quick motions knocked three of their captors about—while the Colonel and Mr. Wilson remained uselessly uninvolved, staying in place on the log.

The gang quickly dispersed, running for their horses—pursued by the loggers, who managed to rescue several mounts for use of the now liberated prisoners, the two cavalrymen remaining with Fogg at the campfire. Phileas Fogg was less interested in apprehending the miscreants than he was restoring Passepartout to their party, a resolve to which the others in Fogg's group (slated for $1000 each reward) found themselves tractably persuaded.

Before they had a chance to discover the two dead men on the snow, though, Robur quickly inspected their pockets and coats, finding wallets with money on them both (which he left)—and a small card tucked in the one of the man called Farley (which he retained):

Stuart Special Services Company

Refer Inquiries to **DAY's HOTEL**
Daytona Beach ~ Florida

Something Aouda should know of, Robur thought as he and Master Xie quickly returned to the *Deimos*. Being far enough away from the campfire and in the opposite direction from the way back to the Elm Creek depot that Fogg's band of rescuers would likely be taking, Robur did not immediately bring the craft to flight.

After Xie helped him wriggle from the gun harness, Robur telegraphed Aouda: *A. PASSEPARTOUT RECOVERED BY FOGG. XIE & I KILLED 2 LEADERS, FOUND CARD FOR STUART SPECIAL SERVICES COMPANY, ADDRESS GIVEN AS DAY'S HOTEL AT A DAYTONA BEACH SOMEWHERE ALONG FLORIDA PENINSULA. SIGNIFICANCE UNKNOWN. REQUEST INSTRUCTIONS.*

Aouda's reply was again rapid: *R. FOLLOW FOGG & PASSEPARTOUT HERE. KEEP EYE OUT FOR AIRSHIP & TRACK AFTER IF SAFE. A.*

This seemed right and reasonable to Robur.

29. IN WHICH THE EMPLOYMENT OF NOVEL CONVEYANCE BECOMES A HALLMARK OF PHILEAS FOGG

The sun had not yet fully risen to flood the dawn on Monday, December 9th, when at seven o'clock gunshots were heard, fired by the soldiers and lumbermen in celebration of their arrival at the Elm Creek station, exhausted and hungry, certainly, but also joyously successful in their mission. Aouda and even Mr. Fix were overcome with much emotion as the horsemen dismounted.

Aouda embraced Passepartout with such affection that the valet appeared to blush, a most unusual condition for him. Then she turned, "You always do as you say, Phileas. Yet again."

The wind was gusting, a biting cold chill—and, were one to listen very closely, a whining sound whooshing somewhere high and away might be discerned.

Fogg motioned to the riders, "Gentlemen, let's go inside the station, I owe you a reward. Aouda, the carpetbag please." Aouda handed the bag over to Phileas as they made for the depot. Once inside, the stationmaster offered them all warming tin cups of coffee—while, true to his word, Phileas Fogg extracted fifty £20 notes, presenting ten to each of the men. "Bank of England notes, transferable to your American currency at whatever fiduciary establishment you may arrange. I hope that is acceptable."

It was, most dearly so.

Mr. Fix winced at still more of what he believed to be the robbery money flowing into the pockets of those Mr. Fogg happened to encounter on his way.

"Are you all right?" the stationmaster asked, misinterpreting his pallor.

"All fine, thank you. Have you heard any word on Colonel Proctor, and his injuries?"

Colonel Moran startled to hear that, listening more attentively as the stationmaster replied, "Nothing so far. It was rather funny, though—him being shot by Indians before he could be shot in a duel. Pardon my humor."

While the lumbermen in the rescue party discussed whether either of the two banks off in Columbus would exchange their reward for spendable money, Fogg checked his watch, then observed to Aouda, "I see no train."

"Returned, and gone, I'm afraid, Phileas," Aouda revealed sadly. "None expected until this evening."

Fogg arched an eyebrow. "Not from the west, surely—nor any through trains the other direction, I'd hazard. Not unless someone had a folded bridge in their pocket at Medicine Creek."

"Oh, yes, the *bridge*. That would shut the entire line down, except for our train pressing east."

"Or any short service trains, which I'd hoped they'd have mustered from the Omaha end." Fogg lowered his voice, "What about your magical chariot?"

"*Deimos* is just going south of us now. My wish is for it to look for that airship, in case it's lurking about. It was only by accident that the attack on the train had to move down the track—I can see that now. So, I wonder what their plan was, if it had happened the way they wanted, miles west of where Colonel Moran and his friends ended up, and whether they kept their airship available to do it."

Fogg was nodding, "Yes, *I'd* like to know that, too." Then he smiled, "It would surprise them all, though, wouldn't it, if you brought the *Deimos* down here, to fly us off in it, right in front of them all? That would make for some excited newspaper copy."

With another smile, Aouda silently agreed.

All the while, Colonel Moran would have fidgeted, were he of that temperament, for he had someplace to go as well, and was uncertain how he was to accomplish it. "These horses, we've been given—are these ours for use now? Forfeit of the kidnappers?"

"I should think so," the cavalry Lieutenant said. "I can put that in my report. Won't accuse you of horse stealing," he smiled.

"You'll want to be shipping the horse with you, on the train?" the stationmaster asked, mentally toting the car needed and the rates applicable, surcharges and fees that might be appended. That's how the railroads made their money.

"I was thinking of *riding* on it. Not waiting for the train. All I'll need is my luggage." Moran turned to the young man in the blanket, "Would you care to accompany me, Mr. Wilson?"

"Sure," Wilson said, expressing some surprise. Then he sneezed.

"Not yet not acclimated to the cold, Mr. Wilson?" Passepartout asked.

"I've been warmer." Which was quite true.

Colonel Moran and Mr. Wilson were soon riding off east down along the railroad track. Phileas Fogg and Aouda watched them go with some suspicion, uninformed as to their destination or further purpose. Passepartout, meanwhile, began to wonder what he could do with the horse he had rode away from the rescue. Fogg's steed was on loan from the Elm Creek telegrapher, he discovered, and none to spare for Aouda, of course—meaning such an equestrian option was not easily open to Mr. Fogg's party.

"There's a resident here who told me he could blow us to Omaha on his wind sled," Mr. Fix put in. "Should the wind hold for it—it's been a brusque westerly all while we've been here." And was still, gusting even now.

Phileas Fogg was skeptical. "I know there's been snow, but is it nearly flat and firm enough for that, all the way? It's two hundred miles to Omaha."

"Mr. Mudge's sledge is good for short distances, but I agree with you, Mr. Fogg," the stationmaster said, adding off-handedly, "It would work better on a handcar."

"How so?" Fogg asked.

"Oh," the man answered, having to think about it. "It would be on rails."

Phileas Fogg looked at Passepartout, and Aouda, all evaluating whether the eccentric idea might be worth a try.

"Do you have one of these handcars available?" Fogg asked the stationmaster. "One to purchase, or rent?"

"As it happens, we do. An old one, discard when the pump gearing broke, dangerous piece of sh—," the man did not finish his disapproval, there being a lady present. "Given your disappointing experience with our line's service this trip, Mr. Fogg, I think we can let you have that old car for gratis."

When approached in his hut, the inventive Mr. Mudge proved agreeable to adapting his rigging to the handcar, installing the mast at the central hole once the now redundant failed mechanical equipment were removed, and taking care not to disable the small handbrake, whose control lever now stuck up beside the mast.

The benches resting on the sledge's skids were transferred to the sides of the handcar, overhanging considerably, but securely enough by stout nails. Mudge had only a bit of room left for his pilot's seat at the rear, which he needed to adjust so that he could guide the sails from this modified relative position, but he pronounced it rail-worthy in the end, and at eight o'clock in the morning, Phileas Fogg, Passepartout, Aouda and Mr. Fix set off down the Union Pacific tracks, powered by the Nebraska breeze.

The propulsion soon had them rolling along at forty miles an hour, causing the passengers to huddle close in their coats and blankets. A quarter of an hour down the line they passed Colonel Moran and Mr. Wilson loping along on their horses. Passepartout doffed his little round hat at them as they passed. They did not look happy.

Though the wind stung some on the skin at this velocity, riding out in the open as they were, prompting them all to keep scarves up over their faces for comfort, the progress of the little car was surprisingly smooth. They rode through a switching junction with the *Burlington & Missouri River Railroad* that ran off to their right, and soon after passed the town of Kearny at a clip.

The metal cable rigging of Mr. Mudge's contrivance vibrated as the strings of any instrument might, singing at times in the wind, causing Mr. Fogg to conclude, "Those chords give the fifth and the octave."

Aouda squeezed Phileas' gloved hand with her own, adding a warm smile, finding herself increasingly pleasured by the curious ways in which this man's mind curled, and under the oddest of conditions.

They had been on the track over an hour when Fogg shouted back to Mr. Mudge, "None of us have eaten properly of late. My *Crofutt's* says there is a dining stop at Grand Island, which we should be reaching soon."

Oh yes, yes!" Mudge yelled back. "I'll stop us there," then wagged a finger at Fogg whimsically, "You'd better make sure the wind keeps up. Not my guarantee, the longer we take."

"Understood, Mr. Mudge. And accepted."

At nearly half past nine, Mr. Mudge pulled his actuators and the sail furled in. The car began to slow as Grand Island came into view, a community moved inland some years ago by the railroad from its original location on the actual island in the Platte River. Since then, over a thousand hearty settlers, including not a few fond of German arts and music, quickly displaced a vaster population of those prairie dogs.

With a firm tug to the handbrake, Mr. Mudge brought their wind car to a precise halt in front of the Grand Island depot.

The stationmaster raced out to them, "What is *this*?"

"We're a remnant of your last train, sir. The one that left us back at Elm Creek." Fogg descended from the car, offering a hand to Aouda, while Passepartout and Mr. Fix stepped from the other side of the mast. "We are finding our own way forward, no thanks to the Union Pacific Railroad."

The railroad man looked harried. "Well, you can't stay *here*!"

"Are you expecting any other trains?" Fogg asked, "For the next hour—two?"

"Well, no. The No. 2—" he began, then shook his head, as he realized which train the visitor was talking about. "None right now."

"And I think you won't, for a while. The engineer of your last transcontinental tore out one of your bridges, in Wyoming." Fogg turned back to the wind car, plopping his carpetbag down on the frame, rummaging inside as he called to their pilot. "Will you not be joining us, Mr. Mudge?"

"I ... should stay out here. Guard my gear." He held up a paper-wrapped thing, "I have a sandwich."

"Nonsense. I shall at least send food out for you. What would you favor?"

"Ham, eggs, coffee, toast—all should do." To Mudge this was a feast, as the Grand Island station cook was known to be fairly competent.

"Consider it done." Fogg declared, having by then extracted $25, which he presented to the fretting stationmaster. "I am confident of your dedication to keep our little car undisturbed while we visit your fine domain."

The man's attitude now turned into smiling cooperation, and he even rushed ahead to open the restaurant door for the generous Mr. Fogg, Aouda now on his right arm, the carpetbag suspended from the other. Fix and Passepartout followed.

"The train stop is normally a half hour," Fogg said as they entered. "I think we have earned the luxury of setting our own schedule."

Mr. Fogg's party stayed at the restaurant for almost an hour. And the food was not half bad. All told, the Fogg quartet constituted an imposing and atypical sight there at their table in the Grand Island depot diner, ordering and then ably consuming a substantial array of breakfast nourishment.

Aouda was in the process of cutting a slice of ham, when she stopped, donning a most satisfied smile. When she saw Fogg looking at her, she tapped her left wrist twice, directly over where her bracelet lay under the sleeve. Then she took her fork in the right hand, and holding it like a dagger, plunged it theatrically down into the meat, declaring as she waved the skewered piece of pork in the air, "You know Phileas, it is such a comfort to know something that was *missing*, has been found." When it was clear from Fogg's expression that he caught her meaning, that the *Deimos* had located the mystery airship, she bit the meat from the fork tines, and smiled once more.

Passepartout watched this exchange, both informed and amused, realizing how deeply linked a pairing Phileas Fogg and Aouda were becoming, mile by mile, day by day.

With everyone thus properly fortified, and settled again out in the wind car (the stationmaster even giving them a hearty salute), Mr. Mudge unfurled the sails to set them off down the tracks.

The wind continued to hold up, fortunately, and soon they had regained their previous brisk pace, the rails along this stretch being especially straight and true. About twenty minutes down the track, though, all aboard were surprised to encounter *Major General McPherson* UPRR Locomotive No. 2, and its train, stopped dead on a siding by the hamlet of Lone Tree. Passengers and porters who happened to be looking out the train's left side windows (fractured by bullet shot or not) had only a few seconds to gasp at this apparition zipping by.

As they passed the locomotive, the curls of oil-soaked steam leaking from sections of the engine not normally intended for such release testified that old *McPherson* had finally been pushed too far.

"If they have not removed the passengers," Passepartout suggested, "it must mean they have sent no train."

"Clear track ahead, Mr. Mudge, it would seem," Fogg said.

"Colonel Proctor must still be aboard," Fix put in, as the train receded in their view.

"Most likely," Aouda said.

ଓଃ ଛ

The airship with the dark red gas envelope had come to rest the day before in a wilderness stand of trees some twenty miles south of Plum Creek. It had been a good place to land, since there were no homesteaders anywhere nearby to see it. Hardly invisible, but secluded enough unless some wandering autumnal hunter happened by, to see the inexplicable thing, and tell a tale or two that maybe no one would believe anyway.

But Robur was no wandering hunter. The airship was far larger than a horse, and had been so much easier to spot against the snow from high above, in the bright of day. Its very bulk was a hindrance in seeing anything above its gondola, so Robur could have flown by at the head of a parade of *Deimos* terror ships without any fear of observation from their quarter. But *Deimos* did make a noise, so to minimize any risk of auditory disclosure, Robur brought the vessel down nearly half a mile to the airship's stern, hoping the prevailing wind would further mask their descent. Robur even found a spot where the airship's envelope could be glimpsed, peeking above the trees from the height of the pilot's cupola.

Robur wore his electric rifle when he crept with Xie on foot through the woods until he could get the craft in his full binocular sights—its starboard side, this time, to supplement what had been learned telescopically of its port face four days previous. None of the propellers on this side of the vessel were turning, and the absence of their sound suggested likewise for those on the other side. They could not see any entry, at least from this side of the craft, and there were no guards about it on foot. Robur could see some small internal compartments through the windows, but the gondola was hardly spacious enough (nor the lifting capacity of the envelope sufficient) for elevating more than a small band of intrepid aerial adventurers.

It was possible they relied on taking flight quickly, if needed, in the event of trouble. Or, they were overconfident.

But under what flag? And to whose allegiance? There were no

identifying marks or insignia anywhere along its surface, no banners flying—nor even masts for such a purpose. Whoever they were, or served, these were not the figures of extrovert advertisement.

"It's much bigger than anything Giffard made," Robur mused to Xie while looking through the lenses, recalling the blighted French airship pioneer, whose creation twenty years before lacked sufficient motive power to be more than a floating novelty, difficult to propel or steer. But the French did admire being *first* at things, even if only marginally successful at it, so that nine years ago, Baptiste Henri Jacques Giffard had been made a Chevalier of the *Légion d'honneur* at the age of but thirty-eight, a *succès d'estime* as the bitter inventor's eyesight and spirits diminished in equal measure since.

"Those engines must be *excellent*, powerful and light," Robur assessed deliberately from their hide. "They're placed out away from the ship, lest cinders ignite the fabric. I see no signs of armament. Weight again, perhaps, and concern for the gas. I don't see any ballast bags—it's possible they use water. Yes, that would make sense." He turned to Xie, "You see, as they flew through the mountains, they'd need to drop ballast, then regain it once they'd vented gas to drop lower. *Deimos* is not buoyant in that way, so doesn't need to do that."

"You are dedicated to make an airman of me, aren't you?" Xie smiled.

"I have no illusion of that, Master Xie." Robur returned his attention to the airship, studying the surface along its top. He spied two vents, at either end of the craft, but none along the middle. He couldn't be certain, but Robur thought he could see the merest shimmer over those vents, where heated air might be escaping. "Niru spotted some latent heat up there when they dropped off that Moran fellow. I *wonder* ... hot air compartments? Fore and aft, maybe heated electrically. That would be a very good way to ballast. A clever science here."

"All to what end? If it is not a warship of the air, Robur, what is it *for*?"

"Transport, and reconnaissance. Prestige, and intimidation. We have already seen the first, dropping off the man in the desert. A dirigible airship would be of much use for the second. It may remain in the air, expending little fuel unless it uses its airscrews. As for the third and fourth, they would have to throw off their anonymity for that."

"So, they are not trying to impress anyone. Yet." Xie thought further, "They are practical men, content to be secret. With a secret to be kept."

While Xie was no airman, he was a swift judge of the circumstance of the actions of men, getting to the point of things with clarity, even with so novel a thing as a flying machine. That was another point beyond even his sharp blade, as to why Robur had made a point of including him when they left the confines of the Diadem.

☙ ❧

The wind had begun to die down by three o'clock (and the temperature warming into the forties Fahrenheit, melting the snow) as Mr. Mudge's wind car reached Omaha, a sprawling collection of broad muddy streets on the western bank of the Missouri River that had grown by dint of effort and fortuitous location into quite the gateway to the East or West, depending on which way the cowcatcher was pointing.

Grand ambitions were all about this Omaha. The *Union Pacific Railroad* had expropriated the city's major hotel for their offices, impelling construction of the even more imposing five-story Grand Central Hotel which had yet to open after $130,000 expenditure. Then there was Omaha's railroad depot, as unprepossessing as any on the Union Pacific line, though company surveyors had plotted out the boundaries for an ambitious open-ended arcade that would cover all the several tracks here—in a few more years.

Mudge's wind car had no choice of track, however: they could only blow along the path for which the switches were thrown, and Mudge's furling of the sails and tugging on the lines brought them to a halt right behind the platform of a waiting *Chicago & Rock Island Railroad* train, now boarding and about ready to depart for points east.

As one might expect, the vehicle brought looks of astonishment from most about. A few bystanders of an entrepreneurial bent even questioned Mr. Mudge on whether he planned to make and sell his device, presenting their agent cards and shaking his hand optimistically.

Phileas Fogg, meanwhile, awarded the inventor $500 in appreciation of his efforts, while Passepartout saw to the honoring of their through tickets to New York with a hasty arrangement of accommodations in one of the Rock Island Line's sleepers. Fogg's exploits were known from the newspapers hereabouts, and that continuing celebrity accelerated their acceptance for the trip. Mr. Fix had to fend for himself, but was equally successful in finding a berth in another car.

The Rock Island train left Omaha eastward along a new marvel: a bridge across the Missouri to the major railroad junction at Council Bluffs over in Iowa. Because the river here was as much mud flat as water, it had been challenging to span (one earlier project to build on the *frozen* river had proven uniquely absurd). The solution now was a very long concatenation of ten box trusses laid on tubular iron piers, reached by climbing steeply embanked approaches. A commemorative arch decorated each end with description of its specifications and import—though the railroads were not waiting for the formality of the bridge to be officially opened next spring before using it.

Nor was Mr. Fogg attentive to the splendor of the many iron girders flashing by the windows. "We still have our cards. All we need is a board or table. See what you may find for us, Passepartout, for whist, after dinner. And, if Mr. Fix is agreeable to play, he can be our fourth again."

☙ ❧

Robur and Mr. Xie had returned to the *Deimos*, waiting to see what might happen with the mysterious airship, dawdling so long in its isolated Nebraska nest. Niru presented some delicious pork dumplings and tea from his tiny electric kitchen, then whiled away the time with Xie sliding the red and blue discs of *Xiangqi*, the venerable Chinese chess (centuries older than its distant European cousin). Robur would have enjoyed a few games, knowing both Xie and Niru to be worthy players, but he remained in the cupola to keep watch on the red envelope.

Just after dusk, the airship's four engines sputtered to life, one by one—a rattling commotion they could hear even inside the *Deimos*, so far from them, the wind having stilled so here. Almost immediately, the red gasbag began to rise above the tree line, higher and higher into the air, barely visible in the receding light. When it had reached several hundred feet altitude, the airship began to pull away to the east.

Robur waited several minutes for the dirigible to get far enough ahead before he took *Deimos* aloft to follow them. While Niru busily activated a variety of instruments (any one of which Robur might request be turned to the craft), Mr. Xie cleared away the *Xiangqi* tokens, returning them to the hinged board that served as the box for the game pieces.

The airship had only flown for an hour into the dark when it came to a stop below them, over an abandoned cavalry fort, two miles south of the Platte River and the railroad stop at Kearney. Located to protect the emigrant wagon trains of former decades, it had become redundant in this age of steam, and closed the previous spring. It lacked even defensive palisades, as it had never been attacked by the Indians.

Once again, one may note the intriguing inaccuracy of Mr. *V.* inflating the military contribution in the rescue of Passepartout and the two other gentlemen (also suspiciously unnamed in his account) to the cavalry of Fort Kearney that had by that moment no existence there—even adjusting the reward to reflect the thirty men involved in his fiction, as opposed to the five who actually participated (ironically, substantially cutting Fogg's *per capita* generosity by this contrivance). Was this another misdirection? Or just another sop to turn attention away from what had gone on under, beside, or passing by the noses of the actual garrison consolidated well west at North Platte? More questions to be resolved by the diligent historians of the future.

An empty flagpole pointed up from the middle of what had been the old Fort Kearney parade ground—a row of bare cottonwood trees on one side, the remaining three perimeter lines fronted by many buildings, from substantial wood frame barracks and residences of two stories, to others little more than low sod huts. It was in the middle of this once martial field that the airship settled to the ground, carefully navigating clear of the flagpole beside it.

Niru adjusted the thermal lenses, and called Robur's attention to two warm spots beside one of the smaller buildings: switching magnification revealed them to be tethered horses. On the pilot's repeater screen, Robur then saw two warm figures striding from the structure nearby, disappearing beneath the airship's darker shadow. In the reverse of the delivery back in Nevada, the craft quickly rose and set course off to the southeast at fifty miles an hour.

Robur steered *Deimos* likewise.

ଔ ଊ

A porter was just announcing the Rock Island train's six o'clock dinner stop at the town of Atlantic, an Iowa location oddly far from that body of water for the name to be credible.

"How will these little stops suffer," a regular passenger lamented to his wife in their seats across the aisle, "if the Rock Island puts on dining Pullmans like the Burlington and Chicago & Northwestern? A whole livelihood threatened, Sarah."

"We'll still suffer indigestion, Roger, just at thirty miles an hour," she half-joked in reply.

Fogg smiled at this grim assessment of railroad cuisine, having found the fare overall not as disagreeable as some travelers' hysterical accounts had led him to expect.

Aouda, meanwhile, was working with her bracelets again. In due course, she announced quietly to Fogg and Passepartout, "Two men—and we may imagine who—were swept away in the night by the, ah, *ship*. My loyal friends are following them, southeast."

"Southeast?" Fogg closed his eyes, recalling maps. "Just the heading for Florida."

"Will they go after them that far?" Passepartout asked.

"You'd rather they stay by us?" Aouda replied.

"I do not know. Florida is far away, even for *your* craft."

"Five hours. Ten, out and back," Aouda conceded.

Fogg interposed, more gravely than he was typically, "I think, this stage of our journey, *Deimos* should be close at hand."

This stage of our journey, Aouda thought. "You have something planned?"

"I shouldn't be at all surprised, Miss Aouda," Passepartout smiled. Tomorrow, they were to be in Chicago.

"I'll pull Robur off the scent then," Aouda said. "*Deimos* should catch up to us in about an hour."

Phileas Fogg and party managed over three hours of whist play after the Rock Island train resumed its way east, using a small table with folding legs that was certainly more convenient than the board on the Union Pacific, though Fogg noticed one of the supports was slightly short, causing it to wobble sporadically were undue pressure placed on that corner.

Mr. Fix seemed anxious to best Fogg and Aouda at the game, though found this increasingly difficult as Aouda began to second-guess his bids and thwart them to their partnership's benefit.

The contest was involving enough that Fogg persuaded the porter (via $25 culled from the carpetbag) to delay the lowering of the berth over his and Aouda's seats, affording them further time to play quietly even after the carriages were turned to sleeping. While they spoke very little except to convey their bids, the shuffling of the cards between hands had to be effected with special attention.

They finally quit at ten o'clock as the Rock Island train stopped briefly at Des Moines. While Passepartout nimbly slipped into his upper berth adjoining, the porter pulled down Phileas' bed as carefully as he could to avoid any mechanical squeaks that might awaken those behind the other curtains. His proficiency earned an appreciative smile from Mr. Fogg.

The remainder of Iowa occupied the train till the first glimmer of dawn on Tuesday, the 10th of December, when they reached Davenport on the Mississippi, and crossed the stupendous new bridge there, only just opened for traffic last month. The river (even here, 900 miles from its mouth), being both navigable and wide, had been a particularly challenging feat for engineering. A first great rail bridge using Rock Island as a stepping stone had been smashed by a steamboat sixteen years before; the second had been rendered so much kindling by a tornado in 1868. Wood was thus eschewed in favor of steel for this third span, a much larger double-decked version of the Missouri River trusses at Omaha, allowing wagon traffic to shunt underneath the locomotives chugging independently on the upper deck.

The bridge could be built low over the water because one of its sections rested on a giant pivot, its pier protected from arrant steamboat impact by solid stone abutments, allowing this part of the bridge to swing perpendicular to afford boats unobstructed passage regardless of the height of funnel or mast. A bronze eagle sculpted to life size perched proudly on the filigreed entrance decorations over the trusses at either end of the bridge, a visible reminder of American ingenuity triumphant, undaunted by obstacle or multiple prior failure.

Passage across the bridge was slow, though, as it was not razor straight like the one at Omaha, but featured a gradual curve to start, while the huge pivoting truss could only be crossed unless it was aligned with its neighbors, for which they had to wait while some last straggling boats passed. Once reaching the Illinois end of the span, the Rock Island train pressed on to Moline, where they made a breakfast stop.

The carriage was restored to its day coach form while they ate, allowing the card table to see further service once the Fogg party were again aboard and the train underway. They were now working on that second deck, the first having finally succumbed to nicked corners and consequently inconsistent shuffles (neither of which were consonant with the precise sensibilities of Mr. Phileas Fogg).

The next interruption was their luncheon stop at the small station at Bureau, Illinois, where a branch line split south to Peoria. Once moving again, though, it was a steady pull across the rural plains of Illinois, Phileas Fogg and Aouda taking their hands with increasing ease as Passepartout's mind seemed less on the game, even Mr. Fix noticing his distraction.

When the line turned north just before four o'clock, heading for the final stretch into Chicago on the southwest shore of the vast Lake Michigan, Fogg declared, "Well, that's the end of our card play this day—at least on this line. We'll see what we can manage later on, on the next train out." Fogg was smiling then straight at Passepartout.

Unlike the other cities the Fogg party had visited these last two months, where construction represented optimistic expansion or corrupt civic improvement, Chicago was a metropolis whose central business district was in the process of frenzied and necessary *reconstruction*— the entire core of the city having been reduced to a scattering of jagged brazed masonry and teetering smokestacks in the conflagration just fourteen months ago.

Three hundred people had perished in the disaster, and twice that again more that deadly October in the fires caused by sparks from the Chicago blaze blowing into the forests of Michigan and Wisconsin to the north.

So it was no surprise that signs of building were everywhere to be seen as the train approached the station, the city away to their left, the lake off to their right. Stacks of brick and lumber were on almost every street, in the midst of mounds of dirt in the process of being excavated or carted off, with scaffoldings and ladders and cranes of various heights protruding block on block as buildings arose to equal (or, better yet, *greater*) height than before the flames. For any who wanted an inspiring tableau of American optimism and tenacity, Chicago that December of 1872 offered it.

All the competing railroads serving the city were temporarily using the *Lake Shore & Michigan Southern Railroad* station at the corner of LaSalle and Van Buren Streets. It had been severely damaged by the 1871 fire, but was nearly rebuilt now and definitely busy when their Rock Island train pulled in under the long covered platform arcade.

Aouda noticed how anxious Passepartout appeared as they disembarked, heightened further when Phileas Fogg ascertained from the ticket booth that their connection to New York on the *Pittsburgh, Fort Wayne & Chicago Railway* would be leaving in just over an hour. Mr. Fix, meanwhile, had come to hover nearby.

"More than enough time," Fogg reassured Passepartout, adding, "We have a package to claim."

Fogg then handed the tickets man a slip of paper from his pocket, "Could you tell me where I might find this address?"

"Very close, sir." Motioning the directions: "Out the front, left two blocks to Fifth Street, southwest corner."

"Very good, thank you," Fogg smiled. Leading the way through the echoing main hall towards the station doors, he detoured around a scaffolding supporting some artisans painting a busy Victorian molding on an upper cornice, and headed to a newspaper stand beyond to ferret several of the latest editions. "We have been away from the news. Something to read on the way, to catch us up with today." Fogg pointed down to a summary placard that proclaimed: **Barbicane Party Found! Daring Explorers Rescued at Sea. LATEST NEWS**.

There were a few scaffolds still to be seen on the exterior, as well, especially on the still incomplete caps to the tall side piers and central mansard-roofed clock tower, and along the sides of the station beyond the immediacy of the frontage. But Fogg's party was not strolling that direction, and the weather outside struck them all as altogether comfortable, just about forty Fahrenheit. Indeed, Fogg seemed quite ebullient (if not actually smug) as he led them along the instructed path.

Passepartout took notice of Mr. Fix following after them, of course, but could see no other characters of immediate suspicion. Letting Fogg and Aouda step ahead a bit, he put down the carpetbag, removed his hat for a moment and gave his hair a good combing. With nothing troubling close about, Passepartout plopped his hat back on, and swept the carpetbag up to trot ahead beside Fogg and Aouda. Their prior experiences of unexpected encounters with personages of dubious character were paramount in his reflection, so Passepartout was taking no chances.

"Robur's signaled that he's landed *Deimos* out in the lake," Aouda said as they strolled along, "until our train leaves. He'll submerge as needed to avoid ship traffic."

Rounding the corner onto Fifth Street, the "Wabash Depot & Warehouse" occupied half of the block up to an alley. Fogg didn't immediately enter, though. Stepping past the door, he looked at the two larger freight portals farther down the street to the right, then went all the way down to the alley, peeking around the corner to see a door opening on to it from the warehouse. He crossed to that, taking special notice of the door's knob and key lock.

With a smile, Fogg quit the alley and led the parade back to the street, catching a wink of Mr. Fix stationed across the way, and went on into the company office.

A stolid gentleman of middling age looked up from his figures to ask, "Afternoon. How may I help you?"

"I am Mr. Phileas Fogg. I believe you are expecting me?"

"Indeed we are. Though the instructions were quite specific, I understand the need to keep new industrial processes from the prying eyes of competitors. Oh—and this was left for you," the proprietor gave Fogg a small wrapped package, light and easily held in the hand, but which Fogg promptly stuck in a pocket.

"Our inspection won't take long," Fogg said. "But we do need to be undisturbed for it."

"As arranged. You're in luck. The delivery boys are away on a shipment, so no one else about to interrupt you. They'll be back in a half hour, though. And we do close shop at five."

"Oh, we'll be done by then. Thank you," Fogg smiled.

The manager escorted them to a side door, opening onto the warehouse proper. Not following them in, he declared, "We left clearance all around, as your man specified. Let me know if you need any assistance."

The warehouse was filled with many crates of various dimensions, but the two Phileas Fogg was interested in were placed directly in front of the large freight doors. Each were not quite ten feet long, and almost eight feet wide and as tall. They had open space roundabout both of nearly five feet, with unobstructed access to the front facing the warehouse doors some thirty feet away. Address labels and signs identifying the contents as "Machine Parts" were prominent on all the sides.

Phileas Fogg crossed to the box on the left, took out an odd looking brass key inlaid with some dark but shining metals. He was about to insert it into an aperture along the front corner when he paused, waving the key at Passepartout and Aouda, "My special locks would have alerted me had anyone tried to open the cases without this."

Once unlocked, the front of the box could be lowered to the floor, forming an angled ramp to the interior, on which rested a tarped object nearly filling the container. Fogg reached inside to flip levers on either side that released spring grips holding what looked to be metal rails on the bottom.

Passepartout's heart was racing now, setting the carpetbag to the floor, while a more simply puzzled Aouda did likewise with her case.

Fogg lifted the front of the tarpaulin up over the top, revealing a bit of what looked like a giant crystal egg, enclosing some mechanisms dimly visible in the low light of the warehouse streaming through small windows up along the rafters, and the few dim gaslights shushing from standards on the walls.

"If you will assist, Passepartout," Fogg motioned to a handle on the right of the egg, while he grabbed its mate on the left. Together, Fogg and Passepartout pulled the thing out from the box and down its ramp to the warehouse floor. Passepartout found it rather lighter of weight than he expected from its size, and the evident density of its transparent encasement.

Once the object was clear of the ramp, Fogg pulled the tarp off completely, tossing that back into the box. Shutting the ramp again, he locked the crate with the key.

Now the entire thing could be seen. It did indeed resemble a crystalline egg, smooth apart from the leveling support rails protruding along the bottom, and the handles Fogg and Passepartout had used to extract it from the crate. The front hemisphere comprised a hatch, hinged internally just above where the handles were. Inside, in the middle, there was a dusky-red leather upholstered bench, with arms and high back. Behind that angular settee, a metallic disc of slightly over three foot diameter was cradled by (but did not touch) four forklike armatures, each about the size of a hand. The disc's axis was attached on either end to several tubular and boxy contraptions of not obvious function that together filled out the rear of the egg. In front of the seat, a tubular console attached to more mechanisms, a lever along its right side, and assorted lamps and switches running beneath a display of some sort, but presently all unilluminated and revealing nothing.

Aouda knew this *object* was important because of Passepartout, his breathing and expression and rapt silence as they both angled to get a look at it. The device—for clearly it was a mechanism—showed a degree of artifice and attention to detail that could only invite admiration. But what did it *do*? There were no wheels under it, or tubes or screws or other obvious indicators of propulsion. It was a smooth and beautiful thing, elegant and simple and ... purposeless.

Stepping around to the left side of the egg, Fogg called to Passepartout. "We need to push this over *there*," pointing over to the space in front of the other box. Passepartout then helped Fogg ease the thing to that location, as far in front of the second container as it had formerly been before the first.

Fogg then circled around to the right side, where he began to spin a combination lock on the frame of the hinged cowl. Passepartout recalled its similarity to the one barring his way back at the courtyard of No. 7 Savile Row. Thus unlocked, the hatch easily swung up, prodded by a tug on a small indentation above the lock, affording access to the bench. Stepping inside to slide all the way over to the right, beside the lever, Fogg waved for them to follow.

"Time to take a short ride. I think there's room for the luggage, on our laps."

Aouda entered first, shifting her case over on its side so that part of it rested on Phileas' legs. Passepartout followed, the carpetbag handle just grazing his chin. He could feel the bulge of the gun case within pressing on his ribcage—or Aouda's electric engine box, it being about the same size.

Fogg reached up past Aouda to pull the hatch down by an interior handle, securing it with a lever where the edge mated with the roof. A faint humming *thump* sounded when he did that. They were crowded in so tightly it could have been seen as an occasion for amusement, but none found it so.

The interior was now *very* quiet. Phileas Fogg began to switch on and adjust the works. As he did so, a chorus of low hums commenced, accompanied by a strange vibration that seemed more *felt* than heard. The display on the cylinder console began to light, revealing sixteen spaces where numbers and characters might appear. At first it showed **1872 AD OCT 02 PM 07:48**—but after only a moment, the symbols for date and time spooled on their own, stopping at **1872 AD DEC 10 PM 10:32**. There was a click, followed by more humming, and some low pulsations, running like the subliminal plunk of a dripping faucet.

Curious scintillations of light were now glinting from several places in the crystal cowl, though not regularly, like some will-o'-the-wisp or St. Elmo's fire. When a green lamp lit on the console, accompanied by another throbbing sound, Phileas Fogg smiled at Aouda and Passepartout, flipped a switch beside the lever, and gently began to pull it toward him. The disc behind them began to turn slowly clockwise, blueish-green glows coming from the pronged armatures through which they spun.

For an instant, images of their own selves standing by the machine could be seen, along with the object itself back in front of the other box. But as Fogg continued to ease the lever down, the disc behind increasing its rate of rotation commensurately, those wraiths and the machine disappeared, the *minutes* counter on the console soon becoming an illegible blur, and the *hour* beside it marching backwards. The warehouse's freight door was suddenly wide open, shadows outside visibly shifting as the sun moved back into the morning, then the door was closed again, the room falling dark.

Most of the sound pervading the space within the machine emanated from the armatures, which throbbed and clicked at increasing frequency and intensity the faster the disc spun. There were also vibrations and hums from the mechanism that supported the control console, and still others from the machinery at the rear of the device, behind the disc assembly. They were *like* electrical and mechanical sounds—and yet unlike any Aouda or even Passepartout had ever heard.

None of this was terribly loud, being far quieter than the background rush of her own *Deimos*. One could have easily conducted an effete conversation with such an ambiance—but neither Aouda nor Passepartout had anything to say. And Phileas Fogg wasn't talking.

Fogg continued to move the lever down, though more slowly now. The *hours* gauge was almost a blur too, and after only a few more seconds the *day* counter was decrementing at a rate of one every second and a half. Fogg had stopped moving the lever now.

The gaslights puffed on and off to this second-and-a-half beat. The warehouse doors continued to flap open and closed, shadows flying, though nothing at all could be seen of any living thing outside or in, even as crates jumped in and out, or seemed to move by themselves. Only once was the ghost of a stationary wagon seen outside, just for the merest fraction of a second—anything not staying put for longer than forty minutes falling far below the human eye's ability to perceive it.

The flickering of light and dark was at once disorienting and intoxicating, and the sounds the machine made—however gently low they were—seemed to pervade the universe. Passepartout could also feel his comb resonating oddly down in his pocket, physically moving and feeling at times to float, as if invested by a spirit of self-animation.

The *day* marker had just clicked past **NOV 22** when Phileas Fogg began to slow the machine, easing the lever back up again towards its neutral position, till only the *minutes* continued to change. When the disc behind them had almost ceased all motion, the console now displayed **1872 AD NOV 18 AM 09:25**. Another thrumming commenced, accompanied by a different lamp signaling green. At that, Fogg notched the lever to its toggle, and flicked the switch beside it. In quick succession, he flipped and poked and adjusted several controls, then the machine fell completely silent.

The whole of this "trip" had taken but forty-five seconds.

"Welcome to the 18th of November," Phileas Fogg said, "Yet again."

22*bis*. REGARDING HOW PHILEAS FOGG FOUND A FECILITOUS PASSAGE TO STONE'S HILL

Phileas Fogg opened the glass hatch of his Time Machine, and wriggled out from under Aouda's luggage to step onto the warehouse floor, taking her case and placing it beside him. At once, Fogg's watch began to chime, playing a sequence of four notes different than any previous. Opening the case, he could see the hands shifting until they now read 9:25, calibrating to Greenwich time as it was *now*, on the 18th of November.

Passepartout heaved the carpetbag over the sill to the floor, then disembarked himself, while Fogg offered a helping hand to Aouda on the other side. Once everyone was out, Fogg pushed the cowl down, then crossed around to the other side to lock the compartment with the combination dials. There being very little light from the small windows, and the gaslights dimmed to a glimmer, Aouda brought out a small electric torch, which she flashed around the room.

"Take care with that," Fogg warned, "we wouldn't want anyone to notice the light outside, but thank you."

Fogg had stepped to the second box and was using his key to open it, when Passepartout asked, "When did you arrange this? You were rarely from my sight."

"It was on the day we left, Passepartout, while you packed. I used my Machine to travel forward a day. I sent myself two watch chimes to signal my arrival." He turned to Aouda, "The chimes take advantage of a peculiar entanglement that occurs whenever the watches are simultaneous."

As he began to lower the ramp on the second box, Fogg continued, "By then, we were in Paris. I consulted maps and gazetteers regarding Chicago and San Francisco, burned your letter as requested, wrote out instructions for Dupin, went out to send a telegram or two, then hire crews to assemble and ship these crates. While I awaited the first gang, I adjusted my watch to accommodate Barbicane's Power X. The rest was quite mundane. Once the crates were on their way, I signaled three further chimes to myself—we had reached Italy—and returned a minute after I'd left. I have a switch especially for that."

Aouda was trying to take all this in. The reality of it—the chill of the darkened warehouse, only blackness visible out the windows—could not be denied, nor what she had just seen from inside the Machine, this slipping through Time from one "now" to another. An impossibility, which had just happened. She would make sense of it.

"You have a car that can move through *time*. You went into the future in it, and then shipped it here. How did you return?"

"Ah, the key was to pull the Machine to one side before leaving."

Fogg stopped his actions at the crate to explain, relishing the elegance of it, "The moment I started forward, when I saw my Machine reappear beside me, I knew I must have been successful. When I stopped, I had the Machine I traveled in, and the second one beside—the same Machine, just a bit older, its own future, there to be shipped away, returning in the present one I still had. Once back in the past, I pushed the Machine back where it was—which I knew I must have done, since I had just packed it off. A bit of a magician's trick, I admit, but it's the sort of thing you can do in Time Travel—and it worked, as you can see."

Aouda had to stop and think about that, feeling a bit like Lewis Carroll's Alice just then, facing an even stranger looking glass.

Passepartout had worked up another question. "If you can signal with your watch, using it as a telegraph—why not *longer* messages, back and forth?"

"Good thought. Which will not work in practice, unfortunately. This is not my first watch," Fogg smiled.

Fogg now opened the small package the warehouse agent gave (or rather, *would give*) him. It contained a key (a familiar kind this time), which he put in his pocket, tossing the box and wrapping into the back of the open second crate. "Would you please help me, Passepartout, the Machine into the box? We can't put it into the other one, since my Time Machine is still in it. Hence, *two* boxes."

Up the ramp with the Time Machine.

As Fogg locked the second crate, Aouda asked, "How did you make this ... *wonderment?*"

Fogg leaned back against the box side. "My father was an amateur scientist of considerable means and technique. He stumbled on its secret quite by accident, perishing in pursuit of it. I inherited—or rather *will* inherit—his copious notes and technical speculations. My curiosity eventually got the better of me, I confess, and I continued his work, to its obviously successful completion. Thanks to my grandfather, Lord Albermarle, I had ample resources, having settled quite a fortune on me after my father's death. The family legend said the legacy stemmed from a great sum he had won in a wager, years before. Only lately have I discovered the wager concerned Mr. Fogg's venture around the world." He tapped his own chest, highlighting the irony.

"So, you and your family are alive now?" Aouda felt a still more intense sympathy for this strange and amazing man, "Have you thought to approach them?"

Passepartout winced. "That, I would suggest, might be most ill-advised."

"True enough, Passepartout. Much worse than playing with watch signals. For many reasons, I strive not to cross any of their paths. Some, I don't have to worry about—not in 1872." Fogg had a troubled look in his eye, thinking of his own mother's death in his childbirth, but he shook that off. "The luggage, please," he waved at Passepartout, and while the valet picked up the cases from the warehouse floor, Fogg headed away to the small door that he knew opened out onto the alley.

Fetching out the new key from his pocket, "This is so we can come and go unobserved."

Door unlocked—out they go—door locked.

The temperature outside was only in the twenties, but for so early in the morning it was ten degrees higher than Chicago would be at this time of night twenty-two days later.

"Now, Passepartout, please take us to your Maker."

Passepartout nodded. Although the region around Chicago was interlaced by a plethora of independent railroads (indeed, it was the common municipal ambition to acquire a station as soon as practicable), no trains or streetcars went where they needed to go. Leading them around the corner onto Van Buren, and up the two blocks to the railroad station, Passepartout sought out a carriage there on this chill Sabbath dawn.

"Good sir," Passepartout awoke one slumbering driver. "We have need to travel some distance from town, out past Summit to the southwest."

"That's a long way," the man said.

"Whatever you need for recompense," Fogg put in. $20 turned out to be persuasive.

Although it was an open carriage, they were still well bundled—and the ride out into the rural countryside was certainly more comfortable than the arctic breezes they experienced "yesterday" (three weeks in the future) aboard Mr. Mudge's car in Nebraska.

On the ride out, Fogg asked Passepartout, "I supposed the reason why you would never tell me more about this savant in Chicago, was to make yourself indispensable."

Passepartout shrugged agreement, and Fogg added, "Logical. I did likewise with my boxes. We both had a long way to jump from London, before knowing we could trust one another. But I have yet to steer you false, have I."

"No, *monsieur*, you have not."

Aouda was following their conversation and manner with great curiosity, and Fogg told her, "Just as with the shipping of my Machine, dearest Aouda, we are about to do something we already know we did: deflect the *Columbiad* into the Pacific. The fun of it is, none of us know anything now about what it is we are going to do. Only, that we succeeded." Fogg's smile was genuinely impish—there was such a side to him, after all.

"Except for Passepartout," Aouda perceived. "You have been here before, so know more than any of us."

"I have been imagining—yes. It may well be, as Mr. Fogg says, 'fun'—but until we are done with it, I cannot say."

The dawn light was on the flush when their carriage pulled up at some well-fenced ground, which at first glance appeared to be farmland. There was a substantial farmhouse of two stories to the left of a locked gate blocking the way to the property's rutted dirt road. A good-sized red barn lay off to one side, all as one might expect on a farm of this acreage, and there were fallow fields and orchards which in the warmer months would certainly have been verdant and productive. Farther on down the road, another smaller house sat next to a more modest brown barn.

But where the way led was to a pair of brick buildings with chimneys and vents, all abutting an even larger masonry edifice where the ribbed edges of an oddly arched copper roof might just be seen in the morning light.

On the center of the gate, a small but professionally made sign announced:

T. Maker
Foundry & Works
Ring Electric Bell if so Obliged

Hours: Strictly to Suit

The bell in question consisted of a button on a small metal box atop a wood stanchion providing the left pier of the gate, which when pressed by Passepartout (once long, then three short taps afterward) made a thin ringing sound via a real bell present somewhere within the box.

At length, an older woman appeared on the farmhouse's covered porch, every inch the farmer's wife—casually holding a shotgun, which she kept in hand as she came to the gate.

Recognition brought a smile as she neared enough to see who had rung, "Well, well, well, Frenchman! We'd begun to think you'd flown away to the Moon, all on your own."

"No, I have no *wings*," Passepartout spread his arms wide, then indicated the carriage, "Greta Sax, may I present my friends, Phileas

Fogg, and the Princess Aouda. We are here to *play*—if we may pass the gate."

The woman unlocked the barrier.

"How is Axel, and your fine children?" Passepartout asked as she swung the gate wide.

"He gets by—day by day. Best we can." Greta quickly withdrew such thoughts of her husband (that dearest heart and love who had returned from the War much diminished in body and spirit), to alight on brighter things. "The kids miss your stories. Grenadier, too—though not so free to admit it."

Passepartout stepped back to the carriage, hauling down Aouda's luggage and the carpetbag. Motioning down the road, "A short stroll, if you will."

The carriage driver was now free to return to Chicago, paying no further attention to his eccentric (but well-paying) passengers who trod away down the rutted path toward the brick enclave.

As the Fogg party passed the other house, a lean black man in his forties stepped out to its porch, clothes hastily donned, coat not yet buttoned, sizing up the strangers accompanying Passepartout. Whatever he thought of Fogg and Aouda was not showing on his face, scarred by not a few sabre encounters earned in a dangerous youth.

"And here is Etienne Dufoy, formerly resident of Haiti," Passepartout declared. "A man of great scientific want, long delayed by grim military history. Fair summary, Grenadier?"

The man smiled grudgingly.

"I am Phileas Fogg. This is Princess Aouda. We are honored to meet all who count themselves friends of Passepartout."

"Amazement here, to find Passepartout has friends." Grenadier was not disparaging, just honest. "He is not a man who talks of it."

"That, I can believe, sir," Fogg replied with a smile, patting his shoulder.

Those must be quite special people, Grenadier decided, as he watched Passepartout lead them on to the foundry.

Activity could already be heard within the buildings, from the chugging of some machinery to the characteristic hum of something electrical—though there were no wires visibly running from anywhere the Fogg party could see. A door in the smallest of the brick buildings had a sign over it, not professionally made, but nonetheless carefully drafted onto a plain wooden plank: **T. MAKER**. Its weathered condition suggested it had been long exposed to the elements, though not necessarily on that current portal.

While Passepartout knocked on the door, Phileas Fogg took out his watch, opened the back case, and caused two chimes to sound—not in the same pitch as previous, but notably lower, and distinctly resonant there in the rural quiet. The jeweled bezels had adjusted also. As he faced east, toward Maker's door, the "**?**" remained at *X* and a yet to be lit "**B**" had fallen beside *VI*. "**N**" and "**O**" were both off by *VIII*—Nemo being in the Pacific, and the *Deimos* beyond it. As for "**A**" at *XII,* its jewel glowed very bright, since they were all but on top of it.

The door was finally opened by a black woman, in her late thirties by age, of average height and build but most distinctive demeanor—not highly beautiful, yet with a face featured in a way few would willingly let go of, and a smile one would despair to forget.

"Jean, you scoundrel!" She immediately embraced Passepartout, still holding onto the luggage (and not letting go of it), their familiarity and enthusiasm not lost on Phileas Fogg or Aouda. "And you brought guests," whom she beckoned inside.

Passepartout laid down the luggage. "Phileas Fogg, Princess Aouda—may I introduce Thomasina Maker."

"You're the Around the World man," Maker pointed. "You've been in the Chicago papers for months. Didn't know you'd got *this* far," then turned to Passepartout, "They didn't mention *you*, either—is *that* we're you've been? When I didn't hear from you, I thought you'd changed your mind."

"Guilty, Miss Maker. It proved advantageous to make a stop in London—the rest has been Mr. Fogg's doing. I could not write or telegraph, without drawing undue attention to you, and imperil your safety."

"You're being ominous again." Maker let a shiver. Then her eyes narrowed, evaluating, "Since you're here now, though—and have brought them along with you, do you folks have something to do with his plan? If so, you're cutting it rather fine, Jean. Barbicane goes in two days."

"That *is* why we are here," Passepartout nodded.

"I understand you have quite an extraordinary conveyance, Miss Thomasina Maker," Fogg put in, arching an eyebrow at his valet, "about which, Passepartout has been continuously reticent."

"He must have decided you didn't need to *know*, Mr. Fogg, hmm?" Maker chided lightly.

Passepartout shrugged innocently.

"I was about to have some breakfast. Have you folks eaten?" Maker asked.

"Our last was a luncheon," Aouda said.

"You must be starved then, come along."

Aouda realized now how easily her statement had been misinterpreted—a meal eaten but four hours ago didn't sound that way told to someone at six in the morning. Clearly, one had to watch one's tongue when Time Traveling.

Maker took her to a small kitchen, which was not only lit with electricity, but equipped with a variety of novel electric gear, including a small cook stove. Aouda appreciated such invention, having helped in the design of *Deimos*' galley, but it was Passepartout who actually assisted Maker in preparing some fresh eggs, taking them from an electrically cooled box.

"No need of the iceman here," Passepartout said.

Aouda could see it worked on the same principles she had used for the similar cooling boxes at Diadem and in *Deimos*' galley. Watching Maker warm some meat in an electric pan, while bread browned on a toasting grid, Aouda thought of the many men and women she relied on at Diadem besides just her machines and said, "Is this how you make do with so few people? Science and machinery. We met only the woman at the fence, and the Grenadier gentleman."

Maker did not turn away from her pan, nudging the meat with a fork. "I used to be a slave. The machines I make have no soul to crush, or shackle. It's the way things *should* be." Then she brightened, "I *do* have others who help—they just don't live *here*. Grenadier and the Saxes stick around to protect the land, and my work, not to do my dishes."

Later, as they sat at her table for their breakfast, Maker explained, "Before Passepartout joined your expedition, Mr. Fogg, we thought my flyer might grab onto the *Columbiad* magnetically—I have plates along the keel that can do that. It must have some alloy other than just aluminum, otherwise it would melt shooting up through the air."

"Steel and titanium," Passepartout interjected, "I was able to ascertain more about its metallurgy after meeting with you."

"Oh—well, that would be fine then." Maker munched on her toast.

"What are its capabilities?" Fogg asked, "Your craft."

"I call her *Kestrel*." Waving her toast about as she gestured, Maker said, "It can fly, it can go under water, and it can go out into the Aether."

"Using *rockets*, for that last?" Aouda asked.

"Yes—you've worked with those?"

"Not for propulsion, but the principle's clear. Heating the particles even beyond vaporization?"

"Yes, more impulsion that way. I inlet the gas too, when down in the regular air—burn *it* instead of fuel."

"How high have you gone?" Aouda and Maker were now completely absorbed in their mutual science.

"Two hundred and eight thousand feet—just briefly. Had to test the engines." Maker turned to Passepartout, "They'll be getting a bigger test if we do what *you* want."

"Once we finish this fine breakfast," Fogg said affably (but which he hoped would be soon, being anxious to get on their way).

Maker even had an electric device for the washing of her dishes, which was rumbling away when she took Fogg, Passepartout and Aouda back into her facility. Aouda was set to compare the range of equipment to what she had assembled at Diadem, but there was surprisingly little in the spaces they passed, going down an open walkway between supporting piers and walls, lit by admirably proficient electric lamp.

It was clear from her kitchen that Maker ingeniously (if not wantonly) combined mechanical and electrical, but only a small collection of machinery and tools could be seen on their left, through the gaps in the columns, filling out large tables. There was at least a lathe and press, combined with gauges and electric switches, everything neat as a pin. While off to their right: a row of metal tanks, each about the size of a man and labeled with their contents, piped by valves and tubes away to the neighboring equipment in a room beyond, whose functions she could not immediately ascertain from so swift a glance. Aouda smiled to see "Oxygen" and then "Acetylene" on two of the vessels. Rapping her knuckles on the latter, the container thudded dully.

The end of this passage opened into an amphitheater of science, occupying the largest of the buildings, the one with the arched copper roof—which turned out to be the retractable covering over the space where the *Kestrel* lay. Passepartout (who had seen it) and Maker (who had built it) were the only ones not surprised by how *small* it was.

From front to tail the car was not quite twenty-two feet in length, its width less than nine, and in height a mere five—so low that Aouda could easily see over its roof, which was of curved glass set on a frame arching over the center of the machine. The passenger compartment was not large, only half as wide as the vehicle itself: two well-upholstered seats, high backed with cushions even for the head, one in front of the other, their curvatures fitted to accommodate four travelers in reasonable comfort, but hardly more than that. A flattened area above the lateral vanes on port and starboard provided a step up, reminding Aouda of that detail she had put below her own *Deimos'* side hatches.

Where the middle of the ship curved down from this passenger dome, an array of closely packed vanes stuck out laterally, with two larger ones in circular rotatable nozzles of about a foot in diameter on either side. Scorched areas on the cement of the pavilion directly under them testified to their propulsive function and power.

The body of the *Kestrel* was smoothly shaped at all points to cheat the wind, from its foremost oval air intake and bulging cowl, to its thicket of propulsion tubes filling out the rear deck, where a pair of tall fins with adjustable sections were attached. Aft of the dome, a thin reinforced metal tube extended vertically, its lower parts shielded by the glass and rear cowling—this and other protrusions along the surface suggested to Aouda the presence of instrumentation sufficiently vital to need protective covers. While the machine's surface color was similar to that of the *Nautilus*, a rusty brown, the consistent lack of seams confirmed for Aouda what Maker must have been making of all that acetylene.

Aouda was already walking around it, noting things. "Your engines are laid out for speed. Then they'd have to, to fly forty miles high."

"You'll find Florida is but a stroll, ma'am," Maker grinned.

Phileas Fogg checked his watch, "May we go now?"

Maker laughed. "Let me flip a few switches first."

Knowing the limited confines of *Kestrel*'s seats, and having just shepherded the carpetbag on his haunches in Fogg's Time Machine, Passepartout suggested, "Should we find someplace to keep our luggage? A strongbox for the carpetbag?"

"No, we'll take the carpetbag with us," Fogg replied. "But we can remove what we don't need, the coats obviously—Florida will be warm. And Aouda may add from her case whatever she will. Travel light."

While Maker dashed off to "flip a few switches" (activating a variety of electrical measures that assisted Grenadier and the Saxes in their protective roles), contents of the valise and bag were rapidly shuffled, leaving Fogg with the carpetbag—Aouda, of course, retaining her small shoulder clutch and cache of pocket gear.

When Maker returned, she had changed into brown leather pantaloons, coat and cap, close-fitting and efficient, with many practical pockets, and carrying a small traveling case. "Open up the starboard casement, will you Jean?"

Passepartout crossed around to that side of the craft, lifting up the section of the glass roof on a hinge that ran its length down the top of the dome, Maker doing likewise on the other, tossing her case on the seat beside. Aouda, the carpetbag and Fogg fit neatly along the rear seat, though Fogg and Aouda had to remove their hats (the lady carefully locating her pins) reflecting the limited vertical space inside. Passepartout sat beside Maker in the front.

There was no need to haul the doors back down, though, as Maker flipped a toggle on the control console in front of her, causing whirring motors in the frame to lower them mechanically, after which they locked without intervention, forming a tight seal with the frame.

Maker turned back to Aouda and Fogg, "There are belts on the seats to hold you in. You will need them." She was already buckling the one on her seat, across lap and chest, tugging both for snugness, Passepartout following suit.

As the others managed their harnesses, Maker took a pair of metal goggles from a compartment beneath a central screen. It had a small cable, the end of which she attached to a hole near the cover, and a diminutive set of earmuffs attached, so that together things could be seen or heard by the pilot to the exclusion of the other riders.

Maker then began to bring *Kestrel* up to power. Unlike Fogg's Time Machine, Aouda recognized the surge of compressors and pumps sounding around and under them, gauges on the pilot's console measuring the increases.

"Passepartout, please keep a hand on my case, and Mr. Fogg, you best hold your carpetbag—and your hats." Maker touched another switch, which caused the roof above them to part and create a wide opening to the increasingly blue sky above.

Realizing there had been no connection by wire to signal the retraction, Aouda said to Maker in admiration, "I see you've mastered Maxwell Waves!"

Maker nodded back at her.

With more switches thrown, *Kestrel*'s engines sprang to life: a high pitched roar emanating from the four thrusting nozzles, less so from the tubes in the rear—a process, Aouda realized, taking roughly the same time as Phileas Fogg's machine had to move them twenty-two days into the past.

The blasts from the nozzles finally began to lift *Kestrel*, the ascent almost level, apart from slight buffeting from the air disturbed around them in the confined structure, but also as they cleared the roof. When they were some twenty feet above it, Maker flipped the switch to close the panels again. Adjusting some more controls, gasps from the side vanes gently heaved the ship around counterclockwise, such that *Kestrel* now faced more to the south.

Increasing roars from the engines accompanied the change to forward motion, which escalated as the four nozzles tilted back more, causing *Kestrel* to climb even faster. Aouda and Fogg found the view from this broad windowed glass bubble extraordinary. As the rear thrust took over the effort, the side nozzles were dampened down, and Maker caused a pair of small wings to extend some three feet out the aft sides, whose surfaces could be tilted to further the craft's maneuvering. They were now easily flying faster than the *Deimos*, and at already several thousand feet—still climbing.

And then, they *accelerated*.

Pushed back into your seat acceleration. Laboring a bit to breathe acceleration. Ground falling away frighteningly fast acceleration.

The engine roar was intense, exceeding *Deimos* at its loudest, penetrating the body as much as the ear. Faster—higher, faster—higher, faster—higher. It never seemed to stop, the rush of air outside adding to the noise, shaking the craft at times, while pumps compensated for pressure changes inside their compartment. Aouda found it all *wonderful*.

Maker shouted over the din, "I don't know if men can take such accelerations as well as we ladies can, Aouda." Fogg was not disagreeing; Passepartout was noncommittal.

Aouda was by now trying to apprehend as much as she could of the instruments. One meter showed their still rising altitude to be just over twenty thousand feet. Another dial gave their speed as nearing 700 miles per hour, though that gauge was also increasing. The clouds a *Deimos* could only fly *through* were now far below them, even great storms she could see in the distance. This was a whole new perspective on the world and its weather.

A mild shudder was felt across *Kestrel*, and a strange cloud puffed into existence behind them for a moment, like a giant ball of cotton.

"We're now moving faster through the air than sound can," Maker noted. "On the ground below, or so I've heard tell, a loud thunderclap follows us as we fly. Brings no end of puzzlement, especially in a cloudless sky."

All the while, the speed measure had continued to rise: 800 ... 900 ... 1000—on and up until finally leveling off at 1500 miles per hour, their altitude some forty thousand feet, when Maker said matter-of-factly, "We should be in Florida in another thirty minutes, give or take."

Aouda took notice of a long white cloud generated by *Kestrel*'s progress through the atmosphere, trailing back as far as she could see behind them. Turning around as best she could while wearing the safety belting, she found the plumes appearing behind the craft's propulsive nozzles both scientifically interesting and quite beautiful, as though they were painting a long white ribbon in the night sky.

Seeing the object of her interest, Fogg asked, "What do you make of it?"

"Condensation around the particles burning us along, I suppose. I've never seen anything like it around *Deimos*. But then, we don't fly this high, into the cold."

Kestrel was racing across Indiana, then into eastern Kentucky, when Passepartout felt the moment opportune to proceed along a new course of his own, peeking around the head cushion to address Phileas Fogg. "You know, Mr. Fogg, we are flying to Florida in this way, solely because of *you*. I'd have used my own vehicle for this, but whatever it is your Machine does, mine does not tolerate it, and has not lifted since."

"Really?" Fogg thought a bit. "It might be the gravitational anchor. It's what keeps the Machine from floating away, or sinking into the Earth, when you move."

"*Unh, possible*," Passepartout mused. "You may understand then, how fitting it was to enlist your help, you being the cause of my quandary."

Maker had been listening to their chatter, and cut in, "So you wouldn't have involved me if your machine were working?"

"What we undertake could be dangerous," Passepartout answered. "I would easily have spared you that, if I could."

His sentiment appearing to satisfy her, Passepartout continued with Fogg, "Is your watch a little cousin of your Machine?"

"Only very distantly," Fogg smiled.

"That's what I spotted, you know, your watch—years ago, back in Alsace."

"Where *your* machine must be buried, yes," Fogg said, thinking of the "?" on his watch. "Are you troubled, to see Alsace has changed flag, the Imperial German eagle now?"

"As you say, well-buried, Mr. Fogg. Though getting to it may be more difficult in years to come." Passepartout pursed his lips.

Aouda continued to be enthralled by the sight of the landscape from this great height and passing at twice the speed of sound, trying to make out signs of human presence amid the natural features that dwarfed so much of it to insignificance. Aouda brought out her glasses, looking through them occasionally as they flew along. The threads of railroad lines could be seen even without the glasses, the towns they linked looking like so many gossamer cobwebs. So much of the land appeared as an indistinguishable mat of green, though, Tennessee looking not that much different than the state of Georgia that quickly followed.

And then came Florida—flatter, widely spaced settlements penetrating the trees hugging a land of lake and swamp, teased by yellow fever and isolation.

A five-hour journey for Aouda's *Deimos*—swallowed in less than an hour by Thomasina Maker's *Kestrel*.

Maker brought *Kestrel* below the speed of sound as they neared

Tampa Town, where Impey Barbicane had transformed the sleepy bayside community into a bustling industrial metropolis constructing the components for the great cannon assembled nearby at Stone's Hill. Dropping altitude as well, *Kestrel* remained high enough not to be easily seen from any on the ground.

They were flying more in the realm of *Deimos*' speed when Maker activated a telescopic viewer that displayed on the central screen. Aouda found its resolution comparable to that aboard her ship—though with the practical improvement of being actuated by controls on the pilot's wheel. She did not ask Maker whether it could register the heat of objects at night, as *Deimos*' could (though if she remembered to, she planned to inquire later).

Stone's Hill proper was an afterthought outside Tampa Town, a collection of buildings that had accumulated about a quarter mile from Impey Barbicane's enormous *Columbiad* cannon, its dull dark gray alloyed steel shaft poking up hundreds of feet in the air from the low hilly protuberance, buildings and sheds close to it, clusters of houses farther on. Both village and cannon precinct appeared thick with people and wagons, even seen from *Kestrel*'s altitude. Beyond the confines of Barbicane's industry, however, the terrain quickly reverted to thickets of pines and palms.

"Ah, something interesting over yonder," Maker declared. Flipping a control lever on her wheel, the image on the central screen changed to a grid of circles centered on *Kestrel*, a blinking dot on the left edge, which a geographic indicator showed to be east. Without warning, Maker banked the ship over to the left and accelerated towards it, the rings on the screen rotating so that east lay dead ahead.

Phileas Fogg and Aouda now completely appreciated Maker's warning about the advisability of wearing the belts.

The dot represented an aerial object off on the horizon, about a hundred miles distant at this altitude. The *Kestrel* sped across the intervening peninsula of Florida, jumping back up to supersonic speed.

"Are you expecting some flying machine down here?" Maker asked.

"Yes," Aouda and Passepartout said in unison, Phileas Fogg offering a more verbose, "Actually, yes."

Ten minutes later, Maker slowed *Kestrel* to *Deimos* speed, and switched to the telescopic image as they circled above it: a dirigible with a reddish gasbag, pointed front and stern, two propeller nacelles on either side.

Aouda had to rely on the screen magnification, since the width of the hull outside the glass obscured the view directly below for her own glasses, but could see enough to decide, "If not the same craft Robur followed, it's a sibling."

"Robur is Aouda's Grenadier," Passepartout explained to Maker. No more need be said.

"I wonder if it uses hydrogen for lift," Fogg speculated.

"Whatever else?" asked Aouda.

"If helium, it would be incombustible," Fogg replied.

"Helium is only known on the Sun," Maker objected.

Utterly true, in 1872—the element having been named for a constituent isolated only recently in the spectrum of that orb. Chastising his lip for the blunder, Phileas Fogg extricated himself with a carefully worded response: "Ah. There *are* terrestrial sources, though I concede not properly known presently." Tossing a knowing wink at Aouda beside him, he leaned in to whisper, "Found in *lavas*, eventually—and even a variety of *pitchblende*, ironically."

Maker's attention had worked ahead, detecting further signals via her goggles. "And not *alone*, either." Again without warning, *Kestrel* spun around for another sprint east, some eighty miles farther out to sea. "Something big's out there, friends, on the water," she cried.

Something big, indeed.

"Good heavens, that's the *Great Eastern*!" Phileas Fogg exclaimed when they arrived over it.

One didn't need telescopic magnification to see and recognize the Great Iron Ship. It was the largest vessel in the world, nothing like it on any sea: six hundred and ninety feet of iron and steam, giant paddlewheels amidships, four tall narrow tan funnels and six black masts rigged for sail crowding its vast flat wooden deck, a great white stripe girdling its hull between the black upper hull and the red by the waterline. The bane of its diminutive and hubristic Prometheus, Isambard Kingdom Brunel, builder of tunnels and bridges and railroads, oh so successfully (or usually so)—and then he tried to build that boat.

As heavy a smoker as any of his locomotives, Brunel was spared the indignity of enduring its prolonged failure by a fatal stroke at fifty-three, just before his Leviathan was to make her maiden voyage, one immediately plagued by mechanical teething and passenger displeasure despite the opulent carpets and mirrors. Its posthumous saving grace in the years to follow, but one: it was the only thing afloat capacious enough to hold the gargantuan spools of cabling needed to link continents by the ephemeral sparks of oceanic telegraph.

So, what was the *Great Eastern* doing off the coast of Florida, this fine November morn?

"Look at that crane," Aouda remarked of a formidable triangular finger of metal perched on the stern of the ship, jumping in and out of focus on *Kestrel*'s screen. "That's not for laying cables."

"They have an escort," Passepartout said, peering out first to the east, then to the west, where maybe a mile away black spots curling smoke could be seen on patrol.

"Hmm," Maker said, and flew *Kestrel* over to the western one, which on approach proved to be a double-turreted ironclad warship, of a type familiar to anyone knowing the designs favored by the Union Navy during their late internecine conflict.

To the south of this vigilance lay yet another ironclad, this one of more peculiar configuration. Resembling the largest of the Confederate breed, sloping iron battlements protecting its central guns, the prow and stern had been amended to support broad flat elevated platforms, clear of obstruction. The front one was unoccupied, but the rear sported the most unusual of residents: what looked like a small wood yacht, its upper deck stabbed all about with what seemed by glint of morning light to be half a dozen white metal palms.

On closer telescopic inspection, though, these proved to be the tubular pylons of a mechanism, the topping "fronds" of each being six-bladed propellers. The height of the poles varied from one to the next, such that the blades of one might rotate unencumbered by contact with any of its immediate neighbors. A pair of horizontally directed propellers and steering rudders occupied what was presumably the stern of this evident airship. None of its motivators were presently turning.

"I'm amazed if they can make that fly," Maker huffed at it. After another circle of observation, she asked, "Seen enough?"

Assessing the collective expressions of Passepartout and Aouda, Phileas Fogg said, "I think so."

Maker headed *Kestrel* back to Florida at six hundred miles an hour—that way avoiding any transonic thunderclap when they passed over the coastal airship on the way. Twenty minutes later, Maker recessed *Kestrel*'s flight wings and scouted around for some secluded clearing to land, near enough to Stone's Hill to walk, but not so close that they would run the risk of being overseen.

"That looks a good spot, over there to the left," Passepartout said, gaze fixed on Maker's viewing screen.

"Pegged, and down, Jean."

The clearing proved suitable, flat and dry enough (landing on open ground, *Kestrel*'s lifting nozzles had to be vented carefully to avoid setting fire to their destination). The tall trees about provided additional concealment, while a rude old footpath offered a not too strenuous way into the village. The temperature hovered in the middle sixties Fahrenheit, rendered still more sultry by the palpable humidity.

"That navy out there, did you know about them?" Maker asked

Phileas Fogg, as she powered down her ship, the dome hatches opened and Aouda putting her hat back on.

"No—and I don't like the looks of them."

"*Kestrel* has no arms to take on gunboats."

"Nor would we ask it," Fogg assured her. "I shall have to think about this. We have to get into the town. Is this safe, left unattended?"

Passepartout volunteered, "I may remain behind, to stand guard. That is best anyway, as I have been here before, and might easily be recognized again by people I would rather not."

"That would include the *Columbiad* trio," Aouda added.

"Who we know by sight," Fogg reminded.

Fogg did *not* add: and who we apparently never do meet close up here in Stone's Hill—otherwise they would have recognized us all, back aboard the *Nautilus* (three weeks ago, in two days' time). One must pay attention to such temporal contingencies.

Aouda asked Passepartout, "Do you need any weaponry? I have one to spare."

"Not imprudent. But you forget, our Colt revolvers, in the case."

Maker added, "There are a few pistols in the *Kestrel*, too. You'll find them under the instrument bar."

"*Merci.*"

Setting off down the path, Maker striding behind by politic choice not command, Aouda obliquely asked Fogg, "Speaking of things unattended—your 'Machine Parts'."

"They are impossible for any but me to use. I am more concerned about the reaction our local inhabitants will have about us. The prejudice of these rural regions being what they are."

Maker advised from behind, "Florida is not the worst place, but there's no Freedmen's Bureau anymore so I will feign quiet as far as my inclination allows."

Phileas Fogg surmised that might not be limitless.

"We shall both look demure, and harmless," Aouda winked back at her.

The path finally broke beyond the trees onto a road going into town. Confirming what they had seen earlier from the air, Stone's Hill was surprisingly crowded, and with disparate sorts. Merrymaking spectators were passing to and fro from the *Columbiad* enclave, running through a gauntlet of tradesmen hawking overpriced food and refreshment, commemorative trinkets, and lofty "educational" pamphlets declaiming on the work and its many implications. *Impey Barbicane and America's Manifest Destiny on the Moon* proclaimed one, while another queried: *Aluminum: The Metal of The Future?*

Not that the idea of flying to the Moon struck everyone there in

Stone's Hill as something to be welcomed. Some of religious inclination took it as an opportunity for hellfire proselytizing, inviting passersby to Repent on account of the End being Nigh. Phileas Fogg was understandably skeptical of that eventuality (at least out to his acquaintance, the bleak year of 802,701), even as he knew Mr. Barbicane would not actually be reaching the Moon in any case, but held his tongue as he bypassed their sincere superstition.

Phileas Fogg and Maker were mindful of the racial mix of the people they encountered. There were black faces among them—the native Indians as well—men and women, some well-dressed but more in laboring garb, so that Maker's presence was not on its own provocative (though her outfit, all so functional for piloting *Kestrel*, was rather farther from the standard attire for those operating at ground level). Still, Fogg made a point of remaining in the street, staying off what few wooden boardwalks there were. This might be a jurisdiction where people of color were not permitted to pace on a walk reserved for those of approved lighter complexion. It would not do that morning to provoke any altercations or ruffled sensibilities to cloud their purpose—which, for Fogg, was to locate Auguste Dupin.

In due course, Fogg encountered a busy boarding house and restaurant, vomiting newspapermen and those seeking business with Barbicane. Stepping up onto the porch and entering, he was about to seek out the manager to ask about Dupin when he spotted the dining area off to their right, and saved himself the trouble. Dupin sat by himself over against a wall, there taking a broad and leisurely breakfast.

Dupin quickly caught Fogg's attention, standing up and waving for them to join him, though preemptive as they approached, declaring, "As your global notoriety precedes you, formal introductions may be discouraged in favor of *anonymity* while here in Stone's Hill, good stranger. I see you have exchanged your valet for new traveling companions, and neither in turquoise."

Fogg smiled, "That lady fell away from us in Suez. She played a quite adequate hand at whist."

"I must caution, I do not think our proprietor will serve all your companions."

"We have just eaten, actually," Fogg replied, "so a seat at your table will suffice."

"I *think* they will not object to that," and Dupin pulled out a chair for Maker by the wall, while Fogg did likewise for Aouda on the aisle side. Dupin returned to his own seat, in front of the breakfast.

Indicating Aouda, Fogg said, "Now, this fine jewel is responsible for those rooftop indentations you identified in Paris." Turning to Maker, "And here is an engineer and scientist of no less skill. As for my valet, he is nearby, but engaged in some necessary ... bird watching."

"Many avian specimens for that hereabouts, to be sure," Dupin joked, "but I assume you are interested in more high flying fowl."

"What all have you learned?" Fogg asked.

Dupin checked to see no one was close enough to overhear easily. "I must say, you set me to a most fascinating assignment. It has not bored me in the least. As you instructed, I travelled to Baltimore where I ascertained all I could regarding Mr. Barbicane's ingenuity and means, both of which are formidable. The secret of his Power X he guards most closely, but otherwise he and his company have been publically boastful over all obstacles overcome. His need to have precise ephemeris for his venture led him to consult all the leading minds of our age, Newcomb of the Naval Observatory here in America, for his vital recalculation of Lunar positions, and two of your British scientists: James Moriarty after his work on *The Dynamics of Asteroids*, and William Clifford on his recent translation of the German Reimann's daring speculations on the possible curvatures of space. All most stimulating to my own scientific curiosity. Barbicane even constructed a giant Difference Engine based on the late Mr. Babbage's design, all to corroborate in perfect accuracy their many calculations. Mr. Barbicane is serious and thorough. And, as far as I could determine, his Baltimore employees are a band most loyal and trustworthy."

While a Negro waiter attended to the nearest table, giving their own a quizzical look, Dupin paused to take a long sip of juiced orange, dapping his lips with the napkin after until the servant had moved on.

"Florida is much more interesting. It did not require supreme observational acuity on my part to notice the abundance of *agents provocateurs* humming like bees around this nest, of many nations, though none so adroitly posted as my own countryman, the poetic photographer and correspondent Michel Ardan, whose diplomacy prevented a duel between the hot tempered Barbicane and his competitor Nicholl, and is now scheduled to accompany them both in the very capsule. *Parfait!*"

Dupin leaned closer, "Ardan happens also to be a most competent agent of our new *Deuxième Bureau*, and he took prompt notice of my arrival." Phileas Fogg startled a bit at that, but Dupin allayed that concern, "Out of mutual respect, and on our own initiative, we have taken the liberty of consulting. Thus did I learn from Ardan that one of your countryman has also come upon the scene, Sir Augustus Moran—lately ambassador to Persia, a region increasingly falling sway to *Russian*, not British, influence. Ardan's *Bureau* surmises that persistent international rivalry may have been the impetus for Moran to assemble a veritable armada presently stationed off the far coast."

Phileas Fogg, Aouda, and Thomasina Maker perked at that.

"It includes the *Great Eastern*," Dupin went on, "justly famous for its telegraphic cable laying, hired abruptly out of Wales to be outfitted with a Brobdingnagian crane, capable of plucking the heaviest of objects that might plummet into the waves, such as any vibrating with Power X. More gregarious still are the several decommissioned American ironclads that have joined them, not exactly vessels one would select for a purely scientific or commercial expedition, do you think? This suspicion is further supported by interview of the many fishermen who frequent the area, all intercepted and brusquely warned away by those still-turreted gunboats. I agree with Ardan's assessment that something, how do they say, 'fishy' is in the works." Dupin paused to dismember a biscuit.

Aouda asked, "Have you heard of a 'Stuart Special Services Company', operating out of a hotel in a place called Daytona Beach?"

Dupin smiled, "Ah, most astute! That is among their supply conduits, a small settlement over on the Atlantic coast. Its figurehead, Felix Stuart appears to be a subordinate of the Ambassador—conjoined history back in India, as far as Ardan could tell. How did you hear of them?"

"An associate of mine acquired one of their business cards."

"They do not seem the sort to be advertising," Dupin mused.

"They weren't," Aouda replied.

Sensing she would not be explaining further, Dupin continued, "There is something I did *not* share with agent Ardan, though I was sorely tempted. Traveling incognito on one of those fishing boats, before they were flicked aside, I spied by glass several very large *airships*, not balloons, though I suspect of more rudimentary capability than your own," nodding to Aouda, who with Maker were growing most impressed with what Dupin was telling them, illuminating so much of what they had seen earlier from the *Kestrel*. Fogg, of course, only found this to be expected from the proficient Parisian.

"What to make of all this?" Dupin leaned back, took in a breath. "So expensive a concentration of salvage and wondrous aerial reconnaissance would seem profligate to the point of stupidity unless they were certain of their prize, which suggests some imminent act of sabotage to plunge *Columbiad* into their waiting arms long before it can reach the Moon, their vessels I assume stationed at a distance consistent with however far the capsule will travel in its interrupted journey." Indicating the ladies, "Your scientific acquaintances may infer those measurements better than I."

"Sabotage," Fogg said darkly, through clenched teeth.

Dupin nodded, wanting the implication to sink in. "How to *effect* a sabotage? For that, one needs at least one technically proficient confederate, motivated by greed or revenge yet with intimate access to all Barbicane's facilities."

Shrugging his shoulders, Dupin enumerated the suspects: "Excluding Barbicane, his son Victor, and passenger Ardan, that leaves only Captain Nicholl, Barbicane's bitter Philadelphia rival whose seemingly impenetrable armor was rendered impotent in a flash by Power X, followed by such an implausible effusion of his ancestral southern charm that he managed to insinuate his way aboard almost at once. And yet, while here, where should he be spending a surprising amount of his unattended time, stealing off from his apartment in Barbicane's grand house at the oddest of hours and taking great precaution (though insufficient to elude my observation), to a hastily improvised machinery set up in the last few weeks in a disused livery, by none other than *Sebastian* Moran, son of the same Ambassador whose vessels presently haunt this coast."

Fogg and Aouda straightened more upon hearing Sebastian Moran's name. Dupin noticed.

"Ardan's *Bureau* determined Moran *fil* was little more than a ne'er-do-well serving as Colonel in India—that *India* connection again—yet obtained suddenly a lengthy leave, turning up here at once to perform the role of *estate agent* and *metallurgical procurement officer*? *Incredible!*"

Dupin leaned in again, "Ardan and I agree to suggest, if sabotage is the object, Nicholl is its likeliest essential conspirator. Neither Ardan nor I were able to investigate their continuously guarded machine shop, nor do we possess sufficient engineering knowledge to otherwise interpolate the composition or placement of whatever they may have contrived, limitations I imagine afflict neither of you," wagging a finger at Aouda and Maker.

"As Nicholl ceased his nocturnal visits some days ago, I assume whatever it is they have needed, is finished. It is relevant that there is a regular inspection of the cannon and its projectile, hence any saboteur may well delay its installment until the last possible moment. If these deductions are anywhere near correct, less than forty-eight hours remain for my hypothetical villain to complete such a mission." Dupin smiled, and resumed his meal.

Aouda couldn't help recalling the reaction of Captain Nicholl aboard the *Nautilus* three weeks ago (though now two days in the future). "*Where are we?*" he had said. Aouda now realized his surprise was not to be in the middle of some ocean, but to be landed on the

Nautilus and not dangling from the crane of the *Great Eastern*. This moment also made her recognize how deeply she liked this Auguste Dupin, even though only at first meeting—his manner, along with the clarity and method of his thought—all meshed with how deft Phileas Fogg had been in bringing him here.

"Most concise, clarifying much we knew by other means," Fogg declared. "Whatever may happen next, my friend, you must arrange to be in New York *on* the 13th of December, where my boxes are to be shipped by the liner *Pereire* the following day, the 14th, arranging again to be aboard to supervise their safe transit to LaHavre and then London. This *must* happen."

Maker cocked a brow hearing this. What manner of "boxes" was this Phileas Fogg so concerned about? She suspected she would not be told much further about them.

As Dupin nodded, Fogg continued, "Once your fast is broken, I think we need a tour of the *Columbiad*."

Not long after (and before the management had more of a chance to decide whether to chuck this racially-mixed quartet out of their establishment), Dupin conducted Fogg and the two women out of the boarding house to stroll among the crowd, which increasingly had a carnival atmosphere to it—further fortunate circumstance, as so many of the visitors were accompanied by servants and guests, that they appeared less conspicuous than they might, were they making their way down an empty thoroughfare.

"We shall all keep our eyes keen to detect any culprits of our acquaintance, particularly Colonel Moran," Dupin cautioned as they walked.

Fogg was sterner. "We have seen that unworthy before."

Impey Barbicane's expedition to the Moon supplied much to look at. The way ahead led first to the *Columbiad* itself, which rested on rails under an open barn on a specially built wide railroad carriage. A small locomotive was parked ahead of it, ready to push the car down to the launch tube when needed. Although no one was allowed to touch it—a roped perimeter and armed uniformed guards conspicuously discouraged that, *Columbiad* could be observed freely all around.

Recalling how the *Columbiad* had looked out in the Pacific, its heat-scorched hull perched horizontally on the *Nautilus*, Aouda studied the vertical shining surface in its pristine condition. There were four strips barely visible, flush with the metal but reflecting slightly different from that around it, running up from just above the bottom to stop where the hull started curving toward its ballistic point. Aouda pointed those out to Maker, "What do you make of those lines along the surface? Passepartout's drawings suggest a different alloy was used."

Maker pondered. "Radially symmetrical. I'd guess some sort of magnetic guidance, to both propel it up the launch tube and keep it aligned to avoid spinning like a turkey rifle bullet."

Aouda nodded, "Agreed."

Fogg stood in admiration of the two women's intellects, just as Dupin was assessing how the three of them worked in concert.

Dupin motioned down the track, "Now, ladies, to the cannon itself."

The rail line was wider than standard gauge, laid level smooth the eighty feet to where it disappeared into the tunnel excavated into Stone's Hill. Off to the left, a pavilion was built atop a wooden stockade in which much machinery hissed and churned, while ahead the towering cannon cast a large shadow west across the hill.

People were coming to and from the tunnel, at the end of which could be seen the hatch of the cannon, open for spectators to marvel at the launching barrel within. The cannon itself was a cylinder sixty feet in diameter, though its internal bore was only as wide as the fifteen-foot machine it would be launching. The gap between the thick inner and outer casings was filled to every interstice by a maze of mechanical and electrical mechanisms, humming and clicking and rattling subtly in the dark, threaded by narrow gangways and ladders.

Visitors to the cannon hatch stepped underneath an intimidatingly massive set of steel gears that would incline the cannon for aiming once the capsule were in place (a mating array balanced the other side, though not visible from where they were in the tunnel).

As the hatch opening was above the track, a temporary stoop was installed, so people could step up to the level of the actual aperture, and out onto a balcony protruding into the space beyond. More guards were on hand to maintain civility and prevent the overly curious (especially rambunctious youths) from climbing over the railing and dropping onto the rest of the moon ship, possibly damaging the many connecting linkages visible on the topmost canister of the four that had already been deployed in the shaft, and only awaited the *Columbiad* to cap them.

"Once *Columbiad*'s brought up, day after tomorrow, all that will be lowered to the bottom, nine hundred feet!" a guard was enthusing to some guests at the rail. "Then, whoosh!"

Dupin and friends were next, and less impressionable. The two gentlemen stood back, letting Aouda and Maker step to the rail for the best view. From this spot, strips similar to the ones on the capsule could be seen to run all the way up to the top of the barrel—a diminished patch of blue several hundred feet above.

"Look, the guidance rails, all the way up," Aouda pointed. "I'm sure you're right, a magnetic induction."

Thinking of the open shaft, the ever-pragmatic Maker turned to the guard, "What happens if it *rains*?"

"Oh, there's an umbrella up top—steel. Opens and closes by some electrical thing. Used it most last summer, on and off since," the fellow replied. "Heard some thunder this morning. Some north, some west—no rain here."

Maker glanced down at the floor of the balcony, suppressing an embarrassed grin.

Dupin interjected, intentionally on the loud side, "You *must* see where the monstrous gears to tilt this beast are controlled," and led them all back down the tunnel, and out to the pavilion.

The building resembled a plantation house, with many windows that could be shuttered should a hurricane come up. Its ground floor being a lair of machinery, stairs on one corner went up to a porch that encircled the whole of the second story, affording observation in all directions. Holding court inside, Victor Barbicane, scion of the lunar explorer, proudly disported on the many devices the father had brought into existence for this room, a warren of gauges and switches to manage the great cannon looming out the windows.

Dupin and Fogg looked about noticeably, while Aouda and Maker attentively assessed the displays with carefully aimed glances.

Grandest of the instruments was a brass panel occupying the center of the room, its row of enumerated rings denoting the declination of the gun by not only *degrees* and *seconds*, but on down into *thousandths* of a second—at which Victor Barbicane radiated expectation.

"Here is where we aim the cannon. I sorely wish I were going with them, but am needed here to make certain all occurs smoothly. Once the projectile is loaded, and the hatch sealed, we'll enter the exact angle needed to fire the *Columbiad*. A flip of a switch and the clockwork will move everything with precision, followed by the firing automatically."

Aouda skillfully donned the eye-fluttering innocence of an ill-informed woman, "However does it do that?"

Victor used a key on a chain to flip open a small hatch on the side, "Gears, ma'am, plenty of gears."

But before Aouda could see much of what lay inside, the young Barbicane had slapped the plate shut and relocked it. Maker commiserated with Aouda by a frustrated shrug from the other side of the panel.

Outside, and down the steps to the ground, Fogg turned to Dupin, "We shall take leave of you for the time being. Remain on hand, following your own instincts and if anything should transpire that we should be made aware of—."

"Take this," Aouda interrupted, thrusting the snuffbox into Dupin's hand. "There is a button inside, acting as a wireless telegraph when the switch is turned to the right, under power so long as the crystal in the cap glows. It will also flash silently for any signals I reply to you. You do know Morse?"

"*Oui*," Dupin said slowly, a mix of insulted confidence. "The International Telegraphy Congress was in Paris, after all."

"*Bon*," Aouda smiled. Recalling how they had never exchanged any names, at his request, she whispered, "As you have kept us all anonymous, I am Aouda, A O U D A. And you, I believe, are Monsieur Dupin."

"I am no other. D U P I N." His eyes widening for a broad smile, "Now we know how to *spell*, for signaling."

23*bis*. IN WHICH ACTIONS ARE UNDERTAKEN TO ENSURE THE TRANQUILITY OF CONDITIONS IN FLORIDA

As Phileas Fogg strolled back to the *Kestrel* that warming Monday afternoon in Florida, he said to the two ladies beside him, "I have my own idea how *Columbiad* might be sabotaged using something that could be machined so quickly, but it pleases me to hear your evaluations first."

"The barrel is a waste of time," Maker jumped in. "No way to climb inside, poor chance of attaching anything that could guarantee putting the capsule where the ships are."

"Yes, all too obvious and clumsy," Aouda agreed. "It's the aiming that must be affected, that means the little box of gears."

"We tread the same path," Fogg said.

When they arrived, Passepartout was sitting comfortably on the side of the *Kestrel* by the opened port entry door. "What have you discovered?"

"Dupin has convinced us there is to be sabotage of the *Columbiad*," Fogg said. "Barbicane's passenger Nicholl is the likely villain, but we are debating precisely when or how."

"Sabotage!" Passepartout hadn't considered that possibility, any more than Fogg had.

"Yes," Aouda added, "those boats out in the Atlantic are there to intercept Barbicane's craft, in the pay of Colonel Moran's father."

Passepartout's brow went up at that. "So, for *our* plan to succeed, *theirs* mustn't."

"I agree, it's got to be the gears," Maker said.

"Gears?" Passepartout had lost the trail.

"Yes, the mechanism that aims the launch tube," Aouda answered. "All someone need do is replace some gears that turn the main ones— bigger gear, more turning. Only we don't know exactly which gears, I couldn't get enough of a look at it."

On a moment's reflection, the way was clearer for Passepartout, "Oh, I know what you mean. But I have complete specifications."

Aouda was puzzled, "How?"

"They're in the plans I gave you," Passepartout smiled.

"I should think *not*." Aouda's memory was not that poor.

While Aouda retrieved the papers from her bag, Passepartout reached into his pocket to hold the comb. His eyes shut briefly, then his hand came out again to take the plans from Aouda. Unfolding them on *Kestrel*'s front cowl, he flipped the sheets over so that one lay on top, showing in great detail all the control mechanism, "*Voila!*"

Aouda's eyes narrowed. "Those drawings were not among what we studied at Diadem."

"No, they weren't," Passepartout admitted with a wry smile.

"Special paper, indeed," Fogg muttered, but turned to the matter at hand, glancing at Maker and Aouda, "What do you think Nicholl would choose to replace?"

"Those two there," Maker pointed. "It's all he needs."

Aouda nodded agreement. "Any increase in radius would translate into less elevation, simple, elegant. They'd only know they were directed on a false trajectory after the firing, and no alternative but to seek safety in the Atlantic."

"And small enough to be made in a hastily assembled machinery, yes." Fogg turned to Passepartout, "According to Dupin, Moran put together a facility for Nicholl to fabricate, *something*."

"That *must* be new. I need to see that," Passepartout said.

Fogg was lost in thought for a moment. "Assuming we would not want the conspirators to *know* they had failed, there would seem only two obvious ways to proceed. One would be to extract the gears and substitute them for the ones Nicholl made, so that he unintentionally puts the correct ones back in—*or*, we make a counterfeit set of our own, switch them out beforehand, and after they have inserted their fakery, we return the originals."

"That first involves not merely knowing where the substitutes are held, but our ability to switch them unobserved," Passepartout said, "not impossible, given my particular skills."

Fogg looked troubled, "But more risk attached."

"I like the second," Maker said. "Since we have the exact specifications, it would only take me a few hours in the shop to turn out copies. They wouldn't even need to be tested for tolerances, since we'd be putting the correct ones back. All I'd need was stock that looked and felt right to the touch."

"We have only then to confirm that Nicholl made *those* parts." Passepartout pondered, "You agree he would keep them on his person, until ready to install them?"

"*I* would," Maker said.

"Then we must establish Nicholl still has them," heaving a sigh, Passepartout went on, "Again, not impossible, given my particular skills. Though it does mean a trip into the village."

While Aouda returned the *Columbiad* plans to her bag, Fogg volunteered, "As a superfluity, this time, I shall remain behind to guard *Kestrel*."

Fogg watched Aouda and Maker stroll away with Passepartout, whereupon he fished out from his carpetbag the newspapers he had bought in Chicago earlier three weeks from now. He thought it advisable not to peruse his December 10th papers in front of Maker.

◯₈ ₈◯

Progressing down the path, Passepartout asked, "Do we know where Moran's machinery is supposed to be?"

"Dupin said it was in a former livery," Aouda replied.

"Ah, I think I know the place."

Passepartout was especially wary as they skirted around the open streets to avoid being seen too much. The transformed livery was enough on the outskirts of the village to abet that purpose, Passepartout approaching along the back wall first. There proved no entry here (the doors of the former livery being boarded over) but Passepartout took out his comb and held it up. The tines splayed out, accompanied by the merest of tingling pops. "No one inside," he announced, "but someone up front."

Coming around the corner to the main street, they could see wide doors presently padlocked, and a man dozing on a chair whose back leaned up against the wall not inches from the regular business entry.

"I recognize the fellow," Passepartout told Maker and Aouda.

Seeing no one else nearby, Aouda signaled for them to wait, and with the utmost stealth crossed in front of the entrance to wave a vial that puffed blue vapor briefly under the man's nose. Aouda then motioned for Passepartout and Maker to come forward, whispering when they neared, "He'll sleep for several hours."

Giving a quick glance to confirm there were still no observers, Passepartout tried the doorknob with his other hand. When it proved to be locked, he took out his comb again. A needlelike probe began to extrude from the top of the comb, which he inserted into the keyway. A swift high pitched sound accompanied the door unlocking. The needle retracted and Passepartout beckoned them to follow.

"Where *do* you find your grooming tools?" Aouda asked.

Maker whispered to her, "You don't know the half of it!"

Once inside, Maker and Aouda took the lead in looking over the works. Maker inspected the settings at a lathe, the stocks that had been affixed, and the shavings still abundant on the bottom of the machine and the floor below. "They were tooling a small part. Could be our gears."

Aouda found several metal blanks on a nearby table, holding them up until Maker noticed, who smiled and nodded, prompting Aouda to slip them into her shoulder bag. They wouldn't need their own raw stock back in Chicago.

Passepartout, meanwhile, sought out any papers or other signs of what the mechanics had been doing there, but found nothing.

Once they were outside, Passepartout relocked the door with his comb, noting the guard was still fully somnolent, and led the way back into the cover of the trees.

"We must surveil Barbicane's house," Passepartout told them. "This will be the most perilous, since there are so many more people there—and ones we are obliged not to be noticed by. Fortunately the Americans have their front porch, and their back door more for the refuse. We will play the *trash*."

The houses lived in by those working on Barbicane's project fell along a row up the way from where Aouda and Maker had visited the *Columbiad* shed earlier that morning. The paths through the brush and trees behind the buildings passed water pumps and wood piles and wagon barns—all further obscuring them from being seen by those more naturally interested in what was going on in the front. Impey Barbicane's residence proved the grandest, sufficient for Nicholl and Ardan to remain close at hand for conference and company.

Aouda spotted Captain Nicholl at a second floor window and called this to Passepartout's attention. Out came the comb again, this time for longer, some of the tines swinging back and forth several times. Aouda witnessed this extraordinary (albeit quiet) spectacle with a mixture of puzzlement and a resolve to make full sense of it. Altogether too much of novel character had happened since they'd arrived in Chicago that afternoon, three weeks from now.

When it was restored to a comb, Passepartout led them away from the house, back towards *Kestrel*. Once they were far enough away to speak easily, Passepartout said, "Nicholl has the two gears, separate coat pockets to preclude rattling, I imagine, which means we may proceed."

Once back at *Kestrel*, Passepartout directed to Maker and Aouda: "While Fogg and I stand watch on the faux gears, you both may return to Chicago to fabricate our counterfeits."

"You'll hear us coming," Maker promised.

Aouda blanched somewhat as she suddenly realized, "I'll be too far away if Dupin signals me while I'm gone."

"A risk to be taken," Fogg said, and unexpectedly kissed Aouda's hand.

Maker fished out a pair of binocular glasses from a compartment, which she presented to Passepartout. "Here, just in case you need to spy something."

Phileas Fogg and Passepartout watched in admiration as the amazing *Kestrel* lifted away, then the pair set off toward Barbicane's crew house, a thunderclap soon sounding in the cloudless afternoon sky.

☙ ❧

Aouda found her second flight at supersonic speed no less

exhilarating than her first. The sun was still high, illuminating the landscape marching by so far below. As *Kestrel* raced along to Chicago, Aouda strove to be heard over the noise of the cabin, "How long did it take you to build this?"

"Off and on, fifteen years. My friend from the Underground Railroad, Barton Swift, saw I had a quick mind right off, let me all I needed, books—lots of books, at first. Then tools, metals, rare rocks from Europe even, costly things I suppose. *He* reckons all that, not me. I made the engines first, didn't work out a hull to fit them in until the War was near done. Glad of that, really, I've had enough of blood, don't want my flyer to be used for that."

"But you do carry pistols."

"Tired of bloodshed, not stupid."

Aouda smiled, "I admit I couldn't resist putting some teeth to my *Deimos*, that's my flyer. I've made great strides over the years in energized crystal optics."

"I'd like to see your designs."

"And I yours," Aouda smiled. Then she changed the topic. "Those clouds behind us—condensation?"

"Yes. Unavoidable up here, like my thunder. I wonder sometimes what uneducated people might make of them down below. Nothing like it in Nature."

Aouda considered that a moment, then had another question, "How did you meet Passepartout?"

"He turned up on my door soon after I began my serious work, like as not following his comb, which I haven't seen him use in *that* way before. He used it to assay minerals, mainly. Warned me on the hazards of refining pitchblende. Never asked anything in return, save room and board, till *now*. Kindred spirit, I guess."

                                                              ଔ ଓ

Stationed in the secluded foliage behind Impey Barbicane's residence, Passepartout intended to use his comb periodically to confirm the presence of the counterfeit gears on Captain Nicholl's person, but with Phileas Fogg standing by, Passepartout was compelled to request, "If you could please stand back five or six meters. It is your *watch*."

A smiling Fogg paced away that measurement, whereupon Passepartout used his comb. Once finished, the valet joined Fogg, "Nicholl's gears remain reassuringly static."

"How does that work?"

"What radiances it uses, you mean?"

"No, how do you know what it means? I heard no sound from here. I have chimes and dials to signify what I want to know on my watch. You divine just by holding it, not even looking at it."

Passepartout thought how he wanted it say what he would of it. "I see what I need in my mind's eye."

Fogg seemed satisfied at that, and he and Passepartout whiled away the day exploring what they could of the region roundabout Barbicane's house, returning every few hours to their spot behind the building to keep track of Nicholl's gears. They found that Sebastian Moran had apparently taken a house not far from that of Barbicane, where he and several of his band presumably could keep an eye on their quarry of Barbicane and presumed confederate Nicholl. Passepartout and Fogg observed what could be seen of them through the windows, trading the binocular glasses off between them as needed, before moving on to more exploration of the environs of Stone's Hill.

At one point late in the afternoon, Fogg and Passepartout saw Auguste Dupin strolling amiably along the dirt road on which these homes were aligned—and bumping into (or was it by stringent prearrangement?) Michel Ardan. Passepartout used Maker's glasses to observe them more closely. They stopped to converse awhile, looking pleasant and unconcerned, then parted.

Towards dusk, Fogg made a solo excursion into the Stone's Hill maelstrom to buy some portable food for them both. Fortunately the crowds were thinning down, visitors staying at Tampa Town boarding carriages, Barbicane's tunnel and *Columbiad* barn being closed to public view at night. For that reason, one vendor was happy to offer discounted value on his remaining skillet of fried chicken, which smelled very tasty and seemed a shame to let waste—though the bottled beer stayed at regular price. This proved adequate for Phileas Fogg, who conveyed the repast (wrapped in recent newsprint) back into the woods, where Passepartout had found a downed log some distance from the houses for their rustic dining interlude.

By the waning twilight, just about seven o'clock, Fogg was just finishing his last chicken part when he said to Passepartout, "Those chameleon schematics, your comb, your craft you would have taken into space had only I not appeared, the provocative allusion to 'Beings' in your letter of introduction that I must burn, and your positively inhuman immunity to narcotics in Hong Kong—all these suggest to me you are a traveler, too, from farther away than any map of mine can trace. Am I correct?"

"Very. Just as I have come to think your father's scientific experiments involved contact with something beyond this Universe, *outside* it, using forces I do not understand. Yet *you* do, and *use*."

Fogg bit the last of the flesh from the bird's leg in his right hand. After swallowing, and flicking the bone over his shoulder to wherever it would land behind them, he said, "My father's journals had much detail, but then many entries like, 'Learned more about Higher Dimensions today.' So you may be right on that."

"Have you used your time car to go back and look?"

"I've considered it, but I'm not ready to do that yet. Time is a field I'm still learning the rules of. Or, if there *are* any rules. So far, I've stayed well away from myself, or people close to myself. I don't know whether there's any danger in doing otherwise. One thing I *can* say, together we are performing a perilous experiment *here*, outcome unknown. You see, in my time, Barbicane's flight to the Moon was successful. We have made it (*are* making it) *not* successful."

Fogg looked melancholy, "I have visited the year 802,701. From what I saw there, Passepartout, I do not want Time to be an immovable stream, however many of its local currents seem to run deep and fixed."

Passepartout said, "If your Machine had never appeared, I would have followed Barbicane's craft, using instruments on my own to shield it from observation by the lunar sentinel. He would have been successful." Then he turned gravely thoughtful, "Or not. How did they *describe* their voyage?"

"They encountered an asteroid along the way, whose gravitation interrupted their path, so they never ... landed ... on the Moon," Fogg spoke more slowly, the import of things dawning. He concluded tersely, "They barely made it home, and were recovered at sea—but in the Pacific, off the coast of California, not the Atlantic. And they were launched in December, not November."

"Hmm, different yet so similar. You vex me with your temporal conundrums. Together, we may have *changed* very little."

After that, Phileas Fogg and Passepartout made their way back to behind Barbicane's place, Fogg standing back sufficient for Passepartout's comb not to be plagued by the interference of the timepiece. Once the valet nodded his completion, they took a seat on a nearby fallen log.

"Keeping an eye on your charges?" It was Auguste Dupin, who appeared at their side from the dark as if by magic.

Passepartout startled, "You *are* a quiet one. I never heard you approach."

"My joints do not yet snap with age," Dupin declared, kneeling close. "Ardan asked me who I was escorting this afternoon, having seen our stroll from afar. I replied, some ladies and their gentleman companion, giddy with enthusiasm for American industrial initiative. We both pretended I was sincere. Once I was alone, I attempted to report this by that exquisite jeweled telegraph, but received no response, so I decided to verify *your* whereabouts and wellbeing."

A curt rumble of thunder sounded just then from the northwest. Fogg arose, "Most diligent, my friend. As you see, we are well, and should be on our way, in fact, before the alligators set upon us, don't you think, Passepartout." Passepartout nodded, and they were starting off when Fogg turned back, "Oh, one thing, Dupin. I assume the *Columbiad*'s aiming room is sentried through the night?"

"Two men, armed, patrolling from dusk till dawn, the same pair since I have seen, no others, circuiting the projectile and cannon as well on their rounds. Do you require their particulars?"

"Not necessarily," Fogg decided after some thought. "Thank you, Dupin." And they each went their separate ways, out into the dark.

Arriving at *Kestrel*'s nest, Maker turned on a small electric lamp built into the central supporting strut in its roof to show Passepartout and Fogg what she and Aouda had crafted on their jaunt to Chicago: shinning metal gears of not quite two inches diameter, each with the finest of serrations comporting to the specifications of Passepartout's changeable "paper".

Phileas Fogg once more engaged to stay behind with the *Kestrel*, since Passepartout (and his comb) were required for their task ahead. Some ten minutes after the valet and the two women departed for *Columbiad*'s pavilion, though, Auguste Dupin appeared out of the dark.

"I can't say I'm surprised to see you," Fogg said.

Dupin looked over *Kestrel* admiringly, "Is this the Negress' vessel?"

Fogg nodded.

"You attract ladies of genius making flying machines, with an ease I am envious of. This must travel *very* fast and *very* far, should it not? For were you and your companions not somewhere in the farthest East, not that many days ago? Or have the newspapers wholly lapsed in their reportage? You see my reasoning, not calling you by name earlier. You play a risk here, Phileas Fogg."

"Unavoidable. I appreciate your caution."

"Caution? My cowardly temperament may not be up to *this* game. As you know, *puzzles*, not cannonades, are *my* pleasure."

"What about your Mr. Ardan? Is he more extrovert?"

"I don't know. He is circumspect, and clever. A man not easily thrown, I think. Do you plan on getting in his way?"

"Not to my recollection," Phileas Fogg declared.

ଔ ଛ

The moon was still bright, only a few days past full, when it rose at half past eight o'clock that evening, affording fine illumination for Passepartout, Aouda and Maker as they worked out where they should conceal themselves to best observe the Barbicane launch building and the guards tending to it. They eventually staked out a spot where they could see the pavilion on their left, and the rail from the now closed cannon tunnel leading to the *Columbiad* shed on the right, whose folding doors had been shuttered around it.

Maker got perhaps the best view wearing her goggles, able to superimpose telescopic images over her regular vision with a twist of a dial or flick of a switch on the frame. Aouda had her glasses, too, as did Passepartout using the pair Maker had given him earlier.

Two uniformed men, armed with rifles and pistols, patrolled together, checking the ground of the pavilion roundabout, up the stairs to confirm the entrance door was secure, then down again to march all the way around the *Columbiad* barn, going down the rail track to the closed doors of the tunnel, and back to the pavilion to retrace their course.

The guards did not move at the quickstep, taking from fifteen to twenty minutes to make the round, but appeared to stick to the same routine each time, except for once, when one of the men stopped for a smoke while they were over by the tunnel entrance.

And something else which Aouda and Passepartout noticed, but which of course would have been unknowable for Thomasina Maker: that the smoking guard was Thomas Wilson, the non-polygamist who would be boarding the Union Pacific Train at Ogden in a few weeks.

"Now we know what he was doing before Salt Lake," Aouda whispered to Passepartout.

"And why he was so disposed to tremble," Passepartout responded, "He'd been here in the warmth."

Then Aouda said, "Two things stand out for me. They follow exactly the same path—and once they go around the *Columbiad* shed, they cannot see the control pavilion, until they emerge around the other side."

"There is a stand of trees down by the building, a mere ten meters from the other side," Passepartout observed. "Near enough to dash across, perhaps—up the steps, and inside, before they see? If we are fleet, and quiet."

"I've been listening for floorboard or stair creaks," Maker said, "Haven't heard any, from here—means *they* probably won't either, with the barn in the way."

They carefully worked their way down to the trees Passepartout indicated, from where they could see the side of the pavilion ahead, although the stairs on the other side were now invisible to them.

"At least we can see when they disappear around the barn," Maker said. "The moment they do, we *rush*. I'm assuming you'll be using your comb to get us in, right?"

"That will be the easiest part," Passepartout promised.

"Next time they make their pass, we go," Aouda resolved.

In due course, young Mr. Wilson and the even younger other guard appeared around the left side of the pavilion's ground level, pacing to the right, looking occasionally at the machinery within, some of it still chugging and huffing behind the wood gates. Finally, but in about the amount of time they were expected to, they turned the corner to go along the side of the building. Despite the stillness, no sound of their footfalls could be heard up those stairs Passepartout, Maker and Aouda could not see.

Not long later, the pair emerged on the left side of the second floor veranda, circuiting slowly around to the right, looking around, even out towards the woods where Passepartout's band stood, but too cursorily to apprehend them in the moonlit shadows. Disappearing around the right side, more anticipated time elapsed before the guards emerged on the ground and headed off to the right towards the *Columbiad* shed.

At the instant they were eclipsed by that structure, the three adventurers moved.

Sprint forward, sharp left turn, up the stairs more slowly, step to the entrance. Passepartout already had his comb at the ready, its needle inserting into the lock. In a moment the door was open, in they went, Passepartout locking the door after they were within.

Passepartout stepped back from the windows a short distance. "We'll be able to see them cross to the tunnel entrance from here." While Aouda stayed at that spot, Passepartout darted over to the control console and used his comb to unlock that, then resumed his position by Aouda at the windows.

"They're in view," Aouda said.

While the moonlight illuminated parts of the room, the mechanism of the console was too complex to be seen clearly without a good light—except that Maker's goggles magnified that more than sufficiently. She opened the door, flipped a lever on the left side, and pulled out the metal mechanism along a drawer. More springs and levers required loosening, at which point she was able to remove the two critical gears from their spindles, placing each into separate pockets on her leather coat. From two other pockets, Maker extracted their counterfeits, easing them into place and restoring the mechanical tensioning.

Drawer pushed back, cover closed. "Ready to relock, Jean," Maker called quietly.

Passepartout crossed to accomplish that, then they waited for the guards to climb up the stairs. There was enough of a footfall for that to be heard inside the room, and while the guards performed their circuit of the veranda, Passepartout, Aouda and Maker hunched down against the instrument cabinets, swallowed by the dark.

Wilson tested the door, confirming it was still locked, then the two continued on. Once the guards had descended the stairs to the ground, Aouda, Maker and Passepartout stood up again and positioned by the window, Passepartout's comb once more unlocking the door.

When they saw the two guards disappear behind the shed again, Maker and Aouda rushed out, not even waiting while Passepartout relocked the door and quickly followed them down and off into the safety of the trees, and then away towards *Kestrel*.

From a carefully positioned vantage behind a tree some distance away, Auguste Dupin evaluated their actions and judged them exemplary. Should they not pursue their temporary careers as preventers of sabotage, Dupin thought, they could easily find employment as *voleurs extraordinaire*.

24*bis*. ON THE MANNER BY WHICH THE FIRST HUMAN TRAVELERS TO THE MOON FOUND THEIR DESTINATION SO UNEXPECTEDLY CHANGED

It was shy of midnight when Passepartout, Aouda and Maker rejoined Phileas Fogg at the *Kestrel*, the valid launch gears safely sequestered in Maker's pockets.

"You'll never guess who we saw, guarding the *Columbiad*," Aouda said to Fogg.

Not waiting a reply to this rhetorical question, Passepartout supplied the answer, "Mr. Wilson, of the train."

"Now there is a coincidence to strain credulity," Fogg said.

Maker might have puzzled on how they could have known the young smoking guard, but the matter at hand pressed their attention.

"If they are to switch the gears out, tomorrow most likely, having someone like him at that post would be most opportune," Passepartout ventured. "The other might be a confederate as well. In any case, I must stay to keep vigil around Nicholl." He turned to Maker, "You, though, need rest and preparation, so I suggest you fly back to Chicago. All of you, freshen up, sleep in a real bed. Eat a meal not on a log."

"Are you fine to be alone? Log-eating." Aouda asked in concern. "Dupin has my only small telegraph, and it is of limited range. How would we know if there is trouble?"

Not telling Aouda of Dupin's recent failure to telegraph her, Passepartout said, "As you already know from Yokohama, I have a way to signal you, we have but to agree on a new frequency." Taking out his comb, he motioned with the hand gripping it for Fogg to move away, "Your watch."

As Fogg stepped away, Aouda began to work fittings on her right bracelet, while the tines of Passepartout's comb splayed and shifted in the moonlight. Finally she settled on a channel and tapped out, *CAN YOUR COMB REACH SO FAR?*

Without seeming to do anything, Passepartout responded, **WILL USE SOMETHING MUCH BIGGER**. Aouda's arched eyebrow and expression showed his message had been received.

Passepartout was correct, though—the rest in Chicago did them all good, time to get an untroubled sleep, deposited in spare rooms on the second floor of the Sax farmhouse, and awakening on Tuesday, the 19th of November, for a relaxed breakfast and some much welcomed bathing and personal grooming. Aouda even had a chance to use her electric engine to invigorate all her devices, Maker finding the little machine both ingenious and amusing to see pistoning away on a table in the Sax's parlor.

This was also the most distance between his comb and Phileas

Fogg's watch since their paths had separated on the *Carnatic*, and Passepartout made the most of it. With the Moon not setting until eleven the next morning, he had all the night to reconnoiter around the buildings under its wan glow. He pressed as close as he could from the trees to Barbicane's cannon complex, just to ascertain any changes not covered in his previous visit. But other than Captain Nicholl and his two gears, Passepartout's main focus that night was Colonel Moran's house and those living within it. The men there—and they were all men—were variously armed, but nothing beyond what one would expect people of this era and region to possess.

San Francisco was certainly better supplied with domesticated firearms than all of Stone's Hill.

There were also no objects within Moran's house of any sophisticated technology, making that airship all the more anachronistic a tool to employ—unless that was the right word, *employ*. The airship a contraption they did not *own*, but merely rented, possibly from some underfunded but ambitious inventor.

Passepartout thought about all that when he returned to the vicinity of the Barbicane house, his comb confirming Nicholl's presence and the gears still in their separate pockets. Retiring some ways into the woods, Passepartout settled on a large stump, comfortably flat across the top, crossing his legs and shutting his eyes, working down into what often passed for sleep in his metabolism.

He wondered what thoughts were going through the duplicitous Nicholl's mind right now, a fellow about to be shot into space on a craft whose trajectory he was conspiring to corrupt. That required a certain steely resolve, wouldn't it?

In such a manner, mentally bobbing up and down, in and out and around awareness of his surroundings, Passepartout consumed the next eleven hours on the stump. What noises there were, fell nowhere close—until he heard a rustle of the grasses. Opening his eyes, he saw Victor Barbicane strolling around the back of the house, smoking a cigar. As the young Barbicane was not among those plunging into the Pacific Ocean twenty-four hours from now, he decided he did not need to avoid all interaction with this one. Besides, he had a curiosity about the Barbicane heir, whom he had only observed at a distance before, although among those surveyed by his comb in the house, and so made no effort to move away when that personage ambled in his direction.

It was not every day one saw a man in a somewhat worn suit and comical round hat, perched casually on a block in the middle of the unsawn forest, like a weary elf that had lost his way. Except this man did not look tired to Victor, who called when near, "You look pensive, sir."

"It has been said of me, before. I am Jean, a French visitor, here for the great concussion tomorrow."

Victor extended a hand, not the one with the cigar, "Many of your tribe here. Victor Barbicane, grounded adventurer."

"I have heard of you, and your father's audacious ambition. Grounded, you say. You are disappointed at not being included?"

"I can't say I'm not curious to go, just for what they'll see, but more than that, not to be there to help, in case anything goes wrong. I faced greater dangers in the War. I don't feel right being down here."

"What skill and sense of purpose you must have, to have fought so, and come to be here now, successfully. But, I think, your father may also travel with an easier conscience, knowing a child such as you remains safely behind."

"Now you sound like him."

Passepartout smiled. "I will take that as a welcome compliment of common humanity."

A rumble of thunder startled Victor, who puzzled, "There's been more *thunder* lately, but not any rain."

"An eccentricity of the Florida season, perhaps. I shall leave you to enjoy your cigar."

Passepartout rose from his stump, and departed for *Kestrel*'s clearing, feeling inspired and yet saddened by his words with Victor Barbicane. So loyal to the father, resolute and honorable—and Passepartout, setting himself (and Phileas Fogg and lady friends) squarely against their intent. No chance at all of Barbicane reaching the Moon in *Columbiad*, futility foreseen.

As Passepartout arrived at the *Kestrel*, Fogg called, "I assume everything remains in order here."

"So far as I may judge. All the Barbicane expedition are resting at their house—the Moran gang likewise. I chatted briefly with the Victor Barbicane—seems a pleasant child."

"Any encounters with Dupin?" Fogg asked.

"None," Passepartout answered. "I imagined he was at the boarding house, but did not check."

"Aouda has volunteered to accompany Maker on her flight tomorrow," Fogg said then. Passepartout could not tell how much of Fogg's tone tempered a recognition of her bravery with concern over the lady's safety.

"She can use an extra eye in the seat. There will be much acceleration," Aouda added.

"*We* will be attending to the carpetbag, Passepartout," Fogg said dryly, "while we watch the *Columbiad* fire from the ground, attending to any eccentricities."

Maker brought out a lunchbox for Passepartout. "Mr. Fogg said you seemed to like fried chicken, and I recalled what you said about mine."

Passepartout bowed as he accepted the handle, smiling warmly. He *was* hungry.

"We also made some sandwiches, for later," Maker added.

While Passepartout dug into the lunchbox contents, Fogg asked, "Do you play whist, Miss Maker?"

"No, can't say I do. Not much for games."

"Too bad," Fogg said. "We have a few hours to fill before dusk, when you make for the pavilion again to follow those false gears to their destination."

"Does he get nervous when he's not on the move?" Maker asked Aouda and Passepartout, who both chuckled at the truthfulness of her snap character assessment. Even Phileas Fogg was smiling.

"We have yet to see him not moving," Aouda joked.

"Jean could tell us stories, where you've all been these last months," Maker said. "I'd like to know that."

And so Passepartout showed a side of himself neither Phileas Fogg nor Aouda had seen from him before. Not merely recounting what had happened since he had been taken on as Fogg's valet, but skillfully editing out all those aspects that might trouble a smooth or politic narrative. Such as, that the three of them were at that very moment in the Pacific Ocean on the SS *General Grant*, where it was already November 20th. Or anything at all about their travels across the American wilderness by rail, none of which had happened yet. Or, of course, a little nicety like Phileas Fogg's Time Machine parked in a Chicago warehouse. And certainly no lurid incidents they had occasioned along the way, from tossing men overboard or throwing them down stairs on ocean liners, to firing electric guns at presumptuous stalkers in Japanese gardens.

The result was an entertaining travelers' *tour de force* that held Maker's interest admirably, from too much architecture seen only in passing, to Aouda's indisputably exciting rescue in India. Both Phileas Fogg and Aouda were impressed with how much he managed to tell entertainingly and extensively without saying anything that wasn't true.

The shadows of dusk were embracing Stone's Hill, around six o'clock, when Passepartout commenced copious descriptions (with bounding physical reenactments) of the rehearsing he had to do for the Tingou acrobats in Yokohama. Aouda smirked and shook her head, but not because of the valet's ingratiating show, but something else altogether.

"I just got the signal from *Deimos*," Aouda whispered to Phileas

Fogg, "the one about their leaving Diadem. I almost answered him—*again*," she winced.

She realized how confusing Time Travel could be, unraveling very quickly the skein of temporality. No wonder Phileas Fogg had so often kept his own counsel on it, to avoid exactly that muddle of duplication.

C3 80

By the time the Moon rose over the Florida glades, just on half past nine, Passepartout, Aouda and Thomasina Maker had deployed themselves once more at the spot in the trees where they had initially reconnoitered Barbicane's launch pavilion the night before. They could not be certain from where the saboteurs might approach tonight, so stayed well back from the scene, relying on Maker's goggles and the moonlight to assist their observation. They watched as Wilson and the other man went about their rounds as before, around and around, thrice to the hour more or less.

Such care in choosing a location proved wise, as just before eleven o'clock Sebastian Moran showed up, carrying a shielded lantern, accompanied by Captain Nicholl and a third man from the house Moran had let. Moran's gang had obviously assessed the terrain and had arrived at the same tactical solution, positioning themselves in the trees just north of where Passepartout's trio had stood the night before.

The critical element for their scheme—and why they needed at least one man on the guard route—turned out to be the *time*. When the guards progressed down the pavilion stairs for the *Columbiad* shed on their first cycle after 11 PM, as they reached the far side of the barn, Thomas Wilson stopped, and invited his companion to indulge in a smoke. This delay allowed Moran, Nicholl and the other to sprint across the open ground on the north side, and up the stairs.

Reaching the door, the third man pulled out implements and quickly unlocked it. Once inside, Moran unshielded the lantern so that their cracksman could open the cover to the timing console, whereupon Nicholl effected the replacement of the gears as Maker had. The flashing of the lantern light, though slight, was still visible enough to show why it was the innocent second guard who needed to be kept out of the way while the work was done. They all did their job expeditiously (though hardly at the speed of Passepartout's team). When Nicholl had finished, the third man relocked the cover, and the door outside as they left.

While Nicholl and the cracksman made away without delay, Moran went south far enough to be able to signal Wilson at the shed with brief flashes from the lamp (the other guard having been maneuvered so as to keep his back to that direction). Wilson putting out his cigarette on the ground confirmed the message was received.

Moran at once closed the lantern, and headed off to follow Nicholl and the other into the night, while Wilson and the hapless dupe continued on their rounds.

Once they were done, Passepartout, Aouda and Maker prepared for a repeat of their actions from the night before, which they began on the next pass the guards made around the shed, and accomplished with equal agility this time. Maker gave Nicholl's fakes afterward to Passepartout, "Here, as souvenirs."

And, off in his place of skilled concealment, Auguste Dupin had taken in both these purloining shows with his customary clinical detachment. In his opinion, Passepartout's team were clearly superior on counts of speed, grace and stealth.

ɞ ʂɔ

While Phileas Fogg and Passepartout stood sentry beside *Kestrel* later that night, Maker and Aouda slept inside, one to each seat, curled up somewhat from the narrow width, but not uncomfortable. When the Moon reached the zenith around quarter past four on Wednesday morning, the 20th of November, Fogg climbed up onto *Kestrel*'s afterdeck to lay down on it and gaze up at the lunar circle.

"A quarter of a million miles away," Fogg said quietly to Passepartout when he came over to see whether he had fallen asleep. Keeping his eyes on the Moon, "How long would it take for your ship to reach it? Before my Time Machine arrived, to hobble it?"

"That depends on a great deal, Mr. Fogg. That moon is actually so close, it is harder to get to than some things much farther away. Let us say, under mediocre conditions, we could easily be there in a few hours."

"And have you done so?"

"Near enough, several times." Passepartout shrugged, "It looks about the same from the other side, in case you were wondering."

In due course, Fogg did slip into sleep, there on the back of the *Kestrel*, to be awakened five hours later by a poke from Aouda. The Moon was now on the horizon, near to setting, while the morning sky was clear and bright all about.

"Good morning, Phileas. Less than three hours from the firing."

The sound of a brass ensemble could be heard faintly when Fogg sat upright and slid off the back of *Kestrel* to the ground, stretching and tempering arms and back and neck.

"They brought in a band?" Fogg asked.

"Yes, been practicing all morning," Aouda said, "if you can call it that."

"It may be the best they could find—Tampa Town's not very big, is it?" Maker was ever mindful of the laborer along with the labor.

The next half hour was filled with preparation for the interception. Maker reminded Aouda of the workings of the hoods she had brought in the case, and which they would both be wearing to protect them while at such high altitude. "Just breathe normally, as if out on a slow stroll."

"They will be turning *Columbiad*'s engines on soon," Passepartout warned Fogg. "We should be leaving."

Fogg nodded, then turned to Aouda and Maker, doffing his hat, "Ladies, you both look fetching in your cowls. We shall see you here, once our deeds are done."

Phileas Fogg, Passepartout and the carpetbag departed for the cannon—or at least a forested glen near enough to catch good sight of it, and the quite large crowd of people who had gathered around for the firing. The band was blaring away, cheers were heard. Somewhere in the throng they supposed Dupin would be milling—or perhaps not. And likewise for Sebastian Moran and his company—or not. There were so many people about, even Passepartout's comb might have been taxed to tease them out, and Fogg's watch was a most proximate distraction.

Passepartout climbed one tree to catch a better view, assisted by the glasses. He could now see the *Columbiad* capsule had been rolled out in front of the tunnel entrance, and Impey Barbicane mounted it to give a short speech, not easily heard from where Fogg and Passepartout were. Impey Barbicane gave Victor a final warm embrace, before he, Nicholl and Ardan climbed a temporary ladder and through the hatch, which was then sealed.

The locomotive surged to life to roll the car down into the tunnel, the band serenading all the way. Within that dark seclusion, the temporary visitor observation balcony having been removed, machinery below the turning gears were brought around from either side to ease the capsule into the opening of the barrel, and the connections to the lower canisters made. The railcar then rolled back down the tunnel, far enough to allow the cannon hatchway to be closed.

A deep low quavering hum began to throb all around, and three distinctive chimes rang on Phileas Fogg's watch—as was happening simultaneously out on the deck of the *Nautilus* a quarter of the way around the world. Here, though, the sound of Power X was pervasive—hair pricking on the back of the neck strange, intense. The gem labeled "**B**" glowed brightly on Fogg's timepiece, owing to their proximity to it, and the ring came to settle with the letter by *XII* as Fogg faced the cannon, where inside its confines, the now lengthened *Columbiad* was being lowered by magnetic ratchet down to the bottom of the shaft.

A long thunderclap joined the thrum of the *Columbiad*'s engines, a persistent rumble that discerning ears could hear circling the cannon at considerable distance. A few thought the cannon had fired—but no, Victor Barbicane was just now entering the launch pavilion to supervise the aiming. Shortly after, the scrape and wrenching of giant gears were added to the symphon of Power X and *Kestrel*'s invisible roar. The cannon slowly angled from vertical—just enough, and then no farther.

When *Columbiad* was finally fired, the bone-shaking detonation caught everyone by surprise—even Passepartout, almost falling out of the tree. The capsule and its attached train of service canisters shot from the barrel, racing into the air, an eerie yellowish-green glow burning at the end like embers of some atomic cigar. All eyes were on this unprecedented spectacle, trying to follow its course with or without lenses.

Who among them would have noted that inconspicuous brown smudge in the sky moving so hastily after it?

ଓ ଛ

Kestrel was climbing higher and faster by the second, Aouda and Maker in the protective rarified altitude masks, tubes connecting them to air tanks. The very air began to ionize not only around the glass dome, but across the front cowl, even as the atmosphere grew thinner as they chased after *Columbiad*. The acceleration was crushing, with the firing rockets screaming to match.

As they navigated to intercept *Columbiad*, they had to fly up and over it, dodging the aft canisters as they were broken off during the climb—one burning up from the friction of the air over the mid-Atlantic, the other cascading in flames five minutes later above the Canary Islands. Finally Maker had brought them up to the front capsule, dropping to it and turning on the magnetic attachments emanating from four angled plates that extended out from the hull on pivots, temporarily making the two crafts one.

"We have to follow that yellow arc on the center gauge," Maker yelled, "just till the end, slowing them and us down, until nothing can prevent their drop."

They were high above the atmosphere in space, scarcely a quarter hour since leaving Florida, and they had already crossed the Atlantic Ocean. The forced hybrid of *Kestrel-Columbiad* chased the night, as the sun set on the north of Africa below them, the Mediterranean Sea beyond wine dark to their left.

The roar inside *Kestrel* was too intense to hear by shared vibration any of what went on inside the *Columbiad* below them: the scrambling in an arc of topsy-turvy gravitation, alarms going off as the next canister broke from the fourth (disappearing in another fiery streak above the Sahara Desert) because of the strain caused as *Kestrel* continued to force the craft off its trajectory. Their plight finally compelled those inside to let the fourth one go prematurely, watching from the window (which faced down towards the Earth) as it plummeted into the atmosphere, flashing into incandescence as it burned up over Egypt, a brief artificial shooting star over the Pyramids.

The next twenty minutes took them across Arabia, Persia, and Afghanistan, then on to glide over the Himalayas, their impassable peaks wrinkling the Tibetan plateau below like a crumpled white carpet. Having now reached their disengagement point, Maker let go of *Columbiad*, leaving the metal bullet to continue on across the black expanse of China, compelled by their curtailed ballistics to drop away towards the Pacific, and whomever Passepartout had arranged to be on hand to receive it.

Kestrel had to slow too, diving keel first, blunting its ablative descent with blasts from its angled lifting nozzles, incrementing them towards a more familiar supersonic speed. They were now seeing a second dawn, the islands of the Hawaiian ridge now discernable on their right, so many brown volcanic dots poking up from the Pacific blue.

ೞ ಐ

The crowds were dispersing rapidly now that the *Columbiad* had departed. While Passepartout wriggled down from his tree perch, Phileas Fogg signaled three chimes on his watch. Handing his valet the carpetbag, Fogg led them out of the trees and into the human current towards the boarding house in the village. But before they reached it, Fogg spotted Auguste Dupin and jogged ahead to him, patting his shoulder.

Dupin glanced back, and stopped, "Ah, you *are* about. I could not *resist* seeing the thing go off, but I *was* looking for you."

"I have one last mission for you, before your trip to New York," Fogg said. "But there should be just enough time for it."

ೞ ಐ

Once *Kestrel* reached lower altitude and speed, Maker extended the side wings. Then she disconnected her cowl and pulled it off, Aouda doing likewise. "We still have about three thousand miles to go, Aouda, across Mexico and the Caribbean. We should be back in Florida ... three?" Then Maker sighed, "I'm glad it worked."

Just as they knew it must, Aouda thought, recalling their morning aboard the *Nautilus*, taking place at this very moment. How much all their lives had changed since then.

Kestrel did indeed land in Florida at three that afternoon, Phileas

Fogg and Passepartout waiting for them in the clearing, Maker retracting the side wings as they descended.

Aouda felt drained by their flight, but utterly thrilled. The moment she had the glass door open, she cried as she climbed out, "Around the world in *a hundred and eighty minutes*, Phileas! Not eighty days."

Phileas Fogg took both of her hands in his, beaming a smile at her as he assisted her step to the ground, and then they embraced, there in the languid humidity of Stone's Hill.

"You seem well by the experience," Fogg decided. Then he turned to Passepartout, "We have done what we set out to, have we not?"

Passepartout could not argue with that.

"Will your *Kestrel* need to cool off for a time, Miss Maker?" Fogg asked, "Or may we return to Chicago now?"

"Goodbye, Florida!" Maker jokingly saluted, and soon were on their way again.

A half hour later, flying over the Cumberland Mountains of Tennessee at forty thousand feet, trailing another plume of white cloud behind them, Phileas Fogg turned to Aouda, "Now we may recall your concern about the Barbicane party's safety on their return."

Passepartout and Aouda both realized where this was going.

Fogg leaned over to hail Maker, "Would you oblige us another flight in your *Kestrel* next month? There is more to learn about those vessels we spied at sea, and several of our own whose safety I am anxious to guarantee."

"Your friends from the Pacific?" Maker asked. When Fogg nodded, Maker said, "How long, and where?"

"It would involve a day or two, flying around the Atlantic—another stop in Florida. We would call upon you round about midnight, on the morning of the 7th of December."

"I'll keep my lanterns burning," Maker told him.

The *Kestrel* settled down through the copper roof panels of Maker's foundry around four o'clock, a half hour before sunset. After rearranging their luggage contents, Maker signaled Grenadier and the Saxes that they'd be using the big carriage. Grenadier soon brought the landau, and Mrs. Sax waved them on their way from the gate.

Rocking slowly down the dirt ways northeast toward the city, Aouda joked, "This seems rather dull compared to *Kestrel*."

"Not as exciting as being seen in that when I don't want to be," Maker replied.

"We know *that* well enough," Aouda agreed, especially with *Deimos* being so much bigger.

As they entered Chicago in the dark, memories of its recent destruction flashed through Maker's thoughts. "We flew *Kestrel* out during the Fire, but couldn't see any safe way to rescue people. God help me, the blaze looked grand from the air."

When Maker brought them up Sherman Street along the west façade of the railroad station, Fogg called, "You may let us out here, I think. Thank you again."

"And see you on the Seventh," Maker said.

As Maker and the quiet Grenadier drove away, Fogg said amiably, "Imagine how much quicker life will be once everyone has motor carriages."

26*bis*. IN WHICH PHILEAS FOGG AND PARTY ARE DRAWN TO EMULATE THE METHOD OF C. AUGUSTE DUPIN

The Wabash Warehouse was closed and locked for the night when Phileas Fogg, Passepartout, and Aouda entered by the alley door. Knowing now Fogg's procedure, Passepartout was at the ready to help lower the ramp door of the second crate, pull the Time Machine out onto the floor, and close the box afterward.

When Fogg turned it on, the dials displayed **1872 AD NOV 18 AM 09:25** but quickly adjusted to **1872 AD NOV 21 AM 12:18**, it already being the next morning by Greenwich Time.

This time, when the Machine commenced its "motion" Aouda and Passepartout noticed Phileas Fogg pushed the lever *forward* rather than back, and the disc behind them rotated in the opposite direction, anticlockwise. Otherwise, the phenomena were comparable, even down to the slow wagon visible through the briefly open street doors amid the sliding shadows and flickering light.

Fogg's destination being only fifteen days in the future, they arrived at **1872 AD DEC 7 AM 03:07** in slightly over thirty seconds. It was a little after 9 PM there in Chicago, and still December 6th in Illinois—Fogg's watch again chiming as it adjusted to the current GMT.

While Passepartout and Fogg opened the second box to slip the Time Machine into it, Aouda sadly admitted, "Traveling through Time seems improperly banal compared to *Kestrel*."

"Should I have added deafening rumbles to it, like the *Columbiad*?" Fogg asked dryly, locking up the crate. "Or organ choirs, perhaps?"

Passepartout smiled at the humor, but recognized a deeper significance, "The ease of it is a puzzlement to me, too, *mademoiselle*. But the *quiet* means it wastes no energy—the purest efficiency. Beyond that, I have learned in my many years, not to fret too much over a science one does not understand—," shooting a wry look at Phileas Fogg, "—still less to meddle with."

The travelers' routine next was expected: venture the blocks to the railroad station to hail a carriage, which was much easier this early time of night, passengers in volume still coming and going. Clip-clopping down the dirt roads to Thomasina Maker's country foundry afterward, they arrived just as the half Moon was about to set. Mrs. Sax was waiting for them on the porch, bundled in a voluminous coat and nursing the shotgun in her lap before rising to step to the gate, which she had already unlocked but pushed open for them as courtesy.

"She's expecting you, Frenchman. And she's been busy."

Passepartout rapped on Maker's door, and opened it on his own.

Maker was drinking a cup of coffee, lost in thought over a collection of maps strewn across a table near the middle of what passed for a parlor off to their right. Hearing them enter, she put down the beverage and strode towards the door to greet Passepartout, Aouda and Fogg.

"I've been thinking about your enemy ships," Maker said. "Provisioning, crews. It takes a lot of people and parts to put on a show like that. Half of *Great Eastern*'s crew—two hundred men, just to shovel coal. These are trails your Frenchmen might not have spotted because they were looking from the top down."

She gestured back towards her parlor, beckoning them to follow to the maps. A large one of Florida was topmost. "With apologies, I talked with Mr. Swift, told him what I saw out in the ocean. Don't worry, I said I was on another testing flight, never mentioned any passengers, but I did say I heard the big ship was hired by that Augustus Moran, just to give him a name to chew on."

Maker paused for them to think about that before continuing. "No one knows better than Mr. Barton Swift who to ask about where to buy this or that, or who might have just bought this or that. It didn't take long for the agents at his shipping line to catch the scent, starting with the victuals: they've been buying volumes of food for the crews, more lavish fare, too, for at least a few aboard. And then there's all that *steel*: one of the ironclads was Confederate surplus, and one of their Union double turrets was bought all the way from France—lots of middle steps on that one. Three large coal tenders have been hired too, from three ports. But I didn't see any roundabout *Great Eastern*, did you?"

Passepartout, Fogg and Aouda could recall none, and remained silent. "Which means they must have an anchorage somewhere, likely on the east coast," Maker waved a hand along the map.

Phileas Fogg was nodding agreement, "Something *temporary*, sailing out and back as needed perhaps."

Maker paused again, the look of someone who hated not knowing something. "The airships are the cipher. Whoever built those did so on the sly, like me—not even the Weldon Institute in Philadelphia had heard of them, though Mr. Swift couldn't get *too* pokey on his questions." She leaned back against the table, facing her visitors, her features cast into relief by the glow of the plain electric chandelier above.

"And then there's the *armament*, lots of it: shells for the old ironclads, plenty of small arms, and those new Gatling guns. Money has been thrown around, my friends. Swift caught whiff of several London bankers, but suspects they were just middlers. All that makes sense. What raised Swift's eyebrows—and *mine*—were Whitehead torpedoes, at least a dozen, shipped on the quiet through Charleston, and signed for by that Colonel Sebastian Moran."

Fogg was surprised: "By *name*?!"

"Yep," Maker replied.

Aouda offered, "They may not have realized anyone might be looking that far afield."

Passepartout turned most quizzical, "Naval torpedoes do not belong on an airship, do they?"

"No, the weight would be a burden, even regular ordnance would be heavy," Aouda said.

"They certainly weren't thinking to sink *Columbiad* with them," Passepartout went on, "not when the whole object was to seize it intact."

Maker got a notion, "Maybe barter, a price demanded by somebody in their gang for service tendered."

Fogg leapt at the inference of that, "Someone with a submarine boat, equipped to take them, yes. Moran hires some jobbers with an experimental submersible, potentially very useful for their salvage, but they'll only do the deed in exchange for the torpedoes, enabling them to take up marauding after."

Aouda joined the chase, nodding, "Something they might not be able to acquire on their own, at least not openly, so they're persuaded to cooperate, leaving the getting to Moran. If that's true, Moran could be relying on many mercenaries, clever and desperate ones—dangerous, perhaps, for him or us."

"*Mon dieu*," Passepartout exclaimed, "we're all beginning to ratiocinate like Dupin."

"There are worse fates," Phileas Fogg said. Seeing a map of the Atlantic Ocean peeking out from under the Florida chart, Fogg pulled that out and set his watch down over near Iceland. Pointing to the timepiece, he asked Maker, "How long will it take to fly *there*?"

"That's a long way from Moran's ironclads. Three hours maybe, faster if I rush."

"No, that should do," Fogg decided.

27*bis*. IN WHICH MATTERS OF GRAVE CONSEQUENCE WERE INSUFFICIENTLY APPRECIATED AT THE TIME

The *Kestrel* exited the foundry's copper roof and headed out northeast across Lake Michigan just after one o'clock on Saturday morning, December 7th, Fogg and Aouda switching their seat positions from last time (Fogg now to port), so each might get a different view. A small food basket rested between Maker and Passepartout, while Fogg rode herd on the carpetbag. Aouda still had to remove her hat.

Their smooth acceleration traversed the hundred miles of water in under ten minutes. The next quarter hour was occupied crossing the Michigan peninsula, followed by the waters of Lake Huron. At this dead of night and no Moon up, not much of scenic inspiration could be gleaned from forty thousand feet.

The next hour took them a further thousand miles across Canadian Quebec, to shoot over Labrador and on to yet another thousand miles of restless Atlantic waves. Maker brought *Kestrel* below the speed of sound as they glanced right of the tip of Greenland. "We'll creep on the rest of the way," she explained, "so we won't rattle your *Deimos* when we pass."

"They're up ahead, well over the horizon," Fogg said, tracking the whereabouts of Aouda's flyer and the *Nautilus* with his watch. Turning to Aouda, "Is there any danger of your craft noticing us?"

"Not at this height. For obvious reasons, my instruments were honed to detect things flying alongside or below us, like the airship. Had I any idea something so small as this could be darting high above us ... well, I'll have to adjust the sensitivity," Aouda smiled.

Deimos still had another hour of flight to reach Nemo's rendezvous when *Kestrel* shot over it in the first glimmerings of dawn, some hundred miles off the Greenland coast. Not long after, Aouda reported, "Srikar's signaling *Deimos* that they've surfaced. We must be close."

They were. Maker's special goggles afforded her broad views of the area below. She addressed one telescopic image to her central screen, revealing the submarine's saw-ribbed prow and fins, "So that's the devil boat!"

Maker gently settled *Kestrel* down on the sea a safe distance from the *Nautilus*, partially submerging her craft so that they could ease closer. With the interior illumination turned to a minimum, only a light reflecting directly off the glass dome might betray their presence, but the lapping waves dissuaded that. Maker elevated a tiny viewer from the tube on the aft deck, giving a fairly clear (though unavoidably bobbing) view of the submarine ahead.

When *Deimos* glided smoothly into view to land beside *Nautilus*' portside, Maker cried, "That's a beauty."

"Thank you," Aouda said, "though it's nothing so fast as this."

Those aboard the *Kestrel* watched on the screen (or used their glasses to see) as Impey Barbicane, Captain Nicholl and Michel Ardan were transferred to Robur's care. Then a pantomime ensued as Nemo and Robur grappled with how best to load the Berthon collapsible boat from *Nautilus* to *Deimos*. While it would fit inside well enough, getting the curved wood frame through the narrow dorsal deck hatch proved a topological jamb.

Aouda surmised from Robur's gesturing that he was suggesting they could bring *Deimos* up in a hover and take it through a side hatch, but that her brother found this impractical. Nemo evidently suggested the boat be unfolded and lashed in its open position on *Deimos*' afterdeck, his expression showing nods of satisfaction when this was done by several of *Nautilus*' crew.

Deimos had flown away and the sun was just rising when the propeller on Nemo's ship began to churn the sea, *Nautilus* soon submerging and continuing its southerly course.

Maker decided to do likewise, curious to see the notorious scourge of the sea close up. Coming up behind it, the *Nautilus* first reminded Maker of a giant rust-red tuna. Light was streaming from the great window to starboard amidships, but not from its mate to port (the covering iris being closed), so Maker piloted *Kestrel* along that side of the hull to avoid being seen. They were passing where the skiff was docked when Maker steered *Kestrel* lower, down below the midline rib that extended laterally all along *Nautilus*' length, to a gap in the keel underneath the viewing port, where a hatch (also understandably closed) allowed the submariners egress when in their diving gear.

Coming up above the midline rib, *Kestrel* was just below the pilot's bubble, where the merest glimpse could be had of Nemo at the *Nautilus*' wheel, intent on the sea ahead and not the tiny craft pacing them that morning. Aouda looked up at her brother, welling with emotion, smiling with commingled admiration and regret for Srikar's accomplishments and the price both siblings had paid for their dangerous achievements.

Maker slowed *Kestrel*, allowing *Nautilus* to pull ahead of them, the submarine's propeller wake jostling them somewhat. "If she keeps on that heading long enough, they may bump into Moran's boats down south."

Aouda perked at that, but said nothing of it.

Maker steered *Kestrel* around to the north, then pushed the engines to accelerate them up and out of the water, into flight. As the side wings extended, Maker turned the vehicle about, to shoot off on a southwesterly tack. The sun was rising now, bathing the trackless sea ahead in a welcoming roseate glow.

"I'm steering around your ship," Maker shouted to Aouda behind her. "Where are they headed, back to Florida?"

"Yes. Barbicane and the others will be dropped off in their boat, to row ashore. They'll be there in … fifteen hours."

"Umm, well, we've already passed them," Maker reported. "We'll go above sound now. Plenty of time for us to take a longer look at the Moran flotilla before they get there."

Over the next hour, *Kestrel* chased the dawn, skirting the Newfoundland coast off to their right. Forty-five minutes later, a tiny island could be seen in the vast sea. "Bermuda," Maker called out, and began to slow *Kestrel*, dropping altitude somewhat, "Somewhere off ahead we should find the *Great Eastern*."

‹๓ ๏›

Aboard the flying ship *Albatross*, a lieutenant pointed out the window to a long thin cloud streak off to their west, high in the morning sky. "Look, Commander," he yelled over the roar of their six lifting rotors, "the *Columbiad*?"

Dapper in his uniform of no official capacity or national jurisdiction, Commander Blake raised a spyglass to the spot. The cloud grew even as he watched, lengthening to the south. He thought he could see *something* to the left of it, at the point where new cloud seemed to be appearing, a dark little spot. "Could be. They're already overdue." The cloud smudged beside the spot, and no more cloud formed. "Odd, if a meteor. Mark it in the log," he ordered.

‹๓ ๏›

Thomasina Maker was bringing *Kestrel* lower and slower after her instruments detected the flying machine below them to the east. Once close enough to identify it as the rotor craft they had seen on the floating platform last month, Maker said, "Quite a good range for patrol. Think they're looking for Barbicane?"

"They should have no idea where to *look*," Passepartout said.

"Then they're either playing busy, or watching who's looking at *them*," Maker decided. "Which ever, we'll leave you, little boat."

Kestrel headed southeast, towards some vessels on their horizon, which turned out to be some warship of the American navy, and the other at some distance (possibly following), one of Moran's ironclads. Much farther on, the *Great Eastern* and the other ships still lay about where that had been when Maker had first flown over them, though both of the platforms on the former Confederate ironclad were empty.

And nestled by the *Great Eastern* was another boat. "Coal tender," Fogg noted.

"They do need to *feed*," Maker joked. Checking over her longest

280

ranged instruments, she mused, "I wonder where the other airship is."

"To the northwest, or so we have reason to believe," Aouda said, then pointed to the long and short vessels she could see down on either side under the edge of the platform, now more visible with the deck above no longer filled by the propeller-festooned flying ship. "Look what's docked at that barge."

"Submersibles," Passepartout hissed. "You were right, Mr. Fogg."

"We'd better go look, then." There being only one ironclad escorting *Eastern*'s starboard flank, Maker dived *Kestrel* into the sea an appropriate distance away in that direction, and headed back under the water, passing beneath the keel of the iron giant, her great paddles sitting idle, to find that platform ship beyond, and the submarine vessels moored there.

The one on the starboard side they reached first was an oval gunmetal gray tube of about a hundred feet in length, its front quarter tethered to the ship, a structural bulge along its top protruding above the water and ringed by a low railing. It was a design that looked familiar to Phileas Fogg.

"That resembles the older French submarine work," Fogg said, turning to Aouda, "The same experiments your brother studied almost twenty years ago, improving on when he built his *Nautilus*."

Maker was spinning *Kestrel* around so they were facing the prow of the craft, where four circular hatches could be seen. "Going on what I know of the dimensions of a Whitehead Torpedo, I'd say there's the covers for four."

Passepartout had brought out his comb, closing his eyes and moving it to and fro, up and down, some of the tines occasionally moving a little, accompanied by a tiny crackling hum. He opened his eyes, "There are tubular shafts behind the covers, all empty. As near as I can tell—in such proximity to Mr. Fogg's watch."

Maker brought *Kestrel* closer to the surface, pulling away from the vessel and extending her viewer from the rear deck tube. This gave them a panorama of the ship where the submarine was docked. The airship landing platform above put much into shadow, but enough morning light cast underneath to reveal half a dozen Whitehead torpedoes, square blocks affixed to either end so they might be stacked as they were now, three high and apparently two deep.

"Available, but not installed," Aouda sighed. "May we see the other submarine?"

Maker nodded, and submerged *Kestrel*, gliding under the keel of the platform ship to the other side, where a much stouter vessel lay: half the length of its partner, but bigger around, more of a *Nautilus*-red iron color, with only an observation turret and two small railings on its top surface. It too had four hatches on its front, in a bulging segment of its hull that suggested it had been modified subsequent to its original construction. Passepartout's comb confirmed these were just as empty—and a periscopic assessment of the deck storage beyond showed a similar array of Whitehead torpedoes, though less easily spied as this side of the ship lay in morning shade.

"This reminds me more of the recent French submarine design," Fogg said. "But identical torpedo fittings—there we have separate engineers adapting to a common specification."

"And we may imagine by *whom*," Aouda said. "I should like to see more of that *Great Eastern*, if you would, Miss Maker."

"As would I, Princess," and Maker piloted them away from the platform ship and over to the Leviathan.

The coal tender was just finishing loading through a side hatch aft of the paddle wheel as they neared the *Great Eastern*'s port side, the hull looming forty feet above the waterline and thereby easily filling *Kestrel*'s periscopic view as Maker adjust the angle to play along the side of the ship. There was a smaller steamboat docked by an open hatch nearer the bow, which Phileas Fogg thought might be used as packet runners to and from the coast. Two small cannon barrels could be seen poking through openings in the bulwarks towards the stern, while the barrels of ten Gatling guns peeked from under canvas covers over the rail from stem to stern. All aboard *Kestrel* assumed the starboard was equivalently armed.

As for the crane built onto *Great Eastern*'s stern, it was as large as Dupin had described, with a ratcheted grappling fixture dangling from its frame, ideally suited for picking up something of the dimensions and weight of Impey Barbicane's *Columbiad*. Had it had only been given the chance.

"Dupin was right—this is a profligate venture," Fogg said. "Two weeks now after their failure, I wonder if any among them are having pangs of doubt."

"Or frustration," Passepartout countered, "a fuel for clumsy reaction."

"It is still the morning," Fogg said, "*Deimos* won't arrive on the scene until nightfall. We may as well make for land, and see what's what at Stone's Hill."

Maker kept *Kestrel* submerged another ten miles before launching into the air, racing to the coast and across Florida once more to land in their now familiar clearing just after nine o'clock local time. Phileas Fogg decided he needed a shave, so fished out his grooming case from the carpetbag and attended to that, borrowing a dash of moisture for his shaving powder from the flagon of water Maker had brought along in her basket.

Checking his watch afterward, Fogg now knew his other temporal self was awake back on the Union Pacific train, whereupon he triggered two chimes on the timepiece.

While Passepartout and Maker remained at *Kestrel* to share her basket of meats, cheeses, bread and wine, Phileas Fogg and Aouda set off into Stone's Hill. The town had quieted down considerably from the hubbub of the Barbicane launch a fortnight before, though many newspaper correspondents and the scientifically curious had remained on hand until the *Columbiad* explorers were either returned to Earth, or their grim fate revealed by some observant astronomer.

From the porch at the boardinghouse, Auguste Dupin saw their passage, Aouda and Fogg arm in arm, confidently striding down the dirt avenue because so many people they worried they might have run into before weren't there to run into now.

"We were just going to see what had happened at the cannon," Aouda said as Dupin joined them.

"It does hold the imagination and landscape, doesn't it?" Dupin said. The tip of the cannon dominated the view east.

"Not easy to overlook an iron mountain, Dupin," Fogg said. "Even buried nine hundred feet in the earth."

"What do you think they'll do with it?" Aouda posed as they continued on to Barbicane's enclave.

Dupin smiled, "Put up a little sign: Slightly Used Moon Cannon, to Let."

Looking Aouda and Fogg over, and recalling their identical attire at the boardinghouse the fortnight before, Dupin asked Fogg, "Did you pack no change of clothes?"

"We seldom have the time, my so observant friend," Fogg replied.

While Stone's Hill was less busy, the Barbicane cannon facility was funereally calm. The windows of the control pavilion were all shuttered, the machinery below silent. A lonely stray dog trotted around the empty paths. The doors were shut at the entrance to the cannon tunnel, too—but one on the *Columbiad* shed lay open, and Aouda led Fogg and Dupin to it.

They encountered Victor Barbicane inside, sitting on the empty railcar platform where *Columbiad* had rested before its departure. Looking up at their approach, the visage was clearly disconsolate.

"What troubles you?" Aouda asked most sympathetically.

"It's five days out to the Moon, and as many back. Even adding a few for exploration, they're days overdue. And no way to communicate. Any number of ways to die out there."

"The presence of this exotic lady may be a true omen for you, I think," Dupin offered.

Fogg smiled. "You may be correct on the omen. I feel beneficial news impends."

"Have you dined?" Dupin asked Fogg and Aouda.

"Not this morning," Fogg replied. "Though my valet and his friend are, I think, enjoying a fine repast as we speak. They may benefit from our finding our own meal—and taking a good time doing it."

"An opportune suggestion, then." Dupin turned to Victor, "Would you care to join us, young Barbicane?"

"No, thank you," Victor answered. "Solitude suits me just now."

At the boardinghouse dining room, Dupin was relieved to find Aouda (a woman of slightly dusky complexion) proved acceptable as a customer in a way the plainly blacker Maker might not. It was not that the detective would have minded her inclusion—indeed, he would have relished it, finding her charming and intriguing—but he also recognized the social inconveniences that might have escalated, and how not having to cross such a prejudiced Rubicon that day simplified the task of ordering and subsequent digestion.

"Ah, I forgot to return this to you," Dupin declared once their orders were placed, handing the small wireless over to Aouda, "I assume it will no longer be needed by me here."

As Aouda returned the device to her pocket, Dupin discoursed slyly, "It requires the most precise tools to open its inner casing, where I am sure one would marvel at the shear precision and elegance of its tiny constituent parts, so many being of perplexingly uncertain function to any unschooled eye. Were one to do that, of course."

"Of course," Aouda smiled.

28*bis*. IN WHICH EVEN THE MOST FELICITOUS OF AERIAL TRAVEL FAILS TO COMFORT ALL ABOARD

Deimos had skimmed past the coast of Newfoundland by early afternoon on December 7th. They had been in the air over seven hours, time enough for the three passengers and those they took for the crew to come to terms with one another. Robur spoke little from the pilot's cupola, Niru even less while monitoring the flyer's banks of instruments, and nothing at all from the contemplative Mr. Xie compacted on the floor.

The two folding seats were made available for their guests' use, but as there were *three* to accommodate, Barbicane and Ardan ended up there. This was abetted by the preference of Captain Nicholl, who found the view of the grizzled Chinaman Xie nearby sufficiently distempering that he far rather sit on the floor back in the side hatch area, where he only needed to glimpse the equally non-Caucasian Niru's shoulder occasionally.

Impey Barbicane had studied what he could of *Deimos'* engineering, though dissuaded from doing too much tactile inspection by a wagging finger or shaken head from Niru. Barbicane noticed in particular the electric lamps aboard—much cooler to the touch than those on Nemo's *Nautilus*. Michel Ardan assessed his curiosity, which stood in notable contrast to the dyspeptic Nicholl.

Niru had made them a lunch. Cooking for disparate cultures could be a chore, but the man prided himself on the ingredients he could juggle to satisfy most every palate. Each elegant black lacquered square plate bore a cup of tea in the center, orbited by tender blocks of *Babi Kecap*, a pork slow-simmered in a sweet soy sauce; small *Lontong* cubes of compressed rice wrapped in banana leaves; spears of *Acar Ketimun*, a spicy pickled cucumber—and a European fork atop a tightly folded napkin, further concession to the travelers' practical expectations.

"These are tastes of my native land," Niru said as he presented the meal to each, who nodded appreciatively—or feigned it, in the case of Captain Nicholl. Despite the unfamiliar seasonings, all the food was splendid and filling. Even Nicholl found it nourishing, however undisposed he was to admit it—and drifted off to a satisfied nap afterward, the empty plate beside him on the deck.

Later on, and only after arching a glance back to see that Nicholl was still sleeping, Ardan softly asked Barbicane, "Will you be building another *Columbiad*?"

"No," Barbicane answered coolly, also keeping his tone private.

"But are you not still curious to explore the Moon, or beyond?"

"Oh, yes. There is much to learn, but not at the price I was too willing to pay."

"It *was* expensive," Ardan conceded.

"You misunderstand. I opened Pandora's Box a crack, and thought what I pulled out was all there was to it, a more intense fire, something to be harnessed as you might a new patent engine. Nemo and this craft opened the box far wider, I know that now. I commend their brilliance, and forbearance. They know what Power X can do; I didn't think that far."

Until Barbicane mentioned it, Ardan hadn't thought about what motivated this strange vessel that carried them along thousands of feet in the air. Although he kept his voice low, there was apprehension to it, "It is propelling us *now*? What *danger* is there to it?"

"In the manner they use it, very little, I imagine. But the amount of fuel powering Nemo's submarine (or this craft, I suspect), if fashioned differently, and by less benign hands, would be more than sufficient to obliterate a city in an instant—say, Paris." That elicited a twinge from the French correspondent, and Barbicane leaned forward to whisper, "And then poison the ruins with an invisible rain to put to shame all the nightmare plagues of old. Better to keep Pandora's Box shut, Mr. Ardan, as long as we can."

Ardan's blood had run cold. He swallowed, and ventured a half-hearted optimism, "Perhaps entrust the secret at least to *democratic* governments, your own, or mine, as a defense should some autocracy come across this terrible knowledge by their own efforts."

Barbicane shook his head, eyes widening over a darkening smile, "Oh, I am sure that will happen eventually. But I will do nothing to hasten it. Such power is far too dangerous to be entrusted even to a government *of the people*. Better everyone think *Columbiad* rests at the bottom of the Atlantic, lost forever to Science." Then Barbicane asked deliberately, "Will you keep our secret, help us sit on the lid of our deadly box?"

Ardan fell silent, and reflected on Barbicane's fearsome admonitions as *Deimos* flew on.

ʚɞ

Kestrel flew out after dark to observe *Deimos*' arrival from on high.

"Your flyer is steering towards that American warship, the one we saw earlier," Maker said.

"That is Robur," Aouda smiled. "Dropping them right on top of a rescue ship, sparing them the long row to shore."

"Moran's ironclad is still behind them—and that rotor ship is appearing on the horizon." Maker rotated a control to put her goggle view of the concentric circles on the central screen, the airship's dot to the east. "We're going to have a crowd."

Maker turned her attention back to the *Deimos*, which had settled down to the water.

Robur prudently did not turn on any external lamps, lest they draw attention to themselves, but there was still some light from the half Moon, low to the west and an hour from setting. Barbicane, Nicholl and Ardan clambered out of the top hatch, working to unlash the collapsible boat, Niru collecting the ropes as they removed them. Robur peered back at them all from the cupola, minding their safety and progress.

The naval steamer, a certain USS *Susquehanna*, was nearly upon them when *Deimos* dropped lower into the water, allowing the boat to float free. Barbicane pushed his oar against one of *Deimos*' fins, nudging them further away, and Niru closed the upper hatch. *Deimos* immediately sank from under them, an action which the captain of the *Susquehanna* witnessed by spyglass but reasonably misinterpreted to be a foundering *Columbiad*.

Thus submerged, the *Deimos* slipped away underwater, though another adjustment of her instruments allowed Maker to trace its departure, following them until *Deimos* was far enough away to break the surface and fly away at full speed to the northwest. Once Aouda's flyer had disappeared from range, *Kestrel* had just enough time to dive down from the heavens and into the waves themselves, to slip close as *Susquehanna* slowed her engines to ease nearer to rescue the Berthon collapsible, heaving in the cold December swells.

Kestrel's periscopic view showed the activity on the *Susquehanna*: rope ladders hurriedly tossed down from the deck aft of the paddle housing, which Barbicane, Nicholl and Ardan quickly ascended, then sailors hanging from those to haul the little boat up after them. Much comradely shoulder touching and handshakes ensued on the deck, testifying to the enthusiasm of the navy men who had found the intrepid spacefarers safely brought to earth—or water, at least.

Then a loud steam whistle blasted, coming from the Moran flotilla's ironclad appearing out of the dark. A crewman on the ironclad began signaling by lamp, using a device of the sort becoming common in the British Navy but not yet adopted by the Americans. Lacking a response by such means, the ironclad had to press closer, to within shouting distance. While this maneuver was done, Maker tried to slip *Kestrel* nearer, though in any case not close enough to overhear anything from inside the flyer's cabin.

Whatever was said between the captain of the *Susquehanna* and the well-dressed but freelance master of the ironclad, the result was the American warship steaming off west unescorted.

The ironclad remained, and just after midnight on that Sunday, the 8th of December, the *Albatross*' Commander Blake brought them beside and landed in the water, its boat-like hull exhibiting its full seaworthiness. The airship's many rotors slowed but did not stop, and the Commander appeared on the open railed deck topside to conduct his own conversation with the ironclad's lamp.

Aouda focused on the ironclad's signalman, while Maker kept her eye on the airship.

"They offered to assist in any way to retrieve *Columbiad*," Aouda reported of their Morse, "but were told it had sunk. Ship taking the rescued men to St. Petersburg." Aouda looked puzzled, "The capital of Russia?"

"The port for Tampa Town," Passepartout interjected.

Recalling her study of the Florida peninsular map, Maker reckoned, "That'll take a day, at least." The airship's lamp flickered again. "Airship is replying, ordering them to lay here 'til *Eastern* comes."

"Marking the spot," Passepartout said.

Maker smirked, "They must think it'll bob up like a cork."

"Or float within reach under water, point of neutral buoyancy," Aouda mused.

Maker nodded in reflection of the viability of that possibility.

"Either way," Phileas Fogg interposed, "a recipe for much wasted time, since it isn't here at all."

The *Albatross*' engines then roared into full power, pulling it up and away off eastward. Maker steered *Kestrel* slowly in that direction.

"You agree, the Navy may be trusted to bring them safely home without our meddling?" Fogg asked. All nodded affirmatively. "Then I think we may bid primeval Florida adieu."

"Fine with me," Maker said. "I'm hungry, tired, and can use a pee."

Kestrel slipped away far enough to burst from the waves and fly northwest at speed, many a slumbering American along her course awakened in the dead of that night by an unexpected room rattling thunder. They reached Maker's foundry just before 4 AM, Fogg and Aouda rearranging their luggage contents once more. But instead of rousing anyone in the other houses for a carriage, Maker swore, "Oh hell, let them sleep. We'll take *Kestrel*."

Even flying well below the speed of sound, it was the merest jaunt into Chicago for *Kestrel*, Maker bringing them down first into Lake Michigan, submerging before heading up the Chicago River, which emptied into the lake just north of the working railroad terminal. Newly built bridges crossed the river at several streets: a truss swinging bridge near its mouth, its pivot built on an embankment in the middle, and another conventional truss upstream. The river turned left and south just beyond that second bridge, and Maker navigated *Kestrel* toward the left bank, surfacing beside a small boat pier at the back of one of the buildings, where a stair led up to the street above. They were now only a few blocks west of the railroad station.

Maker released the port dome door, which hissed up wide, the cold morning air brushing against them. Aouda and Fogg exited the rear with the princess' case; Passepartout stepped out with the carpetbag, allowing Maker to slide over to tender their partings.

While Aouda reaffixed her hat, Fogg bowed to Maker, "I am sure I speak on behalf of us all, how much we appreciate your assistance these last weeks, as well as the singular pleasure and honor of being allowed to travel in your amazing craft."

"It was a memorable adventure, Mr. Fogg. We all learned a thing or two, I think. And had a bit of fun, too."

Passepartout declared to Maker, "I shall not lose track of you."

Maker smiled, "You know how to catch the attention of my Maxwell Wave detectors, Jean Passepartout, Knight of the Comb."

As they watched *Kestrel* turn around and disappear down into the river, Fogg took out his watch to ring three chimes upon it. Already they missed Thomasina Maker. Much like Aouda, she had that effect on people of discernment and good character.

But yet no delay as Phileas Fogg led Aouda and Passepartout back to the Wabash Warehouse, where the extraction of the Time Machine was accomplished with a now practiced ease.

This time Fogg was last to enter his Machine, giving a final pensive look around at the collection of crates and boxes. "There is a certain serenity to a warehouse at night, I find. A human utility to it, different from the silence of a cathedral. Perhaps it's the lack of stone."

Then he took his seat in the Machine, Aouda's case propped on his left leg, and fussed with its many controls as before.

From behind a crate by the warehouse's outer door, a rat was aroused by this modest commotion. There was the crystalline egg, scintillating tiny rainbow spectra for a moment, each visible particle of itself seeming to fold and melt into translucence.

The rodent emitted a small annoyed squeak at the disturbing low hum accompanying the egg's legerdemain show, followed on its disappearance by a gentle exhalation as air popped into the evacuated void. The rat then lost interest in what was now an empty space on the floor.

29*bis*. IN WHICH TALES FALSE AND TRUE ARE SPUN IN FLORIDA

Monday, the 9th day of December, 1872, brought exciting news to Stone's Hill, as the telegraph reported that the USS *Susquehanna* had rescued Impey Barbicane and his voyagers at sea, delivering them safely into St. Petersburg harbor, where a carriage was taken to convey them on to the cannon site. The estivating newspaper correspondents still on hand at the *Columbiad* enclave were instantly aroused, and anxiously awaited the returning heroes so they could extract all marketable reportage for dispatch to their assorted banners.

When their carriage arrived at the Barbicane house, Victor rushed down the steps to embrace the father with the greatest emotion. Turning back at the porch before entering, Impey Barbicane brightly promised to give all the correspondents the fullest accounting of what had transpired since they had left the Earth nineteen days before.

As the two Barbicanes disappeared into the house, going upstairs for a secluded emotional reunion, Michel Ardan and Captain Nicholl remained on the porch. Ardan waved and smiled, rather enjoying the unaccustomed adulation of the throng. The Captain appeared more bilious, glancing about at the people gathering around, and looking still less enthused when he spotted among them Moran's cracksman associate, the sullen but intense Mr. Stevens.

Someone else outside was Auguste Dupin. When Ardan and Nicholl finally quit the celebrants, Stevens set off for the Moran rental house, whereupon Dupin darted up the steps to take his fellow Frenchman by the arm. After a brief conversation in the foyer, the pair approached Captain Nicholl to cordially invite him into the parlor for a moment. Dupin pointedly did not introduce himself, nor did Ardan make such honor.

Once they were all settled into comfortable armchairs, Nicholl sitting opposite, Dupin brushed flat a segment of his trouser crease, then looked the Captain dead in the eye and began:

"I am called upon on occasion to conduct independent investigations on matters involving great mystery or a need for extraordinary discretion. This present inquiry entails both. If it is your intention to deviate in any way from the tale your traveling companions in the Aether are about to recount, interjecting any of your actual adventures these previous weeks, let me apprise you of information that may completely discourage you."

Dupin pulled the two sabotage gears from his pocket that Phileas Fogg had Passepartout surrender to him the day of the *Columbiad*'s departure. Nicholl tensed as Dupin held them up for a good view.

"These you may recognize. They are imperceptibly larger than their counterparts employed successfully last month. On the night before the *Columbiad*'s firing, you accompanied Colonel Moran and his gang to the aiming chamber, where you installed these counterfeits with the object of redirecting the projectile's course into the waiting arms of Moran's superiors out in the Atlantic."

Nicholl looked in the process of suppressing a nervous facial tic, Ardan now assessing his every gesture.

"No need to deny it, you were well observed," Dupin continued, "including your many nocturnal visits to the machinery where you fabricated them. Many relevant samples have been recovered from the detritus there, which I have little doubt will corroborate the specific metallurgical provenance of these unique pieces. Not only do you risk disgrace and possible imprisonment should these details be revealed, it is not impossible that Barbicane would immediately challenge you to yet another duel to extinguish his most righteous fury at your insidious betrayal. This time, I assure you, Monsieur Ardan will not intervene."

Dupin turned to Ardan, who nodded gravely in corroboration.

"Do you understand now the gravity of your situation, and how your behavior is rationally constrained?"

A checkmated Captain Nicholl could do nothing but nod lamely, in silence.

"I leave you then to the charade with Barbicane," Dupin concluded affably, and departed.

The "charade" in question being Impey Barbicane's enthusiastic and fictitious recounting a few hours later of their launch and journey, which he declared had occurred without flaw until their path was disturbed *en route* to the Moon by an unexpected encounter with an asteroid. His narrative of that gravitational perturbation held the newspaper correspondents in utter thrall, hearts racing at *Columbiad*'s subsequent blazing around the Moon off course, their very survival in the balance—only to be saved by levelheaded American ingenuity and quick collective effort (whose boring technicalities he mercifully spared them), whereby they were returned after further perilous days through the welcoming atmospheric embrace and into the ocean so conveniently adjacent to their point of departure.

All who heard Barbicane's riveting story sighed that the *Columbiad* capsule itself was lost, of course, both to posterity and the paid admissions of all those citizens who surely would have lined up to observe it in some traveling Theater of Science. But in all, the melodrama sounded eminently believable, certainly entertaining—and uncontradicted by either Michel Ardan or Captain Nicholl, who stood silently shoulder to shoulder with the Genius of Baltimore.

のめ

Later that night, after a large restorative dinner and a chance for the hubbub of the return to die down, Impey and Victor Barbicane shared a lengthy smoke and private conversation in the library. Michel Ardan took that opportunity to invade the parlor to rifle through what there were of recent newspapers, catching up on something of the world (or narrow slices of it, at least) since their Pacific plunge and its unprecedented submarine and aerial interludes, while thinking on what he might do next, now that they were back on *terra firma*.

When the doorbell jangled at 7 PM, the butler opened the door to Mr. Stevens, who asked to speak with Captain Nicholl.

Ardan lost no time in secreting himself behind the opened parlor door, from where he overheard Moran's flunkey tell Nicholl that he was to accompany him. Not a request.

"Do I need to bring anything?" Nicholl asked.

"Guts," Stevens said without a trace of humor. "You're on summons, from the nabob."

Nicholl did not wait to inform anyone and left with Stevens at once. Ardan waited a suitable time and followed after them. One advantage to Florida in December: no need to take a coat.

Stevens and Nicholl headed out east of Stone's Hill, off down a winding path into the brush and trees a good quarter of a mile, to a clearing where the *Albatross* had landed. Ardan of course knew naught of the vessel's identity (and Auguste Dupin had not included mention of it in their collaboration) but the last few weeks with Barbicane on, under, and above the sea had cured him of a great deal of surprise no matter what he chanced upon.

A section in the middle of the boat-like hull had dropped to the ground as ramp to a door hatch, open with a uniformed man on guard, rather harshly silhouetted by an electric illumination within. Two closed gun ports flanked the hatch higher on the hull, and a low railing circled the deck above, where lit windows harbored their pilot and its few crew.

The various rotors on the flying machine were turning slowly, but Ardan assumed they would not be staying that way for long. There were enough rough paths roundabout for him to skirt around to reconnoiter the other side of the vessel, which he reached just as Nicholl and Stevens were entering the craft on the other side.

The starboard was the mirror of the port side, though with its hatchway sealed—a quick tug of its handle revealing no obvious means to unlock it. The machinery spinning the rotors began to sputter and increase, quickly racing in intensity. and Ardan jumped at an opportunity—literally, as he used the hatch handle as leverage to leap up to grab the vertical strut of the railing on the deck above, and haul himself up and over the side just as the vessel began to be sucked away from the ground.

The wash of air and noise of the lifting rotors were not an experience Ardan was enjoying, but he had made his choice and would work the best from it. He quickly crawled around the polished wooden deck—it being folly to stand—and looked for somewhere to position himself. White metal shrouds encased the rotor mechanisms, so at least there were no flailing machinery to threaten him at this level, and Ardan eventually found a place to wedge himself behind the windowed deck, next to one of a pair of small lifeboats, and out of view of a rear hatch whose small window looked directly aft.

Once he had settled on a location, Ardan could take notice of the fact that the airship had risen hundreds of feet into the air. And while the view of Florida passing by him in the half moonlight was not without its beauty, keeping himself from slipping off the deck to his doom was more prominent in his consideration.

Unlike the flyer that had ferried him from the *Nautilus* in such fleet comfort, this machine did not maintain nearly so level a course, often heaving and tilting as steering rudders adjusted behind the two horizontal propellers—a condition easily compensated for by the passengers inside with a steadying hand placed against a bulkhead, but which threatened to dislodge Ardan out here on the deck. Moreover, the combination of their speed and the blast of turbulence from the rotors was as strong as any hurricane, and gave Ardan cause to regret not having donned an overcoat to cocoon himself in before leaving Stone's Hill.

As the flight continued, Ardan found if he braced his legs just right against the lifeboats or railings or deck housings, he could amble around the deck well enough to reconnoiter more of the windowed section ahead, glimpsing Nicholl and the others occasionally. The noise of course made it impossible to understand anything being said, but what Ardan could see of their expressions appeared unalarmed.

Two hours brought the airship across Florida and then out over the open sea for an equal duration before the *Great Eastern* armada came into view.

Some manner of electric lamps were shining around the crane mounted on *Eastern*'s stern (looking quite pretty there in the dark), which was just hauling a dripping spheroidal diving ship from the water on a cable. Two craft Ardan recognized as likely submarine boats floated nearby—one long and thin, the other shorter and more rotund. At first he supposed Ambassador Moran's men might be working around the clock, but a check of his watch showed 9 PM and he concluded it was just as possible he was just witnessing the end of their evening's labors. He wondered wistfully whether he'd be staying out here long enough to see which surmise was correct.

The airship angled again in its descent to the landing platform on the ironclad, prompting more stiffened legs and frantic hand gripping by Ardan. He let out a sigh of relief when the machine finally came to a stop on the platform, its engines slowing but remaining on.

Two well-dressed gentlemen stepped up onto the platform from an opening in the ironclad's slanted gun housing and approached just as the port gangway began to lower from the airship's hull. Judging from the descriptions Ardan had obtained from the *Deuxième Bureau*, the stouter older fellow was most likely Sir Augustus Moran, and his thinner and handsomer associate possibly Felix Stuart, member of the engineering clan whose expertise and resources had been drawn on extensively for this show of naval might. Ardan sidled around to see and hear what he could.

"Have we been too dependent on the loyalty of hirelings, Stuart?" Sir Augustus challenged, both watching as the *Albatross'* hatch lowered, its sill thudding to a stop on the platform deck, and the inner door swinging open.

"Have Commander Blake dampen the blades, I do not intend to *shout*," Sir Augustus barked at Stevens as he escorted Captain Nicholl out.

The former Ambassador to Persia did not much like these mechanical contrivances, useful though they may be to his enterprise. They made too much noise, and relied on people of low or independent character for their operation—ambitious jump-ups who did not always accept their station with sincere deference to their betters.

Fortunately Sir Augustus had no occasion to have flown in either the *Albatross* or the *Aurora*, eluding the stress of being so elevated or having to acknowledge dependence on their mere expertise. His son was more obstreperous, of course, braving the *Aurora*, but Sir Augustus was not at all convinced these machines were even *safe*. Railroad engines blew up or derailed—it stood to reason floating in the air only compounded the insanity of it. He'd let the more expendable among them make use of these noisy toys—even his son, since the boy had so insisted on volunteering.

Stevens ricocheted back inside and Sir Augustus waited until the propellers slowed further, the engines dampening sufficiently, before inquiring with clipped enunciation: "What—went—wrong?"

"*Nothing* went wrong," Nicholl drawled. "I *made* the gears, you son *watched* me do it. We put them in place. *Everything* went to plan. But somebody else was watchin' all this: some Pinkerton Ardan set on me."

From his position of concealment, Michel Ardan winced wryly at that.

"He had the gears I made in his *hand*," Nicholl went on, "threatening dire consequences if I didn't play along with the fiction Barbicane told the press. He knows all about your son's involvement, too."

Sir Augustus considered that, his expression souring. "You did not, by chance, ask this oracle his name?"

Nicholl wasn't backing down. "No, I didn't. Nor was he disposed to volunteer it. He looked familiar, but there've been so many foreigners at Stone's Hill I couldn't tell him from Adam."

"What did he look like?" Sir Augustus pressed.

"Same height as Ardan, older. Sixties maybe."

Stuart leaned into ask Sir Augustus, "Could he be the man Fogg met in Paris?"

"Someone else we don't have the name of," Sir Augustus grimaced.

Ardan cocked his head, taking note of that new name. The only "Fogg" Ardan had ever heard of was the Englishman Phileas Fogg—but that seemed a connection too peculiar to imagine.

Sir Augustus decided to leave the issue of the mysterious detective for another more pressing one, "What happened to *Columbiad*?"

Nicholl laughed bitterly, "We weren't minutes past the firing when some other flying ship came along side and forced us off course. This was out in *space*. All the aft cars fell away, Barbicane was near panic. Couldn't catch a good look at it out our windows, and not long after we splashed into the Pacific."

"The *Pacific?!*" Sir Augustus was close to a wide-eyed, mouth-agape incredulity.

Stuart confined his reaction to a raised eyebrow, while Stevens began to listen more intently from his spot in the airship's open door.

"Yes, there were two vessels waitin' to pick us up," Nicholl explained. "One was, I believe, that *Nautilus* submarine boat, or something very near to it.

Stuart's eyebrow arched more at that, while Sir Augustus glowered at the deck as Nicholl continued.

"It was outfitted with a rig special to fit Barbicane's bullet. We were plucked out of the water by the other one, much smaller, but it could *fly*. No screws like this thing, don't ask me how it worked—I'm a metallurgist, not an engineer. The crews were a mongrel lot, too, coloreds and whites all mixin'. Some Hindu woman seemed to command the flyer, crew full of *chinee*. Can you imagine such a thing? There were two white men with her, too, didn't seem part of either crew: a stiff Englishman and a frog, dressed like a servant but not actin' like one. There's you're conspiracy, Sir, if you're looking for it."

Sir Augustus was now taking Nicholl's tale much more seriously, and had stopped looking at the decking.

"Anyhow, Ardan and I were taken below deck, so I can't say what happened to *Columbiad* after that. We sailed for many days, usually under water. We were treated all well enough. Nemo—or so I assume. He's got an 'N' on his pipe organ, played that almost every night, Bach and Mozart mainly." Nicholl let a disapproving snort.

"He barely spoke to us, though Barbicane seemed more friendly with him, called him by name, something besides Nemo—I forget."

If Stuart's eyebrow could have lifted further, it would have. Instead, his lips began to purse.

"For the last week all I could see was ice above us, there's broad windows amidships. Finally we broke surface, somewhere freezin' cold. It was in the morning near as I could tell, but still dark so I suppose a pretty high northern latitude. The smaller flying ship appeared almost at once, so they sortie like clockwork. We flew to where we were found by the Union navy in *fifteen hours*. Higher and much faster than your lumbering *Albatross*, if you want the truth. And that's as far as I know. I'll tell you plain, nothing would have pleased me more than to see Barbicane fail, even if it meant my own destruction, so I am not at fault here."

Sir Augustus began to pace around the deck, his mind's gears racing. Finally he turned back to direct Stevens, "Until Sebastian gets back to tell his side of things … return Nicholl to his associates." Pointing a commanding finger at Nicholl, "*You* play along with them."

An unbowed Nicholl strode back into the airship, hands clasped behind his back. Stevens followed, and while a crewman closed off the door and hauled up the hull hatch, a fuming Sir Augustus turned to Stuart.

"The *Pacific*! We've been gulled, tricked, like a magician show, made to look at one hand while the other picks your pocket. This Passepartout didn't bolt from Florida only to be dragged along by Fogg, flotsam. He meant to be where he was. *Damn*, if you hadn't failed to break that insolent wog years ago, his iron wouldn't be beating us *now*."

Was this indeed about the Phileas Fogg so fixated in the press, Ardan wondered.

Stuart accepted Sir Augustus's chastisement with a stiffening stance, the best he could muster given the plain truth of it. But by now the ambassador's disapproval had turned in on itself, seeking to contort frustration into some practical course of action.

"Ardan ... and his stranger. Too many people who we clearly know too little about." Sir Augustus wheeled about, absolute resolution on his face. "*No!* We are too close to our prize, Stuart—it belongs in Her Majesty's Imperial crown, *and in no other*. It's time to change the game!"

Albatross' engines now begin to roar, causing both their coattails to flap, and Felix Stuart motioned Sir Augustus to step back from the craft to the comparative safety of the steps down to the ironclad's deck, where they held onto their hat brims to watch the machine lift up and away towards the west.

Still clinging to the deck, his apprehension no less diminished but still successfully concealed to all, Michel Ardan had much to think about on the four hour journey back to Florida and land.

30. IN WHICH THE IMPETUOUS AMERICAN CHARACTER METAMORPHOSED A DARING BUT PERILOUS SCHEME

It was after three in the morning on Tuesday, December 10th, and the Moon just setting, when the *Albatross* came to ground outside Stone's Hill, disembarking its passengers (known and stowaway).

The airship left almost immediately afterward, but Ardan tarried a bit to watch it fly off. He did concede it looked extraordinary.

While Captain Nicholl and Mr. Stevens hurried back into the village, parting company to go to their separate residences, Ardan took his time—and not only to recover his wits after that exposed eight hours aboard the flying machine.

That he and Nicholl had been shown a world of superior scientific understanding aboard the *Nautilus* and the other craft was one thing—that Nicholl's conspirators in the Atlantic now knew of it too was quite another. Ardan already was torn over how much of the Power X story he could (or should) honorably convey to his superiors in the *Deuxième Bureau*. Now he had a further complication to evaluate and accommodate.

Whatever he worked out, Ardan had come to be more than casually invested in achieving the best outcome. His difficulty now was in distinguishing what was desirable for the French Republic, serving its people and national interests, and whether that differed from what was the ideal for all peoples, their safety and future. Could there even *be* a future if anyone opened Pandora's Box?

Before he had swept along on the voyage to the Moon, Michel Ardan had thought those two goals lay not far distant from one another, the needs of France and those of the world, easily reconciled by the universal promise of *Liberté, Égalité, Fraternité*. Now he was far from certain they were even close, or could ever be made so—not while the world's borders were still subject to the ambitions of violent temper.

Ardan entered the Barbicane house with the utmost quiet, but even when safely in his bed upstairs, it took some time for sleep to finally come.

Understandably, both Captain Nicholl and Ardan slept in late that morning, missing breakfast entirely. Nicholl was satisfied with some coffee and toast, appearing even jaunty of spirit, before taking a stroll around eleven—in search of further conference with Mr. Stevens, as it happened, to try and find out when Colonel Moran might be returning (and from where, if at all possible). Nicholl's confidence stood in contrast to Victor and Impey Barbicane, who were more contemplative that morning.

When Ardan finally arose, he had resolved what it was he needed to be frank about with the Barbicanes, and happy that Nicholl had already left the house. He found the Barbicanes in the library, hunched over a map of the world they had spread out on a table.

"Ah, Ardan, Victor and I were just mulling over where we went after Nemo picked us up. We must have sailed under the Arctic ice. Isn't that amazing?"

Ardan smiled wanly, a rare knot in his stomach testifying to how unaccustomed he was to speak so plainly on matters he was trained and committed not to.

"There are some things I must tell you. A few you may suspect already. Captain Nicholl, acting with confederates here locally, attempted to sabotage *Columbiad*." Impey and Victor's attentions fell away from the map at once.

"What?" Barbicane challenged. "Is that what brought us down?"

Ardan held up a contradicting finger, "I said *attempted*. A corruption of the cannon aiming, before we even left. That scheme was thwarted by compatriots of our Pacific rescuers." Ardan could see they weren't aware there might have been such people here, under their noses, and he waved a hand, "I know, too many plots at cross-purposes. In any case, I observed firsthand who it is commanding Nicholl. They summoned him last night. I know this because I followed them. They have a mechanical airship; comically primitive, I now recognize, but sufficient to ferry them across the state and out to sea, where a private navy had been assembled to snatch us all—and would have, had only those others of more agility not interfered. His masters suspected he had betrayed them, which Nicholl countered at once by telling them what *did* happen—Nemo, *Nautilus*, our flight in his sister's craft. A quite observant summary."

Ardan scratched the back of his neck, then shook his head, "Nicholl cannot be trusted further, not a moment."

Victor was fuming at these revelations; stalking back and forth, unable to put feelings into words as yet. The father was still more conflicted, for he had begun to like and even admire Nicholl, finding a courage and enthusiasm beneath that intermittently oily manner. Now he had to rethink everything.

"Does this viper in chief have a name?" Impey asked severely.

"Sir Augustus Moran, a British ambassador with grand ambitions for his Queen, if not his own career, that include gifting her arsenal with that dangerous power you are now in fear of."

The elder Barbicane blanched, "Fool."

"Hasn't there been a *Colonel* Moran hanging about among the spectators here?" Victor asked.

"Son of the same. It was he who helped Nicholl tool gears they hoped to use to misalign the cannon on our launch." Ardan paused. "I further overheard the elder Moran fulminate over his failure 'to break' the inventor of the *Nautilus*. I have no doubt such virulence could, and likely *shall*, be vented on any of us, if he gets the chance."

Victor looked sharp, "Unless *we* vent first."

"Just we *three*?" Impey asked.

"Unless some of us are in the confidence of Nemo and his clan," Ardan shrugged, "we could hardly count on their aid."

"Many in Pa's company are veterans, like me," Victor said. "Itching for a good fight, maybe, if the cause be proper."

Ardan thought of the resources available to him on requisition via the *Deuxième Bureau*, including arms and men if necessary, but also how far removed those might be from the here and now of Florida. "I'm not sure any worthwhile assault could be mounted on such short notice, or that we would know what to attack if we did. They have several ironclad warships, armed with cannon."

"If you want to stop a snake, you chop off his head," Impey declared.

"Moran *père*? I assume he has a suite somewhere aboard the *Great Eastern*—that's the main vessel they have—but I have never been aboard it, so would have no idea where to look."

"The *Great Eastern*?" Victor expressed some surprise. "That's a pricy cabin to rent."

Impey's eyes narrowed, as an idea began to kindle. "Do you play poker?" he asked Ardan slyly.

"Baccarat or euchre are more my preferred vices," Ardan replied warily, gauging that Barbicane had more than cards in mind.

"If you want to entice a gambler, for our American poker, you place a bet they can't resist calling. If Moran had a chance to *buy* Power X, wouldn't we be *brought* to him?"

Victor quickly caught the father's drift, "Then it would just be a matter of getting you all back out."

"Not saying *all*," Barbicane replied darkly.

Ardan was trying to keep up with the Barbicane pace, considering all the implications and objections regarding what he imagined they might be considering. "If using his air machine, I cannot operate it."

"I was thinking of something else," Victor said with a sly smile.

※ ※

When Captain Nicholl returned from his rendezvous with the Moran gang (where he had learned nothing of benefit from Mr. Stevens regarding Colonel Moran's whereabouts or itinerary) he found Victor Barbicane rocking on the porch, smoking a cigar.

"A question for you," Victor called, not quite casually, "Was the story my father told yesterday, the *whole* story?"

Nicholl took the chair beside him, "Why ever would you think not?"

Victor offered him a cigar, which Nicholl accepted. While the Captain prepared it, Victor ventured, "The time you spent away was longer than any I could calculate for you, and it seems a puzzle to me that you should plop down so convenient to where you left."

"Coincidences are the hazard of life," Nicholl said as he lit the smoke.

"True. Did Power X work as expected?"

"*You* know I'm not a technical man. Didn't your father give a full report?"

"Not to my satisfaction. This has been a costly enterprise. It occurs to me my father might not have been forthcoming if there were ... *defects* that compromised the process. It's a matter of profit and loss."

"Yes, your own inheritance. Sellin' Power X might be a pig in a poke now, like *Crédit Mobilier* paper. Do you still seek a profit?"

Now that the fish was on the hook, Victor began to gently reel him in. "Most assuredly, if not by licensing, perhaps even sell the patent outright and be done with it."

"Certainly your father would not agree to that, givin' up his ambition to fly to the Moon?"

"I don't sense the fire in him on it anymore. That's why I wanted to know what happened out there."

"So you'd advise him to sell Power X?"

"If the deal were good, yes. Better still if it were splendid."

Nicholl now looked disinterested, innocence incarnate. "Well, I'll ask around. See if there's anybody in the market for your pig. Would I get a commission?"

Victor smiled with great conviction, "Find such a buyer and you will *definitely* earn your reward."

30*bis*. IN WHICH PHILEAS FOGG AND PARTY RESUMED THEIR COURSE OF TRAVEL, AND WHO AMONG THEIR ANTAGONISTS CAME TO NOTICE

When Phileas Fogg pushed the lever forward on his Time Machine on the morning of December 8th, Passepartout and Aouda noticed him removing his hand from it almost at once, and engaging a button on the console which now glowed yellow. They also perceived they were moving through Time more slowly than before, such that only five hours were flashing by each second at speed (less than a third of that they had witnessed previously).

But even at this leisurely pace of temporal displacement it was only possible to get the most shadowy flickering glimpse of living motion, of horse drawn wagons or warehouse workers who took half an hour or more to carry out their tasks in about the same place—all just a blur on the perception. And at even this slower rate it still only took twenty seconds to progress forward the sixty hours from the early morning of December 8th to the late afternoon of December 10th.

Having engaged the button, the handle on Fogg's Machine slowed of itself to arrive at the recalled moment of **1872 AD DEC 10 PM 10:33**—one minute after they had left three days before.

Had anyone other than a few familial rodents been present in the Wabash Warehouse to witness it, they would first have heard a low pop as a point in front of the second crate quickly expanded into a shimmering bubble, expelling all atmosphere from its space, immediately to be filled by infinitely many shards of the Machine's existence unfolding back into normal temporality, spectrum glints flashing around the lowly thrumming device like so many prismatic fireflies. And then it was just a large crystalline egg, resting silently on the floor.

Phileas Fogg's watch began to chime differently, as the mechanism encountered no simultaneous counterpart, and so began to consult the Time Machine itself and comparing its findings against the master chronometer humming along in Fogg's London laboratory, deciding between the two when it was supposed to be and resetting to GMT.

As Passepartout helped Fogg push the once more tarped Time Machine back into the first shipping box, he asked, "I understand why we cannot *hear* anything outside your Machine when we move through Time. But I am puzzled how we can *see* things. And do observers see a black spot where we are, as we intercept the light on the way?"

"Oh, that *would* be inconvenient," Fogg smiled as he latched the machine in place and sealed up the box. "I performed experiments, with a miniature—no black spot. But all the waves passing through where we're moving *are* perceived, but only by their higher dimensions. The waves themselves pass right through. We actually *do* hear sound too—some of the hum of the Machine is that. But light is so much faster than sound, our eyes can't tell the difference between the higher dimensions and what we take for regular light. I was surprised myself at first, that it looked so normal."

The packing formalities done, Fogg and his two companions returned to the Wabash Warehouse offices.

"Well, that didn't take long," the manager said.

"You have kept my property in most excellent safety, sir," Fogg smiled. Retrieving $2500 from the carpetbag, which he lay enticingly on the desk beside a stack of blank paper, Fogg took one of the sheets along with a pencil and began to scribble out *No. 7 Savile Row, Burlington Gardens, London.*

"Having found a customer for my wares, and establishing their perfect condition today, you will arrange for both containers to be shipped to this address, via the *French Transatlantic Company* liner *Pereire*, which sails on the Fourteenth from New York." Fogg slid the money over to the fellow. "This should cover all your expenses. Any remainder, you may of course retain as most appreciated gratuity."

With all the details settled to his satisfaction, Phileas Fogg, Aouda, Passepartout and their luggage set out for the railroad station, followed by the attentive Mr. Fix, uncertain why Fogg had visited the warehouse or why their time there had been so fleeting.

"Just out for a constitutional stroll," Fix burbled as he caught up to Fogg.

"Your dedication to fitness, Mr. Fix, is an inspiration to us all," Fogg responded dryly as they paced along, then added, "And your interest in whist, undiminished?"

"Invigorated, Sir!" Fix promised.

"Then we shall see you for cards on the train, after dinner," Fogg decreed.

As there were so many railroad lines vying for the same station access until their own terminals could be rebuilt, finding the right departing train involved more effort outgoing than the Fogg party had expended alighting from their arriving an hour before—or three days earlier, depending on how one wanted to measure it.

Both Passepartout and Aouda were far from reconciled to the strangeness of how they felt about Time Travel—the abruptness of weather change, bouncing from December to November and back again, further compounded by their to and fro excursions to sunny warm Florida and chilly Atlantic.

More to the moment, they had to maneuver around one particularly long incoming westbound train that not only featured the expected complement of Pullman sleepers but also several boxy immigrant cars, carriages resembling more the sort employed for shipping livestock, but well crowded with human cargo guarding their meagre belongings and nervously seeking solace in their native tongues. There was also a day coach especially segregated for a contingent of Negro passengers—a widespread practice not legally sanctioned in this land despite the theoretical equality cascading from their tumultuous civil conflict, and provoking many a pending lawsuit as yet unresolved by their discomfited Federal judiciary.

For anyone looking for injustice to fly over in *Kestrel*, America in 1872 offered a surfeit of destinations to be reminded of their righteous ambition by Maker's artificial thunder rolling in a cloudless sky.

When Phileas Fogg's party found their *Pittsburgh, Fort Wayne & Chicago Railway* train, they discovered it had two carriages of interest (neither immigrant nor segregated, as none of those marginalized persona were passengers among them). The first was that marvel of American ingenuity: a dining car—which was actually a regular Pullman sleeper with linen-draped tables between the seats and to which a small kitchen was amended in the front. The other was a drawing room car where freestanding chairs were arranged, some around small tables. Phileas Fogg informed the conductor of his intention to spend considerable time there for whist, and that he should apprise passenger Fix of their plans.

Once they were settled into their seats and the train beginning to move, Aouda rummaged in the carpetbag for her electric pillbox. "It may be more difficult for Robur to distinguish one train from another in this settled area, so I will signal him of our location as needed with this," and the device disappeared into one of her manifold dress pockets before she began to rap upon her left bracelet.

The train sped southeast around the lower coast of Lake Michigan and into neighboring Indiana, a land of low hills and many tiny lakes, somewhat discernable in the moonlight. They were almost across the state, nearing Fort Wayne, when the Fogg party experienced their first railroad dinner. Passengers were seated in shifts, but Fogg's ever-radiating notoriety served to bump them to first call.

Aouda ordered a breaded veal cutlet, Passepartout decided on a porterhouse steak with mushrooms, and Phileas Fogg took lamb chops, plus potatoes prepared in various ways, coffee and tea for their beverages, and some bread. Seeing champagne wines on the menu, Fogg inquired "Might we have a bottle of your Krug over cards later, served in the drawing room car?"

Fogg was pleased to learn this could be arranged, and added an assortment of fruit preserves (apricots, blackberries and cherries) to accompany the wine. All that came to just under eight dollars (half that being the champagne), which Fogg attended to with two American five dollar notes from the carpetbag.

The food and company proved eminently agreeable for those three that evening.

☙ ❧

Florida time being an hour advanced from Indiana, the ship's clock aboard the airship *Aurora* was just then reading 9 PM as Commander Tremaine approached their landing berth straddling the prow of the platform ironclad. The *Albatross* reposed on the aft deck, lanterns glowing from below as workmen on both sides labored over small hoists to load the long torpedoes out and down into the upper deck hatches of the submersibles.

Sebastian Moran and Mr. Wilson were waiting by the gondola door until they were safely landed and the mooring lines affixed to deck stanchions. Both had weathered their first aerial voyage tolerably enough, eased by a dearth of storms to evade or plow through along the way to Florida, but neither gentleman would have marked down flying across a continent anywhere on their list of persistent desires.

A steam launch was at the ready to convey Moran and Wilson over to the looming bulk of the *Great Eastern*, where a long floating dock extended aft from the great paddle housing. This was held by cables from winches along the bulwarks above, such that it could be drawn up from the sea for sailing. A pivoting gangway led to a fixed stair up to the paddlewheel housing, where a still longer railed stair angled up to the bulwarks—these, protruding some four feet all around the deck, required a makeshift staircase from the edge down to the polished wood deck (covering a ladder to what had formerly been purely a crew egress). The same docking arrangement had been installed on the starboard side, but not easily observed on so expansive a deck.

Once to the top of the stairs, one could see dim light from the six windows along the angled roof of one of the low skylight sheds, eighteen of which dotted the *Eastern*'s vast open deck. Behind it towered the third of the ship's four narrow tan funnels, no smoke emanating from it at present. To the left of the skylight shed, a staircase led up to one of the two great transverse gangways that bridged the ship from one paddle housing to the other, this one crossing to the exposed wheel.

Sir Augustus Moran stood at the bottom of the makeshift bulwark stairs, hands clutched behind his overcoat, legs astride, and looking not at all pleased with things.

"Much has transpired while you two were seconded to the American wilderness," Sir Augustus commenced as soon as their feet reached the deck.

"Yes, we heard Barbicane turned up, the papers were full of it when we stopped yesterday at Birmingham for provisions," Sebastian replied.

The father at once set off forward, continuing as they strode under the paddle bridge, "I don't hold you responsible for the failure of the kidnap—it was a risk, suitable enough, without further arousing their suspicion. From what I know now, it was doomed. Passepartout is a man of many secrets. Thanks to Nicholl I know a few of them."

Sir Augustus veered right to avoid the rigging stays and stopped at the corner of the huge engine skylights, a shallow white arched arcade that spanned most of the deck. A few lamps below showed the monstrous pistons within were under no motivation, and the *Great Eastern* overall was mostly still.

"I've suspended the salvage work," Sir Augustus said. "Barbicane's *Columbiad* isn't here to find. Passepartout picked it up in the Pacific on the very day of its launch."

His son was aghast, "*How*? Wasn't he on the *General Grant* with Fogg and the others?"

"They apparently have a flying machine, and the *Nautilus* submarine boat. Or so Nicholl swears. Did you find him a man prone to fantasy, or confabulation?"

"Nicholl? *No*, he's clear as glass."

"Unfortunately, I am inclined to agree. Which means we have a problem. *Columbiad* has been spirited away somewhere, and the only people who might possibly know where, are God knows where themselves, and slippery as eels. I've trebled the pace of our steam launches to the coast to keep abreast of telegraphs...."

Sir Augustus cast a look upward at the masts and funnels, fretted by a thought, "How do they communicate at *sea*?" Then he cleared his head with a shake, and continued to his son, "Proctor fell behind them in Omaha, promises to catch up now that he's free of Hospital. As Boyd is back from Suez, I sent her to New York to monitor the incoming trains and outgoing ships. No expense spared, she can hire whom she pleases."

"You think he'll keep to Fogg's coattails all the way to London?" Sebastian asked.

Sir Augustus's eyes narrowed, "Fogg has kept to the *Daily Telegraph* plan from the start. If he continues, we'll have a chance to catch them."

All the while, young Mr. Wilson had followed the pair, trying not to fidget or otherwise appear useless. Finally he offered tentatively, "Did you have anything to ask *me*, Sir?"

"No," Sir Augustus replied flatly.

31. IN WHICH MOST UNWELCOME DISTURBANCES OCCUR AT THE ST. NICHOLAS HOTEL

Phileas Fogg and his whist partners enjoyed the champagne over long rounds of cards that Tuesday evening, as the *Pittsburgh, Fort Wayne & Chicago Railway* train left Indiana for the farmland of Ohio.

"The champagne is almost chilled," Fogg observed agreeably as the town of Sandusky passed in the night. "I wonder if they store the bottles in the baggage car, to avoid warming."

"Better to hang them over the side, in this cold," Mr. Fix quipped, as he played to the next trick.

"Phileas needs a *seau à glace*," Aouda smiled. "One we fill with snow, plucked from a mountaintop—by a balloon, perhaps ... or some other."

"Or better, an icebox *ala* Maker," Fogg replied.

Although the detective found this exchange quite confusing, Passepartout took the trick, and Mr. Fix let the topic drop.

The sleeping berths were all prepared for them when the whist players finally relinquished their table, and the Fogg party were well rested when they awoke on Wednesday, the 11th of December, to the southeastern portions of the state of Pennsylvania. There was a dawn stop at the burgeoning industrial city of Pittsburgh (accounting for some half of the nation's steel and a third of its glass produced), where breakfast might have been had at the station were they not already being served in the restaurant car.

Aouda chose an omelet in rum, some bacon and toast, with English breakfast tea. Passepartout favored a ham omelet, toast and French coffee. Phileas Fogg decided to try a scrambled egg, also with bacon and toast, and the same tea as Aouda. This repast totaled $2.80, which Fogg recompensed with a $5 bill, cleaving the train staff even more closely to his satisfied attendance.

Pennsylvania being a horizontal state of some spread, there was scenic variety in its breadth. Admittedly, the Allegheny Mountains were not as rugged as the crags of the Sierra Nevada or Rockies, but nonetheless warranted schemes to cheat the grade. Just before the town of Altoona the line followed a huge horseshoe roundabout half a mile in length and thirteen hundred feet across to manage the summit without strain. Their train was just long enough for those in the caboose to glimpse their locomotive heading in the opposite direction farther along.

The Fogg whist party was back at it after luncheon, catching sight of the wide Susquehanna River outside of Harrisburg around three o'clock, as they went over its 3800 feet on a series of wooden arch truss spans marching on two dozen stone pilings, light snow and ice ringing them and the shore. It took three further hours to reach the historic city of Philadelphia, by which time Phileas Fogg was checking his watch.

"At this rate, I am not certain we will reach New York in time for our Cunard connection, SS *China*."

Mr. Fix shook his head in disappointment. "No one wants you safely on your way to Liverpool more than I, Mr. Fogg."

Fogg retrieved his Bradshaw from the carpetbag while Passepartout shuffled the next hand. "The *Pereire* won't be leaving New York until the Fourteenth," Fogg winked at those of his partners who knew of his "Machine Parts" that Auguste Dupin would be accompanying aboard that vessel. "The Hamburg boats sail to Havre, not Liverpool or London, more delay that way. Inman steamer tomorrow ... uh, too slow to cross the Atlantic in time, I fear. Well, we will see. We have not missed the sailing *yet*."

The cards got their full use as they trained across New Jersey, past Trenton and on to Jersey City to catch the railroad ferry across the icy Hudson to New York City. A small squad had been watching all the incoming passengers for just such a trio as Phileas Fogg's distinctive party, and one of their number raced to the telegraph office to report their arrival, and embarkation on the Cortlandt Street Ferry that was departing every fifteen minutes at this time of night. A counterpart band performed the same duty on the terminus side, and a trio of fleet followers kept on their carriage as it set out for the Cunard Line pier, wending past the southern terminus of New York's latest experiment in advanced urban movement: a new cable-driven elevated railroad, whose single track perched on a line of pylons that disappeared up Greenwich Street like an orderly stand of steel trees. It was not running at this hour.

At quarter past eleven o'clock, Fogg's party arrived at the Cunard dock, to discover that the *China* had sailed for Liverpool forty five minutes before.

"Bad luck for you, Mr. Fogg," detective Fix said.

The absence of a liner was juxtaposed with the presence of the three men who had tagged along from the ferry. Passepartout found that an improbable coincidence, and while Fogg considered his transportation options, the valet stepped away some distance to give his hair a comb. The three men were armed with guns and knives.

When Mr. Fix stepped away far enough, Passepartout sidled back to Fogg and whispered, "I think we may have been followed from the ferry."

"Either that," Fogg agreed, "or three not very prosperous looking characters minus all luggage felt obliged to visit an empty pier in the middle of the night."

"Time for a hotel?" Aouda asked, adding with a gesture to her left bracelet, "Or call on a friend?"

"Given those following us, a mattress and pillow might be desirable tonight over a flying machine landing in front of them, so a hotel," Fogg said. "We shall consult about what is best tomorrow. Come."

An inquiry of a cabbie outside the Cunard pier revealed most notable hotels fronted Broadway. The Astor House was nearest, but rather dated, while most of the newer establishments were considerably farther up that avenue. The best available and closest was the St. Nicholas Hotel, which occupied the full block between Broome and Spring streets, and that is where Phileas Fogg directed their carriage, followed by the three rough men in a cab of their own.

The million dollar St. Nicholas Hotel was not quite twenty years old, but had set a standard for luxury and appointment all rivals had to match. Its main building was six stories high, with a five-floor expansion filling out the block, all faced in elegant white marble done in the Italian style. Those most favored posteriors within had $125,000 worth of carved rosewood furniture upholstered in the finest satin damask to sit on, while carpets specially woven for the hotel fell to foot.

But there was more than just opulent decor. The hotel was a seething microcosm of American technical innovation, from their gaslight fueled by vapors refined on site, to a factory of machinery washing and drying their laundry in volume. Safety was minded by thousands of gallons of water kept in an attic reservoir, to extinguish any conflagration in minutes via a labyrinth of interstitial piping.

Five tall gas lamps presented puddles of light at the hotel's entrance on Broadway, a somewhat understated classical pediment over four fluted marble columns, flanked by the doors and windows of the shops leasing their lower perimeter, purveying hats and such, long since closed for the night. The foyer soon opened onto an expansive lobby gleaming in marble, topped by an Italianesque frescoed ceiling springing from pilasters with gilded capitals, all of which Passepartout gawked at as they crossed to the reservations desk.

Following behind with his modest traveling case, Mr. Fix gulped a bit to imagine how expensive even the most basic room might cost this night.

Passepartout kept a tight hold on their two pieces of luggage despite the proffered assistance of several insistent porters, all the while casting an eye on the three men following them, who had crossed off left to saunter down a side hall affording access to the reading room and gentlemen's drawing room beyond, joined by a connecting door.

Whereupon they faced a social impediment: none of these laboring classes were dressed apropos either room—marble-floored sancta with bronze chandeliers lit under now dark domed skylights. As the reading room opened also onto the lobby, that proved their best venue for loitering, rifling through the papers arrayed there, trying to look as though they were properly waiting for someone—which, in fact, they were.

At the desk, Phileas Fogg held up fingers on his right hand as he addressed the hotelier, "Three in our party, separate chambers."

"We have parlor suites with two bedrooms. As for your man, the fifth floor is reserved for our guests' servants, with their own dining room on the third."

Fogg glowered, "My valet should be close to hand, a room on the same floor—adjacent if possible, or at least near."

The clerk looked Passepartout up and down, including his odd round hat. "As you wish, sir." He consulted a map of rooms and their occupants. "We have a parlor suite on the third free, two bedrooms, and another standard room two doors down. Satisfactory?"

"We should hope," Fogg smiled. "We are also likely to be leaving early in the morning, hours of our own election, so will be paying fully in advance." He turned around, "Oh—Mr. Fix, permit me to include your accommodation on my bill."

Fix combined embarrassed gratitude into a shamefaced nod.

"When is breakfast served?" Fogg inquired.

"From six to eleven, sir."

Passepartout, meanwhile, was minding as one of the three pursuers broke from his company to cross the lobby to another of the hotel's unusual amenities: its own telegraph office, down a hall by the main staircase, next to a railroad ticket office and a cavernous barber shop (its mirrored walls and skylight in darkness at this hour). Passepartout maneuvered himself far enough from the desk to catch a look at what the man was up to in the telegraph office. As the fellow began penning a message, he surmised someone was in the process of being apprised of their presence at the hotel. And doing so nervously, biting his lip, a manner which Passepartout did not like at all.

When Fogg finished signing the register, and the desk clerk turned the volume around to read the names, he blurted, "Not *the* Phileas Fogg?"

"You have an infestation of us, here in America?"

"Oh, no," the clerk flustered, then turned to the Princess of Bundelcund with an obsequious bow, "I hope Your Highness will enjoy her stay at our modest accommodation."

Passepartout abandoned his spying position to stay closer to Fogg and Aouda, and continuing to fend off efforts by porters to take possession of their luggage to be escorted to their rooms once Fogg had signed for their keys (Mr. Fix being attended to separately).

While the latest New York hotels were being equipped with elevating rooms by their inventive Mr. Otis, stairs were still the mode at this venerable address. Proceeding up the grand white oak staircase to the first landing, an $1100 chandelier illuminated a painting of St. Nicholas dispensing gifts from his stocking, the jovial portrait hanging above a rosewood piano positively exploding with carved flower wreaths, the keys of shimmering pearl rather than pedestrian ivory.

The moment the Fogg party had disappeared up the stairs, though, the lip-biter darted from the telegraph office to nod his head to direct one of the other two standing by the reading room entrance to head after them, keeping back but finding out where their rooms were.

As the Fogg party passed the second floor, the porter nodded off to their right. "Dining room there, tea room adjoining. Supper's still being served till midnight." And indeed there were still many diners within its long hall, capable of seating four hundred at a go.

"I could see my way to a dessert, or some wine, perhaps," Fogg said, "if we have time." It was presently a quarter to twelve, but both Aouda and Passepartout appeared agreeable to this proposal.

Phileas Fogg and Aouda's parlor suite occupied a corner on the third floor in the new section of the building, its windows looking north onto Spring Street and eastward down over Broadway. Poking his head briefly around the corner of the long transverse hall, the man sent to follow them caught sight of the porter and Fogg party entering that corner, and withdrew like a circumspect turtle to avoid being seen by his quarry far down the passage. The moment all were inside the room, he dashed down the hall to secrete himself along one of the closer side halls.

Inside the suite, the porter turned up the gas, then called attention to a small knob on the wall near the door. "Press this for any requests to the office," adding portentously, "It is *electrical*."

"How amazing!" Aouda smiled coyly, evoking a smirk from Passepartout, which he suppressed as the porter turned to him.

"Now sir, to *your* room."

"You may find us in the dining hall, Passepartout," Fogg called after them, then turned to Aouda, "I'll be locking the room, but will be carrying the carpetbag. What about *your* luggage?"

"Locked, my case should be fine here while we're absent. All the valuables are on my person or in your bag."

As they departed, they chanced to run into the spying man, poking his head around the corner. He swallowed, put on a lame smile, and sped away down the hall to disappear into the side hall stairs.

"We may assume they know our rooms now," Aouda told Fogg.

"And know we're onto them, if not excessively stupid," Fogg replied.

Arriving in the dining room just shy of the midnight hour, Phileas Fogg and Aouda were taken down the rich carpet runner to be settled near the entrance at the head of one of their long communal tables, each seating twelve, but this one otherwise empty. The twenty jets in the gas chandelier hanging over Fogg's right shoulder were being dimmed on account of the hour, but not yet enough to make reading the menu difficult.

"Just a dessert and wine for us," Fogg told the waiter. "And we are expecting a third, momentarily."

Looking over the menu, Fogg grew intrigued, "Cranberry pie. I wonder how that tastes compared to the condiment of it we had aboard the *General Grant*."

"We must try it then," Aouda smiled.

Fogg examined the wine listing next. "I see they have an amontillado sherry. Would that appeal to you?"

"Let us be adventurous, Phileas."

"Then amontillado it is."

Passepartout arrived shortly thereafter. "The rooms are most luxurious. Especially having a bathroom all to oneself. *America!*"

"It will become a common practice for hotels, not long from now," Fogg said. "We ordered a sherry and some cranberry pie. What would you have?"

"You will like that, tart but interesting." Passepartout said. "I see they have the pumpkin pie. Mrs. Sax makes a good one—I shall compare with hers." Turning to the wine list, Passepartout's eye fell on one of their most expensive entries, sighing, "Ah, there's a cognac, vintage 1843."

"Then by all means have it," Fogg nodded.

The pies arrived on plates warmed by steam, the silverware glinting in the gaslight, while another waiter poured Aouda's sherry, then Fogg's, followed by Passepartout's cognac into a snifter. But Fogg stayed the waiter when he began to take up the tray on which he'd brought the wine.

"We'll be taking the bottles to our rooms, thank you," Fogg smiled, "and the glasses."

Their two bottles of wine and pie came to $10.50, which Fogg paid by three five dollar notes, causing their waiter to lesson concern for the tray and glasses, or show haste in easing them from their seats even as the dining room clientele thinned after midnight, ushering them into

Thursday the 12th of December.

"Did you notice our gentleman from the dock, sending a telegraph from the office downstairs?" Passepartout asked as the waiter departed. "He looked apprehensive."

"They do rather stand out," Fogg said.

"One of them was in the hall when we left our room," Aouda said, "So they're aware of our suites."

Passepartout frowned at that. "All three are armed, by the way."

"No surprise there," Fogg said. "Now, how liable are they to use them?"

"They're running low on opportunity," Aouda said, "this being our last night before taking to sea."

"Quite true," Fogg agreed. "Do you think he was just telegraphing our presence here, or requesting reinforcements?"

"If the latter, we may have a busy night," Aouda warned.

"This is quite good pie," Fogg said then, prompting a smile from Passepartout.

"The pumpkin spices are no match for Greta, but mine is good enough," Passepartout said of his slice, then sighed, "I will sleep most vigilantly until we are safely on our way tomorrow. The plan is to be at breakfast at six?"

"That should suffice," Fogg replied. "I'd like to be at the docks by seven. We have a boat to hire. Will that be enough sleep for you all?"

"No deviation from our rush this entire trip," Passepartout quipped.

"Before I retire, I will pay a visit to the hotel reading room," Fogg said, "a chance to pass through the lobby again. Observe its occupants."

"I shall escort Aouda to your rooms," Passepartout promised firmly.

As Fogg rose, Aouda took his arm, "Do not delay, Phileas."

Fogg smiled, and lay the room key on the wine salver. "*In vino veritas*, I leave to your custody."

But Passepartout returned the key to him, "Retain the key. I will use my comb." When Fogg looked puzzled, the valet added, "Aouda understands."

Fogg quickly made his way down the grand staircase to the lobby, where he found the three men deployed roughly as before. This surprised him regarding the one at the telegraph office—it increased the likelihood that the fellow was waiting for a reply. As for the other two, they looked at Fogg with "what are we to do about that?" expressions as he confidently strode by them to the reading room.

There were still a few late readers within even at this hour, several looking up when Fogg appeared, only to return to their papers after the glance. The folding connecting doors to the men's drawing room were now shut. Without taking a seat, Fogg looked through the assortment of local newspapers, some of which were apoplectic over the difficulty of bringing to justice a local corrupt politician, William "Boss" Tweed, whose imaginative graft in the Tammany Hall Democratic administration had set benchmarks for innovative accounting (such as ringing up construction expenses for the New York County Courthouse totaling twice what the American government had paid Russia for the entire Alaska Territory).

☙ ❧

Aouda and Passepartout were just then reaching the door to the corner parlor suite. Dropping the carpetbag to the floor, he took out his comb and quickly opened the portal, pushing it wide for Aouda to enter with the wine tray. After shifting the carpetbag inside, Passepartout swept up the cognac and snifter with a nod, "Six o'clock, in the dining room, *mademoiselle*."

"Relock the door, if you please, so only Phileas may make proper entry."

"You do not mind, no key to exit on your own?"

"He should be returned presently. And I do have tools of my own," tapping her dress pockets.

Passepartout smiled, relocked the door with his comb, but used the actual key to unlock his own farther down the hall. Once inside, he set down the wine and glass to bring out his comb again, for his slow rotational waltz to ascertain what he could of their environs—Fogg and his watch being propitiously removed most of the way down the block and two floors down. With the black blob of Fogg's timepiece registering in the reading room, Passepartout was able to confirm the presence of the three men together in the telegraph office down from the lobby, as well as a general configuration for the building. Because of his previous probing, he could even place Mr. Fix (in a room on the floor above, only across the hall and not so far down).

That surveillance accomplished, and with a mostly full bottle of cognac and a tub in his bathroom, Passepartout worked out how to occupy at least the next hour.

☙ ❧

Down in the reading room, Phileas Fogg noticed out the corner of his eye one of the two men had sidled along to stand by the reading room door again. Randomly flipping through a stack of older issues of *Harper's Weekly*, Fogg came upon a November 16th issue telling of an outbreak of horse distemper that had briefly brought the city to a halt—Fogg thought back to realize he had then been aboard the *General Grant* in the Pacific, the one occasion during their trip when they had been free of the hovering Moran gang.

Continuing down through the older issues, one from February 3rd illustrated the Grand Central Station that the shipping millionaire turned railroad magnate, Cornelius Vanderbilt, had just built up in the wilds of distant 42nd Street, as depot for the many rail lines he had bought in a plan to corral every rail from the city to Chicago for his New York Central Railroad. Since they had come into the city by an independent line and would be departing by boat, though, the drawing of the impressive terminal was the closest Fogg and party would be getting to it. If the picture were accurate, that towered cathedral to steam monopoly was very large, with a covered track arcade far exceeding the Chicago station they had visited.

Fogg took out his watch, just to check the time, which read 5:22 GMT. But he did take note of the bezels: "**A**" resting before *I*, the now inactive "**B**" still at *VI*, while Passepartout's "**?**" was beside "**N**" nearing *V*. Nemo must still be sailing southward in the Atlantic, Fogg thought—though of greater relevance was the reassuring nearness of "**O**" bright by *X*, which by his reckoning put Aouda's *Deimos* just out in the harbor.

CB ΒΟ

Aouda had set up her electric engine on a table in the parlor when Phileas Fogg rapped gently on the door before unlocking it and entering. "I must oversee my pistons. If you want to use the bath in the meantime, now is the perfect time."

"I shall *steep* a bit then," and Fogg repaired to the bathroom, where he bathed and shaved.

Aouda had concluded her electrification when he emerged. "*Deimos* is laying out in the harbor, by one of the low islands. I signaled our location with the pillbox." Aouda smiled, "Now I have my own toilette to do."

Pouring a sherry, Fogg considered their situation: the need to find ocean conveyance to the British Isles in the morning, and forestall any trouble should the Moran gang become unduly aggressive while they were still on land.

"What was this about Passepartout's comb?" Fogg asked when Aouda emerged from the bath.

"We know he uses it to extend his senses somehow, but it also has a probe that neatly unfastens locks. He used it on the Moran machine shop, and again when we had to gain entry to Barbicane's gear room."

Fogg raised an eyebrow, "His surname is well chosen."

"I should dearly like to learn some of his tricks, Phileas." Aouda had Passepartout's ability to invoke unconsciousness uppermost in mind, though having one of those combs would not be remiss either.

"I fear many are things he cannot *teach*." Fogg considered it imprudent to elaborate on matters relating to that extraordinary visitor from afar.

That extraordinary visitor from afar had by then settled into a warm bath, his cognac snifter close to hand on a table he moved nearer to the porcelain tub. Passepartout was annoyed at the prospect of this latest contingent of villains making trouble for them, interrupting what was so far a most satisfying and comfortable interlude in a journey seldom punctuated by sybaritic repose. He resolved to enjoy himself here, at least, as long as he could.

After his bath, Passepartout settled down for what passed for sleep in his nature while he kept the comb active in his right hand as he lay on his back. He remained thus for two hours, relaxing and yet not, until around three that morning.

He popped awake, alerted to the presence of figures already known to his observation who had come within the perimeter of his comb: the red-bearded man and half a dozen others, down on the ground floor in the rear of the building, conveyed evidently by an enclosed wagon—and another comparable body down at the lobby, including that woman from two months ago, Mrs. Hammond, whom he had thought would be one personage at least he would not be encountering again. His instrument had no way to detect whether she was attired in turquoise or rose.

Passepartout sat upright on the bed, closed his eyes and sent an intentionally strong signal to Aouda down the hall: *AOUDA. ALERT. PROCTOR & OTHERS AT HOTEL. I COME TO YOUR SUITE NOW. JEAN P.*

After a few moments, a reply: *PASSEPARTOUT. UNDERSTOOD & AWAITING. AOUDA.*

Shoes, coat and hat quickly donned, Passepartout, cognac bottle and snifter soon appeared at Fogg's corner suite. He tapped the bottle against the door and called, "*C'est moi*."

An incompletely attired Phileas Fogg opened the door, "Aouda is dressing. What have you discovered?"

"Colonel Proctor and Mrs. Hammond are back amongst us."

"Her? You're sure?"

"Once I measure a form, its characters are retained. The machinery of my ship recognized them both."

The door to Aouda's room was ajar, and her voice rang out as she adjusted some of the wires that led from her bracelets up the arms to batteries she wore in her undergarments, before getting into her frock, "I've sent for reinforcements of our own. *Deimos* is only minutes away. They'll have to land on the roof, as we did at Aronnax's. If there are any locked doors, you'll have to clear the path, Passepartout."

"I think I know the way, but there are two roofs, one a floor higher. The lower one is first to reach, by a side stairs in the older part of the building, second cross hall before the main staircase."

"I'll signal Robur. Go on ahead, and we'll follow to the stair."

"Wait a moment," Fogg said, and retrieved the gun case from the carpetbag to give Passepartout one of their remaining four revolvers and a box of ammunition. "To cover eventualities."

Trading his cognac bottle for the weapon, Passepartout was gone, Fogg locking the door after him. Then Phileas returned to the case to pull out two more of the firearms, along with two boxes of ammunition, which he laid on a table for himself and Aouda. After replacing the case to the carpetbag, Fogg turned to their wine. Making sure the corks were secure on the sherry and cognac bottles, he added those to their carpetbag booty, before crossing to his bedroom to finish dressing.

CS SO

Passepartout reached his target staircase in short order, quickly tucking the pistol under his belt and the bullet box in a coat pocket as he went down the hall, not wanting to alarm any guests or staff he might encounter (however unlikely that was at three o'clock in the morning). Three flights up the stairway terminated in a side passage with the door to the newer wing's roof—which was indeed locked, though not for long, thanks to his comb.

A draft of bracing night air sucked in as Passepartout pushed the door open. A short stair dropped to the roof, which resembled an inverted "F" where the bulk of the building on the right branched into two westward oriented room wings. Though each section was as wide as two rooms with intervening hall, *Deimos* was not a small craft, and Passepartout was concerned how the structure would respond under its not trivial weight.

A light frost coating the roof boards shimmered white and gave the spot a bleak or magical cast depending on one's temperament. Five stories was tall for a structure in the city, so the view from the roof of the St. Nicholas Hotel was considerable—or would be, were it daylight and the sky not hung low by clouds and dank with coal soot. The dense grid of streets marched up Manhattan Island between the tangle of ship masts crowding Hudson River on the left and the East River on Passepartout's right, the dim lines of municipal gas streetlamps broken only by the even darker rectangular patch of the barely begun Central Park well to the north.

CS SO

Phileas Fogg and Aouda were dressed and packed by then, and entering the hall. As Fogg turned back to lock the room, though, Aouda took in a tense breath: down at the far end of the cross hall,

Colonel Proctor and three men appeared out of a stairway door.

"Phileas," she called, nudging his shoulder and nodding down the hall. Nursing his recent groin injury, Proctor's men were fortunately proceeding at his measured lead.

"Drat," Fogg said. Pushing the door to their room back open and entering to remove themselves from their line of sight, Aouda now took note of yet another band of people coming into view from the other direction: far down the main hall, near where the grand staircase was.

"Might that be our other miscreants?" Aouda asked.

Fogg peered down the low-lit passageway, seeing a woman accompanying them, in fur collared coat and of a bearing consistent with his recollection of her. "Mrs. Hammond, I think, yes." Fogg shut the door before they might take notice of the activity at the corner suite, and twisted the key to lock it once more. "Cornered on both ends, by large numbers. Not a good place to be. My apologies, Aouda."

"Bosh. Not your fault, Phileas—nor are we without resource. Robur will be here shortly, so here … we need … a defilade." Aouda began to look around the room, lips pursing as she thought. Going to the tall parlor windows, she pulled back the drapery, but was hardly attending to the view outside, such as the signage of the book dealers who were now offering photography from the five story block catty-corner.

"If we can step off moving ships at sea, we should be able to exit out a stationary window, don't you think?" Aouda checked the sash, "We can give it a tug together, if we do this," but grimaced, "It would make *Deimos* rather conspicuous in the street, though. But, if it has to be done—devil take the hindmost."

CR ʃɔ

On the roof of the hotel, a piercing whine emerged from the clouds above as *Deimos* dropped down into view, Passepartout wincing as he watched to see if the vehicle would stay put, or crash through the ceiling below. As the engines powered down and the craft's weight came to bear, there were distinctly creaking timbers, the vessel's skids pressing down into the thin frost coating the roof boards. To Passepartout's relief, the machine remained supported—though in the Fifth Floor guests' servant rooms, a few stirred briefly at the heaving, until the rooms grew quiet again.

Passepartout stepped around to *Deimos*' port hatch just as Niru was opening it, Robur emerging with his electric rifle pack strapped on. Followed by Xie with his sword at the ready.

"Mr. Fogg and Aouda are to be coming up *that* stair," Passepartout pointed back to the roof door.

Robur nodded to Niru, "Hold fast," and led Xie and Passepartout into the building to rendezvous and escort them as needed.

ଔ ଚ

A rattling could be heard at the door lock of Fogg's parlor suite, as someone proficient in picking set to work out in the hall. Aouda got a determined look and crossed to the casing. Taking out her electric gun, she activated it, adjusted some dials upon its handle, waited until it hummed in a particular way—and fired at the lock. The dazzling yellow-green bolt quickly fused the key and lock, and jumped along the lock pick to throw its handler down onto the hall carpet, unconscious and hands singed.

Mrs. Hammond and her cohorts were startled, to say the least. She recognized that some sort of electric phenomenon had occurred, but had no inkling how it could have been accomplished there in the hotel, or how it might have been improvised in the moment.

"Clever chap," she muttered, then a bit more loudly addressed the door, "Will the management approve of your vandalism, Mr. Fogg?" When no response or sound followed, "Come, come—don't feign no one's home."

"This is not the hour for *whist*, Mrs. Hammond," Fogg finally declared from his side of the panel.

Hammond smiled, gratified at the recognition, so many weeks having passed since they had last met in distant Suez. The appreciation of honed adversaries.

Approaching (slowly) from down the hall, Colonel Proctor reported the negative result of his team's efforts at Passepartout's room, "The Frenchman's gone. What's the problem here?"

"Fogg used some electric trick, jammed the lock," Mrs. Hammond explained.

"Damn, we'll have to break the door," Proctor glowered.

Mrs. Hammond nodded, "But quickly—otherwise we'll be rousing the whole floor."

"Our wagon can't wait much longer, either," Proctor amended.

ଔ ଚ

Just as he was about to open the door to the Third Floor, Robur stopped. Flipping open a leather flap on his wide left coat lapel, he tapped out a message on a set of keys concealed beneath. "Aouda has locked the intruders out, but blocking themselves in. We need to find the room above theirs."

Robur turned to Xie, "Relieve Niru, who will be joining us."

While Xie raced up the flights, Robur and Passepartout retraced their steps to come out on the Fourth Floor, Passepartout leading the way.

On the floor below, Colonel Proctor had just then selected the burliest shoulder among their men, who proceeded to ram into the portal with a solid thud. Neither the door nor jamb budged.

"This hotel bought the highest quality doors," sighed Mrs. Hammond.

Behind that testament to architectural integrity, Phileas Fogg hauled one of the hotel's fine chairs to prop its back up under the knob, just in case the next blow successfully breached the hinges. "Waste of decent furniture."

"Give it one more try," Proctor directed to his man. The impact was a bit louder this time, but the outcome was the same.

No one had appeared from any of the rooms yet, so perhaps their commotion had awakened no one, but neither Proctor nor Mrs. Hammond were confident that could continue much longer.

"Are there any other exits? Connecting rooms?" Proctor asked.

"I can't be certain," Mrs. Hammond answered. "I don't think so."

Rubbing his groin absentmindedly, Proctor shook his head, "I can't imagine they'd seal themselves in without a strategy. These people are damned sharp."

"I'm not about to pitch a tent out in the hall all night to find out," Mrs. Hammond said, but had begun thinking about that herself.

She decided to reveal a perhaps impolitic confidence, "My briefing suggests they may have some sort of airship, though whether it's nearby or how it could be used I have no idea. If you can find your way to the roof, have a look around, see what you can see. Meanwhile, we'll use your battering ram here, till the door breaks or we wake up the floor—at either point, we will be going."

Proctor, his cracksman, and one other man set off down the hall toward the nearest staircase. Soon discovering the stairs ended at the Fifth Floor, he quietly led his team out into the guest servants' floor to find another way up.

◈ ◈

Arriving at the corner parlor suite on the Fourth Floor, Passepartout pulled out his comb and determined that the rooms were unoccupied—which Robur perceived only as the valet standing silently, eyes shut, and the comb tines inexplicably quivering. Passepartout's then using the comb to unlock the door brought a more overtly raised eyebrow from Robur.

Niru now rushed out of the stairway onto the Fourth Floor, wearing an electric gun and leather tunic with communication flap as Robur did, but also carrying *Deimos*' rope ladder. He proceeded quickly but silently to their location.

Passepartout was waiting at the door, which he kept slightly ajar. Once inside, Niru handed the ladder to Passepartout. Then he and

Robur donned goggles, which they kept on the top of their head while they turned on their weapons and adjusted the controls on their barrels.

Eying their preparations, and how they positioned themselves about ten feet apart in the middle of the room, Passepartout began to pace along a section of the floor beneath where several nozzles protruded from the ceiling. "There are fire drainage pipes along here, gentlemen, which you may wish to avoid. The gas pipes are only on the walls."

Robur nodded, relocating himself a few feet to one side, Niru mirroring. Tapping on his lapel keys once more, Robur warned, "Best look away."

He and Niru pulled the goggles down over their eyes.

In their suite directly below, Aouda turned to Phileas Fogg and took his hand, "Come, Phileas. Let us admire the view over here, by the window, our backs to the room, eyes shut." She tapped her left bracelet.

With another nod, Robur and Niru fired the guns for a fraction of a second. The broad simultaneous blasts vaporized a hole in the floor, a coronal shock wave washing over them and leaving the edges smoldering and dropping flaming debris onto the floor of Fogg's suite below.

Outside in the hall, the Moran gang were certainly startled by the unusual sound, but took it as some sort of tactical incendiary and did not lose their heads.

"Upstairs!" Mrs. Hammond cried, directing some to go back down the hall to the stairs there, while she sortied the rest of them to the nearest stair along the main hall. Along the way, her right hand pulled a rapier blade from her dark burgundy parasol (once again of a match with the color of her dress beneath her coat), while brandishing the umbrella portion in the other, its handle raised as a club.

ↂ ↃↃ

Turning around and seeing the burning mess descending on the carpet, Phileas Fogg dashed into his bedroom to grab a blanket to dampen down the curls of smoke already coming up from the carpet. Aouda meanwhile located the luggage nearer the opening, just as the rope ladder rolled down through the hole, up which Aouda immediately began to climb. After handing up his carpetbag to Aouda, followed by her case, Fogg began the ascent himself.

As his head cleared the floor of the room above, Fogg saw Passepartout sitting on the floor, straining on the end of the ladder, Robur and Niru kneeling on either side of his spread legs, holding his thighs and knees fast, bracing the exceptionally strong valet until Fogg was clear.

That accomplished, Passepartout gathered up the ladder, and Robur expeditiously led the way out into the hall, Fogg carrying the carpetbag in his left hand, a drawn revolver in the other (which he was reluctant to use given the noise another report would entail). Aouda held her luggage likewise, but with her electric gun at the ready. Passepartout had his gun out as well, although keeping hold onto the rolled rope ladder meant more grasping the firearm than actively aiming it. Niru held the rear point with attentive head sweeps.

Fortunately, by the time a few guests poked their heads out from their rooms to assess the disturbance (including detective Fix), Phileas Fogg and escort had already disappeared from view down the main hall. The second contingent of the Hammond-Proctor pursuit party were just progressing up the side hall, however, and sought to hide their weapons as they raced along.

Robur was about to pass the next cross hall when Mrs. Hammond and her men began to surge out into the passage from the adjacent stairs, proficiently brandishing their guns and knives. One of the more defensive men fired into the approaching Fogg brigade, striking Passepartout in the shoulder (though this did not cause him to lose hold of the ladder). Robur coolly returned fire, slaying the man, while Niru spun around to fell another just as he threw a knife, which buried itself in the hall's decorative wainscot molding.

Faced with such unusual opposition, Mrs. Hammond pulled her men back into the hall. "Must we use our guns, Mr. Fogg?" When none of those around the corner spoke, she added for the benefit of the woman she reckoned to be among them, "Or leave it to us ladies? Dueling hatpins?"

Aouda couldn't suppress a smile at that, and recognition of its implication. Mrs. Hammond could only have known of that if some of Colonel Proctor's team had told her of it.

Just then the second contingent appeared around the corner behind Niru. Another shot was fired, though not striking any of Fogg's party in the dim hall gaslight. Aouda had already spotted that group out the corner of her eye, and quickly brought her electric gun to bear to take that fellow down with a lethal pulse, causing his comrades to retreat behind the corner, wide-eyed and suppressing some panic.

Back around in the side hall, seeing and hearing matters turning serious, Mr. Fix shut his door to give him time to fetch his own gun before resuming his investigation.

Robur assessed the inadvisability of remaining where they were, and "spoke" for them all.

Striding slowly forward, he held the electric gun trigger to produce a continuing bolt that he strafed along the hall wall, which arced farther along it as Robur stepped ahead and turned right, exposing more of the wall to his fire.

"*Sheiße!*" Mrs. Hammond swore, urging her men back into the stairwell to avoid the deadly electric beam inching nearer.

Fogg and the others could now proceed, and Robur concluded his covering fire by melting the stair door knob, disabling their egress. Those men still at the far end of the hall decided to quit the field of battle altogether, running by Mr. Fix when he reappeared in the hall. Down in the blocked stairwell, Mrs. Hammond likewise abandoned the hunt, and led her men downstairs to flee while still able.

The gunshots and electric fire had roused several on this side of the hotel, though most were drawn to the three bodies cluttering the carpet runner, prompting gasps and one squeaked cry of alarm. Fewer were paying close attention to the backs of the strangely attired people heading swiftly down the hall in the other direction, and soon disappearing around the corner into the stairs.

೦೩ ೮೦

What sounds the electric blasts and gunshots had made were still less perceived where Proctor and his men were, finally arriving at a stairway that opened onto the roof. And the door was unlocked.

That unlocked status put Proctor on his guard. Pushing the door open slowly, the sight of the *Deimos* on the roof instantly heightening that apprehension.

None of the three men had ever seen the like. *Deimos*' windows faced them, the electric light within glinting off the various metal surfaces, fittings, and instruments—whose purposes they could hardly imagine—while the smooth gray hull with its apertures and vanes looked unlike any contrivance of their experience. Though the low hums and gasping exhalations from its vents certified to them of its human artifice, if not its threatening power.

And then the stern Chinese man appeared from the port side of the craft, right hand on the hilt of his sword, legs spread. No one could mistake him for other than a determined and formidable guardian.

Prejudiced fantasies of an implacable Yellow Peril now invaded the thoughts of Proctor and his men, whipping up their suspicions that the enemies of their distant employers were indeed a dangerous conspiracy of foreigners and malcontents who would not know their place.

With no hesitation, Proctor pulled out his pistol, and raised it to fire at the Chinaman. But in the time it took to lift his arm for aiming, and for his companions to begin to follow his lead, Master Xie broke into a run forward, sweeping out his blade and slicing first one then the other of Proctor's aides just as the Colonel pulled the trigger.

Neither the report nor the bullet delayed Xie's course or intent, and the Colonel fell in turn only a moment after he had used his gun.

Xie looked down at his tunic, where a large blood stain was already appearing. He closed his eyes briefly, girding his strength. Then he turned to hobble much less quickly back to the *Deimos*, to settle at its entrance hatch, seeking to rest even while remaining at guard.

Mere moments after, Robur and his charges appeared at the door, frowning down at the three bodies splayed around the short stairs. Then he sighted the trail of blood spatters, dark spots against the white frost on the roof. Aouda noticed them too, and raced ahead to find Xie slumped, eyes closed, hand no longer on his sword hilt, yet with a most peaceful look on his face.

She tried to rouse him, and when she could not, Aouda laid her head on his shoulder and began to sob.

Finally Phileas Fogg took her shoulders and gently prodded her to rise, while Robur and Niru lifted Xie's lifeless body and with the greatest of care took him into the *Deimos*, to lay him out on the deck in his favored station by the windows. Once the hatch was sealed, Niru fetched his most beautiful and comforting blanket from his stores to shroud the body.

Passepartout placed the carpetbag by Xie's feet, and Aouda's case by his head, like improvised sentinels at a shrine, then took a place on one of the folding seats, to evaluate his own gunshot wound with eyes shut and breathing calm.

Aouda could not bear to look upon the body of her old dear teacher, so settled on the hatchway bulkhead—ironically in the same spot Captain Nicholl had occupied on his flight from the Arctic, not wanting to see Master Xie when alive, though for reasons utterly opposite of Aouda's respect and grief.

Phileas Fogg sat beside her, his right arm cradling her shoulder, feeling every shudder of Aouda's silent weeping.

Robur was now in the pilot's cupola, and *Deimos* revved to life, departing the roof of the St. Nicholas Hotel and flying out to land in the harbor, where they might have time for them all to decide what to do next.

Aouda could muster only one spoken sentiment during that brief journey, a genuine lament uttered with voice choking, "He never liked flying."

Phileas Fogg hugged her closer.

32. IN WHICH PHILEAS FOGG AND OTHERS TAKE TO SEA IN PURSUIT OF THEIR PURPOSE

None aboard the *Deimos* that Thursday morning were able to do more than nap for a few hours, fitfully, too troubled by the loss of Master Xie. Robur, who kept up in the cupola to his own silent counsel, had submerged them in the Hudson River off away from the shipping lanes. The gentle swaying of the vessel as their position was maintained against the current helped a bit to lull them to slumber.

Passepartout remained in the folding seat almost motionless, eyes shut, striving for repose while the bullet in his chest could be worked out, which it did at a quarter past five. Fishing it out when the projectile slid down under his shirt to his pantaloons belt, he placed it atop the sill of the *Deimos*' windows, another offering for the makeshift Xie shrine.

Roused by Passepartout's motion to and from the window, Niru began to busy his hands by making omelets for their breakfast, which he completed just after 6 AM as the others began to awaken. Robur brought *Deimos* to the surface then, the first glimmers of dawn showing from the windows of the pilot's cupola.

"Xie must be taken home for his funeral," Aouda told Robur as Niru made the rounds with his plates of food. They both knew rites had to be done, in the proper order and at the proscribed time. Aouda absolutely owed him that. "That will be a long journey, for you both."

"We will manage. We'll cross the Pole to save time. Tanseem will have fresh provisions ready, and we'll return as soon as we can," Robur promised.

Phileas Fogg was especially downcast as he took the breakfast plate from Niru. Finally turning to Aouda, "Why don't you hate me?"

"Hate you? Why?"

"No chimes on my watch, Aouda. I never used my Time Machine to save your Mister Xie. I must never even have tried."

Aouda paused her breakfast to reflect deeply on that. The import of what having such a tool truly meant struck her deeply, Phileas so honestly insisting on bringing it up.

"We're not gods, Phileas. And Time isn't just something to be changed—even if we can. It's the sum of all that we *do*, what we stand for. Master Xie lived a good life, honorable and true. I knew him to carry no spite or hatred. He died with a smile on his face, Phileas. I think he regretted nothing. So, no—I do not hate you, Phileas Fogg."

Then Aouda donned a steely resolve. "I reserve my fury for those who deserve it. Those who spurred Proctor and that woman on. They should stay out of our way, if they value their lives. Once *Deimos* is done with laying Xie to rest, and your wager won in London, I'd be obliged if you'd help me close the book on Sir Augustus Moran, and whomever his friends are in this affair. Whether you may use your Machine in this, or not—no matter. I just want your alliance, and presence."

"That you have. Fully."

‌ ෴ ෨

Mr. Fix was in the dining hall of the St. Nicholas Hotel, awaiting his presumed breakfast appointment with Phileas Fogg and company, and so did not catch sight of the new contingent of police who arrived to investigate the night's disturbance.

The constable who had arrived a few hours before reported that six men had been found dead, leading the chief detective up first to see those on the roof. Sheets had been laid over the three bodies there.

"All were armed with guns and knives, and all killed by sword slash, very precisely delivered," the policeman explained. "Only this bearded man seems to have fired his. Maybe hit someone—there's blood drops," pointing off across the roof.

The detective followed that trail until it ended, next to two parallel furrows in the frost. Returning to the three victims, one turned out to have lock picking gear in his coat pocket. "Was the roof door normally locked?"

"According to the manager, yes."

That made sense, the detective thought, explaining the opened door, but puzzled, "Seems an odd place for a duel."

"It gets more interesting below," and the copper took the detective down to the Fourth Floor.

Two bodies had been sheeted by the side hall, and the policeman indicated the knife imbedded in the wall nearby. But it was that adjacent passage that drew a gasp from the detective, where a charred burn line ran along the south wall for a good twenty feet, as if some lightning bolt had worked along it. The stairway door lay on its side, leaning up against the north wall. The doorknob had been melted, requiring the door to be dislodged by the hinges.

The detective sucked in a breath as he looked at the burns on the body nearest the wall charring.

"All three down here are like that," the policeman said.

"St. Elmo's Fire, indoors?" the detective wondered, though without much conviction.

"Come see *this*," and the policeman circumnavigated the remaining shrouded body to enter the corner parlor suite, the one with the hole burnt in the floor.

The detective whistled. "Some kind of bomb?"

"There was no sound of one," the policeman said. "The gunshots were what woke some up. This room was unoccupied."

"What of the one below?"

The policeman consulted his notebook. "Taken by a Phileas Fogg—the one from the newspapers, going around the world. A Hindu Princess was traveling with him, and his valet—who Fogg insisted on having in a regular room, just down the hall. They're all gone, though they had told the desk they'd be leaving early."

Looking at the hole, the detective huffed, "I don't blame them."

The policeman pressed on concerning Fogg's parlor suite, "The door to their room had to be taken off the hinges too, like the stair door. Same melting of the lock."

That set the detective to pondering. Finally he asked, "You weren't here eight years ago, were you?" The constable shook his head. "Secessionists tried to burn down this hotel, and some others. It could be some plot, like that. Aimed at foreigners, maybe—or Fogg just the coincidental guests downstairs."

The hole still held his gaze. "That's some incendiary. The War Department would want that."

ଔ ଓ

Robur used considerable discretion to find a suitable place to surface to disembark Aouda, Passepartout and Phileas Fogg. Aouda took this as her last opportunity to give her respects to her old friend Xie. Kneeling by the body at the window, she noticed the bloody bullet on the sill when she looked up.

Where did *that* come from? She looked about, noticing the empty folding seat, and recalling who had sat there. In the fearful business last night she had forgot that Passepartout had been struck. But now the valet seemed completely recovered, conversing in hushed tones with Phileas by the port hatch. She reached out to take the bullet from its spot, thinking to deposit it in one of her pockets, but stopped and left it where it was. It had been placed there for a reason, she decided, and would leave it thus.

Just before seven o'clock, Robur finally found a pier empty of boat and observing people to slip into, lifting up long enough for them to dash out the starboard hatch and continue out to the streets. *Deimos* then dropped back into the water, to continue south out of the harbor before taking flight for China.

With the task of hiring a boat before them, Fogg and party could take their minds off the loss of Master Xie. The sun was just coming up, the temperature just hovering near freezing, the climate and sky utterly fitting their mood.

As in Hong Kong, the problem was not merely engaging a boat that reliably displaced water, but one with engines sufficiently robust to transit them across the Atlantic in time to fulfill Phileas Fogg's wager. Sailing vessels (of which there were an abundance) were out of the question as too slow. That left steam alone.

Nearing the end of the Hudson River docks around eight o'clock, down by the open Battery Park, Fogg spotted a craft with some prospects: iron-hulled with steam screw, good lines with wood decks above. The SS *Henrietta*'s pennant was up, indicating an impending sail. Her commander, the auspiciously named Captain Andrew Speedy, of Cardiff, was a thick-set red-haired man of fifty, and freely answered Fogg's inquiries from the gangplank.

Speedy was set to sail for Bordeaux in an hour, carrying no freight but also averse to passengers. Her speed would suit: though lacking the latest Holt compound engines, at eleven or twelve knots *Henrietta* fell not that much shy from the White Star's *Adriatic*, current Atlantic crossing holder at 14½ knots.

Except Speedy would not be diverted to Liverpool, nor sell the ship (which he owned outright). As for passengers, these he would not accept even for $200. So Fogg offered him $2000. Apiece—for four people (he was still not forgetting Mr. Fix). That sum finally surmounted the captain's reluctance, and £1600 were withdrawn from the carpetbag.

"We have to fetch our fourth from the hotel. Here is my quarter," Fogg handed him £400, "the remainder once we're all aboard and on our way."

"We sail at nine," Speedy reminded tersely, waving the pound notes, "Forfeit if you're not here."

Speedy's flagging of a wad of cash (the English banknotes being ever larger than the American paper money) caught the attention of several of *Henrietta*'s crew, securing hatches and preparing to unmoor the ship. Hard currency often had that effect on people, even in this American bastion of gold and silver coin.

All of which amused Aouda (who sorely needed it just then)—a further indication of how accustomed Mr. Fogg was to getting his own way. At least as long as he had the money to throw at it.

Passepartout had wandered far enough from Fogg's watch to make use of his comb, which revealed no familiar bodily vibrations anywhere close about. Still he did not feel calm about things, uncertain whether any of the people milling back and forth on the docks might be there to take notice of them.

His concern was not unfounded.

Unbeknownst to the Frenchman's instrument, their activities down on the Hudson piers had not gone unnoticed by the spider threads of men Mrs. Hammond still had turned to that purpose. After the nocturnal battle at the St. Nicholas Hotel, word had been passed around to show the utmost caution in tracking their progression. As a recognizable figure, Mrs. Hammond initially stayed back from the docks, operating out of the Stuart company's New York warehouse over on the East River (where they had planned to hold Fogg's party, had it but come to that), but once her runners had located the Fogg group down on the piers, she had relocated to a nearby hotel—and where a runner was even then dashing to report the development at the SS *Henrietta*'s mooring.

With only a half hour before sailing, Fogg considered sending a messenger for Mr. Fix, but decided instead to bundle them all into a coach and so set off for the hotel together, Passepartout up with the luggage, warily surveying their course. Down within, Phileas Fogg and Aouda rode without conversation, holding hands.

Swinging around toward Broadway, off to their right the round roof cupola of Castle Garden occupied the southernmost tip of Manhattan Island—that former theater now turned terminal for the rising tide of immigrant traffic. Passepartout noticed the place was already busy that morning, a portal for European immigration that stood in such contrast to the haphazard arrival of the Chinese laborers back in San Francisco.

Threading north, Trinity Church's narrow spire thrust up over the financial village of Wall Street, where fortunes were made and lost both in person and via the marching lines of telegraph poles that linked all the world's commerce to this suburb of New York City. That too was a place already busy that morning, but Fogg and Aouda gave it scarce notice, enjoying the pleasure of one another's company as their carriage wended up Broadway, thick with the traffic of coaches, public and private, the Trinity tower receding behind them.

ଔ ଓ

Not ten minutes after the Fogg carriage rolled away for the hotel, Mrs. Hammond appeared at the dock to ask after them. She had changed into a sedate blue-gray dress, again with matching parasol, and made a striking figure as she strode across the gangway to the *Henrietta*'s deck.

Captain Speedy was finishing his inspection rounds, and intercepted this latest distraction before she had an opportunity to step farther. One of *Henrietta*'s crewmen looked up from the bow mooring line.

"I understand you've taken on some passengers this trip," Mrs. Hammond declared.

"What is it to you?" Speedy asked.

"I'm anxious for their safety. Indeed, so much so, were you to be met at sea, and your passengers safely conducted to a still larger vessel, would that be agreeable to you?"

"That seems *complicated*." Speedy was more suspicious now.

"Only insofar as your passengers might not initially consent to the transfer. Could you see through to that? Whatever they arranged to pay for passage, by the way, we are prepared to recompense you double further."

That diverted Speedy's suspicions more onto the lane of greed. "They're paying ten thousand dollars."

Nary a flinch from Mrs. Hammond, who smiled, "Then you will earn twenty thousand more with your cooperation."

"Who are these people to you?"

"They are on an around the world voyage, quite famous. *Phileas Fogg*," she emphasized slowly. "Our newspaper is anxious to see a successful conclusion to it, but they have not always been receptive to outside assistance, even ours. You know how stubborn some people can be," flicking her umbrella at him with a conspiratorial wink.

"Any advance on that twenty?"

"But of course. Here's a thousand now," which Hammond fished out from her bag. Hesitating before tendering it, "The remainder on their safe embarkation to our vessel."

The sailor at the mooring line was uncertain when he'd ever seen so much cash money being tossed around on a morning.

"Fair enough," and Speedy accepted the cash.

"Good voyage to you then, Captain Speedy." Mrs. Hammond added, "You will know the ship when it comes. Very big. Quatermass commanding."

And with a nod, she was gone, pleased that he had asked neither her name nor the newspaper for which she purported to act as agent. She had offered what he wanted to hear, and counted upon the fact that he would be in a hurry to finish his tasks before sailing.

ଓଃ ଌ

Arriving at the five gas lamps fronting the St. Nicholas Hotel on Broadway, Passepartout was dispatched to fetch Mr. Fix, "Move quickly, Passepartout," adding to Aouda, "No idea what the police might have done here since we left."

Passepartout fulfilled his task. The detective had left a message at the desk for them, indicating he would be languishing in the reading room with his traveling case, which he was.

"I thought we were to meet in the dining room at six," a peeved Mr. Fix demanded of Fogg soon after as he stepped into Fogg's carriage.

"There was some sort of pipe rupture in the room overhead," Fogg replied. "We declined to stay the night."

Fix accepted that. "There *was* a commotion last night, gunfire and bodies. You must have left by then. I saw some fire damage down one of the halls when I left for the dining room—where I paid for my own breakfast," he grumped.

"I hope it was worth the money," Fogg said.

Fix's begrudged expression suggested it had.

Once more the distinctly terse treatment of the St. Nicholas Hotel stay in Mr. *V.*'s account may be evaluated for what it did not discuss. As in the Hong Kong episode, all active action on the docks in search of a ship were attributed to Phileas Fogg alone, relegating Passepartout and Aouda again to clock-watching passivity. There is of course the possibility that the management of the hotel (and even the municipal police and authorities) preferred that concise banality to the broadcast of violent parties running unchecked in a major hotel, with all its potential depressive impact on tourist confidence.

Beyond that most dramatic omission of the hotel fight, though, it remained that Phileas Fogg, Passepartout, Aouda and Mr. Fix arrived at the dock to clamber aboard the SS *Henrietta* just as it was about to sail at 9 AM. Away to the Atlantic and Bordeaux.

☙❧

Sir Augustus Moran's ironclads had fallen low on coal and tenders were busy topping up their store that morning as another boat arrived from the mainland with the latest telegraphic messages, conveyed at length into the hands of Mr. Stuart, who dispatched them to Sir Augustus and waited by his desk for instructions.

"Nicholl says the Barbicanes are open to selling Power X," Sir Augustus said of one message.

"That's a turn. He never let any of us get within a mile of it."

"Nicholl thinks they're in need of money now and discouraged about its difficulties, which might be true."

Stuart was more cynical. "Or it's Nicholl, seeking to stay central to the game now that he's superfluous."

"Also a possibility," Sir Augustus nodded. "If it *can* be bought, though ... send *Albatross* over, that's a gadget to dazzle the Barbicane sort, and have Blake accompany my son to put further braid on the invitation. We must all look serious and not too eager."

Later that afternoon, Sebastian Moran and Commander Blake duly strode into Stone's Hill from their preferred secluded clearing to invite the Barbicanes and Captain Nicholl to meet a prospective buyer for the scientific discovery of the century.

Once seated in their drawing room, Moran began, "Good afternoon, I'm Colonel Sebastian Moran. My father, Sir Augustus has heard about the investment possibilities of your work here, which I've been following while my father conducts his oceanographic studies, rather boring to me."

"Yes, I've seen you hereabouts," Nicholl dissembled. "Didn't know you were related to his Lordship."

"And this is Commander Blake, who operates one of my father's experimental flying machines, which we used today to come here. We'd be most honored if you would fly with us out to meet my father on his steamship, just a few hours journey, where perhaps some good business may be conducted."

"A flying machine! My word." Barbicane glanced over at Nicholl, gauging his implausibly bland reaction, given their mutual experience aboard the astonishing *Deimos* only the week before.

Nicholl had other angles on his mind, "Your son, is he at hand to accompany us?"

"No, Victor is off to Baltimore, on a company errand. But we are of one mind on Power X and all that needs to be done about it."

Michel Ardan chose that moment to enter the room.

"Ah, what luck—we've been invited onto a flying machine, belonging to Colonel Moran's father, a business excursion that may have much pleasure to it." Barbicane turned to Moran, "You wouldn't mind if Ardan joins us, would you?"

While Nicholl hid his discomfort at the idea, Moran smiled, "More than enough room."

At the door, Barbicane instructed his butler, "You may say we are traveling now." The servant nodded.

It was dusk when they arrived at the airship in its clearing, an almost full moon just rising. Ardan had tried not to act familiar with the path.

Moran waved a hand as they advanced into the clearing where the airship lay, "Gentleman, the *Albatross*."

"Well that is *grand*, don't you think?" Barbicane said to Ardan, then asked Moran, "How ever did you keep news of it out of the papers? The correspondents have all hung on us."

"My father is interested in the work itself, like a monk, not courting public recognition."

While Michel Ardan had flown aboard the craft before, being inside it this time was not only more comfortable (there were several leather upholstered benches built into the hull for seating), it afforded him an opportunity to see how it was operated. Though he was not at all confident he could recall whatever switches were thrown or dials consulted were he forced by necessity to try and fly it himself.

As the engines were brought to power and the *Albatross* lifted away, Barbicane was ebullient, "It's like one of our old Union balloons, only bigger—and noisier." He turned to Nicholl, to goad a bit, "It sure takes a lot of mechanical to make *this* machine fly, wouldn't you agree?"

The pitching of the craft required some care in walking, but Barbicane made his way to Blake at the wheel. "Are you the builder of this craft?"

"A big part of it, yes," the Commander beamed. "The rotors were designed by several others, but I pioneered a way to angle them while they turn to enable better steering."

Ardan stepped up by Blake's other shoulder, "You must have assembled quite an accomplished team. Only the one ship, or a factory to build more?"

Moran careened in, "Our Commander needs to concentrate on his navigation. I hope you don't mind."

Thus rebuffed, Barbicane drew Ardan aside by one of the port windows to declare softly, "We're taking quite a circuitous course, to avoid being seen by any settlements below."

"They did likewise to my experience," Ardan replied. "I had quite a view from the *roof*."

The *Albatross* reached the Florida coast just before sunset, when a crewman made the rounds of the ship, lighting their small electric arc lamps, which sputtered and glared the gondola into brightness. Barbicane followed this process with some amusement, smiling to recall the more perfect *Nautilus* lamps, and the still more impressive ones aboard *Deimos*.

ଓଃ ଛୋ

The *Henrietta* was just then reaching the eastern tip of Long Island, bearing northeast for the stretch of open sea to pass Massachusetts. The cold sea air discouraged deck promenading, but a small ward room had a table and chairs that Fogg quickly commandeered for whist. The quartet found the distraction most relaxing, though their playing cards (bought on the train last week passing through Wyoming) were beginning to show compromising signs of wear on the corners.

A sympathetic crewman spotted their plight and said he might have a pack or two of new ones somewhere below deck. When he returned with them later, Fogg insisted on giving the man $5 in trade. "Card playing is our religion, so consider it an offering."

Aouda almost laughed, which given the last day of troubles Fogg counted a fine progress.

ଓଃ ଛୋ

Sir Augustus Moran was taking dinner with Stuart when the next shore packet arrived, which the ambassador worked through while he ate, beneath the six lamps of the massive chandelier.

"Ah, news from New York," Sir Augustus said of one envelope, but soon looked most displeased. "Damn! They've failed to catch Fogg or Passepartout—lost half a dozen men in a melee at the hotel, including that Colonel Proctor."

Stuart exhaled, "They were veterans of their war. Two men and a woman should have been no match for them—especially since we'd warned them how dangerous Passepartout could be."

Sir Augustus read on. "They'd been joined. Two new men, one possibly European, one definitely Asian. They carried some kind of electric guns. Blasted a hole in the ceiling for them to escape, then kept Boyd and her men at bay in the hall. The police found Proctor and two of his men on the roof, killed by sword. She'd sent them up there to check on any airship. They may have found one."

"The same that ferried Nicholl off *Nautilus*?"

"I hope so—otherwise it means they have more than one."

"Nicholl said it was fast." Then Stuart mused, "Electric guns. That smacks of Nemo."

"It does suggest what they're capable of when not playing *whist*." Sir Augustus continued to read Hammond's report. "Boyd's at least identified the ship they hired, bound for Bordeaux. She's offered their captain twenty thousand of *our* dollars to look the other way if we pick them up at sea."

"*She's* free with the expenses."

"Maybe not, this time. Fogg paid him ten thousand for passage, so she was just sweetening the stakes. She already had a thousand in hand. I might have done the same."

"Open invitation to catch them at sea, at least," Stuart looked more positive, "where they'd be most vulnerable and alone."

"*If* they're alone. I hope so." Sir Augustus leaned back in his chair, flicking the fingers of his right hand back and forth, "You know, Felix, I think we have rather underestimated Mr. Phileas Fogg. *He* may be our true nemesis, standing back, observing—planning from a distance, much as I have here. He's certainly *very* well protected."

"As are we," Stuart reminded.

ଔ ଛ

The new decks of cards were being well serviced in the *Henrietta*'s ward room when Phileas Fogg recalled something of utility he'd forgot in all the tumult of the last sixteen hours.

"Ah!" he cried, burrowing into the carpetbag to fetch the bottles of sherry and cognac salvaged from their ill-fated stop at the St. Nicholas Hotel.

Passepartout smiled. "Now, all we need are glasses."

A search of the ward room's cabinets recovered four adequately clean ones, Mr. Fix not averse to sharing the cognac (even as he felt the Fogg warrant chafing in his coat pocket), while Aouda and Phileas Fogg resumed their amontillado.

Fogg raised his glass and offered a toast across the table, looking in Aouda's eyes all the while, "To friends gained—and others lost."

Clinks ensued.

"Here, here," Mr. Fix said, affably dim as to what they were talking of.

○3 ♊

The *Albatross* arrived at the Moran flotilla around nine o'clock, giving a splendid view of the scene, bright in the moonlight.

"Isn't that the *Great Eastern*?" Barbicane asked from the window as they descended toward the landing platform.

"Yes," Moran smiled.

"Laying a cable?" Barbicane asked, with a tinge of sarcasm.

"No," Moran replied, "but they still have the runners for it."

Seeing the *Aurora* on the platform over on the bow as they dropped, Barbicane said, "Another airship. Quite a collection. What do you do with them all?"

"Fly about," Moran said.

Once they were moored, there was the boat ride over to the *Eastern*. "I saw her dock in New York once—never sailed on her," Barbicane told Ardan as they approached the towering hull.

Mr. Stuart met them at the stairs by the port paddle housing, "Commander Blake, you are wanted for consultation with Sir Augustus. Colonel Moran and I will keep our guests company in the meantime."

While Blake scurried off to the charthouse (a structure nestled behind the second funnel, just forward of the great paddlewheel engine skylight), Stuart introduced himself, then led Barbicane, Ardan and Nicholl off forward, under the second elevated inspection bridge, all the way past the first funnel to enter a stairwell in a little deck building.

"One does get one's exercise aboard this vessel." Stuart motioned for them to enter, where they worked down stairs to reach the bar salon, a long lavish room set around the mirrored funnel casement that extended from the boilers below. The gas chandeliers (fueled by pipes from its manufacture down in the bowels of the vessel) were lit, reflecting off the panes of the extensive skylights that ran parallel along the hull on either side of the funnel, a hint of moonlight glinting off them.

There was a fine setting of food laid out as a buffet on a marble-topped side table, while a barman attended to drinks from across the room, purveying everything from coffee and tea to stiffer beverages. Stuart indicated a darkened room adjoining the saloon aft, "We have that hall set up for dining. Our expedition operates on so diverse a schedule, breakfasts, luncheons and dinners are laid out there, but we put out a lighter night supper here."

Colonel Moran and Captain Nicholl had an appetite and promptly set to filling their plates, as did an initially hesitant Barbicane and Ardan. Stuart, who had eaten, took a whiskey and sat down at one of the small circular marble tables arranged around the room, appearing the most casual and affable of hosts.

Taking a seat beside Stuart, Ardan asked, "Are these the original appointments of the ocean liner?"

"I imagine so. I never sailed on her before. The rooms are quite cheering when the light's streaming down from the skylights. Brunel had an unusual inspiration for it all. Pity it never did well as a liner."

☙ ❧

Up in the *Great Eastern*'s chartroom, Sir Augustus Moran hunched over a map of the Atlantic, the chandelier casting shadows on the wall of those assembled around the table: himself and Captain Quatermass, Commanders Blake of the *Albatross* and Tremaine of the *Aurora*.

"My agent in New York learned the Fogg party has bought off a vessel from the piers, the light steamer *Henrietta*, single screw and funnel. That's all the description I have."

Captain Quatermass raised an eyebrow at that—Fogg? Did they mean the Phileas Fogg of the newspapers? He held his tongue, though, as Sir Augustus continued with the briefing.

"They're sailing for Bordeaux, which should take them along the Grand Banks," Sir Augustus swept his hand along the track their navigators had plotted. "Quatermass will be putting *Eastern* to steam for an interception, the others following, but that's still six days to cover fifteen hundred miles and more. *Albatross* and *Aurora* will do that in thirty hours."

Sir Augustus looked up at Blake and Tremaine, "Whichever one of us locates the *Henrietta*, *Aurora* will stay on to pace her, while *Albatross* returns to the *Eastern* with exact position and course." Nodding to Blake, "If needed, you'll refuel the *Albatross* with full haste, and return to our target to put your Gatlings to best effect. If we can stop the *Henrietta*, all the better, but any delay brings *Eastern* and the ironclads closer to snap the trap for good." Then he frowned, "They're in league with Captain Nemo, though, so his submarine boat may be lurking. There may also be a flying ship present, so we'll all have to keep watch on the skies, too."

"Armed or unarmed?" Blake asked.

"Their crew have electric guns, strapped on their backs," Sir Augustus said. "Beyond that, I don't know. It's a small machine, and apparently can fly quite high and fast."

"They may be sacrificing speed for power," Tremaine suggested.

"If you're up for the game, gentlemen, we'll set off," Sir Augustus concluded.

The ambassador looked grim as he rode over to the platform ship with Blake and Tremaine. Moran carried but one traveling case, in which he'd stashed £3000 and $4000 intended for the captain of the *Henrietta*.

Too many mistakes had been made by subordinates while chasing Passepartout and Phileas Fogg these last months, so even though it meant actually flying in the lead *Aurora*, Sir Augustus reined in his trepidation. He intended to be on top of things this time.

As the two airships lifted off and headed north, the *Great Eastern*'s horn blasted once long, then once more. The paddlewheel engines started up, impossible to ignore vibrations rippling through the giant vessel as it began to move forward.

"*That* is interesting," Michel Ardan brought his arm up on the chair back, looking aft toward where the engine rumble emanated.

Barbicane turned to Moran, "Your invitation didn't mention an *ocean* voyage."

Stuart was promptly apologetic. "There are so many circumstances at sea that might occasion a change of plans. But we do have airships, as you know, so your time away from shore should only be brief, and we have adequate accommodations for impromptu guests," Stuart spreading his hands wide, reminding them they were aboard a ship capable of cabining thousands. He then rose to take Sebastian Moran aside to whisper some instructions, occasioning the Colonel's departure.

Barbicane and Ardan exchanged silent glances. Plans would need to be revised.

03 80

Some distance away from the *Great Eastern*'s stern, a small steam sloop (hull and sails darkened to render them still less visible among the waves) dogged the Moran flotilla, keeping just at the limits of a good telescope held to a keenly observant eye.

Such a one as Victor Barbicane, who now swore, "Damn, they're moving off." To an anxious Mr. Danielson standing beside on deck, "Tell Grady to bring up more steam, we can't lose their trail."

Their ship was fleet and piloting proficient, but Victor knew it would not be easy keeping up with the Great Iron Ship at speed.

ଓଷ ଯ

When a steward appeared in the *Great Eastern*'s saloon, Stuart announced, "I believe your rooms are ready. If you gentlemen will follow me."

They went out to starboard, across a small bridge straddling the skylight overhangs, where railings ringed a second set of frosted skylights set down into the deck floor. The bridge led to further halls connecting the liner's passenger cabins, some fronting the outer hull, others facing inward to the skylight area. Ardan took notice of how few chandeliers were full lit in this space, which he surmised was for economy in little used rooms.

Nicholl lagged behind, observing Barbicane and especially Ardan with measured suspicion.

"A shame this old paddler's not outfitted with your airship's arc lamps." Barbicane joked to Stuart.

"They do hiss a great deal, though, don't they? And cast rather a harsh light, in my opinion, compared to gas." Stuart motioned ahead to the steward, who had stopped at one of the cabin doors, "We keep several rooms at the ready for visitors, with provisions for the bath under the settee in the connecting parlors, all of which I hope shall be to your liking."

As Stuart opened the door, the steward flitted in to raise the gas lamps to sufficient brightness. "Mr. Nicholl, this should suit you."

Continuing on to the next door, "Here, Mr. Barbicane, please," and the steward repeated the lamp lighting, the room revealed to be a fairly small eight foot square.

Regarding the third chamber's intended occupant, "My apologies, I don't think I know your name."

"Ardan," the Frenchman smiled, as the steward did his duty with the lamp.

"Ah, yes, I recall from the newspapers. You had a most narrow escape from disaster out there in the airless space, didn't you?"

Ardan shrugged, "Newspapers so often embellish."

"Let me know at breakfast of any inadequacy," Stuart said, then disappeared back around the corner across the skylight bridge with the steward.

Ardan turned around to inspect his cabin, which while compact was not poorly appointed, a Turkish rug atop the oilcloth flooring, space for a chair and small table beside a settee. Lifting the cushion revealed there was indeed a small tub within its base, with tiny faucets dispensing hot or sea water. Over on one well, an adjoining door opened onto a similarly sized bedroom.

Though Ardan heard no locking of the door to the hall over the churn of the ship's engines, a check confirmed it was not barred, and he discovered Barbicane had come out into the hall on the same surmise. Captain Nicholl had apparently kept to his room.

"We seem not to be prisoners," Ardan said.

"Except we're on a moving boat, headed Perdition knows where."

Ardan pulled out a compass, "Northeast."

"If we're not prisoners, let us explore this great vessel."

Which they did into the night, following the path of the working passage lights.

"The lamps tell us which sections of the ship are in use, otherwise they wouldn't be wasting the gas," Ardan observed as they proceeded back into the bar, where the barman and a steward were just cleaning away the evening's buffet, nibbling on bits of it until they spotted Ardan and Barbicane.

"Do not mind us, gentlemen," Ardan said, adding with a wink, "And it would be a shame for that food to go to waste."

"We weren't yet ready for sleep," Ardan called to them as he nipped a piece of cheese himself. "I take it the night work crews dine elsewhere?"

"Down aft, yes," the barman said. "You two gentlemen just visiting?"

"A check on the progress of the expedition seemed in order," Ardan said. "Have you found this voyage entertaining?"

"Boring, mostly," the steward said as he put covers on salvers and moved them to a rolling cart. "Weeks here, floating with nothing happening, then a dash to another spot. Now we're moving again."

"We don't get told a lot," the barman added.

"Such is the way of the laboring man. But you do your duty," Ardan complimented. "I would ask which way is the most interesting walk, fore or aft, but imagine the crew behind us would be wanting their sleep, without disturbance, no?"

Barbicane smiled to see how quickly Ardan had contrived to be mistaken for some officious inspector, as well as how deftly his questions were eliciting the lay of the land, and followed as Ardan headed off forward, retracting some of the steps they had followed behind Stuart and Colonel Moran earlier.

The *Great Eastern* was nothing if not cavernous, whose size was brought home to the nocturnal strollers when they encountered a doorway that opened onto one of the three sections of the ship that had been converted to cable storage, extending several decks from one bulwark to the other.

"One of the old cable holds," Barbicane said, his voice echoing a little. The chamber was empty now, though a tiny sliver of moonlight beamed down from a shuttered cap where the cable would have been fed up to the deck machinery.

"The world hums from messages sent on cables laid by this ship," Barbicane told Ardan, before securing the hatch door.

ಚ ಸು

Though Captain Speedy's practice was not to carry passengers aboard the *Henrietta*, the vessel had enough compartments for their accommodation. The arrangement for suitably fresh bedding and linens proved more challenging. Fogg's party played cards long into the night, fortunately, giving the crew considerable time to rehearse the pretense of being a passenger liner.

"Don't fret over them too much," Captain Speedy advised his First Officer from the wheelhouse. "With some luck, we won't have them staying all the way to Bordeaux."

"You going to throw them overboard?"

Speedy laughed, "No. But there may be a boat to pick them up in a few days. A big one."

The seaman didn't know what to make of that as he oversaw the preparation of the Fogg party's cabins, one room for Phileas Fogg and Passepartout, one each for Aouda and Mr. Fix.

"We hope not to inconvenience any of your crew," Aouda told the First Officer later as they were shown their quarters.

"We don't have fancy fare on board," he cautioned.

"Good sturdy food, fit for a seaman's needs, will suit us fine, sir," Aouda smiled. She did not add that her experiences with dining drawn along in the Fogg vortex meant very little could be a genuine disappointment.

Passepartout meanwhile noted Phileas Fogg's casual reaction to all this. How unlikely this scene would have seemed, concerning the punctilious and demanding Mr. Fogg who had hired him as valet scarcely two months before. But then, so much had happened for them all in the meantime.

ಚ ಸು

It was just after midnight on Friday, December 13th, when Barbicane and Ardan worked their way back up the stairs to emerge on the *Great Eastern*'s deck, by the second mast. There were still a few crew up top going about their rounds, but all quite oblivious to the nocturnal visitors.

"For a cabal, they seem a casual lot," Ardan thought as they headed toward the bow.

"It may be there's nothing aboard ship they need to *conceal*."

"Apart from things like this," Ardan stepped to port and one of the small platforms where one of twenty Gatling guns were stationed.

341

After peeking up under the cover, Ardan hopped back onto the deck. "No sign of ammunition, those may be locked away below."

"Meaning it would take time to bring them up and load, should there be alarm," Barbicane offered.

"Just so," Ardan replied.

They couldn't easily go beyond the first mast, since the old cable-laying equipment occupied the forepeak, with a trough running like a viaduct about at bulwark height to the bow, so they turned back, past the skylight housings flanking the first and second funnels.

Catching sight of plumes of smoke off to port, Barbicane crossed to the bulwark between two of the lifeboats dangling over the side, and pulled a spyglass from his coat pocket.

"That would be some of their ironclads, I imagine," Ardan offered from behind Barbicane's shoulder.

"Right you are, sir," Barbicane said, "a cheese box and our airship dock." Turning back to Ardan, "This ship can steam at over fourteen knots. But I don't think those can."

"So because they are keeping up, we are not at speed. Very good." Ardan listened to the engine throb aft, "We should hear and feel then should we add speed, eh?"

Barbicane collapsed his glass and resumed the deck survey. They could just see the edge of the bar below through one of the skylights off to their left. Continuing past the second funnel, they could see the pilot's wheel up at the center of the aft transverse gangway, a crewman tending the giant wood and brass wheel, connected to a web of cables and gears that signaled the course to the rudder a hundred yards behind them.

"Our captain is no doubt asleep," Ardan said, "Though I think we will want to converse with him, before this voyage is done."

Directly aft, the transverse skylight straddled the hull over the four engines propelling the *Great Eastern*'s two fifty-foot paddlewheels, whose efforts now overwhelmed any sound of the sea. The moonlight glinted off the giant pistons and shafts heaving relentlessly below—quite a sight, beautiful and fearsome in only the way the machinery of man could be, and not even at their full speed.

Barbicane and Ardan continued on beyond the third and fourth funnels, where the longer main cable laying conduit ran clear to the fantail, again at about the same height as the bulwarks. One either had to walk around it at the third funnel's end, or duck down under it if one wanted to see the starboard side of the ship, but the investigators stuck to port.

Nearing the stern, Barbicane and Ardan encountered several small cannons, pointing through openings in the bulwarks.

"I think these were put aboard to protect the cable laying," Barbicane patted one. "They traveled in some perilous seas at times."

"As may we, my friend," Ardan ventured.

The pulleys and wheels of the cable equipment at the end of the trough were still a sight—their retention a testament to the contingent profitability of the *Great Eastern* in that regard (the ship being the only one on earth capacious enough to hold the incredible mileage of cable needed for transoceanic submarine telegraphy).

But the great crane at the fantail was definitely *not* part of the cable laying gear.

It had its own steam engine, and a proud embossed label identified it as the work of "A. Stuart & Cie, Glasgow."

Ardan, long aware of the *Eastern*'s crane, was more intrigued by the diving sphere on the deck beside it. Tapping its thick metal casing, "I wonder who aboard operates *this*."

Just then a crewman came upon them, patrolling from down the starboard side, "You're out on a late stroll, sirs."

"Curious temporary passengers, insomniac to avoid the *mal de mer*," Ardan announced, then waved at the crane and sphere, "This is *most* impressive."

"Be careful, though, don't play with any winches or tackle," the crewman cautioned. "Not for untrained people."

"We promise not to make a nuisance on your watch," Barbicane smiled.

After the crewman set off, Ardan said, "There went a sailor, wouldn't you say? Not armed apparently. Not a ruffian with seaman's skills recruited to act *as* a seaman, but an actual seaman, doing his patrol. There are implications to that."

By now Barbicane had turned away, to pull out his glass again to anxiously survey the horizon aft, the Moon high over his left shoulder.

"It will be difficult to see anything at this distance, even with the Moon," Ardan said.

"That's what I'm hoping. Whatever I can't see, maybe they can't either." Having failed to catch any glimpse of Victor's pursuing craft, Barbicane took in a breath. "Well, I suppose we may as well get some sleep," and both gentlemen returned to their cabins.

33. IN WHICH PHILEAS FOGG IS NOT ALONE IN BEING EQUAL TO THE OCCASION

When Sir Augustus Moran awoke on the modest crew cot aboard the *Aurora*, that Friday morning, December 13th, the airship's progress was so smooth, so unlike the perpetual heaving of a ship, even the giant *Great Eastern*, that for a moment he forgot he was in the air. But the omnipresent drone of the airship's engines rumbling away out on their nacelles soon reminded him of his suspended isolation.

Emerging from the crew carrel, Sir Augustus turned right down the narrow hall that ran from the aft entry hatch to open onto the windowed pilot's deck, where Commander Tremaine and the two day shift crewmen were already at their stations. Moran squinted for a moment from the morning light, so turned to the port windows facing west. The trackless sea looked even more so from several hundred feet height.

"Good morning, Sir Augustus," Tremaine greeted brightly. "Sleep well?"

"Surprisingly so," the ambassador replied.

"Unless we're in a storm, we can often fly dead level, smoother than any water ship. Shows the superiority of not trying to use *wings* to fly. Since we left last night we've covered five hundred miles. I suggest Henson's old Aerial Steam Carriage would have crashed by now. Even Blake's *Albatross* proves you don't need wings—they may not even be desirable."

Sir Augustus was not especially interested in such minutia.

Tremaine had taken out a special day signal lamp and a pair of goggles with polarized lenses suited to their use. Cranking a small handle on the side of the lamp, which whirred electrically within, he said, "Speaking of *Albatross*, I'm about to signal that all fields here are clear ahead."

Sir Augustus stepped closer to the window casements to both watch the commander operate the device, and to snatch a glimpse of the sea below, until his nervous breathing and shaking hand compelled him to step back from the precipitous view. He could also hear the gentle rattling of the glass in the metal frame (so much of the ship being crafted in a king's ransom worth of the light metal aluminium), buffeted by the artificial gale as they sped along at a locomotive's rate.

Seeing the signaling procedure, the ambassador thought the mystery flyer in the Pacific might use something like those lamps for communication. But unless Phileas Fogg and Passepartout packed around their counterparts (which seemed implausible given reports of their limited luggage) he could not see how they could have utilized such means to signal from the *General Grant* in the Pacific.

Tremaine shut down the lamp and removed his goggles, which he lay on a bulkhead table, beside a small portable chessboard. He and Commander Blake had been playing a game before they left their Florida station, and since they would be in signaling contact on this venture northward, decided to continue the match by appending their moves to their necessary messages. Blake was the better chessman, but Tremaine was holding up his part so far.

Resuming the wheel, Tremaine reported to Sir Augustus, "*Albatross* is progressing smoothly, all clear at their end. We're still south of the trans-Atlantic lanes anyway, won't see much till tomorrow. Together, at this altitude we can survey a swath a hundred miles wide."

Sir Augustus turned to Tremaine, putting his back to the windows. "I wonder what my wife would have made of this. It might have been a sight to amaze her." Then he sighed, "My great regret, Tremaine, not having her by my side, now—when we're nearing our goals. I miss her still."

"These last fifteen years have taken their toll. Voices in the wilderness, you most of all. But now, we're flying into a new age. Imagine a fleet of airships like this, patrolling the Empire. Descending on the colonial subjects, White Gods of the Air." Tremaine's face showed a fierce conviction as he held the wheel firm, "And if we build them large enough, we can drop bombs from them, too. The aerial navy is the future, Sir Augustus. Whoever controls the air, controls the world. Borders, fortifications—all obsolete."

Moran caught a mental chill from that declaration, the sort one gets when recognizing something not previously considered, and dangerous. He had wrestled enough with trying to imagine how inferiors like Captain Nemo could contrive machines better than any European engineer, and on less resources. But now his own subordinate Tremaine was sprinting ahead beyond anything the ambassador had surveyed, into a world transformed by limitless speed and power ... into what?

All those lines so carefully drawn on the globe, and the armaments assembled to defend them—could these really be eclipsed by an airship's shadow? Was Tremaine the harbinger of a world to come, a wasteland of global warfare? Was Moran helping to make an age where these mechanics of science inevitably raced out of control, perhaps so far that they too forgot their place, confidently tending wheels and levers their "betters" could never hope to master? A time when aristocrats like himself were swept aside as ... *obsolete.*

But Sir Augustus was not yet auditioning the role of superfluous Dr. Faustus, nor yet heed the warning playwright Marlowe once emblazoned on that character's arm: "*Homo, fuge!*"

A deferential crewman appeared with a plate of breakfast for Sir

Augustus, a Spartan repast of ham, toast and coffee, carefully prepared in their miniscule galley but unavoidably deficient compared to what the ambassador was used to aboard his floating *Great Eastern* palace.

Balancing the plate on his lap as he sat on one of the bulkhead benches, Sir Augustus asked Tremaine, "Is this what you have in store for the Air Age? Rations without even a table?"

Mistaking that for humor, rather than a disapproving prophecy, Tremaine smiled while keeping tight on the pilot's wheel.

ଓଃ ଛ

Abiding by her nature, especially when traveling, Aouda woke quite early, dressed with determination, her bracelets and other devices of interest electrified and at the ready, and took an early morning stroll around *Henrietta* before breakfast. The crew going about their work were of course unaccustomed to passengers, but responded to her smile and ingratiating visage with generally similar reaction. If some fretted at the presence of a woman aboard their ship as the direst of bad omens, the jinx of jinxes, they were not showing it as she explored the decks.

Captain Speedy was up at the railing outside the wheelhouse, surveying the seas with a spyglass. Not looking ahead, where the *Henrietta* was sailing, but more to the south and west, which Aouda found peculiar. More so still when Speedy caught sight of Aouda standing below him on the main deck, and tried turning a frown into something passing for a smile. Aouda nodded graciously at him, and the captain stiffly disappeared into the pilothouse.

Not long afterward, Aouda found Fogg and Passepartout in the galley. The crew had eaten at dawn, but the ship's cook was providing the unexpected passengers with a banquet of pancakes, bacon and toast, with coffee and even tea.

Seeing no Detective Fix as Aouda took a place beside Phileas Fogg, she joked, "Mr. Fix's sea legs left ashore again?"

"He was indisposed when I knocked on his cabin door," Fogg replied, "I hope he recovers them before our cards tonight."

Glancing at the cook busy some ten feet distant, Aouda leaned across the table and lowered her voice, "I saw something odd out on deck. Our captain had a glass on the horizon—*very* intently. He had the look of a man expectant to see something, and disappointed not to."

"He was looking to sea—not up in the air?" Fogg put down his toast.

"Good point—no, the horizon. And not in the direction we're going, either, back around and behind us."

Passepartout put his elbows on the table and his fingers together. "If we presume the worst, which has been rather necessary this trip, I suppose someone may be chasing us, and the captain knows it. If so, which of their ships—the ones we've seen? Or ones we haven't?"

"Depends on how much money they have to waste." Fogg resumed his toast, adding after a swallow, "How far away can your comb detect them?"

"Line of sight, to the horizon. Except in the direction of your watch." Passepartout pondered, "That would give an hour warning, at the speed ships go."

"I'd considered trying to persuade our captain to divert to Liverpool." Fogg took a knife and fork to the pancake on his plate. "This may warrant a change of plans beyond that. We need to know what sides there are—and who among the crew may be nudged, if needed."

"I think I should pay a visit to the engines after breakfast," Passepartout decided. "See what the valves look like, compared to the *Rangoon* and *Carnatic*."

"This time, I think I shall go with you," Aouda said. Turning to Fogg, "And what will you do?"

"Finish these pancakes," Fogg retorted. "They are fairly filling."

ଔ ଓ

In the dining alcove of the *Great Eastern*, Captain Nicholl and Colonel Moran were partaking a fine breakfast buffet, while the main paddle engines rumbled away somewhere on the other side of the elegant bulkheads, close enough to rattle the table settings.

Nicholl took a seat beside the Colonel. "Any idea when your father will be returning? I'd like this matter of the sale settled."

"No doubt. My father will return as he will."

"How long do you think Barbicane and Ardan can be stalled?"

While he owed an account of himself to his father, Moran felt no call to explain anything to the Captain, and shrugged, "Not my concern."

Captain Nicholl looked unsatisfied.

Over in the passenger cabins, Michel Ardan was just then knocking on Impey Barbicane's room, who appeared at the door only partially dressed.

"Good morning," Ardan said, "I have availed myself of their bathing amenities, which are satisfactory, if not opulent—hot water from a couch, amazing! Moran and Nicholl have gone on ahead to the dining salon, where I would rather not be alone with them. At least not yet."

"I'll be dressed shortly," Barbicane promised.

Once they had arrived in the dining room, perfunctory good mornings were exchanged and food willingly marshalled. Though Nicholl and Moran had finished eating, both had remained. Nicholl had lit up a smoke.

What else had they to do, thought Ardan, save to attend to himself and Barbicane?

Landing his plate on the table across from Moran, Ardan asked, "What plans does your father have for Mr. Barbicane's Power X?"

"I couldn't say," Moran replied.

"Ah." Ardan turned to Barbicane, who had sat down beside the Frenchman. "I had a most interesting conversation after our return to Stone's Hill, before you recounted a version of our adventures. Captain Nicholl will recall it." He shot a look at Nicholl, who was now on guard.

"Its full import only struck me now, though. The nature of the discussion bore many signs of a government's distant hand. I cannot say the gentleman we met there was in service of the *Deuxième Bureau*—that's the Second Bureau of the French Army, set up to gather and act upon intelligence—but it is not impossible that by now all that we discussed has found its way into some report, to be carefully read by those for whom the acquisition of Power X might be deemed a significant *matter of State*. Do you think that possible, Nicholl?"

Nicholl had to admit how very discrete Ardan was about that meeting with the mysterious third party, but said nothing as Ardan added, "Something to think about."

Barbicane was faster to catch the play, "Well, I haven't been approached by any government, even my own." He turned to Moran, "*Is* your father acting on behalf of the Crown?"

Moran shrugged—an honest one, since Sir Augustus had by no means confided all his plans or connections to him.

Reading Moran's gesture correctly, Ardan pressed ahead against the surmise that the son may not have fully appreciated the scope or peril of his father's designs. "Well, if he is not, he may be swimming in deeper waters here than he imagined. Governments, especially very large and powerful ones, craft policies with great care, and are often mercilessly ungrateful to those acting in a rogue manner without their consultation or consent." Glancing at Moran, "With apologies, Sir Augustus has a clouded past, does he not?"

Ardan didn't wait for a reply, nor was Moran quick enough with one, as the Frenchman turned again to Barbicane, "I had heard his wife, the Colonel's mother, was slain most brutally in the Sepoy Rebellion, leading to incidents of temper and retribution that exceeded even the British Government's inclinations for repression. A posting to Persia would have been a natural way to … cool him off."

Turning again to Moran, Ardan asked slowly, "Do you think your father has cooled off?"

Moran had no ready answer to that, either, but was interrupted anyway by Stuart entering with Captain Quatermass.

"Good morning, all." Stuart was the hail fellow well met. "I thought you'd like to meet our Captain Quatermass ... Impey Barbicane ... Michel Ardan ... Captain Nicholl."

All rose for the ritual. Quatermass did look impressive in his braid.

"You're the news of the moment, it would seem," Quatermass said, "next to that Fogg fellow racing around the world. We get papers from shore."

"Sir Augustus not with you?" Barbicane asked.

"I'm afraid he has been called away *urgently*," Stuart affirmed.

Ardan pounced. "Whisked away by airship?"

"Exhilarating, isn't it, the age we live in?" Stuart smiled.

Barbicane had crossed close enough to put his arm around Quatermass' shoulder, "Tell me Captain, are you with the ship's owners, or were you brought on just for this expedition?"

Chafing somewhat at the American's familiarity, Quatermass replied, "I knew the ship from the repair days at Milford Haven."

"Is everything turning out to your satisfaction?" Barbicane asked.

Quatermass was beginning to sense the American's direction, "A seaman always keeps an eye on the horizon, Mr. Barbicane."

"On which there are so many hazards," Ardan appended. "We were just discussing what governments might have become interested in what's been going on out here."

"Governments?" Quatermass' interested was rising.

"Oh yes," Ardan explained, "Even I couldn't help hearing the many foreign accents back at Stone's Hill. I suppose it was only a matter of time before some of them noticed one of your airships, or boats."

Stuart didn't appreciate where this conversation seemed to be going. "What would *we* be of interest to them?"

"Oh, *monsieur*, dissembling at this late stage, when so many of us know so much already." Ardan turned to Barbicane, "Except you, my friend, presuming so easily a loyalty and friendship where it was unwarranted." Ardan pointed as he accused, "Colonel Moran and Captain Nicholl conspired to bring down *Columbiad*. That's what that conversation was about, at Stone's Hill. An agent had all the evidence of their perfidy. We might all have been *killed*, had others not intervened. Isn't that correct, Nicholl?"

Ardan's throwing this gauntlet in front of someone who he hoped was an independent witness, Captain Quatermass, had its effect. Nicholl's temper immediately boiled, and forgetting Dupin's warning of only a few days before, blustered, "There was no *danger*. Barbicane built his craft all right."

Barbicane was ready to play his part, fanning up an honest indignation of his own, "So you don't *deny* you are a traitor, and a cur?"

Captain Nicholl directed a nasty smile to Barbicane, "It has taken all my stomach to abide being in your company, sir. I can do so no longer."

Barbicane slapped Nicholl's cheek, "I demand satisfaction. You're my witnesses, gentlemen."

Felix Stuart felt the situation spiraling beyond his grasp.

"I stand as second," Ardan called, waving at Colonel Moran to indicate that he could be Nicholl's second, "You, Moran?"

By now concluding that Nicholl was both superfluous to Sir Augustus's needs and enough of a liability that a duel might not be an impediment, Stuart turned to facilitation, "We certainly have ample space, unless you'd prefer on deck."

"Makes no never mind where," Nicholl said.

Stuart turned to the Captain, "Any qualms on dueling at sea?"

Quatermass was disdainful, "Damage to the vessel all on your bill, Mr. Stuart."

Stuart seemed agreeable to that. "Your choice of weapons, Nicholl."

"You have pistols, Moran?" Nicholl asked.

"I can find some," and Moran set off to that purpose.

"You may as well return to the Bridge," Stuart told Quatermass. "I'll supervise the field of honor here."

Quatermass was happy to take leave of this absurdity. Barbicane and Nicholl began pacing out the space along the skylight railing, the bright light streaming down contrasting so with the dark humor of what was being planned. Stuart took up a spot between them by the railing.

Ardan joined Stuart by the skylight banister. "It is troubling, is it not, how quickly the American temper can flare, and things spin out of control. Perhaps Sir Augustus should have tendered offers *before* there were bullets flying."

"You find too much amusement in such things, I think, Mr. Ardan."

"Perhaps," Ardan replied. "Others find too little."

"What if the amusement were shooting *you*?"

Ardan failed to be ruffled. "Ah, none of us are immortal, Mr. Stuart. But have you identified *all* the Ardans of the world, and who all may lie behind them, that you could make such sport of this one? Do not forget Nemo and the mystery airship. You'd agree their activities were too opportune not to be coordinated. If I were playing for such stakes as you are here, I'd be worried I'd seriously misjudged the casino."

When Sebastian Moran returned with a case of pistols suitable for dueling, Barbicane and Nicole were positioned back to back where Stuart had stood.

"Twenty paces, turn and fire?" Stuart proposed.

Both antagonists nodded their ascent.

It proved not at all easy to aim on the *Great Eastern*'s deck, a ship years of disapproving passengers had already found too prone to rolling in the waves despite its great tonnage. Still, Barbicane and Nicole performed their dueling duties with precision. Firing simultaneously, Nicholl was seriously winged on his left shoulder. Barbicane was not struck at all.

"Honor served," Ardan called out, while Moran ran to the injured Nicholl.

Stuart stood where he was, weighing whether he was relieved or disappointed Nicholl was still alive.

"Was your aim true?" Ardan whispered to Barbicane.

"The boat rocks," Barbicane scowled. "I aimed for his heart. Pity I missed."

"Get Nicholl to his room," Stuart said. "I'll send Doctor Lawton down to him, at last something to earn his pay."

Once that trio had departed, Ardan became the embodiment of calm. "Well, I haven't quite finished my meal," and returned to his place at the dining table.

Barbicane followed, smiling, "That's because you talk instead of eat." After he was seated, he added, "I apologize, Ardan. You play poker very well, just not with cards."

Ardan nodded a smile, but continued to eat.

"So, our Sir Augustus has flown away, leaving his taciturn son and affable factotum Stuart behind. To where?" Barbicane wondered.

Ardan sacrificed civility by speaking with his mouth still somewhat full, "Something more attractive than buying *you* off, I'd say."

"Could he be hunting *Nautilus*?"

"Nicholl deduced we were let off in the North Atlantic, so that is possible."

"The *Nautilus* sunk ships by ripping their hulls—*wooden* ships, not iron ones like Moran's."

"Thinking like a tactician," Ardan approved. "Yes, *Nautilus* could be at a disadvantage."

"Could a submarine boat be seen from the air?"

"You mean, if only slightly submerged? I don't know. Neither of us were on *Albatross* during the day."

"We'd better survey the alternatives, in case things go bad. It's possible they still don't know Victor's behind us. If we stop, he'll try to slip in at night."

"You are sure he is behind us?"

"That is a *guarantee*, Mr. Ardan."

Ardan thought about what a nocturnal rendezvous would entail, "It would mean our conspicuously loitering by the paddlewheel gangway."

"And then there's the crew," Barbicane stressed. "How many friends, how many foe."

"They seem, so far, utterly professional," Ardan said. "The Captain doesn't strike me as sinister, either."

"Only a few dozen would be needed for the Gatling guns, special pay, people the Morans could trust. The rest might not be itching for a fight at all, or like to prevent one."

"We have not been hindered in any of our perambulations, so far. Perhaps this will extend to a discrete canvass of the denizens of the steamy dark," and Ardan pointed a digit downward.

ॐ ஓ

Passepartout and Aouda's incursion into the *Henrietta*'s engine room drew only favorable reactions from the engineer and his crew, which surprised them a bit.

"We hope you don't mind intruders," Passepartout apologized. "I am much interested in the mechanical side of ships."

As the engineer wiped his hands on a cloth before shaking hands with the valet, Aouda observed of their outfitting, "They have an excellent engine. Return connecting rod, laid horizontally to keep deck clearance down without sacrificing power."

"Ma'am, you sound like an engineer," the *Henrietta*'s engineer said.

"I have learned from the finest."

"So long as we make steady progress across the ocean," Passepartout told the engineer. "It would not do if we had to *stop*."

"We're fine at this speed, fuel enough for Bordeaux," the engineer smiled.

When the crew returned to their duties, Aouda told Passepartout, "I don't think they have any plans down here to stop."

Passepartout turned his attention from the cycling pistons to grunt an assent.

Aouda smiled, "Your fascination with our machinery, it's real, isn't it? A bit like what a naturalist like Mr. Darwin feels, coming on a particularly ingenious termite colony?"

352

"I admire your inventions more than that," Passepartout replied. "You have all come so far, and fast. I appreciate the industry in it."

Aouda paused a moment before telling Passepartout, "I left the bullet on the window casement, where you must have placed it for a reason, out of respect and care."

Passepartout raised a brow, pleased by her perception and discretion. "I thought it appropriate."

"You may never let me or Phileas see the inside of *your* machine, Passepartout, but I am sure it would be most interesting. I wager it would have very few moving parts."

"Not many, true," Passepartout smiled. "Perhaps after the voyage is done, all our journeys settled, we should take a trip to Alsace, to anchor all your curiosity. It may be as disappointing as Mr. Fogg's Machine."

"A disappointment I will risk," Aouda replied.

03 80

Several decks above, Phileas Fogg surveyed the sea from the railing of *Henrietta*'s wheelhouse walkway. Captain Speedy remained at the helm but the First Officer came out to see what might be the matter.

"You look bemused, sir."

"Is it not rather rare to see another vessel passing at sea, let alone approaching? Would your Captain be expecting such a thing this voyage?"

Pursing his lips, the First Officer acknowledged softly, "The Captain told me a boat may be coming for you. A big one, he said."

"He mentioned none of that to *us*. Do you find that *odd*?"

"A bit, yes. Now that you mention it."

Fogg continued, "Did he give you any particulars on this 'big boat'?"

"Nothing beyond that, sir."

"You should know, we have arranged for no boat to come for us, and would resist most strenuously removal from this one without our consent, for which secure passage we have paid honestly and generously." When Fogg noticed the officer reacting to that mention of generosity, he added, "Did Captain Speedy not discuss bonuses with you?"

The officer glanced back at Captain Speedy in the wheelhouse, then out to sea rather than answer.

"Another oversight on his part." Fogg went on more severely, "There *is* a large vessel I am aware of, serving no government or authority save their own. *My* only object is to reach London, on my wager, but enemies of Princess Aouda will likely be aboard that ship, and I am obliged to protect her, come what may. They made an attempt on our lives in New York. If that ship comes ... are you up for an altercation at sea?"

"Seems we've steered into some bad weather, taking you aboard."

"That was not our desire nor intent. Your captain may not have planned to share any of his windfall with you, but I am not so constrained. A hundred pounds to each among you (Speedy excepted) who will stand, should the time come, in protection of her passengers. And," Fogg looked the First Officer in the eye, "see us safely ... to Liverpool."

At length, the officer said sympathetically, "I'll let the crew know of your offer, and your need."

ଓ ଯ

Although there were many passageways for Impey Barbicane and Michel Ardan to follow and ladders to descend aboard the *Great Eastern*, finding the furnaces was inevitable, since half of the ship consisted of boilers and coal bunkers, all raging busy as the liner plowed along at nearly full head.

A stoker foreman spotted the new arrivals in gentlemen's attire. "Are you two *lost*?"

"Oh, no, we are explorers, from above," Ardan said. "If we are in your way, we will remove ourselves."

"You're the first of the *passengers* I've seen down here," the foreman had to admit.

"We're recent arrivals," smiled Ardan.

"I'm an engineer," Barbicane said. "I appreciate *all* the hands that go into making the machinery sing."

The foreman glanced away, "You can let the nobs above know we're doing our part."

"Has it been a trial, earning their appreciation?" Ardan asked, and the foreman nodded. "That's our impression, too. What a difference a few decks can make. Well, we will leave you to your work ... *we* notice."

Ardan and Barbicane stepped briskly through the hot inferno of coal dust and smoke, smiling appreciatively at the workmen and staying clear of their shoveling, out of appreciation for their needs not to bang into passersby rather than any effete disdain for the labor.

At the aft end they reached the hatch into the lair of the monster engine driving the paddles, the morning sun painting a skylight grid of shadows across the enormous reciprocating pistons. As the *Eastern*'s engineer came over to them, Ardan slipped a small writing pad and pencil from his coat pocket and began to look around at the machinery.

The engineer straightened his uniform and asked, "Here on an inspection, sir?"

Ardan replied, "Running smoothly enough for you?"

"Yes, sir! Even the propeller is behaving."

"Excellent," Barbicane put in. "Confident she can stay the whole course, then, no let up?"

"The Captain's told us we may have to steam full head for a week, no worse than any Atlantic run. Not sure those shallow draft gunboats can keep up with us, but that's their problem."

"Do the crew speak much about the gunboats?" Ardan asked.

"They rumor some on whether it's some country they're protecting us from, Spain or America are the favorites."

Ardan chuckled. "Good we have further protection, the Gatlings on the bulwarks. Their stations anxious to get some shooting in, you think?"

"Not that I've heard, but they're hired former soldiers, not sailors—keeping to themselves, doesn't surprise me."

Ardan scribbled gibberish notations on his pad, and with a concluding positive nod quit the engine room, Barbicane following as the Frenchman came upon a stairs. Once they'd ascended far enough to be sure of seclusion, Ardan stopped. "I think we should pay a call on the Captain, up on the Bridge."

The stairs led up to a deck building just forward of the third funnel. There was enough of a reflection in the window panes once they were outside that both adventurers could see they had some coal soot smudging their cheeks, and handkerchiefs were retrieved to clean that away.

The *Great Eastern*'s wheel was directly over that structure, and they could see Quatermass standing by the helmsman. A quick sprint brought Barbicane and Ardan around and up the steps to the bridge gangway.

Quatermass looked welcoming, calling to Barbicane as they approached, "Mr. Stuart tells me you grazed Nicholl."

"Yes." Barbicane smiled, "The woodwork escaped without a nick."

Quatermass leaned toward Barbicane, as though not wanting to be seen to be showing such interest, to ask softly, "What was it like, flying by the Moon?"

Barbicane calculated his reply, since in truth they had never got anywhere near the Moon, but he felt he owed the sailor more honesty. "To experience what no one else has ever done, that was the deep thrill of it. Very dangerous, though."

Ardan gently tapped the edge of the wheel, "Are you ready to trade in your wheel for navigation in space?"

"If I were twenty years younger, maybe yes. Traveling company might be improved, too."

"Stuart and the Morans not the most congenial passengers?" Ardan asked.

"Passengers!" Quatermass snorted. "Being a Captain is supposed to carry proper responsibilities and respect at sea. To them, I'm of no higher station than a stoker."

"That is *most* inappropriate," Ardan said. "I sympathize, sir."

"I'm impressed with the array of equipment that has been assembled," Barbicane said. "Ardan was wondering who attends to that diving sphere we saw aft on the crane."

"A pair of inseparable Swiss brothers, I think," Quatermass replied. "They've kept rather to themselves, and speak only French."

Mr. Stuart noticed the gathering up at the wheel and hastened to join them, "Ah, I'd wondered where you'd got to."

"Barbicane and I have become the explorers, so much to see on this great ship. No one of curiosity could be kept from it. Have you seen the engines and boilers yourself?"

"The engine is amply visible from the skylight. The boilers I leave to those best suited to attend to them."

Ardan pressed close and whispered to Stuart, "I have done my best to calm Barbicane down. Hopefully there will be no more dueling."

Stuart startled a bit. "Obliged."

Barbicane leaned back against the bridge railing, to face Stuart. "Poking around in the ship's corners is about all we have to do, since our host, Sir Augustus, has *literally* flown the coop. I suppose we can do nothing on negotiating until he returns? You have no authority or instructions on your own?"

"None of a financial character, no."

"Regrettable." Ardan sighed, "Watching others toss great sums of money about can be most diverting."

೦೩ ಏ

Late that morning, the *Henrietta*'s First Officer sought out Phileas Fogg, who he found strolling on deck with Aouda and the carpetbag. The servant Passepartout was off some distance away, fussing about his hair it seemed.

After a small bow to Aouda, the officer asked, "If I may, Mr. Fogg. How much did you pay our Captain for your passage?"

"Two thousand per passenger. Sixteen hundred pounds all told, *in cash*."

The officer drew in a breath. "Speedy told me you paid two hundred each. I learned from one of our crewman, Speedy told the woman of the boat you'd paid *ten* thousand—and she promised him *twice* that to look the other way, once you were taken off."

"*His* head is easily turned," Aouda snapped.

Fogg raised a brow. "That's even more for him not to share with your men, isn't it?"

"I apologize for all this, Mr. Fogg." The officer turned to look out to sea as he vowed, "The crew is with you, through to Liverpool."

Passepartout was drawn to the trio by the railing, sensing something was up. "Our seas are clear, for the moment," he told them.

Fogg and Aouda recognized the full important of that, as the officer did not.

"If the Captain cannot be persuaded to change course," Fogg posed, "what are our alternatives?"

"Lock him in his cabin?" Passepartout suggested tentatively, gauging their reactions before moving onto the idea of throwing the man overboard.

The officer laughed, "I'm not sure we *can*. The doors have locks, but no keys—none that *I've* ever seen. And we don't have a brig."

"No key." Fogg tossed Passepartout and Aouda a knowing glance, then turned back to the First Officer, "If you will give us a few moments alone with the Captain, to see reason—or not."

With a short bow, the officer remained outside by the railing while Fogg, Aouda and Passepartout entered the wheelhouse.

Phileas Fogg crossed to the small chart table to survey the track to Bordeaux plotted there, and what marginal northerly deviations were in order to aim for Liverpool instead. Aouda and Passepartout had stationed themselves to either side of Speedy holding the helm, where Fogg joined them, plopping the carpetbag down by the wheel to ask, "Captain Speedy, tell us about the woman who offered you so much money to see us off this ship."

"She said she was from a newspaper, wanted to help you. Seemed concerned."

"What newspaper was this?" Fogg pressed.

"She didn't say."

"What was her name?" Passepartout asked.

"Didn't say that, either. That's all I know." Speedy adjusted the wheel. "You should leave me to my piloting now."

"We have some ideas on that," Fogg smiled. "It would suit us better if we sailed to Liverpool, not Bordeaux. And not stop for any big ships that come."

"Not while I'm captain."

"We have some ideas on that, too." Fogg summarily socked Speedy on the chin, forcing him off the wheel. Fogg quickly grabbed one of the spindles to keep it from spinning free.

Aouda had stepped around the wheel from the other side and tapped the captain's shoulder to catch his attention. When he turned about, he faced her electric pistol.

"What's *that*?" Speedy cocked his head back in puzzlement, since there was no familiar barrel that made him think of it as a gun.

Aouda fired, bringing Speedy to the deck unconscious. She turned to Passepartout, "No key," then nodded at Speedy sprawled out.

Passepartout understood, and picked the captain up as he might a rag doll, carrying him down the short back stair to the captain's quarters. With Fogg remaining at the wheel, Aouda followed to open the door so Passepartout might enter with his burden. Plopping the captain down on the bunk, Passepartout returned to the passage, shut the door and took out his comb. After the mild snap and hum of the device had locked the door, he smiled to Aouda, "No key."

When they returned to the wheelhouse, Fogg declared from the helm, "I've changed heading for Liverpool, just a slight turn to port at this distance. Do signal the engineer for full speed, and ask our First Officer to put up sails, if possible. We'll need our best if we're to outpace the *Great Eastern*."

While Aouda attended to the engine room by calling down the speaking tube, Passepartout went out to marshal the crews' assistance on the sails. Fogg now appeared quite accustomed to the wheel, revealing yet another side to his kaleidoscopic expertise.

os so

Aboard the *Great Eastern*, Michael Ardan and Impey Barbicane ventured up to the aft observation bridge connecting the paddle housings, from where they could see the wheel off to their left, and survey much of the deck and sea beyond. Smoke plumes curled up into the afternoon sky from the liner's four funnels, as did thinner tendrils from Moran's several ironclads patrolling in the distance. Closer to hand, the rumble of the paddle engines vibrated the platform.

Ardan leaned back against the railing and crossed his arms, looking aft with a calculating eye. "Consider this assessment," he began, voice raised to overmatch the machinery and paddle flaps. "We have the invisible Sir Augustus and the more corporeal Stuart ... Moran's son, who if capable of spontaneous anger or enthusiasm, has yet to manifest either ... and the volatile Nicholl at the nadir of his self-control. That puts three genuine adversaries aboard—the rest, many hundreds, evidently just crew."

He paused. Barbicane was attending closely.

"I'd love to meet some of those Gatling gunners," Ardan continued, "but so long as they are cocooned below, we can only surmise their motives as more financial than Imperial. The *Albatross* is a precious rental, and we may assume likewise for the other airship and gunboats. I can't imagine how much money was poured on all this, but money is all I smell here, not fervor for a cause. We are not isolated in a floating den of conspiracy, it's our trio who are alone, utterly dependent on the provisional loyalty of the contract and pay chit. This is a plot done on the cheap, Barbicane, a true *bon marché*. I contend it is tactical folly to have mounted so massive a campaign with so few of one's partisans on the field. And now, so many of them have flown away. Your critique?"

Barbicane looked off behind them to the south, "If only Victor's squad were here, we might outnumber them."

34. IN WHICH PHILEAS FOGG IS LOCATED IN THE ATLANTIC AND WHAT ENSUED

When Mr. Fix's stomach had settled to the point where he could forage from his cabin and look forward to a good diverting game of cards, he found sustenance readily provided (despite being after the ship's regular dinner hour) but the second unexpectedly denied him. Learning the cause—that Phileas Fogg was occupied being captain *ex tempore* of the *Henrietta*—took him unawares. Finding (or rather *hearing*) a vociferously uncooperative Speedy yelling a mixture of threats, expletives and pleadings from behind the locked door against which the seaman occasionally pounded shoulder and fist, only magnified the detective's disorientation and puzzlement.

"The captain disapproved of changing course to Liverpool," Aouda explained pleasantly, standing near Fogg at the wheel. "The crew rather likes the idea."

"*You* want Monsieur Fogg to reach England, don't you?" Passepartout asked from a chair, a partially consumed plate of dinner perched on his lap. "You have vowed thus, remember." Passepartout flirted with thoughts of punching Fix again, just for the spirit of it.

"So I have," Fix acknowledged, wondering what to make of this apparent mutiny and whether he, as an officer of the law, ought to take some stand on it. Then again, what of practical effect could he do? Fix shook his head as he left for his cabin, "The strangest things happen around you, Mr. Fogg. You are aptly named."

"Purpose served," Fogg smirked softly once Fix had gone.

"Whenever you need a rest, Phileas, I can take the helm," Aouda offered.

"Ah, yes, I think that would be fine. Give my arms a stretch, finish my dinner," and Fogg surrendered the wheel to Aouda's most capable hands, while he took a chair beside Passepartout to down the remainder of his ham and bread.

"What a pity none of Moran's machines are propelled by Power X," Fogg mused. "I could easily track them then."

That reminded Fogg of his watch, which he hadn't checked recently, caught up in so many other distractions. He set his plate down on the deck and retrieved the timepiece, finding it just on 11 PM Greenwich Time, which when adjusted for the locality fell reassuringly within a few minutes of *Henrietta*'s wall clock. Fogg waited for the bezels to finish spinning.

The "?" of Passepartout's buried interstellar treasure settled just past *XII*, the "**O**" of Aouda's *Deimos* dimmer, far away around the globe by *IX*. The "**A**" of Maker's *Kestrel* was not quite to *VII*, crowding the inactive "**B**" at *VI*—all as expected. But not so Nemo's

"N" bright by *III*.

"*Nautilus* is out *there*," Fogg called, standing up and crossing to the dark windows to starboard. "Very near—three, four hundred miles, at most." He went to Aouda at the wheel, "He's chasing Moran, isn't he? Are you steering him with your bracelets, as we learn whereabouts?"

"I will if I can. Srikar isn't waiting for us, though. Once *Deimos* is returned, that should help."

Passepartout got up and waved Fogg to the Atlantic chart, which Phileas had oriented with the Canadian coast along the lower border. Pointing a left finger south of them where Nemo's submarine was sailing, then a wave of his right hand in the general area where he imagined Moran's boats might be now, Passepartout marched the fingers together to a spot roughly between, pulling his hands up to clap, "A day or two and they will be *bumping*."

"*Deimos* will be back by then, to play together," Aouda's tone suggesting what manner of grim amusement lay in store.

☙ ❧

As the *Aurora* flew on through the night, Sir Augustus Moran kept his back to the windows, despite the beauty of the sea shimmering so far below in the full moonlight, made even more visible as the gondola's interior lamps were kept low. Without that exterior perspective, apart from the shuddering of the panes and drone of the engines, there seemed less indication they were moving.

When a crewman left to scurry up a ladder into the bowels of the envelope to check the tightness of fittings, the commander at the wheel was the only other on deck. With all the windows reflecting his own face back at him, wherever he looked, Moran felt boxed in, and began to contrast this aerial greyhound with what Nicholl had revealed about the mystery flyer.

"How would you make this ship fly twice as fast?" he asked Tremaine.

The commander thought a bit. "Bigger engines—more gas to lift the bigger engines, more fuel. Twice as fast would not be easy."

"So four times faster, harder still."

"Is *that* the speed of the mystery ship?"

Sir Augustus nodded with a grunt.

Tremaine was impressed, "That *is* fast."

"Do you think *Barbicane*'s engine could move a thing that way? Without shooting it out of a cannon first?"

"A little flying *Nautilus*, you mean? Maybe. What I saw of his machinery in India didn't seem nearly small enough for that. As for what Barbicane worked out, I will repeat: we need to see the innards of

Columbiad firsthand. My men can't make any sense of it without that."

"We may yet be able to buy the designs, at least," Sir Augustus said. "In any case, I'm as interested to hear what Mr. Fogg and his friends may be made to tell us. They have taken *Columbiad* somewhere, and I mean to find out how and where."

"Remember what happened with Nemo. With due respect, sir, do you want Stuart poking at yet another hornets' nest?"

"Stuart relaxed his guard and the wog slipped away, to nurse his insolence," Sir Augustus said sourly. "We are all more vigilant now. Even Felix. And we have assembled greater means—Stuart's cousin and his banker friends have seen to that. We have gunboats. *Two* submarines to their one, with the latest armament. Iron boats, not wood. And very possibly two airships to their one. They may be swift, but we are strong, and resolute. And *patient*. We will *not* give up."

"The question is," Tremaine responded, "what will their electric guns not give up?"

cs so

The Moran armada's progress north was steady but uneventful through the rest of that Friday. The only excitement aboard the *Albatross* occurred in the evening, on Commander Blake's receipt of the chess play by Tremaine, appended to the end of the latest polarized lamp report from the *Aurora*. Tremaine was making good use of his Queen's Knight.

After moving the piece on his traveler's chessboard, Blake fretted over one of the ship's gauges. High on a bulkhead, its needle had dropped below two thirds. "I hope we find our quarry soon," he told his helmsman. "I want a good reserve for our return to *Eastern*."

"Any chance to un-hatch the guns?" The helmsman appeared to relish such a prospect.

"Only if they take to shooting first. And we don't know that they're armed."

"Some *spies*, if they don't shoot back."

"Don't be too quick on the trigger," Blake huffed, and paced to the forepeak window, muttering under his breath, "Not my wish to have guns at all. Better to fly on exploration, for the joy of it."

Blake stared out over the night sea, to the full Moon rising off to starboard, thinking back to the Frenchman who'd flown around that very celestial body, and being asked by him only a few days before whether they had a factory to build ships like this. He wished he'd said yes—though not for any with guns.

cs so

That night Sir Augustus Moran experienced a striking dream.

He was in his old mansion in India, before the Rebellion. Edith was there, holding out a hand to him, smiling. But he couldn't reach her, lightning bolts barred the way whenever he stepped closer, their bright flashes forcing him to avert his gaze from his beloved wife. And yet she stood, calmly beckoning, arm outstretched. He felt almost able to brave the lightning and reach her, when a great airship propeller invaded the room behind, larger than those motivating the *Aurora*, attached to a bulbous motor nacelle. Spinning relentlessly, it began to devour the walls and floor and ceiling, menacing ever closer.

Edith seemed oblivious to the approaching danger, the great noise and hurling debris of splintering wood, ripped carpets and drapes, of no concern to her, looking Sir Augustus straight in the eye and upholding her smile. The blur of blades was almost upon her, his apprehension at full pitch, when Sir Augustus awoke in a sweat.

The *Aurora* had encountered turbulent air, and Commander Tremaine labored to level the ship high in the clouds. Sir Augustus decided the shift in the engines' intensity he could hear and the altered level of the floor must have contributed to his vivid reverie. It was now early on the morning of Saturday, the 14th of December, when Moran went to the little washroom to splash his face, annoyed at the rationing meter he had to twist to release a calculated trickle.

Sir Augustus wondered whether they would carry more water and have proper tables to dine on, should Tremaine make good his stupendous ambition of bomb-carrying airships.

෪ ෫

The dawn lacked lightning for the *Henrietta*, but not thunder.

"All right, I was greedy! Wouldn't share. Is that cause to take my *ship*?" Pounding followed on the cabin door.

"The captain is awake," Passepartout redundantly declared with a smile toward Phileas Fogg, whose hand held steady on *Heinrietta*'s wheel, eyes ahead on the ocean expanse. "I will go fetch some food for him."

Passepartout skirted around Mr. Fix, briefly perambulating on deck in the cold morning air. The detective's expression appeared preoccupied, and not just from *mal de mer*. Assailed by the turmoil of his reluctance to intervene on behalf of the beleaguered Captain Speedy, on account of its irrelevance to his present unshakable purpose: getting Phileas Fogg successfully to British soil, where the warrant still aching in his pocket could at last be made good.

Once Fix had paced away out of view, and glancing quickly about to see no crew watching, Passepartout conducted another comb sweep of the sea, from the southwest round to as far to northeast as could manage from that position on deck. No ships at all, let alone one of the *Great Eastern*'s bulk.

With a not entirely satisfied sigh (since he only knew their enemies were not upon them, not from where they might be springing next), Passepartout went below to find a comparably pensive Aouda taking breakfast herself. After requesting suitable nourishment for their incarcerated seaman, he plopped down beside her to wait.

"*Deimos* left Diadem early this morning. The rites are underway. I didn't get much sleep. Ran my little engine, to keep me busy. How did you fare, Passepartout?" Aouda brightened a bit. "Or is versatility there another part of your, shall we say, *nature*?"

Passepartout waved his fingers from his chest up to his head, "It suits this package. I doze as needed."

Sensing an openness in his manner, Aouda continued, "Have you always looked the way you do now?"

"No, mademoiselle. Though I think I did a good job making something that looks the part."

"Would I be shocked, or amused, to see your native form?"

"It depends on when you catch us. We go through several metamorphic stages, none as pretty as butterflies. Adapting that allowed me to take on a form like this. We are very small. I have enjoyed the strength these muscles have," Passepartout flexed, smiling, "And improving on a few of their connections, to match the pace of our nerves."

Aouda marveled at the idea of intellects who could engineer physical form the way her own crafted brute machinery. "Are you exploring on your own, or here on behalf of your people?"

"More the Sir Richard Burton here, than the Magellan. Though there are Beings who make a campaign of it. Not many in your neighborhood, fortunately—for you. But one of them does leave little alarm bells. There's one on your Moon, in fact."

"Which the *Columbiad* would have jingled?"

"*Exactement*."

Aouda nodded to reflect her increasing understanding. "I suppose our world will have to get used to knowing we have such neighbors."

"Not unless more are able to react with the equanimity you show, Princess. With apologies, your people are often rather skittish."

"That we are, Passepartout. That we are."

Aouda accompanied Passepartout back to Speedy's cabin. Laying the food tray down on the deck, he checked what lay beyond the door with his comb, finding Speedy sitting on the bed. The moment Passepartout unlocked and opened the door, though, the captain lunged for the opportunity. Aouda intercepted him, bending Speedy's arm behind him with one hand.

"Vixen!" Speedy protested.

The captain's opinions stopped when Aouda pinched a nerve on his neck, inspiring him away from the table where the valet landed the tray. Passepartout turned and grabbed Speedy's neck tightly, causing the captain's eyes to bulge.

"You are annoyed at this present situation," Passepartout stared him down. "Most understandable. But you are in no danger, here in this room. Beyond it, no guarantees."

With Passepartout holding the captain's neck, Aouda released Speedy's arm and stepped away to the door, smoothing the folds in her dress after the swift exertion.

When Passepartout let go of his windpipe, Speedy accused, "You're pirates now?"

"The ship after us is," Aouda said. "We do not mean to be taken by them. Had you not agreed to help them, you would not be in this predicament now. And knowing how dangerous those people are, believe me, captain, you are safer in here."

Speedy had recovered enough presence of mind to ask, "Where did you find keys to lock the door?"

"*Magic*," Passepartout replied. "So behave, lest we turn our wands on you, umm. Poof—not so speedy then."

As Passepartout shut the door and relocked it, and recalling what little he could remember of the scorpion's sting from Aouda's electric gun, Speedy was unsure whether he oughtn't to take that supernatural threat seriously.

Rejoining Fogg at the *Henrietta*'s wheel, Aouda gave his shoulder a friendly caress before laying her head up against it to declare, "I'm glad you followed your watch to find me, and Passepartout for his daring rescue."

Without taking his eyes from the sea ahead, Fogg smiled and replied, "Thank you, for staying close enough for all that to happen."

Seeing them thus pleased Passepartout, and it moved him to a gesture for Aouda's benefit. He closed his eyes for a few moments, clutching his comb, then crossed to ask her, "Are the *Columbiad* plans still on your person?"

"Yes, in my shoulder purse."

"There's something interesting on one I should like to show you."

Aouda retrieved the papers and began to lay them out on the chart table, but startled when she saw one of the images was no longer anything like a schematic of Barbicane's craft. The sheet was black as night, save for what appeared to be dot-sized globes of light arranged around a central sun, and tiny inset pictures along one side bearing characters in no human language.

"This is a map of your planets," Passepartout said. "You will find if you touch the little pictures, they will alter the scale of the images, and navigate your perspective. Touching the discs themselves will call up a larger picture of that place, allowing you to see what I studied of them when I first came here. Touching them twice quickly will make them as they were. The text is in my language, which perhaps you will be able to decipher. Think of it as a puzzle gift, for you and Mr. Fogg, to better know your neighborhood."

Aouda placed a finger on one of the planets, which enlarged to reveal the distinctive ringed Saturn. Other pictures cascaded to represent that body's many moons (those known and others as yet unknown to the findings of terrestrial Science).

"Thank you, Passepartout."

But he wasn't done. Passepartout turned the sheet over. "And this is a little taste of my ship, some basic drawings, still in my language. Something to whet your curiosity, until the someday should we visit Alsace."

Aouda was immediately intrigued to pour over the views of the small spheroidal space vessel, surprisingly limited in its internal compartments—or so she surmised, since recognizable dimensions were wanting, and with nothing immediately revealing as to what propelled it or how it was navigated. This would occupy her attention for many hours, certainly as Passepartout intended.

ଔ ໑

At breakfast that morning aboard the *Great Eastern*, one of the seeds Ardan had planted was germinating into a question Sebastian Moran had for Felix Stuart. "I know my father had to call in favors to bring me here. But to pay for all this, who does he owe for that?"

Stuart glared across the table, "Did you do the accounts for your Company, too?"

"I'm not a stupid man, Mr. Stuart. I know what debts are, and how rarely they are forgiven. If I'm being drawn into an obligation my father has taken on, I'd rather like to know the scale of it, before we're all in too deep."

"You've gone from 'I' to 'we', Colonel. Have no fear, you are not that central. You may incur your own debts fresh—of which I'm sure you're most capable—once you're back at your post in India."

"And when will that be? We're still going north."

"Patience, Colonel. You should take up reading, to occupy your time."

Moran rose, tossed his lap cloth down on the table with a dismissive flourish, and left for some solitude up on deck.

Stuart wondered what Sir Augustus would make of that—a bit of cold feet, perhaps? Or just pique, a conflict occasioned by their abrading personalities? Something to think about as he left to while away his own hours aboard their paddling iron hotel.

For their part, Impey Barbicane and Michel Ardan bumped into the *Great Eastern*'s Dr. Lawton on the way to breakfast that morning. Nicholl was still bedridden, or so the doctor averred, with food taken to him in his quarters.

Coming into the dining room, they saw a waiter cleaning away two place settings, which they correctly surmised were those of Moran and Stuart. Being spared their company suited them both quite fine.

"Not even the Captain dines with us," Ardan observed. "By choice, or prevented by our hosts' rigid class distinction? Given how many people are aboard this ship, it feels like a tomb down here."

"One I'd gladly be off of," Barbicane sighed.

"We have only to *stop*. But what happens when we do?" The waiting and uncertainty were beginning to wear on Ardan too.

After dining, Barbicane and Ardan found a surprise up on deck: the secretive gun crew were taking air *en masse*, pacing or exercising as to their nature, feeling the breeze as the *Great Eastern* pressed ever northward. Though keeping together aft on the starboard side, that was no discouragement to either Ardan or Barbicane strolling among the uniforms, radiating good fellowship. Both were looking for whoever might be their leader.

One among the men was Thomas Wilson, late of the *Columbiad*'s guard and regretful airship passenger. Not wanting to risk being identified by either man, Wilson cut short his deck leave and ducked into a staircase housing by the fourth funnel.

Barbicane and Ardan were casting their net for the best braid anyway, and finally an epaulet caught their eye.

Waving at the vast expanse of the *Great Eastern*'s deck, Ardan joked to the young officer, "If any of your men are up for foot races, this is the ship for it."

The Lieutenant chuckled. "We have to make the most of our Saturdays. You're the men from the Moon, aren't you?"

"Out and back again," Barbicane smiled. "And now here, for further adventure."

"There is much new here." Ardan pointed at the shrouded Gatlings, "Was it a challenge recruiting for these special guns?"

"Training on those took a bit, but they're quick lads. I knew most from the Army, and the rest by good recommendation."

"With so much untried, you can see there's concern on that." Barbicane put a hand on the Lieutenant's shoulder, "May we have a word with you?"

"We can use the lounge over there," the officer gestured at a deck structure built around the ship's fourth mast.

That turned out to be chamber thick with the plushest of curved settees, flowered upholstery and drapes and carpet, oddly fussy but undeniably comfortable.

"Have you enough coverage?" Barbicane asked as they sat. "Twenty guns to man, and the cannon, to run smoothly if action runs hot."

"You're expecting some soon?" the Lieutenant inquired seriously.

"Anchors were pulled quickly," Ardan reminded, "and the escorts are kept close."

The Lieutenant nodded agreement. "I urged taking on more men, but a platoon cost a lot as it is. I broke up the ammunition running and sleep breaks so we can keep two on most of the Gatlings. Remaining squad's assigned to the cannons. Those came with the ship, and aren't as critical to repel boarders anyway, compared to the ordnance we can aim easily."

"Your care with limited resources is most appreciated, at least in our view." Ardan paused, "Your men know there may be much ahead that is ... unusual?"

"That's why we have the flying machines, isn't it? God, those are amazing! Reconnaissance from above, and the submersibles, to cover below."

Ardan and Barbicane traded quick concerned glances, hearing that "submersibles" were involved too.

"We are confident all will be up to their tasks," Ardan smiled.

"Thank you for time, and honesty," Barbicane said, giving the Lieutenant leave to depart.

As the Lieutenant closed the door after him, Ardan leaned back and interlaced his fingers behind his head. "*Bon marché*—the gunners too."

"But submarines, *plural*," Barbicane countered. "That's news to me. If they're able to keep up with the ironclads, they could be formidable."

"Hmm, you are always one to notice the *speed*." Ardan winked, "It is an advantage, having an engineer to chat with."

Out on deck, while the gun crew continued their exercising and relaxation, Felix Stuart had come to stand by the port bulwarks, looking down at the rolling sea, already considering the logistics of their intended rendezvous with the *Henrietta*. That vessel might prove too large to safely employ the floating pier by the paddlewheels, but either of their submarines could manage it, conducting Passepartout, Mr. Fogg, and his lady friend to them—all the while in the sights of the half dozen gunners along that stretch of the *Great Eastern*, to guarantee their sanguine cooperation.

"Behold, the sea, itself," Michael Ardan called from behind, Impey Barbicane stopping close by.

Stuart turned at the interruption of his tactical planning. Not a reader of American poetry, least of all Whitman, he regarded Ardan's comment as merely a florid description of the scenery.

"Barbicane and I were marveling at the enthusiasm of your gunnery crew. Proud and ready to confront any eventuality." Glancing about, Ardan continued, "Having seen no winged chariots settling in our midst, we may assume the Ambassador has yet to return?"

"Quite right, Mr. Ardan." Increasingly suspicious of the pair's shipboard tourism over the last few days, Stuart asked, "Have you mapped out all the ship's personnel and facilities, to your satisfaction?"

"Oh, *we* do not matter. It is whether they will meet *your* satisfaction that would seem more salient. I assume you are familiar with at least some of the ferry ride Barbicane, Nicholl and I were given from the deck of the *Nautilus*. What do you make of that?"

"I would value *your* opinion first, sir."

Ardan was happy to give it, and Barbicane equally keyed to hear it.

"Have you flown on the *Albatross*?" Ardan asked Stuart.

"No," he replied.

"It is an amazing craft. Unless you have journeyed on that 'ferryboat'. After that, your *Albatross* was a disappointment. I know very little of the capabilities of the *Nautilus*, or the 'ferryboat'—or the minds behind them. But you lack even that. There are people here on earth flying about in a craft that puts everything around us to shame. I, for one, would be very reluctant to tangle with such people, by choice."

Barbicane detected a flinch in Stuart's reserve, and pressed to ask, "Have you been tangling with them, Mr. Stuart? Or seeking to? Come, one gentleman to another. You tried to pluck us out of the sky, you owe us that."

"I owe you *nothing*," Stuart snapped. "You Americans, and now the French, smitten with everything republican. Speaking of what is *owed* you, without the *duty*, the obligation of tradition." Feeling his own temper getting away from him, Stuart shook his head and stalked off in silence towards the bow.

"That man will never make a good salesman," Ardan joked.

"I doubt that's ever been his profession," Barbicane replied darkly.

CR SO

A quarter past one that afternoon, Passepartout's latest comb sweep of the aerial horizon encountered a response. His eyes still shut, he moved his hand side to side across that spot of the sky several times to be certain of what had been detected. Drawing in a long breath,

Passepartout strode into the wheelhouse to inform Fogg and Aouda, "We have visitors. But not by sea. One of the airships, the gyroplane one I think. It will be spotting us within the hour, unless they are very stupid."

"*Deimos* is still a day away," Aouda frowned.

"They're a long way from their ships," Fogg called from the wheel. "They must be on reconnaissance, and knowing more or less where to look."

The *Albatross* did indeed come upon the *Henrietta* shortly thereafter, the rumble of her engines drawing not a few crewman out on deck to gawk at this approaching apparition. Mr. Fix, below with the seasickness, missed this opportunity to witness so momentous an aerial marvel.

"What in *hell* is that?" the First Officer cried, as the craft flew directly over them, clipping just above the mast heights.

Passepartout had rushed out on deck to brandish his comb at the machine, which the First Officer found most eccentric. After that, the airship turned to fly away southeast.

The First Officer followed Passepartout back into the wheelhouse, and waved at the departing craft visible out the windows, "Anything to say about *that*?"

"It has guns, but they are not stopping to fire them," Passepartout reported.

Aouda smiled. "Tight on fuel, I'd bet. Like we were, chasing after you in Yokohama, Passepartout. Forced to turn around if they're to make it back safely."

"You weren't kidding about your enemies, were you?" the First Officer asked.

"No, sir," Aouda replied. "And that flyer is, I think we may all agree, on its way to warn their ships of our location."

"How long do we have?" the officer asked.

"Thousand miles maybe, to their ships," Fogg declared.

Aouda estimated the slower speed of the vessel, "A day at least for them to reach them. Another two for the ships to reach us."

"You keep saying *ships*," the officer worried.

"The big one has escorts, old American ironclads," Passepartout explained. "We may be in for a time."

The First Officer made a face. "We don't have a lot of guns."

"We're not yet at the Rubicon," Fogg declared, adding with a nod to Aouda and her *Deimos*, "A great deal may happen in the next few days to tilt the balance."

ଔ ଓ

Aboard the *Aurora*, the nearing of the *Albatross* later that afternoon signaled something was afoot, and lamp communication soon established that the *Henrietta* had been located.

"At last!" cried Sir Augustus. "We'll tag after her while Blake does his part, and brings the fleet."

"At this range, still several days before they can close the bag," Tremaine calculated as he stowed the lamp gear, then quietly performed Blake's latest chess move.

Tremaine reported to Sir Augustus, "The *Henrietta* appears to be a standard freighter, no guns in sight when Blake flew over. Still, we'll be careful."

"Careful? How so?" the ambassador asked.

"Those electric guns reported. We have no idea of their range, or how many they might be carrying."

"Can they penetrate this metal?" Sir Augustus asked. "All this costly aluminium—are you telling me it's as vulnerable as a wooden hotel floor?"

"It's more the suspension envelope that concerns me, sir." When Sir Augustus looked rather blank, Tremaine added, "Hydrogen gas."

"So?"

Tremaine looked like a schoolteacher confronting a pupil who had failed to study his lessons. "Hydrogen is highly combustible. Weren't you aware of that?"

Apprised of that now, Sir Augustus reached for something to steady himself as he felt a trifle faint.

ଓ ଚ

There was another crew commotion aboard *Henrietta* when the *Aurora* appeared off ahead to the east, drawing Passepartout and his comb outside to investigate, which he tucked away when the First Officer appeared to survey the craft from his spyglass.

"This one's different. How many flying machines do they have?"

"Just the two, as far as we know. That one is staying well back, you will note." Passepartout pointed, "See that big red part on the top? That contains their lifting gas—it can explode, if agitated properly. So best it stays far."

The First Officer winced, "And my mother said the *sea* was a perilous profession."

Aouda stepped out, pulling her coat tighter around her, "Did that one slip past you?"

Passepartout shrugged, "It was not above the horizon when I looked before."

After the First Officer departed to enthuse the crew back to their work, and away from invading airships, Passepartout asked Aouda, "What is the reach of your electric pistol?"

"A lot closer than that is now," Aouda sniggered. "Without knowing their covering, I can't even say whether a flash might occur unless we were right on top of it—which could be bad for us, under it. If your Mrs. Hammond has told what we did at the hotel, though, they may stay away for exactly that reason."

☙ ❧

Of all the people in that antagonistic band on the Atlantic Ocean that evening, in pursuing airships and boats or aboard the *Henrietta* with Phileas Fogg, only Sir Augustus Moran could be accounted genuinely nervous. Ever since being informed that the means of elevation that held him trapped hundreds of feet in the air consisted of an invisible vapor capable of bursting into flame under conditions he only poorly understood, he could not help but be more mindful of the *Aurora*'s gondola ceiling, above which the omnipresent gas lay hidden.

When the crewman assigned inspection duty was about to open the hatch to climb up into the envelope, Sir Augustus caught his shoulder, "Does it frighten you, boy, going up there?"

The lad misunderstood, not realizing the older man was obsessing on the hydrogen gas, and replied on a different concern. "No. You get used to stepping carefully, not trip and fall through the canvas. You get to know the fittings, almost like people, the bolts that turn easy or the ones that balk. And the sound's comforting, too, like a low organ kind of."

"I see." Actually Sir Augustus didn't, but let the fellow go about his work.

The ambassador had never been one to easily imagine a life and interests other than his own, or credit them with any spirit or attraction save that of begrudged labor and necessity. Not even the *Aurora* and her crew's evident enthusiasms could change that in his nature.

☙ ❧

By dawn that Sunday, December 15th, the *Henrietta* and her aerial escort were passing the Grand Banks, about a third of the way to Europe, the wind biting icy in their billowing sails, heaving to supplement the steam to make the best speed.

Commander Tremaine had eased the *Aurora* to the south of the ship, where by keeping pace they could assess their mutual rate. Lowering his glass, Tremaine stepped to rap knuckles on a wall instrument showing their own airspeed. "With sails up, they're doing fourteen," he told his helmsman. "At that rate, *Eastern* will never catch them."

Sir Augustus, who was not yet awake, would not like that.

Twelve hundred miles to the south, the *Great Eastern* and her flotilla were paddling and propeller screwing just west of Bermuda, enjoying the balmier zephyrs of that latitude.

Where Mr. Fogg could have used a good game of whist, were he not resolved to his steerage task, those aboard the *Great Eastern* were elevated by a proper Sabbath service—mandatory or by conviction, no matter, as the crew and gunners bowed in their several meeting rooms.

Captain Quatermass being a Unitarian, and hence of heretical disposition to any of correct Church of England proclivity, Sir Augustus had supervised the Sabbath service for the officers and their elite passengers until his departure. That morning, Captain Quatermass, Sebastian Moran and Stuart were present, but still no Captain Nicholl. In the absence of the ambassador, Dr. Lawton was impressed to this duty, hesitatingly delivering in the alcove between the bar lounge and the dining room a truncated homily suitable for a marine setting: on the disobedience of Jonah, delivered from the great fish to spur the repentance of sinful Nineveh.

"Does the *Great Eastern* suffice the role of fish or Nineveh, do you think?" Ardan asked Impey Barbicane with a smile.

"I'd wager our Mr. Stuart could play an Assyrian tyrant without much rehearsal," replied Barbicane, eying that gentleman seated close to Dr. Lawton. "Your guess is as good as mine, how best to cast our spectral Sir Augustus."

"Aim high, for the Almighty, my friend."

A fine and leisurely luncheon was served afterward, during which Stuart, Sebastian Moran, Barbicane and Ardan successfully avoided confrontational banter—perhaps due to the fact that Ardan had accomplished pretty much what he'd intended to in the way of mental bomb throwing, so could let natural digestion take its course unimpeded. And besides, it was the Sabbath—a day of rest even an agent of the *Deuxième Bureau* could endorse.

The *Great Eastern*'s steam whistle suddenly blew, then again, and this blast-pause-blast sequence was repeated twice more.

"Excuse me, gentlemen," Stuart all but jumped to his feet, and sped aft for the staircase leading to the wheelhouse, quickly followed by an expectant Sebastian Moran.

"Excuse me, gentlemen!" Ardan mimicked, rising himself, waving for Barbicane to join him in finding out what all this was about.

They were working their way up the stairs when the paddlewheel engines eased to a stop. The sudden comparative quiet was most disconcerting.

Emerging up on deck, the sight of many crew (with Sebastian Moran among them) gathering along the port bulwark flagged what direction to look. Pulling out their glasses, Barbicane and Ardan soon homed in on the *Albatross*, just then settling onto its landing platform.

Tapping Barbicane's shoulder, Ardan waved his attention to Stuart and two crewman (one carrying a signal lamp, and both wearing curious goggles) climbing the stairs to the paddle bridges, obviously to gain preferential height. From there, the lamp man was soon signaling the *Albatross*, the other penning notes on a pad, but neither Ardan nor Barbicane could see any flash in return.

"Either it's a one-sided conversation," Barbicane said, "or they're using some lens or filter we can't see."

"A pity, I so enjoy eavesdropping," Ardan replied.

From the look on Stuart's face, any intelligence just received was favorable—and so presumably not what the *Columbiad* veterans might have liked.

Unbeknownst to Ardan or Barbicane *père*, the unexpected cessation of motion among the Moran boats required Victor's steam sloop to engage in an abrupt change of course to avoid veering too close and thereby risk detection, crying "Hell's bells!" and spinning the wheel while barking orders on sail settings and engine speed, trying to keep down in the troughs of wave swells to minimize even a masthead's protrusion.

The *Albatross* stayed on its platform an hour for refueling and provisioning—but was no more than in the air, though, when the *Great Eastern*'s whistle blasted their cycle again, followed by the paddlewheel engines' resumed action. Clearly there were honed procedures in place, and efficiently adhered to.

Barbicane directed Ardan to follow him up to the paddlewheel bridge, from where a better view of their wake could be seen. Observing its gentle leftward curvature, Barbicane suggested, "We're changing course. The *Albatross* brought *directions*."

"To what?" Ardan posed, his expression taut.

At dinner, Stuart and Moran were clearly in brighter disposition. Stuart was almost swaggering when he entered the dining alcove, while Moran hung back in the manner of someone looking forward to seeing fur fly, and wanting a good vantage for it.

"Did you enjoy the air spectacle earlier?" Stuart asked Barbicane and Ardan once all were settled.

"They did not stay long," Ardan observed.

"No," Stuart taunted, "were you hoping to hail a ride?"

"They weren't flying to Florida," Barbicane said.

"No, quite so."

"Where, then?" Ardan asked flatly.

"I am not a man for navigation. North is all I can say."

Ardan turned toward Barbicane, but kept an eye cocked on Stuart, "We missed our opportunity—Canada."

Stuart dispensed a little smile, every flickering detail of it falling to Ardan's cool assessment.

Once they had food before them, the pleasantries of chatter were minimized even more than previously, save Ardan pointedly complimenting the proficiency of the ship's cuisine.

Afterward, when Stuart and Moran had gone their separate ways, Ardan and Barbicane took some drinks in the bar and sat at one of the diminutive tables.

"I saw your eye at work," Barbicane said. "Catch anything of note? Beyond that they didn't say anything."

"Oh, but they wanted to tell us so much. They were itching to— even young Moran, whose lips were sewn. That they did not, means it is something very important. If you are right about our course change, and I have no reason to disagree, what they found is not in Canada—or on land at all, I think. Have they cornered *Nautilus*?"

"How do you corner a submarine?" Barbicane wondered. "Without sinking it."

CS SO

The *Deimos* arrived back from its sad journey to Diadem around half past eight o'clock, and Robur was in telegraphic converse with Aouda for some time. Passepartout could see her tapping on her bracelets, pacing to and fro in the *Henrietta*'s wheelhouse. Both the valet and Fogg knew she would speak afterwards of whatever they needed to be told.

As it was just the three of them in the room, she could speak plainly.

"Damn your Time Machine, Phileas. So many things I knew, and I couldn't say how *or when* I knew them. In the end, I've sent *Deimos* on to follow the gyroplane's heading, warning that I suspect the *Great Eastern* of steaming north against us, let slip the name of our enemy Moran—that he should find them if able, and that there were warships and submarine boats to account for too."

"The gyroplane had a long head start," Fogg said at length.

"Robur had a similar concern. They could fly all the way to Florida in that time, so we must gamble they are dull, and kept to a narrow heading."

"Dull," Fogg said. "That may spell their downfall."

35. IN WHICH AGENTS OF VENGEANCE SETTLE GRIEVANCES LONG DELAYED

Aouda was helming the *Henrietta* while Fogg seized a hard-earned nap, when about half past ten that Sunday night she began to work her bracelets—while still holding the wheel, a juggler's dexterity Passepartout could only admire. Realizing she must be in telegraph with *Deimos*, he stepped up to intercede as temporary helmsman to allow her to focus fully on that communicative task, which leave Aouda accepted with a grateful smile.

"*Deimos* has passed the gyroplane," Aouda said afterward. "Six hundred miles south of us, dead on the heading, but going *north*. Robur agrees they must be flying back from the *Eastern*, so he's keeping on that tack until we know where they are."

"Not tempted to knock the flyer down right then?" Passepartout asked.

"Tempted, yes. But they're twelve hours away. Robur can swat that fly on the way back here, if needed."

"Regrettable we cannot swat that *other* fly," Passepartout said, nodding in the direction of the red airship, pacing them out in the dark.

He would have to think a bit more on that.

ଓଃ ଚ୍ଚ

Just after midnight on Monday, December 16th, the *Deimos* reached Sir Augustus Moran's splendid armada. There were some clouds, but even without their extraordinary instruments, the view by the light of the nearly full Moon was exemplary. Smoke streaked back from the four funnels of the *Great Eastern*, the sea churned by the paddlewheels and propeller; lesser plumes from the two ironclads to her port and the one patrolling to starboard.

Robur focused first on the large ship, passing over it while Niru directed their telescopic lenses on the deck below. There were only a few crew patrolling this time of night, plainly visible when the thermal filter was actuated, though due to the moonlight Niru kept mainly to a direct image.

"Regularly spaced tarpaulins, interesting," Robur said of the bulwark shrouds reflected on his pilot's viewer.

"Could be guns," Niru said.

As they traversed the stern, Robur could see the small cannons—those did not impress him. "Let's see what the other ships are about."

Deimos veered west to check out the port ironclads. The airship dock lay nearest to the *Great Eastern*, but showed only three small barrels of obviously lesser poundage poking from each side of the canted deckhouse between the empty mooring platforms. The armament on the flat warship they studied next was more to brag about:

two heavy guns per turret there (both rotated to threaten further west).

Flying eastward, back over the Great Iron Ship, Robur found the starboard ironclad to be the mate of the double-turret to port.

"I don't see any submarines, do you?" Robur asked.

"None," Niru shook his head. "Though there is one small boat, to the south, seven miles. But it looks like a steamer, with sails. We could sound for the submersibles if we dive."

"If we had the time. Their main position will have to do," and Robur telegraphed Aouda: *A. MORAN SHIPS FOUND 35 22 N 62 5 W. NO SUBMARINES SEEN ON SURFACE. SEEK THEM OR GO? R.*

Aboard the *Henrietta*, Aouda was still holding the helm. She glanced over to Passepartout, who had nodded off a bit in his chair. So as not to catch his attention this time, with special care she positioned her left hand so she could steer while signaling with her right, first in reply to *Deimos*: *R. GO. A.*

After receiving Robur's acknowledgment, Aouda adjusted the setting on her bracelets, to telegraph at another frequency—that reserved for her electric gift to the *Nautilus*. Tears were welling as she signaled her brother: *KALAPANI MOVING NORTH FROM 35 22 N 62 5 W. REPEAT KALAPANI 35 22 N 62 5 W. BLESSINGS & WARNING.*

Whether her message would be received depended on the *Nautilus* being on the surface. Five minutes later she obtained knowledge of that: *SO BITTER JOY, WILL & MUST CONCLUDE. BLESSINGS RETURNED.*

Aouda closed her eyes briefly, head bowing slightly. It was done.

At last, Srikar had a place to sail to confront those who had once cast him into the pit still active in the Andaman Islands. She and Phileas Fogg had passed so near the very place, only seven weeks before, on their journey to Singapore aboard the *Rangoon*. It was officially mapped as Ross Island, but known to its many victims by another name: *kalapani*—black water.

ଔ ୬

Had anyone aboard Victor Barbicane's steam sloop been exploring the airways above the *Great Eastern* and her consorts that night, the glint of the Moon on *Deimos*' several fins and windows might just have been visible in a good glass. But no one was looking up.

Nor were they looking down. Otherwise Victor or the two others on watch might have seen the brief wash of water off the back of Sir Augustus Moran's shorter pet submarine, as it breached the surface several hundred yards to the north, only to slide beneath the waves and disgorge one of its Whitehead torpedoes at the intruding ship. By the time the bubbling wake of the weapon could be seen by those aboard, it was too late.

The *Deimos* had turned north and was accelerating to her working speed when the explosion flashed on the south horizon. Taking place far to their stern, neither Robur nor Niru took notice of it, but its acoustic concussion reached the flyer a little over a minute later, and triggered a reflexive alarm.

Niru tracked that to the source, "It must be that little ship." Viewed telescopically with the thermal lens, it appeared now to be on fire. Without any word, Robur swung *Deimos* around to investigate.

The blast had caught the attention of the *Great Eastern*, too, her whistle bellowing thrice to awaken their crew to the disturbance, loud enough for it to be heard even within the *Deimos* over her own cabin vibrations as she flew nearby overhead.

The warning bell had awakened the *Deimos*' third crew member, Tanseem, who arose from her shift slumber to emerge from the little sleeping birth by the kitchen, buttoning her leather flight tunic as she asked, "What's the air fluctuator caught?"

"Possibly a submarine torpedo," Robur called from the cupola. "Unless the boat chose that moment to have a boiler accident."

Niru's expression suggested that was unlikely.

It only took *Deimos* a few minutes to reach the burning ship, already in the process of foundering. Its descent to the sea level was an apparition none of the sloop's crew were prepared for, though when the port side hatch was thrown open by Niru, the light within offering a warm halo as he waved for them to board, the two men carrying the third readily accepted.

Robur held *Deimos* as precisely to station as he could, his gaze flashing from one instrument to the next, along with his view out the cupola and down at the flyer's deck.

"We've got a man hurt here, bad," the lead carrier warned as they stepped up onto the deck.

Tanseem noticed the sailor carrying the other from behind had a bloodied arm and shoulder, and she pressed in to relieve him of the burden. After closing the hatch, Niru quickly fetched blankets and pillows, laying out a temporary place by the main windows for the injured one to be gently placed.

"Must be flyer father described—grand." Victor Barbicane tried to smile.

Robur brought *Deimos* to rest on the sea, the sundered ship sinking before them out the windows, like some grim Barnum spectacle. While Tanseem donned a pair of listening earmuffs and consulted several devices to keep vigilance regarding any submerged threat while they were in the water, Robur descended quickly from the pilot's chair to kneel by the injured sailor shuddering under the blankets, already nodding groggily.

"I am Robur, custodian of the *Deimos*."

"Victor Barbicane. Luck ran out, torpedo blew us, lost Danielson and Grady—" consciousness fled.

"Perform what medical aid you can on these two," Robur told Niru.

Tanseem interposed, "I think your torpedo spitting fish has turned north. We should leave the water, lest they swim back."

Robur frowned, knowing she was right. Turning to the third uninjured sailor, he barked, "You, whatever you may know, tell now."

As Robur climbed up into the pilot's seat, Walt Kinnard set aside his understandable disorientation and wonderment at the *Deimos* long enough to recount the intent and disposition of their late expedition: "Ah, Vic's father and the Frenchman wrangled their way on board the villains' ship—had us follow so we could slip in later and...."

ଔ ଛ

The clarion siren of the *Great Eastern*'s whistle had roused enough observers that the *Deimos*' ascent from Victor's sinking craft was seen by several, including by spyglass, providing sufficient detail to categorize it as a flying machine of no trivial accomplishment.

By the time Impey Barbicane and Michel Ardan appeared on deck, coats and trousers hastily donned, rumors were flying among the crew almost as swift as the *Deimos*' departure into the heavens. The moment Barbicane heard that one of Moran's submersibles appeared to have sunk an intruder, his face palled in the moonlight. Ardan placed a comforting hand on his shoulder, realizing the dire implications of this naval intelligence.

Felix Stuart was out on deck now too, attired in a long green silk dressing gown, and queried an officer, "An airship, you say? Where is it now?"

"Too high or far now to tell, sir. It was only visible for a few moments. Gad, it was fast."

Sebastian Moran appeared next, and Stuart snapped, "Their airship's down *here*, and no way to inform your father."

"I thought there was some ship sunk?" the Colonel asked, half awake.

"There was. Torpedoed apparently—someone knows how to follow their brief. We won't know the report 'til we stop and they can dock. Which we will not. On to the *Henrietta*." Nodding to the Colonel, "You'd better muster the gunners, keep watch from now on for that flyer. Warn the ironclads, too. All may fire at their discretion."

Stuart returned to his cabin then to get dressed, since this could well prove a busy morn.

ଔ ଛ

Robur had brought *Deimos* to a comfortable altitude and was heading north at speed when Niru climbed as far up the pilot's ladder as he could to report discretely on the condition of the injured sailors.

"I've done my best for the two," he told Robur gravely, then whispered, "Mister Barbicane's wounds are serious, needing a proper doctor and hospital ... and, he also is not a *mister*."

Robur raised a brow at that. Shaking his head to consider what to tell of these new developments, he finally telegraphed Aouda: *A. BARBICANE & ARDAN ABOARD EASTERN TO FIGHT MORAN & NICHOLL. OUTCOME UNKNOWN BUT SUBMARINE TORPEDOED BARBICANE SHIP FOLLOWING. RESCUED 3 SURVIVORS, VICTOR BARBICANE BADLY INJURED, NEAREST HOSPITAL BERMUDA. ADVISE. R.*

That message struck Aouda like a knife. She was concerned about the injured sailors, but that a torpedo had sunk them meant her brother was sailing into peril. "Bloody damn!" she swore softly, and signaled Nemo: *WARNING SUBMARINES WITH TORPEDOES PROTECTING GREAT EASTERN.*

While she waited for the *Nautilus* to acknowledge her message, Aouda replied to Robur: *R. BERMUDA CERTAINLY, BUT NAUTILUS COMING AFTER EASTERN. TORPEDO DANGER NOW, WARNED & AWAITING REPLY. A.*

Robur knew what it would mean for Aouda should *Nautilus* be struck by any of Moran's submarines—an outcome he could not abide either. He looked down at the blanketed unconscious Victor, glimpsing with great sympathy a shoulder and foot of the rescued comrades holding vigil there, and weighed the alternatives of swinging south to rush for Bermuda now, or do so after attending to the threat to Nemo's vessel—and the uncertainty of how long either might take. He could well imagine the similar turmoil raging in Aouda's heart.

A. WILL ATTEND TO THREAT HERE THEN TO BERMUDA. R.

R. TAKE CARE. A. Leaning her chin down on the *Henrietta*'s wheel, Aouda closed her eyes briefly, berating herself for her haste in sending her brother *Eastern*'s position.

SRIKAR REPLY, TORPEDO DANGER AHEAD, Aouda called once more to *Nautilus. Henrietta*'s clock marked off the minutes with no response.

"Passepartout!" Aouda called sharply.

"Yes?" The valet shifted in his chair, his right foot reflexively scraping the carpetbag beside him.

Aouda didn't take her eyes off the window ahead. "I have blundered. Please awaken Phileas, and have him bring his watch."

Passepartout wasted no time in carrying out her request.

Fogg quickly appeared, the watch in his right hand. He had thrown on his clothes, vest and coat buttons left undone, and cravat forsaken. "I take it, something has happened."

"Robur has reached the *Great Eastern*. I sent Srikar the position at once. That was a mistake. They've sunk a ship by torpedo—they've put them on the submarines. *Nautilus* is sailing straight into it. I tried warning them, but Srikar must have submerged. Robur will do his best, but—," only now did Aouda turn, looking Fogg eye to eye, "I thought you might tell how close they are, with your watch."

Fogg stepped to the starboard window and opened his watchcase. 4:18 GMT, which he could not help himself checking against the accuracy of *Henrietta*'s timepiece—having to wait a moment anyway for the rings to fall into place. Passepartout's "?" settled near *VIII*, Maker's "**A**" by *IV*, and "**B**" inactive at *VI*, but none of these concerned Fogg. Only the "**N**" and "**O**" mattered now, off ahead at *XII*, their jeweled illuminations indistinguishable bright.

"If not on top of one another, they will be soon," Phileas Fogg said. Turning back to Aouda, he asked, "Does your *Deimos* have any way of detecting them, under water?"

"Yes, but if one of their submarines encounters them first, with their torpedoes, that won't count a difference."

Snapping shut his watch, Fogg crossed to the wheel and displaced Aouda to pilot again. "I won't be able to fall asleep, not now."

Passepartout was crestfallen, furious at his present uselessness—even his comb could not help, unable to discern what peril lay in wait for the *Nautilus* so many hundreds of miles distant.

ଓଶ ଛ

As Robur flew *Deimos* south toward the *Great Eastern*, he swore at the inadequacy of their instruments on this night. In the dark there might have been a chance of seeing the lights of an approaching *Nautilus* from the air, provided the ship were sailing close enough to the surface. But in this moonlight, the sea was all beauteous reflection, the surface waves betraying no clue to what might be sliding beneath.

Robur actuated several switches on his pilot's controls, causing a small display of twelve vertical bars to glow green, though from the bottom of each the color began to change to red, and crept up along each gauge as his mind raced trying to think where best on the expanse ahead to land and submerge.

"Tanseem," he called, and when the woman's head poked into view beside his left leg, "We'll have to listen for all the submarines." After her silent nod, Robur advised, "*Nautilus* will sound a bit like us, a bit piston—not necessarily louder than the *Eastern*, or the gunboats. The submarines will be electric, or something just as quiet—no choice but to resonate for them. Not that they'll understand what they're hearing."

Tanseem slipped away, to be replaced by Niru, "Five minutes to finish crystal charging. Should we adjust for preference?"

Robur smiled at Niru's ever-reliant sagacity. "Yes, prime front and ventral first."

Settling *Deimos* on the surface of the Atlantic Ocean, Robur donned a pair of viewing goggles, linked by a wide black cable to machinery at his left, and set various switches there so he could control what measurements they would display. That done, he could attend to their underwater hunt.

As *Deimos* began to submerge, Niru told the two sailors by Victor, "We have a patrol to perform. Then fly your mate to a doctor."

No sooner were they beneath the waves than the low pulses of *Deimos*' resonator could be heard, by which they could judge the location of the metal vessels thereabouts by their distinctive reflections. Tanseem monitored that by her gauges and ear pads, interpreting the signals Robur in mirror above. "*Nautilus* is the one four miles to port, moving fast. Smaller submarine, the one not quite a mile south of them, good as dead in their path."

Robur performed a mental calculation and realized immediately no time could be wasted. He brought *Deimos* to the surface and, once they were in the air, accelerated as quickly as he could, skimming low over the surface flashing by below. The sloop's sailors could hear the difference in the *Deimos*' engines, and had to brace themselves against the bulkheads as they sped forward. Even at that clip, though, it took three minutes to reach the spot between where *Nautilus* and the enemy submarine were coming into closing proximity.

Robur brought *Deimos* back below the surface—not exactly plunging in the manner of Thomasina Maker's lithe *Kestrel*, but with a splutter of the propulsion vanes to drive them to depth quickly. More shifting of the cabin for Victor's mates to steady against. Tanseem resumed her view of the resonator viewer.

Deimos was barely a hundred yards from the *Nautilus*, and a greater distance from the other submarine back to port—but it had launched one of their Whiteheads at Nemo's passing left flank. Robur forced the ship to its limit, furiously flipping switches, which roused another sound to accompany the engines: a fiercely escalating energetic whine, simultaneously of high and low pitch, whose crescendo caused the ears to pop just as a greenish-yellow bolt pulsed from one of *Deimos*' forward apertures.

It was only on for a fraction of a second, but that was sufficient to vaporize the water, resembling an incandescent sausage. The torpedo instantly detonated, safely premature of its target. The shockwave sphered outward, though, even as the *Deimos* plowed through its periphery, convulsing the ship and causing Victor Barbicane's blanketed frame to slide on the deck, stayed at once by the gentle but firm touch of the panicky guardians to either side.

Their anguished looks to Niru affirmed their fears about the effect of such lurching motion on the condition of their injured charge, which they had to repeat as the *Deimos* was still at speed, forcing Robur to turn the ship tightly and climb to avoid ramming into *Nautilus*. They approached so close that Robur could glimpse Captain Nemo up in his pilot window, flinging the wheel to steer *Nautilus* away from the unintended menace.

By the time *Deimos* arced back around to once more face the oncoming vessel, they had fired another Whitehead. Robur responded with a second plasma blast, producing another wave through which they buffeted, steering around the debris on the way to the submarine. Robur was now most intent.

These blasts pluming in the night had not gone unnoticed by those aboard the *Great Eastern*, of course, especially the Gatling gun crews assembling on deck nearest the bow, uncovering their weapons and affixing ammunition. The repercussion among them was to redouble their efforts to defend the ship.

Impey Barbicane and Michel Ardan were following their preparations as well.

Aboard *Deimos*, Robur's magnifying night lenses revealed that a third torpedo hatch was opening on their antagonist's prow. Robur fired again, directly on the submarine.

The torpedo prow exploded, magnified by the detonation of the two remaining Whiteheads—while sections of the vessel behind imploded, all as the concussion sphere radiated outward and rattled the *Deimos* again, stressing even the superlative engineering of Aouda's craft.

All aboard with Robur knew the terrible drowning death he had brought upon the submariners in these dark depths.

That bigger eruption of foaming water was even easier to see (and hear) from *Great Eastern*, nearing the spot by the minute.

Robur knew Victor needed medical attention, but he also could not ignore the second submarine still posing a threat to *Nautilus*. Beyond that, the armada itself posed a threat to Aouda aboard the *Henrietta*. So here he was, together with them—now, not at some future prospect. Informed by these facts, Robur's resolve was clear: he must defang this snake to the extent he might, before he could quit the field and fly away to the palliative ministry of a Bermuda hospital.

Checking where the other submarine was on his instruments,

Robur pulled *Deimos* out of the water so he could fly there quickly, never mind that he was darting right past the *Great Eastern* and her gunboats. Several of the port Gatling gunners took aim and fired as they passed, including Thomas Wilson (who averted his gaze when a worried Barbicane and Ardan passed nearby), though the range was such that none hit their mark.

The port ironclad was swiveling one of their turrets toward the east, but *Deimos* was moving far too rapidly for it to range and fire— and at an altitude where, even had they shot, they'd have as likely struck the *Great Eastern* instead. Such are the perils of haste in the fit of conflict.

Once he was within range of the southern submarine, Robur returned *Deimos* to the sea. Approaching the craft from its stern, it was dimly visible by the light of their interior lamps. He called down to his temporary passengers, "Gentlemen—that is the vessel that sank your ship and slew your comrades."

The two sailors rose to their knees—not wanting to let go of their fallen commander—and looked at the trail of bubbles from its churning screw.

"Can they see us?" the man on the left asked.

"Doesn't matter if they do." Robur targeted the submersible's propeller with precision. It took only a modest pulse to disable it, a greenish-yellow arc that reduced the screw and rudder to a useless tangle but without rupturing the hull beyond it. That soon brought the craft to the surface, where Robur joined them.

"Niru, keep station," Robur commanded as he climbed down from the pilot's seat, and ascended the ladder to open the upper entry. Spying several sailors clambering out of the submarine's hatch, Robur withdrew an electric pistol from a pocket on his leather tunic, which he held below in case it might be needed. "Who is in command?"

Their captain protested, "Was it you who wrecked our propeller?"

"Yes, and if you find conversation not to your liking, I can do more than that. What orders were given you on flinging torpedoes?"

"We weren't to let any vessels near the *Great Eastern*."

Seeing ten men altogether now on the deck of the submarine, Robur asked, "Is that all your crew?"

"Yes," the captain replied.

"You're about to abandon ship," Robur bellowed. "Jump aboard and grab hold. We will convey you to *Eastern*, where you may tally your failures."

When their Captain reluctantly nodded agreement, Robur closed the hatch, watching through the porthole to see the men leaping over and finding handholds either on the fins or the few protruding stanchions roundabout. Once he counted all aboard, Robur replaced Niru at the helm.

None of the submariners were expecting their transport to the *Great Eastern* to involve *flight*, so their reaction as *Deimos* lifted into the air mixed a genuine wonder at their novel experience with muscle-tensing panic that tempered their appreciation.

Robur swung *Deimos* around to the submarine's bow, all the while pulling up to give good distance from any blast. When he reached a hundred feet, Robur fired a tight bolt, the ionizing air momentarily flashing as bright as a dozen fireworks. The front of the ship exploded, followed by additional concussion as the three remaining Whiteheads detonated. What remained of the submarine sank.

Those explosions engendered more alarm aboard the *Great Eastern*, where even Captain Nicholl had roused to join the marshalling forces, brandishing a pistol in his free right hand, his left in a shoulder sling. But the nearer ironclads patrolling on their port flank were equally vigilant, alarm whistles blowing and the crews laboring to elevate and target their ordnance on the strange gray craft flying east— an action they could only account a threat to those aboard the *Great Eastern*.

One of the turret gunners had the best chance, since they could rotate their weapons, and for a brief span the *Deimos* was to the right of the *Great Eastern* and so could be fired upon without fear of striking their comrades. After a quick aiming at where he anticipated the machine would be when the shell arrived, he fired. But by that time Robur was taking the flyer lower, approximating the height of *Eastern*'s bulwarks, so the shell flashed overhead without harm, to arc down into the water beyond with an ignominious *splat*.

Several of *Eastern*'s Gatling gunners tried to strafe the *Deimos* as it neared the stern, but stopped once they heard the protesting yells of the submariners clinging to the fins. The crane obscured their line of fire as well when Robur swung the ship around and lowered to the bulwarks, tilting slightly to the left and shaking a bit to encourage them all to disembark without delay.

Trotting toward the stern from a hundred feet away, Nicholl stopped to point his pistol at *Deimos* and roar at Stuart by his side, "*That* is what took us off *Nautilus*!"

Stuart was aghast, knowing Ardan was right. That craft was haughtily more sophisticated than either *Albatross* or *Aurora*. In its smooth terrible elegance it was *beautiful*.

Once all the seamen were tumbled onto the deck, Robur lifted *Deimos* vertically, past the crane and up above the mast height, too high for any of the Gatling guns to be trained upon them. Though some of the men had brought rifles and small arms, it was difficult to aim past the mast rigging. A few marksmen of keenest eye managed the target, but at a range of nearly three hundred feet, those stray bullets that reached *Deimos*' hull dinged off to little damage.

Colonel Moran had raced in to take the submarine's Captain by the shoulders, "Is your ship lost?"

His expression told enough in the moonlight, but added what was on all their minds, "I fear the other's gone too."

Up in *Deimos*, Robur called to Victor's guardians, "A lesson on *aerial* war for you, should you live into such pitiless times. However strong they seem, weapons intended only to fire at others on the flat, are useless when attacked from *above*."

Those men could see only what was visible out the main windows, which at this altitude showed the tips of the masts ahead, the smoke roiling up from the funnels between them, and the forward stretch of the *Great Eastern*'s hull, marked by the rectangular glow of the skylights ahead of the paddle engine dome.

Activating a downward telescopic view, the night lenses toggled on, Robur positioned *Deimos* directly over the stern-most Gatling on the starboard side. Nudging the ship to put the gun in crosshairs, a quick pulse of the plasma was all it took for the barrel to flash asunder, along with the ammunition stored beside as the melting slag struck them. The two gunners leapt back in terror with burns to body and face. Cries to fetch Dr. Lawton rang out from the crew near most.

Robur eased *Deimos* forward to the next Gatling, repeating the process. That second gun crew had withdrawn from their station far enough to sustain lighter injuries. A few pings and clunks on *Deimos*' hull verified that marksmen were continuing to try and fell the flying monster with small arms, but Robur and the gunners were on their game. The *Great Eastern*'s small cannons were in like manner dispatched, throwing quite a cascade of shrapnel in the concussion that ensued.

By the time Robur targeted the third Gatling gun in line, their crew had prudently stepped back with resigned shrugs, not waiting to stand close enough to be splattered by melting barrels or exploding ammunition.

Over on the port side, Mr. Stuart watched with mounting dismay the incremental disintegration of what had seemed, given its cost and effort, an unassailable protective screen.

Michel Ardan stepped up, "So you have annoyed after all those you should not have been meddled with."

Stuart wheeled around with the intent of punching Ardan in the face, but the *Deuxième Bureau* agent jumped back agilely, with a smile, to evade the blow.

Barbicane truculently interposed, "Come the dawn, will you have much left?"

Robur continued gun by gun all along the starboard bulwarks, as unstoppable and coolly conducted as one might rub out the exposed top of an ant's nest with a firm boot heel twist. The flashes and resultant Gatling puddles from the guns forward of the paddlewheel brought the direct attention of Captain Quatermass from the wheel, holding to his duty even as the gun crews were running about below in rout.

As if all that were not enough, the discerning ear soon heard another whining machine sound joining that of the flyer menacing from above the masts. This time, from the sea.

Captain Nemo knew the *Great Eastern* had no vulnerable wooden keel, but the saw tooth prow of *Nautilus* had something to sink its blades into: the paddlewheels. And at that moment the submarine was bearing down on that tempting point, its engines screaming at full attack speed. As *Nautilus* ripped through the starboard side, the shattering paddle vanes were thrown up against the housing such that the main axle momentarily seized up. That dangerously strained the engines inside, forcing *Great Eastern*'s engineer to disengage power on his own authority—and for both paddles, lest the ship veer to starboard from the port side continuing to churn.

The end of the main engine rumble would have been more noticed had the blasts of *Deimos*' weapons and the exploding Gatlings not filled so much of the night, and so many of the crew not been running about, shouting, pointing, or otherwise wondering what it was they were supposed to do next. But Captain Quatermass knew what was what, and let blow *Eastern*'s steam whistle—four steady blasts, repeated, to signal to their ironclad escorts that they were slowed to only their single propeller and in distress. Their ironclad escort heard and responded, steering to their aid.

The *Deimos* was over *Eastern*'s bow, and swerved over to the port quarter, floating as effortlessly as a leaf on the breeze, to clear the Gatlings there. Thomas Wilson was among those on that port line. With all he'd been through over the last month, from complicity in the sabotage of the *Columbiad* to shivering in the plains of Nebraska, and seeing the *Deimos* approach, incinerating the guns one by one, he teetered away from his post, crying to his mate, "I just want to get back to my wife."

Away to the *Great Eastern*'s stern, Captain Nemo took *Nautilus* around in a tight U-turn to starboard to position for a second attack, on the ship's port paddle. The sound of that approach was now familiar to those aboard, and what few Gatling gunners remained fired rounds at the passing submarine—though as only the upper serrated arch was near the surface, and *Nautilus* raced by at thirty feet per second, the bullets had little impact.

Once Robur had disposed of the last of *Eastern*'s Gatlings, he flew out to port to the double-turreted ironclad, making a point of staying along a heading where they could only fire on *Deimos* at the risk of hitting *Eastern* beyond. When he was in range, Robur fired a powerful bolt from a forward aperture, straight at one of the turret guns. The effect was to detonate its shell, the turret exploding, which sent a plume of water high as the flat deck was breached and the warship began to sink by the head.

The crew were scrambling for their lifeboats as *Deimos* scouted overhead, some trying to strike the flyer with pistols as it passed. But Robur had done what was needed there—hitting just the one gun had proven sufficient—and set off for the platform ship. Their ordnance were subjected to a blazing electric blast along one side of the angled hull, which pierced their bulkheads, and caused several more of the cached Whiteheads to explode. Once more seamen strove to deploy their lifeboats before the craft foundered to port.

That left the lone escort ironclad to starboard. It barely took a minute for *Deimos* to fly back and over the *Great Eastern*, which her defenders watched, impotent to interfere, and another minute to reach the warship, where a properly-aimed blast to a turret gun similarly removed that craft from the Moran armada. The *Great Eastern* now lacked all naval accompaniment.

While inspecting the ruined port paddle from the overhead gangway, Quatermass set his glass to see some of the lifeboats rowing from the sunken ironclads. Shaking his head in dismay, he trotted down the bridgework to the wheel. Stuart ran after him.

"Full stop," Quatermass ordered, flinging the lever to signal the engine room below of the command.

Stuart nervously objected, "We cannot stop for *pirates*."

"Are you *mad*? Our paddles are smashed, leaving us with one propeller, about which I have little confidence. We are clearly in no condition to continue your chase—*and*, we have boats approaching with what's left of *your* hired warriors. We signed no contract for Armageddon, Mr. Stuart. It's time to gather survivors and assess our damage, then work out how to make safe port—if we can. I advise you, have your men stand down."

Quatermass ordered crew to both of the floating dock winches, to lower them for the lifeboats already on their way. He then sought out Dr. Lawton, who agreed to set up a temporary infirmary in one of the lower lounges for those injured from the molten metal and shrapnel thrown off during the invader's strafing run.

All the while, Quatermass kept shaking his head, appalled and frustrated by how this "scientific adventure" of Sir Augustus Moran had escalated into a military disaster that threatened the life and limb of all aboard. And to what purpose?

☙ ❧

Robur had one more task to accomplish before he could quit the field for Bermuda. Flying northwest from the sinking starboard ironclad, he sought out *Nautilus*, which had surfaced and was heading toward the *Great Eastern*. Seeing *Deimos* approach, Nemo pulled to a stop and was out on deck when Robur landed beside.

Robur flung open the top hatch to tell Nemo, "Aouda tried to warn you of the torpedo threat, but by then you had submerged. We've attended to them, and the other ships, for you. Was there any damage to *Nautilus* from the concussions?"

"Nothing serious." But Nemo indicated some steam fitfully spurting from some of the nozzles in *Deimos*' hull, "Do you need repairs?"

"Some, yes. There was small arms fire. We also have injured, rescued from a ship they sank. Mr. Barbicane's … son among them. The father and Ardan are aboard the *Eastern*—after the same quarry as you. Whether they're prisoners, or other, I have no idea—and no time to search that giant. If it's your plan to board, check to their safety, and tell Barbicane we're taking Victor to hospital in Bermuda. It is serious."

Nemo nodded gravely. "I will carry your message."

☙ ❧

Aboard the *Henrietta*, Aouda received a telegraphic report from Robur, sent as *Deimos* flew south: *A. MORAN SUBMARINES SUNK. NAUTILUS SAFELY IN AREA, SRIKAR TO BOARD EASTERN, ALL SUPPORTING ORDNANCE BLOWN. THRUST REDUCED AS SEVERAL VANES DAMAGED, STILL AIRWORTHY. ALL CRYSTALS INTACT BUT CAPACITORS DRAINED. PROCEEDING TO BERMUDA. R.*

All that greatly relieved her, and she quickly replied: *R. MOST GRATEFUL, TAKE CARE. A.*

She was even happier to receive a message from her brother soon after: *NOT YET USED TO SINGING FAR AWAY TO YOU, SISTER. FOOLHARDY TO SAIL IN WITHOUT CARE, BUT THE OAK HELD ALL FIRM. BARBICANE & ARDAN MAY BE ALLIES THIS DAY. FINAL DICE TO ROLL.*

YOUR SONG SHALL BE HEARD. BLESSINGS TO YOU, NOW MOST OF ALL, Aouda responded.

While she disliked being so far from her brother's efforts, at this most critical time, no longer even by proxy via *Deimos*, she was not unhappy as she looked over at the resilient Mr. Fogg at the wheel, or the extraordinary stranger Passepartout, poised still on his chair in a manner of sleep. All had become linked in a subtle friendship that seemed as though it always had been—and could never have been other.

☙ ❧

With the commotion of *Deimos*' attack concluded, and the engines of the *Great Eastern* shut down for inspection, the sound of the approaching *Nautilus* could be heard off to port—its strange low resonance unlike any engine save that of the fiercer *Deimos*.

Barbicane waved Ardan to follow to the bulwarks, where the glow of *Nautilus*' bulging wheelhouse glass marked it clearly in the water, gliding a hundred feet away from where the ironclad lifeboats were being unloaded at the floating dock and tethered temporarily to the paddlewheel housing. *Nautilus*' propeller stopped, then reversed, and by turns the vessel's thrusting nozzles sidled the tail beside the lifeboat at the dock, the wash from the submarine's screw pushing the other moored boats away like children's toys on a pond.

The remaining men in the lifeboat were thus spurred to leap out and up the gangway and ladder to the deck. Word of the *Nautilus*' proximity was dispatched to the bridge, of course, which brought Mr. Stuart out to the bulwarks, looking down at the submarine in some agitation.

But it was Captain Nicholl who sought to rally the dispersing throng, "We must muster what guns we have, meet any boarders in force!"

Aroused by his own revived martial fervor, Nicholl scouted around for Sebastian Moran, intending to enlist him in his campaign. Thinking he spotted the Colonel away aft, Nicholl set off after him.

"A man who refuses to give up," Ardan offered caustically to Barbicane, "even with one arm."

Felix Stuart frowned down from the rails as the *Nautilus* shifted so close that it squeezed the lifeboat against the floating dock, and that in turn up against *Eastern*'s hull, the screel of wood creaking near to the breaking. The pulse of the waves raised and lowered the iron submarine and the still larger Leviathan in an undulating roll, leaving the floating dock and the abandoned lifeboat to jostle this way and that.

Giving a quick glance back around the deck, as if looking for something or someone, Stuart turned and headed away to the stairwell building beneath the Bridge wheel.

Nicholl returned with Colonel Moran and a dozen of the now less occupied Gatling gunners, including their stalwart Lieutenant, all brandishing rifles and pistols, most of them hot to display their mettle—and the remainder not wanting to seem otherwise.

Barbicane caught Moran's arm as he was about to lead the charge up and over the bulwarks stair, "Are you sure of this, Colonel?"

"Join in—or stand back, Mr. Barbicane."

From off behind Moran, Ardan gestured in favor of the latter, and Barbicane let go of Sebastian's sleeve.

The sliding hatchway on *Nautilus* was slowly retracting as Moran cautiously inched down the paddlewheel stairs, at the head of a line of firearms pointing every which way on account of the steepness of the incline preoccupying their descent. Slower progress still on the lower steps, slippery from the sea wash. By then, *Nautilus*' hatch was fully open, but as yet no crew emerging in the moonlight.

One by one, Moran and his band jumped from the floating pier to the lifeboat and then across to *Nautilus*' hull. The most adept of them kept their footing—Sebastian Moran and the Lieutenant were no laggards there. But a few stumbled in the process, and tried to keep hold of their weapons while scrambling for a handhold with the other. Some of those were helped back on their feet by a quick hand from their comrades, such as their Lieutenant. A few, of such temperament that they had gained no friendship among their fellow recruits over the last weeks (whether by active antagonism or mere indifference), had to fend for themselves. The world in microcosm.

Colonel Moran's boarding party had landed well back on *Nautilus*' length, dispersed between the central dorsal fin and the submarine's covered skiff. The Lieutenant and one of the men tried to undue the hatch there, but found it secured from the inside. Moran and two of their more confident fellows were exploring ahead of the fin, heads bobbing side to side to catch what they could of the stairs leading down into the halo of electric light.

By now, quite a number of *Eastern*'s gunners (including Thomas Wilson) and some of the liner's crew were gathered along the bulwarks to witness this courageous venture, many embodying a fatalist curiosity more than bystander enthusiasm of the sort the truculent Captain Nicholl radiated. A considerably more circumspect Impey Barbicane and Michel Ardan were there, too. Even the mysterious Swiss diving sphere aquanauts had surfaced on deck, initially concerned about the security of their prized machine, but now drawn to the *Nautilus* show. Felix Stuart was nowhere to be seen.

One of Moran's men was a marksman of no small accomplishment, having demonstrated his deadly skill on many occasions with the Union Army. When a uniformed shoulder slipped into the limited angled view available up on deck, he nursed the trigger forward and a bullet struck the spot. The cloth target instantly recoiled and disappeared from his sights, followed shortly after by returning "fire" of another sort.

Electric sparks spat from every metal surface between the opened hatch and the closed skiff. Leaping to gun barrels and singeing their uniforms, dancing up legs and arms causing numbness and palpitations, it took scarcely seconds for Moran and his men to throw aside their weapons and be purged from the *Nautilus*' electrically invigorated plating like fleas from an infuriated dog.

A few were lucky enough to fall into the lifeboat, but most had only the water to welcome them. The Lieutenant was one of those. The least favored were those diving off *Nautilus*' starboard, putting them on the far side of the submarine, which they had to swim around once their wits were sufficiently recovered.

Viewed from the *Great Eastern* above, this was no tableau of heroic resistance, but a pathetic bowing before an implacable technology beyond most of their comprehension. Some of the witnesses gasped at the jerks and fits of those attacked, but not a few were moved to laughter by it, a dumb show of human puppetry. Such titters enraged Captain Nicholl more than if any of the men had been killed.

Nicholl spun around like a dervish, waving his pistol. "Stupid cowards," he screamed, "afraid of sparks!"

With a fleet and firm motion, Ardan grabbed the weapon from Nicholl's hand and flung it over the bulwarks, "Enough of guns for you this trip."

While Sebastian Moran and his men swam to the dock where they might board the *Great Eastern*, emerging dripping wet and colder for it, Captain Nemo and a squad of his sailors marched from the open hatch stair of *Nautilus*. Nemo wore the electric gun harness Aouda had gifted him in the Pacific Ocean over a month before; the others carried electric rifles of Nemo's own contrivance—not so sophisticated nor compact as his sister's, but barely less formidable.

Several of those armed crew were stood on guard, while the rest accompanied Nemo for the hop and jump from submarine to lifeboat to dock. Those of Moran's team who had made it to the pier put on a quickstep to rush up to the *Eastern* ahead of them, save for the Lieutenant, who stayed below on the dock, watching as Colonel Moran climbed onto the boards.

The sight of Captain Nemo and his men brandishing their unusual weapons reminded Moran of the reported fate of Colonel Proctor and company at the hands of such devices. Not privy to such sinister intelligence, the Lieutenant looked upon the machines with more puzzlement than apprehension.

"Naval engagements are not your forte," Nemo frowned at Moran. "Do you have a name?"

"Colonel Sebastian Moran." He reared what pride he could manage while dripping so much water, and suspecting what he did of the weapons Nemo and his guardians carried.

Nemo stiffened. "Are you a relation of Sir Augustus Moran, satrap of this great navy?"

"My father." Moran would not show fear or flinch.

Nemo waved the butt of the electric gun leftward to indicate he would be escorting the waterlogged Moran over to the Lieutenant, and the pair of them up to the bulwarks.

As Moran, the Lieutenant, Nemo and his men proceeded up the paddlewheel stairs, the gunners and crew were not of one mind about whether to resume their defense or stand down. No command had come, from the now absent Mr. Stuart or any other. Nicholl looked about to burst into exhortation again, but Ardan kept close to him, ready to act as the occasion warranted, reflexively feeling for his small flat pistol tucked in his left inner coat pocket.

Barbicane was seized with a countering indignation of his own. Climbing a few steps of the paddlewheel bridge access, his voice rang out, plain and sure.

"I am Impey Barbicane. This is Michel Ardan," he pointed out each, "along with Captain Nicholl—a traitor, and deserving of no respect. You may have heard of we three—we attempted a flight to the Moon. Whatever you may have been told, make no mistake, this is no scientific expedition—not with a guard of warships and guns. You fine men have been duped, lied to. Your employers are *thieves*, who tried to steal *my* ship, and failed." Waving back to the stern, "That was what that crane was for—no honest salvage. And now, riddled with failure, they've been steaming north, chasing after the brave men, and women, yes—*women*, who thwarted their design. Or trying to, until those who helped save my ship came to stop them. That vessel and her captain do not warrant your fire. They deserve your *salute*."

The sincerity and intensity of the Great Barbicane was having its effect, plucking strings of mounting doubt about the nature of their mission that only needed his clear reminder to gather into resonant chords.

Ardan wondered whether Nicholl would fly off the handle at that, but was relieved to see the grimacing Captain stalking away for the moment without escalating to another duel. Having seen the behavior of the other soggy gunners who had slunk aboard, Ardan intercepted the Lieutenant to gently recommend, "A dry set of clothes for you, sir." Then he turned to Moran, "You too, Colonel, drying off now could do you great good."

Both men conceded the wisdom of that and departed, serving the *Deuxième Bureau* agent's preference to have Moran off the deck for the time being.

Behind the briskly formed cordon of the *Nautilus* guard, Barbicane took Nemo by the arm, "Have you been following us long?"

Nemo shook his head. "A social call today. I'm here to see Sir Augustus Moran."

"He's not aboard—though I see you've met his son," Barbicane answered. "The father flew away in one of his airships four days ago."

Nemo swore under his breath. "Fled?"

"No. We thought they were chasing *you*." Barbicane turned to Ardan, "Stuart would know his plans, if anyone does."

"Stuart?" Nemo asked.

"The Ambassador's second in command," Ardan said. "One of his associates from India, who remained behind with Colonel Moran to simulate maritime hospitality."

Nemo's eyes narrowed, "He may do." The mention of Moran's son and hospitality reminded him of his messenger duty. Now it was Nemo's turn to take Barbicane's arm, "Robur rescued some men from the sea, including your son Victor. Seriously injured, but *Deimos* is flying them to Bermuda to seek hospital."

Barbicane visibly shook. "As I feared. Flying—that won't take long, at least. Do you know more detail?"

"No, my friend." Srikar returned the subject to his own immediate concerns, "Where then do we find this Stuart?"

"It is a big ship, and he wears no bell." Ardan turned to those milling about to call loudly, "Has anyone seen our Mr. Felix Stuart?"

When no information was forthcoming, Barbicane said, "Odd of him to turn shy on us."

"Perhaps the Captain will know." Ardan waved for Barbicane and Nemo to follow.

Nemo set three of his men to guard the ladder stairs, the remainder to accompany him, but before they left, Barbicane pointed Srikar to the nearest Gatling fragments, then indicated the line of identical debris back along the bulwarks. "Did you know your sister's machine had such bite?"

Nemo was impressed. "I only saw it used underwater, and was ... preoccupied." With a shrug, he turned with Barbicane to stride along behind Ardan. "Aouda said she'd made advances. Always given to modest understatement," he smiled.

As they passed the paddlewheel engine skylight dome, the *Nautilus'* master could not resist a glance down at the machinery, earning a nod of respect for its scale and evident excellence—even if far eclipsed by what he or Aouda were capable of.

Their expedition found Captain Quatermass in the chartroom, hunched over a map, discussing course of action with two of his officers. All looked up at the visitors.

"I apologize for disabling your ship," Nemo ventured, "but I am at war with your Augustus Moran, and offer no apology there."

"Not *my* Moran, I assure you." Quatermass sighed, "Though, thanks to you, it will be a slow limp, to Milford Haven." Eying the *Nautilus* men's gear, he asked with a nod, "Further strange weapons?"

"Correct, sir," Nemo replied. "Not aimed at you."

"We are looking for Mr. Stuart," Ardan pressed.

"Ah, I should like a word with that gentlemen, too," Quatermass said. "After this night's ruckus, our contractual obligations are due for review. Perhaps he's holed up in his stateroom. We'll check there first."

Captain Quatermass led the way, followed by Ardan, Barbicane and Nemo, and the *Nautilus* guards, vigilant at every turn, first to the nearest stair house, then trotting down the steps with determination. When they turned to the right, toward the portside cabins, Barbicane and Ardan realized they (and Captain Nicholl) had been deposited in rooms as far from the nabobs as practicable.

"Curious, not an outside cabin facing the sea," Ardan observed when Quatermass stopped at Stuart's door. The three of the *Columbiad* party had been assigned exterior facing rooms, and as he couldn't imagine Mr. Stuart not having a broad choice of compartments aboard, Ardan could only conclude that this claustrophobic outcome was intentional and desired.

After a rap and a call of Stuart's name elicited no response, Quatermass barged in. All that activity drew the attention of Colonel Moran in his cabin just down the hall, where he had finished slipping on dry clothing. Opening his door ajar, he tried to hear what he could, though the men in Stuart's rooms made little noise and spoke even less.

Stuart's cabin was in some disarray, with a suitcase thrown open on the settee, clothes and other contents helter-skelter, exposing an open gun case at the bottom, its long pistol cradle empty of the revolver.

"Less *Felix* now, more threatened, I think," Ardan punned apropos the retrieved weapon.

A search of the adjoining bed chamber confirmed Mr. Stuart and his gun were elsewhere.

"Where next?" Ardan asked once they were out in the passageway.

"I'd put the coal gang and crew quarters low on the list,"

Barbicane offered. Nemo smirked at that.

"I know where I'd go," Quatermass said. "Follow me."

Sebastian Moran eased shut his door and leaned back against it as the parade passed.

⋘ ⋙

Felix Stuart stood behind the bar, exploring a whiskey at some depth when he heard the voluble Captain approaching from the passenger cabins. Stuart was alone, the barman's shift having concluded hours ago. The bottle was obtained by his copy of the liquor cabinet key—his revolver lay beside it. When he discerned the shuffle of many feet moving from the ship's carpeting to the bare floorboards adjoining the bar, Stuart picked up the gun and turned to face the oncoming party.

All friend? Or other?

Ardan and Quatermass came around the corner of the mirrored funnel casement first, and Stuart remained cool. But the moment Nemo and Barbicane appeared, Stuart raised his pistol and took a shot at the *Nautilus*' captain. He hit the mirror beside him, shattering several pieces, the consequence of too many whiskey swigs to compensate impromptu for the *Great Eastern*'s notorious roll.

Quatermass immediately shouldered the others back behind the funnel housing, but two of *Nautilus*' men went forward on their own and fired their electric rifles at the bar. Those bolts were different from the greenish-yellow arcs of Aouda's weaponry—these more resembled genuine lightning, white hot and crackling through the air. Both struck the bar, blasting the mirror and woodwork. But by then Stuart had sprinted away toward the next funnel housing. He turned back to let off another shot at the *Nautilus* men, nicking one's arm by accident, and was able to send a third while the men's guns whirred as they charged again.

"I didn't think Stuart could move that fast," Quatermass said.

Ardan tapped Barbicane's shoulder, holding up three fingers to remind him of the number of shots Stuart had fired.

"That man we *know*," Nemo swore darkly, meaning other than a royal "we" by that. He meant himself and the crew of his *Nautilus*. Spitting the name, "*Stuart*, you say."

Nemo was now on Stuart's trail, and would not be deterred. He and his men took the point, leaving Quatermass, Ardan and Barbicane to follow out the bar and through the dining room. As they headed for the still partly open door at the end, Quatermass explained, "That leads to the side passage over the engines. Just a few old Second Class public rooms now, the rest were ripped out for the cable drums."

The passage was about eighty feet in length, dimly lit by *Eastern*'s flickering gas. An opening to their left led away to a staircase straddling the keel, which one of Nemo's band went to check to hear for footfalls while they pressed on. The man quickly reported all was quiet at the stairs—his task abetted by the absence of the rumble of *Eastern*'s paddle engines, now stilled below. There were a few doors along the way, to storage and other service rooms, which Quatermass knew ought to be secured but shook the handles anyway as they went along, to preclude Stuart having slipped into any of them.

As they reached the end, Nemo's man ran down another hall to a central stairway, but soon returned when a shot rang out. Stuart had lain in wait behind the third funnel in the lounge beyond to ambush whoever emerged from the passage.

Barbicane raised *four* fingers at Ardan.

Nemo fired a swinging volley from his electric rifle (unwittingly imitating Robur's tactical sweep four days previous at the St. Nicholas Hotel), arcing across the deserted room to rake the effete spindle columns and mirrors decorating the funnel casement. Parts of the shattering glass ended up as molten blobs smoldering on the carpet, while the panels and trim preserved the beams' traverse in palm-width blackened scorch marks.

The *Great Eastern* damage bill owed by one Captain Nemo of the *Nautilus* (address necessarily fluid) ticked upward.

Stuart had not tarried after firing, though, dashing to the end of the disused lounge, tossing open a door into the service ways around the mid-ship cable laying drum. The problem he faced now was that, truth be told, he was not all that familiar with the *Great Eastern*'s lower warrens—at least, that beneath the crane and Gatling guns, or the bar and dining table. He would have to *speculate* his way along, room by increasingly unfamiliar room. And he'd have to think about it fast.

Captain Quatermass was not so constricted, but neither was he in the vanguard. The door opening was heard, however, and Nemo broke into a trot across the silent room, accompanied by the grim submariners. What a counterpoint they were to the better days of the great ship, when travelers and crew (merry or seasick) had tried to enliven its vast unprofitable chambers.

"Is your makeshift infirmary near?" Barbicane asked the Captain as they passed another dusty sheet-covered plush settee, concern growing in them both for the safety of any bedded there should Stuart reach them in his present belligerent condition.

Quatermass shook his head as they tried to keep up with Nemo and his men, "Farther, past the fourth funnel."

Wary of plunging through the door, lest he face another volley from Mr. Stuart, Nemo nudged it open with his weapon barrel. Silence.

Nemo entered the passage first, which turned out to be the corner of a right angle split: one long way leading aft, following the line of skylights, the other turning left. The lower internal skylights had been gutted away, along with segments of the deck, so that the circular cable drum could fit into that and the two floors below. A few new chambers abutted the curving drum wall, filling out some of the corner spaces.

There was no pretense of Victorian elegance here, the refit of the 1860s left only the most functional of decking and walls, plain gas jets hissing small pools of light onto the dark floor.

Had Stuart continued aft, or taken the starboard way around the drum? No sign of him, either way. Could he have moved so quickly as to recede from view around the farthest corners?

Nemo waved them all to silence. The ship had quieted down remarkably from the hubbub of barely a half hour before—would some stray creak or rattle betray Stuart's whereabouts?

Or something other than *sound*. Nemo looked down at the flooring. "When were these decks last swabbed?" he asked Quatermass softly.

"Not this voyage—no traffic here."

"Some of the carpet dust has gone a-walking." Nemo pointed down at a few faint blotches of gray on the leftward passage, spaced as a fast-moving gate might have scattered.

While Nemo led the way forward, some of his men checked the abutting chambers, which proved still locked. As they neared the broadest curve of the drum, Quatermass stepped ahead to the access hatch, an entry without lock that may have proven too tempting for Stuart to forego. With a resigned look, the Captain did his duty and pushed it open. The space behind was very dark save for only a few perfunctory gas jets in the ceiling.

The door hinges showed their reliable oiled condition by not squeaking—and the immediate report of Stuart's gun affirmed how that quiet had worked to his advantage when he sought refuge there.

Quatermass pulled back, his left shoulder stinging from Stuart's grazing bullet, which pinged high off the metal wall a few feet beyond. Nemo noticed the steep angle of the shot, meaning Stuart had fired from well below. By these Nemo could surmise much about the unseen space within.

Ardan flashed *five* fingers at Barbicane, who nodded.

"Only one bullet left, Mr. Stuart," Ardan shouted. "Will you waste it on one of us, or find a more deserving target, so closer to hand?"

"What makes you think I didn't bring fresh ammunition, Mr. Ardan?"

As Stuart had, and was even then adding bullets from his pocket to the emptied chambers. But in the cavernous metal drum, clicking open the revolver carriage echoed with a great snap. Captain Nemo instantly seized that moment to step into the doorway and fire at where he reckoned Stuart was temporarily preoccupied reloading, his eyes unavoidably averted to that task.

Not loudly, but with the gravest of resolve, Nemo swore, "For Himadri and Ajit!"

Nemo's aim was true, the greenish-yellow beam striking Stuart's gun, momentarily throwing the whole cable chamber into searing relief. The energy cascaded along Stuart's left arm and back to his lower torso. With a brief scream, Stuart was thrown back against the iron plating.

Several of Nemo's men pulled out pocket electric lamps to light the way as their Captain stepped through the door onto a railed landing, from which a stair descended to their right. Nemo noticed that it was just by happenstance his gun's beam had missed hitting the railing or the landing floor. They found Stuart sprawled beside the central drum spindle, below a tall frame box of girders, suspended from a closed hatchway above, the frame for the spooling out of the cable that had come to signal the calls of many nations.

Stuart still had the last lingering breath of life in him as Nemo's glaring face loomed in his blurring final vision. It was a bitter pleasure for Srikar to see the man eye to eye, even if only for a moment, before he died.

Nemo turned to the others, "This man gave the orders, at the prison of *Kalapani*." He turned back to Stuart, his voice breaking, "You wanted my secret. You tortured my wife and son to death, for just the ambition of your master. I could have forgiven what you did to me— you spurred me to create so much after we escaped. But I cannot forgive you for my wife and son. I cannot forgive you that."

With a last eyelid flicker, and what could almost have been taken for a final ironic defiant smile, Felix Stuart was dead.

Two of Nemo's men donned their gloves and bore Stuart's charred body out of the drum. Ardan became custodian of Stuart's partially fused pistol (the distorted cartridge wheel blown and melted so that he couldn't be sure whether Stuart had successfully reloaded it or not before his electric demise). When they passed through the lounge, a stop was made to pull a sheet from one of the unused settees. The residual dust was fluffed from it before wrapping Stuart's body.

The stairs they took came up under the wheelhouse, where some rope was obtained from a small stockroom to affix the sheet more rigorously. Then a short but oddly solemn procession bore the white shroud to the bulwarks. Only a few straggling crew and Moran gunners were on hand to witness this strange ritual.

"For a man who brought such grief," Nemo announced flatly, "may he be consigned to his rest."

Nemo's sailors balanced the body on the bulwarks, then flipped it overboard.

Stuart had seaward-facing quarters at last, Ardan thought, and tossed the now useless revolver after him.

Turning away from the railing, Nemo said, "I regret not being able to question Stuart about Sir Augustus's whereabouts. My temper, the heat of passion overruling judgment. Though I imagine he'd have been no more forthcoming than I."

"Sir, *I* know his plans," Quatermass said. "He flew off in the *Aurora* after a steamer, the *Henrietta*, bearing someone named Fogg—I think, it's the Phileas Fogg going around the world. He was certain they were in league with you."

"Fogg!" Ardan dropped into musing, then berated himself aloud, "Stupidity! I forgot his name was mentioned, back on the *Albatross*. And some other ... with a P." Ardan put a palm to his forehead, which didn't help the recollection.

"Passepartout, his name is Passepartout," Nemo declared. "And you met them both, though not by name. They were aboard the *Nautilus* when we retrieved you in the Pacific, along with my sister, Aouda, the creator of the *Deimos* whose caresses you have felt. She has told me much of them both in the last weeks, I almost feel I know them as deep as she. Their danger sets my course. *Nautilu*s will sail north, to be where needed."

Which is what Captain Nemo did, the *Nautilus* slipping away into the night with far less fanfare than its arrival.

As for the *Great Eastern*, the separate smaller engine driving the propeller was started up, and Brunel's injured Leviathan hobbled forward, now on altered course to eventual repair (and losing of much prior construction history by parties best left forgotten) at Milford Haven in Wales.

36. IN WHICH THE *HENRIETTA* STAYS HER TRUE COURSE WHILE OTHERS FIND THEIRS

Deimos arrived at Bermuda just after three o'clock on the morning of the 16th of December. The elongated hilly islands that comprised the Royal colony stood out against the moonlit sea like tracery, its northeastern most one linked by a new causeway south. As they flew over the strips of land girdling a line of shallow harbors, Niru and Robur scouted for their largest settlement. The island bulged wider ahead, into a hook bending westward around the Great Sound. A telescopic view revealed a fort of some sort on the western tip of the hook, while the main town of Hamilton nestled to the east of that, on the sheltered northern corner of the bay. Robur brought *Deimos* down on its periphery, submerging to the cupola to navigate inconspicuously through the scatter of tiny islets toward an inviting empty pier at the town.

Both of Victor's attendants had nodded off down on the deck, as had Tanseem back in the alcove bunk—a condition shared by so many on the island at this hour, lulled by the pleasant warmth, just about sixty Fahrenheit. Still, one elderly black man was up, out smoking his pipe, plopped on a small crate, accompanied by a wiry attentive dog that let a few echoing barks at the oncoming *Deimos*, until stayed by the man's petting hand.

As the *Deimos* surfaced to expose the aft hatch, the man rose and approached the pier with wary curiosity. Robur eased open the cover, the warm air of the Bermuda night invading the cabin. With a nod at the man on the dock, "Is there a hospital near abouts?"

Mindful of the diseases that could be borne by men on boats, especially ones so unfamiliar and strange as this metallic craft, he queried, "What be the ailment?"

"Explosion, at sea. We have just come from a battle. Some American sailors are in want of aid."

"Just Navy beds here, two hospitals, *British* ones, over at their dock." His left hand pointed off in the direction of the fortification Niru had spied earlier.

"We will take our chances with their mercy, then. Thank you."

The hatch closed, Robur cast caution aside and lifted *Deimos* directly into the air, to the marvel of the old man and his dog, and flew west toward the naval base. Having no idea which of the provincial buildings might be their hospitals, and recognizing the imprudence of setting down inside their likely patrolled perimeter, Robur found a wooded spot on the beach some ways to the south to land. He did this so gently that neither of Victor's men awoke.

Robur climbed down from the cupola to retrieve half a dozen £5 notes from a box, which he slipped into a leather wallet that went into one of his inner tunic pockets. Fetching next a collapsible stretcher from a cabinet, he told Niru, "Once we're gone, take the ship out into the bay and await my signal. I don't know how long this will take."

Unlocking the port side hatch, a slight breeze brought the sweet scent of the island's native cedar. Robur stepped out to unfold the stretcher on the sand a few feet away, then returned to awaken the slumbering men, "We've reached Bermuda. Time to find a doctor."

Mr. Kinnard helped Robur carry the unconscious Victor out to the stretcher. "We're at the edge of their navy yard," Robur said. "Somewhere in there are hospitals."

Niru had climbed into the pilot's seat and, as soon as the stretcher team set off, brought *Deimos* up and out over the water, settling and submerging to the cupola height. To wait.

Robur held up the front of the stretcher—he felt he owed them that, given the delays at his hand between the torpedo blast and Bermuda. Not regret, not for Robur, but a sense of what must be done at the moment.

They found a road threading toward the base, and pressed three hundred yards down past a few buildings, dark in the night, and across a bridge to the naval precinct on Ireland Island, before finally encountering a sentry.

"We understand the only hospitals on the island are here," Robur said. "Some Americans need your help."

The sentry came forward to inspect Victor under the blanket, suspecting some ruse. "Where are you from?"

"We came over sea. These men were attacked by pirates. I helped rescue them."

"Vic's hurt bad … please!" the injured mate Jack Trainer pleaded.

"Where's the hospital?" Kinnard demanded from his end of the stretcher, quietly but with an unmistakable firmness and honesty, warrior to warrior, that overcame the sentry's qualms.

It turned out the nearest such facility was not far: a white wrought iron box atop the hill ahead, overlooking an embayment where an unusual floating dry dock was moored, an innovative necessity brought to the island three years before after it was realized the underlying limestone stalled plans to deepen the yard's repair needs. That limestone figured in the hospital, too. Built half a century ago as a quarantine, its ingenious prefabricated design had been combined with local blocks, embellished since with ambitious veranda galleries along its third floor. It looked almost palatial in the moonlight.

The hospital had fewer patients these days than during the time just past, when convict labor had been so often mauled while expanding the dockyard, or when victims trickled in from the naval engagements between disapproving Union blockaders and the several Confederate gunboats serviced here not quite on the sly.

But now the Atlantic was all tranquility (apart from the wake around the *Great Eastern* that morning), and the American consul, Charles Maxwell Allen, had done much to dampen the recent wartime animosities, such that the doctor and nurses on duty turned to the foreigner on the stretcher with proficient sympathy, not coiled resentment.

The sailors and Robur provided self-censored particulars of how they had come to be at their door. No mention was made of the *Eastern*, of course, or submarines, or flying machines descending on all as fiery Nemesis—the story they spun impromptu, a dissembling equal to the lunar yarn Impey Barbicane had offered the press back at Stone's Hill.

As Victor was borne away to a bed, Robur chose his words to a recording clerk with care, "You may mark down the name as V. Barbicane. I. Barbicane, of Baltimore, and the flight to the Moon, is the most concerned *parent* here, bear that in mind regarding your discretion and care."

The staff did their duty, leaving Robur and the third sailor alone in a waiting room. Neither spoke, but Robur stepped away to put his back to the other so that he might flip open the leather flap over his telegraphic controls. Niru was soon informed of their successful arrival at the hospital.

A quarter hour on, the attending doctor appeared to tell Robur, "Compliments to your ship's medic. I could not have done better on the dressings. A follower of antiseptic."

"I will tell him so," Robur said, wondering whether the man had the slightest inkling that the medic in question could be someone like *Deimos*' Asian chef of many trades.

Once the doctor was gone, Robur turned to Mr. Kinnard. "I must return to my ship, lad. I don't know when Barbicane, or others, will come, so you may be stuck here for a while. We must leave, but you are not abandoned." He pulled the wallet from his coat. "This should tide you over for any expenses. It's the least you are owed."

"I'll do my duty, sir."

Robur placed a hand on his shoulder, "I know you will."

The sailor watched stoically as Robur stepped outside and disappeared into the moonlight.

☙ ❧

Half an hour later, aboard the *Henrietta*, Aouda had received Robur's report of his actions in Bermuda. She glanced at Passepartout, still evidently napping beside her, while Fogg appeared immune from fatigue at the wheel. Dropping her left elbow on the chair arm, she rested her head on the fingertips, worrying the scalp. Finally she rose and crossed to the chart table, frowning down at the grid, mentally calculating.

"A thought?" Fogg asked softly, so as not to awaken Passepartout.

Aouda matched his tone. "Not a good one, I'm afraid. Robur brought the men to Bermuda, good news there. But they are low on supplies, gases need replenishing; repairs to do. That means Diadem—nine thousand miles. Two days out, two days back. We'll be close to England by then. But even without that, *Deimos* couldn't reach us before the gyroplane does—which Srikar tells me, is called the *Albatross*." She nodded at the ship's clock, which they had kept adjusted ahead to local time as they sailed east, "Ten, maybe eleven. *Nautilus* is sailing toward us—too late there, too. And he can't rip the keel from an airship, anyway. Srikar did find and kill his torturer on the *Great Eastern*—that man Stuart. But his master, the Ambassador Moran, lives—and is aboard that other airship, Phileas, the *Aurora*. So near and so far."

Fogg pursed his lips, "The *Aurora*. They'll stay away from us to spare the hydrogen. Unless we can lure them close, or go to them. That leaves us to work out the vulnerabilities of the other, *Albatross*." The way he said it suggested Fogg did not approve of the name. "What are the limits of your electric gun? Passepartout's comb has *Albatross* with four guns, two to the side."

"I could hurt one on a charge, not sure two. Even then, they'd just have to flip around, and train two more on us. I could keep the generator attached, but it can't cycle fast enough from full discharge. I should have taken one of the bigger guns, from *Deimos*, when we were there."

"None of us were in a sharp calculating mood, right then." Fogg looked at the clock, "Five hours to *not* prepare."

Aouda stepped away from the chart to peer out at the sea. The light in the wheelhouse was dim, but still she sheltered her eyes with the palm of her right hand to get a clearer view. "Are those storm clouds out there?"

"Yes, ahead, and well to the south. We'll be sailing straight into it. Mr. Fix will likely stay in his cabin."

Aouda had something other than the detective on her mind. "I wonder how seasick their airships get."

Fogg nodded appreciatively.

ଓଙ

Commander Tremaine's officer on the watch awoke him to warn

of approaching bad weather. After assessing the extent of the storm ahead and the danger it posed, he ordered *Aurora* to head north of the clouds. He knew that would turn them away from the *Henrietta*, and put the squall between them and the *Albatross* (which he had no doubt was bearing toward them even as they steered). He further recognized the *Henrietta* might take advantage of this, since they knew they were being tracked, but Tremaine could not risk *Aurora* staying so close to the winds and lightning.

"What are you going to tell the Ambassador?" his officer asked.

"That we did what was necessary. I hold no shame in that."

03 80

The storm raged for several hours as the *Henrietta* sailed along its northern edge, rolling and heaving in the waves a bit differently than if the ship had been carrying cargo to weigh the keel. Water sloshed over the gunnels spectacularly, and the window panes shuddered, but overall the *Henrietta* proved a stout vessel.

Down in his cabin, Mr. Fix awoke to feel tossed about like a ragdoll, and yearned for a bed on a ship larger than the *Henrietta*.

Her Captain, meanwhile, honed by years of experience to every shift and sway of what had been his command, was likewise made awake down in his locked quarters. Speedy yelled a few times to be released, to at least be present and of use so long as his ship needed him—but feeling how well the usurpers were handling the helm (still Phileas Fogg, at that moment), realized he had been supplanted there, too. Finally he curled back to sleep.

03 80

Captain Quatermass took breakfast that morning with Impey Barbicane and Michel Ardan in the *Great Eastern*'s dining alcove, the gentle throb of her lone propeller engine barely felt up here. When Colonel Moran arrived, he was surprised to see the ship's officer present, and a bit more not to see the early-riser Stuart.

"If you are looking for Mr. Stuart, he will not be joining us," Ardan said. "He was unavoidably, and permanently, and righteously, *delayed*. Would you like details?"

No one could accuse the younger Moran of being slow. "Who did the deed?"

"Captain Nemo," Ardan replied. "Did you know the two had met before?"

"No." Which was not entirely true. You don't grow up in a family and not catch wind of certain breezes, or be unaware of numbers that would have added up clear enough, had one only stopped to do the sums. But Sebastian Moran hadn't thought that far back. He'd only considered the factors that involved *him*.

"Your father is responsible for what Stuart did to Nemo and his family. Had *I* lost a wife and son thus, *nothing* would stop me from avenging them." Ardan asked the Colonel, "Do you think the *Nautilus* will not rest until Sir Augustus is brought down too? Or that his sister, who has a flying machine that melts Gatling guns and sinks ironclads as casually as one winds a watch, will retire to weave tapestries, rather than help her brother to this vengeance? I offer my condolence in advance, Colonel, on your becoming an orphan."

Distilling disapproval, Barbicane told Moran, "Given what your father has enlisted you to do, you seem altogether late, coming to the history of his scheme. I wonder what pages you'll find missing from your future story."

Sebastian Moran ended up assembling a full plate but took it back to his cabin for solitary ingestion. Captain Nicholl did not appear for dining that morning at all.

❧ ☙

When Sir Augustus Moran stirred awake that morning, and learned that the *Aurora* was no longer in visual proximity of the *Henrietta*, he was furious. Not quite face red as a beet, perhaps, for apoplexy was not his manner, but no less uncompromising for it. It's not that he berated Commander Tremaine for his judgment in moving the airship north of the squall. Sir Augustus recognized that was a prudent call, mindful only of their safety. And indeed, Tremaine had already steered *Aurora* back onto a southern heading, now that the storm was breaking up, intending to restore their track on the *Henrietta*.

But still, he was not where he wanted to be—and, not dissimilar to Phileas Fogg, Sir Augustus was a man who liked to get his own way.

"We cannot coordinate with the *Albatross* if we are not *there* to do it," Sir Augustus pointed out the window ahead. "I don't want Blake arriving at a rendezvous where we are *absent*. *Henrietta*'s Captain Speedy is committed to surrendering Fogg to us, and if that can be accomplished before the *Great Eastern* arrives, all the better. I will have this purpose *done*, Commander. Bring us within sight of *Henrietta*."

Sir Augustus returned to the side bench again, to finish his modest breakfast plate, though without so much appetite now.

❧ ☙

Around nine o'clock, Captain Speedy was awake again and bellowed, "Can a man be *fed*?" Passepartout roused from his wheelhouse slumber. The storm was fading and the sun had just come up, trying to peek around the many slanting shafts of rain still harassing the sea all about. Aouda now stood at the wheel.

"Breakfast calls," Passepartout smiled, and asked Aouda, "I see

Mr. Fogg has finally taken to rest? He should not push himself too far."

"He's worried about the *Albatross*, as am I. *Deimos* can't help us, and they'll be here in a few hours, with their guns. They won't know their navy isn't following—that we could use as a lever. *If* they stop to chat, which I assume they won't. Our best hope now is the weather holding bad."

Thus reminded, Passepartout brought out his comb to perform a sweep of their surroundings. "The *Aurora* has gone. Our cloudy skies are clear."

"For how long, Passepartout?" Aouda sighed.

"My I fetch you any breakfast?"

"A porridge I should fancy, some oatmeal. Reminds me of my old English school. Is that silly?"

"Nothing you have ever done is that, *mademoiselle*," Passepartout smiled. But his thoughts grew more pensive as he went down to the galley, working to keep his footing on the rocking deck and stairs—a sudden amusement for him, the acrobat with reflexes of such inhuman temper.

Henrietta's cook grinned as Passepartout entered, enjoying the ritual of learning what it was the Fogg party up top would be having, at any and all hours, along with the set fare the cook continued to turn out for their trapped Captain.

"Oatmeal, you say? Did the lady want plain, or fancy?"

"She did not specify."

"Well, I have some cinnamon," the cook smiled. "I'll set that in a little jar on the side, beside the sugar."

While the cook worked away, Passepartout dropped to a bench with a frown. Then he began to think, holding up his right hand, spinning the index finger in imitation of *Albatross*' many propellers. Gradually the digit spun off kilter to stroke the philtrum of his lip, as he pondered what it meant to be suspended in the air by so many spinning blades, and by nothing else.

Passepartout took out his comb, clutched it in both hands on his lap, and closed his eyes. The comb tines flaring out much as they had in Yokohama, with the tiniest of electric snapping few could hear beneath the sizzle of the cook's bacon frying, in far off America the telegraphic gear in Thomasina Maker's laboratory began to spark receipt of a very powerful and repeating signal: *JEAN NEEDS MAKER ... JEAN NEEDS MAKER ... JEAN NEEDS MAKER ...* with a five second delay between each call.

This went on and on, and the cook thought Passepartout had fallen asleep when he lay a breakfast tray before him on the table, "Friend, your food."

Passepartout did not open his eyes nor move. "Busy. Thank you."

It was absurd and embarrassing, sitting there thus, while the food got cold, but now that he had committed to it, he could not abandon the overture. He realized it must be only about five o'clock in the morning there in Illinois, so he counted now on Maker's habit for greeting the dawn already at work.

Five minutes later, which seemed an awfully long time, Maker came into her works bearing a hot breakfast of her own, but raced to the mechanism once she heard the insistent snapping. Plopping the plate on the table, she spun control levers, and replied in the next gap: *MAKER HERE WHAT TROUBLES.*

Passepartout heaved a very relieved sigh. **MORAN NAVY DESTROYED BY DEIMOS, BUT CANNOT INTERCEPT THEIR FLYER ALBATROSS HEADING NORTH TO LIKELY ATTACK OUR SHIP. COULD KESTREL COME FOR ANOTHER WINDMILL?**

Maker bowed her head, torn over what she was being asked to do. She thought back over what she had seen of the gyroplane, considered how that might figure in what Passepartout had just proposed, and replied, *FOR YOU, AND BECAUSE THEY HAVE LIFEBOATS.*

KEEP FREQUENCY OPEN ON KESTREL, Passepartout concluded. Now he could open his eyes, deposit the comb in his pocket, and convey a regrettably colder breakfast up to the wheelhouse.

"Your bowl is a bit cooler, Princess, *pardon* my delay," Passepartout set the tray at the chart table. "I'll explain after I feed the Captain."

Aouda still had the wheel, so could not have her oatmeal anyway until Passepartout returned. Performing his duty with Speedy below, he bounded back to the bridge to displace Aouda at the helm.

She decided a sprinkle of sugar and cinnamon would do the trick on her porridge, and sat down in one of the chairs. "Warm enough," she decided after a taste. "What did you need to 'explain'?"

"I asked Maker to deal with the *Albatross*. She can fly to it in under an hour."

"What can she do? The *Kestrel* is unarmed."

"A weapon is just a tool used to violent purpose. Bullets and bombs—or gaseous rays—are not the only way to make trouble. *Kestrel* has a hidden talent your *Deimos* cannot match." Sitting behind him, Aouda couldn't see the cryptic smile cross Passepartout's lips. "Once you've finished your oatmeal, either you or Mr. Fogg will have to regain the wheel. I will have to stay by my comb."

ങ ഔ

Half an hour later, in Thomasina Maker's landing hall, the Grenadier knelt by a fluid conduit attached to a nozzle on the tail of the

Kestrel, while Maker attended to its pumping on the corresponding gauge of her control panel. Both were dressed in leather flight gear, and needed only that last provisioning before taking wing.

"Done!" she yelled, and Dufoy disconnected the tube, rising and stepping back to swing the conduit around like a whip, then coil its length into a manageable clump by the canister.

Maker had lowered her side of the glass roof, and Dufoy paused for a moment, leaning on his opening before entering, an expression of wry resignation marking his silent doubts about the rightness of their course, buoyed by his own long-earned confidence in her judgment.

"How like Jean to remember our old windmill," Maker shrugged, and the Grenadier climbed in.

"Ours didn't have people hanging on it," Dufoy said as his door sealed.

Maker powered up the *Kestrel*, opened the roof doors, and they ascended into the cloudy pre-dawn sky, to scream due east at speed.

ය ඏ

Phileas Fogg had dressed to his customary standard when he returned to the wheelhouse after his brief slumber. Aouda was at the helm, but Passepartout sat on his chair clutching his comb, eyes shut. Fogg passed him in silence and gestured back with a quizzical look at Aouda.

"Passepartout has called on Miss Maker's *Kestrel* to deal with the *Albatross*," Aouda explained softly.

"Did he say how?"

"He set it as a puzzle—something *Kestrel* could do that my *Deimos* could not. I've been turning over both crafts in my mind, trying to figure what I've missed. We both can ram things."

Passepartout grinned, and called while eyes still closed, "One of *Kestrel*'s testing flights fell too low and fast. Their windmill didn't like it."

"The thunderclap," Aouda realized, delighted to be made privy to the magicians' secret. "*Deimos* is slower than sound. Can it be that severe?"

"We will see," Passepartout said. "By the way, the *Aurora* has returned on the horizon. The storm has not brought *them* down."

Another consideration came to Fogg's mind. Tapping the coat pocket where his watch lay, and with no special chimes forthcoming, did it herald *Kestrel*'s success in advance, just as with the *Columbiad* in the Pacific? "Very good, Passepartout, very good."

ය ඏ

Kestrel flew high and fast that morning, riding their long white condensation cloud at supersonic speed, circling past a few light storms. Grenadier waited until they were out over the Atlantic to switch on the instruments to search out the offending *Albatross*.

"They're only going fifty miles an hour. Jean's coordinates should be close." Maker peered out at the far horizon, "On this side of that big storm, I think. Once we find them, we'll have to do a long turn."

"We'll be blind for a bit," Dufoy warned.

"I'm assuming they don't jump up and down like a grasshopper. Hundred feet should be clearance enough."

Dufoy got the first return of the airship on their detectors a quarter of an hour later. There were scattered clouds, but as Maker anticipated, the ship was flying outside the main storm.

"They're going north," Grenadier reported. "Coming from ahead would compound the blow."

"But *behind*, less to see coming, less time to turn or dive. In for a penny, in for a pound," Maker added with a determined sigh.

Maker aimed so that they flew by the *Albatross* well to the south of them, then began a wide slowing descent, turning clockwise, dropping below the speed of sound. Heading gradually south and then west, *Kestrel* was soon several hundred miles behind them, and only a few hundred feet higher than the airship's altitude. Thus positioned, Maker nodded at Grenadier and they accelerated, intensely so.

Up past the speed of sound, beyond 1000, and 1500, and still faster. Gently easing their trajectory so they were dropping ever so slightly, *Kestrel* put on a final burst of speed, such that the air streaming over them now glowed red hot, blinding their physical and instrumental vision in a shroud of ionized gas.

And behind, a shockwave wake slapped the sea like a deadly oncoming razor.

The *Kestrel* was so small and moving so quickly, Commander Blake would have had no chance at all seeing its approach, even had he set men to survey their rear. *Kestrel* flashed over *Albatross* like a silent dart, followed some moments later by the shockwave. All it took was for a few of her rotors to twist, the pylons to bend, just enough, so that the tips of some struck those of the ones above or below. In that brief concussion half of *Albatross*' lifting vanes were smashed to bits—that cacophony buried in the overall roar of the pressure wave.

Commander Blake and the crew on the bridge could see the shockwave racing ahead even as the convulsion of the ship signaled they were losing all functional lift and were in great trouble. Angling toward the sea, those aboard grabbed what they could to hold on as the deck careened downward to port, splintered propeller vanes shooting away to slice the waves like white knives.

It was a saving grace that *Albatross*' main hull had the properties of a boat. They splashed bow first into the waves, the stern settling down behind. Unfortunately, the damage to the engines was only amplified by the slam into the sea, causing an explosion to blow out part of their aft to starboard, flipping the lifeboat there out to the water, and breaching the hull causing them to take water.

The other lifeboat was still in place when Blake led his crew up top. Incredibly, they had suffered no fatalities, though two men nearest the exploding engine took injuries of consequence.

Concerned over the ethics of what she had just accomplished, Maker braked below sound (which took almost as long as her acceleration) and flew back to the wreck to see what had happened. Sight of the crew boarding the lifeboat lightened her spirits.

Both Maker and Dufoy were wearing their leather altitude masks, obscuring their faces, and only Maker's window was facing the wreckage as they passed. Whether his reaction might have been different had he known them to be personages of color, Commander Blake offered a grudging salute as *Kestrel* floated by on its whining carpet of combusted air. One honest combatant to another, battle well fought.

Maker nodded in response, and took *Kestrel* up and away to the south.

As the noise died away and he had better chance to survey their predicament, fractured smoking parts littering the waves and what was left of *Albatross'* prow sinking fast, Blake lamented accurately, "What a mess."

Blake then began to think of where to take their small boat, heaving in the Atlantic swells, and no sign of land. Northwest was their superior bet. "Well, men—Halifax, I think. Long row ahead."

Kestrel was by then over the horizon, but Maker was not returning to Chicago. She telegraphed Passepartout: *ALBATROSS BROUGHT DOWN, CREW TOOK TO LIFEBOAT, BEST OUTCOME. FLYING TO EASTERN TO OFFER APOLOGIES TO BARBICANE. AND JUST DAMNED CURIOUS. ANYTHING WE NEED TO KNOW?*

From his chair in *Henrietta*'s wheelhouse, Passepartout smiled, and responded: ***MORAN SON STILL ABOARD, CHECK AFTER NICHOLL TOO, UNCERTAIN DANGER. BARBICANE SHOULD BE TOLD DEIMOS BROUGHT VICTOR & OTHER INJURED SAFELY TO BERMUDA NAVAL HOSPITAL.***

The course set, at a more leisurely pace and scenic altitude, Maker pulled off her mask and turned to her travelling companion, "You're going to get to see the *Great Eastern* after all."

The Grenadier likewise removed his gear and grinned. He'd heard it was quite a sight.

They arrived at the *Great Eastern* around eleven o'clock, finding it somewhat east of their expectations. Maker's instruments soon confirmed the absence of all Moran's ironclad escorts. *Deimos* had swept the field clear, indeed.

The arrival of the *Kestrel* brought another flurry of alarm aboard the *Great Eastern*. What was this next aerial harbinger? Had they not endured enough?

But by the time the little craft glided down toward the deck, many aboard were not so sure it posed a threat at all, especially when Maker maneuvered around the rigging by the second mast, just aft of the bow cable laying equipment, to gently glide over the lifeboats to land in one of the few spaces open enough for its footprint.

Maker and Grenadier were just raising the dome doors when they were met by Captain Quatermass, "I believe you missed the party. That was in the wee hours."

"No sir," Maker said. "I'm here to speak with Mr. Barbicane. If he is aboard, and well."

"Correct on both counts, ma'am." Quatermass dispatched a crewman to fetch Barbicane. Looking at the craft and the two aeronauts' unusual leather attire, he asked, "Are you from the Moon?"

"No," Maker laughed with a shake of her head, "Illinois, presently. Though I should like to *go* to the Moon—and *all* the planets, if I had a chance."

"I've seen some mighty strange vessels lately," Quatermass explained. "Yours is the first to be peaceable."

Given what *Kestrel* had just done to the *Albatross,* Maker averted her gaze for a moment.

Quatermass was now bristling with curiosity. "How do you make it float in the air like that? The other machine did that, too—no propellers. Is it like a steam whistle, pressure?"

"Of the highest quality," Maker nodded.

Impey Barbicane appeared by them, accompanied by the ever-protective and interested Ardan. Neither knew what to make of the newcomers, strangers to them both.

"So, who might you be, to come down from the skies for me today?" Barbicane asked.

Maker, who had not previously seen Barbicane up close to recognize him on sight, sized him up favorably. "My name is Maker. Not sure how to set my bona fides. Met a Dupin here, from France—he knows Mr. Ardan, who should be here, I've been told."

"As indeed I am," Ardan interposed quickly, being the only one present privy to that gentleman's identity, and preferring the subject move on, "Tell us your purpose."

"I have a message, and an apology. Message first." Maker looked

Barbicane in the eye, "Your son and his friends are safe in Bermuda, at the hospital there."

Barbicane shuddered backward in relief at that news, "Thank god!" All consideration of any Dupin was forgotten.

"I don't know their condition," Maker cautioned.

Barbicane accepted that. "And the apology?"

She waved at her craft, "*Kestrel* is what brought down your *Columbiad*. I'm sorry for vexing you that way, but we had a purpose to accomplish."

"That little thing!" Barbicane shook his head, in admiration, not disapproval. "No, you didn't vex us. Scared the shittin' hell out of us, yes. But you spared us from *being* vexed, here on this ship—so I can't count that against you."

"How does it launch?" Quatermass asked.

"Just up and away. Doesn't need a cannon." Maker turned to Barbicane, "Me and my friends saw your three men picked up north on the *Nautilus*. How did things go before, on the Pacific side? Was it hard? If so, I'm sorry."

"Was a bit. We landed heavy." Barbicane smiled, "Nemo's sister and Mr. Fogg handled it well. Nemo just supplied the boat."

"Fogg?" Maker startled. "Phileas Fogg?"

"The same. Nemo's sister Aouda flew him and his French servant down for the recovery—hard to remember, funny big name." He turned to Ardan, "What was that?"

"Passepartout," Ardan obliged, adamant not to forget it again.

"That's it! I'm not sure how they got involved—Nemo didn't tell. Quite a detour for Fogg, in any case, running around the world."

"So Mr. Fogg, Nemo's very beautiful sister, and the funny named Passepartout helped you out in the Pacific Ocean *on the day* I knocked you from the sky? What an adventure they must have had."

Ardan at least was puzzled at Maker's tone, and slipped it into a little mental compartment, to think more about sometime.

"It would be an adventure to see this ship," Grenadier reminded Maker.

"May my friend have a tour?" she asked the Captain.

"Certainly. Though we're in rougher condition than we were yesterday."

When the Captain motioned whether Maker would be coming with them, she said, "I'll stay here, mind the *Kestrel*." Looking at Barbicane and then Ardan, "Perhaps you gentlemen would remain with me, jaw a bit."

Barbicane and Ardan were fine with that.

Quatermass pointed out the cable machinery to Grenadier, then turned to lead the black visitor aft.

Once they were gone, Maker asked, "I know about Colonel Moran and Captain Nicholl, the part they played in all this. Passepartout said Moran was aboard, and Nicholl might be here too. Any trouble from them?"

"You *are* on top of things," Ardan smiled.

"I shot Nicholl in a duel. Winged his arm. Intended more fatal. He's been half a nuisance with one arm in a sling."

"Colonel Moran got a bath when he led an attack on *Nautilus*," Ardan added. "He almost took breakfast with us this morning. We were happy it was almost."

"Nemo's sailed off after Moran's father," Barbicane said. "Final score to settle."

Ardan sensed Maker was owed a clarification. "Nemo's family were killed at the behest of the Ambassador Moran. His subordinate Stuart was the instrument of that outrage. Barbicane and I witnessed a rough justice Nemo exacted on him this morning. We now have one less passenger."

"We have yet to actually meet Sir Augustus Moran," Barbicane confessed. "But knowing the suffering he's caused, I could throttle his neck myself."

News of the *Kestrel*'s arrival had filtered out among the crew, and a small crowd had assembled to gawk at the machine—though not approach closer, as Barbicane, Ardan and Maker somehow together radiated an imposing cordon that kept them all at bay.

CS SO

The giant deck of the *Great Eastern* was quite the promenade for Captain Quatermass and the Grenadier. The Haitian had never been aboard so tremendous a vessel—a circumstance true of most everyone, save the five thousand who had sailed aboard her as passengers since 1860, and of course her crew of four hundred.

They passed the ship's skylights, Grenadier stepping to them, peering down at the grandeur below. He did the same with the paddlewheel engine.

As for the paddle housings, Quatermass explained, "Our paddles looked better yesterday, before Captain Nemo paid a visit."

Dufoy had seen the melted Gatlings they passed by the bulwarks, and finally asked, "What are those slag heaps all along the deck?"

"Those are what's left of the guns Ambassador Moran bought. They were the *best*, until the flying machine came over this morning. If this is the war of the future, they can have it." Quatermass stopped to reach out and lean against the bulwarks, looking out to sea, rocking back and forth a bit in mimicry of the *Eastern*'s natural motion.

"What's it like, to fly?"

"Maker's the one that loves it. I help her. It's a fear at first, then you get used to it. Start looking at the sights. The world looks so different from high up. Can't see any hate, or envy."

"A Philosopher. Are people surprised at that, your skin?"

"Those who are, Captain, don't usually bring up philosophy."

Quatermass disengaged from the railing, and escorted Grenadier further aft, by the long cable trough, all the way to the crane.

Coming back along the starboard side, they encountered some of the idle Gatling gunners, and their Lieutenant. A few looked askance at the Captain's black guest; others paid him no mind.

"How are your men holding up?" Quatermass asked.

"Well enough. Looks like we'll have nothing to do till Milford Haven. At least we have food, and plenty of room to exercise."

"If our propeller fails, we'll invite your men to help row." Quatermass was only half joking.

The Lieutenant grew more serious, "Is it true, Captain Nemo killed Stuart?"

"Yes."

"And Stuart tortured Nemo's wife and kid?"

"So I heard him say."

"Bastard," the Lieutenant swore.

"At least that." As Quatermass and Grenadier strolled on, the Captain's spirits flagged. "This has been a sad voyage—another in a long decline. Truth is, this grand ship is being passed by. It was built to carry thousands to the Far East, but that never happened. And on the Atlantic run, the smaller ships were always more profitable. The cable laying made money. You can see they've never taken any of that out. Now it's a ship without a service—decorated with dead guns. I wonder how long before she's just scrapped."

Quatermass turned to Grenadier, "Do you think someday flying machines will replace ships altogether?"

"Not for cable laying," Dufoy decided.

ଓ ଛ

Impey Barbicane's enthusiasm regarding Maker's *Kestrel* was contagious for anyone with a scientific imagination. Michel Ardan could see that, watching the faces of the crowd gathered around them, even as he or they understood little of Maker's answers to Barbicane's many questions and observations on its features, from its rotatable lifting vanes to its battery of rocket nozzles. When Barbicane ran his hand along the smooth glass roof, it was with almost the sensuality one might reserve for a romantic encounter.

"This astonishes me. *You* astonish me, for building it. So small—

so powerful. If you figured a whole Difference Engine into a matchbox, I couldn't be more amazed, or impressed. Harnessing pitchblende like this—"

"Is this what it's come to? Niggers with wings?"

It was Captain Nicholl, who had come up to look at this latest aerial wonder, only to find the leather-clad black woman talking with Barbicane as an equal. No, worse—as a friendly mentor, purveying superior knowledge to someone avidly receptive of it.

Thomasina Maker stepped up onto *Kestrel*'s front cowl, proud like an ebony angel. "Yes, wings. *My* wings, built by *me*. Nothing of its like on all the earth. Honest labor, to be proud of, by daylight—not like you, sneaking in by night to steal those gears. Saw you. Except they weren't Barbicane's gears. Me and my friends made a false set for you to take. Watched you do it. Then we marched the right ones back in." She winked at Barbicane, who smiled in return. "Worse than a thief," Maker leaned toward Nicholl, "you didn't even know what you were pinching."

A flash of understanding darted across Ardan's face, as he realized this woman must have been one of the band he had seen Dupin with back at Stone's Hill, from so far removed. She had been part of a greater enterprise that had taken place under his very nose. What an agent Dupin might have made for the *Deuxième Bureau*, had he only a bit more the blaze of discipline about him, a duty to the Republic, and less a yearning for comfort and ease while playing with his detective puzzles.

Nicholl tried to jump up onto the cowling after Maker, a clumsy maneuver with one arm in a sling altering his balance—and Impey Barbicane aborted the maneuver anyhow by seizing that injured arm and yanking Nicholl to the deck. Captain Quatermass and the Grenadier had completed their circuit of the *Great Eastern*'s expanse, and witnessed this from the edge of the crowd. Dufoy rushed forward to stand beside *Kestrel*.

"If there were any doubt what a *stupid* man you are, Nicholl, this settles it," Barbicane was disdain embodied. "A craft of genius flies here, and all you can see is the hue of her skin. How much genius has been ignored by people like you? How much of our potential, *wasted*? Well, Nicholl, we're not going to wait. *We* are the future. *She* is the future. We don't care what *this* looks like," Barbicane pointed to his own cheek, then touched his forehead, "We only care what's up here," and then his heart, "And *here*. I don't know when our future will come, but Lord help us if it doesn't."

Nicholl had managed to regain his feet, and outright screamed, "*Future*? What future, when all Honor's gone? Nothing left but cold mongrel equality, *science* and things that fly fast."

"You want Honor met?" Grenadier slapped his own chest twice sharply, "Name your weapon."

Nicholl doubled over in laughter, then reared to tell the crowd, with the manner of an exasperated headmaster explaining a privileged truth to simpletons, "You see? He thinks he can challenge my Honor, like some equal. That's what their world means."

"You're right, we're *not* your equal," Grenadier said. "We were never that *low*."

Grenadier pulled out a pistol and aimed at Nicholl's heart, but Barbicane stepped up to push his arm down. "No more bullets. He's not worth it, after all."

Barbicane spun around and landed a firm fist on Nicholl's cheek, sending him to the deck again—this time, unconscious.

"We'd best go, before we cause a scandal." Maker said. "But not without an invitation, to make amends." She turned to Barbicane, "I can fly you to Bermuda."

Barbicane shook, knowing the need of it, and nodded. "Would you like another ride, Ardan?"

"And leave these hundreds of men to the subtle mercy of Captain Nicholl and Colonel Moran? In a heartbeat." Ardan turned to Quatermass, "Enjoy the rest of your voyage, Captain. It was one to remember."

"Nicholl's too near," Maker decided.

"Give us the honor." Barbicane enlisted Ardan to pick up Nicholl and carry him some ten feet from the *Kestrel*. "Far enough?"

"More than enough."

Grenadier had already opened the starboard door, and Maker set about the port one. Barbicane climbed in on that side, but crossed to take the seat behind Dufoy. Ardan paused just a moment at the entry, swallowed his doubts, and slid in beside Barbicane.

"Nicely upholstered," Ardan joked to quell his suddenly queasy stomach.

Maker switched the doors to seal, and began to fasten the belt harness, as did Dufoy.

"You're sitting on your safety buckles, gentlemen," Grenadier scolded the two rear passengers. "Don't."

Both remedied the deficiency, a bit clumsily, but satisfactorily in the end.

Having experienced the *Columbiad* and *Deimos*, and while neither saw the *Kestrel* land on the *Great Eastern*, Barbicane and Ardan had different expectations as Maker powered up the machine. Barbicane's mind raced as he tried to imagine what conduits and shields were involved to transfer the volatile energy of Power X into the directed blasts needed to move such a craft. Ardan, meanwhile, felt especially exposed under the glass roof, realizing that the enclosed space of both *Columbiad* and *Deimos* had proven a comfort to him. This flyer seemed altogether too much *window*.

Once the engines had escalated to their necessary whine, *Kestrel* eased up into the air, and when high enough to clear the bulwarks and lifeboat stanchions, glided laterally out over the water. Although you couldn't see directly down on account of the curving sides, enough of the *Great Eastern*'s hull dropped away to leave Ardan no doubt how high they were in the air.

Putting *Kestrel* under forward thrust and climbing, the unprepared Barbicane and Ardan were pushed back into their seats with a jolt. Over the next three seconds, they flew up past the port paddlewheel, revealing the extent of the damage wrought by Captain Nemo that morning, dangling bits of the paddle flopping on their own from the leisurely impetus of the ship's propeller—and back along the hundreds of feet of lifeboats and skylights and funnels and ambling men, looking smaller by the moment, finally to leave the long cable trough and competent Stuart crane behind.

Ardan squirmed around in his seat as much as he could under the harness, to catch a final glimpse of the receding *Great Eastern*. After not many more seconds they were a mile from it, and the Great Iron Ship looked like any other dark flotsam would bobbing on the gray Atlantic waves.

❦

Aboard the *Aurora*, once more pacing the *Henrietta* within manageable telescopic range, the skies continued to clear but there was cloudiness on another front. The chronometer had reached Noon. The *Albatross* was overdue.

"Could they have been lost in the storm?" Sir Augustus Moran demanded of Commander Tremaine.

"Anything is possible. Blake's not a reckless man." Tremaine glanced over at their interrupted chess game. "They could have been delayed at *Eastern*, though I could only speculate why—fueling accident, rotor repairs, take your pick. Or—they could have fought with that flyer, and lost. All we know is, no *Albatross*. You'll have to decide: do we remain here, or fly south back to the ships?"

Sir Augustus stared out the starboard windows to where they knew Speedy's ship steamed. "The *Henrietta*'s been staying exactly to course, hasn't she?"

"Like a metronome."

"The *Great Eastern* should be here Wednesday—when?"

"Morning, thereabouts. May I remind, a lot can happen in two days."

Sir Augustus replied with confidence, "We have the fox in sight. We'll stay here, to mark his tail. Await Quatermass and our guns."

☙ ❧

Michel Ardan kept his hands together down on his lap as *Kestrel* flew along, trying to conceal their shaking. He was terrified of this height and speed, more than even his first ride clinging to the outside of *Albatross*, since he had been too focused, muscles straining then, to feel his own relaxed bodily reactions so directly. Nor did he want to be ill, soiling this incredible machine and its fine interior with rude spittle or vomit.

Barbicane, by contrast, seemed quite at home, leaning forward with his arms crossed on the frame of the seat ahead, shouting in conversation with Maker. By now, she had confessed her connection to Barton Swift, a businessman of sterling reputation not unknown to Barbicane's circle. "Ships like this would revolutionize transportation, abolish distance. Don't tell me Swift didn't suggest building more?"

"Mr. Swift entertains all possibilities—and their troubles." Then Maker asked, "Would you like all the world tinkering with engines like mine? Doing God knows what with them then?"

"Probably not. You dampen my dreams, ma'am. But you've faced more the hard end of life than any I have," Barbicane admitted. "I admit to blundering ahead too easy, not thinking through all the consequences. But a world where things like *this*"—slapping the side of the compartment—"are as common as wagons is something to imagine."

From his position, the Grenadier could see the other passenger's condition. "Mr. Ardan looks like he'd rather be in the wagon."

Barbicane turned to see. "So, something unsettles you, after all. Don't know whether to be disappointed or relieved." When Ardan didn't look pleased, Barbicane reassured him, "Buck up, my friend. I don't know what I've have done without you, these last few days. I'm all obliged."

Ardan strived tried to smile in thanks.

The reality of their speed struck home when not long after, just before one o'clock, they were slowing and descending for their approach to Bermuda Island, a thin green arc inviting in the warm azure sea.

"The naval station's on the south end, to your right, Tom," Grenadier reported. "Not that I'm so good with it from this height, remembering from the ground. If it's their old hospital, it's up on a hill, far side, beyond the slips."

From high overhead, Maker scouted the location with her instruments, watched by an admiring Barbicane (and even Ardan, whose stomach qualms could not completely allay his curiosity about her surveillance skills).

Grenadier spotted the huge floating dock and nodded his appreciation of it, but spoke only to identify the hospital building. He and Maker soon agreed on a secluded spot to land by a cliff among the trees to the west, within walking distance of the structure. It was just a matter of bringing *Kestrel* down into the water, sailing up by the cliff, where Maker would disembark with Barbicane and Ardan, leaving the Grenadier to drop the flyer back into the sea to await their return.

The fragrant air, about seventy Fahrenheit that time of day, came as an invigorating balm when *Kestrel*'s doors reared open. "We'll wave from the cliff when we're done," Maker said.

"This water's so clear, a keen eye will see *something*," Grenadier sighed. "Hope no fisherman sails by and tries to net me."

The mysterious patients dropped on the hospital that night had become both an issue of jurisdiction (stray Americans in a British facility) and cause for some celebrity, the name of "Barbicane" fast circulating among the rumors. Two men among those gathered at the place were there on the first account and personages of import: the American Consul, Charles Allen, and the commanding Admiral, Sir Edward Fanshawe. The latter's concerned wife Jane and artistic daughter Alice (proficient in watercolors of that and other islands) tagged along from their Admiralty House over in Pembroke Parish, in some deference to the second circumstance, as curious about the "V. Barbicane" in their midst as any there.

Even the sailors' spiritual needs were volunteered by a personable but insistent Negro minister, ready to evangelize on the Methodist denomination he was committed to spreading beyond the local black inhabitants, all trying to find their way in a world freed of the scourge of overt slavery, though far from devoid of the covert prejudice and greed that had so lately sustained it.

None of that gaggle interested Impey Barbicane when he strode into the hospital with Ardan and Maker in tow. He was not immediately recognized, but he at once spotted Walt Kinnard sitting by a mended Jack Trainer and crossed to them, who rose with anguished expressions Barbicane could not miss.

Barbicane sat down between them, "What's happened?"

"Torpedo hit," Trainer said. "Blew the engine sky high, Grady and Danielson were down below. Never saw 'em again. Magic machine flew us here, after destroying everything in sight." He shook his head, speechless.

"Victor caught shrapnel," Kinnard added. "The doctor's not saying much, to us."

"We'll see what he says to *me*." Barbicane left to find the physician in charge of Victor. Ardan and Maker followed.

The doctor was relieved (and somewhat surprised) to learn Barbicane himself was on their island, but did not inquire how he had arrived. Soon the Consul and the Fanshawes were coalescing around the renowned adventurer, though deference to good manners stayed them from intruding beyond sympathetic and prayerful looks. The doctor had a delicate line of his own to tread, and took Barbicane aside to vouchsafe, "We were all uncertain about what to do about our patient—called Victor by her friends. The man who brought her here warned us to caution, and we've held to that. Listed her only as V. Barbicane, at his suggestion. Was this some masquerade?"

"Victoria. She was always up for a good fight, you see, and wouldn't be kept from service on account of her sex. You've never met a better shot, or a greater spirit. I backed her *masquerade*, and would again." His voice could hardly be contained free from the deepest emotion, "So, how is my *Victor*?"

"I wish I could bring good news. She hangs—*he* hangs by a thread. We've stanched the loss of blood, but our surgery can do nothing for the organs hit. We've given some morphine by syringe for the pain. It's good you arrived when you did. *Victor* could be gone in a moment."

"Let me visit." Barbicane gestured that he wanted Ardan and Maker to continue with him. He needed these not quite strangers beside him.

One could not have hoped for a more tranquil and comfortable setting for a sickroom, the warmth of the island, a gentle breeze coming in from the sea, the crisp sheets and bedding, and a measure of antiseptic practice to put the facility up at the better end of what counted for competent medicine in the second half of the 19th Century.

Ardan and Maker stood back at the doorway while Barbicane pulled a chair beside Victor's bed, trying to be as quiet with that as he could, and took his audacious daughter's hand.

The father was so pleased when a flutter of recognition came across Victor's face. "Made a mess of things," she wheezed.

"Nicholl and his gang have been brought down. We *did* that."

"Wish I had been awake more for the flyer. Looked grand."

"It *is* that." Barbicane, who knew her every manner, could sense Victor slipping away, the hand growing colder, and in just an eyelid flicker she was gone.

Impey Barbicane bent low, sobbing quietly—and would not let go of his daughter's hand for the longest time. No one witness to his grief could be unmoved by it.

☙ ❧

When Thomasina Maker waved for *Kestrel* to come up to the cliff edge, she was alone. Barbicane and Ardan had remained behind at the hospital, to attend to all that needed to be, and arrange for eventual passage for them and Victor's men back to America and work out their course for the future. None were at all clear about what that might be.

Once in the air and flying north, but before rousing to full speed and altitude, Maker said to her companion, "I think it's time to expedite things." She relished the sound of that word, *expedite*. "*Nautilus* is slow, we'll be passing it soon. *Deimos* has flown away for repairs—leaving Aouda on their ship, minus her knife." She pointed off at the horizon ahead, "And there, the villainous Moran must be floating in his airship, just out of electric gun range I'd bet, waiting for his *Albatross* and the *Great Eastern* to show up, so he can play the king. What should *we* do? Climb on the high ground, Grenadier, assess the field and divine our play."

Dufoy didn't have to ponder long. "We pick up Captain Nemo, fly him north to add Aouda, and bring them both to *Aurora*, where they may do what they will with someone who deserves little mercy."

"Plain enough," agreed Maker. Soon she had communicated her plans to Passepartout, who relayed how Aouda had arranged set times for *Nautilus* to surface in order to send or receive messages. In due course their coordinates were conveyed and *Kestrel* sped to them, not quite two hundred miles ahead of the *Great Eastern*. Even adding the distance from Bermuda, *Kestrel* reached Nemo's submarine in a quarter hour.

The *Nautilus* presented a most striking sight from the air, a serrated shape unlike any plowing the seas, threatening and beautiful at once. When Maker dropped *Kestrel* down to circle the pilothouse, Nemo had not been advised how small the craft was, surprising him somewhat. But he had brought his submarine to a stop already and Maker landed beside the covered skiff. Nemo emerged from the hatchway behind the pilothouse carrying the electric rifle case Aouda had given him. His First Officer accompanied him around the dorsal fin to where Maker was opening the port door panel.

"I hope you appreciate how unaccustomed I am to leaving my ship," Nemo told Maker. "And my sister has warned me about the belt harnesses," gesturing across his chest.

Nemo jumped across to the rear seat with the gun case and set about buckling into the safety harness, as the panel whirred closed to seal.

The First Officer remained on deck to watch as the *Kestrel* rose and flew away, at a rate far eclipsing that of Aouda's splendid machine. He could never admit it to his Captain, but after seeing those vessels come and go, the iron plating under his feet now seemed most rudimentary.

Nemo had obviously discussed the *Kestrel*'s capabilities with Aouda, as he kept an eye on their aft quarter until the puff of cloud appeared. "We are flying faster than the speed of sound, now?" he turned to ask them.

"Yes, Captain. What do you *think* of that?" Maker called back.

"I would not have thought it possible to fly so smoothly at such speed. It reminds me how unexpected the science can be, thwarted by experience."

When they had climbed so high that the white cloud plume formed in their wake, Nemo smiled to see it, with the innocent pleasure of a child—another side of himself he was glad to know he had not completely buried.

CS SO

The *Henrietta*'s engineer came up to the wheelhouse that afternoon to apprise Phileas Fogg of a disquieting circumstance: due to their steaming along at full head, they were running low on coal.

"How long do we have before we're scraping empty?"

"At this rate, two days." The engineer gave an odd look at Passepartout, in seeming meditation in his chair, comb held like a sacred relic. "That would be three days shy of Liverpool, sir."

"All correct," Fogg conceded. "I will consider."

When the engineer left, he paid no mind to the tiny dark red dot to the south, descending from a thin tracery of cloud dissipating in the high sky. But Passepartout was well aware of *Kestrel*'s approach. He put down the comb and opened his eyes, "Maker is here. I'll awaken Aouda from her nap and greet our guests."

Those crew up on deck initially showed some alarm as Maker flew about looking for a good place to land, but were calmed when Passepartout and Aouda appeared and waved *Kestrel* to a spot between two of the cargo hold covers aft of their funnel. The *Henrietta*'s First Officer shook his head at this sight, the friends of Phileas Fogg apparently held no bounds for surprises.

As soon as the cowls were opened, Nemo bounded out to embrace his sister. "We could see the airship on their instruments. Lying in wait, they think." Then he quaked, "My heart almost burst when I saw the man they called *Stuart*, face to face again. He ran, Aouda, and hunting him down was an awful pleasure for me." He reached down to pull the electric rifle case from the seat, which he handed to her, "He died by this, so by the two of us, together."

"Poor Victor Barbicane died, down in Bermuda," Maker told them. "At least the father could be at the bedside. I took him and Ardan along from the *Eastern*."

Both Passepartout and Aouda were much moved by that sad news. Even though having met Victor only so fleetingly, they felt bonds of sympathy for that one. For Aouda, it further kindled her purpose.

"Phileas wants to come with us," Aouda said. "Mr. Grenadier, would you stay behind with Passepartout to hold the wheel while we complete our journey?"

"Honored," Dufoy replied.

Nemo turned to Passepartout, "Don't you want to see the man who's been plaguing you all this time?"

Passepartout smiled. "He became nothing to me the moment we saved *Columbiad*. But you two, you have a just call against him. And Phileas Fogg shall be there because of Aouda. That makes my fifth a crowd, and unnecessary."

"Keep your comb attuned to my bracelets, Passepartout," Aouda directed. The valet nodded.

Relieved by Passepartout and Dufoy, Phileas Fogg joined the trio beside *Kestrel*. Maker had laid out a signaling lamp to have handy on their excursion, while Aouda decided to bring the electric gun with them, and had opened its case to check on the charge. She smiled at her brother when she found its gauge reading full, and Srikar nodded in response.

Fogg turned to the First Officer, "You and your men have seen *nothing* unusual this voyage—especially *this*," and slapped the *Kestrel*'s cowl.

"That's a pile of seaweed, isn't it?" the man winked, "Thrown up by the storm."

It took *Kestrel* only a few minutes to reach the *Aurora* hovering on the horizon. None of those aboard had seen that craft before, or the *Deimos*, and Commander Tremaine took some time to realize the nearing shape was something other than an unusually dark seabird.

Those aboard each craft had ample chance to spy the other from almost arm's length as Maker circled *Aurora* several times anticlockwise, to see what they could of the airship and its inhabitants. Maker minded staying wide of the four side propellers and the aft rudder ones, but showed her piloting proficiency by hovering *Kestrel* nose toward the gondola windows like an iron hummingbird, even as the *Aurora* continued to fly forward at a steamer's speed, and the shadows grew longer from the approaching dusk.

Since Maker was not wearing her altitude gear, it was impossible to miss the color of her skin, or the hues in the woman beside her, and the surly male visage behind that one. Only Phileas Fogg carried the familiar look of a European. And turnabout: *Kestrel* darted in near enough to the gondola windows to see the uniformed men within, along with the older fellow in gentleman's attire, all gaping at the noisy apparition—and several (including the older man) pointing in Maker's direction with looks comingling disdain and astonishment.

"If the white-haired gent ain't your Moran," Maker observed, "they've got the oddest crew."

"Let's ask," Aouda said, and took up the lamp beside Maker to signal in Morse at the uniforms on the other side of the glass: **HELLO MORAN. YOU WANTED FOGG AND NEMO MY BROTHER. HERE WE ARE.**

Tremaine was on the receiving end of this, and he evidently relayed its contents to Sir Augustus beside him, while bringing out a signal lamp of his own to respond as directed. The Ambassador's acid expression at this point suggested a message correctly received and understood.

"What do I reply?" Tremaine asked. But Moran was momentarily at a loss for words.

Aouda was not so reticent, continuing: **ALBATROSS NOT COMING, NOR YOUR NAVY, ALL DESTROYED. GREAT EASTERN SAILING HOME WITHOUT YOU.**

Upon hearing Tremaine's précis, Sir Augustus yelled, "Liar!" That's impossible."

"Do you want me to signal that?" the Commander asked.

"Yes!" Sir Augustus ordered.

Seeing Tremaine's Morse of Moran's arrogant delusion, Maker shook her head.

"Any of you know how Stuart's name is spelt? Like the royal clan?" Nemo asked from the rear seat. Aouda supplied that, from her remembrance of Robur's reportage of the company card, and Nemo took the lamp to send a message of his own: **STUART DEAD AT MY HAND.**

Hot on Tremaine's translation, Sir Augustus reared back, blanching and biting his lip. Feeling suddenly frail, he looked up at the ceiling and thought again of all that gaseous hydrogen above.

"Your past has caught up with us, I see," Tremaine told Sir Augustus, quite unsympathetically.

From the hovering *Kestrel*, Fogg nudged Nemo, "Suggest they deliver Moran to the *Henrietta*, then leave in peace."

Still holding the lamp, Nemo obliged Fogg's request.

"Deliver *me*, like a parcel?" Sir Augustus fumed, then turned to Tremaine, "Would you like to drop me out a door, then fly back to

Ireland? Am I alone here, or still among loyal friends?"

What a choice Tremaine now faced, and so wished to avoid. He waved at the machine floating so reliably out the window, and played the best and most obvious card available to him. "How do we evade *that*? It isn't the flyer you were thinking of, is it? Not the description I've heard. So we have another one. How fast does it go? What weapons does it have? What powers are behind it? If even a bit of what we've just been told is true—and where *is* Blake, if not?—then your plans are dross. Tell me, how long are they going to wait for us to make up our minds?"

Sir Augustus rubbed his cheek and thought. "All right. We abandon the field. Bring us up to speed and head away from *Henrietta*. See if they'll accept that. Throw the dice."

It took only a second from the moment when *Aurora*'s rotors sped up for Maker to reflexively pull *Kestrel* backward and down to draw clear of the blades threatening their right—done more by sight than sound, on account of their louder engines masking most of the acoustic increase.

"So much for diplomacy," Fogg said as the gondola and its supporting red envelope plowed away leftward overhead.

"Do they suppose to outrun us?" Nemo wondered incredulously.

Maker turned *Kestrel* around and eased the thrust forward to keep pace with the airship, its tail looming around fifty feet ahead and somewhat above their track.

Aouda looked back to her brother, "They're buoyant, even striking their engines won't bring them down to *Henrietta*'s deck, unless they want to."

"Hit the envelope, they come down—in flames," Maker said. "Terrible, and beautiful—like the Chicago Fire. Only they're hundreds of feet in the air. That'll be a crash like the *Albatross*. I don't see lifeboats on this one."

"*Henrietta*'s close to pick up survivors," reminded Phileas Fogg.

"If, if, if," Maker called. She glanced at Aouda and Nemo, "Moran's not alone on that balloon. You weigh the lives. Decide what we do."

Aouda reached back to clasp her brother's hand, eye to eye.

"Here. Now," Srikar's voice quavered with fierce emotion. Aouda understood, and agreed.

She turned to Maker, "If we can raise the glass in flight, it will only take one bolt to detonate the envelope. The wind shouldn't be too bad at this speed."

"If that's what you want, we won't need your gun," Maker said. "Or open a window."

Without a word, Maker dashed the *Kestrel* ahead to parallel the main gondola windows again, which those aboard *Aurora* could plainly see. But instead of pulling toward the gondola, *Kestrel* swung around counterclockwise, bringing her battery of aft rocket nozzles to face them. Then the flyer lifted up, out of their view.

Captain Nemo, Aouda and Phileas Fogg turned around to watch the great red surface of the envelope become a panorama, right and left. When the *Kestrel* was even with the central axis of the balloon, Maker had only to fire its engines to shoot away from the *Aurora*'s side. The searing gas ripped through the envelope covering behind them, breaching the hydrogen bags within, and setting them ablaze.

Maker brought the *Kestrel* around and began to settle toward the water as the *Aurora*'s lift disappeared in an inferno darkened by the burning cover fabric. As the gas in the middle over the gondola was consumed first, the airship began to buckle even as it plunged toward the sea, the propellers still turning. The rear rotors were now pointing upward at an angle, further unbalancing the descent. Then some internal fire caused several explosions at the rear of the gondola, throwing debris in all directions, and changing the balance of the disintegrating *Aurora* yet again.

In the short time it took for *Aurora* to reach the Atlantic, it had become a tangle of burning girders and compartments, smoldering fabric raining down, the propeller nacelles slamming into the waves at varied angles, to break or explode in their turn. And something else: unlike the *Albatross*, *Aurora*'s gondola was never intended to be a *boat*. It began taking water immediately.

Two crewman were scrambling around the wreckage, another man and Sir Augustus Moran were paddling in the water, as Maker brought *Kestrel* low to survey the disaster. Commander Tremaine bobbed face down beside a smoking propeller nacelle, one of three in the water that afternoon, all severely burned. The swimming crewman went to the Commander's, turned the body over, but there was no sign of life. The young man who knew all the bolts and fittings of *Aurora* so well, was another of the three fatalities. A few scorched chess pieces floated in the water too.

"*Henrietta*'s on her way," Aouda reported as *Kestrel* glided toward the water.

Ambassador Moran had somehow managed to retrieve his suitcase and was clutching it as a floating assist, though the burns on the luggage and his body did not bode well for either's survival. Only he knew of the £3000 and $4000 in waterlogged bills inside, intended to lease the ethics of Captain Speedy. It would do him no good now.

Kestrel settled into the water, putting Moran on their right and the other survivors behind or to their left. Maker extended the winglets, adding surface for those swimming to take hold of. After judging the degree of the swell, she reckoned they'd be swamped by opening the panels, so employed an electric enunciator to announce, "Climb aboard by the fins, men, up onto the afterdeck. We'll fly you to the *Henrietta*."

Landing as they had, Aouda and Srikar were on the side facing Moran. The Ambassador was either too weak to move from his baggage float, or had no desire to be rescued in such manner. Nemo and his sister watched him with grim resolve from behind *Kestrel*'s dome.

Fogg and Maker watched as the three other survivors clambered onto the winglets, and then use them as a platform to work up onto the back cowl by the fins. None of them seemed disposed to help Sir Augustus either.

Rearing up to get a look at this Sir Augustus Moran, Maker's black face rising beside Aouda's in Moran's line of sight was just one more affront to his blurring vision.

Maker forgot she still had the enunciator turned on. "So that's the thief," her voice rang outside, "Thought you could shackle ideas, and wear them like a patch."

Moran's eyes closed. His hands slipped from the charred case. He was dead.

Maker switched off the enunciator. "No, you can't."

37. IN WHICH IT IS SHOWN THAT PHILEAS FOGG GAINED NOTHING BY HIS TOUR AROUND THE WORLD, UNLESS IT WERE HAPPINESS

Thomasina Maker flew *Kestrel* very slow and carefully toward the approaching *Henrietta*, staying low over the water on consideration of the three rescued *Aurora* crewmen hanging onto her fins for dearest life. Down in his cabin, a brooding Mr. Fix could have briefly seen Maker's flyer slip past the porthole before rising up to land on deck, its odd whining noise heralding its passage plainly enough. But he was too preoccupied with his own queasy stomach, aggravated by his inability to reconcile his own unease over accepting Fogg's benefit so many times even while holding the warrant for Fogg's arrest. He would give neither up.

While the three damp *Aurora* airman dried out, Maker and the others gathered on the bridge to decide what to do with them. Fogg relieved Grenadier at the wheel, thanking him for his help.

It was the common judgment of Maker, Fogg, Aouda and Nemo that the three survivors seemed more confused than fearful or angry, and it was soon discovered they worked at a secluded factory in Ireland where Tremaine had built the airship. They were as anxious to get back to what passed for home as any aboard the *Great Eastern*, and Maker thought returning them to their workplace would be a suitable move—not just as an act of compassion, but as the simplest way of finding out where it was.

"They'll likely clear it out once its known they've been compromised," Passepartout said.

"But not the trail of receipts, deeds of ownership, provisions shipped," Maker said. "Barton Swift will be a bloodhound there, as he was with the *Great Eastern*." She leaned back in her chair, "I still have to take Nemo back to *Nautilus*, too—who wants first ticket?"

"I could remain here with Aouda for a while longer. I imagine it won't be a long trip for you, in any case, to Ireland and back."

"An hour on the flying part," Maker admitted. "Probably longer, unless they're crackers on giving directions in the dark while in the air. Grenadier will come along, to keep us company."

Before Maker and Grenadier could leave on that task, Aouda offered a very heartfelt parting, "I thank you for all you have done, for me and my brother. It's help lift a great burden from us. And I hope we meet again someday, under brighter skies."

Nemo did not speak, but all knew he shared his sister's sentiment.

After they'd gone, Nemo told them, "*Nautilus* would be near tomorrow evening, to accompany this ship as far as I dare into British waters. But the torpedo concussions left more damage than we thought at first. We're stopped for repairs. That could take forty-eight hours, or more. I'm sorry to shirk my duty, sister."

"The villains and their toys have been smashed one by one. We should have clear sailing now, Captain," Passepartout said. "You may contrive your repairs with a calmer conscience."

"Were as close as our telegraphy now, Srikar. And for the first time in all these years, my *Deimos* can mean just a name for a ship of travel, not a mission." Aouda rested against Fogg's right shoulder, pressing close, but not so hard as to distract his steering.

Fogg smiled. "When I first started looking for you, Captain, some years ago, it was more as an intellectual exercise. Wondering why certain paths weren't taken, or if new ones could be hewn. I never imagined our lives could be twined together like this. And I'm the better for it."

~ ~

It was a tight squeeze, five aboard *Kestrel*. The Grenadier sat beside Maker, and the three *Aurora* crewmen filled out the back seat. Because there were only two safety harnesses available, the smallest of them was placed between, and those on either side advised to link arms with him and hold fast. They soon discovered why, as it took all their might to keep him from sliding around as the *Kestrel* roared up into the night sky—especially as Maker made a point of adjusting their course periodically, so the craft would drop slightly, sending the hapless center body toward the ceiling panel.

Ardan's disquiet at his voyage was trebled in them, and in such manner their attentions were kept focused on the short dash to the Irish coast with scarcely a thought given to resisting their rescuers on the way. Occasionally some would close their eyes, or mutter prayers of some sort. None lost their bowels or vomited, which could be counted in their favor.

The airship base lay by the sea. There was a large barn obviously for the lost *Aurora*, and several buildings for machinery and construction, but not as imposing as either Maker or the Grenadier were expecting. After a quick pass over the place, true to their word, Maker landed the men safely some short distance from its fencing.

"Stay out of trouble," Grenadier advised them (even while largely doubtful it would take), and the men broke into a run for their camp even before *Kestrel* lifted away.

Staying out of trouble was, in fact, the desire of all those aboard *Henrietta* when the *Kestrel* settled down on the deck again forty-five minutes later. The stress and violence and worry of the last few days put the lot of them on a track yearning for sheer domestic tranquility, whether it be settling down to a good hot cup of tea by a fire, or curled under the covers of a warm bed without care of when they got up.

Captain Nemo was anxious to supervise the successful repairs aboard his precious submarine, and Maker hoped her role in the destruction of *Albatross* and *Aurora* would not come to haunt her own dreams. But that was not the theme of her final parting with Passepartout down beside *Kestrel*.

"Next time we meet, Jean, we're going to have to have a little talk about *Time*," she whispered, "and what Phileas Fogg does with his, *twice*." A quick kiss on his cheek and she was off to her pilot's seat, and soon the *Kestrel* was gone.

Passepartout speculated how Maker and Nemo must have been sharing their experiences. Cat out of the bag there. Not unexpected—inevitable, even, knowing Maker as he did. He couldn't help adoring her all the more for that.

CR SO

The wind that had been to their backs all the way from New York began to stall on the 17th of December, and threatened headwind. On the First Officer's advice the sails were furled. That slowed *Henrietta*'s pace, even as the depleting fuel threatened to stop them altogether.

"Do you think Nemo will give us a tow?" Passepartout asked Fogg, still on the wheel that morning. "Should *Nautilus* appear, of course."

"That would be a contrivance. And a dangerous one, for Nemo, hauling us into Liverpool harbor on his tail. Can you imagine the reaction of any British naval patrols? No, sir. We must work something else out."

"*Kestrel*?"

Fogg shook his head. "We've stretched her aide enough, already. No, we have to reach our destination in this ship, and be known to do so."

The slower rate helped Mr. Fix settle his tummy and he began to venture out from his cabin for longer times that Tuesday, finally going all the way up to the Bridge in the evening to tell Fogg how much he'd enjoy another hand or two at whist. Only it was Aouda at the helm just then.

"This is not a self-steering ship, Mr. Fix. So I think our card playing days are done this trip."

Mr. Fix was roundly disappointed, and left to take a constitutional around their more slowly rolling deck.

The following morning, Wednesday the 18th of December, *Henrietta*'s engineer reminded Phileas Fogg of his coal prediction. They would be running out that afternoon.

"Do not let the fires go down," Fogg said. "Keep them up to the last. Let the valves be filled."

The engineer shook his head in bemusement, but would do as Fogg asked.

After the engineer left, Fogg turned to Passepartout. "Take the wheel a moment." Once Passepartout had the helm, Fogg stepped to the chart and began to calculate their position, glancing at his watch and the ship's timepiece. Then he stepped back to replace Passepartout. "Please release Captain Speedy. I have a proposition for him."

Passepartout's eyes widened. "He'll be a madman!"

"Very possibly." But Fogg seemed utterly calm and serious.

Passepartout unlocked the Captain's cabin and let the door swing wide. "Mr. Fogg would like to see you."

Speedy fulfilled his name by racing out of the cabin and up to the Bridge, demanding of Fogg, "Where are we? Where are we?"

"Seven hundred and seven miles from Liverpool."

Captain Speedy now knew Fogg had been serious in his intention to divert to that destination, come what may. "Pirates!" he cried, an altogether accurate description, legally speaking.

Passepartout stood at the ready should Speedy turn physically belligerent, but was also puzzled by what Fogg was about, as well as amazed by his absolute imperturbability.

"I have sent for you, sir—"

"Pickaroon!" Speedy grimaced.

"—*sir*, to ask you to sell me your vessel."

Speedy reared back as if struck by a blow, "Sell? No! By all the devils, no!"

"But I shall be obliged to burn her," Fogg said, calm as you please.

"Burn the *Henrietta*?"

"Yes; at least the upper part of her. The coal has given out."

"Burn my vessel? A vessel worth fifty thousand dollars!"

That was as inflated a value for the ship (built twenty years before) as Speedy had given in his life. But Fogg was in no mood to haggle. "Sell her then for *sixty* thousand. I have the cash."

"Passepartout, the wheel," and while the valet took that post, Fogg retrieved from the carpetbag almost all of what remained of the pound notes, wincing ever so slightly at the depleted reserve, beside a slim remnant of American dollars left over from his San Francisco currency exchange.

Waving £12,000 in front of the Captain, Phileas Fogg showed himself no less skilled than any snake charmer staring down a surly cobra.

"The thousands in bribe you were expecting from the 'big ship' aren't coming, Captain. But this is *real* money, here and now."

Captain Speedy's grievances of naval mutiny and illegal incarceration vanished before that enticing fan of tangible Imperial currency.

"And I shall still have the iron hull?" Speedy was much calmer now.

"The iron hull and the engine," Fogg promised. "It is agreed?"

"Agreed." Speedy snatched the wad from Fogg's hand, and began to count it.

The First Officer was called to the Bridge and apprised of Fogg's resolution of the Speedy matter.

"We'll start with the interior seats, bunks, and frames. Pull them out and burn them." Fogg turned to Passepartout, "Do let Aouda know what is pending, if the hammering doesn't wake her first."

And so it was, while still some seven hundred miles from the British Isles, the *Henrietta* began to lose weight to keep her engines burning bright. The furnishings were consigned to the boiler first, but pry bars and saws were working on the poop and the cabin paneling generally before the day was out. Aouda quite enjoyed helping to tear the ship asunder, venting pent up energy brought on these last few days, and even Captain Speedy got into the spirit of the thing, helping to ferry wood chunks down to the engine room. The engineer was shocked to see Andrew Speedy in such a novel mode. Mr. Fix thought everyone had gone mad.

Hearing how set Fogg was on reaching London in time to win his wager, and being $69,000 the richer on account of his and Mrs. Hammond's remunerative exuberance, Speedy begrudged some admiration for the Englishman's hard effort. Swinging by what was once his own cabin to carry off the door that somehow had been locked by the French valet, he tendered what for him was a great compliment: "Captain Fogg, you've got something of the Yankee about you."

The work continued from that moment on, in shifts and spurts, turning the *Henrietta* into a reverse beehive, compartments disappearing by the hour. When Fogg needed a rest from the wheel, a blanket and pillow were laid out on the Bridge deck, and Aouda whispered, "*Deimos* has reached Diadem, more repairs to do than Robur thought at first. Just like Srikar and the *Nautilus*. How like some men, to wait to the last minute to admit such things."

Fogg chuckled at her jibe, knowing it was directed as much at himself as at Robur or Nemo. And not without a little merit.

On Thursday, December 19th, the masts, rafts and spars were being burned. As the wind was no longer favorable, losing that rigging was not so critical—though it struck Mr. Fix as the ultimate folly of Mr. Fogg's obsession. He was about to tell Aouda so, when he noticed over her shoulder a strange dark shape cutting through the waves some distance to the south of them, and moving as swiftly as they. He stepped over to the railing and peered out at the sea, trying to identify it.

"Something wrong, Mr. Fix?" It was Aouda, carrying a plank destined for the furnace.

"What do you make of that?" Fix pointed out at what Aouda knew to be the *Nautilus*, repairs concluded and now in place as her brother had vowed, to escort them.

"That is a sea serpent, Mr. Fix."

"You think so?" Fix stared out at the spot again. "So you see it, too?"

"Oh, yes. You must set down your observations on the monster. Letter to *The Times* later." And Aouda resumed her way to the engines below, plank in hand.

The *Henrietta*'s railings, fittings, and much of the decking were laid siege to the next day, Friday the 20th of December. By this time the amount of Captain Fogg's purchase had become widely circulated, and the First Officer led a delegation to Andrew Speedy to "persuade" the man to part with a third of that, to share among the crew. Even $40,000 made a fine profit on the old ship, and the crew were of one mind that they were owed their fair share of the remainder. Speedy would need their testimony to corroborate any tale of mutiny—which could so easily be turned on its head, were the crew to swear how he had gone all *non compos mentis* and ordered the ship dismantled. Speedy saw reason and shared his spoils on their terms.

Around eight that evening, the Irish coast and Fastnet Light came into view, forcing Captain Nemo to pull away from the *Henrietta*. Mr. Fix turned over in his mind whether he should recount anything of this serpent of the sea. In the end he decided against it, believing himself insufficiently the descriptive writer for a convincing narrative.

Two hours later the increasingly skeletal ship was passing Queenstown, and as soon as Fogg learned that, he directed they should put into port. Speedy objected that they could only do that on the turn of the tide, which wouldn't take place until one the next morning. Fogg still ordered them to a stop.

"What would you need in Queenstown," Speedy wondered, "since your haste was to get to *Liverpool*."

"The mail express to Dublin," Fogg replied. "I had forgot about it. Their fast packet would get us to Liverpool by noon, well ahead of us trying to steam on our own, even waiting until one."

So, on the turn of the tide, *Henrietta* (or what was left of it) steamed into Queenstown Harbor (or Cobh, as the place was known to its Gaelic constituency). It was now Saturday, the 21st of December, and Phileas Fogg must make his way to the Reform Club by 8:45 that evening—or forfeit the wager to Misters Stuart *et al.*

Those at the docks at that hour did not know what to make of the gutted Flying Dutchman steaming to the quays. Fogg and party had to balance carefully on what was left of the footing, many of *Henrietta*'s crew visible through the gaps in the decks below, like so many mice peeking through the holes of a motorized iron cheese block. It was not something one saw every day.

True to his plan, Fogg left *Henrietta*'s husk to Speedy and the crew, and the travelers made at once for the railway station to catch the next train to Dublin. The size of the Cobh station testified to the volume of mail traffic the port generated. Built right by the harbor, the building was charming in an angular way, its entrance marked by a row of five triangular awnings. The weather was helping, too, a pleasant forty degrees.

As Detective Fix followed Fogg, Aouda and Passepartout inside, to arrange passage, he rubbed his coat pocket where the warrant lay. Yet he did not pull it out, even though now standing on British soil at last. Was there some strange impediment to his intent, an unrecognized feeling that however English the place names might be presently, this town signed as "Queenstown" was still *Cobh* in its heart, the brogue being heard too "foreign" for his ear, and so not quite "England" after all?

Such preoccupations kept Mr. Fix from noticing something at the ticket purchase that might have attracted his detective's eye otherwise: how carefully the clerk marked down the name of Phileas Fogg, making sure to repeat the name to confirm its accurate recording. And while they waited for the next train's departure, how the factotum penned a carefully worded telegraph to be dispatched at once to an interested desk specified at the Foreign Office in Whitehall.

On the train north, once Mr. Fix had nodded off, Aouda whispered to Phileas Fogg, "Did you jump to land here solely to bypass to the Dublin-Liverpool ferry? Or are you scheming a detour out to see that airship station up on the coast?"

Fogg sniggered softly, "No time for that, though it would likely be of interest. It's been a tiring trip, and now my object is just to be at the Reform Club at the appropriate time. I think we are all due a rest."

Knowing the sweat they all gave dismantling the *Henrietta*, Passepartout could not argue with that.

The mail express arrived in Dublin at dawn. It had been five years since the failed Fenian rebellion there, and proper British administration was once more in place. Or at least going by appearances, where who knew what barely quenched embers of resentment yet seethed beneath perfunctory deference, awaiting some new spark of outrage to ignite disobedience and barricades in the streets.

Fogg's party followed the mail bags to the Liverpool ferry.

The rising sun warmed the waves as the boat chugged east, but not so much their spirits. Passepartout thought back to that first ferry ride he and Fogg undertook over two months before, across the English Channel in the dark, with the dangerous Mrs. Hammond on their tail. It seemed like an aeon ago.

He looked over at Phileas Fogg and Aouda, leaning on one another, shoulder to shoulder, eyes often closing for a bit. Both seemed exhausted—but as a *couple*, far from a pair of strangers thrown together by amazing circumstance.

And then there was Mr. Fix, and that unserved warrant. Had he finally decided to let it go? Passepartout admitted his own often limited grasp of the nuances of human behavior gave him no easy answer there.

The trip across the Irish Sea proved routine, and they were passing George's Dock on the Mersey estuary about half past eleven, slowing toward the ferry slip. All entirely to Phileas Fogg's satisfaction.

As with Ireland, a history crouched behind the commercial hubbub arrayed before them, unexposed in the beams and brick of the docks and warehouses. Because of their great dependence on the American cotton trade, Liverpool had been the most vociferous of any in Britain in support of the Confederacy. Now that peace prevailed, their merchants and investors had to encourage a renewal of affection for the triumphant Union. Would that process be faster or slower, and more or less bumpy, than the disposition of municipal signage in Érie across the sea?

It was twenty minutes before twelve when Phileas Fogg and party stepped off the ferry. Where Queenstown and Dublin had failed to stimulate Mr. Fix's warrant pocket, the pavement of Liverpool had that instant effect. Placing his hand on Fogg's shoulder, he arrested him in the Queen's name.

In short order the Around the World man found that world to consist of a locked holding room at the nearby Customs House, a grand classical edifice of dark stone pediments and tall central dome, where Phileas Fogg would be kept until he could be taken on to London the next day.

Passepartout and Aouda were disconsolate, frustrated, angry—and remained in a nearby waiting hall to consider whether comb or electric gun should be called to action to effect Fogg's release.

And yet, Mr. Fogg himself seemed reconciled to his imprisonment. It was a legal warrant, after all—and had he not taken full advantage of the law himself in posting bail back in Calcutta, or brazenly flaunt its provisions in suborning mutiny from the crew of the *Henrietta*?

It was at this point in his narrative of Mr. Fogg's adventures that Mr. *V.* dropped the first of two notable anomalies concerning *timepieces*.

When the Custom House clock struck one, Mr. *V.* reported that Fogg checked his watch, and found his own running two hours ahead. No explanation was offered for how someone so meticulous as Phileas Fogg could have so inexplicably lost track of the time, and it may be wondered whether this was another subtle clue interpolated deliberately to excite the reader's puzzlement or suspicion that something was *amiss*—even if Mr. *V.* himself lacked full familiarity with the facts to venture anything beyond his own disquiet. Or, perhaps still more likely, was not at liberty to be more forthcoming on what he did know, or suspect—or fear.

Was it purely coincidental then that Mr. Fogg happened to have a visitor at just about that time? One left unrecorded on any official log, even if occasionally rumored among those who made it their avocation to keep note of such clandestine comings and goings.

Phileas Fogg first heard doors being opened, then the one to his own chamber, to permit entry of a well-dressed gentleman in his middling twenties, somewhat portly and disinclined to strenuous effort, beyond arriving unseen by either Passepartout or Aouda outside. Fogg was about to rise and offer him the only chair, but the man remained standing. He fastidiously removed his gloves to hold them in his left hand, but did not remove his fine silk hat.

"I would offer you a 'good afternoon,' but given the inconvenience of your incarceration, I'll spare you that. My name is Holmes. I am here, entirely unofficially, to convey the concern of several diplomatic parties who have come to take a peculiar interest in your plight. One is the French government, ostensibly on behalf of your servant—Passepartout, isn't it?"

Fogg nodded.

"Their consuls and our own in Tokyo have been much tasked cleaning up after you. Then there are your man's escapades in India, where complaint and bail records had to be carefully misplaced on your behalf, for which you should be exceedingly grateful. Likewise for police reports and hospital records in San Francisco, keeping both the French and British consuls there burning the midnight oil. And your latest: a rumored conspiracy to mutiny on the high sea—beyond our jurisdiction, fortunately. These are but clerical adjustments in the view of certain nervous members of Her Majesty's Foreign Office, who have followed with mounting alarm the renegade initiatives of one of our recent Ambassadors. As the whereabouts of this diplomat have turned elusive, your own continued discretion and silence on this matter would be most appreciated by them, now *and in future*."

Mycroft Holmes looked most grave. "That executes my brief, but my own curiosity has compelled me to take note on my own of the many striking particulars swirling around your frenzied circumnavigation, aspects of which exceed, I suspect, even the most unfettered imagination at the Foreign Office, or the *Deuxième Bureau*."

Fogg's brow went up at that.

"While international travel is not without its peril, Mr. Fogg, the disproportionate litter of mishap attending you and your servant would pique, I think, even Mr. Galton's actuaries. I have my own suspicions regarding the part your servant may have played in the misadventures of three of SS *Carnatic*'s passengers *en route* to Yokohama—more men with shadowed links to particular associates of that certain Ambassador, hardly a coincidence. And there are those four dead men found along the Union Pacific Railroad right of way, casualties of that suspiciously pretended 'Indian' attack involving your servant and the Ambassador's *son*, who unaccountably decided a journey on the same train with *you* through frigid Nebraska was just the holiday respite he needed from his post in balmy India. I acknowledge, the bridge collapse was not your man's fault—accidents *do* happen. But I need not remind you that even the New York police are not such dullards to overlook *all* the attendant circumstances of the carnage at the St. Nicholas Hotel—a frightening application of scientific violence some at our War Office have an envious eye cocked on too."

Holmes sighed, "I dread, sir, to envisage what might happen, were you to remain in a hostelry more than *one night*. But, so long as you elect to remain reticent about all this, and my own Government sanguine in turn, who am I to speak otherwise." A thin smile leaked. "If that is all acceptable to you?"

Phileas Fogg nodded once more, "It seems so."

"For all our sakes, then, Mr. Fogg, I pray our paths never meet again. Good day to you, I have a return train to catch."

As abruptly as he had arrived, the terse fledgling diplomat Mr. Holmes was gone, leaving Phileas Fogg in solitude once more. That lasted for almost an hour and a half, when at 2:33 PM the door rattles were heard again, this time joined by Passepartout's animated voice, followed by something less joyous from Mr. Fix.

Passepartout, Aouda and Fix were vying to bolt through into the holding room as the door opened.

"Sir, sir—forgive me," a winded and disheveled Fix struggled to confess, "unfortunate resemblance—robber arrested three days ago—you—are free!"

Fogg stood up, looked the detective in the face, and without a word knocked Fix to the floor—his punch delivered "with the precision of a machine," as Mr. *V.* described.

"Well hit!" Passepartout said, thinking of his own fight with Fix on the *General Grant* on November 22nd, and how the expenditure of physical energy improved his own spirits. "*Parbleu*! That's what you might call a good application of English fists."

"The robber, James Strand, was caught in Edinburgh on the Seventeenth, while we were at sea," Aouda said with a withering expression that kept Fix on the floor. It was likely that the detective would be in a fix of his own on account of this obsessive mistake.

Fogg lost no time departing the Customs House, heading at once for the *London & Northwestern Railway* terminal most plainly visible up Lime Street. The original entrance was one of England's oldest railway façades, but its classical splendor had been greatly expanded in 1867 by the addition of a massive iron arch track arcade, among the largest in the world.

Fogg inquired about the next express to London, but found the last had steamed out thirty-five minutes before. He then asked for a special train. There were locomotives and cars free, and Fogg paid out fees and inducements to facilitate the impromptu scheduling. Both Passepartout and Aouda were surprised Fogg had the money for this left in the carpetbag.

"We're as low now as the *Henrietta*'s coal bunkers," Fogg admitted as they set off. It was just three o'clock, less than six hours from the wager default and as many hours away from London should they average a commendable thirty miles an hour.

The engineer pressed ahead as quickly as they could, but there were inevitable short delays as the special train threaded through the network of lines between Liverpool and London. It was only an hour to sunset, and by the last light of dusk at six Fogg and Aouda had come to be holding hands, smiling and sighing at one another repeatedly. There was little in the way of necessary conversation, and Passepartout took vicarious pleasure seeing them settle so closely in the increasing dark.

ଓଃ ଥିଓ

When the latest scheduled express from Liverpool arrived at Euston Station at 7:23 that evening, Mycroft Holmes disembarked and made for the Great Hall at a waddle commensurate to his nature. As he appeared in the echoing space, a lanky young laborer stretching in exercise on the stairs beside the giant marble statue of railway pioneer George Stephenson, descended past the elegant Mr. Holmes to plop down on one of the benches there.

Mycroft slowed to a stop and sat beside him. Their gazes did not meet. "You're becoming very proficient with disguise, brother. That you accost me here so theatrically means news of Fogg's arrival in Queenstown must have reached our delinquent engineer, and his reaction ... *untoward*?"

The young man smiled. "The bodyguards. Whatever security Mr. Stuart thought to hire after learning of New York City, dissipated in a rage on receipt of the Queenstown rumor. But more a revelation, his Reform Club and wager associate Samuel Fallentin visited him in like disposition, and left with several of those toughs to armor himself."

"Did he now?" Mycroft hardly moved a muscle nor turned his head, but his left index finger absently drumming on his pant leg signaled a heightened interest. "Stuart's honest panic appears to have tugged that loose end Whitehall wanted clarified—which bankers were putting pen to check to underwrite this fiasco."

"Perhaps only the one required," the younger brother proposed. "Fallentin never served in the military, least of all India, but weren't some of his millions cobbled from ventures with the East India Company? A common passion."

"Good memory. He's made and lost several fortunes on railroad ventures here and abroad, loves the inside trade. There may be a familial addiction to it, too. Decades ago his father was keen to cut a canal across Nicaragua with the American Vanderbilt, but failed to incite a revolution to countenance the scheme. Mr. Barbicane's strange science may have been just the latest irresistible honey pot." Holmes pursed his lips. "But if only *his* fortune lies behind it, failure here may entail his ruin. Money wasting has been a hallmark of this affair. We should be thankful to be spared that curse of great property and ambition."

The younger brother relaxed a bit. "Following them all has held some novelty for me, distinctly more interesting than academic studies. Gaining the confidence of Stuart's servants in their off hours, finding street habitués of pluck and guile sufficient to keep track of their movements outside my own observation—all these have an appeal equal to the most intricate of chess problems."

"I did not invite you into this merely to spur your own personal amusement. Whatever diversion you took from it, though, we are not unappreciative of your assistance."

Young Sherlock understood that "we" meant Whitehall, not Mycroft's rhetorically waxing royal.

"I should prefer to follow this temporary distraction until term resumes. It would be a pity to quit the pier just as the boat was about to dock. I pledge to keep you informed as needed."

Mycroft arched a brow, "At the Diogenes for a change?"

"A pure tedium—but, if necessary."

଼ଷ ଛ

As the "Phileas Fogg Special" was clearing Bedford, about eight o'clock, Fogg was considering how (not whether) to ask for Aouda's hand in marriage. When two chimes clinked on his watch, all three of them were startled to a degree.

"What has popped into *your* head, Phileas?" Aouda asked.

"Or *will* do so," amended Passepartout.

Fogg shrugged and checked the time, and the bezels, none of which surprised him. Passepartout's "?" lay close to *XI*, Aouda's "O" was at half past *IX*, and the inactive "B" occupied *VI*. Maker's dimmer "A" jostled with Nemo's brighter "N" beside *V*, suggesting *Nautilus* was sailing north for the Arctic passage.

"I'm not at all sure right now," Fogg smiled. "Though what I was thinking of works best now that Mr. Fix isn't here to observe any of it."

All were more mindful of the passage of time as they neared London. When they finally drew into Euston Station, it was 8:50 PM, and the second of Mr. *V.*'s temporal oddities arose, as that narrative reported how "all the clocks in London were striking ten minutes before nine." This was more than merely a peculiar, or implausible, thing to happen—but actually preposterous. No clock, public or private, would have been chiming on such a schedule, so was this not another deliberate idiosyncrasy?

With Phileas Fogg arriving seemingly too late to have won the bet, Mr. *V.* could then roll out his ingenious and famous resolution: that somehow Fogg had blundered accounting of their eastward progress, such that he thought himself a day later than the fact, leading to a dramatic denouement where the traveler only learned of his mistake the following evening, and almost too late to rectify it.

But once Mr. Fogg landed in San Francisco, having jumped that "lost" day in the Pacific, how could he have so failed to notice what *day of the week* it actually was anywhere along the way? True, he was spared the clue of Sabbath church bells failing to toll on what Fogg would have taken to be a Sunday (or hear their calling the faithful in the distance only the next "Monday" morning) because that weekend the Union Pacific was traversing a spiritually barren region of Nebraska. But in Fogg's enthusiasm for newspaper intelligence, could he have consistently failed to read *any* of the dated headings on the latest copies in the hotels or restaurants or railway stops?

Whatever day Phileas Fogg thought it was, he seemed in no hurry whatsoever to get home to Savile Row that night, stopping in the Great Hall of Euston Station to tip his hat (still bearing its small hole courtesy of Robur's electric rifle back in the forest of Bundelcund) in admiration of Stephenson's statue, acknowledging the critical role locomotives had played in moving them from one adventure to the next. Once outside, Fogg grabbed Passepartout's arm as he was about to dash for a cabby.

"It is a mile and a quarter from here to No. 7," Fogg declared. "Making that trip on *foot* this evening, without any cabman to remember our hiring of him, will suit our purpose to the T."

Fogg already knew Aouda's tireless walking stamina from their trek in San Francisco, and that was with her case that he now carried. Passepartout bore the carpetbag, itself lighter by nearly £20,000—no one doubted his ability to keep up.

Strolling between the great Doric columns of Euston Arch, that imposing *propyleum* marking the station forecourt, Fogg set a pace neither tiring nor dawdling, meandering south to the merchant row along Tottenham Court Road. There were fewer pedestrians out as their many shops were shuttered at that hour, but still many carriages rolled by.

Catching what glimpses they could of their occupants from the curb, Aouda mused, "One wonders where they're all going."

"That one?" Fogg said of the latest, "An aged roué, off to an assignation with an ingénue soprano from the Opera."

"He's dressed for it," Aouda agreed. "And as it's too late for the Overture, you might be right, that he wasn't going for the fa-la-la."

"Why a soprano?" Passepartout queried.

"Really, Passepartout, would you risk domestic scandal for a contralto?" Fogg joked.

And so it went, block on block of London pavement at night, as the Fogg trio occupied their wit conjuring amusing lies about the carriage occupants.

Turning right when they reached Oxford Street, Fogg continued west toward the imposing façades of Regent Street. As they crossed south at that intersection, Fogg's watch chimed thrice. Fogg put down Aouda's case beside a streetlamp and opened the timepiece. It was just past ten o'clock Greenwich, but this time he paid no attention to the wandering bezels.

Tucking the watch back in its pocket, Fogg turned to the lady at his side. "Aouda, would you do me the honor of marrying me?"

Aouda smiled matter-of-factly, "Yes."

"Passepartout, you are the witness," Fogg returned the pleasurable look, and they continued on.

It did not take too much longer to reach Savile Row. All the tailors were shut for the night, of course, and Passepartout found himself heaving a sigh of relief to see no Mrs. Hammond (or any of her like) lurking about.

The door of No. 7 was soon unlocked, and Fogg led them into the foyer, where a solitary gas lamp had been turned up to bathe a hall table. Passepartout took notice of that illumination, but Fogg seemed unconcerned, crossing to take up the single envelope placed in its middle.

"P. Fogg" it declared on its face, in a hand Phileas well recognized. Inside was one small slip of paper, which he read in silence as Aouda began to explore the other still blackened rooms:

> *A Wedding Present:*
>
> *The Reverend Samuel Wilson has been engaged for an 8 PM ceremony,*
>
> *Marylebone Parish Church*
> *Monday the 23rd*
>
> *Brother of the bride etc. have been informed & keen to attend; transportation arranged.*

Fogg smiled broadly, and dropped the missive into his coat pocket. "The side bedroom opposite mine should be suitable for the Princess, till the wedding," he told Passepartout, then called to Aouda, "I'm thinking Monday, if agreeable?"

Aouda turned from the drawing room entry, "Can it be done that soon? In India, our nuptials can become quite a production."

"Simple, and prompt, for me, ma'am," Fogg smiled.

Passepartout went upstairs to prepare Aouda's room, then up to his own on the top floor, which he was surprised for a moment to find dark, having to turn up the very gas lamp he'd left burning eighty days before. *Two* lamp keys were turned between the latest of Fogg's watch chimes, Passepartout realized with a grin. But twisted by whom?

There was something a bit disconcerting about that, not knowing whether it was by his own hand, or some other. Fogg's Time Machine allowed one to play at being one's own ghost.

As it happens (or, rather, *would* happen and already *had* happened), it was Passepartout himself who turned down the gas, during a brief stop Phileas Fogg arranged on the morning of the Fourth of October, meaning the gas had flamed unchecked a mere forty hours. On that future/past occasion, Passepartout wore quite a grin as he attended to that trifling domestic mission.

☙ ❧

Regarding the temporal sequence as Passepartout continued to experience it in London, Sunday, the 22nd of December, proved a quiet day at No. 7 Savile Row. Passepartout awoke earliest, playing the part of functional valet for the first time in his eighty days of employment. With no train or boat or flying machine to catch or intercept, he discovered Aouda and Fogg had slept in. Understandable, but certainly amazing concerning Phileas Fogg, who in that departure from his set routine showed how much his inner clockwork had been reset by their entwined experience.

When Fogg did rise, he instructed Passepartout to get Aouda breakfast, and a cup of tea and a chop for himself. Checking the pantry confirmed their lack of supplies, and Passepartout took some of what little cash remained in the carpetbag to fetch sufficient victuals.

Stepping out onto the front steps, Passepartout found the morning air quite bracing, despite the inevitable contamination of coal soot. His pleasure was buoyed by a survey of the street, where no one suspicious seemed about. He confirmed this with a quick comb of his hair.

Passepartout made his way up to Oxford Street, and then east toward the market district. Along the way he passed a newspaper placard heralding **FOGG LATEST! WAGER WON! EXCHANGE REELING!**

If only he knew how they did it—or would do it, or had done it. He would have to think about which tense to properly employ in the age of Time Travel.

Oxford Street merged onto the new Holborn Viaduct, which spanned the ancient vale there to bridge the way down to St. Paul's Cathedral. But Passepartout did not remain on that elevated route long, taking the stairs to Farringdon Road and thence south to the market. The once thriving Farringdon Market had fallen on hard times recently, eclipsed by the new Borough Market across the Thames by London Bridge, and the remaining butchers and grocers scraping by in the shadow of the splendid viaduct were most appreciative of his trade that Sunday.

☙ ❧

Breakfast and even luncheon accomplished, Phileas Fogg and Aouda stood facing one another, arm in arm, by the drawing room windows, enjoying the afternoon light. The mantle clock ticked softly.

"Aren't you going to go to the Reform Club today, to confirm you won the bet?" Aouda asked.

"I suppose I should. But I'm trusting in my chimes. Right now, I'm more content being here with you." Fogg paused. "You know, I would have proposed to you even had I lost the wager."

"I know. And I would have accepted, in any case. We do have my resources at Diadem to rely on, after all."

"Oh—you are a rich widow, aren't you? I hadn't appreciated that."

"Not troubled about how I got to *be* a widow?" Aouda was serious.

Fogg smiled. "I'm confident it won't be a habit."

CB ED

Phileas Fogg did not go to the Reform Club the following day, either. Monday, the 23rd of December, was his wedding day and that preoccupied his attention quite adequately.

The charming Neo-Classical Marylebone Church faced north onto Regents Park, about a mile northwest of Savile Row, and Fogg's carriage arrived in advance of the ceremony, about half past seven. The Reverend Wilson greeted Passepartout with ebullient familiarity, pumping his hand before nodding towards Fogg and Aouda, "Ah, and now at last to meet the bride and groom you told me of, to be joined by the rings you left."

Passepartout's eyebrows lifted, wondering what he had said about any of this and whether his unawareness of it would turn an embarrassment. But the minister's attention flashed away from such details to three strangers who entered: Srikar and Robur on either side of Thomasina Maker. Somehow all had managed to don conventional attire, though in Nemo's case the suit appeared of a cut somewhat removed from current fashion.

"Friends of the bride," Passepartout told Rev. Wilson as Aouda dashed to silently embrace her brother, then touched Robur's arm with like affection, before pressing Maker's right hand between her own two, "Thank you for coming, and bringing them."

"I should add Ferry Service to my sign," Maker joked, though not without a moistness in her eyes.

The three witnesses who had flown in from around the globe settled on the front pew in the otherwise empty church, the minister's voice resonating as the requirements of the ceremony were attended to. Passepartout proudly gave the bride away, rings were exchanged and vows affirmed.

Phileas Fogg and Aouda were married. No one had thought to bring rice or other grains to hurl in deference to fertility myths long forgotten in the ritual.

"Where did you leave *Kestrel*?" Passepartout asked Maker after, as they congregated to leave.

"Grenadier's minding it, submerged in a little boat pond in the park just north. Or *almost*—it's only four feet deep, so the dome sticks up a bit. The park isn't open at night, it seems, and he found shelter under a small suspension bridge across an inlet, where he'll sit tight for our return."

Aouda was about to commiserate over poor Dufoy, kept from the wedding of his great friend by his duty, but Fogg turned the mood by recalling of the boating lake, "It used to be deeper. Some ice broke five years ago and two hundred fell in, forty died—they filled in the depths to preclude such tragedy in future."

"I'm sorry to hear that," Maker said. She thought how ill-equipped Phileas Fogg might be to adapt his chatter to suit the social context, even on his own wedding day, unable not to toss in the bleak statistics of those pond fatalities, the moment it crossed his mind. As she could be like that, at times, Maker would not judge him too harshly for it.

"If only that were the worst of things, Miss Maker," Fogg muttered darkly, "for London and the world to endure."

With a shiver—and not on account of any cold that evening—Maker realized what a terrible burden such foreknowledge might be for Mr. Fogg. What ghastly things had he seen, or learned of by future History, using that Machine whose existence she had so skillfully inferred? Still she chided him, "You may know much of the shape of things to come, but you don't always have to tell us about it."

"Point taken," Fogg answered without offense.

The newlyweds, the valet, and their three wedding guests kept together for the walk across Marylebone Road, passing between the ends of the long residential blocks of York Terrace, to the edge of Regents Park proper via the short York Bridge that pointed toward the Inner Circle road within.

Captain Nemo addressed them, "Fifteen years ago, when all seemed lost, I could not have imagined a scene like this for me. With friends, beside a tranquil garden, and my sister wed in happiness. More than just a world was traversed in your eighty days, Mr. Fogg—*brother-in-law*," Nemo amended with a smile. "I thank you all for it."

Aouda stayed put, watching until Nemo, Robur and Maker disappeared into the dark garden. Still she did not move, holding up a finger to delay them going. She was waiting to hear the characteristic whine of the *Kestrel*'s engines, proof of their safe departure. Some five minutes later, Mr. and Mrs. Fogg and Passepartout heard that telltale sign, and caught a fleeting glimpse of the red flash of the craft's engines, marking its ascent above the trees ahead of them, only to shrink quickly to invisibility as *Kestrel* slipped higher into the soot smudged skies of London.

"*Now* we go," Aouda decided.

☙❧

Up in their Savile Row apartment on Tuesday, December 24th, Aouda and Phileas Fogg savored at considerable leisure their first nuptial morning.

"So this is Christmas Eve!" Aouda stretched under the bed covers. "Isn't it the English practice now to have a tree, weighed down with little glass bee-bobs? And candles, to burn the house down?"

"I confess it's been years since I've kept a Christmas. It's the sort of thing one does with children about—then it's quite sweet." Fogg shook off that thought with a witticism, "Though the candle fires are one way to find out who is too stupid or inattentive to be trusted with an open flame. Unfortunately, such people can take their neighbors with them." Fogg took up Aouda's hand, "If you *want* a thoroughly Teutonic Christmas, next year we will do one."

A mounting clatter of horse hoofs and dray wheels sounded on the pavement outside, followed by a ring of their bell. Although he knew Passepartout would be attending to it, Fogg got up and crossed to the window anyway to see what it was about. Or, rather, what he knew and expected it *ought* to be about: Auguste Dupin had arrived with Fogg's "Machine Parts."

Phileas Fogg donned a most satisfied smile. Without turning from the window, he called to Aouda, "Father Christmas will have to wait. We have a trip to take."

☙❧

As the hour approached on December 21st for Phileas Fogg's wager to be met or forfeit, great crowds had gathered along Pall Mall and neighboring streets, as excited as a carnival. Some of those were anxiously hoping for the latter outcome, as they had bet against the eccentric Englishman. A very few were like Lord Albermarle (who of course was not present on account of his aged infirmity): staking Fogg would succeed.

Rumors ricocheted among them—no news by correspondent or police report of Fogg's whereabouts since his release from the Liverpool Custom House that afternoon, or what had happened to the indefatigably wrong detective Mr. Fix. Watch had even been put on No. 7 Savile Row all through that day, but as no Fogg was seen, those on vigil there abandoned the street by eight to join those waiting at the Reform Club.

Had they only but known who came and went by another way altogether: the unprepossessing side gate of that old former residence just one street over from Savile Row, whose slim courtyard abutted Mr.

Fogg's back door, and whose locks were impervious even to Passepartout's comb. While Passepartout slipped away to arrange for a certain ceremony at Marylebone Church, Phileas Fogg and Aouda casually strolled down the block where they might hail a carriage for the ride to the Reform Club.

With so many people about on Pall Mall, no effort at concealment was needed for the young Mr. Holmes (now changed into more customary—and thus inconspicuous—street dress) to wander among the throng and look for the arrival of Stuart and Fallentin on behalf of that demanding sibling as yet not officially associated with the Foreign Office.

The parties to Phileas Fogg's wager began to arrive just after eight o'clock, each by separate carriage and in varied temper.

It being a Saturday, the bankers had the least reason not to arrive early. The more elderly Bank of England director Gauthier Ralph set the standard by being first to slide through the gauntlet mob (to which he seemed oblivious) and tread up the eight steps of the Reform Club, his gait measured as one might expect from one of such substance and means. His fiduciary analog John Sullivan appeared not long after, throwing a wan smile at the noisy spectators, feeling the transient celebrity.

The arrival of Andrew Stuart was more dramatic. His carriage disgorged three bodyguards who had to survey the field and pronounce it benign before the engineer would set foot to pavement. A fourth guardian sat by the coachman as further defense. When he did emerge, two of the men fell to station on either side of him—tall men both, against which Stuart appeared suddenly rather small. Barreling expeditiously through the crush on the sidewalk up to the door, they did not accompany him inside the exclusive precinct, but returned to the carriage to wait.

The banker Samuel Fallentin similarly tarried in his closed carriage until satisfied by his two resolute guards that there were no assassins hiding among the milling hundreds. While one of the men held the carriage door, Fallentin bolted out and sped up the steps into the club as if pursued by wasps.

One of Fallentin's protectors sauntered over to the gang at Stuart's carriage. "Keep a special watch for the Frenchman. He's the most dangerous."

Attending from barely ten feet away, the young Mr. Holmes deduced they were confident overall in their mission, innocent of grave apprehension. He was not at all sure such calm was warranted.

The brewer Thomas Flanagan was last to reach the Reform Club, after evidently fortifying his courage with some of his own product, careening up the steps to some sympathetic cheers from the crowd, and definitely showing less concern for the impending resolution of the wager than he might have *sans* imbibing.

By twenty past eight the five bettors were simmering by the library fire.

Andrew Stuart rose from his chair to proclaim, "Gentlemen, in twenty minutes the time agreed upon between Mr. Fogg and ourselves will have expired." Only Fallentin properly caught the tension in his voice.

"What time did the last train arrive from Liverpool?" Flanagan slurred.

Gauthier Ralph had that information at the ready, "At twenty-three minutes past seven, and the next does not arrive till ten minutes after twelve."

Stuart marshalled confidence. "Well, gentlemen, if Phileas Fogg *had* come in the 7:23 train, he would have got here by this time. We can, therefore, regard the bet as won."

But Mr. Fallentin was unpersuaded, "Wait—don't let us be too hasty. You know that Mr. Fogg is very eccentric. His punctuality is well known. He never arrives too soon, or too late; and I should not be surprised if he appeared before us at the last minute."

Fallentin's glare spurred Stuart to a nervous ramble, about how he'd checked the passenger list of Cunard's SS *China*, which had docked yesterday with no Fogg aboard, and suggesting Fogg might not even have reached America. By this dissemble Stuart tried to stay as far from admitting any of his own knowledge of Fogg's actual movements as he could. By the end of it, "I think he will be at least twenty days behind-hand, and that Lord Albermarle will lose a cool five thousand."

Out on Pall Mall, the carriage bearing Phileas Fogg and Aouda maneuvered among the bodies milling around the Reform Club. Just as they were slowing to a stop, Fogg realized the anachronism of his wedding ring. "This won't happen for another forty-eight hours," slipping his off, and Aouda removed hers to a secure purse pocket.

A few recognized Fogg (or thought they had) as they alighted from the cab, and murmurs and cries commenced, loud enough to be heard up in the Reform Club's library—though insufficiently appreciated as yet. Sherlock Holmes also identified Fogg correctly, and felt a twitch of puzzlement by it, as he couldn't fathom how the man had managed to reach London without being on the 7:23 from Liverpool along with Mycroft. A resourceful man, indeed, he decided.

Adding the lady on his arm, they seemed not what Holmes expected such fearsome and innovative buccaneers to look like. But he was only seventeen, with a lot of the world yet to know, and put it down to his own inexperience. As Fogg and Aouda entered the building, Holmes concluded his evening's reconnaissance, and set off for his own modest rented room.

Phileas Fogg had crossed the marble foyer of the Reform Club and ascended its stairs for so many years that he knew exactly how long it would take from front entrance to library, to open the doors precisely as its clock marked the three-quarter's hour. "Here I am, gentlemen!"

There was surprise on five faces by the fire—and grimmer pall besides on two of those.

Being the drunkest of them, Flanagan acknowledged Fogg's triumph with a hearty handshake, soon emulated by Ralph then Sullivan, who promised to write his check on the spot.

"I'm in no rush. You all may settle your accounts with Barings come the Monday," Fogg said, then introduced the three to Aouda.

Stuart and Fallentin waited for Flanagan, Ralph and Sullivan to sulk away before tendering their begrudged congratulations.

"Aouda, may I introduce Mr. Andrew *Stuart*."

Her thoughts raced. "Might you be any relation to a *Felix* Stuart?"

The man tensed. "A peripheral cousin of mine. Do you know him?"

"By reputation only, second-hand," Aouda was casual affability itself. "I've been told of a shipboard encounter he had with my brother recently—news of which, I think, has yet to reach you."

"Your brother?" Stuart felt on a precipice.

"Yes, he was out sailing, and stopped for a final chat, on their *big boat*. They had met years before, you see, under most trying circumstances, and my brother was anxious to repay the degree of *kindness* shown him on that occasion. He settled that debt, mister cousin Stuart, in full measure."

The smile Aouda put on cut Stuart like a knife.

That was not unexpected, but Phileas Fogg's eye was on Fallentin, and the banker's merest flinch when Aouda mentioned that "big boat" put him on a fresh scent.

"Did you insure the ironclads and the *Great Eastern* against damage or loss, Samuel?"

"No, should—," The banker instantly realized he'd blundered an admission.

"Yes, Samuel, you *should*," Fogg smiled sharply. "There have been some substantial accidents at sea. More bulletins you have yet to learn of. Your channels of communication are tortoise to our hare. I think that may have been chief among your insurmountable disadvantages here."

"What an irony for us all." Fogg faced Stuart and his banker, "When you took my wager, neither of us knew of the other's involvement, tugging at opposite ends of Sir Augustus Moran's long conspiratorial rope. I would have thought slightly better of you had either shown any interest for the politics or philosophy of what you were doing—still more for the science. But in all that, you lack the imagination. All you wanted to do was make *money* by it, am I right?"

"There was a *lot* to be made," Fallentin mused sadly.

"Built on how many bodies?" Aouda spat. "Did you ever account that?"

"Of course not," Fogg said. "These are not men of conviction, but of convenience and personal advantage. Remember, I've partnered with them both at whist—no better judge of a man's character than how he handles the play."

"Well, we won't be *played*, Phileas. We're not about to be waylaid by your man—," Stuart began, then glanced around, "And where is he, by the way, that Passepartout? Has he quit you at last?"

"Passepartout seems to be where he needs to be," Aouda said. "But he didn't sink your ironclads, gentlemen, or bring down your airships—something else did that."

Stuart and Fallentin's expressions showed how that came as a surprise.

Fogg now played his ace. "You really do need to assess you situation. Sir Augustus failed to take *Columbiad*—you've known that for a while, certainly. All *your* money and *his* effort, for naught. How that must chafe. And now, Sir Augustus failed to take *us*, for here we are, safe and sound. Do you know where Sir Augustus is?" Fogg waited a moment. "I thought not."

"News may eventually come to you of the tragic drowning at sea of a former ambassador to Persia," Aouda declared. "Whether they mention the unusual wreckage will depend on the luck of the sea. The *Aurora* made a frightful mess when it crashed, but was sinking fast even as we saw it. I won't be giving interviews to the press on it, though—unless you insist."

"You are not going to take us!" Stuart swore, looking about as he realized his voice may have risen to a threshold of volume sufficient to provoke the annoyance and censure of the other club members.

Gauthier Ralph overheard fragments of their exchange with Fogg and Aouda, and completely misunderstood the import of Stuart's outburst, "You do owe them the money—."

"Be good chaps, pay up like gentlemen!" Thomas Flanagan blurted, still in his cups.

Andrew Stuart looked most sour, while Fallentin was merely

deflated, and the two departed the club without another word said.

Fogg was about to follow, but Aouda stayed him with a tug on his sleeve.

"Let them go, Phileas. We can scribe their doom at our leisure." Aouda chided him, "You, of all people, should know we have the *time* for it." Then she beamed, "Besides, they all have *roofs*, don't they?"

Phileas Fogg couldn't dispute that.

FINIS

APPENDIX I

Letter of Introduction presented by Jean Passepartout to Phileas Fogg in London, 2nd October 1872

> Monsieur "Fogg"
>
> Pardon, but I know of your other & truer identity as a journeyer through Time. I pray <u>silence</u> from you now, for I <u>pen</u> this entreaty rather than <u>speak</u> it aloud, on concern that our conversation may somehow be overheard (by means overt or covert) by persons whose interest in the topics disclosed herein are far from benign.
>
> I have no desire to trespass upon your privacy in this matter of your Machine, or your Intentions being among us presently because of it, but all your skills are urgently needed to prevent a most undesirable event: the intended journey to the Moon next month by M. Barbicane of Baltimore, America.
>
> If you are aware of the true Nature of the "Power X" Barbicane employs to facilitate his Lunar Expedition, I shall not reprise its insidious potential. But far more is at issue than even that perilous trespass into the most fundamental Secrets of Nature, M. Barbicane's recklessly public display of a Lunar navigation threatens to bring undue attention to this World among Beings whose interests are, at this time, best left <u>unaroused</u>.
>
> To safely prevent <u>Columbiad</u>'s journey to the Moon will require the concerted efforts of many, including a most skilled engineer of my own prior acquaintance, T. Maker of Chicago, America. Having contrived an apparatus uniquely capable of operating beyond the confines of our Terrestrial Atmosphere, as well as in the air and even underwater, it would be possible by this means to intercept <u>Columbiad</u> <u>after</u> its departure from Florida, diverting it from its intended trajectory (per calculations of a still preliminary character, I acknowledge) sufficient for a successful Marine retrieval of the projectile shortly thereafter in the <u>Pacific Ocean</u>.

This Marine scheme would most greatly benefit from the participation of a speedy & highly maneuverable <u>submarine boat</u>. Here I am further aware (again with due deference to our own disparate sources of information & the need for reticence regarding them) of how closely you have followed the late exploits of a certain vessel of exactly that capacity, in your own manner and to your own presumed purpose. I implore you, if at all in your power & inclination, to at once contact its troubled Master and entreat his full cooperation in what I profess to be our collectively beneficial endeavor.

If you are not already aware of them (though I suspect you are), there are those in the most privileged of positions who have sought (so far fortunately in vain) all secrets involving Atomic/Etheric energies, and I assure you they are equally dedicated to obtaining the parallel knowledge of M. Barbicane. You are likely also aware of the recent unpropitious disappearance of Prof. Aronnax from his apartment in Paris, an occurrence very possibly relating to the very matters on which I appeal to you today.

If you accept the verity of this summary and wish to pursue this matter through to its appropriate conclusion, simply assent to my employment (and destroy this resumé at the earliest opportunity).

Your intended Servant (and also in due course, I hope, a most dedicated Friend)

"Jean Passepartout"

APPENDIX II

Letter of Instruction by Phileas Fogg to C. Auguste Dupin in Paris, 3rd October 1872

> *My great friend:*
>
> In the next days two sealed crates (of roughly 12 cubic meters each) identified as "Machine Parts" will be sent to Paris to your care. You will not open (nor allow any other to open) either container, but will arrange (by funds provided) their safe shipment to New York, along with your own passage to accompany them aboard ship in whatever state of luxury you deem appropriate. Absolute discretion is needed for this, however, and although there is no reason to suspect any will be attending to your activities, nonetheless, from this point on, you will maintain the utmost vigilance in the event any persons of a suspicious nature do chance upon any of your preparations or your activities *en route*.
>
> Once you arrive in New York you will further relocate the containers to Chicago, arranging for a suitably secluded establishment (warehouse or other business) in convenient proximity to the working railway terminus there, where they may be stored undisturbed but accessible for two months minimum, making it known to its managers that I, Phileas Fogg, will be calling in due course to personally inspect their condition, and so the crates must be positioned to afford easy access on all sides.
>
> Whatever facility you obtain *must* have an entry that may be opened from inside or outside as needed and at all hours by key (rather than one locked by purely external fastening, such as bar or padlock). As the crates will not be removed on my inspection, the keyed entry need only be suitable for human egress. Your possession of a copy of that key must be part of the arrangement for the crates' storage (with whatever bond or surety is required to obtain the proprietor's nominal compliance).
>
> Once you have the key you will have a copy of that secretly made, packaged up and addressed to me, to be left with the proprietor to be given to me when I come for my inspection (its content of course not disclosed to him). You will inform me telegraphically only regarding the following increments of your travels: (1) your receipt of the containers, (2) the day you actually sail for New York with them, (3) your confirmed

arrival in that city, and (4) your successful deposition of the containers in Chicago, with the identity of its specific location noted (the key being a necessity, its packaged presence will be assumed). Your telegraphs may be sent to the next appropriate destination on my itinerary:

>Brindisi RR terminus—to be reached on 5 Oct
>Suez P&O line—to be reached on 9 Oct
>Bombay Great East Indian Peninsula Railway—to be reached on 22 Oct
>Allahabad & later Benares GEIPR—to be reached on 24 Oct
>Calcutta GEIPR terminus—to be reached on 25 Oct

By this time I am confident the containers will have been safely positioned, and you will have embarked on the next and more interesting stage of your investigation: Impey Barbicane's celebrated <u>Columbiad</u> project, first journeying to Baltimore and his factory facilities there, then to Florida to observe the expedition's final preparations. Having gained whatever intelligence you can of who may be involved directly, or indirectly, in this undertaking, you will remain on hand in Florida until I arrive (before the <u>Columbiad</u>'s scheduled ascent on 20 Nov Noon) to hear your full report in person (which I am certain will be far too extensive and likely impolitic for any mere telegraphic précis).

I will next see you then in Florida, esteemed chevalier, where I may encounter you as that inconspicuous foreign traveler Dupin staying at whatever hotel or boarding rooms may be available in so rustic a settlement as "Stone's Hill" (most logically at whatever establishment where the various reporters already covering the scheme may have assembled). At that time I will give you further specificities regarding your eventual return to Parisian seclusion.

Yours, P. Fogg

Printed in Poland
by Amazon Fulfillment
Poland Sp. z o.o., Wrocław